PAUL MENDELSON

APOSTLE LODGE

Constable • London

CONSTABLE

First published in the UK in 2017 by Constable

Copyright © Paul Mendelson, 2017

1 3 5 7 9 10 8 6 4 2

A CIP catalogue record for this book
is available from the British Library.

ISBN: 978-1-47212-188-2

Typeset in Bembo by Photoprint, Torquay
Printed and bound in Great Britain by
CPI Group (UK) Ltd, Croydon CR0 4YY

Papers used by Constable are from well-managed forests and other
responsible sources.

FSC
www.fsc.org

MIX
Paper from
responsible sources
FSC® C104740

Constable
An imprint of
Little, Brown Book Group
Carmelite House
50 Victoria Embankment
London EC4Y 0DZ

An Hachette UK Company
www.hachette.co.uk

www.littlebrown.co.uk

PROLOGUE

She descends the steep Bo Kaap cobbled street cautiously, glancing to her left between terraced cottages at the sparkling silver water beyond the glass skyscrapers, dazzled by the intensity of the light. She pauses in a pool of shade, pushes her veil a little forward so that it is low over her eyebrows, wishes that she had water. Even now, before nine in the morning, the heat is settling heavily in the City Bowl, buildings and pavements still exuding warmth from months of unrelenting, unprecedented heat. Even the wind, the theoretically cooling Cape Doctor, is hot and breath-stealing. She leans against a white-painted wall under bright scarlet bougainvillaea, looks at the topographical arms embracing the city: Devil's Peak ahead of her, Signal Hill behind, Table Mountain itself, sharply defined, free from cloud, augmented only by the revolving cable car, refracting the sun like a jewel as it approaches the summit.

She adjusts her backpack, her shoulders stiff, wipes sticky hands on the coarse black material, steps out down the hill.

She crosses Buitengracht Street, congested with cars, engines turning over fast to power air-conditioning, pumping fumes into the low smog, which forms earlier as each week goes by. She finds little respite in the shady narrow confines of Shortmarket Street: a line of cars is backed up, hawkers and porters weaving between them with carts and trolleys. She studies each of them as they

1

approach her, registers their fatigue, the narrowing of eyes as they take in her veil and heavy black robes. She is panting now, the exertion wearing on tired limbs. She looks up to find that she is almost at Long Street, one of Cape Town's central avenues, a Mecca for tourists and locals alike, fronted by bars and restaurants, hotels and backpackers' lodges, African artefact emporia and independent clothing stores. Commuters and visitors jam the pavements. She turns at the sensation of ice-cold air seeping from the opening door of a fluorescent-tube-lit tattoo parlour. Ahead, she sees the building that was described to her. She stops, composes herself, checks her backpack.

The small white truck drifts up the right-hand side of Long Street, pulling out around double-parked cars without warning, ahead of the slow-moving traffic. It accelerates past two youngsters on scooters, picking up speed. The driver sees the traffic lights ahead change to red, registers the Metro police car to his right, brakes hard.

From two hundred metres up the hill, she hears the brakes squeal, turns into a thunderous blast, glimpses the first second of the vast explosion, tongues of fire, like the arms of an anemone, human mouths wide, screaming silently, arms raised, lifted from their feet away from the invisible core of the detonation. She finds herself jolted backwards, head hitting the pavement hard, eyes scalded, vision gone, a siren in her ears, consciousness seeping away, her last coherent thought for what would be forty hours: her long-sought, hard-fought interview appointment missed.

PART 1

The hall at the Inns of Court in the centre of Cape Town is grandly proportioned, ceiling high and elaborate, tall leaded windows running its length overlooking dusk descending on the Company's gardens. On the opposite wall hang huge oils, dark portraits of white men who carry their gravitas heavily.

At the lectern, Dr Grace Bellingham says:

'The belief in Manichaeism is that the battle between good and evil – God and Satan – was not external to the human race, but intrinsically located within us. The human was the battleground in which these powers fought: the soul defined the person. Nothing about us was assumed good or evil, but rather that we possessed both light and dark, that the battle was ongoing and never-ending through the reign of humanity.'

Colonel Vaughn de Vries of the South African Police Service opens one of the heavy wooden doors, slides inside, glances down at his cheap, tarnished shoes against the shiny parquet floor, eases his way to the back row of seats, slips into a chair on the centre aisle. He glances around, sees the sides and backs of heads he senses belong to the distinguished – a larger gathering than he had expected – inclined slightly upwards to face, in the dusty funnel of light, the raised lectern at the far end of the room.

'If it is true, as many studies suggest, that every one of us has, at some point, considered an act of extreme violence, including murder, what but our own brain can possibly be considered in our search for the source of an evil that allows us to commit such a crime? And whether our actions induce remorse or we remain unmoved is surely only determined by our own moral barometer, and how it might have been set.'

De Vries ducks his head, clears his throat, looks back up. Only the monotonous insistence of SAPS bureaucracy has made him late. He is embarrassed, though he has little interest in the subject matter, dreads the socializing with his fellow audience members.

Her voice is clear and deep. He stares at her face, smiles, re-membering their late-night conferences, their faces close, lips almost touching. The intensity between them not from the dead-lines of a murder investigation but their own physical attraction, her smell, her touch. In three years of working together, he can remember every expression that crossed her face, but not one word that was discussed.

'There is, naturally, one other consideration: influence, and the hypothesis of learned or inherited behaviour. Can our innate, inbred control mechanisms be manipulated, or are they truly set within us?' She looks out across her audience as if applying her question to each member. 'We might, I suppose, be grateful to Charles Whitman. In 1966, at the age of twenty-five, the former marine killed seventeen and wounded thirty-two in a mass shoot-ing at the University of Texas. That morning, he had murdered his wife and mother. At this first crime scene, he left a suicide note.' She looks down at the lectern and reads, '"I do not really under-stand myself these days. I am supposed to be an average, reasonable and intelligent young man. However, lately (I cannot recall when it started) I have been a victim of many unusual and irrational thoughts. Pay off my debts and donate the rest anonymously to a mental-health foundation. Maybe research can prevent further tragedies of this type."'

She looks up at her audience. De Vries is suddenly aware that there is silence. He has been meditating on how their life together might have been and how, now, both have two children, both have left their spouse, both are alone in the city they call home.

'Did Whitman sense that evil had infested his brain, disoriented his previously balanced moral compass? Is the concept of evil nothing more than a distortion of our brain function? And, if that is so, can evil – as a human concept – actually be said to exist at all?'

She bows minutely, takes a step back from the lectern. The applause sounds strident in the cavernous room. The audience begin to shuffle and chatter, rise from their seats, greeting one another with noncommittal smiles, firm handshakes. Double doors between portraits open and slowly people move towards the tables laid with glasses of Champagne, sweating canapés, sad tumblers of orange juice.

'Vaughn . . .'

De Vries turns to see the director of his Special Crimes Unit, Henrik du Toit, in full uniform.

'Sir.'

'I had no idea you were attending this evening.'

'I have some interest in the cerebral, sir. When time allows . . .'

'After the events in Long Street last week, to contemplate such questions must be considered timely . . .'

'Is it just the quantity, do you think?'

'Quantity?'

'Of victims,' De Vries says, 'that make it headline news. That many die every day around Cape Town. Every newsman loves a bomb, or a plane crash.'

7

Du Toit leans towards him. 'They were tourists and professionals.'

De Vries snorts. 'Does the differentiation of victims lack humanity?'

He feels Du Toit's hand in the small of his back, permits the gentle pressure to rotate him, finds a photographer, knees bent, lens pointing. The man snaps, turns away.

'Now I see why you're here, sir.'

Du Toit is media friendly. At least he protects De Vries from them, allows him to work.

'The entire city is afraid. Eleven dead. What is it? Forty-something injured?' He lowers his voice. 'Nobody knows who these people were, what they hope to achieve. We can't even identify the driver. No one's claimed responsibility.'

Another photographer attracts their attention. Du Toit stands to attention. De Vries turns away, walks towards alcohol, takes a glass, moves to a corner by the doors. In his pocket, his cellphone vibrates. He reads the message, smiles. He drains his glass, takes a final glance at the self-congratulatory gathering, slips out between the doors into the cool of the stone stairwell, descends, strides into the street.

Mlungisi Solarin walks through the tall bronzed doors of the anonymous SAPS building into the hot Pretoria air, across the pavement, into the waiting people-carrier. His small bag is loaded into the boot. The driver slams the door, gets into his seat, starts the engine. Solarin glances back at the austere, castle-like structure, still in awe that this is his workplace. He turns to the man beside him.

'Good to be getting out of the city.'

'Hot down south too, my friend.'

The vehicle sets off; the air-conditioning accelerates. He sits back, digesting the three-hour briefing they have just been given on the explosion in Long Street, Cape Town. In the seats ahead of him, two officers speak quietly; the man next to him rests his head against the frame of the vehicle, his eyes closed. This is his first assignment outside Gauteng, his opportunity to be part of a taskforce, to travel his country. This is why he studied, worked weekends through university, excelled in the ranks of the SAPS, aced his promotion exams. So that he could be sitting here, en route to Wonderboom National Airport, Pretoria, on the flight down to Cape Town, no longer to be merely the child of an illegal Nigerian immigrant and a South African mother. No longer Mlungisi. He is, he reflects, as he sees his face in the copper-hued window, Lieutenant Mike Solarin of the Major Crimes Unit Taskforce.

De Vries stands as she reaches the table.

'You won't be missed?'

Grace Bellingham embraces him, kisses both cheeks, allows the waiter to place her to De Vries's left.

'The speeches I can give, the glad-handing defeats me.' Her voice is husky from years of smoking; her posture is confident; her eyes are wary – perhaps, he thinks, afraid.

She surveys the ornate dining room, part of a grand former banking hall now the Taj Hotel at the top of Wale Street.

'I can't imagine this is your local?'

'You said you wanted Indian food. This is, I'm told, the best. And, no, I have never been here before.' He looks curiously at the waiter who is spreading his napkin across his lap. 'There's a good takeaway just around the corner from my house.'

'We could have gone there.'

9

'This place has air-con.'

They order drinks, balance heavy menus on their laps.

She says: 'Did you hate everything I said? I can almost imagine you rolling your eyes . . .'

'I was late, as you know.'

'Were you?'

'You saw me slip in.'

'Did I?'

'I know you, so I know you did. Why are you trying to trap me?'

She smiles at him. 'Because this is the game we play.'

He nods. 'I've missed it.'

They eat ornate, refined Indian food, converse happily. De Vries stares at her, hair untied, eyes no longer occluded by dark spectacles, still wearing barely any make-up. He thinks that she still exudes the beauty of the precociously intelligent woman he met over twenty years ago, after he had joined the SAPS. Over those years, their paths have crossed sporadically, including 2003 to 2005 when she worked with his previous Major Crimes Department, building profiles of rapists and murderers. A six-month placement with the FBI in Quantico, Virginia, has propelled her to the forefront of criminal profilers in South Africa, an author and private consultant in the States.

He watches her eat, lay down her cutlery, speak; there is a delicacy to her hand movements, her posture, a style that he, and his circle of friends, wholly lack. She always had control over him: his awe made him her puppet, his lust juvenilized him. He wonders why she has contacted him now.

'I'm coming home. For good this time, I think.'

'To do what?'

She sits back, sighs. 'Little, I hope. Write, probably teach. Maybe sit on a sunny stoep. Semi-retirement.'

'Brace yourself. It's been the hottest summer on record. The dams are dry. No sign of respite.'

'You're as bad as the Brits. I couldn't believe them. Obsessed by the weather.'

'In case you've forgotten, we have much more weather than the Brits.'

'As if you care . . .'

'You've been away from Cape Town for too long.'

She picks up her glass, toasts him. 'And now I'm back.'

'Leading a discourse on the nature of evil. You've picked an apposite moment. Everyone is jittery.'

'No word on the bombing, who, or why?'

'The powers that be are characteristically tight-lipped.'

'They don't know?'

'So I'm told.'

'Terrorists like to claim responsibility, so I'm surprised.' She eats a couple of mouthfuls, lays down her cutlery. 'And the lecture, it's just publicity for the book, a way to announce my return, to the select few.'

'You'll be in demand.'

'A demand I may not meet. I'm tired, Vaughn. You should know: dealing with the people we do, you can rationalize all you like, but there's a tangible cost. It reroutes your brain. They have destroyed all joy in me.'

'They're welcome to whatever I have left. Go to waste otherwise.'

'Those who use us think that we study them to learn and that we remain untouched, but the truth is that they eat away at us, they feed on us.'

He pats his stomach. 'I have flesh to spare.'

She doesn't smile. 'Be careful,' she says. 'Before you know it – before I knew it – you live only in their world. You lose yourself entirely.'

'My wife lives happily in Jo'burg with some media type, my girls have finished university, starting work. It's just me and my house. I live for the work. Nothing else does it for me.'

'Nothing?'

He smiles, remembering their history, a meal together in more modest surroundings than this, a flirtation that nearly evolved. 'That was then. I was just married, faithful. You were taken. I used to see you with your kids, your husband, wonder what it was we had . . .'

'Or didn't have . . .'

'We had something, Grace. I was never sure what.'

'We're both older, Vaughn.' She looks up at him. 'Just because a girl loves a puppy doesn't mean she wants a dog.'

He shunts piles of rice with the back of his fork, pushes them into thick, sweet sauce. He senses she is watching him.

'What do you want, Grace?'

She shrugs; a half-smile creates a dimple in her right cheek.

'I don't know . . . Company, a familiar face, something to ground me back into my life here . . . Love, sex, friendship.'

'Apparently I was only ever good at one of those.'

'And have you considered,' she says, head tilted, 'perhaps, now, you aren't my type?'

He does not raise his eyes. 'Women often say that before they sleep with me.'

She does not laugh, even smile. 'You're very sure of yourself, aren't you?'

He looks up. 'I don't care any more. When I was young, being rejected was the end of everything, so I was nervous, but now . . .'

'Now you're used to it?'

12

They stare at one another, each keeping a straight face, until he laughs first. 'It never happens.'

The bright dark sky reveals the stars blurred through the almost viscous warm wind. They battle uphill, tired and intoxicated. No one sits outside. Smokers press themselves against the walls of restaurants and bars, watch sparks fly as they flick tips. They climb the stairs to 15 On Orange Hotel, amid up-lit white right-angled pillars, the lobby level illuminated brightly beneath a hazy glow from the upper storeys of the tinted-glass rectangle.

Arm in arm, they cross the lobby to the lifts.

'Three nights,' she says, 'courtesy of my publisher. I need to find an apartment.'

The lift doors part. She steps in ahead of him. His cellphone rings. He snatches it from his pocket, squints at the screen.

'I have to take this.'

She cups the edge of the lift door, preventing its closure, watches him listen, his eyes close.

'I have to go.'

She sighs. A philosophical smile forms beneath fallen eyes.

'You know there are some things I can't ignore. I'm really, really sorry, Grace.'

She lets the doors close, says: 'So am I.'

Sweat forms over his entire body. He feels feverish and disoriented from the downhill jog back to his car. His back hurts, neck aches. He battles the car aggressively across town, honking and flashing at the slow and weaving populace, crawling on wheels or foot. He joins Kloof Nek Road, runs through the gears of his under-powered car to climb the steep gradient towards the cable-car station, crests the humpback mountain pass, follows the main road down above Camps Bay.

Twenty-five years ago, this area was still considered wretchedly windblown and sun-bleached; properties were ramshackle, the vertiginous land cheap. Now, the view down to the blue bay, the white-sand beach fringed with palm trees, overcomes concerns about inhospitable terrain and the blistering wind. Every portion of land that can be built on has been. The seafront has morphed from traditional town thoroughfare to neon-lit strip of high-priced cafés and restaurants, boutique hotels and a promenade for the rich to cruise in their imported supercars, to lunch and dine and club the night away. He rarely comes here now.

From high above, the crescent of beach is dimly lit by the multicoloured beams of light projecting from the bars and cafés, the sky and sea battleship grey, the water crowned by the start-lingly white crests of the waves being blown back on themselves into sheets of spray. To his left, the Twelve Apostles – the peaks at the back of Table Mountain, running almost as far as Hout Bay – are deep purple, fringed with translucent, elongated wisps of cloud.

He brakes hard at the first sharp corner in the road, fighting the adverse camber, strains to see the black on white signposts indicating side-streets. He free-wheels down the hill, tapping the foot-brake, finds Plumbago Lane, notices that it runs on both sides of Camps Bay Drive. He instinctively turns left, sees flashing lights at the end of the narrow street, his choice vindicated. He slows before he reaches them, takes out a cigarette, lights it, inhales deeply. Within the chaos, the tragedy and fear, he must focus only on what he can see and feel about the crime scene. To him, the politics, the regimen, are unimportant. He drifts down the slight incline, noting that the substantial properties at either side of the road are built on wide plots. There are no cars parked on the street, save for the SAPS vehicles.

As he draws up behind a marked patrol car, he sees a small group who are residents, he assumes, craning their necks past a uniformed officer. He takes a final drag on his cigarette, pushes it hard into the ashtray, one among a hundred *stompies*, opens his door.

The wind, driven up the side of the Mountain, funnelled up ravines, squeezed between buildings, hits him. He holds his door as he stands straight, steps away, lets the wind slam it shut.

He looks behind him. The lane is dark, the small streetlights off. Gnarled trees, mostly leafless, lean back like limbo dancers; spiky hedges in front of electric fences mark boundaries. Lights glow dimly behind drawn curtains. As he turns back, he sees his warrant officer, Don February, walking towards him, his arms wrapping his oversized suit jacket around his small, slender frame.

'Be careful, sir. I was almost blown over.'

De Vries smiles. 'That's because there's nothing to you.' De Vries pats his stomach. 'Alcohol anchors me.'

'Yes, sir.'

'We have one body?'

'Yes, one.'

'Old?'

'The victim is not old. Nor is her body. But, sir, I do not know what you will think.'

'Think of what?'

'What you are about to see.'

They start to walk, past the gathering of neighbours, as far as what appear to be the final houses on each side of the lane. The sandy tarmac road opens up to form a turning circle, beyond which there is a thicket of contorted trees and long grasses leading to a rocky escarpment.

Don gestures ahead and to his right.

'Down here, there is one further property. It is called Apostle Lodge.'

He walks ahead of De Vries, produces his torch, illuminates a turn down a steep incline, leading to large garage doors at the base of a cast-concrete structure, featureless and dark. To its right, the entrance hidden by an overgrown evergreen shrub, Don indicates a narrow raised walkway, which runs around and over the driveway. He gestures for De Vries to take the lead.

A coarse metallic screech startles him.

'What the fuck's that?'

Don points to the roof of the house. Against the dimly glowing sky, De Vries can just make out the angular form of the bird-shaped chimney cowl. It turns again in the wind, squealing mournfully.

De Vries exhales, looks down at the narrow walkway above the deep caldera of the garage area.

'What is this place?'

'All I could discover is that it was built by a young female architect in the 1970s, one of the first houses on the street. The windows are all black from the outside. You will see, sir. It is a very odd house.'

'Who lives here?'

'Nobody. It is for sale. I have contacted the real-estate agent, but I have received no reply. According to the neighbour, it has been on the market for many years.'

At the end of the walkway, a uniformed officer stands at the door under an opaque glass globe, its light grey and dim. Within, De Vries sees a whiter, colder glow. He steps into a hallway panelled in dark bare wood, lit by recessed fluorescent tubes above each wall. The light is cold and sickly. He is immediately aware of a minute rapid flickering, which makes him feel nauseous, of the pervasive chill, many degrees cooler than the hot night air from which he has come. He lets Don overtake him, lead the way through a Spartan kitchen – more concrete, dark wood – into a wide living room, floor-to-ceiling windows overlooking a garden and, in the distance, far below, the bay and the vast expanse of shadowy sea beyond. The angle to the ocean means that he can see no moon, no horizon.

The back of the room is also clad in wood, the same flickering lighting. There is an oversized silver free-standing lamp, with a wide, curving arm, ending in a chromed globe. It is not illuminated, hanging over nothing but the highly polished grey and black terrazzo floor. There is no furniture but for a narrow, almost Z-shaped, chrome and black leather chaise longue, facing out to the view, and a single dining chair. As he approaches, the smell of excrement and urea begins to intensify. He sees the back of Harry Kleinman, the department's senior pathologist, bent over the couch.

'Harry?'

Kleinman does not move. 'Give me a moment.'

De Vries rarely sees Kleinman outside his lab, let alone the building itself. He turns to Don. 'Why is Dr Kleinman here?'

'I asked him to attend.'

'Why?'

Don opens his mouth, closes it again. 'I want you to see, sir.'

De Vries steps forward.

'Sir, wait.'

He freezes. 'What?'

'Look down at your feet.'

On the floor, De Vries discerns movement. He squats, sees Don offering his torch, takes it, points it. A wavering line of ants, dark orange-brown against the almost black floor, meanders between his shoes.

'Ants.' He shrugs his shoulders. 'So what?'

'There are two other trails. One heading towards the corner of the building there.' He points towards the far right-hand corner. 'The other leads towards the door in the wall to the left.'

'There's a body. There are always bugs.'

A deeper, more certain voice says: 'They're not interested in the body.' De Vries turns towards Kleinman, who stands straight, arching his back slightly. 'Flies, maggots, cockroaches, many other what you call bugs, but the ants, they have a different destination.'

'Can we talk insects later? Let me see the victim.'

Kleinman smiles grimly, glances at Don. 'Of course.'

He steps aside. De Vries finds himself staring into the black, bloody, empty eye sockets of a woman's face, her mouth wide open, distorted, screaming. Dry rust-coloured blood stains her face, like tears. He feels a cold shiver pass down his back, a feeling like static electricity reacting with his damp skin. He takes a breath, tries to retain his dignity.

'Shit.'

He forces himself to study the body. She is probably in her late thirties or early forties, dark hair curling around her face, bound to the chaise longue by her wrists and ankles. Her blouse is raised over her breasts, her bra still in place; her skirt is pushed high to her thighs. De Vries ascertains that she is wearing no underwear, looks away again, wishes she was covered, knows that this cannot happen until he has borne witness.

'Where are her eyes?'

'Follow the ants, Vaughn.'

De Vries looks up at Kleinman, back at the floor, sees the two trails converge on the dining chair. On the black leather seat cushion, two eyeballs sit apart, smothered in crawling ants, moving tentacles of insects stretched out behind them. One is nearly at the edge of the chair.

'I imagine that they were placed next to one another,' Kleinman says, 'possibly lined up to give the impression that they are looking

18

back at her. The ants are attempting to move this one.' He points with a pencil at the eyeball near the edge of the chair.

De Vries exhales, wipes his face, feels both chilled and suffocated; wonders how Kleinman and Don February can seem so calm.

'Her eyes: before or after she died?'

'Afterwards.' Kleinman studies him. 'Are you all right, Vaughn?'

'No. Why are you?' He looks accusingly at both of them.

'I should have warned you, sir.'

De Vries examines the room. The low ceiling, exposed concrete and dark panelling make the space seem barren and hard. He turns back to the scene, determined to study it dispassionately.

He works his way up from her bare feet, past the light summer dress. Her skin is lightly tanned, smooth, healthy.

'Sexually assaulted?'

'You don't like speculating and neither do I,' Kleinman says, 'but, from a cursory examination, I would say yes. I've taken swabs already but, once you're done, we're going to transport her and the chair back to the lab – still attached.'

'Time of death?'

Kleinman folds his arms. 'There are so many factors at work here, I'm guessing. With that understood, I'll say that life probably became extinct between twenty-four and forty-eight hours ago. When I examine her and calculate exactly, based on the readings provided, I can be more accurate . . . No obvious cause. Something frightening, agonizing – but that's your department, isn't it, Vaughn?'

'Then why are you here?'

'Because,' Kleinman says firmly, 'I was intrigued by Warrant February's call to me, his description of, and his initial reaction to, the scene. It's good that I've seen her *in situ*. I can tell you now: she is dehydrated, the wounds beneath her bindings old. I think she has been here a while. She was bound to this chair, raped, terrified and, over a period of perhaps several days, she was left to die.'

De Vries stands still, his back to Don February. It is his ritual to absorb the atmosphere of the scene, to study details, to commune with the victim, to devote himself to them. He wishes that he could be more objective, more disinterested, but that is not how he operates. The victim, helpless and unknowing, naked and exposed, has taken him into her confidence, and he vows never to betray it, never to give in.

He turns from the interior to the dark garden, the rising moon beginning to backlight the bent branches of the surrounding trees. After a couple of minutes, Don squats with his torch, produces an evidence bag and a folded piece of white paper. He scoops up several ants, tips the paper into the top of the evidence bag, seals it. He stands, puts the bag in his jacket pocket.

'What do we know?'

'We have not even begun house-to-house yet,' Don says. 'There are neighbours outside, but I have not spoken officially with any of them. We have a team ready.'

'Who found her?'

'All I have been told is that the neighbours' children discovered the body and their father raised the alarm.'

'They saw her from outside?'

'No, sir. We can see out of the windows but, from the outside, you cannot see in. On the outside, the glass is black. There is a side door from the garden into a utility room, and another door into the house. Both these doors were open when officers arrived.'

'They touch anything? The kids or the officers?'

'The Camps Bay guys say no. I have not spoken to the children yet.'

'No ID?'

'Nothing apparently belonging to the victim. Caucasian. No jewellery, but maybe she wore a wedding ring, and an engagement or eternity ring. I have not touched her fingers but, if you look, you can see a wide, pale band on the fourth finger of her left hand.'

'We need to find out who she is. Who called us?'

'The Camps Bay guys said that they called in what they found to their captain and he called our unit immediately. Everywhere is short of men because of the bomb in Long Street. As you know, everyone has been called in.'

'Because we must be seen.' De Vries rolls his eyes, finds his gaze upon the woman's eyes on the chair, stops, swallows hard. He nods in its direction. 'Look at the chair. It's facing the chaise longue.' He walks gingerly over to stand behind it. 'Did he place it there after he killed her, took her eyes?' He turns on the spot, scrutinizes the room from the far end and back again. 'No one can see in . . . No one nearby to hear anything . . . Or was he sitting there?' He looks up at Don February. 'Watching her die.'

The forensic technicians assume control of the scene. De Vries observes them, head tilted back on his neck, studying their scrutiny, follows what they retrieve, from tweezer prongs to evidence bag. In his mind's eye, he divides the room and stares at each section.

The chaise longue – with the victim's body still attached – is wrapped and carried through the hallway, down the narrow walkway to waiting transport. De Vries follows it outside, thankful to be out of the room, of the dwelling itself, for the wind in his clothes, drying his face. When Don February is at his side, De Vries says:

'Talk to the neighbours out here, then start house-to-house. Wake people up if necessary. Anyone not at home, come back tomorrow and check again. Try to find out who everybody in the street is, even on the other side of Camps Bay Drive. A complete layout of Plumbago Lane.' Don moves away. 'And the kids: are they next door?' He points at the house along from Apostle Lodge. Don nods, waits, then turns towards the small group still waiting behind a non-existent line.

Before De Vries reaches the gate at the boundary of the house next door from, and above, Apostle Lodge, it buzzes open. He walks to the front door. A broad, middle-aged man stands in the frame. He is wearing nothing but shorts.

'You in charge?'

'I need to speak to you and to your children, sir.' De Vries holds out his ID.

'Who was she?'

'We don't know yet. Can I come in?'

The man does not relinquish his position. 'They were playing with another boy, Thomas Vermeulen, from number thirty-four, across the way there.' He points. 'It's not the first time that boy has got my sons into trouble.'

'They're not in trouble.'

His voice is deep and harsh. 'They broke into that house. Far as I'm concerned, that's trouble.'

De Vries shrugs. 'I need to talk with them now, sir.' He steps forward, still finds the man unmoving.

'You should talk to the Vermeulen boy first. He's behind this. My boys wouldn't do that. Not without being influenced.'

'Influenced?'

'His parents. They're no good. Especially the wife. She can't control the boy.'

'What is your name, sir?'

'Marten Cloete.'

'Right, Mr Cloete. I want to speak to your children now. Then I'll speak to Thomas Vermeulen.'

The man stretches his shoulders, pushing out his hairy stomach. De Vries smells body odour and beer. It is not a combination unfamiliar to a policeman.

Cloete says: 'Why not the other way around?'

'This is the deal, Mr Cloete. You want me to talk to your children in their own home,' De Vries says quietly, 'or will you make me take them down to Camps Bay police station and interview them there?'

'What's your name?'

'Colonel Vaughn de Vries.'

'So, Colonel, this is how it should be – if you are being fair. You can talk to my boys after you have interviewed Tony Vermeulen and his *kak* son. He's responsible.'

De Vries grits his teeth, speaks quietly but firmly: 'Don't tell me my job. I'll speak to whoever I want, when I want. I'm not interested in what your children, or this Thomas Vermeulen, did. Let me in now, or I will make trouble for you. Next door to you, a woman died a very painful death. You are interfering with my inquiry.'

Cloete stares at De Vries, takes a step back inside his house. De Vries moves forward.

'I've brought up these boys myself. Mother left years ago. They're good boys. This is nothing to do with them.'

De Vries opens his mouth, about to turn and call for officers to back him up. Cloete turns, walks into his home. De Vries sighs, shakes his head, yawns, follows him.

In the centre of town, Long Street bustles but for the taped-off area three-quarters of the way up the street, guarded by uniformed

Metro officers, a void in the melee of tourists and locals, like a knot in a piece of wood.

The scene is a hundred hours old. Plastic hoardings have been erected so that the passing public cannot see the mangled vehicles, broken glass, bloodied tarmac. Even so, Mike Solarin observes the morbidly curious staring from distant office windows, even from the balconies of restaurants and bars lower down the street. Reporters and photographers have finessed their way into the nearest vantage points, although most have tired of the mundane routines. Their every move will be scrutinized, analysed and judged. Whether Cape Town can quickly regain the confidence of tourists, both domestic and international, will rest on their ability to solve the case and apprehend the perpetrators. The Christmas season is already upon them; most will visit anyway, but the Easter season might be decimated by the attack. All the taskforce agents have been warned that politicians, media and public await results: they are not to fail.

Most of the taskforce gather in the shade from a cast-iron balcony that has defied the destruction. The death toll stands at eleven, the critically injured number sixteen, the remainder are out of danger or have already been discharged. As he has done on the two previous visits, he walks slowly around the scene, observing the forensic technicians still at work, imagining the build-up to the explosion and the effect it would have had on human flesh and man-made structures. The question that has been posed, yet to be answered, is: was the explosion intended at that moment, at this point on Long Street, and, if so, why?

He approaches Gugu KwaDukuza, a forensic technician he has worked with before, with whom, he believes, there is the beginning of a connection.

'Howzit, Gugu?'

24

She looks up, smiles broadly. Her face is flushed, wet with sweat. 'Hey, Mike. *Ja*, tough, man.'

'You find out what these marks are?' He points with his toe to a patch of gooey, blackened gel. 'I see more and more of them each time I'm here.'

'Look more carefully, Agent Solarin.'

He gets to his knees in front of a patch, studies it; puts his head over it, sniffs. 'I don't get any smell. It fruit?'

'*Ja.*' She squats next to him, points with a narrow metal scraper. 'See there. Grape pips.'

'There were grapes in the vehicle?'

'Maybe. It's not where I'm working. We're all taking quadrants. Everything gets fed into the system but we don't know much about what anyone else is finding.'

'Anything else I should know?'

She stands, stretching her back, looks around her, says quietly, 'They tell you about the explosive?'

He shrugs. 'There was a lot . . .'

'*Ja*, that's true too.' She turns again as part of a renewed stretch, covers her mouth casually with her hand as she speaks. 'It's old. Forty, fifty years old. You can see the residue everywhere. Modern explosives don't leave this shit around.'

'Mining explosive?'

'Good call, but no. More like military. The explosives team are working on it.' She faces him. 'You have to be careful, man. You heard the boss. We're not supposed to be talking . . .'

'*Ja*. What is that?'

'The paparazzi out there have their cameras aimed. They film us, get in lip-readers, find out what we're saying, quote us in the press.'

'Shit.'

'And the politicians want it all locked down, like yesterday.

So, keep your head down and your mouth shut. That's what they told me.'

'You gonna be here longer?'

'Long as they want us,' she says. She unscrews a litre bottle of water, downs half of it. 'Not offering you any. You guys probably going out to lunch, eh?'

'I get to see you one evening?' Solarin says. 'Early dinner?'

She smiles at him. 'You not working?'

'Being given nothing. They tell us you guys haven't turned up anything.'

'Do they? Maybe we have dinner and I give you something.'

He raises his eyebrows. 'I was hoping you might say that.'

Brigadier Henrik du Toit pushes his hand between the closing doors, enters the lift sideways, waits until the doors close.

'Sorry you got the call so quickly last night. Shortage of personnel generally.'

'So I heard.'

'Didn't disturb any plans, I hope?'

'I never have any.'

Du Toit studies him; sees nothing. 'I gather it was coming our way anyway.'

De Vries nods. 'Anything difficult ends up here. Better it comes immediately.'

'It's difficult?'

'We'll see this morning. Maybe there are fingerprints from a guilty husband, a spurned lover, incriminating DNA all over her. Then we sign it off and move on. That would be easy, good for business, wouldn't it, sir?'

'But you don't think so?'

The lift slows at their floor.

'You don't want to know what I think.'

'Why?'

'Why not enjoy the next hour? I may be wrong.'

Du Toit holds his gaze.

De Vries shrugs. 'Empty house, two pieces of furniture, one agonized body with her eyes gouged out. Prolonged torture, murder. Doc Kleinman thought she hadn't died quickly.'

The doors part, their paths diverge.

'Nine a.m.,' Du Toit says.

The Special Crimes Unit is divided into four teams. De Vries is the most senior team leader, the others a lieutenant colonel and two lieutenants. Most officers of the rank of colonel and above are administrators. De Vries insisted otherwise. Here, he has his own fiefdom; regular colleagues whom he has chosen, form his core team.

Shortly before nine a.m., they gather in the squad-room. As well as Don February, there is Sergeant Sally Frazer, the collator who co-ordinates and disseminates information received; Constable Ben Thwala, who leads house-to-house enquiries and backs up Don February. There are four other junior officers and a civilian office manager. Also present is Dr Steve Ulton, De Vries's favoured in-house forensic supervisor, and Dr Harry Kleinman, one of the three unit pathologists. Every department on these three floors of the building has priority access to the in-house forensic, ballistic, technical and pathological information. This is what, in theory, gives them their edge; outside here everything moves slowly, inefficiently, requiring layers of bureaucracy, which serve only to hinder the pursuit of justice. The standard waiting time for SAPS detectives to receive forensic results is eight months. Limited budgets prevent more than a select few of those samples being fast-tracked to private laboratories. Henrik du Toit fought to create and retain his Special Crimes Unit but, in the new SAPS, in the new South Africa, the number of old white officers in these elite units, many having served during apartheid, has caused resentment and animosity within the hierarchy.

Du Toit arrives astride a wave of silence, stands straight, arms behind his back.

'As you all know, events in Long Street last Thursday have changed everything. Remain aware that the public are in a state of shock. That will make your jobs harder. We will attempt to withhold the more gruesome details of this new crime from the press, but do not be surprised if word spreads quickly. Everyone is nervous, everyone is watching us. They are looking to us to be guardians of the city. Expect the pressure to grow and, when the opportunity presents itself, reassure the people you interact with that we are in control and that they are safe.'

De Vries waits for a moment, says quietly, 'Because Drs Kleinman and Ulton and their colleagues have worked through the night for us, we will hear the key elements of their reports now, act on this evidence and get moving immediately. As you know, these first few hours are our time. Do we have an ID for our victim?'

Sally Frazer raises her hand.

'A woman named Bethany Miles was abducted on Friday last week from the car park of Rose's nursery and garden centre in Constantia. The description given matches our victim. As soon as you tell me, I'll visit the husband, ask him to come in for a formal identification.'

De Vries writes, 'Bethany Miles?' on the whiteboard.

'Did we know about this abduction?'

'Constantia SAPS distributed a description and alert to every station. The Camps Bay officers should have been briefed to be aware.'

'Aware?' De Vries echoes.

Frazer says: 'It was the day after the bomb, sir.'

De Vries turns to Kleinman. 'Doctor, can you précis the relevant findings of your post-mortem?'

The pathologist stands. '*Ja*. As we suspected yesterday, the victim was seriously dehydrated. Taking into account all the elements, including excretions, I estimate that she had no access to food or water for a period exceeding ninety-six hours.'

'That would match up with an abduction on Friday last week,' De Vries says, counting days on his fingers.

'The building, as officers who attended will recall, was extremely hot and dry. I am estimating time of death as between six p.m. Tuesday and ten a.m. Wednesday. It is not as narrow as I would like, but there are reasons for doubt.'

'Cause of death?'

Kleinman says slowly, 'I make no apologies for prevaricating. The provisional cause of death is asphyxiation. This conclusion is not without problems. I have examined her body extensively and can find no evidence of pressure applied to it other than, obviously, where she was tied to the reclining chair, and possibly where she was leaned upon while she was being raped. There is little to suggest that her windpipe was obstructed or constricted. Nor is there any evidence of smothering in her nostrils, sinuses or oesophagus.'

'So?'

'So something caused her to stop breathing . . .'

'The dehydration?'

'Possibly. There is evidence of damage to her organs but not to such a degree that I would expect them to fail. Certainly not her lungs.'

'So what, then?'

Kleinman takes a deep breath, staring at De Vries. 'I know you

29

want answers. Sometimes there aren't any. Further evidence may point to a more certain conclusion.'

'What details on her rape?'

'She was raped, probably on two or three occasions. There is damage to her internal organs, which leads me to believe that the rape was rough, but beyond the act itself, not violent. There was no ejaculate, no foreign pubic hair, but there is evidence of a slight secretion of spermicide, which would suggest that he wore a condom.'

'The removal of her eyes?'

'. . .Was post-mortem, immediately or very soon after.'

'Anything else that might help us at this point?'

'Dr Ulton will tell you more about how you found the body. Gruesome as it may seem in the pictures, her mouth has been posed post-mortem to suggest a scream. There is no reason to suggest that her death would have been especially terrifying . . . no more terrifying than for anyone facing death, raped, bound, and at the mercy of a sadistic killer.' He looks around the room. 'I don't mean that in a flippant way, just that when you see the pictures you may be shocked.'

In the silence, De Vries says: 'I have attended many scenes. This one . . . I tell you, it was fucking horrible – the house, the room, the state of the victim.'

'I will say one more thing,' Kleinman says, 'so that you do not underestimate what this victim suffered. Beneath the blood that flowed from her eye sockets, I found a build-up, probably from many days, of saline evaporate – salt from tears. Bethany Miles cried many times while she was held in that house, and her tears poured down her face, covered only after death by her own blood.'

De Vries looks out numbly at the gathered officers, the heat and silence suddenly suffocating him. He nods at Steve Ulton, the scene-of-crime supervisor.

Ulton rises, calm, controlled. 'We have many prints and DNA markers from around the scene, but none on the chaise – or whatever you want to call it – apart from those of the victim, who is not in the system. There are none on the single dining chair. These surfaces have been cleaned recently.'

'The house was for sale, apparently for some time,' De Vries says. 'We'll have to track down the agents, find out who was shown around the property, and anyone else who had access.' He observes each member of the team writing notes. Don February will divide up the workload and second other officers to assist. 'Access to the building?'

'The back door leads into an anteroom and a second door onto the living area. Both these doors can be opened by the keys the children used to gain access to the building. According to the report, they found them in a terracotta pot by the back door. These were generally used by the gardener.'

'The three boys,' De Vries states, 'the two Cloete boys and the Vermeulen boy, claim that only Thomas Vermeulen entered the room, glimpsed what he thought was a body but, more importantly, retreated because of the smell and the flies.'

'There's no evidence to contradict those statements,' Ulton says. 'However, neither is there much to indicate who else might have used that means of entry. We checked the doors, walls of the anteroom, surrounds to the door and the keys themselves, but there isn't anything we can use. Unless the killer had access to a full set of keys, it seems unlikely that he used the front door, and the garage, while empty, would be risky to use due to the noise of the automatic doors and the narrowness of the staircase leading from the garage to the entrance hall of the house.'

'So we conclude,' De Vries says, 'that the killer used the same entrance as the boys?'

'We can't be certain. It seems the most likely scenario.'

'Don, who has keys? The estate agents?'

'I left two messages last night with the estate agent on the land-line number. I called the cellphone number of the manager, but there was no answer. The cellphone was not switching to voice-mail. I have called again this morning and there is still no voicemail. The phone just rings.'

'Someone needs to get down to the office after this meeting,' De Vries says. 'Is it a Camps Bay business?'

'The company have four offices,' Don says, 'with head office registered in Camps Bay.'

'Until we speak to the agents, we're in the dark over keys and access, even what was in the house. Was there an alarm?'

'There's no working alarm system,' Ulton says. 'The one in the house is old and was disconnected.'

'Right. I spoke to the three children last night. The two younger boys . . .' De Vries looks at his report '. . . Robert and Patrick Cloete – they're eleven and twelve – were following the older boy, Thomas Vermeulen, aged fifteen. They climbed under the fence from the Cloete house, which shares a boundary with the garden of Apostle Lodge, to snoop. It was an adventure. If you haven't seen it already, I can tell you, the place is weird. Not surprising no one wants to buy it. The children independ-ently assert that they found the keys in a terracotta pot by the back gate, tried the side door, opened it and went inside. The other key opened the inner door. The Vermeulen boy entered the main body of the house, smelt something bad, saw the woman on the chaise longue and got the hell out of there. The younger boys told their father and he called Camps Bay. They had officers there within fifteen minutes.' He pauses. 'Be aware, Marten Cloete, the father of the two younger boys, at number thirty-four, is very defensive, to the point of being obstructive. He's a single dad, big chip on his shoulder. He doesn't like the Vermeulen boy or his parents.' He looks at both Kleinman and Ulton, but neither volunteers any further information. 'Sergeant Thwala, Ben, what have you got from the neighbours?'

Thwala towers above everyone else, speaks in a clear, deep voice.

'We have two officers still in Plumbago Lane following up residents who were not at home last night. All those who we talked to have stated that they have not seen anything suspicious in the last few days. No strange cars, no one on foot. No one reported having seen lights on at Apostle Lodge, or having seen anyone enter or leave the building. The Vermeulen household say that the house has been on the market for over four years and that they cannot remember when they last saw anyone viewing the property. In other words,' Thwala looks up, 'no information.'

Don February says, 'Would you see lights through those windows, even if they were on?'

De Vries glances at Steve Ulton.

'We haven't done a specific analysis, but there was no obvious light showing at any of the windows when we were inside last night. My previous experience of this tinting process is that, if you put your face right up to them, cup your eyes, you can see a faint lightness, a glow, but it wouldn't be observable from afar.'

'So anyone could have operated in the house without being seen.' De Vries turns to Sally Frazer. 'I want a layout plan of all the properties on Plumbago Lane. It continues over the main road too, *ja*?'

'Yes. Just seven houses on the other side.'

'All right, I'm going to ask Warrant February to bring in Bethany Miles's husband. I'll keep you here, Sally. We need to speak to him on the record, so keep it silent or, at worst, neutral in the car. I'll come down to Camps Bay once I've spoken to the husband, assuming the victim is Bethany Miles. Warrant February will assign as required . . .' He turns away, then back again. 'Team four are signing off on their last case and have personnel free. I've already cleared it with Lieutenant van Zyl, so we'll get the extra bodies.' He looks at them. 'We break this now or it gets sticky, as you know . . .'

The officers disperse quickly. De Vries returns to his office at the back of the squad-room, glass walls fitted with cheap blinds providing little privacy. He sits down, adrenalin pumping, running through what he will have to accomplish in the coming hours. The air-conditioning has been programmed to a low setting throughout the building and the office is already hot, even before the afternoon sun hits the thin windows. Who takes a woman, starves her, perhaps watches her, rapes her and takes her eyes out? His fear rises; he swallows it back down.

Jaw locked, Luke Miles identifies the victim's body as his wife, Bethany. He shuffles from the mortuary to the lift, leans against the wall of the tiny car as it rises slowly, stumbles into an interview room. Fighting for breath, he gulps a large glass of water, sways in his chair, vomits across the table, head thumping down into his excretion, neck limp. Every last muscle in his body has crumpled. He stays there for a full minute, before he hauls his head up above the table-top and howls with grief.

De Vries watches from the other side of the long mirror in the interview room. The display of grief is ostentatious. He thinks of Oscar Pistorius in the courtroom, puking into the wastebin. He observes Luke Miles, unmoved; has long ago accepted that, professionally, it is impossible to empathize with others' grief. His sorrow is always for the victim; it is she whom he represents now.

He instructs Don to move the man to the second interview room, call a medical officer, ensure that he remains supervised. He walks slowly back to his office, ruminating on Luke Miles, on what he must have been shown of his wife to complete the identification, of his own reaction.

The report from the Constantia officers – operating out of the Rondebosch hub – on the abduction of Bethany Miles is brief, investigation thorough but fruitless. All investigations in the days after the Long Street explosion will have been foreshortened.

Rose's nursery is less than a kilometre from Constantia village shopping centre, widely known and used by Constantia residents. A long-established, popular garden centre with a large gravelled car park, it sits amid old London plane trees, surrounded by lush hedges. Other than the one above the cashier's till inside the low building, there are no CCTV cameras. No witnesses among the staff or customers have been discovered or have volunteered information. At eleven forty a.m. last Friday, a female customer discovered the tailgate to Bethany Miles's SUV open and a young child crying and screaming. When a parent or nanny could not be located, staff called the police, who attended the scene, traced the vehicle registration and contacted Luke Miles. From that moment on, no evidence had been found of Bethany Miles's whereabouts, how or by whom she had been taken. A cursory interview with Luke Miles noted some marital stresses, probably due to bringing up two energetic toddlers, and a vague suggestion that Bethany was depressed, could have suffered a breakdown of some kind, and just walked away. The child, aged three, was unable to recall what had happened, just that her mother had put her into the child seat in the back of the car and then disappeared.

After twenty-four hours, Bethany Miles's picture and details were circulated by the Missing Persons team, notices were displayed at Rose's car park and also at Constantia village shopping centre. No pertinent calls had been received.

The voice is more angry than sad. 'I've been asked this already, more than once.'

Luke Miles's demeanour has changed from shock to nervous belligerence. De Vries sits casually, to the side of the table in the interview room, observing the widower.

'I want to be with my children. They're only young, Josh has his leg in plaster. Lucy hasn't stopped crying all weekend.' He makes a cursory attempt to stand, sits back the moment De Vries speaks.

'Mr Miles, you spoke to local officers about your wife's disappearance. This is now a murder inquiry. Two different things. So, I ask you the questions, you answer them, I watch you answering them, and then you go home. It's just the way it has to be.'

'You watch me?'

De Vries nods.

'You're going to ask me if I killed my wife?' Miles meets his eye. 'No, I didn't. Of course I didn't. I was at work on Friday. All day, like every day. You can ask anyone at my offices.'

'I will.'

'Nothing was different that day, nothing was different in the days and weeks leading up to it. We've been married for nine years. We occasionally argued, mostly about the kids. All our friends argue, fight. Bethany hadn't told me about anybody or anything that was worrying her. She said she might go to the nursery because the heat had killed some bedding plants outside our stoep. What else? We always went to Rose's nursery, in the same car. Jesus, I don't know.'

'In your statement about her disappearance, you mentioned the possibility that she had been kidnapped, for extortion. There was no contact with anyone?'

'Of course not. I would have been on to you guys immediately.' He shakes his head. 'I've been successful, but I'm not super-rich or anything. We have a couple of staff, Beth looks after . . .' He sighs. 'She brought up the children herself. There are no nannies, no child-minders. She devoted herself to them, to the family.'

His face crumples. He covers his mouth, eyes squeezed shut. De Vries studies him silently. Miles has a high forehead, curly dark hair, slightly greying, long, neatly shaped sideburns running down to well below his ears. He is lightly tanned, dressed in casual but expensive clothes. He wears a simple broad gold wedding band, with no watch, no other jewellery. When he raises his head, sniffs, De Vries says, 'Did Bethany wear a wedding ring? Other rings?'

'*Ja*. A wedding band, like this.' He holds up his left hand. 'Her engagement ring. Big stone. They're gone?'

'Can you provide a description of the engagement ring?'

'I have photos. The insurance guys have photos. I'll get them sent to you.'

'What is your business, Mr Miles?'

'It's a software company called UnityAveco. I started it a few years after leaving uni, still own seventy per cent of it. It rationalizes warehouse to wholesaler to retailer orders, deliveries and payments.'

'Doing well?'

'*Ja*. I have two hundred and fifty staff.'

'Have you or your company received any threats?'

'No. Listen to me. It's not possible whoever took Bethany knew her. Anyone who knew her would know that she was beautiful and loving and strong . . .' His composure fails once more. 'People who do business with me know how I do it. I'm tough and ambitious and fair, and if I piss anyone off, they take it up with me. They know that.'

'Happen often?'

'What?'

'You piss people off?'

'No. Look, business is business.'

'Piss anyone off badly? Piss anyone off who didn't know the rules – about taking it up with you?'

'No.'

De Vries waits. Luke Miles meets his gaze.

'You mentioned before that Bethany might have been depressed . . .'

'Nothing that would make her abandon the kids. Her mum got sick in the summer, probably won't live much longer. Jesus . . . She was upset.'

'Was there anyone your wife mentioned from her past? An old boyfriend?'

'No one long term. That's what she told me. I never met any previous guys.'

'A lover, an affair?'

'No. She had everything she wanted.'

'We don't always know that . . .'

'I do.'

'Sometimes couples have secrets. Do you have any suspicions at all? Any behaviour that seemed odd, out of character?'

Luke Miles seems to regard himself. 'Think what she had. Why would she want anything else?'

On the Camps Bay side of the Mountain, a bleak, blinding sun refracts from a billion grains of sand, windblown up hundreds of metres of slope, across the dark, matt tarmac. That wind is now a breeze, the sea black. At Plumbago Lane, De Vries slows, makes the turn, pulls in immediately. He walks back to the junction, studies a bent metal stump in the cracked tarmac pavement, then looks up across the road, sees a cul-de-sac sign with a bullet hole in it. He ambles back to the idling car, glancing up each side of the street, then, with just one pump of the accelerator, drifts down the gently sloping road almost to the end. He pulls up behind two other unmarked vehicles he recognizes as belonging to members of his team.

'Did the husband confess?'

He turns, sees Don February behind him.

He snorts. 'Not yet. Ostentatious show of grief, immediate recovery, looked positively excited when I asked him about his business. Commented on the size of the diamond in his wife's engagement ring, the value of his company, his financial status. Got the feeling he only has eyes for one mistress – his job.'

'Their house is grand. One of the best roads in Bishopscourt.'

'An "ambassadorial-level residence" . . . Isn't that what the estate agents call them?'

Don shrugs. 'I have called the estate agent for Apostle Lodge again, but there is still no reply. I will go and visit the office just now.'

'Good.'

'And I have been thinking, sir . . .' He begins to walk towards the end of the road, De Vries following. 'Anybody could drive along here, drive down into the garage area and, even without actually entering the garage, their car would be hidden from view.' He gestures down into the hollow, overhung by trees. 'There are steps up the left-hand side to the level of the garden and the back door. Dr Ulton's team have examined them. I do not know what they found.'

'If they haven't told us anything, they have nothing. You know how it is: either a great big fingerprint, a pool of DNA, or nothing at all. The moment we saw the scene, we knew what this would be.' He turns away from the steeply dropping driveway, stares down the narrow street, jumps at the metallic screech. He turns, stares up at the metal bird-cowl on the top of the chimney, silhouetted now against the clear blue sky. The bird turns again, faces him.

He swallows, swivels back to the street. 'Any of the neighbours have anything to say?'

'Nothing. A few extra cars drive along here since the sign at the end of the road was knocked over. The cul-de-sac sign.'

'The one on the other side has been used for target practice.'

'They say people turn off thinking it is a short cut towards Clifton, turn around at the end here. It's been down since the winter.'

'Anyone see the estate agent or people viewing the property?'

'Not that I have heard. No one comes to see the house. There is no board, no open-house afternoons. None of the neighbours like it.'

'Who lived here before?'

'A German family. They left about four years ago. They are asking twenty million for it.'

De Vries shakes his head. 'Why?'

Don knows how many of his superior's questions are rhetorical. He waits and usually De Vries starts talking again.

'We still have guys in there?'

'Yes. There are forensic technicians, and a uniform at the gate to the walkway.'

'I'm going to take a look. What are you doing? The estate agent?'

'I must speak to the neighbour almost opposite, Mrs Vermeulen, then I will go.'

'Good luck. Ben Thwala said she was pissed. Didn't care what her son was doing, didn't know where her husband was. Have fun.'

De Vries moves towards the officer standing by the gate to the concrete walkway over the driveway, up to the front door. Apostle Lodge looks no less bleak this morning than it did the previous night. The cast concrete is patchy and water-stained, the windows black and hollow. He thinks of Bethany Miles's eyes, reflects that the windows are like them: blank, unseeing sockets. He walks on, stops, remembers that he cannot see in but the windows can see out; what Bethany Miles could see is now the subject of the investigation.

At the end of the walkway, he turns right, edges past the blank front wall of the house into the garden to the side. Between Apostle Lodge and the neighbouring property there is a tall, thick hedgerow of windblown trees and spiky shrubs. A lush lawn runs down to the far boundary, maybe thirty metres away. From here, De Vries can barely see the horizon on the ocean. He walks the boundary, sees broken branches and light from the next garden, squats and observes that ground and lawn both reveal faint scuffing. This is where the children entered the property. He stands, follows the light depressions in the grass across the garden, towards the opposite side of the plot where, again, trees and shrubs form a high but less dense hedge, beyond which there is a shallow ravine, overgrown with leafier trees. He realizes that this is one of the run-offs that carry water down the Mountain in winter. Now all he can hear is the rustle of dry leaves, whistling grasses, the distant sound of cars decelerating on Camps Bay Drive.

He turns back to the house, walks the gentle incline to the side door, examines the pot in which the boys claim they found the keys, looks around. The back door is invisible from the street or any other property. The moment the killer brought Bethany Miles to Apostle Lodge, he would have been safe from observation. De Vries stands still, imagines the man carrying the woman from his car, hidden in the dip from the lane, up the stairs on the left of the house, to the narrow paved path at its side. Here, he could enter the building, lock himself in, be certain that he could neither be seen, nor likely be disturbed . . . The killer knew the house was empty, that there would be no viewings, no visits. This means that he surveyed the property over a period of time, or had contact with the estate agents, even the owners. He walks up to the rear windows, peers into them, sees nothing but a darkened reflection of himself. He cups his hands against the glass, still sees nothing. Suddenly, there is a thump on the glass. The pane vibrates. He jumps back. From inside, he faintly hears a voice.

'You want to come in, sir?'

He gulps, barks: 'No. You gave me a fucking shock.'

'Sorry, sir.'

He hears laughter from the crime-scene technicians. It evaporates in a gust of wind. Something about this cold, empty house consistently unnerves him.

He returns to the side door, glances back once at the garden, follows the path to the stairs, which take him back down to the parking area and garage doors.

He calls up to the uniformed officer, who is staring at his cellphone, probably sending an SMS.

'Hey! Have these garage doors been opened?'

The officer leans over the railings. 'I don't know, sir.'

'When you see Warrant Officer February, ask him to come here.'

Before he looks back down, a tall, broad silhouette appears at the top of the driveway.

'I have the remote for the garage door, sir. It was on the sideboard in the hall area.' Ben Thwala jogs down the steep drive until he is standing next to De Vries.

'You've checked what's in here?'

Thwala presses a button and the double-width metal door begins to rise.

'There is nothing, sir. An old foot-pump, but otherwise it is empty.'

The door rises slowly, accompanied by a cacophonous metallic grating. De Vries recoils. When it is fully risen, slotting into place on the ceiling of the garage, the screeching ended, De Vries says: 'I'm guessing our killer didn't garage his car.'

Thwala turns to him. 'I asked all the neighbours if they had heard anything. None mentioned the garage doors.'

They walk into the dusty, dark space. De Vries scrutinizes each of the three walls. At the back, there is a bare metal door, fitted with two heavy bolts and a lock.

'Is there a key for this?'

'Not that we have found. There are stairs down to the other side of it. There are bolts on that side too.'

'Any other keys to anything?'

'No, sir.'

'How did we get the front door open last night?'

'The locks on the front door can be opened from the inside without a key. There is no mortise lock. The officers who answered the call were directed to the side door. When the scene was secured and we arrived, I suppose they opened the front door.'

De Vries pauses. 'Go back up there and look down. I want to know what you can see from the street.'

He watches Thwala bound back up the stairs to street level, step away from the railing. De Vries waits until he reappears.

'Nothing until you are right here, on the walkway. Even then, you have to lean over.'

De Vries gives him a thumbs-up, slowly follows his constable's steps up the concrete staircase back to the street.

'If you wanted to abduct someone, tie up, rape and starve them to death,' De Vries says to Thwala, 'this seems a really good choice.'

The serpentine Camps Bay Drive down the side of the Mountain into Camps Bay is the one stretch of road that makes De Vries feel sick. The adverse camber, sharp turns, jolting gear changes all conspire to make him ill. Don February drives carefully and slowly, allowing more aggressive drivers to overtake him on the bends. Below him, De Vries sees the white-sand beach deserted; even the bergies – the homeless and drunk – and hawkers are absent from the grass between the palm trees. Once the season is over, the town will become normal again, the preening city folk and tightly costumed lobster-pink tourists gone for the duration of the winter. But now it is too hot for tourists on the beach; sand blows inland onto the roads; locals stay indoors, windows open, curtains drawn.

The offices for Nobuhle Estates are located on the first floor of a weather-beaten white courtyard development, one row back from the seafront, above a tired sushi restaurant. A display of properties for sale takes up the far left window of the restaurant, next to which is the door that leads to the upper floor. De Vries scans the properties, does not see Apostle Lodge, pushes open the door and leads Don upstairs. In the upper hallway, there is another display of real estate, which, on the bottom row, advertises Apostle Lodge. The paper and photograph are faded, but the price is shown on a white label, which has obviously been added more recently.

The office itself appears open plan, and when they enter the air-conditioned space, three heads look up eagerly. One white, one Cape coloured, one black: the Rainbow Nation. Within seconds, they have been assessed as unlikely purchasers and all three heads drop back to their desks. Reluctantly, the Cape coloured woman closest to them hauls herself up, greets them.

'I want to speak with Miss . . .' De Vries frowns, turns to Don.

'Miss Dlomo Nobuhle.'

'Miss Nobuhle is out of the office today.'

De Vries produces his warrant card, pushes it up close to the woman.

'We have been trying to contact Miss Nobuhle since yesterday evening. Call her and tell her that we need to speak with her.'

The woman sits, slides her cellphone towards her, presses a key, holds the phone to her ear. After a few moments, she says: 'There are police here, Miss Nobuhle. They want to speak with you. Please return this call as soon as possible. Thank you.' She looks up at them.

'Where is she?'

'I don't know, sir.'

The white man at the far desk stands up, strides over to them, his voice loud, assertive. 'Is this about Apostle Lodge?'

De Vries stares at him. 'You are?'

'Greg Harrisson.'

'What do you know about Apostle Lodge, Mr Harrisson?'

'What happened, *ja*? Everyone around here is talking about it.'

'Are you involved with its sale?'

The man laughs, glances at the two women in the office.

'The company is, *ja*. Sure. We've been trying to shift that place for the last . . . I don't know, three, four years. We're all involved, I guess.'

'Mainly you, Greg.'

De Vries looks at the black woman. 'Mainly Mr Harrisson?'

Harrisson blushes, smiles. '*Ja*, I guess, mainly me.'

'When did you last show a client around the property?'

He looks to involve the women again, then says, 'In the

spring. September, October? It was before the vendor put the price up again.'

'And who is the vendor?'

'I'm not allowed to tell you that.'

'I think you are, sir.'

Harrisson glances at the women yet again, says: 'You'd better come to my desk.'

He leads them to the back of the office, invites them to sit in front of his immaculate, almost empty desk. As he sits, he smooths the collar of his jacket, which is hung on the back of the chair, ensuring that he does not crush it as he leans back.

'Some clients are easy, some not. The vendor for Apostle Lodge moved his family to Germany, won't sell for any less than his asking price, and that keeps rising every six months. We keep advising him: lower the headline price, get potential purchasers through the door, but he has his figure, and each time I speak to him, it's the same thing. No negotiation.'

He smiles at De Vries, glances at Don. 'It was a dead woman, *ja*?'

De Vries ignores him. 'How many other agents work from this office?'

'This is it. The four of us, including the queen bee, Miss Nobuhle.'

'Where do you keep the keys for the properties?'

'Sometimes we don't have keys. Some clients always want to be there when we show purchasers around, but when we do . . .' he stands up, twists on the spot, swings open a key safe mounted on the wall behind his desk '. . . they're kept in here.'

'Who has access to those?'

He shrugs. 'Just us.'

'Nobody else?'

'No. The safe is locked at night. We change the combination monthly.'

'What about the keys to the side door?'

Harrisson frowns. 'Side door?'

'To Apostle Lodge.'

'I don't know.' He opens the safe again, scans the paper index on the inside of the door, retrieves a heavy set of keys from the hook marked '13', examines them. He holds out individual keys to De Vries. 'These open the front door. This is the remote for the garage. I don't know what these two are for. Maybe these?'

De Vries looks at Don, who says: 'They are similar to the keys used to open the side door.'

'Does anyone else have a set of these keys?'

'No. I mean, possibly the vendor, but we haven't seen him.'

'What about a gardener or domestic worker?'

'There is a guy who comes in to look after the garden, mow the lawn, sure.'

'Does he have these keys?'

'I don't know.'

'You have his contact details?'

'No. We don't employ him. He worked for the vendor. As far as I know, still does.'

'I need the vendor's details.'

'I need to talk to Miss Nobuhle first.'

De Vries dislikes the self-assuredness of Harrisson, his creaseless fitted shirt, tight suit trousers.

'Where is Miss Nobuhle now?'

'I don't know.'

'She doesn't contact me within two hours, I want those details from you or you'll find yourself in court. You clear? Give me a card.' He takes the card Harrisson proffers. 'She open up the office this morning?'

Harrisson plucks a set of keys from his desk.

'I have keys. If Miss Nobuhle isn't here, I open and close up the office. If I'm out on call or on vacation, one of the girls does it.'

De Vries turns to the two women, their heads bowed over their desks. 'So, you all have access to this office and the clients' keys.'

The black woman says, 'Only Greg holds the keys. If he is off sick, and Miss Nobuhle is not available, one of us must collect the keys from his home.'

'Unless I'm away,' Harrisson says, 'then I leave them with Mary,' he nods at the black woman, 'or Anita.' The coloured woman by the door raises her head, but does not turn it towards them.

'So you and Miss Nobuhle have access to the office and the keys at all times. You have an alarm here?'

'*Ja* . . . Just a basic one. We have no valuables here overnight. We take our own laptops and tablets with us.'

'You've had any break-ins this last year?'

'No.'

'Any enquiries about Apostle Lodge? Anyone who asked about it, but didn't want a viewing?'

Again, Greg Harrisson looks over to the two women before answering.

'No. You can see for yourself, it's an odd property. It's over-priced. It's the kind of place you either fall in love with or you don't. And no one has.'

De Vries says: 'I think someone did.'

The briefing room is full. Mike Solarin estimates that there must be in excess of thirty officers sitting, perhaps another forty on their feet at the sides of the space.

The next speaker stands before them, a computer display projected onto the screen.

'The vehicle containing the explosive material has been

identified as a 1999 Nissan Cabstar 3.2 diesel, manual, four by two, grey engine unit, fitted with a white load box body. This was reported stolen five nights ago from a warehouse yard located in Farm Valley industrial estate, Oudtshoorn . . .' He peers behind him. 'The picture on the screen now is the actual vehicle, photograph taken approximately two years ago. We're sending officers to interview the owner, check for possible CCTV or witness reports, but the local SAPS sergeant who took the report says he's known the guy eight years. Owner's been there since the units opened in the 1980s. Never reported a theft before, no criminal record.'

Mike Solarin raises his hand. The speaker points at him.

'What is the business of the vehicle keeper?'

'Business is called . . .' he looks down at his notes '. . . Build It For You. Sells, delivers and assembles low-cost kit furniture for small offices, clubs and residential.'

He looks out across the room, continues: 'We're looking for any sign of this vehicle on the N1, N2 freeways or the R62. It's anonymous – probably cannot travel fast anyway – and speed cameras have not picked it up in any of the usual places. We'll be sending guys out to every garage between Cape Town and Oudtshoorn. Some have auto-plate recognition but we expect records to have been expunged.'

He nods at the room, stands to the side.

Colonel Brent Juiles walks to the front.

'We will focus our primary search for the perpetrators between Oudtshoorn and Cape Town, a distance of some four hundred and sixty kilometres, with a breadth of a hundred kilometres, but we cannot discount the possibility that the ordnance was transferred at Oudtshoorn because another vehicle was failing, or for security, en route from another location. Taskforce officers will report to me immediately following this meeting, as accorded in the schedule you have before you. Time is against us. Those above want results, answers, explanations, above all reassurance. It's our job to give them that. Let's go.'

De Vries drives back up to Plumbago Lane, in control of his stomach contents.

'Any of them could have lent keys to be copied, but if the gardener just leaves them in the pot by the back door, then it doesn't really matter, does it?'

'The owner could have extra sets of keys also.' Don says.

De Vries nods. His stomach rumbles. No dinner, no breakfast. 'I don't like Greg Harrisson,' he says. 'I think he's been questioned by the police before. Look him up, *ja*?'

'You think that?'

'I think *ja*. Just by his manner. Find out.'

As they turn left into the opposite end of Plumbago Lane, De Vries says, 'You been along here yet?'

'No. Ben Thwala has taken names and talked to owners, but there are only seven houses there.'

'Anyone show any interest in Apostle Lodge?'

'I do not think so.'

The narrow lane is almost identical in feeling and architecture to the longer section on the other side of the main road, a mixture of sleek modern buildings and old-fashioned, often single-storey dwellings with tiled roofs. Three houses face one another across the narrow lane, with a two-storey Victorian-style villa on the right-hand side overlooking another shallow ravine, umbrella pines and tall grasses disguising the topography. Only the occasional whine of a car decelerating down the mountain road disturbs the almost silent breeze, the rustling branches of dried and dying shrubs and trees.

De Vries pulls up, exits and stands next to the car, facing towards what little breeze there is. After a while, he sits back inside the cabin of the car, angles the air-conditioning vents towards himself. Don stays silent.

De Vries says, 'I'm thinking . . . a crime like this . . . No evidence, no witnesses. This is planned, and I'm telling you, it doesn't feel like his first.'

'You need to see this,' Sally Frazer says, as De Vries ambles across the squad-room. She indicates the plan she has prepared of Plumbago Lane. 'I've transcribed and cross-checked all the names Ben Thwala and his team have provided from the house-to-house and there's an interesting one. Leigh Finnemore, at number one. It's on the other side, but look . . .' She gestures De Vries to a computer on the desk nearby. 'He has a section-eighteen mark against his name.'

De Vries frowns. 'Restricted to the highest level. You don't see those every day.'

'I've only ever seen a handful in all my time,' Frazer says. 'What is it? A mental illness warning? Potentially dangerous suspects not arrested? Can we see what it is?'

'I don't know what the definition is, but it's serious. I'll have to talk to Brigadier du Toit. It'll need a joint approach from both of us. I'll call him just now.' He looks back up at the plan of the lane. 'No one else of interest?'

'Just the usual selection of minor stuff. The family on the opposite side from Apostle Lodge, in number thirty-four, Tony Vermeulen – his son, Thomas, was one of the boys who found the body – he's been arrested for punching a neighbour, another guy called . . .' she runs her finger along the line of houses on her plan '. . . Mackenzie. Something to do with him reprimanding Thomas for skateboarding. Went all the way to a hearing, and

Vermeulen was fined and warned. Two or three neighbours didn't seem to like the Vermeulen family very much at all.'

'I thought the father was a shit,' De Vries says, 'but that's my default impression of the public. He's done well, but the whole dysfunctional family seem out of place in surburbia, probably gets loud when he's pissed. The wife's clueless and the son's a little shit version of Dad, a bored teenager with too few friends.'

He glances over the squad-room. Everybody present is looking busy but, he senses, busy to no end, stalled. 'I'm going to find out about this Leigh . . .'

'Finnemore.'

'*Ja*, him. Right now, a section eighteen looks the closest thing we have to a clue.'

'We will be called upon this afternoon.' De Vries follows the line of Du Toit's finger to the chair opposite his desk, and sits. 'That is what I've been told. A closed meeting. I got the impression it may be someone from the medical profession, but they're telling me as little as possible.'

'It seems a section eighteen enquiry does, at least, produce a reaction.'

'A resented one, yes. What else is happening?'

'Everything and nothing. Legwork's done already. Nothing, but you only have to look at the scene to know that. It was planned. Unless the killer was focusing solely on Bethany Miles . . .' he runs the heels of his palms from his forehead across his hair '. . . I have a feeling that it may not be a unique event.'

'Don't say that out loud, for God's sake.'

'You haven't seen that house. Something about it that reeks of misery. You read the report? There was a chair facing the chaise longue, like he was watching her die.'

52

'You don't even know COD yet.'

'We have a provisional cause of death. Kleinman said there was nothing wrong with her heart, that dehydration would have been unlikely to weaken it sufficiently. He takes her eyes, displays them, poses them, distorts her body post-mortem. That is someone taking a lot of care. Then he steals her rings. That's something different.'

'A memento?'

'Perhaps . . . But you know what it suggests . . .'

Du Toit holds up his palms. 'Don't even mention it, Vaughn. We all have enough to worry about.'

De Vries sighs deeply, shuts his eyes.

'You all right?'

'I was in the army. I've seen bomb victims, torture victims, mashed-up corpses, but yesterday, Jesus, when I saw her there, in that place . . . Not good. Couldn't sleep last night, lay awake. All I could see were Bethany Miles's black eye sockets and that gaping, screaming mouth.'

'I saw the pictures.'

'You know me, Henrik. I get up in the morning to find evidence, but this . . . There's something about it I especially don't like. I hope I'm wrong, and maybe in a few hours' time I'll know I am, but whatever reason this man had to kill Bethany Miles, he took his time. He made it just what he wanted it to be. I'm telling you, I think he did it for fun.'

Henrik du Toit's office door is closed, blinds lowered. The air-conditioning trickles tepid air onto the sweaty crowns of heads, each man in shirt sleeves. Around his desk sit De Vries and the Special Crimes Unit's advising attorney, Norman Classon. The fourth man, Stephen Jessel, represents the Department of Section Designation, responsible for the issuing and monitoring of vulnerable and dangerous people in society. He sits upright in his chair, angled towards them, neat moustache above a creased tartan tie.

'Leigh Finnemore,' Jessel begins, 'is thirty-one years old, lives alone at number one Plumbago Lane, Camps Bay, Cape Town. The house belonged to his paternal grandfather and was passed on to Finnemore in 2009, since when he has resided there following supervised relocation regulations under the section-eighteen mandate.'

'As we explained,' Du Toit says, 'a murder investigation is under way following the discovery of a body at the opposite end of Plumbago Lane to Mr Finnemore's house. As with all residents, we have tried to make contact with him, without success, although we believe that he is at home. We need to know why Mr Finnemore has a section-eighteen flag in his record.'

'As you are aware, Brigadier,' Jessel says, 'those covered by a section-eighteen order are being supervised and, on some occasions, their movements are restricted to protect the public.' Jessel folds his arms, cosseting the file on his lap.

De Vries shuffles.

Du Toit says: 'We require the terms of the section eighteen.'

'I understand, but those are not available unless the department deems the reason essential.'

De Vries feels his fists clench. Jessel's stillness, his guarding of the file, his stilted delivery: all these things annoy him.

Du Toit speaks calmly: 'How can we judge that without knowing anything about this man?'

Norman Classon leans forward, his voice booming in the small room: 'The correct procedure has been followed to obtain the contents of the report by suitably ranking officers. It is not, I believe, Mr Jessel, in your gift to grant or withhold it.'

'As the senior case officer in charge of this man, I retain the right to withhold the information if I deem that it is not safe either for Mr Finnemore or for the general public. I will require guarantees that the information does not leave this room, and that, if Leigh Finnemore is to be interviewed, we are given advance notice so that someone qualified, ideally myself, is present when this occurs.'

'Brigadier du Toit is the director and Colonel de Vries the senior officer of the Special Crimes Unit,' Classon booms. 'There is no reason whatsoever to withhold such information from them. They are advised that, unless the information is directly relevant to their investigation, it will remain within this room and it is further understood that Mr Finnemore requires accompaniment if he is to be interviewed at his home.'

Jessel balks, straightens himself. 'Leigh Finnemore is an exception to the usual criteria for such a classification. You must understand that he remains a patient, under scrutiny, both for the scientific understanding we might gain from him, but also for the protection of those around him. We are still uncertain if particular stimuli might lead to an adverse reaction. We are not being obstructive. We have legal and moral responsibilities.'

'We have,' Classon says patiently, 'dealt with those. There is no reason to prolong this process.'

Jessel opens the file, withdraws a sheaf of papers, shuffles them until he has found what he requires. He speaks quietly, in a gentle monotone, showing no emotion:

'In 1996, at the age of ten, Leigh Finnemore killed his four-year-old sister, Susie, by drowning her. Her mother answered the telephone and asked Leigh to supervise Susie in her bath. Julie Finnemore was, according to testimony, tired and angry, deeply frustrated with her daughter, who had been boisterous and noisy all day and in the preceding weeks. Susie continued to scream and shout when she was in the bath and her mother called repeatedly from the living room for her to be quiet. During the inquiry, it was agreed that she may have used phrases such as "You are driving me mad", "I can't cope any more", "I can't go on with you". Leigh Finnemore took it upon himself to quieten her by ducking her head under the water and keeping it there until all movement had ceased.' Jessel looks up at them. 'In the minutes afterwards, it has been established that Leigh had no idea that he had killed his sister, but his mother attacked him, breaking one of his arms and beating his face. In his testimony, Leigh Finnemore recounts his mother saying, "Why Susie? Why my darling, beloved Susie?" and telling him, "I always knew you were the devil."

'Following the incident, Leigh and Susie Finnemore's father, Jonathan, died, also by drowning, in a deliberate act of suicide. Julie Finnemore blamed her son for her husband's death, and refused to see him or speak to him. Within eighteen months of the incident, she had sold her house and moved elsewhere, relinquishing all responsibility for Leigh. It was previously thought she had gone to another province of South Africa, but there is now reason to believe that she left the country and started a new life and career abroad.

'Leigh Finnemore, at the time on the borderline of legal responsibility, was counselled, supervised and accommodated by a specially trained foster family. In this case, he will never be fully free. He will remain under some form of assessment and supervision for the duration of his life.'

'Why is he living in Plumbago Lane?'

Jessel looks at Du Toit. 'His grandfather, on his father's side of the family, was, it appears, appalled by his grandson's treatment by his mother. The home, which would have been left to his only son and his family, was transferred into Leigh Finnemore's name on the condition that he might reside there at a time when it was deemed safe for him to do so. There is also a trust, which finances his living expenses.'

'What do his neighbours know?'

'Nothing,' Jessel says firmly. 'And that situation must remain. When Leigh was moved there, his neighbours were informed that he was an agoraphobic artist who wished to be left in peace. This they have largely done.'

'Is he an artist?'

'Of sorts, yes.'

'Does he work?'

'Not in a traditional sense, no.'

'So, what does he do?'

'He reads. He sculpts. Much of the time, he – the medical term escapes me – meditates or trances, locked in his own thoughts and memories of his life before the incident.'

Du Toit says quietly: 'Is he considered a threat?'

Jessel hesitates. 'I am told not.' He flicks pages, reads from one. 'The most recent psychological report – three months ago – indicates that he remains agoraphobic, afraid that his mother will return to harm him, and locked in a mental prison of guilt and remorse.'

'You are the officer assigned to him?' De Vries asks.

'I am a supervising officer, yes. We try to keep regular weekly appointments as well as unscheduled visits, but it is not always possible. I have been involved in writing a paper on his case and reporting to the Justice Department. For that reason, I see more of him than I might other subjects of cases we handle.'

'Does he leave the house?'

Jessel turns back to Du Toit. 'As far as I am aware, rarely. He has been driven by friends, on the first occasion with me present, to Newlands Forest, to look for wood. The outing was not entirely successful – Leigh's agoraphobia seemed worse – although he did express satisfaction at leaving his house and hoped that he might return to the forest. I am not sure that he has.'

'But he is free to leave his property?'

'Yes. He is certainly able to drive to go shopping or walk down the street. Leigh understands that there are places where his presence . . . could lead to unfortunate or embarrassing situations.'

'Dangerous situations?'

Jessel looks up at De Vries; his mouth twitches minutely.

'For Leigh, yes.'

'I meant for others.'

'No, I don't think so.'

De Vries shakes his head, frowns.

Du Toit says: 'Who are his friends? How did he make friends?'

'For some years, Leigh lived in a supervised hostel for young people where friends were permitted to visit. If you meet him – although I hope you will not – you will find he is an agreeable man, intelligent and, when well, good company. He was befriended by other residents and their friends, as well as his adoptive brothers in his long-term foster home. As far as I am aware, he socializes only rarely and always at his own home.'

'How do you know that he doesn't leave his home?'

'I ask him, and he tells me.'

'But,' De Vries says, 'can he be trusted?'

Jessel says: 'Leigh Finnemore was a child when he did something with a fatal outcome. It is extremely unlikely that he had any awareness of the consequences of his actions, less still what might happen as a result of such actions. But this does not interest me – indeed, *must* not interest me. I am required to supervise his rehabilitation, report to those who study him, ensure that he attends psychological sessions, and help him to lead as normal a life as possible. I have no reason to believe that Leigh lies to me.'

'Ever?'

Jessel frowns at De Vries, looks first at Du Toit, then Classon. He shrugs his shoulders. 'Do any of us always tell the truth?'

De Vries smiles sourly. 'I'm not interested in any of us, Mr Jessel, just Leigh Finnemore, and whether there is any chance he could have committed the crime I am investigating.'

'I am not a medical practitioner,' Jessel says, the calmness leaving his voice. 'I have neither been told nor read any suggestion of a violent element to this man's mental state.'

'But earlier you said that you were uncertain if particular stimuli . . .' he emphasizes the word '. . . might lead to . . . What did you say? "An adverse reaction".'

'He remains under scrutiny. There is no evidence that would occur.'

'But there is evidence, isn't there? When he was ten, he murdered his sister.'

Jessel turns to Classon. 'This man knows nothing about the matter other than what he has just heard. It is irresponsible even for him to express his opinions.'

Classon says: 'We don't censor opinions. This is an unusual situation. Children who have offended like this are either released after rehabilitation or, if they are considered a serious risk, detained. It is Colonel de Vries's duty to examine all possibilities.'

'He knows nothing about Leigh. If there is blame to be attached, it is to Julie Finnemore. She failed to supervise her children and she abandoned her son.'

De Vries stares at Jessel until he faces him. 'I know one thing. When I was ten years old, I knew the difference between right and wrong. I think almost all children would . . . And if I had committed murder, I would expect the consequences.'

'Colonel.'

De Vries turns back, leaving Classon to escort Jessel to the lifts. He waits for the door to click closed.

'Why do you do it?' Du Toit says. 'Why can't you leave these people alone?'

'He annoyed me.'

Du Toit shakes his head. 'He's a glorified social worker, probably with an unsustainable workload. He has a certain power and he wanted to brag about it. So what?'

'I thought we didn't censor opinion.'

Du Toit smiles thinly at De Vries. 'We may not censor it, but we might counsel its withholding – when it serves no purpose. If you want to talk to Leigh Finnemore, you may have to work with this Jessel.'

De Vries sits down in his chair. '*If* I want to talk to him?'

'When, then?'

'Doesn't it annoy you, Henrik? A ten-year-old boy murders his sister, probably because she is the parents' favourite, causes the destruction of the family, and it's him receiving all the help, the money, the attention. What happens to the innocent?'

'He was a child.'

De Vries shrugs. 'Ten? Maybe. Anyway, you know me. I'm interested in the victim. Seems to be a rather unfashionable view.'

'If you're interested in the victim, Vaughn, go away and find who murdered Bethany Miles. If anything points to Finnemore, you can demand anything you want.' De Vries stands. 'And, for God's sake, no mention of patterns. You have nothing. There's enough panic on the streets as it is.'

'The owner of Apostle Lodge,' Sally Frazer says, 'is a Hubert Swartz. His family were originally from Germany and he left Cape Town, with his wife and two children, four years ago.'

'The owner of the estate agency contacted Don?'

'No. A guy you spoke to, Harrisson, asked for you. You were in a meeting so I took the call. He said you expected the details.'

'I did.'

'I called Swartz in Germany, got his wife. She said they hadn't been back to South Africa since leaving, were much happier gone. She sounded frustrated about the house but her husband had appointed Nobuhle Estates, and she had left it to him. Apparently, the architect has made a name for herself in Germany and he bought it from her there. It had cost him a lot of money. Husband calls every three months, still follows the property market out here.'

'And the gardener?' De Vries asks.

'She didn't know about that, but said they had used a Malawian guy and she assumed it was him. He had a bank account so she suggested that her husband probably paid him by transfer.'

'You get a name?'

'*Ja.* Blessings Silumbu.'

'We can find him?'

'Already doing it. He stays out in Mitchells Plain.'

De Vries turns away, then back. 'Did Harrisson say he'd spoken to his boss, this Nobuhle woman?'

'Just that he wanted to give you the information.'

'Sensible man.'

Colonel Brent Juiles has a complexion like worn tan leather in an old car, his hair thin, eyes red. Mike Solarin and a white officer in his fifties, Ray Black, sit in front of him. They have been placed almost at the back of the queue of briefings.

'You two are going west to east along the R62.' He holds up his hands. 'Before you say anything, I know it's unlikely these guys took this road. But our mechanical team said that those vans run for half a million kilometres, no problem. The owner said it was a daily runabout, always reliable. So, we know the R62 has mountain passes and some tough going, but this vehicle could have taken it. And, if they wanted to keep off the radar, it's the quickest route out of Oudtshoorn and they're unlikely to see much traffic, even this time of year.'

'If they did stop,' Solarin says, 'they're more likely to be remembered.'

'I agree. Unless they brought their own fuel, they stopped somewhere. We don't know yet what time the van was stolen, but if it was before midnight they could drive the best part of the way to Cape Town in darkness.'

Ray Black shakes his head.

'Not happy, Warrant Black?'

'They're not driving that truck down the R62 at night. Be crazy.'

'It's just one theory. More likely, the vehicle was stolen, taken to a rendezvous and the bomb was fitted. Then – could have been two, three days later – it's driven to the detonation point.'

'Do we know if it was a suicide run? Remote detonation?'

Juiles turns back to Solarin. 'No, we don't. Guys sifting through the debris say no detonator has yet been identified.'

'No identification on the men in the truck?'

'Again, no. We'll find teeth, maybe DNA, some way to ID them, but they were at the epicentre. They're all over that scene in a billion pieces.'

'Witnesses said two men?'

'Yes. We have agreement from multiple witnesses. Two men. No positive ID on race. Sun was low, windscreen was lightly tinted, may have been dirty. The cab could hold three, pushing it four, sitting across. There were only two. Whether there were more in the back, in the transport box – the trailer – we don't know, but there's no immediate evidence to support that idea.'

'So, two men driving this truck into Cape Town. Why detonate at eight fifty a.m.? Why not wait until more tourists are on the street?'

Juiles stares at Solarin. 'Great you're using your head, Lieutenant, but those aren't questions for you. We have analysts for that. You have your job. You leave first light tomorrow morning. Any sightings of the Nissan lorry, anything suspicious at garages, service stations. It's tedious, but it needs doing. Full reports logged constantly. You can't find the server, you call them in manually. Everything is being fed to us here. We'll tell you if we want you to divert. Otherwise it's a straight line along that road. You detour to anywhere the perpetrators could have stopped. You clear?'

The two men nod.

By the end of the day De Vries has nothing. Each avenue of standard investigation has been exhausted. Sally Frazer has checked Silumbu, found him to be honest and capable, confirmed with him that he had kept the keys in the pot by the side door since the house became empty and he had left them behind at his house one day. The journey in from the township and home again was arduous enough without making it no end. He was emotional and apologetic, confirmed that he had neither seen nor heard anything. He also stated that, although both keys had been left for him, he never entered the main building, only the anteroom, to collect his tools, turn on the water supply to the outside tap, to wash and change. He had been inside the house once, coming up from the garage, helping Hubert Swartz to carry something. He said he did not like it. Did not like it inside, or looking at it from the exterior, with its blank grey walls and black windows.

De Vries's office is tepid, air stale, but when he puts his hand against a window, he can feel the heat in the glass. He looks down to the street, sees the weary gait of tourists looking for cool bars and air-conditioned restaurants. His own two-storey Victorian house is cool downstairs, but hot in his bedroom. He has been sleeping, sporadically, on the sofa in the back room overlooking the garden. He feels deflated and disappointed that no single lead has emerged, knows that his team must be re-energized and encouraged.

Don February appears at his open door, knocks softly, walks in. 'I'm going.'

'*Ja.*'

'You want anything tomorrow?'

'Don't know . . . Don, this morning, why were you talking to Mrs Vermeulen?'

'She had told Ben Thwala that her fifteen-year-old son, Thomas, has been going out at night and she did not know where. I wanted to ask her again what she thought he was doing.'

'And?'

'She did not know. Said he was always back at home in the morning and went to school.'

'That was it?'

'Yes, sir. I did ask her if any of his clothing had gone missing, or if she had seen blood on any items, but she said no.' Don frowns. 'She did not even seem surprised that I asked her.'

'Ben talked with the father, Tony?'

'Last night. Yes. He did not like his opposite neighbour much, the Cloete man. He said that he had never been inside Apostle Lodge, often forgot it was even there.'

'All right, we get Thomas Vermeulen in here – bring his father too, if you can – find out what he has to say. It doesn't seem likely that he'd foul so close to the nest, but you never know. Did Thwala say anything about the boy?'

'He is a teenager, with all the anger and confusion you would expect.'

'But not anything else?'

'Not that Ben said, no.'

De Vries nods slowly. 'We'd better see ourselves.'

De Vries stands in shorts and sandals, one palm flat above the coals, waiting for heat, the other cooled by the side of an icy beer bottle. He has flirted with craft beers, but this is a lager summer. He flips his raw steak in its marinade in the metal tray next to him, drains the bottle, wanders inside for another, returns to the braai. Above him, behind the boundary wall of his garden, the topmost branches of the tall gum trees scarcely move. He feels sweat from the crown of his head occasionally drip on his shoulders, run down the small of his back. His pool is green, despite the chemicals he has thrown in; his skin smelt stagnant as he lay rigid earlier, trying to imagine that he was not so hot.

He arches his back: the pain at its base is intensifying. Finally, he picks up the meat and throws it on the grill, hears the marinade sizzle. He takes two cooked *mealies* and places them carefully at the edge, watches the food cook, tries to dodge the invisible currents of even hotter air, which seep towards him on an imperceptible breeze.

He is agitated by the lack of response from Dlomo Nobuhle, presumably the owner of the estate agency, realizes that she, or any other of her employees at the Camps Bay office, could visit the property at any time and have the perfect excuse for doing so. He recalls the face of Greg Harrisson, his expression both solicitous and dismissive, recollects an impression of aggression beneath a gaudy veil of camaraderie.

The meat sits heavily on him, but he falls asleep in the garden in a white plastic chair, bottle in loose fingers hovering over the hot pink bricks of the pool terrace until it drops, almost silently, rolls away to the base of a bougainvillaea.

At dawn, they meet in the car park of the motel where they are billeted. Ray Black offers to drive first, but Solarin retains the keys, takes the wheel. He wants to be the passenger once they reach Route 62, so that he can scrutinize the surroundings, not for the first hour or ninety minutes as they speed out of Cape Town towards Paarl. He does not tell Ray Black this and the warrant officer does not comment.

The route takes them onto the busy N1 freeway where, despite it being early and approaching the Christmas break, traffic is heavy travelling into town. They pass through the four-kilometre-long Huguenot Tunnel onto De Toitskloof Pass, heading towards the agricultural and industrial town of Worcester, then drop onto the R60, through faded, dusty farmland, as far as the junction with the R62. Despite the air-conditioning in the Toyota hire car, the glass is hot to the touch. Ray Black sweats, filling the small cabin with stale cigarette breath and body odour. Solarin finds that the inadequate engine whines whenever tested; the brakes squeal when he brings the car to a halt. It frustrates him, but he reasons that if the Nissan truck came this route, it too would have been hot, underpowered and with brakes that struggled.

'You want breakfast?'

Ray Black turns. '*Ja.*'

It is their first interaction since the hotel.

De Vries leaves early, but still catches the rush hour into town. Even taking the high road around the Mountain, he is caught in queues into the business district. The weather has created a new schedule for many workers: arrive almost at first light, leave mid-afternoon.

He is first in the squad-room. He throws his jacket over the back of his chair, strolls into the main area to study Sally Frazer's information board. There are brief mentions of negative information received from neighbours, the location of the two known sets of keys, basic outlines of the children's testimony, and the lay-out plan of Plumbago Lane. No witness names or photographs; no evidence.

He must recheck Blessings Silumbu, whether the man could have sent another in his place at any time, whether others knew from him where the keys to the property were. He is all too aware that his department is decried as the 'White Crimes Unit' by many high up in the SAPS, but that is what he knows. It is the reason for his unit's existence. It is a generalization, but the perpetrators of psychopathic crime against white victims are overwhelmingly white themselves; the statistics tell him this.

At seven thirty a.m., a coloured officer he recognizes by sight knocks at his open door. De Vries beckons him in, observes that he is distressed, invites him to sit down.

'I don't know your name.'

'Constable Apolles, sir.'

'What do you want?'

He takes a deep breath, sits up straight on the edge of the chair. 'I stay in Strand, sir. Last night, I met with two friends who are based at Strand SAPS. We have a braai outside. We are talking generally. I mention – without disclosing any details, sir – that we are investigating a woman who has been tied to a reclining chair. That the room is empty. That she has been held for many days. This is the point, sir. They say there is a case like this in Strand. A woman was found tied up in an abandoned block of flats. She was dehydrated and she died after being there many days.'

De Vries sits forward. 'Raped?'

'I think, yes.'

'Her eyes?'

'I did not mention her eyes. Your instruction, but they did not say. I thought you should know, sir. I could not decide whether I should try to contact you last night. My friends said no, that maybe this is not the same . . .'

'When was she found?'

'Maybe five weeks ago.'

'You know who's leading the investigation?'

'My friends say it is an officer called Malgas.'

'I know Captain Malgas.'

De Vries looks up at the squad-room. Two officers are talking with Sally Frazer at the other end from his office. He lowers his voice, fixes Apolles with his stare. 'Never talk about our operations here, not with friends or even colleagues unless they are part of our group. We work in a different field, and you don't know who they will tell. Don't discuss anything where it might be overheard. Do you understand?'

Apolles nods.

'You did well telling me. If it's linked, it could be a break-through. Don't discuss it with anyone here yet. Not anyone at all. If they ask what you were doing in my office, tell them I wanted a coffee.'

'Sir?'

'Get me a coffee.'

Apolles stands, still nervous, relieved, exhilarated. De Vries registers all his emotions in a moment, recognizes himself in the young officer.

They cut through the mountains, turn into the Klein Karoo town of Montagu, find the main street slowly coming to life. They drift slowly down the road towards the sharply angled Dutch Reformed Church at its top. Solarin pulls in on the left, outside a café called Tracy's, window boxes flourishing, flags scarcely moving in the still, clear air. He switches off the engine.

'You want to eat or work first?'

Ray Black shrugs. 'Whatever. No way they stopped here. Not so close to town.'

'Everywhere checked. Pictures shown, witnesses noted. We're ticking boxes, but we're ticking them right. *Ja*?'

Even after forty-five seconds, the cabin is heating up. Solarin wants to be out of this space. He checks his mirror, swings open the door. The heat slaps his face, leaving it wet with sweat. He opens the boot, pulls out his jacket, swings it over his shoulder. 'We'll eat. Get some liquid inside us too.'

He looks over at the café. One pale family of tourists sits outside on the sweltering terrace. Inside, there is a cooler dark dining room, ceiling fans turned up full, beyond that a small courtyard with four tables under umbrellas.

They choose the dining room. Solarin sits with his back to the courtyard, directly under a fan, lets the strong breeze cool his neck. The paper napkins on the table flutter, the menus bow in the draught as they hold them. He watches Ray Black study the laminated card.

'One plate, Ray. Then we go to work.'

The N2 out of Cape Town passes the airport, crosses the Cape Flats, then rises up Sir Lowry's Pass to track the southern coast of Africa for some seven hundred kilometres as far as Port Elizabeth. Fifty kilometres from the centre of Cape Town, the road narrows and hits a series of traffic lights between Somerset West and

Strand. De Vries turns right towards the sea, heading for the ever-expanding conurbation of Strand, meaning literally 'beach'.

De Vries has few colleagues with whom he has worked whom he sees now; fewer still who seem pleased to see him. The elite units are, by definition, exclusive, taking him away from the every-day reality of many police stations, especially in the tougher areas where motives for murder can be as prosaic as one man drinking from another man's glass at a bar, picking up the wrong bottle in a shebeen, teasing the wrong guy, on the wrong drug, at the wrong moment. He has no idea how officers live their lives among such mindless carnage.

Danie Malgas is an exception: a coloured officer close to thirty years on the job, his ethics unimpeachable, his energy if not undimmed then still present, whom De Vries has commanded and, subsequently, worked with casually through the years. He is stationed now at Strand, the town where he was born and has always lived; De Vries sees Malgas as a constant in a sea of change within the SAPS. Some see him, and De Vries, as nothing more than old and tainted by the past.

'Not "captain",' he tells De Vries, when he meets him in the main car park for the Strand SAPS. 'Not since April. Don't you know anything up there in your ivory tower? Captains and majors are phased out, lieutenants and lieutenant colonels expanded. So, the same old Danie is now lieutenant, and don't you forget it.'

De Vries smiles, counts the teeth left in Malgas's mouth when he grins. 'Nothing changes, though, does it?'

'Nothing changes. Only the names and the colours . . . and the numbers. Jesus, did you see the stats?'

De Vries shakes his head.

'You don't want to. Colleague down in Philippi – something like thirty murders a week now. Even coming and going from work is an ordeal. Officers shot at, Molotov cocktails thrown at you. Jesus, it's out of control. You think we close a case down there? You people solve the crimes that reach the press. That's what the middle classes want to know – and I'm talking whites and blacks now. We'll just keep the dockets filled with victims and no chance of finding who or why. And, mind you, Colonel de Vries, that's just the bodies we find.' He opens the doors to his car. 'You going to tell me what we doing, or you going to keep me in suspense?'

De Vries gets into the car, says: 'You've got the docket?' Malgas squeezes into the driver's seat, nods. 'Get out of here and I'll tell you.'

They drive in the slow traffic along Beach Road, past the restaurants and bars, new apartment blocks and old-fashioned, almost Art Deco, low-rise flats, painted pinks and yellows. The traffic is rerouted into narrow lanes as workmen sweat in the sun building a paved promenade, the suburb gentrifying. On their left, beyond the building, the narrow yellow beach is busy, the shallows full of paddlers all the way along from Melkbaai as far as the dunes in the distance. The sky and sea and sand seem never to end, a sandwich of defined colours all the way to Muizenberg and the mountains beyond.

'Eish, man, it is getting hotter than the Mother City out here.' Malgas twists the air-conditioning knob hard to little effect. 'All the money my people have now, they come build these fucking great skyscrapers, drive around in Mercedes Benz cars, flash their toys, and wonder why they're getting treated like you whiteys. All the boys from the gangs are coming in now from Nomzamo, Khayelitsha and Macassar. Robbery rate's up God knows how many per cent, and now they're getting careless and the knives are flying and the guns aren't just being waved, you know? Bad enough being pistol-whipped, but when the trigger's pulled . . . Pulled for fun.'

'It's everywhere – maybe not the tourist areas – and it'll only get worse as the population explodes,' De Vries says. 'One suburb bleeding into the next. Won't be long before everything's joined up between here and Cape Town.' He turns to Malgas. 'You been given more people?'

'Oh, *ja*, more people, *ja*. Quantity, not quality. All I do is train them and watch them pass me by, but none of them know the first thing. Not *fokkol*. I'm telling you, we're breeding a whole generation of slackers and morons.'

'What about you, Danie? You going to get booted upstairs sometime? You going to sit behind a desk?'

'Never gonna happen, man. They want me doing what I know. Donkey work. I can't make a fuss, can't put a line in the sand . . .' He brakes suddenly as a woman pulls out of a parking space in front of him. '*Jeeez*, look at her. Cell in one hand, coffee in another, cigarette on the go. Lucky she's got her fat thighs for steering, eh?' He turns and laughs at De Vries.

'When you got the call,' De Vries says blankly, 'what did you make of the Marie Garsten scene?'

'I knew the moment you said you wanted to talk about a case you thought I'd caught it would be Marie Garsten. That one's branded me, you know. We moved on, but she's still bothering me. Something really bad.'

'Just tell me, Danie.'

'All business today, eh, Vaughn? You haven't even told me why all this interest. You got another?'

'What do you mean, another?'

'I felt all along it wasn't a one-off. Had nothing to back it up, so I kept my big mouth shut. You'll see when you read my report. There's no evidence – maybe a receipt that seemed out of place, maybe a couple of little pubic hairs our guys reckon aren't from her. Like Velcro down there. Good chance something stuck when he pulled out. Might have a follicle to analyse, but we'll get nothing back from the labs for maybe five months. Tried to get it pri-oritized, but they said no.'

'He wear a condom?'

'They think. And there was nothing else. Not a print, not a smudge, not a smear.' Malgas turns from the road to look at De Vries, turns back. 'I felt from the moment I saw her that this was part of something. Jesus, you can tell me . . .'

'It's possible.'

'Shit, man. I knew it.' Malgas bangs the top of the steering wheel impotently. 'He bound Marie Garsten up with ties and raped her. Our pathologist reckoned she'd been there maybe six days. No food, no water. Won't get DNA from her now, but some-times you get other stuff. Disappeared from Somerset West, and no one saw anything. You'd think something, anything . . .'

'COD?'

'Complications from dehydration?' Malgas says. 'Respiratory? Pathology open to opinion.'

He prods the indicator stalk to turn right off the main drag, takes a side road inland for a hundred metres, past a half-finished tower block, turns left, brakes hard in front of two scruffy gates. He pulls himself out of the cabin, his stomach catching on the steering wheel, grips the door frame for support. De Vries gets out on the other side. The heat engulfs him.

Malgas squints at the padlock. '*Ja*, it's the same one. They've just left it, like I thought.' He reaches forward, pulls down on the pad-lock, is left with just the barrel in his hand. 'The foreman admitted it was like this when they set up the gates in the first place. Spend tens of millions building but can't afford one padlock.'

He pushes the gates apart, toes a brick against each to keep them open. They get back into the car and drive into the dusty building site. Above them, the grey untreated concrete skeleton of a tower fifteen storeys high looms dark against the deep blue sky.

At least it throws shade. The structure is windowless, without scaffolding, seemingly deserted.

They get out, sweat forming on their brows even in the darker light.

'They stopped building after Marie Garsten was found?'

'They stopped six months back,' Malgas says. 'Ran out of money. Tried to sell the flats off-plan to raise the cash but, you know, we're just a bit far along out here. Most can't see sea because of that block there – so you're paying to look at your neighbour's washing – and you've got the squatter camps starting just over there. They say they'll be cleared, but you know what happens once they become established. Then there's talk they'll be developing along the dunes there. Could be decades of building. Dust and noise and traffic. Doesn't look like luxury to me.'

They walk towards a pair of doors to the right-hand side of the building.

'Who was handling the sale?' De Vries asks.

'What? You mean the estate agents? I don't know.'

'Not Nobulhe Estates?'

Malgas shakes his head. 'Never heard of them. It was one of the big boys. Some bust-up between them and the developers.'

They reach the doors. Malgas pulls hard at the handle and one opens. On the ground-floor level, the interior is completely bare, the only light leaking from slashes of sun through gaps in the concrete slabs. Malgas takes out his torch, shines it around a large, empty foyer. From above, there is a pitiful scream, which reverberates on the concrete around them.

De Vries has one hand on his weapon, the other clenched tight. 'Shit.'

Malgas shines the torch at his face, making himself look ghoulish.

'It's fucking kids, or druggies. We've tried to clear them but they come back. You go up there, you need protective suits. Even then if they're high they come for you with syringes.'

'Jesus.'

De Vries smells the remnants of bitter, acidic smoke, sees polythene bags and greasy newspaper balled up in the corner opposite the entrance. The howl sounds again. He cannot tell whether it is male or female: it is animal-like, as if something is trapped in a snare. 'This place is a death trap.'

'These people, that's why they come here,' Malgas says. 'They're half dead already.' He turns, pointing his torch at ground level towards an open door, leading to a set of concrete steps down. There is police crime-scene tape over the frame at waist level. Malgas pulls it away, takes the lead down the stairs.

Above them, there is staccato laughter, but it is not happy: choking, coughing, maniacal. The sound follows them down the bare staircase, reverberating from wall to wall as it tumbles ahead into the subterranean space.

'You carrying?'

De Vries nods, takes the final step down, eyes straining in the gloom, heart pumping hard. He follows the beam of light from the torch, jumps when Malgas speaks.

'This would have been the plant room, electrical controls, air-con, security. Watch yourself on the ceiling where you step up. It's low.'

A few steps further, the windowless room opens out on both sides, the ceiling low, the air thick and warm. Within moments De Vries feels claustrophobic; his nostrils itch and burn.

Malgas sweeps his torch beam to the left, then turns right, walks as far as he can go, stops, illuminates a patch of concrete floor, scratches and stains still showing through the dust. 'Right here.'

'What was there?'

Malgas points the torch at him. 'You'll see in the pictures.'

De Vries shakes his head, protecting his eyes with his palms against the glare of the beam. Malgas lowers it.

'What did *you* see? Tell me, Danie. I want it in your words.'

'Okay. It was like some kind of modern art – sculpture.' He moves the torch beam jaggedly along a patch of ground. 'Paving blocks, about half a metre square, laid out, nine, ten blocks high, like a bench, but at an angle, like a reclining chair, a couch ... but hard, you know? Her arms are tied behind her around the back of the blocks, her thighs around the entire mass of the thing, ankles, spreading her legs, to each corner. You should have seen the marks on her. He tied her so hard the blood can't pass. Her thighs were blown up like purple balloons ... He leaves her skirt, bra, no knickers.' Malgas hesitates. 'Shit, piss, blood – the angle she was lying in, man. It was fucking horrible.'

'Black cable ties?'

'Black cable ties, linked together.' He points his torch to the foot of where he has indicated the stone couch to have been. 'And then there was a second pile, about a metre high, kind of a stool, like he was sitting on it, looking at her.'

De Vries feels cold in his palms. The pads of his fingers swim in sweat as he rubs them against one another, pressure growing.

They stand silently, side by side, staring at the bare ground.

De Vries asks quietly, 'What made you think he'd done it before?'

'You know how it is? You don't say so. You don't say out loud. But, Jesus ... You want to rape a girl, maybe you bring her down here, you shove her up against the wall, maybe tie her up, screw her, leave her, kill her, I don't know. But this? He'd had to have planned it out, taken his time, stacked up the concrete slabs, made this place. Some kind of torture chamber. He knew the site was empty, no one around for months. Even if anyone came in, he'd hear them on the stairs.'

'The kids, squatters?'

'Upstairs where it's light, kind of rooms on the lower floors, views from the top, sure, but down here? Why?' De Vries nods. 'Anyway, Crime Scene said the swing lock on the door back there in the hallway could have had a padlock on it. There are scratches. If anyone got curious, they couldn't get in.'

'What about her face?'

Malgas shrugs. 'Tape over her mouth. Not there when we found her, but glue on her lips, on her cheeks.'

'Her expression?'

''Bout how you look when you've been raped and starved.'

'Nothing happened to her eyes?'

'No.'

'No posing post-mortem?'

'Not that was noted. Your vic the same? Different?'

De Vries gestures for the torch, takes it, shines it around the space. Blank, grey, air thick. He swallows, feeling grit in his throat. He wipes his other hand down his face. 'Let's get a drink, Danie.'

They take a table at the back of Ben's Diner, near the padded bar, away from the other customers sitting in the window overlooking Beach Road and the ocean beyond. The waitress moves a fan so that it blows directly across them, brings them two light beers. Malgas seems to know the staff. They leave menus and stay away from the policemen.

'Of course, we're still working it,' Malgas says, 'but you know how it is.'

'A dozen other cases . . .'

'Two dozen, three. Take this copy of the docket. I keep 'em close by in case anything suddenly strikes me but, these days, that doesn't happen so much.' He glances around, sees no one within earshot. 'I know you can't say, but just tell me. You seen this before?'

De Vries nods, jaw locked, voice quiet and tight: 'Bindings, rape, length of time, the facing chair. We need to get the pubic-hair samples back, processed by my guys now. If they find anything on my vic and it's a match, we'll know what we've got.'

'You want me to retrieve it from the lab?' Malgas says. 'And get it to you?'

'*Ja*. My boys can do it overnight.'

'That's just unfair, man. We're up to close on ten months now for standard analysis unless we pay to go private.' Malgas gulps down his beer. 'What were you asking about eyes?'

'He took them out of her. My girl, Bethany Miles. Her eyeballs. Put them on the chair facing.'

'Shit.'

'And her facial expression was posed post-mortem.'

'You going to take this on? Marie Garsten?'

'Looks like it. Who else has been involved your end?'

'Just the team.'

'If you tell them to keep quiet, will they do it?'

Malgas tilts his head. 'I don't know, man. The ones who didn't see her, maybe, *ja*. But you take over the case, there'll be questions. I can try.'

'The press'll get it soon enough. We need time without them. You understand what's happening, Danie? If this is the same guy from before Bethany Miles, he's escalating. The posing of the scene, taking the eyes, adjusting the mouth, it indicates growing confidence. If the books are right, then if it was five, six weeks between attacks just now, it'll be less before the next one.'

Malgas holds up his hands. 'This isn't my playground, Vaughn. That's why we have you guys, in your smart suits,' he looks De Vries up and down, smirks, 'and I know you probably get a whole shitload of hassle when you turn up and take away a case, but you aren't going to get any from me.'

'Just get me the sample, *ja*? Today. Now.'

'Sure.'

De Vries looks down at the docket. 'I'd better go.'

'No lunch? The Greek lamb Athena here . . .'

'Not hungry now.'

'Another beer?'

'Nothing, Danie,' De Vries says quietly, as he gets up. 'I feel like nothing.'

Cape Route 62 used to be the major route from Cape Town into the Klein Karoo, linking farming towns for four hundred kilometres east. The communities on the route became wealthy from the traffic but, in 1958, when the South Coast Highway, the N2, was opened, traffic decreased dramatically on the winding inland road, with its mountain passes and long, flat, narrow plains. As a result, many of the towns are still well preserved, unchanged for almost a century, and although the townspeople may not be as wealthy as they used to be, the farmers largely are.

In Montagu, the photographs of the white truck meet with blank expressions and outright denials. Most townsfolk seem to be in bed by nine p.m. Agricultural lorries are the norm here, but it is still too early in the season for anyone to notice them.

Mike Solarin has sent the results of their visits to petrol stations and businesses back to the Greenpoint HQ, via a secure electronic link, and now, Solarin still at the wheel, they drive the sixty-five or so kilometres past yellowing fields, half-empty dams, dried-out riverbeds. On the other side of the mountain range, in the distance to their right, lies Swellendam, an old and always hot early Cape settlement. The temperature rises to forty-three degrees on the little LCD readout in the car. As they approach Barrydale, Solarin realizes that he has read about this country town, how it is an oasis in the crook of the low mountains that bound the route on each side. Now, late in the morning, he sees a low-lying community just off the main road, largely brown and yellow, with just the odd patch of green grass, and a line of healthy-looking trees banking an active stream or river.

He turns the car off the R62 and drops down into the town. Here, scarcely anyone is on the streets. Black farm workers huddle under tall eucalyptus trees, presumably hoping for some casual work later in the day. Visits to the Caltex service station, and other small automotive-based businesses, yield nothing.

'Why would these guys turn off the highway to come here?'

Solarin turns to Ray Black. 'Because they're running low on fuel – they're maybe three hundred kilometres from Oudtshoorn. The owner thinks the tank of the stolen truck was only half full.'

'They not turning off. No way.'

Solarin is hot, claustrophobic, bored by the repetition of questions, the only variation being language. Here, Afrikaans predominates; the words themselves seem spoken in reluctant, dry, disparaging tones.

'We're just doing our job. You heard Colonel Juiles: we're not paid to think.'

Black snorts. 'This your first taskforce?' Solarin nods. 'Each one you're part of, you'll enjoy it less. Trust me.'

'What is it?' Du Toit says. 'Why are you shutting the door?'

'Bad news.'

'Where have you been anyway?'

'I've been in Strand talking with Danie Malgas.' De Vries sits. 'You remember him? Six weeks ago, he investigated a scene where a woman . . .' he looks down at the report in his lap '. . . Marie Garsten, was found bound to paving blocks, clothes the same, raped, a chair facing her.'

Du Toit's eyes widen. 'How did you find this out? The JOC – Joint Operational Committee – meeting isn't until next week.'

'One of my team was, tangentially, discussing cases with officer friends from Strand. They realized that something similar was on the books there. He kept it quiet, but reported it to me. Captain – Lieutenant Malgas was the assigned detective. I met him, looked over the scene, have a copy of the docket.'

'Her eyes?'

'Not removed, but he raped her and their guys think he may have left pubic hairs. We might get lucky. I'm having Malgas intercept the samples at the lab – if he can find them – and bring them here today. I've asked for a re-examination: maybe our guys will find something more on Bethany Miles.'

'At least we'll know for certain, but, Vaughn, if it is . . . My God . . . This changes everything.'

'Until the press get it, it changes nothing. We link the crimes, we compare. If we can find links, we can find him.'

'It's not that simple,' Du Toit says, already anxious. 'If the press find out we have, let's say, a multiple killer, and we didn't tell them about it, didn't warn the public . . . You see where this goes?'

Du Toit and De Vries's loyalty to one another has been constant, but De Vries resents how his boss always reduces his work to how it will be seen, how it will be judged. To him, this deviates from their only task – to find the killer – but Du Toit has adapted to the new media-friendly SAPS, to the corporate world, and that is how he sees his role.

'Until we have a sample comparison, we know nothing, so nothing need be said. My team will start work assuming linkage, but it'll be kept solely within our group. If and when we know, you or the big boss himself, General Thulani, can make the call on what you tell everyone. Is that fair enough, Henrik?'

Du Toit nods.

'Our esteemed general cannot make his office cold enough right now. Passed over for the Provincial Command in the re-shuffle, the bomb, and now, possibly, this.' Du Toit looks up. 'You'll get in more personnel?'

'Already in hand. I have a contact who might be able to assist with a psychological profile too. I'll talk to her this evening.'

Du Toit smiles. 'The charming Dr Bellingham? Apparently you were seen dining *à deux*.'

'If that's supposed to mean together, then yes. Grace Bellingham and I go back, as you remember, sir.'

'Try to keep it on a professional level, Vaughn. You mix it up with personal stuff, it compromises her position and yours and, far more importantly, the case.' He fiddles with items on his desk. De Vries can see his restless leg twitching, the foot bouncing rapidly on the floor. Du Toit continues: 'I'm going to have to tell General Thulani. I can't let you brief your team on this and keep him in the dark. Just do me a favour: if he asks to see you, behave. I don't know why, but he and David Wertner, the Internal Investigation Unit, are leaving us alone right now. Ever since we started this Special Crimes Unit, they've been on our backs ... Significantly, they're even leaving you alone. So, if they're not on your case, try to keep it that way.'

'I must be a terrible weight on your shoulders, sir.'

Du Toit smiles wanly. 'Without your results you'd be dead weight. Remember that.'

He is intercepted by Don February even before he reaches the squad-room.

'Thomas Vermeulen in the interview room for you, sir. Neither parent would attend, so as he is only fifteen years old, I have a duty social worker on standby.'

De Vries nods. 'I'll talk to him just now. Get the social worker in there, will you? And then, Don, have everyone in here for a meeting at . . .' He glances at his watch. 'Let's say two thirty, *ja*? Everyone.'

'A breakthrough from your meeting?'

'Yes and no. I'll tell you when I'm done with this Vermeulen boy.'

The signs to Ronnie's Sex Shop always startle, even if you know they're coming. The road is featureless in either direction, the mind wanders: people have been known to drive off the road into the Little Karoo until their car hits a tree or rock.

The small, rectangular building is plain and white. To one side there is a dirty concrete foundation on which a deck and pergola in orange wood sit, with a plethora of parasols, providing the merest protection from the blasting sun. Wind, so hot it sucks the moisture from your mouth, gusts across the car park. Inside, curious visitors discover a tiny bar, overhung with autographed brassières, graffitied walls, and Ronnie himself, white beard so long it drags over the cluttered counter. When he first opened here, fifty kilometres from anywhere, no one came until his friends added the word 'sex' to the painted name.

When Mike Solarin and Ray Black park outside, before they have time to open their doors a party of, maybe, thirty bikers arrives, engines revving, dust flying. One parks close to the driver's door of the Toyota.

'I'll take these guys,' Black says. 'You happy with that?'

'Biker at heart?'

'Have a Goldwing.'

83

Solarin raises his eyebrows, watches the warrant officer get out, greet the men as they take off their helmets. Solarin edges over the gearstick onto the passenger seat, then out into the car park. The side deck is full, buzzing with tourists. He moves indoors, speaks to Ronnie and a few taciturn locals, nursing beers disconsolately. The tourists on the deck seem a waste of time, even to him, but he undertakes the task, asking questions and showing the pictures of the Nissan truck. When he has finished, he looks over at the bikers. Ray Black is laughing with them. He does not appear to be questioning them, or showing them the pictures of the truck. When the first group of men start to walk towards the bar, Black goes with them.

'Ray.' The man turns. 'We're going.'

Black's shoulders slump. He breaks away from the group, strolls towards him. 'Thought we could grab a beer, maybe talk to these guys casually . . .'

'No. We have to go.' He tosses the keys at him. 'And you're driving.'

Thomas Vermeulen sits in the interview room looking so relaxed, so self-confident, that the sullen female social worker with him seems the more apprehensive. De Vries sits opposite him.

'You remember me from two nights back?'

Vermeulen shrugs.

'You described how you and your friends entered Apostle Lodge. Have you anything you want to add to what you said?'

'No.' The boy pouts.

'You been in that house before?'

'No.'

'Never been in there? In the garden?'

'Told you. Patrick said he'd seen the gardener with the keys put them in the pot. Never been near that place.'

'Patrick Cloete, from across the road?'

'Yeah.'

'When my warrant officer spoke to your mother, she said you'd been out at night a lot. Is that right?'

Thomas Vermeulen laughs stridently. 'She say that?'

'She did.'

He shakes his head, smile cocky. 'Dunno how she'd know. She's always pissed way before dinner. Usually drops a plate on the kitchen floor. Stays there till the maid comes. I need my food, so I go out.'

De Vries studies him. Behind the swagger, there is something empty in his eyes. De Vries does not know whether it is an escape from a domestic nightmare, or something else, something more defined and premeditated. 'Your parents at work?'

'Dad is,' he says, 'but, you know . . . Mum, some bar with her friends.'

'Do you spend time out of your house at night?'

He shrugs. 'Yes. Course.'

'Where do you go?'

'Places. Down the beach, over the Mountain: Long Street, Green Point.'

'On your own?'

'Sometimes. Sometimes with mates.'

Vermeulen's face is narrow, nose sharp, eyes squinting to focus. His skin is pale and spotty. When he is speaking, he seems relaxed but, when De Vries stops, remains silent. De Vries sees the unease, senses discomfort almost emanate from him.

'When you go out, when you come back, you see anyone around Apostle Lodge?'

He shakes his head.

'Neighbours? A car?'

'No.'

'Where were you? At night, when your mother says you weren't at home.'

Vermeulen says nothing.

De Vries can see the pulse in his neck beating fast.

'I'll make it easy, Thomas. Generally, I don't care what people are doing, where they are. I'm interested in only one thing. A woman was held, raped and murdered in Apostle Lodge, almost opposite your house. I need to know where you were, who you were with, and exactly when, for the last week. You give me that, I leave you alone.'

The boy swallows. 'What if I don't want to say?'

'You can talk to the lady next to you. She's a social worker here to check we're treating you right. She'll tell you that we never repeat what we're told in here unless it links to our investigation. She and I guarantee that we won't repeat what you tell me to anyone. Not your parents, not anyone else.'

Vermeulen's eyes swivel towards the woman, back again to De Vries's neck. Eye contact, scarce before, has now transmuted to none. The boy's demeanour has changed entirely, the brittle confidence cracking. 'What if it's something else?'

'What? What is it?'

'What if it's something that might get someone into trouble?'

'If it's not serious, it won't matter. There's no statement here, no record. We're just talking . . .'

Vermeulen shakes his head, his lips closed tightly.

'The point is, if you don't tell me, I have to consider you a suspect. That means I, or other officers, will have to investigate where you were, what you were doing, officially. Then we involve your folks, your friends, the law. Or you can tell me and, if it's nothing, I can get on with catching the man who did this.'

De Vries sees blood rising to the boy's face, his lips suddenly dry. He has seen these physical reactions so many times, knows now that it is sex or drugs, probably sex. He wishes he did not have to make the boy speak.

'I meet someone. We hang out together. I always come home.'

'I need to know who it is.'

He shakes his head. 'I can't tell you.'

'Why not?'

'Just can't.'

De Vries's way would have been to bang the table, jolt the information out of the boy, but he has watched Don February quietly and gently coax information from witnesses and he has pledged to try this method first. It is an effort to remain calm, keep his voice even.

'Whoever it is, whatever you're doing, it doesn't matter. You have to account for your whereabouts.'

'If I say, he'll get into trouble.'

De Vries hears the male pronoun, knows this makes it harder still, remembers that Vermeulen is only fifteen, fears that this now opens new avenues of investigation, reports to other agencies. All his life, sex has brought him pleasure and pain, the former out-weighing the latter, but, professionally, it is nothing but trouble. It seals people's lips, ferments lies and distortion, results seemingly only in recrimination and misery.

'All right, listen to me. I don't care what you and this guy do together. If you have a problem with it, you're being forced into something you don't want, tell me now. I'll deal with him, and that will be it. But if you're happy with what goes on, just tell me who it is. I'll speak to him myself. Just me. I give you my guarantee, he will be in no trouble. You understand?'

De Vries feels the social worker's stare, ignores her, remains focused on the boy.

'It's about priorities and trust,' De Vries says. 'I have to stop a man who has raped and killed. Who could do again what he's done. That is more important than embarrassment and discomfort on your part. What we do, who we do it with, it's up to you. I don't care. Anyway, you're nearly an adult and you can do whatever you want.'

'You tell my parents?'

'No.'

'You promise?'

'I promise.'

Vermeulen looks at the woman. De Vries looks at her. She shakes her head.

'He's called . . . He's called . . . Tom Stoker.'

'That's good. Where does he live?'

'Flats top of Long Street, across from the baths. The block with the giant ad all over the windows.'

De Vries pushes paper and pen across the table. 'Write down the address for me.'

Vermeulen starts writing. De Vries sees his hand shake, eyes redden. The boy pushes the paper back to him.

'When were you here, at this address, in the last week?'

The boy's eyes widen, his teeth grit. He speaks from beneath the flap of blond hair in front of his eyes, the sides of his head shaven. 'Most evenings. Not Wednesday, not Sunday. That's when we went into the garden, went into the house. Flies everywhere, disgusting. Saw the woman's arm . . .'

'One more time: you've never been inside Apostle Lodge before?'

'Never.'

'Okay.' De Vries stands, thanks him. He thanks the social worker, ushers her out of the room, turns to Vermeulen, who is still sitting, eyes down, says quietly, 'No one's judging you. There's

88

nothing to be ashamed of. But you're young, and there are laws to protect you, whether you think you need protecting or not.' He produces one of his cards. 'Be careful. You want help. Call my number.'

Vermeulen takes the card, meets De Vries's eye.

'I don't need help.'

De Vries knows that his investigation has done what it always does: opens sores, overturns rocks, disrupts and disorients. Every secret in every life with which he comes into contact is laid bare and then – almost always – man, woman and secret discarded.

They stand facing one another, Vermeulen leaning on the table with his fingertips, swaying. De Vries watches as the boy's face reddens, tears form, his body shakes, he begins to cry. De Vries pushes the door closed with his shoe, lets him sit back down, arms curled around his head, face on the table; sits opposite him, waits.

The road from Ronnie's Sex Shop is relatively featureless. Ray Black drives fast, but well. The air-conditioning seems to be faltering, the cabin heating steadily.

'You show your friends the Nissan pictures?'

'Ja.'

'And?'

'And nothing. Few of them said maybe, but they pass a hundred trucks, even along here.'

'You note their IDs?'

Black turns momentarily to face him. 'No one said yes. "Maybe". That was it. That's nothing.' He turns back to the road.

'Next time anyone says "maybe", I want their ID and their statement. When, where, how many drivers? It may not mean anything on its own, but it can build up to form a picture and then we may get a break. You clear, Ray?'

'You're in charge.'

'*Ja*. Slow down to a hundred k.p.h. I want to be able to see where we're going, what we're passing. You may think this is shit, but we'll do it right.'

The report of the investigation into the murder of Marie Garsten mirrors his own team's work on Bethany Miles. Marie Garsten was thirty-eight, married for eleven years, three children, a house in Somerset West not ten kilometres from where she was found. Her car discovered unlocked, abandoned around the back of a small retail cluster on the outskirts of town. No cameras, no witnesses. The search for her began immediately, without recourse to the twenty-four-hour period for missing persons, and continued in earnest for five days, overseen by a sergeant from Stellenbosch SAPS, a friend of the victim's husband, who ensured that extra officers were drafted in to look for her. Their reports show extensive questioning, a roadblock on the main drag from which the mini-mall car park was accessed, flat-to-flat enquiries in the nearby residential area. Just as De Vries's own team had discovered, her abductor had left no trace. A man presumably, unnoticed.

De Vries looks up from the copy of the docket, knows that there must have been a car, a period of time when, even if he is parked right next to his victim's vehicle, he must assault her and then get her into his own vehicle. This involves a high level of risk. That both known attacks have taken place in daylight displays a knowledge of the areas involved and the confidence to carry out the assaults. A plan of the parking area shows that the victim's car was parked to the side of the shops, under trees, presumably to provide shade. They had also provided cover for the abduction.

The post-mortem examination on Marie Garsten indicated severe bruising on the back of her head, consistent with her being struck by a heavy object, probably rendering her unconscious. When she came to, she would have found herself held captive, either in a car or van, or already in the basement of the apartment block. From there, if she were able to cry out, either no one would hear her or she would have been assumed to be just another homeless addict.

The whiteboard is now divided into two sections. One for Marie Garsten, one for Bethany Miles.

'This afternoon,' De Vries tells the meeting, 'Sergeant Frazer and Warrant February will co-ordinate you to build profiles for these two victims, to search for connections between them and, importantly, whether they ever met. Within that search, we hope to find locations, perhaps even people, in common. Until we find forensic evidence on Bethany Miles that can be compared to the pubic hairs taken from Marie Garsten, we won't know for certain that these two murders are the work of the same man, but we will work on that assumption for the rest of today. No word of the possible connection between these crimes is to be discussed outside this room. If these crimes are connected, if they are the developing work of one killer, then we face the possibility that this is just the beginning of a sequence of crimes. We cannot afford to let that information leak to the public and risk starting a panic.'

He looks to the back of the room, sees both Henrik du Toit and Norman Classon observing him.

'No one goes home until after we meet here at six p.m. If you're out on enquiries, Sergeant Frazer must be updated with your information before five forty-five.'

He steps away from the board, walks slowly towards the back of the room. He can hear Don February and Sally Frazer putting his orders into action. The sensation tangibly pleases him.

'What did our great leader have to say?'

Brigadier Du Toit speaks quietly, keeping De Vries between him and the rest of the room: 'General Thulani said what we would expect: we wait until we hear about DNA. If we do. Obviously, anything we turn up between now and that point will influence what we tell the public.'

'The bloody public.'

Classon laughs.

'We are but servants,' Du Toit says.

'I hate the fucking public.'

'And, doubtless,' Du Toit says calmly, 'the feeling is mutual.' He seems unwilling, perhaps unable, to rise to the bait. 'Just get on with it, and report to me before you leave, *ja*?'

De Vries bows. 'Yes, sir.'

'We're running everyone through the system as fast as we can,' Sally Frazer tells him, standing at the corner of his desk. 'Only one hit that may be significant. Gregory Harrisson, works for Nobuhle Estates, was arrested for attempted rape in 2013. The case was moving to court, but the victim changed her mind and refused to testify so the case was dropped.'

'Who was the victim?'

'You'll have to find that out.' She speed-reads a print-out. 'She was a thirty-year-old Caucasian woman, resident in Blouberg. I only have a precis of the statement. She claimed stalking and, after she'd attempted to reason with him, he tried to overpower her in her apartment.'

'Nothing else?'

'That's it. I have the docket code if you want to see the detail.'

'I'll follow that up. Don and I spoke to him. Guy's too smooth for his own good.' De Vries hesitates. 'Does it say what he was doing in 2013 in Blouberg?'

'He was working in real estate there too. AE Estates was the company. He was laid off when he was charged.'

'Good. Do me a favour. Call Nobuhle Estates – Don's got the details – see if you can locate Dlomo Nobuhle. Don and I have tried, but she's keeping well out of the way. I want her at her office or in here today. Maybe a woman's voice will appeal to her more – and, if you do get to her, don't mention Greg Harrisson.'

Frazer tilts her head. 'I'll put on my best woman's voice, sir.'

They cross the Touws river and, after half an hour, come to Ladismith. Every parked car they pass is covered with a thin layer of orange dust; even the palms and jacaranda trees are heavy with it. They take the right-angled turn to stay on the R62 by the Little Karoo Co-op, drive through the quiet Karoo town, its farm shops and cafés largely empty, traffic light, pull into Hicks garage on South Street.

Mike Solarin asks the black attendant to fill the tank with unleaded to the top, walks across the forecourt to the kiosk, feels the cool air from the fans blow across him, drying his sweat. He pulls four cans of cold drink from the fridge cabinets and approaches the cash desk. In broken Afrikaans, he asks if there is anywhere in the town that might be able to recharge air-con. '*Is daar 'n winkel in die stad wat lugversorging kan herlaai?*'

The answer comes back gruffly in English. 'At Larry's.' She looks at her watch. 'But he sleeps afternoons.'

Solarin laughs, pays for the cool drinks, asks about the Nissan truck, showing the photograph. The cashier stares blankly at it. He shows it to her colleague, who shakes her head, returns to checking social media on her phone. He turns, pauses under the fans, exits the little shop and walks briskly back to the car. At the side of the building, next to the entrance to the toilets, he sees Ray

93

Black talking on his cellphone. Solarin squints at him, studies his body language, until the attendant re-holsters the fuel pump, announces the cost. Solarin pays, asks him to clean the front and rear screens, tips him three rand. Ray Black saunters back to the car.

'Important call?'

He looks up at Solarin, meets his eye. 'Girlfriend. Not happy I'm away.'

'I got cool drinks anyway.'

'Okay. We have something to eat here? There's a coffee shop just back there. Give the car a chance to cool, *ja*?'

Solarin wants to drive on, knows there are more towns and villages in closer proximity to one another, that Calitzdorp and even Oudtshoorn itself are within striking distance. It is after four p.m. They have made good progress.

'*Ja*. Let's eat.'

By six p.m., it becomes apparent that there are few connections between Bethany Miles and Marie Garsten. They are both white, in their thirties, married with children. They live fifty kilometres apart, children go to different schools, with no apparent overlap, husbands work in different professions. Marie Garsten had qualified as an accountant, but had never practised, preferring instead to bring up her children. Bethany Miles had worked part-time before she married. If they ever met, no one has so far discovered where; if they have friends in common, no connection has yet been found. De Vries has failed to speak with Mark Garsten, the first victim's widower, as he has moved his children to Durban to be with his parents. He expects to reach him, by telephone, in Durban the following morning at eight thirty a.m. He dismisses his officers by six thirty, tells them to arrive early for work tomorrow and prepare for a long day.

He returns to his office, frustrated, the energy ebbing from him. Sally Frazer appears at his door, waits for him to look up.

'I spoke to a woman at the Camps Bay office of Nobuhle Estates. She said that Miss Nobuhle is not answering her cell and that her answer machine is switched off . . . but, with a bit of persuasion, I did get her to admit that the reason might be because she has been attending a big pan-African real-estate conference from Monday to today, trying to do some big deal for the company.'

De Vries nods. 'Can't let anything get in the way of business. Where is this conference?'

'Up till,' she twists her wrist and glances down, 'just now, it's been at the International Conference Centre, but at eight tonight, there's a reception for delegates at the Grand Africa Café & Beach.'

De Vries raises his eyebrows. 'All right for some.'

Sally Frazer smiles. 'I'll be here until later anyway.'

'You were here early. Get home.'

'Nothing is more important than this.'

'That what I always used to say – and look at me now. Get some rest. I'll see you first thing.'

She backs out of the doorway, moves to her desk, sits down.

Lacy's Coffee Shop is styled like an American diner: light blue leatherette semicircular banquettes, stools up at the counter, two elderly waitresses smelling of nicotine, wearing pale blue paper hats at a jaunty angle, desultorily waiting tables. It is cool, rather than cold, largely quiet, but for a couple both wearing dungarees, sitting in silence opposite one another. The girl has a black eye the colour of her boyfriend's intensely tattooed arms. Solarin stares at her until she sees him and scowls.

They order steak, eggs and fries, sit to wait with coffees and cool drinks. Ray Black's cellphone rings. He glances at the display and stands. 'Be back just now.'

He ambles out of the restaurant onto the forecourt. Solarin studies him, wonders what is so private that he would endure the dry afternoon heat to avoid being overheard. The plates of food arrive, eggs speckled with black burned flecks. Solarin waits momentarily, then begins to eat. Ray Black looks frustrated and angry. They appear to make eye contact momentarily, although, through the dusty glass, Solarin is not certain that Black sees him. Black turns his back to him, continues to talk.

When he has eaten half his food, Black comes back in, sits, sighs heavily. Solarin looks at him. Black says: 'Food good?'

'*Ja*. Okay.' He studies his fork going into the food, to his mouth and back again; does not look up.

The law of the land is that alcohol may not be consumed on a public beach. It is, at least on the fashionable beaches of Cape Town, a rule to which everyone quite strictly adheres. The Grand Africa Café & Beach, behind an unassuming broken-tarmac car park, is a warehouse of a restaurant, also containing a couple of boutiques, which spills out onto a man-made sandy beach, with tables, chairs, umbrellas and modern art, leading down to a geometrical concrete breakwater, permitting little, if any, access to the icy seas just beyond the Waterfront. For New Year's Eve and many balmy summer evenings, it is one of the places for the wealthy of Cape Town and myriad tourists to wile away an evening, with alcohol, right next to the roiling ocean.

De Vries parks several hundred metres down Beach Road, which joins the Waterfront to the newly fashionable Mouille Point, around the dramatic and beautiful Cape Town stadium, a much underused legacy of the 2010 World Cup finals. Even now, after dark, the sea air moves slowly over the land, salt and pollution mingling to form a syrupy breeze, which seems to heat, not cool, all who stand within it.

He ambles down through the rough car park, arrives at the outer entrance to the venue, prepares to joust with the imported security guards to gain access. At the sight of his ID, the guard ushers him inside immediately, along the boardwalk and towards the glowing cavern of the main building. On his right, there are photographers taking no notice of him; to his left, the yellow beach is awash with the well-dressed, violently groomed glitterati of Cape Town, along with, he assumes, estate agents. The sun has set beneath the horizon, but the sky still glows a pinky-yellow above dark water.

He takes a glass of Champagne from the tray held aloft by an aloof waiter at the doorway, strolls into the middle of the warehouse space, its vaulted ceiling providing an escape for the hot air forming around him. By the steps down to the beach, people are posing for yet another photo shoot, watched over by others. A few faces seem familiar, if more lined than he remembers. He assumes he recognizes them not professionally but from the cover of some magazine. He pities these people. The celebrities all look hungry, their clothes too tight, faces shiny, hair metallic. He glances around, loses himself in the cacophony of dialogue. They face one another, listeners with a rictus grin, eyes staring past their interlocutor. He imagines they hear nothing but the slow trickling away of their fragile fame.

He walks towards the beach, sees a group of black African women, heads towards them. When he reaches them, they seem to close in around one another, excluding him. He smiles to himself, quite used to the reaction of those who see themselves as above him.

'Dlomo Nobuhle. I'm here to meet her.'

They turn to study him; one seems embarrassed, an almost imperceptible shudder.

'Miss Nobuhle?'

She detaches herself from the group, smile beaming, gestures for him to follow her away from the group, down the beach towards the breakwater where there are few guests. She turns in the sand to face him. 'What do you want? Who are you?'

'You know who I am, Miss Nobuhle. I am the policeman who has been leaving you messages for two days – until you turned off your voicemail – because a murder occurred in one of the properties your company is marketing.'

Her eyes flare. He sees her lips purse, anger rising.

'How dare you come here! This is a private occasion. I am at work.'

De Vries now has his back to the sea, looks past her to the party up the beach, the coloured lights in strings above the tables, the jazz band on the tiny stage built out over the sand, platters of canapés held above waiters' heads. On the surface, it is a glamorous and beautiful scene on such an evening.

'You think that a party is more important than the life of a woman, bound and raped, perhaps tortured and left for dead?'

'It is not my house and, besides, she is dead now. Nothing I do will bring her back.'

De Vries listens to the harsh voice, each word enunciated individually. Her hair is beautifully plaited into two horns, which are pushed back from her temples, like those of an oryx, her make-up is exotic and immaculate, but her mouth is small and, he thinks, ugly.

'When I have completed my business here, then I will return my calls. That will be on Monday. Now, go away. I have deals to be completed and contracts to sign.'

She turns away from him, begins to stride up the sand.

'Dlomo Nobuhle.' His voice is loud now, his hand stretched out displaying his ID. She stops, turns again. 'You speak with me now, or I will arrest you right here, cuff you, and lead you out across this charming party to my car. And then you will spend the weekend in my cells before you talk to me on Monday.'

She hurries back towards him, ankle turning in the sand as she stumbles, gesturing for him to lower his voice. Already, behind her, he can see groups twisting to look down towards the sea.

'You can't do this.'

'I can, and I will.' She opens her painted mouth again, but he continues. 'If you talk with me now, maybe for ten minutes, then you can return to your party and complete your business. This is your last chance.'

She shudders, overcome with frustration. 'You will show me your ID again and you will hear from my attorney.' She turns. 'Come with me. We will talk in my car.'

She strides towards the entrance across the beach, ignoring the enquiring glances from guests as she passes. De Vries follows at a saunter, out along the fairy light-lit boardwalk into the car park. Ahead, he sees her throw open the door to a black BMW Z4, slam it shut. He ambles to the car, opens the passenger door, gets in.

'If my deals are interrupted because of you, I will sue the police.'

De Vries waits until she turns to him.

'As the owner of the sole agency representing the sale of Apostle Lodge, you are responsible for its security. When I investigate a murder, I expect the co-operation of everyone. If you receive a message from a member of the SAPS again, answer it immediately.'

'Do not lecture me. You think I do not know about our history?'

De Vries stay calm, feels unaffected by her constant threats and barbs. 'There is no history here, Miss Nobuhle. If you want co-operation, threats will not ease your path. Are you ready to answer my questions?'

'Show me your ID.'

He produces it again.

She takes her cellphone, pushes it close up to the pass, photographs it twice. 'You ask what you want now, hope that you still have your job in the morning.'

He smiles again. 'When did you, personally, last enter Apostle Lodge?'

She angles her head down towards her lap, her jaw tight.

'I do not conduct tours. I am the owner of an important business. My job is to supervise and control.'

'So, have you never been inside Apostle Lodge?'

'Of course. High-worth properties receive my personal appraisal.'

'So, when were you last there?'

'I met with the owner maybe four years ago. Since then once, last year, to check that the open house was set up how I had specified. Maybe April. I am not in charge of the disposal of that property. That is the responsibility of Gregory Harrisson, one of my sales representatives.'

'Has anyone contacted you personally concerning Apostle Lodge in the last eighteen months?'

'No. There has been no interest in that property. It is unrealistically priced.'

'Why have you kept it on your books?'

'I told the vendor that I would sell his property, and when he is realistic about the price, that is what I shall do.'

'And it looks good to have a premium property on your books?'

'I have many such properties.'

'There are no other eight-figure properties in your window.'

100

She opens her mouth, hesitates, flicks away the question with her left hand. 'I have many.'

'Apart from the three members of staff in your Camps Bay office and yourself, who has access to the key safe at that office?'

'No one. Apart from me, only Gregory Harrisson has a key. He acts as the day manager for that office.'

'But the safe is left open during the day?'

'That is not procedure. The safe is to be locked at all times.'

'It was open when I visited.'

'Then procedure has been violated. I am not responsible for the failings of my staff.'

'Have you lost or mislaid your keys in the last four years?'

'No.'

'No?'

'I tell you. No.'

'Are you aware of the owner of Apostle Lodge returning to Cape Town since he left?'

'No. He emails me every three months to hear what viewings have been conducted, and tells me at what price I should advertise his property.'

'How many viewings have your colleagues conducted in the last eighteen months?'

'I have conducted none, but my staff have shown the house maybe six times.'

'Six times? You have the details of those you showed around?'

'The details will be in the office.'

'Before you employed Greg Harrisson, did you check his criminal record?'

She smiles, twists to face him, tone sarcastic. 'Oh, yes. I know about Gregory's past. He told me when I interviewed him, but he was not convicted. The woman who accused him was unreliable and weak. Besides, what do I care? This is business and Gregory is my number-one sales representative.'

101

'You are not worried about him showing houses to women alone?'

'No. Why should I be?'

'Because of his past.'

'His past, as you say, was made up by one woman and you, the SAPS. It is nothing.'

'Have you ever met or had business dealings with Luke or Bethany Miles?'

'I do not know these people.'

'Bethany Miles was found dead in Apostle Lodge.'

She shrugs. 'Okay.'

'Have any of your staff ever lent keys to or used properties that you were selling?'

'No. They would be fired if they did.'

De Vries thinks about further questions, realizes that, however much he may dislike Dlomo Nobuhle, she has told him what he wanted to know, the relevant boxes ticked.

'When will that property be available for my people to clean and prepare it for showing?'

'Very soon, Miss Nobuhle.' He opens the door and steps out.

Before he closes it, he hears her say, 'Policeman.'

He ducks down to see into the cabin.

'You are not even saying my name right. It is Nobuhle. Nobuhle, you understand?'

De Vries drives from the stadium back into town, up Long Street, onto Orange Street, stops in a lay-by close to the 15 On Orange Hotel. He dials Grace Bellingham's cellphone number.

'I can't talk now.'

'I wanted to see you.' He can hear that he sounds too casual, too desperate. 'To say sorry for the other night.' In the background, he can hear conversation, music.

'I'm busy tonight. Call me tomorrow.'

'Later?'

'Tomorrow.' She disconnects the call.

De Vries is tired and hungry, does not know whether to eat or sleep. He turns up the air-conditioning, wipes sweaty hands on his shirt, drives through the night towards a bar, towards beer.

The road twists around the low mountains, the sun blinding him in his rear-view mirror when the car faces due west. There are hints of dusk in the sky to the south. Ray Black guides him off the R62, down Hoof Street towards Zoar, then double-backing to the settlement of Amalienstein down Suikerbos Avenue. The roads are dirt tracks here; behind them, they leave a thick dusty trail, which hangs in the air.

'Why here, Ray?'

'Cos this is the kind of place they might come, stop off.'

Mike Solarin looks at the low shacks, each with its own burned-out backyard. There are a few stalls but no shops, no garage. He pulls over. 'There's nothing here.'

'You wanted everywhere checked. Thought we should tick this one off too.'

Solarin points to a tiny superette under a corrugated-iron roof on the corner of the street ahead. 'You go ask in there, Ray.'

Black collects pictures, clambers out of the car, walks along the road.

Mike Solarin gets out also, stretches. They have been driving for only half an hour, forty minutes since eating, and already he feels stiff and sticky. His cellphone rings; a number he does not recognize. 'Mike Solarin.'

'Lieutenant, Colonel Juiles. Where are you?'

'Between Ladismith and Calitzdorp, sir.'

'Good progress. There've been developments here. We're recalling everyone to HQ.'

'Suspects?'

'We've made identifications. I'm not discussing it now. We need
you and Warrant Black back. Turn round, retrace your steps, drop
down to the N2, whatever you want. Get you back tonight, ready
for work tomorrow.'

'You want us back tonight?'

'That is correct, Lieutenant.'

'Yes, sir.'

'Tomorrow, eight a.m., both of you. We have a debriefing and
new assignments.'

He disconnects. Solarin stares at the home-screen of his cellphone.

'Nothing.'

Solarin turns. Ray Black stands on the other side of the vehicle.

'We're going back.'

'What?'

'Back to Cape Town now.'

'Why?'

'Orders.'

Black gets into the driver's seat, slams his door. Solarin waits a
moment. No complaint, no argument, no curiosity; Black's phone
taken out of his left trouser pocket as he got in when, as he left
the car, he put it in his right. He looks down at the roof of the
car to where Ray Black is sitting. Then he climbs into the cabin.

The telephone call between De Vries and Mark Garsten is fruitless and depressing. The man's life has been torn apart. Five weeks
on from the discovery of his wife's body, he seems utterly unable
to cope, to work, to care for his children. At the end of the call,

his father comes onto the line, begs De Vries to find who murdered his daughter-in-law, to make some progress so that his son has some closure to mark the end of one life and the beginning of a new one. De Vries tries not to promise results; has fallen into doing so before now through weakness, left himself with unsustainable pacts and a deeper guilt when failure and the pressure of the next case overcome him.

No sample considered to be from a second party has been discovered on Bethany Miles. De Vries reflects that this, too, may be an escalation. The attacker has realized that he must be more careful, that he must plan more intricately. To his surprise, Brigadier du Toit has concluded that the evidence from the two crime scenes is compelling. As a result, he has met with Assistant Deputy Provisional Commissioner Thulani, and the wheels of the SAPS public-relations machine have begun slowly to turn. De Vries has enjoyed his last few cases, each without interest from the press or requiring interaction with the hierarchy of the elite units. Each quietly resolved, reports complete, charges laid, trials forthcoming.

Work continues on connections between the two known victims. De Vries calls Stephen Jessel, the case-worker who supervises Leigh Finnemore, arranges to meet at his charge's property after lunch. His office is so hot, he longs simply to leave it, and the entire airless, claustrophobic building, to find cool air somewhere. He decides to drive back over Kloof Nek, down into Camps Bay, to talk to Greg Harrisson in the cool of his effectively air-conditioned office.

Before ten at the weekend, traffic is light in Cape Town. He reaches the crest of the pass, waiting only a few moments as the queue of vehicles heading for the cable-car station make their way along Tafelberg Road searching for the already elusive parking spaces. He decides against taking Camps Bay Drive and turns right instead, down the serpentine Kloof Road, between the tall pines and huge boulders, slowing as he takes the sharp turns to enjoy the framed vistas of the bay beneath, the iridescent turquoise sea, the blank, perfectly unblemished blue sky. At the bottom, he turns left to join the strip, already busy with tourists and locals enjoying late breakfasts or cool drinks at the many cafés and restaurants. Stallholders and hawkers block pavements, taxi-vans and minicabs double-park on the street. Everything moves slowly, but, to his delight, when he opens the front windows of his car, a cooler breeze sweeps across him, the air chilled by thousands of kilometres of travel over freezing ocean rooted in Antarctica. On the beach, sunbathers have laid out towels, ice-cream sellers prowl, children run towards the sea and retreat screaming as the ankle-achingly cold water rushes towards them. At some point, probably even earlier this morning, a small group of elderly sun-tanned swimmers will appear with bathing caps, in some cases wetsuits, and wade into the sea for ten minutes. Precious few others will be seen submerged today.

He finds a vacated parking space directly outside Nobuhle Estates, steps out, takes a few paces to the door of the block, climbs the stairs and enters the office. Inside, the cool saturates his clothes. Only Greg Harrisson sits at his desk; otherwise the space is deserted. He sees De Vries, his face struggling to form a smile. He stands up, proffers his hand. 'I'm alone this morning, Colonel.'

'I just have a few questions, Mr Harrisson.'

'Yeah, that's what I'm saying. I can't speak now. I have to keep an eye on everything.'

De Vries's smile contains no more humour than Harrisson's. 'When the phone rings, or a client walks through the door, you can look after them.'

Harrisson sighs, gestures to the chairs in front of his desk. 'You're going to ask me about the girl in Blouberg, aren't you?'

'Why do you think that?'

'I received a late-night call from my boss.'

'Did you now? That was nice of her.'

'Not nice. She doesn't do nice.'

'So, what should I know about the girl in Blouberg?'

'It was nothing. A misunderstanding. I admit I liked her, fancied her. We talked in a bar, I got her number. I called her a few times, she didn't seem keen. I saw her at another bar and went over to her. She was a bit drunk, seemed up for it, so I walked her home. She invited me in, lay on the couch with her legs apart – you know how women can be? I took it as an invitation, but apparently it wasn't. Nothing happened. The charges were dropped.'

'What nothing happened?'

'Nothing. I stopped when she told me to get off her.'

'Just like that?'

Harrisson meets his eye. 'Nobody says different.'

'Well, your victim did, didn't she, at first?'

'She wasn't a victim and she changed her mind, okay?'

'Why was that?'

'She realized I hadn't meant any harm. I'm a red-blooded male. I haven't seen her since. I was happy to move away. It's like another world out there, so far from the Mountain.'

'And Miss Nobuhle grabbed you, did she?'

'I'm good at my job.'

De Vries sees the confidence seep back into Harrisson's demeanour; wonders if he has missed the line of questioning the man had, at first, undoubtedly feared. 'Where do you stay now?'

'Seapoint.'

'Own a place? Renting?'

'Renting just now. Like to feel free.'

'Never know when you're going to be moving on?'

De Vries watches Harrisson's reaction, then sees a shadow in the mirror behind him. Harrisson sits up, expecting the door to the office to open, but the figure moves away again.

'Ever lived in Strand?'

'Strand? *Ja*, for a while. Got one of my first jobs in the industry there . . . 2007. Why?'

'I like to know things. Have you got a girlfriend now?'

Harrisson frowns. 'I don't think I have to discuss my private life with you.'

'You'll find with me, sir, no topic of conversation is out of bounds.'

'Look, I'm twenty-eight. I play the field, go to bars, clubs. Sometimes I meet a girl and I think maybe she could be the one. We bond, you know. Talk into the early hours. But I'm a free agent. I like it that way.'

'What car do you drive?'

'Am I a suspect? Is that what you're telling me here?'

'Yes.'

He answers quietly: 'I have a Sirocco. New model, last year. White. It's around the back in the bay for the office.'

'Have it cleaned?'

'Yes. I expect you have your car cleaned too.'

'When last?'

Harrisson shrugs. 'I don't know. Two weeks?'

'I might just take a look at your car, sir.'

Harrisson snatches up a bunch of keys from his desk, throws them at De Vries. 'Help yourself. Go through the back door. It's right there. I leave the office and the boss sees, shit hits the fan.'

'Tough cookie, is she?'

'You met her.'

'Still have the bruises.'

Harrisson smiles, genuinely this time, stands up as the door from the street opens.

De Vries takes the short corridor to the back of the shop, passing a locked office door, a toilet and a small kitchen area. He unbolts the back door, steps out into the tiny courtyard. The heat slaps his face, the reflection off the white paint of the car stinging his eyes. It stands in one of the two parking spaces beyond a metal sliding gate. De Vries finds the Volkswagen-branded key-fob, depresses the unlocking button and the boot release and pokes inside the sweltering cabin. The back seats are small, the roofline low; access from the door would be difficult even if you were conscious and able-bodied. One back seat is folded forward and the front half of a surfboard is visible. He backs out, slams the door, peers into the boot. Apart from the board, there are flip-flops, a towel, a wetsuit, damp board shorts and half a dozen plastic carrier bags. The carpet is sandy. He studies the gas-struts, trim protectors, cubbyholes, sees nothing suspicious. He closes the hatchback, locks the car, re-enters the back door of the office. Inside, he can hear the agent describing a property to a potential client. He places the keys back on his desk, glances across the surface, walks towards the front.

'That's all in order, Greg,' he says, as he passes him and a young couple. He smiles at them, raises a palm to Harrisson, winks.

'See you soon.'

He drives back up the Camps Bay side of the Mountain. Harrisson's car seems an unlikely vehicle for an abduction, his knowledge of Strand probably no more than coincidental if, at least, marginally significant. He wonders what, on first seeing him enter the office, had so concerned the man, yet, moments later, questions under way, allowed him once again to relax.

The briefing room contains fewer than twenty officers. The lights are on full, the atmosphere flat. Mike Solarin thinks that the ceiling seems lower, that energy has seeped from the space. He sits in the second row of chairs, looks around for Ray Black, but cannot find him.

Colonel Brent Juiles sits on the edge of the table in front of them, casual, as if he is addressing friends.

'Gentlemen . . .' He scans the room, nods to himself, smiles. '*Ja*, just gentlemen. At sixteen hundred hours yesterday, we received positive identification from our labs of the two suspects in the Nissan truck in Long Street. They were Akram Ibrahim Jabouri, twenty-eight, originally from Iraq but from 2013 identified as being in Niger, and known associate Abdu-Allah Baravan, twenty-six. These guys are known to our security services as being loosely associated with al-Mourabitoun, as you should know, also known as al-Qaeda West Africa. They may or may not have had dealings with Abubakar Shekau but, as yet, we have not received a claim for the incident.

'What happens now is that our analysts get to work and try to piece together why these guys should mount an operation in South Africa, Cape Town in particular, and whether their actions were sanctioned or rogue. We're betting on the latter.' He stands, paces from one side of the room to the other.

'No country with corrupt governance has been able to tackle extremists effectively. Resources get diverted before they can be channelled effectively. Bribery is widespread. This is why these people are flourishing in eastern and central Africa and they are moving south. Make no mistake. Authorized or not, this will not be the last we see from these guys.'

He turns to them. 'I want to congratulate all of you. Job well done. I'm standing you down from Cape Town and you'll return to Pretoria in the coming days. You'll be assigned new duties.'

General Thulani's office, so often an icy cave of misery, is today, at least, gloriously cold and refreshing.

'These are dark times,' Thulani intones, looking down from his huge chair at his long-time colleague David Wertner, head of the Internal Investigation Bureau, Henrik du Toit and De Vries. 'Every unmarked van that stops is suspect. The shops in town have reported falls in sales and foot traffic. The bomb has been news in every country in the world, and everyone is concerned about next summer. And now,' he stares at De Vries, 'you bring us this.'

'The two crimes are not centred on Cape Town City Bowl, the tourist area,' Du Toit says.

'They are centred on Cape Town. My city. When we release this to the press, however careful we may be, there will be renewed fear, panic even. And remember this, gentlemen. When there is crime unstopped, we are to blame. No one else. Our new leader has made that quite clear. We cannot blame crime on the criminals, we must bear the responsibility ourselves. That is what the public think.'

'The public . . .'

Thulani stares at De Vries. 'What did you say, Colonel?'

De Vries checks himself. 'Hard to please, the public, sir.'

'Impossible but, nonetheless, it is your job to try.' He draws himself up. 'Let us be candid here. What do we have? A spree killer, a serial killer?'

Du Toit looks at De Vries, who says, 'We have two killings linked only by the modus operandi, what might be considered the natural development of a killer who is escalating his actions. We do not know whether these women are linked in any way. At present, it seems not. If that is the case, there is danger that we have a serial killer and that his timetable will escalate until he is caught.'

'So, we don't know?'

'No. To call two linked crimes by pejorative titles is counter-productive. It will not help us, and the press will frighten people.'

Thulani raises his shoulders in a demonstrative shrug.

111

'Who knows what the press will do?' He turns his attention to Du Toit. 'Knowing how little Colonel de Vries cares for the press, you should be responsible, Henrik. You,' he continues, turning to De Vries, 'stay on the case, to the book, and impress us once more with your abilities, Colonel. And I am going to say this once again, with Colonel Wertner here in front of you: the press will be watching. Pretoria will be watching. Cases such as these reflect not only on you and your unit but on me also. I want only to bask in your success. You understand?'

'He is stealing jewellery,' Don February says. 'According to the docket on Marie Garsten, she only wore a gold wedding ring. Nothing else. Bethany Miles wore a gold wedding band and an engagement ring with a five-star, four-carat tanzanite stone surrounded by diamonds. Her husband emailed the photographs, asked us to sign off on the insurance.'

'After three days?'

Don looks at Sally Frazer. 'Either he is a very efficient man, or the insurance payout has great value to him.'

'Sorry to be the one asking this,' Ben Thwala suddenly says, 'but what about the ladies' knickers?'

'According to the docket,' De Vries says, 'in the Strand killing, Marie Garsten's underwear was discovered at the side of the room. That item was sent to be analysed so it's not missing.'

'But the underwear from the Camps Bay scene?'

'Not found, as far as we know.' De Vries stands up. 'This man isn't leaving messages. If he's staging scenes to tell us something, we don't yet know what. The jewellery could be mementoes, it could be robbery. It could even be to give the perception of robbery. Just check with the husbands where the jewellery was

112

purchased, will you? You've checked dentists, doctors,' he lists these on fingertips, 'obstetricians, gynaecologists, hairdressers, beauty salons, all of that, have you?'

'I don't know about obstetricians and gynaecologists,' Sally Frazer says, taking a note. 'We checked salons, clubs, gyms. I'll get it covered.'

'We need a connection,' De Vries says. 'If there's nothing, we have a man picking victims seemingly randomly. In terms of catching him, or not catching him, I think we all understand the significance of that.'

Mike Solarin enters, sits when Colonel Juiles gestures towards the chair, waits in silence as the CO writes on the desk in front of him. Juiles signs a paper hard, looks up.

'This has been good experience for you,' Juiles says. 'You pick up how we work here?'

'Yes, sir.'

'This is just the start. We are going to be on the front line from now on. You want to be involved in anti-terror?'

Solarin nods.

'There's a problem, Lieutenant?'

'No, sir. Just questions.'

'Ask away.'

'Isn't it unusual that there has been no claim?'

Juiles sits back, surveys Solarin. '*Ja*. But, as I said at the debriefing, we think that this may have been unauthorized. Two young guys frustrated by a lack of action, yet radicalized. Perhaps there is an imam, a religious leader, who inspired these guys. We don't know. That's what our analysts will want to discover in the coming days and weeks.'

113

'Do we know whether they self-detonated or whether it was remotely detonated?'

'We don't know that. The blast was, as you saw, as you've read, enormous. We've brought in the best people, but resources aren't unlimited, even for us. We'll find the detonator soon. We'll piece together what happened. I know what you're asking: is there another guy out there? A man who pushed the button, dialled the number, sent the signal. We don't know, but, in these cases, that would be unusual.'

'And the explosive. I was told that it was old.'

'Who told you?'

The three words warn Solarin. The forced casualness of the question, jarring with the speed at which it was asked.

'No one. The guys were saying it wasn't modern explosive. The residue seemed to suggest old ordnance, although my recollection of the exact science is sketchy . . .'

'These guys aren't state-of-the-art. They utilize what they can get their hands on. It might have been smuggled in but, more likely, it's old stolen material, sold on the black market, perhaps even in the Eastern Cape.'

Solarin nods. 'Yes, sir.'

'As a senior officer, you have the choice of staying here a day or two over the weekend or flying back this evening. Up to you. Chill out on the beach?'

Solarin had been told. Solarin affects casual better than Juiles. '*Ja*. Meeting friends at Fourth Beach, Clifton, tonight. Going to enjoy the Mother City.'

'Good man.'

Juiles studies him. Solarin sits, unblinking. Juiles nods. Solarin gets up from his chair, leaves the office. He books an Uber cab to pick him up, stands in the car park, in the full sun, the heat on the back of his neck causing drops of sweat to fall down the marked ridge between his shoulder blades. He does not feel it. He dials another number.

'Hey, Gugu. You still in town? I need to see you.'

When De Vries arrives at the short end of Plumbago Lane, he sees Stephen Jessel getting out of his white Toyota Prius, waving him down. He pulls up next to him.

'Before we go in, Colonel, I'd like to speak to you. Perhaps in my car?'

De Vries parks, locks his own car, walks over to Jessel's vehicle, gets into the air-conditioned cabin.

'Nicer here than on the street.' Jessel fumbles in the centre console, offers De Vries a sweet from a tin. 'No?'

'What do you need to speak to me about, Mr Jessel?'

'Leigh does not see many guests. As I have explained to you, he does have friends and they do occasionally visit him. The strangers who come to the house are usually there to study or evaluate him and, naturally, he is suspicious. No one likes to be watched, their home life scrutinized. So, I'm asking you to be gentle with him, show him respect, and understand that this will be a difficult encounter for him.'

'It should be a simple matter.'

'But it will not be simple. Leigh's mind is such that he will assume you suspect him for this murder because of his past. That he will always be suspect because of it. It is for this reason he is unable to lead a normal life.'

'Is that it?'

'There is one more thing,' Jessel says. 'While medical professionals are reluctant to categorize it as such, Leigh suffers from a form of dual-personality complex. I have spoken to him twice already today and he seems stable. If that is his mood when you speak to him, you will find him a polite and calm man. However, he can become intensely depressed, surly, difficult. It is not surprising. If this is the case, I would suggest suspending your questioning until another time.'

'All your points are noted.'

'Good.' Jessel lets himself out of the car, waits until De Vries has closed the passenger door, then locks it. They walk slowly along the road, looking down on the mirage that blurs the view of the bay.

'Thank you for coming in an unmarked car.'

'I never drive a marked police vehicle. I prefer anonymity.'

'I'm sure we all prefer that. Although I imagine most people recognize you pretty quickly for who you are.'

They reach the front door. Jessel rings the bell three times.

'You don't have a key?'

'I do, but I prefer to show Leigh respect. It breeds a healthier relationship.'

The door opens on Leigh Finnemore, and De Vries is taken aback by the imposing, slim man who stands before them. He is close on two metres tall, with red hair swept back over his forehead, a light beard, very pale blue eyes and freckled white skin. His wrists are adorned with hundreds of pieces of coloured thread. Around his neck, there are more small objects. He wears a T-shirt, rust-red shorts, and his feet are bare.

'Leigh, this is Vaughn. I was telling you about him.'

Leigh Finnemore stares at De Vries. His eyes narrow, his brow furrows, then his mouth breaks into a wide smile. He holds out his hand.

'Hello, Vaughn.' He looks at Jessel. 'Hello, Stephen. Why don't you come in and have some tea?'

The living room is at the back of the house, doors open to a small, burned-out lawn, which slopes steeply upwards towards a line of

116

bent trees. Over the doorway a cast-iron balcony is supported by iron columns. The room itself is cool, an oversized ceiling fan rotating on the high, ornately plastered ceiling. The room also contains a selection of antique South African furniture made from yellow-wood, stinkwood and mahogany. Underfoot, a light Persian-style carpet lies over aged blond parquet flooring. Books are stacked untidily on shelves, tables are covered with magazines and books, and there is a pile of vinyl records by an old-fashioned music centre. On the walls are three large, brightly coloured naive paintings of the view of Camps Bay from above. The room is elegant and calm.

Finnemore seats them, exits, and then returns, only a few moments later, with a tray holding a teapot, three cups and saucers, milk, sugar and a plate of biscuits. He pours each of them a cup, hands it to them, then offers sugar and biscuits. Everything is formal, his actions precise, mannered, silent. When they all have tea, he sits back in an upholstered armchair, affects a strained smile.

De Vries looks at Jessel, who nods to him.

'Did Stephen tell you that I need to ask you some questions?'

'Yes. About Apostle Lodge.' His voice is quiet and controlled.

'That's correct. These are questions which I and my colleagues have asked every one of your neighbours. Everyone on the street.'

'I understand,' Finnemore says, facing De Vries in his chair, his body language open and unrestricted.

'Have you been inside Apostle Lodge since you moved here?'

'No.'

'Have you walked up to it to see it from the outside?'

'Stephen drove me to the end of the road. The other side. He told me that I should see my neighbours' houses and what the rest of my street looked like. I've lived here all this time and never walked the length of it.'

'You don't go out on your own?'

Finnemore glances at Jessel. 'Not often.'

117

'Have you ever met a lady called Bethany Miles?'

'No.'

'Are you sure?'

'I don't think so. Unless she was in a hospital I was in.'

'Did you know that a lady had been killed in the house at the other end of this road, in Apostle Lodge?'

Leigh Finnemore's face falls. He nods. 'And I know why you're here. Because when I was a child I killed my sister. I drowned her, and everyone knows why except me, and everyone remembers it except me, and that's why you're here.' He stares at De Vries, challenging him to deny his motives.

'But you didn't kill the lady, Bethany Miles, at Apostle Lodge?'

'Is that a rhetorical question?'

'No.'

Finnemore smiles indulgently at him. 'Then no.'

'Thank you.'

'I try to never hurt anyone or anything.'

De Vries sits back, picks up his cup, sips. It is a fragrant Indian tea in delicate china. He looks at Leigh Finnemore, who has sat back straight in his chair. His long fingers hold his cup awkwardly, but he sips his tea, replaces the cup on the table to his side. Everything is calm, under control.

'Are these paintings yours?' De Vries says, indicating the canvases on the walls.

'Is that it? You ask me whether I killed the woman, I say no, and then you ask me about art?'

'My interests are surprisingly broad.'

Finnemore turns to Jessel, shrugs his shoulders. Jessel just smiles. 'All right,' he says, returning to De Vries, indulgent again. 'Yes. I am an artist, a hermit, an outsider. The world outside my window does not welcome me. So I have a house full of paint and canvas. My grandfather liked to paint too. This has always been an artist's house.'

'It's a lovely view.'

'It is what I see from my bedroom at the top of the house. I paint there. I only paint landscapes.'

'Not abstracts or portraits?'

'Never portraits,' Finnemore says. 'I can't paint people.'

'But you've painted your cat, haven't you, Leigh?' Jessel says.

Finnemore glances at Jessel, lips pouting. 'It didn't look like him. I destroyed the canvas.'

'Why do you think you are not welcome outside?'

Jessel sits up, says, 'Vaughn.' He laughs. 'We leave Leigh to make his own decisions, to decide what he wants to do.'

De Vries looks at Finnemore, sees no reaction on his face, just a slightly blank, happy smile. 'I'm just curious. Do you ever go to the beach?'

Finnemore's eyes widen. 'No.'

'You see it every day. You paint it. Would you like to go to the beach?'

'No.'

'Why not?'

'All right, Vaughn,' Jessel says, with a pronounced firmness, despite keeping his voice light. 'No one likes friends to ask personal questions.'

'Because I can't be trusted,' Finnemore says. 'Because I might harm someone.'

'Is that what people tell you?'

'No, Colonel,' Finnemore says, more loudly now. 'It is because I am, and always will be, a killer. I killed my sister and I don't even remember it. So, how will I know if I go to the beach? I might kill again, and still not know anything about it.'

'It's all right, Leigh.' Jessel says.

'So, that is why I stay here, away from people, children especially, because I can't be trusted . . . I can't be certain I can trust myself. Can you imagine what that might be like?'

'I don't know.'

'Look outside at my garden. There used to be a pool there. They filled it in. They even took out the baths and put in showers, because imagine what it would be like to be with me in a pool – or in the sea – knowing what you know about me. Imagine when you're out of your depth and you don't want to be seen moving away from me or swimming back to shallow water, when you check that I'm not coming towards you, when I raise my arms and you think, Maybe, maybe Leigh will put his hand on my head and push me under and not let go until I have no breath.'

'I wouldn't think that,' De Vries says.

Leigh Finnemore smiles, his breathing fast, face red. His hand reaches for the cup and saucer. The china rattles in his quivering hand. He puts it back on the side table. 'That's what people say, but I know what they think. And I know what you think too. You would watch me, Colonel. You would watch me very carefully.'

De Vries speaks to her in his office.

'Number One Plumbago Lane, a Mr Finnemore – the section eighteen – I've spoken to him and I don't think he has anything to contribute. Something of a recluse.'

'I know you can't say,' Sally Frazer says, 'but the section eighteen. It was all right?'

'*Ja*. I'm sworn to secrecy. If anyone wants to talk with him, I need to know, okay?'

She nods.

'You get my note about Greg Harrisson?'

'*Ja*. I've put in requests elsewhere, including Strand, for any information or record on him. So much gets lost even now, and that's if it's even entered in the first place.'

'He's hiding something. So far, he's pretty much all we've got.

Connections to both Camps Bay and Strand, suspicious past, probably pretty insensitive to women, but there's a difference between insensitivity and murder. If it's him, he's very good.'

'Good?'

'He's slick and smooth, and I don't like him. But Cape Town's full of them.'

'You rate our killer as young?'

De Vries raises his eyebrows. 'You're right. I think he's older. We need a profile.'

'Your lady friend?'

'One dinner. I eat one meal with a woman and now she's my "lady friend"?'

'Nothing stays private for very long, sir.'

'No.'

'Whoever he is, he's killed twice already and left nothing. He's clever.'

'He left pubic hair at the Strand scene . . . if it's his. We can't take anything at face value.'

'Why don't we get the idiot criminals?' Frazer says. 'The ones you see on TV robbing a bank disguised as a tree, or who leave their cell-phones behind after a burglary?'

'Because they go to the rest of the SAPS and, if they don't fuck it up, they strike one for the good guys. We just get the clever bastards.'

Don February sees a shadow pass behind the peephole in the door to 35 Plumbago Lane. He can hear breathing. He stands patiently, holding out his ID.

'*Ja?*'

'Police, Mr Cloete. I am Warrant Officer February.'

Marten Cloete opens the door, sweating, his knees dirty, shorts stained.

'I need to ask you some more questions about the incident next door to you.'

'Not a great time now. My sons will be home from their day camp soon.'

'I am required to ask you questions, sir. And I must do this now.'

Cloete seems to look over and past Don, across and down the street. 'What's this about?'

'It is very hot here, sir. Please may I come in?'

'Why don't you talk to the other householders first? Leave me till later?'

'I must talk to you, sir. I can ask my questions here if you will not let me into your home.'

Marten Cloete backs up, watches Don cross the threshold to his house. 'Go on through to the kitchen at the back.'

Cloete leaves Don standing by the table, takes a can of Grapetiser from the fridge, gulps most of it.

'You know, I'm sick of always being the one you guys talk to. I'm a working man, and I come home early so I'm here for my sons when they get back from school. Now you're here again.'

Don opens his notebook, pencil poised over the page, voice quiet and calm. 'What do you do for a living, sir?'

'I'm a builder. I own a building company. Why do you need to know that?'

'And the name of the company?'

'Why?'

'Because it is my job, sir. I am told to ask questions, I report the answers and the murder inquiry continues. That is all I do, sir.'

'Cloete. It's my name. My business.' He drains the can, flicks open a sliding drawer and tosses it inside, then kicks it closed with his toe. The drawer speeds back, halts a few centimetres from its position, glides slowly into place.

'Have you ever been inside the property next door, Apostle Lodge?'

'You could have asked me this when that other guy was here. What are you guys doing? You have any idea who killed that woman? I've got kids. We want to know you're doing your jobs, keeping us safe.'

'Colonel de Vries questioned your sons, sir, but not you. It is procedure.'

Cloete sits at the head of the table, his back to the garden, spreads his legs and places his elbows on the surface. 'Get on with it, then.'

'Apostle Lodge, sir. Have you ever been inside?'

'*Ja*. I saw it when they had an open house about two years ago. It had been for sale for years already. I wanted to see what it looked like inside.'

'Why?'

'I build houses. It's an ugly building, but it's interesting, you know? The vendor is asking a lot of money. I wanted to know why.'

'Was that the last time you were inside?'

'I went into the living room through the back door when the gardener was there. Maybe a year ago.'

'Why was that, sir?'

'Why? My boys flew their remote-controlled plane, helicopter, or whatever it was, into the garden, so I retrieved it. The gardener guy turned up, said he had found a cricket ball on the grass. I said it was ours and he went inside to find it. I followed him in and the door to the living area was open, so I walked in.'

'What was in the room?'

'I don't know. Nothing. It was empty.'

'A chair, or a chaise longue?'

123

'*Ja*, a bed thing, zigzag, like a couch, black leather, chrome.'

'A chair too?'

He shrugs. 'I don't know. Who cares?'

'You walked around the room?'

'I looked in. Maybe took a few steps. I told you this.'

'You haven't been in since?'

'No . . . the garden, *ja*, because footballs, cricket balls, you name it, boys kick it over there. But not in the house.'

'It is just you and your two sons, Patrick and Robert Cloete. Is that right, sir?'

'*Ja*, that's right. Just us, last six years.'

'Anybody else stay here, or go next door to Apostle Lodge?'

'No one goes next door. A girlfriend stayed for a while, but she's gone back to Gauteng now.'

'You didn't hear anything, notice anything strange last week at any time?'

Cloete stands up. 'Okay, that's enough. Another of your guys, big bloke, already asked me this shit, did I see anything, hear anything? Of course I didn't or I would have said, *ja*? I'm trying to bring my boys up well, Officer, and I don't want the police here when they get home.'

Don breathes gently, waits a few beats until Cloete has stopped. He looks at Cloete's knees. 'Have you been next door to the garden since Thursday, Mr Cloete?'

'Why do I want to go anywhere near that place? Fucking death house now, isn't it?'

Don closes his notebook, scans the kitchen, slowly walks towards the front door. On the table in the hallway, he glances at a small pile of mail, sees on top a letter addressed to Apostle Lodge. He stops, picks it up, scrutinizes it.

'These letters, sir. They are from next door?'

Cloete recoils, grabs the envelope out of Don's hand.

124

'I take them in. They're left out there in the mailbox, sticking out, for weeks. The agents are supposed to collect them. It's like shouting out the place is deserted.'

'You are not allowed to tamper with the post, sir. I will take the letters.'

'Help yourself. I drop all of them in to that estate agent down there every month.'

At the door, Don turns back to him. 'When did you last take the letters out of the mailbox?'

Cloete shrugs. 'Last week. Monday, Tuesday maybe?'

'The victim was inside the house then. You are sure you did not see a car, anybody near the house?'

'Ja.'

'If you think of a car, you will let us know, won't you, sir?'

'Ja.'

Marten Cloete stands at his threshold, watches Don walk slowly away, turn right towards Apostle Lodge. He observes him study the mailbox, open the unfastened tin hatch at the back, replace it gently. He watches him walk back to his car, wearing his thick suit, tie fastened, not a bead of sweat on his face.

The restaurant spills out onto the wide pavement, smokers sitting on the outside at the double-sided bar, facing inwards. They have both lit cigarettes. The ashtray, unemptied and smouldering, has ensured that no one sits opposite them.

'You remember when we did this at that place in Seapoint all summer?' De Vries says. 'Talked about cases, got drunk?'

She nods. 'That was twenty years ago. Forensic science is transformed – even the way we assess suspects psychologically is completely different.' She looks up at him. 'And we had other things on our minds . . .'

'Did we?'

'You did.'

He sits back, hands behind his head. 'You were distracting.'

'But we got the work done. I learned from you too, Vaughn. I won't forget that.'

'This city seemed a lot smaller then,' De Vries says. 'Policing seemed simpler. Not in the townships. Not on the Flats but, here, in town.'

'Everyone had been concentrating on the Struggle,' she says. 'Whichever side you were on, whether you said you cared or didn't. When we all became one, that's when we started noticing the trouble.'

'Our kind of trouble.'

Grace Bellingham smiles at him. 'We're not the people we were then, Vaughn. We're older and wiser, jaded and cynical and, frankly, I for one am damaged. I think you are too, if only you could see it. That's what happens to people who do what we do. We live in another world, and it is not a happy place.'

'It's my place.'

She smiles wanly. 'I was so happy to see you the other night but, afterwards, I realized it was a mistake.'

'Why?'

'Because you're everything I'm trying to escape. I left California, I ran away from London, and I came back here, came home. I can't keep going with my old life here. Here has to be sanctuary . . .' She draws hard on the cigarette, sighing her exhalation. 'It was a good evening. My talk went well. I escaped like a naughty school girl to my rendezvous with you. Even that blustery walk through town made me smile. But then, when you got called just as we were about to go upstairs, I remembered who you are.'

'A bad man?'

'A policeman. A policeman chasing the same men I've faced

126

across the table in the cell that could be anywhere in the world for the last twenty-five years. When I flew in, I looked down on the Mountain, and I saw what the tourists see – a beautiful, sunny city, surrounded by turquoise sea, deep blue sky. That's what I want it to be, need it to be, now. You see another city – and I know it's there – but I have had enough of the darkness, the shadows, the evil men do.'

'And you can't look at me without seeing all of that?'

'No, man. You know it's not that. I always knew what you were thinking, and I know now. You told me the other night. You've been a husband, a father, and now it's just you. I know what drives you – and that excited me then, when we were young, but not now. Not any more.'

De Vries waves at a waiter. 'Have another drink. Maybe you'll feel differently.'

She smiles again. 'Sorry. I've spoilt the evening.'

'No. You've just warned me it's not going to end the way I want it to.' He looks up at the waiter. 'Another bottle.'

The man nods.

'You don't know how I felt about you. It's not black and white. I just have to protect myself now. I've been hurt, and I'm not strong enough yet to be hurt again.' She puts her hand on his. 'Be a friend for me, Vaughn. Maybe I'll heal. Maybe things will be different but, just now, be here.'

He drives home along an empty freeway, windows open, the syrupy night air swirling around him, his car taking the slip road to Liesbeek Parkway as if on tracks. He heaves the wheel left at the traffic lights and ambles up his road to the gates of the family home, an old Victorian villa surrounded by pepper trees. He fumbles with the remote control, edges into the driveway, extinguishes the engine, slumps forward, his head on the wheel. He pulls himself up and out of the car, clumsily jams his thumb against the button which closes the gates again. He is drunk, wretched.

He undresses, splashes cold water against his face, opens the windows in the bedroom. He hears a television, loud and tinny. On the side of the neighbouring house, the small rectangular balcony is illuminated – a small screen in a vast dark cinema. He squints through branches, sees a thin black woman with an Afro haircut sitting propped up on a mattress, a dog at her feet. He adjusts his position, cups his hands around his eyes. She sits surrounded by a fridge, microwave, two-ring cooker, a pile of clothes atop an old tan suitcase. She seems relaxed, but not sleepy, as if she is preparing to sit up the whole night.

Inside the house a bare bulb illuminates the gutted interior. He sees a short black man, bald on top but with dreadlocks, cupping a mug, aimlessly checking doors and windows. De Vries looks back at the woman, sees her light a cigarette, her face occluded by a cloud of smoke, the television flickering in the haze, like distant lightning in a night sky. A car accelerates up the road to his side; the dog raises its head, opens its mouth to yawn and yowl, eyes squeezed tight shut.

De Vries turns, yawns, lies on his bed, curls up.

He wakes, head heavy and aching, pulse beating in his temples, turns to the empty side of the bed, closes his eyes and listens to himself breathing. An angle-grinder sends a spasm of pain to the apex of his head. He swings himself upright, showers, dresses, is out of the house within a few minutes. He strides past his car, out of his gates, to the house next door, its own gateway open.

'Hey!'

A coloured guy in blue overalls turns.

'It's seven thirty, man. What the fuck is going on?'

'When we start.' Saws buzz, hammers hammer.

'It's Sunday.'

'We're behind. Only the morning.'

'It's not allowed. It's the law. No building on Sunday. It happens again, you'll find yourself at the police station. Turn off the machines. If you want to work this morning, it's hand tools only. You understand?'

The man nods.

'The girl on the balcony in the night. Who's she?'

'Site guards. A lot of expensive equipment and supplies here. My boss always has them.'

'What's happening anyway?'

'You can come see.'

De Vries doesn't move. 'Just tell me.'

'Clients refurbing everything.'

'Who bought it?'

'The property? Don't know, man. We just do as we're told.'

'Well, just do it quietly. I know the law, so tell your boss he won't catch up if he fucking wakes me up. *Ja?*' De Vries turns away, mutters under his breath, rubs his eyes.

They gather in the same formation as on previous days, each in their place.

'Marten Cloete,' Don February says, 'told me that he had been in Apostle Lodge at least twice. Once when the estate agents had an open day, another time when the gardener went to retrieve a cricket ball he had put inside the anteroom. And, yesterday, he acted strangely. His knees were muddy, his shorts were dirty. I think he had been back to the garden, crawling through that gap in the hedge.'

De Vries says: 'The gardener told me that he never opened the inner door to the house, just the anteroom.' He tilts his head. 'Someone is lying.'

'There is one more thing,' Don says. 'Cloete was taking the mail from the letterbox and keeping it in his house. He told me that he took it to the estate agents' office in Camps Bay, but I do not think this is true. Two of the envelopes had been opened.'

'Could Marten Cloete have carried the body through his house, through the hedge?' They turn to Sally Frazer. 'Or maybe he took the body to Apostle Lodge at night, but visited the victim through the hedge. No one would see or hear that, and there would be no risk. It might explain his hostility, how angry you said he was about his sons being in the garden and in Apostle Lodge.'

'And,' Don says, 'if we had found his DNA, he has already admitted that he has been in the house on occasions. That could protect him.'

They turn to De Vries.

'He certainly knew Apostle Lodge was empty. If he kept in touch with the agents, he might know if or when they would have a showing. I was going to say that it doesn't feel right, keeping the victim so close to where he lives, but we don't know what happened to his wife. He's there alone with his kids. Doesn't like letting people into his house.'

'Self-employed. He can come and go and no one takes much notice,' Frazer says. 'We pay him more attention?'

'We do.' De Vries turns to the room. The officers are focused. 'I want you, Ben,' he indicates Thwala, 'to follow up on Greg Harrisson. Talk to the estate agents in Strand, find the woman who accused him of rape, then dropped the charges. Find out if he tried to tie her up, bind her to a chair. Don't worry if you get in Harrisson's face. He doesn't like it and that means I do.' He turns to Frazer. 'We're looking backwards here. The attack in Strand was almost six weeks ago. Look for unsolved attacks on women involving bindings, plastic ties, eyes, peeping Toms. I'm guessing that we're talking about more than maybe two months prior to the Marie Garsten attack. Anywhere in Cape Town, Somerset West, Gordon's Bay areas, maybe Stellenbosch too. The two victims we know about show that he's mobile. If we find a third victim from earlier, we may be able to triangulate a home position.' He looks up. 'Let's be clear. Unless something is really off here, this is the same guy and, if we don't find him, there'll be another victim, and another . . .'

He trails off, waves them away, stands by the whiteboard. He watches his team work; knows too little is happening.

Henrik du Toit's office is shaded until the afternoon, the air warm but not stifling. His desk is piled high with folders and reports, the stacks moving but seemingly never diminishing. De Vries wonders how he can fill his days with administration, have turned his back on policing, on investigation. Now he seems only to fight for the continued existence of his cherished Special Crimes Unit, solid in his belief that it makes a difference, stoical against the claims that it investigates too many crimes against white victims, that its arrest rate does not justify its budget. Yet both men know that those they pursue are criminals who cannot be allowed to remain free, men – and occasionally women – whom the under-funded, undermanned, inefficient and sometimes corrupt standard SAPS stations, even the Hawks, might not catch without the determination of many older, more experienced officers. That they may be tainted by their time serving the old apartheid regime is a public-relations price that must be paid. Each of the senior officers knows that, within the general pool of officers in the new SAPS, they would be drowned out, eased to desks in central offices, persuaded to retire in favour of the young, up-and-coming, poorly trained, naive.

'You've seen the press?' Du Toit asks. De Vries shakes his head. 'They've taken what we gave them and woven it into a story. We're not quite at serial or spree killer yet, but they've taken the connection and run with it. I know you don't care,' Du Toit says, 'but, for my sake, give me something each day I can pass on to them, even if it's nothing. They are beasts which must be fed.'

'I thought we were here to slay beasts.'

Du Toit sighs. 'I'm not playing that game with you, Vaughn. Just do as I say. You may not like being in the public eye, but you are, so get yourself together.' He moves a pile of papers left and right, then back to its original position. 'If this is a series of crimes, are you obtaining a profile?'

'Cyril Fenner is in Jo'burg. We got hold of him and he's busy.'

'Fenner isn't our only profiler, surely.'

'He's the best we have. There's some new guys, but we get a profile from some kid who's read a few books, passed a few multiple-choice exams, it can do more harm than good.'

'I thought that you and Grace Bellingham . . .'

'Dr Bellingham and I are old friends. The whole team know we had dinner together, and that must be fascinating for everyone, but she's not working right now, and she certainly doesn't want to work for us.'

'What about working for you?'

'Maybe . . .'

'How did your interview with our section-eighteen man go?'

'If he's telling the truth, he stays at home pretty much permanently. Utterly paranoid that everyone will think he's responsible

for anything bad that happens. I can't see how either he or anyone else is sheltered by having him living there, but Stephen Jessel
is very protective of him.'

'That's not what I meant.'

'He's a murderer living a couple of hundred metres from a murder scene.'

'Vaughn. I'm not interested in your opinion of the treatment
of this man. Is he involved?'

'I doubt it, but beyond the veneer of charm, there's a knowing-
ness about him I don't like.'

'You don't like anyone knowing anything.'

'Maybe I'm just not convinced that he's a victim. Everyone
else is.'

'If he's not involved, he's not your problem. What are you
doing now?'

'What we do. Rechecking neighbours' statements, looking
backwards to see if there are earlier crimes, maybe get a description, some idea where he operates.'

'Nothing concrete?'

'No, sir. Nothing concrete. Nothing that would make
good copy.'

'The press are here at six. I want something.'

De Vries gets up, his smile fixed. 'There'll be something.'

De Vries leaves the office, walks to Long Street and the crossroads
with Shortmarket Street, where he enters the cool, sweet-smelling
interior of one of his many regular coffee shops. He orders two
double espressos and asks the so-called barista to heat a cheese and
bacon sandwich in the microwave oven. He drinks one of the
coffees watching the digital countdown, takes the second to have
with his brunch. Whenever he is absorbed in a case, his meal

routine becomes disrupted or non-existent and, as he grows older, he finds that he begins to tire more easily. The first coffee fuels him to walk quickly back to the office, hugging the shaded side of the street. The still, stagnant air hits him the moment he passes through the revolving door into the lobby of his building. The lift car is warmer still, the interior dim, mechanism buzzing. By the time he reaches the squad-room, his entire body is sweating.

He slams the door of his office, throws his jacket over the back of his chair, sits at his desk, shoes on top of a pile of dockets. He realizes that the blinds over the internal windows onto the squad-room are raised, but he does not move to lower them. He unwraps the tepid sandwich, chews with his eyes closed.

When he has finished his coffee, Don knocks at his door, enters. 'I gave you ten minutes. Did you enjoy your sandwich?'

'No.'

'Marten Cloete is not answering his cellphone or his home number. Apparently, the house appears empty and his car is not there. Maybe he has taken his sons away.'

A loud knocking startles them.

'Sir,' Sally Frazer says, 'you should see this.' She beckons them out into the squad-room. Don waits while De Vries struggles to lift his feet from his desk and back to the floor. As they approach, Frazer says: 'We're just starting to look for any possible linked earlier crimes, and one sticks out.' She points to a sheet on her desk. 'It's an attack on a woman in Claremont, back in September. It's in her own home, but she's blindfolded, and the binding of wrists and ankles to a chair with black cable ties is the same. He demonstrates an intention to rape her, and the only reason he didn't is that her son returned home and disturbed him.'

'Either of them see anything?'

'Nothing that's mentioned in the report.'

'Anyone else? Neighbours?'

'No, but I know the road. It's behind Cavendish shopping centre, parallel to Main Road. All the cottages are behind high walls, tall gates. No one can see the street from their house, and there are always people trying to park there to avoid paying – like me.'

De Vries squints at the report. 'You think it's our guy?'

'It feels right, and the timing fits your theory, but you know how it is, we're guessing, hunting for a break.'

'You and me, we'll go now. Can you check she's there?'

'Done, and she is.'

'Good work.'

Frazer smiles. 'Thank you, sir. And I need to warn you. Hazel Calder and her son, they're little people.'

De Vries is already walking. 'Aren't we all?'

De Vries looks right over her into the tiny cottage, then bows his head to her and the smell engulfs him. Her voice is assertive, demanding.

'It's my sauce.'

De Vries stares down at Hazel Calder, broad but barely 1.2 metres tall. 'Excuse me?'

'I make sauces. That's what I do. Little Sauces, that's what they're called. We sell them at markets and food fairs, in cafés and pop-up cafés. Pick and Pay wanted them. They wanted Little Sauces, and I said no. You cannot have it. Today is the last day of cooking for Christmas. I sell three-quarters of everything in December. Makes an original present, uses up turkey, stimulates the taste buds after all that rich food.'

De Vries finds himself staring at her small, puckered mouth, the stream of words delivered in a high-pitched yet husky voice. He is aware that she has stopped.

She stands aside with a flourish, beckons them in, leads them

135

to a lounge overlooking a tiny patio. She walks bow-legged, limp-ing. Over dark floral wallpaper, framed photographs are displayed, each of a tiny man in heavy make-up, engaging in circus acts, per-forming in what De Vries assumes are pantomimes.

'That's Ricki, my son. He's an actor. We keep a record of every-thing he's been in.' She points to a picture of Ricki in a sequined jacket and bow tie on top of a grand piano, apparently tap-dancing. 'That's his current show. It's in town. In the orange tent, like Cirque du Soleil.'

She lowers herself into a small upholstered armchair, De Vries takes a full-size dining chair, and Sally Frazer squats awkwardly on a low, curved sofa facing an enormous flat-screen television.

Hazel Calder picks up what appears to be an oversized plastic tumbler and sips enthusiastically from a tall straw. She faces De Vries. 'Why do you want to talk about September the fifteenth?'

He indicates Sally Frazer, who says: 'We're investigating two further rapes, which sound like they could have been committed by the same man who attacked you.'

'So you didn't catch him?'

'We're a different department.'

'Is that what happens? One lot can't get him so it moves to a different department?'

'No.'

'When we met them – when we spoke to the officers, we knew they wouldn't catch him, wouldn't do anything. They weren't interested.'

Frazer talks over her: 'We've only just heard about your case, and we will catch whoever attacked you, but we wanted to check that you hadn't remembered anything new since the original report. Something that could help us find this man.'

'Something new? I'll tell you what I remember. I came home and found the gates weren't working so I got out of my car, found the handle that disengages the motor and pulled them open myself. It was almost dark. I drove in. I didn't close the gates again because I knew that Harold and Ricki were due back and I thought it was easier to leave them.'

'Harold?'

'My husband. He had the day off and he was picking Ricki up from town and bringing him home. I know that's how the man got in. I know it was my fault for being careless . . .' She trances momentarily. 'I carried the shopping, one bag at a time, into the kitchen, and when I closed the front door, he hit me. I didn't see or hear him, I just felt pain in my neck and the back of my head and I think I must have passed out. When I woke up, I was in this chair – my chair. He'd put something over my head, like a carrier bag, but thicker, bundled up, and I couldn't breathe. He gagged me.'

She sits up, brings arthritic hands to her mouth. 'I was tied up, to the chair, with those plastic ties . . .' She pulls up her skirt and opens her legs, pushes each thigh apart as far as she can manage. 'Ankles to the chair legs here, wrists to the arms, like this.' She poses silently, her body contorted and stretched to reach even to the corners of such a tiny piece of furniture. De Vries lowers his gaze, shields his eyes from her. 'I couldn't call out, couldn't find a voice, but I'm trying to talk to him, trying to make him realize that I'm a human being. I can't breathe through my nose and I want to moan or cry but I can't. I can't move and I can't struggle and I can't call out. He had a knife. I didn't see it, but I felt the tip of it against my body because he started to cut my clothes, down here.' She points between her legs. 'He was breathing hard, and it was strange, but I glimpsed his hands at the very bottom of my field of vision, under the bag. I think he was shaking, that he was afraid. And he whispered to me, almost under his breath, but I heard it . . .'

She pauses, eyes wet, voice breaking, her body still spatchcocked across the chair. 'He said: "You should never have been a mother."'

She freezes. They hear the sound of taxi-vans honking on Main Road, a siren, perhaps at the crossroads.

De Vries jumps when Sally Frazer says: 'What happened then?'

'I heard a car outside, an engine. Heard voices, Ricki's. He'd forgotten his father was fetching him. He'd taken an Uber and he was outside.'

'What did the attacker do?'

'He didn't do anything. He just wasn't there.'

'Where did he go?'

She shrugs. 'I don't know. Maybe into the garage. There's a connecting door from the kitchen. Ricki started opening the front door, calling out. I was trying to make a noise and the next thing I know, he's taken the bag off my head and he's screaming.'

She reaches down for her drink, relaxing her limbs, wriggling back into a more normal sitting position.

De Vries looks up, sees Sally Frazer still listening to her, watching her intently.

'And neither of you saw him?'

'No. Ricki just wanted to hold me, untie me. He went to the kitchen and got scissors and cut me down. Then he called his father and then the police.'

'Did you get any impression,' De Vries says quietly, 'of the man, the attacker? Race or age?'

She puts down her glass.

'I didn't see him, but I felt he was white and not young. Not a child. He didn't speak, just whispered that one thing. "You shouldn't have been a mother." I don't know. I assumed he was white, but he could have been coloured.' She looks up at them. 'He sounded white, as much as you can sound anything when you're whispering. He didn't smell. I suppose I can't say that, can I? He didn't smell black.'

De Vries says: 'You can say whatever you like if it helps us find this man and put him in prison.'

'My mother was Indian,' Hazel Calder says conversationally. 'I grew up there and smell was very important. It's part of my DNA – and a very important facet of a good palate, you know. In India, you could tell how smart someone was by their smell. My mother used to say you could smell a person's caste.'

'I'm sorry to ask this,' Sally Frazer says, 'but can you think of a reason why he should say what he said to you?'

'You can ask, dear. It's not the first time I've been asked. Harold and I – Harold is your size – we thought a long time before deciding to have children. We underwent genetic testing and they told us they did not know whether Harold's or mine would pre-dominate. We knew there'd be a chance that our offspring would inherit my health problems too. Boys, especially, have a shorter life expectancy, but the doctors felt there was a good chance that a child would grow normally. We had three sons, but now we only have Ricki.'

'Your other sons passed away?'

'Jerry was only six and Jack was seventeen. People judged us for bringing our boys into the world. Maybe that's what he meant. Or maybe he just didn't like how I looked. Maybe he was afraid of me . . .'

The squad-room is quiet. No phones ring, no one talks. The people alone do not make it seem busy.

'What is the *New Cape Gazette*?'

Sally Frazer sits in a neighbouring chair, pushes away from the desk, rolls herself next to Don February.

'It's a new tabloid. Someone called it "Berliner-style". I think it's trying to be an independent voice in journalism. No political affiliations.'

'The myth of objectivity.'

They both turn to De Vries.

'Sir?'

'Nothing is objective in this world if it's reported by another person. Think about witnesses: what they see, what they think they see, what they say they've seen. It's all subjective.'

Don and Frazer exchange a glance.

'Sir,' Don says, 'there is this journalist. She works for the *New Cape Gazette*. Her name is Ali Jelani. Look at what she has written.'

He indicates four A4 pages displayed neatly on the adjoining desk. He points at the first.

'This is from November the eighth. The woman you have just been interviewing, Hazel Calder. There is an article about her, about the attack.' He moves his finger to the sheet below. 'She wrote this piece on November the eleventh, about a woman called Michelle Ricquarts. She was kidnapped by a man who blindfolded her and drove her out towards Milnerton Beach. The shacks on the other side of the railway line, he took her to one of those and bound her to a wooden bench inside. He went away, and she escaped because the wood was rotten. In the article it claims that she saw nothing.'

His finger moves up and to the right. 'The articles start as just paragraphs, but they get longer. Look who is here next. Marie Garsten. This article was published on November the fourteenth. That's only two days after she was found. But notice, sir: one every three days. No interview, obviously, but a biography of the victim and, at the end, she states that she was bound with black plastic ties. She actually ends the piece . . . Look.' He reads: '"This is the third attack on a mother involving the victim being bound with

140

black cable ties. An empty chair faced the body of the victim. Did the attacker of Marie Garsten sit there and speak to her? Did he whisper his warning?"'

Don can feel De Vries's hands on the back of his chair as he leans over to read the enlarged newsprint.

'Last. Yesterday. Bethany Miles. It points out that, like the other women, she was bound with black cable ties, raped. She once again describes the crime scene, that she was laid out on the chaise longue, that there was a chair facing her where her attacker may have watched her suffer. She describes that the eyes were removed.' Unable to swivel because of De Vries's hold on his chair, he twists around to face him. 'I do not understand, sir. The crime scene, the detail about the victim's eyes. You were clear that this must not be released. Where does she get this information?'

'A leak,' De Vries says.

'She does not say it clearly but she is making a connection between these crimes.'

'And faster than us,' Sally Frazer says.

'Who is this second woman?' De Vries asks.

'I have been looking into the case,' Don tells them. 'The docket is still open, but no one knows who is leading the inquiry. She was taken from outside the back of Ruby's Lounge.'

'The strip club, off Loop Street,' Sally Frazer says. 'You know it, sir?'

De Vries glances at her. 'I knew Ruby,' he says blankly. 'Until he or she was shot in his or her car at the traffic lights at the top of Orange Street.'

They stand in silence momentarily.

'So we have the Central guys and also Milnerton hub. Something has gone wrong.'

De Vries shakes his head rapidly, runs sweaty hands through

damp hair, his balding crown stinging from sunburn as he passes his palms over it.

'Sally. You need to find out everything about Michelle Ricquarts. We need to know if she's connected, what happened to her and what she remembers. You, Don, and me. We're going to this *New Cape Gazette*. I want to talk to the editor and I want to talk to this Ali Jelani. We need to know how she knows what she knows.'

The offices of the *New Cape Gazette* are located in a former factory at the city end of Albert Road. The raised freeway snakes into town, partly encircling the small, formerly industrial area in a horseshoe bend of smoke and noise.

The office conversion itself is smart, a façade of tall and broad multi-paned iron panels of windows, heavy steel doors and utilitarian fittings. Inside the enormous main double doors, from behind a bare aluminium reception desk, a young coloured man calls the editor's office and, a few moments later, leads them to the ground-floor office housing the *New Cape Gazette*.

De Vries and Don stand in the doorway, unimpressed by sparsely populated, well-spaced desks and the unadorned bare brick walls.

'We've been here seven months and we still don't know how to make it seem more . . . I was going to say homely, but I mean like a newsroom.'

A very tall white woman, perhaps in her late fifties, immaculately dressed in a well-cut navy pin-striped trouser-suit, stretches out a long arm at De Vries, then Don.

'Penelope van Reidel.' She studies each of them. 'I suppose it is good that the police are angry at what we have printed.' She speaks in a low voice, each word enunciated, intonation and emphasis very deliberate. 'It demonstrates our determination to remain independent of the government, the political pressures of globalization, the establishment.'

She seems to study their reactions from above, haughty.

'Why would you think we were angry with you?'

'One of your officers contacted me, discussed your need to speak to me and to Ali Jelani.'

'Yes,' De Vries says. 'But what made you think you were in trouble?'

'Ali warned me that you might come.'

De Vries frowns. 'She will be available to speak to?'

'I've spoken to her on her cell. I think she was expecting it.'

'Then,' De Vries says, 'while we have you, we should talk immediately.'

She turns away from them, walks through the middle of the quiet newsroom, towards glossy blood-red metal double doors. She throws them both open and continues into a large office. Don only just catches the second door before it slowly clicks shut. De Vries enters the room, waits for Don to join him.

Already, she is sitting behind an oversized wooden desk, her head lower than the tall scarlet-upholstered chair back. Behind her, there is a floor-to-ceiling Gothic arch of stained glass, lit from behind. Between towers of papers, the table is highly polished. They stand in front of it.

De Vries says: 'Who is Ali Jelani?'

'Don't you trust Wikipedia?'

'I'm asking you.'

She smiles. 'Exactly. You go directly to the source, if necessary by a trusted third party. This is what we do here.' She points to the two chairs in front of her desk.

'I'm not interested in a sales pitch.'

'Ali Jelani is not employed full-time by the *New Cape Gazette*. She is a contributor. An increasingly interesting one, but a free-lance none the less. What do you want to know? Kenyan descent, attended UCT's first new journalism degree course in 2009, and graduated top of her year. She made contributions to some local and provincial titles here, before spending a year in New Orleans, USA, writing about the plight of those widowed by Katrina, made homeless, unemployed and forgotten. Then she came back here.'

'There are four stories that interest us, Ms van Reidel.'

She watches Don February gently lay the four printed sheets in front of her in a two-by-two pattern. Her hooded eyes study each momentarily; she shrugs.

'This is Ali Jelani's latest project. She may have discovered a sequence of crimes against women, escalating as you can see. I sent a reporter to the press briefings, but there was no mention of a connection. It made me wonder even more. Do the SAPS – what do you call your department? Special Crimes? – have no idea what is happening, or is there some reason you are withholding information from the public?'

'We withhold it so that when secret information comes to light we can judge whether it suggests suspicious behaviour on the part of the person who is aware of it.' She seems to sneer at De Vries. 'Or to confirm that someone who confesses is truly who he claims to be.'

'Is that game-playing with the lives of women?'

'No, it is an attempt to protect them.'

'It seems you haven't succeeded so far.'

'Well, unlike a glib headline, or a half-story, a multiple homi-cide investigation requires great attention to detail.'

She raises her eyebrows. 'A multiple homicide investigation. Is that what it is? You haven't told us that before.'

De Vries feels the soft pads of his palms itch like prickly heat. He grits his teeth. 'Does Miss Jelani claim to have a source within the SAPS?'

'She has a source certainly. I can't confirm or deny from where it emanates.'

'Whoever it is,' De Vries says, 'is compromising my investigation.'

Van Reidel smiles broadly. 'I would say that it seems to be aiding your investigation. Did you know already about Hazel Calder and Michelle Ricquarts?'

'We've interviewed them, yes.'

She gently scratches the right-hand side of her nose, meets De Vries's gaze. He looks away, looks down.

'I spoke to Michelle Ricquarts yesterday. She told me that she had not been contacted since the original investigation into her abduction stalled and subsequently evaporated.'

De Vries bites the insides of his cheeks. 'She is being interviewed this morning, perhaps now, as we speak.'

'After viewing our coverage?'

'I'm not here to play one-upmanship games with you. Several pieces of classified information have appeared in these articles. I need to ask you: do you know your freelance's source?'

'If I did, I wouldn't tell you but, as it happens, I do not. If Ali Jelani were a staffer, I would insist upon it, as a matter of due diligence, but in this case all the information in her reports seems to be accurate.' She locks her dark eyes on him again. 'Doesn't it?'

De Vries stands, stumbles backwards a few centimetres. He feels disoriented.

'If I find that you're withholding information from me, there will be repercussions.'

She holds up slender fingers in a stunted gesture of surrender, gemstones sparkling under the spotlights that illuminate her desk.

'We withhold nothing and, as a token of good will, I am happy to show you what we will be running on the front page tomorrow.'

She opens a drawer, extracts a tabloid-sized sheet, pushes it across the desk, facing De Vries.

THE CAPE TOWN COP AND THE MISSED CONNECTION

Beneath, there is a photograph of Grace Bellingham and himself sitting at the bar on Bree Street, smoking and drinking. He scans the text beneath.

Renowned profiler Dr Grace Bellingham has returned to her home city just in time. Bombs explode, a series of attacks has escalated to torture and murder, but the officer leading the SAPS investigation, Colonel Vaughn de Vries, seems more interested in socializing than finding the culprit. These are the people who should be working to protect us, yet instead relax at a fashionable city-centre watering hole.

De Vries looks up at her. 'This is outrageous. This was taken at eight p.m. on a public street. You want to call yourself a highbrow paper, but you print this rubbish?'

She withdraws the paper, floats it back into the open drawer. 'When you read the entire article, you will see that what we and Ali Jelani have to say is a great deal more interesting than rubbish.'

De Vries bridles. 'Print whatever you like about me, but leave Dr Bellingham out of it. She is not involved in this case.'

'Perhaps she should be. It seems you need help.'

'Grace Bellingham has retired. When you have to deal with the kind of people she has battled to understand throughout her professional career, there is a price to pay. She deserves some respect.'

'She is yet to earn that from me. Have you actually felt the atmosphere on the streets?'

'I understand "the streets" very well.'

She smiles. 'You're almost invented, aren't you? Street-smart heavy-drinking cop, struggling in the new world. Can't quite cope with women, authority, the rules.'

Don February clears his throat.

She ignores him. 'We could interview you personally about this investigation. Would you agree to that? An exclusive? I'm sure that you – and your colleague – could benefit, in more ways than one.'

'I strongly advise you to consider not printing that front page tomorrow.'

'Shall I include that threat in the article?'

'It was not a threat, Ms van Reidel. It was a request to aid the investigation and, possibly, to protect you from charges of hampering my inquiry.'

'I can assure you, I am quite protected.'

De Vries feels his jaw locked. He presses his tongue into the roof of his mouth; the tension reduces minutely. He keeps his voice even, aping her.

'When did Ali Jelani file that copy?'

'For what it's worth, around lunchtime yesterday. It's her picture – she has declined my offer of a photographer – and, although we contributed to your background and reputation, the story is hers.'

'Thorough in her character assassination, isn't she?'

'She claims that a photographer would draw attention to her,' she says, disregarding De Vries. 'Might warn the subject that they were the focus.'

'Where is Jelani?'

'She's not here.'

'Why not?'

'I told her that I would speak to you first. I fear that if you met her now, your attitude would prove most counter-productive.'

'When a SAPS officer asks that someone make themselves available for interview, that is what I expect.'

147

'Ali Jelani has no legal duty to submit to your interview. If you wish to arrest her and take her to your headquarters, you surely better have due cause.'

De Vries opens his mouth, but Don says quietly:

'Please would you provide Miss Jelani's contact details so that we may request such an interview directly?'

'And I am not required to do that. However, I will supply you with her email address, which is her preferred method of contact.' She writes it on a small piece of heavy card, passes it to Don. She stands up. Behind her, the glowing stained glass partly silhouettes her, making her tall, contained features seem darker still. 'Don't make an enemy of me, Colonel de Vries. We've already advanced your investigation once. It may be that we can assist you again.'

'You haven't assisted me at all.'

She smiles, removes her black-rimmed spectacles.

'Perhaps we are wrong about the contribution Dr Bellingham might make . . .' she says lightly.

'You are.'

'Perhaps it is *you* who requires profiling.'

The car seats burn the underside of their thighs even through the fabric of their suits. Every window is misted and damp – the air-conditioning has little effect. De Vries yanks the control to off, winds down his window, elbows Don to do the same on his side.

'Email that Jelani woman now. Tell her that if she doesn't agree to a meeting immediately, the full force of the law will descend on her.'

'I am allowed to phrase that in my own words?'

'You sound like Penelope van Reidel.'

'She is a lady who works hard to create an effect.'

'I'd say that she was a rich wife with a passing fancy to dabble in journalism, but I'm afraid that she is much more than that.' De Vries brakes suddenly as the car in front stops in the middle of the road for seemingly no reason. The car edges forward; there is still nothing obvious to have caused such a manoeuvre. He struggles to retrieve his cellphone from the shiny material of his inside jacket pocket on the back seat. He speed-dials Sally Frazer's phone, which goes straight to voicemail. He drops the phone into the centre cubby-hole, toots his horn as the car in front fails to move forward with the queue of traffic ahead.

'Sir.'

'What?'

'The traffic is merely the lights ahead . . .'

De Vries squints through his windscreen.

'It's a woman, Don. She's on her phone, she's doing her hair. I saw a woman a couple of days ago who had tongs plugged into the lighter socket. Tongs. This is what women mean when they say they can multi-task. Doing lots of things except the most important one.' He turns to the passenger seat. 'And I'll tell you, I'm just about done with women already today.'

Don turns to his window, stares intently at the summit of the Mountain.

It is almost five p.m. before they gather in the squad-room. The air-conditioning does no more than push hot air around the space. The sticky, dusty windows overlooking town reveal a low bronze smog descending below the tops of skyscrapers. It is both beautiful and claustrophobic.

Sally Frazer says: 'Michelle Ricquarts is thirty-four, lives in the Disa Towers. She's divorced, looking after her two daughters, who are eleven and fifteen. The ex-husband has ceased all maintenance payments and gone off radar. She started working at Ruby's

Lounge in January last year and says that she makes sufficient earnings to cover all her costs, but that she fears her time working in that environment is limited.

'On October the fourth, she left Ruby's at eleven thirty p.m. and walked no more than thirty metres down the street to the corner where she usually picks up her cab. A car stopped behind her. She says she glanced back, glimpsed the driver but cannot imagine what his face looked like, other than she is almost certain that he had a pale complexion. The next thing she knew, she was hit around the back of the neck and woke up in the back of a car, her wrists bound together, her right ankle bound to the seat-belt holder. She was blindfolded and gagged. She estimates that she was driven for half an hour to forty minutes and the driver took the freeway towards the Southern Suburbs. She was untied and marched over what she felt was uneven sandy ground. The man was wearing what she felt were leather gloves. Still blind-folded, she was made to sit on a wooden bench and bound by wrists and ankles to it. She says that the man whispered to her: "You left your children alone."'

'She's certain about that?'

Frazer looks at De Vries. 'So she says. She estimated that the accent was white South African, not, she felt, Afrikaner, but it is only five words whispered. She said that the attacker left almost immediately, padlocking the door. She waited a few minutes, then started pulling at her bindings. Her right wrist came free when the backrest to the bench snapped. She removed the gagging and blind-fold, and managed to break the wood holding her left wrist. Then she was able to pull the bench from the wall, turn it at an angle and stamp on it until her ankle bindings could be slipped off. She showed me her wrists. They are still deeply scarred. Black cable ties. The Milnerton boys entered them in evidence. From there, she found more rotten wood in a back corner, split it open with another piece of wood, and made her escape.' Frazer regards each of the officers present. 'My view is that Michelle Ricquarts is a very strong, resilient woman and that her testimony is accurate.'

'Any intent to rape?' De Vries says.

'She states that she is not certain if it was his hand but that she was being touched between her legs. She admits that her mind was racing and that rape was the most likely thought.'

'What about this shack by Milnerton Beach?'

Ben Thwala says: 'I've got a copy of the docket now. Forensic officers found nothing to identify the abductor, or any witnesses who saw the car or Michelle Ricquarts. The cabin was scheduled for demolition, to be replaced with more modern warehousing, and had been empty all year. The area is not well lit and there are many cars parked around it at all times. There is very little residential building nearby.'

Frazer nods, continues: 'She waved down a car driven by a woman, who took her to the station. There was no sign of her handbag or cellphone, which has been off since the attack.'

'What's interesting,' De Vries says, 'are the whispered comments to Hazel Calder and Michelle Ricquarts. Without that, it would be difficult to be certain of the connection. And we don't know what, if anything, he said to the two murder victims, although the placement of the chair suggests he was watching them and, possibly, speaking to them.'

Sally Frazer says: 'We have one crime in Claremont, one in town, ending in Milnerton, one in Somerset West, Strand area, and most recently Constantia, ending up in Camps Bay. This is a really wide catchment area.'

'The perp is travelling. He's driving around the peninsula,' Ben Thwala says.

'Yes, he has local knowledge of the movements of the victims, but, if all four crimes are connected, as we believe, notice the way

151

that, apart from the first victim, Hazel Calder, he takes his victim away from where she lives by some kilometres.' Sally Frazer turns to De Vries. 'I know that Dr Fenner is not available, sir, but right now what we really need is a detailed profile.'

De Vries stands still, expression blank, the knowledge of the next day's newspaper front page suddenly flooding back.

'I'll talk to Grace Bellingham.'

Don February follows De Vries silently, enters the lift after him. De Vries jumps.

'What I am thinking, sir,' Don says, 'is that the connection between Hazel Calder and Michelle Ricquarts could only have been made by someone who had access to the dockets. The attack on Hazel Calder did not receive any press coverage, and from what I have found, there have been only two very small mentions of the Michelle Ricquarts crime. Neither contained any details which could possibly link them.'

De Vries nods slowly. 'But it doesn't make sense. Even if someone from the SAPS was leaking this information, how would he or she have had access to both dockets?'

'Notice that Ali Jelani did not write her articles about the first two crimes until well after the events,' Don tells him. 'Perhaps she, or her source, did not make the link until the third crime, the Marie Garsten abduction and murder in Somerset West and Strand.'

The lift doors open onto the gloomy, stifling lobby. De Vries steps out, walks slowly towards the exit, says nothing.

Don waits, then says: 'I wonder, sir, whether you should speak to your friend, Captain Malgas. It was after that crime that the coverage started, that someone made the connection.'

De Vries's mind is racing. There is a gap in the logic somewhere, but he cannot see it yet.

'Where are you going now, Don?'

'Home. Tomorrow is not going to start well, is it? With that front page. I think I will need all the sleep I can get.'

'Yes.'

'Where are you going, sir?'

De Vries turns to him. Every piece of clothing he wears is damp; his chest aches from inhaled humidity; his pulse throbs at his temples.

'I'm going to where beer is, Don. Perhaps wine, but probably beer.'

The tree-lined roads in Greenpoint are busy with evening traffic, lit lengthwise by deep golden sun, pavements filled with tourists and locals heading to bars and restaurants, walking into town. The World Cup football stadium seems to hover, almost as if preparing to rise from a mesmeric shimmering heat haze. The skyscrapers of the Central Business District are divided in two by the copper layer of smog and glittering dust.

Giovanni's is packed tight, bare-armed strangers sticking to one another, clammy but happy, the cool interior deli populated by workers picking up an easy supper, picnics for the beach. The coffee-bar stools and narrow benches bordering the street are all taken, customers with the sun on their backs or reflecting in sunglasses, ending their day or starting their night with some of the best coffee in the city.

As Mike Solarin ducks inside, a tall bar table at the end of the deck becomes free. He pushes past those standing, lays claim to the tiny circular plane, the single stool. He places his sunglasses on the table, leans out over the wooden barrier, looks down the street. He steps towards the bar, asks for a cold drink, is shown the big glass-doored fridge, told to help himself. He takes a red Grapetiser back to his table, screws it open, downs half; sees in his peripheral vision Gugu KwaDukuza on the street, waves. Her smile is very broad. She squeezes between the other customers. They embrace. He fetches her a drink, before they walk to the counters, wait in the queue chatting casually, pick plates, his carb-heavy, hers leafy and low-calorie. They carry them back to the table, clink glasses, eat.

After a few minutes, she says: 'The way you said, "I need to see you." It did not sound only like a nice supper.'

'No.'

She glances involuntarily around the café, onto the street. 'You want to ask me?'

He feels fraudulent suddenly, their casual friendliness stilted by tension.

'What do you think?' He lowers his voice although, above the happy cacophony, he surely cannot be heard. 'Two Islamic terrorists in a lorry in Long Street at eight fifty in the morning?'

'I think that neither I, nor my friends in the team, have seen anything to suggest that.'

'No?'

'No. But, then, that is probably because, two days ago, the usual teams are swapped over. Some new guys come in.'

'What do you mean, new guys?'

'Just a new team. One we do not know. In any case, this scene, it is not like anything we have worked before. Information not shared between teams. It is all fed into the system, but none of us know what it is.'

'What you said about the explosive?'

Her eyes flare. 'You have not repeated that?'

'No. What we say here is just between us. I will protect you.'

She smiles. 'I do not need you to protect me.'

'I mean, something is not right.'

'No, it is not right. I have studied what these extremists do, what materials they use, how they plan, operate. This is atypical. I think that it is not believable.'

'What in particular?'

'Two things. My friend who specializes in electronics. He tells me that they have found a receiver — what is left of it — and that it is almost certainly the means of detonation. This was not a suicide attack. This was detonated remotely, perhaps by a cellphone, maybe a transmitter of some kind.'

'Could it have been triggered accidentally?'

'Why would you ask that?'

'It was early in the morning. The street was busy, but not crowded. There are other more politically significant sites . . .'

'It is possible. I suppose that there are many signals travelling in the middle of a city.'

Solarin nods. 'What else?'

'You remember you asked me about the sticky gel you saw at the scene? I told you it was grapes. We found grape seeds, boiled pulp. Maybe three or four bunches, no more. Do you know that they can identify a variety from its seed? This was a grape called Souzão. That, my friend, is a Portuguese port grape. A cultivar, they call it, only grown in South Africa for port-style wines.' She glances around her again. 'So, seeing as how the van was taken from Oudtshoorn, I am thinking Calitzdorp.'

'Calitzdorp?'

'"The Port Capital of South Africa."'

'Ja?'

'Why would there be grape residue in the van if it had not stopped on its way from Oudtshoorn?'

'We were heading that way when they called us back.'

'When was that?'

155

'Yesterday. Maybe five p.m.'

'We delivered the report on the grapes to the supervisor. Maybe two p.m. That, as you conspiracy theorists might say, is a big coincidence.'

'Who have you spoken to about these grapes?'

'No one. We don't discuss what is in the reports. We, the technicians, we keep quiet, do our job, keeps our heads down. I know this is not how you are, Mlungisi.'

He smiles at the use of his proper name.

'No.'

'And you are going to challenge them?'

'Maybe. I was put with a white guy, Ray Black. He was not interested in his duties. I think he was talking to Colonel Juiles . . .' he shrugs '. . . to someone about where we were, what we were doing. He's not been stood down. Never showed at the debrief. I do not trust him.'

'But do not go risking your job. It will not bring back the people who died.'

'Don't you ask yourself, Gugu, why?'

'No. Never. That is not my job.'

'They call it Isis when we – you and me – know it is not. What are they hiding? That's the point. This is my job: to ask why.'

'Better I tell you before you saw it yourself, or someone texted you,' De Vries says, watching her body slump, hand shaking as she places the wine glass back on the table.

'Why?' Grace Bellingham says. 'Why would they do that?'

'We have a serial attacker – now a killer – and you are the best. They want to involve you in the investigation.'

'I told you,' Grace Bellingham states. 'No.'

'You told *me*. I didn't know they'd photographed us. How would I have any idea they'd have any interest? We didn't even know what we had until today, and it was their bloody articles that confirmed it for us.' He stretches his arm out, but cannot quite reach her chair. 'I asked the editor to leave you out of it. I pleaded, Grace. They can attack me – they are attacking me – I'm used to it. But this bitch was having none of it.'

De Vries watches her breathing heavily through her mouth, head bowed.

'I haven't even seen this paper . . .'

'It's new. Low circulation, but the *Times* and the *Argus* will pick up on it.' He offers his hand across the cool metal table, but she ignores it. 'The city is in turmoil. The heat, the students' demonstrations, strikes, the bomb, for Christ's sake, and now this. This is what the media love. Ramp everything up, frighten everyone, find scapegoats. You got any idea what I'll face when I go in tomorrow?'

'Take you off the case?'

De Vries snorts. 'Never. They'll back the press, they'll make me dance, and if I don't find what I'm looking for, they'll get me out. It's always the same, Grace. It may be twenty-five years, but there's always a hundred facets to every struggle.'

Grace Bellingham looks around the crowded bar, more popular perhaps for its icy air-con than the claustrophobic metallic cacophony in the small basement room at the bottom of Loop Street.

'Tell them I'll help you.' She holds up a finger as De Vries sits up. 'I won't be seconded, I won't be employed by the SAPS. I'll talk to you, advise you, privately. That's as far as I'm prepared to go.'

'Thank you.'

'You come to my flat. We work. Nothing else. Any hope you had there is burned, my friend. You tell them that I'll provide a profile, advise. That's as far as it goes. No press, nothing official.'

De Vries nods.

She drains her glass, stands.

157

'I'm going now. If I find that any of this was your doing, I'll give them what I have on you. It may be old but, mark my words, they'll love it.'

De Vries is woken at seven a.m. by a summons to the top floor of his building and an interview with General Thulani, flanked by Colonel David Wertner of the Internal Investigation Bureau. After thirty years in the SAPS, he knows precisely how it will play out. For now, he will be backed and protected, but, if he fails, it will all be kept to indict him.

After a wretched night of craving sleep in his bedroom, where the temperature did not fall below thirty degrees, he is strangely calm and sanguine. He meets the scorn of David Wertner, who has long sought to discredit him, with a quietly defiant smile. He has been here before and, this time, he almost feels as if he doesn't care what they do to him. He lets the predictable warnings and repetitive aphorisms wash over him as he quietly calculates what must be achieved today. His mind is tired but clear. He does not counter what they say, does not fight. He agrees with their suggestions, accepts blame, reveals his agreement with Grace Bellingham for profiling services.

Finally, when he stands, Thulani studies him from his raised seat. 'I'm worried about you, Colonel.'

'Why is that, sir?'

Thulani glances at Wertner to his side. 'This morning, you almost seem like a rational human being.'

'Is this it, then?' Danie Malgas says. 'This the cream at the top of the bottle?' He is looking around the gloomy foyer to the Special Crimes building.

'It's no cooler in here than down your place.'

'Great way to save money, eh? Braai your workforce, take away their equipment, throw them into darkness. . .' He shuffles into the lift. 'As if it weren't dark enough already, out there.' He looks at De Vries. 'You should get out of the city, down to the beach.' He chuckles. 'Well, maybe check for the paparazzi first . . . But, you know, at least there's some breeze there. The wind off the water, it's actually cold, man.'

He follows him to his office, stands until De Vries has sat.

'Is it what we thought?' Malgas says. De Vries nods. 'You're too quiet, man. What's happening?'

'We've got a problem, Danie. This journalist, Ali Jelani – we haven't reached her yet, but we've talked to her editor – has information she shouldn't have. I need to know how she got it. Remember I asked you if your guys would keep quiet if I took over on Marie Garsten?'

'You think I'm leaking?'

'Not you. Not you, Danie, but one of your guys. Maybe?'

Malgas tips his head back, wipes sweat from his neck.

'I can't think of anyone. You know, no one said *fokkol* when the Marie Garsten docket went away. I told you, if they didn't see her, they didn't care, and if they did, they wanted to forget. Too much else. I mean, maybe now the press have it, someone might, if the money was good enough, but . . .'

'Keep an ear open.'

'*Ja*, sure . . . You get nothing from the samples?'

De Vries shakes his head.

'He's good. He's careful. He's staked out where he wants to take them, knows they can stay there, knows these are places he's not likely to be noticed. If there's more, I don't want to think what he'll do to these women.'

'You said the eyes . . .'

159

'Eyes, and with the first two assaults, he whispered something to them. "You shouldn't have been a mother" and "You left your kids alone" – something like that. Then we both find a chair facing the victim where she's been tied up, like he's watching her, speaking to her maybe.'

They sit silently a moment, then Malgas says: 'No one reads that new paper anyway, that *New Cape Gazette*.'

'Is it even for sale in Strand?'

Malgas tilts his head. 'I think they sold a few copies today, around the station.'

'Boosting their circulation. That'll make one Machiavellian woman very happy. We've had over fifty media requests already this morning. We didn't tell the public everything, so now they have us two ways. Builders' Holiday next, everyone flooding down from Gauteng, hot as horse shit straight out the arse, and this guy, somewhere out there.' He stands, opens his door. 'Come look at the boards. See if anything strikes you.' Malgas shuffles after him. 'You know what they say about a fresh eye . . .'

The three white Disa Park towers stand starkly against the dark backdrop of the Mountain's face, their cylindrical forms dwarfed by the incomprehensible mass beyond them. Looking up at the Mountain from the bay or Waterfront, they are all that interrupts the contoured plane of matt black rock. In the 1960s, the Murray and Roberts construction company exploited a loophole in the planning regulations, constructing their bases beneath the building line and developing up seventeen storeys. The Pepper Pots – the polite local nickname for them – seem lovely inside, mainly, their critics suggest, because at that moment you do not have to look at them.

Michelle Ricquarts buzzes De Vries into her block, is standing on the twelfth-floor landing as he arrives in the lift. She is dressed in a shortish white dress with bold flower prints, her hair up and back. Her apartment faces almost at right angles to the Mountain, so that one side of the view is just dark, overwhelming rock face; the other, the buildings and roads leading towards the city, with only a glimpse of sea in the docks beyond.

'Four more years on the bond.' She turns back to the window, smooths down her skirt. 'Think I'll make it?'

De Vries frowns. 'Make it?'

'Pay off the bond on here and I'm laughing, well, smiling. Just depends how long I can keep going at Ruby's.' She gestures for him to sit. 'You want a cool drink?'

When he shakes his head, she sits in a yellow velour armchair facing him, her back to the Mountain. De Vries sits forward.

'I wanted to meet you, to introduce myself as the officer who has taken over your case, and assure you that I, we, are doing everything within our power to find your attacker and make sure that he is put away for a long time.'

'Your sergeant yesterday, Sally. She was nice.'

'I'm sorry that the original inquiry fell short. My department was created to follow up these serious crimes and bring them to a conclusion.'

'I thought about that night again. I can't remember anything else. Anything I haven't said already.'

'I wanted to ask you one thing personally. In your statement you recalled that your attacker had whispered to you . . .'

'"You left your children alone."'

De Vries recoils. She has whispered the words, her voice deeper, accent stronger than her light Cape Town inflection.

'That's what he said to me. Like I said, if I was guessing, he was white, generic accent, not that thick. He said something under his

161

breath in the car when I was tied up in the back. A sentence or two, but I couldn't make out the words or his voice.'

'One or two attackers?'

'It felt like two on the street, but I'm sure there was only him in the car. I've thought about that a lot. Maybe it was only him on the corner of that street, and it's just pride makes me think that it took two men to bring me down.'

'When you got home, your children were safe?'

'I called them from the police station, told them not to answer the door, but nothing happened. I've worried, of course, so I take them to school, watch them walk into the building. I'm waiting there when they finish, but they're sixteen and thirteen now. You can't watch them all the time.'

'What happened to your husband?'

'Jerry? He got bored. Had a mid-life crisis at thirty-two. I don't know. He went. The money stopped pretty quickly, the calls to the girls after that. Now they don't even get a birthday card.'

'It wasn't him in the car?'

She smiles. 'I knew Jerry since I was fourteen. Got me pregnant before I was eighteen. That wasn't Jerry. If it had been, I'd have beaten the shit out of him. I don't do what I do because I want to.'

'And the guys at Ruby's Lounge, the regulars. No one there been paying you particular attention? You must have guys coming on to you. Anyone who took rejection badly?'

'Ja, ja and ja. You know what it's like? It becomes normal. You take no notice. I thought about it afterwards, sure. But I couldn't think of anyone. They're all still there, looking at me the same way. Nothing's changed.' She lights a cigarette. 'Do I get to ask you something now?'

'Certainly.'

162

'Is it true? You think this same guy went on to kill two women?'

De Vries appreciates the significance of the question, the understanding that she will realize now that she escaped not just rape and pain and misery, but death. He watches her suck on the slender white cylinder.

'We think so.'

She nods very slowly, exhales. Then she rests the cigarette in an ashtray and stands, gesturing at the view. 'At first I thought we'd made a mistake. I mean, it's cold, isn't it? The Mountain. But it's comforting too. It kind of wraps around us here, keeping us safe. My mother always said to me: "Wrap your home about you like a cloak." You can't trust a man, but four walls . . .'

He stands to face her. Against the black backdrop, she seems very bright.

'I'm pleased you've recovered reasonably, Ms Ricquarts, been able to continue with your life. I find some victims of crime – crimes far less serious than that against you – unable to carry on. I'm very pleased to see that.'

She smiles openly at him. 'The moment my husband left, I knew I had to be strong. Two daughters, living in a dangerous city. I'm still alive, but all those people who died in the bomb in town, and the two women after me . . . And, don't forget, I work as a stripper – and that has its moments. There are horrible things happening out there. We're all frightened but, for me, it just about falls into a day-to-day category I can cope with: an acceptable level of terror.'

'It doesn't matter what you have to do,' De Vries tells them. 'Trace her backwards from her email address. Get back to that condescending bitch, Van Reidel, whatever it takes, but find Ali Jelani.'

163

He strides to his office, slams the door.

Don February says to Sally Frazer, 'Perhaps tread carefully with Ms van Reidel. If we are seen to be too aggressive towards her and her newspaper, it might not look good.'

'You're becoming a politician, Don. You know how Vaughn hates them.'

'You are right but, working with him, one of us must show some tact.'

At five p.m., they gather for the six o'clock meeting. Ben Thwala reports that the sales representative at Nobulhe Estates, Greg Harrisson, was showing two families a house in The Glen on the afternoon that Hazel Calder was attacked, but has no alibi for the time Michelle Ricquarts was abducted. Sally Frazer tells the group that there has been no response from Ali Jelani by email, or any success tracing her current address. Penelope van Reidel's cellphone goes straight to voicemail and, so far, she has not called back.

'We want to talk to this Jelani woman,' De Vries says wearily. 'Tomorrow, Sally, can you co-ordinate all research on the children and families of the victims. On two occasions, this man has whispered to the women referring to motherhood and children – the only thing he said out loud – so we need to look into this. Anywhere their children could have intersected, going right back to their births.' He pushes himself upright from the table against which he has been leaning. 'Get some sleep. Prepare for the long days. I don't have to tell you. Right now, as we speak, he has probably chosen his next victim. We have to stop him.' He raises his eyes, nods at them.

Sally Frazer returns to her desk, sits, picks up her cellphone. The other officers gather belongings, begin to file out of the squad-room. Don February talks to two female officers who man the department at night. De Vries pulls his jacket from the back of his chair, checks the pocket for his cellphone, walks slowly towards the lifts. As he gets in, he sees another officer approaching, then checking himself, letting De Vries descend alone.

The early end to the working day at his office leads to more time spent in the agonizingly slow-moving traffic out of town. The duration and intensity of the rush hour has increased greatly in the last few years, and now even getting onto one of the three freeways out of town takes as long as the entire journey home in years past.

De Vries sits on Nelson Mandela Boulevard staring to his left at the docks, the cruise-liners glittering in the mixture of sea mist and smog. The season is under way: people are flocking to Cape Town from the UK, Germany, the north of the country. And there are people with bombs in the Cape; a man who seems to revel in the slow death of the women he abducts without being seen; rapists and thieves, robbers and muggers, pimps and pickpockets. He looks in his rear-view mirror at his city backed by Signal Hill, the pink in the sky starting early, enveloping the skyscrapers, the streets full of restaurants, bars and clubs, the Waterfront silhouetted against the dazzling pinky-white of Table Bay. Despite what he knows, he thinks it is beautiful.

PART 2

'Renting?'

'Sure.'

'You move quickly.'

Grace Bellingham smiles. 'I always did.'

'But here, out of town?'

'For the moment.'

She stands aside and De Vries walks into her apartment. The entrance hall and kitchen are both small and dark, but the living room opens out onto a terrace overlooking the southern slopes of the Mountain. He looks across towards Fernwood, an old estate, now developed with houses, where his friend John Marantz lives, but he cannot quite see his house. Marantz is an exile from the security services in the UK; he is the one man De Vries can talk to about everything. He reflects that they haven't spoken in many weeks. The sun is low, about to pass behind the crest; hazy sunbeams shoot from between the crevasses. The lush green of the slopes seems to defy the drought, the interminable heat.

'This is all right.'

'Only room in the place. My bedroom looks at downtown Claremont, but at least it has air-con.' She pulls a chair out from the table, gestures for him to sit. 'You eaten?'

'Sort of.'

'Sorry about the furniture. It was here already.'

'Got a fridge?'

'We can have a drink when we're done.'

She sits at the head of the table, looks up from the papers she has arranged in front of her.

'I want you to understand that I spent a lot of time soul-searching this morning. I know it's a mistake. I nearly called you. But I decided to do it for you, Vaughn, because you'd helped me out before and, although I'm not keeping count, this is returning a favour from a long time ago.'

'What favour?'

'You protected me when things went bad.'

'I don't remember.'

'It doesn't matter. Just know that I'm delicate. I've spent the last twenty years being strong, appearing strong, but that costs. It wears you down and I'm down now. So just remember that. Keep me out of it. I need that distance.'

'I will.'

In the silence, he hears her breathing.

'When I started reading these dockets,' she says, her voice clear, as if she has dismissed all that she has just said, 'I realized that I'm doing this for another, more important, reason. Everything we know that this man has done is a classic development of what people like to call a serial killer. He is escalating his action, and the violence that he shows towards his victims is increasing incrementally.' She shuffles papers. 'You must be a nightmare to work for, but I'll give you credit for one thing: you understand what's important.'

'I'll take any credit awarded.' He puffs out his chest and points at one side. 'Pin it here.'

'You write,' she continues, 'that Hazel Calder described seeing her attacker's hand shaking, that he appeared nervous. This is what

I would expect. This is a man who has decided that he will take action against women – or a certain category of women, whether normally recognized or created by himself – and, on this first occasion, or at least an early occasion, he is nervous, clumsy. This indicates a reticence to carry out what he has planned.'

'He was interrupted.'

'Yes, but the impression I gained from Hazel Calder's original statement, and then from your interview with her, is that he was moving slowly, deliberately. He was measuring what was going on, how he felt, what he could accomplish.'

'He intended to rape her, surely? That's why he tied her legs apart.'

'I'm sure he did. That is what he would have planned. But, if this was his first physical encounter with a victim, it may have turned out very differently from the way he had imagined it.' She produces another sheet. 'In her original report, she stated that she kept trying to talk to him the whole time because she felt that would humanize her. She said she didn't get many words out, but that she felt it was disturbing him.'

'Do you have any wine?'

She looks up at him, face serious, mouth set. 'This is work, Vaughn. I told you exactly what it would be and that's how it's going to happen. If we're done before I'm completely exhausted, we might have a glass of wine. If you want water, the tap's in the kitchen.' She slaps the page back on the pile. 'I want to keep going with this and then we may have time to discuss what we think we know and what we can learn from that.'

He sits back, rolls up his sleeves.

'He enters Hazel Calder's home when she is alone. This is easy. He abducts Michelle Ricquarts on an empty street, late at night. There is some risk in this action but, if he were to be challenged, he could always claim that she was propositioning him. He would likely be believed. He takes her to a shack near Milnerton Beach. This setting is industrial and utilitarian, so we cannot read anything into that location other than that he almost certainly knew it was abandoned and that he was very unlikely to be disturbed. The key element here is that he does not tie her up in a sexual position. He deposits her there and leaves. Why?'

'Can I ask a question?'

She nods.

'Have you made a report of this my team can see?'

'Of course.'

'I don't know the answer to your question.'

She smiles. 'I think it is because he is afraid that he has been followed. Possibly he wants time to prepare himself, anticipate what he is about to do. I have no doubt that the intent to rape, torture, kill was there. Thankfully, the victim escapes. There is something of interest there too. The victim escapes and he does nothing about it. As far as we know, he does not harbour anger towards her, frustration. If the reason for her being selected were deeply felt, I think we would see a change to his behaviour. Instead he starts planning his next attack.'

'But he's not picking them randomly?'

'No. Definitely not. He is selecting them but what I am saying is that it is not essential to his plans that he kills these early victims. Perhaps he feels that fear of rape, threat of death is a job adequately done, but – and be clear on this – that attitude will not last. He will increase the violence against his victims and he will kill them.'

'Is Michelle Ricquarts in danger?'

'I would say no, but I can't be absolutely certain. As I say, I think he will feel that she has been punished sufficiently, but he may plan to return to her at a later point.'

'There won't be a later point.'

'He abducts Marie Garsten in broad daylight, albeit in a hidden corner of a car park. The level of risk involved here is far greater, and this demonstrates the escalation of his desire. We don't know for how long he keeps her or what he does to her during the time of her incarceration, but the thing which bothers me – just as it did you, and Lieutenant Malgas in Strand – is the chair facing the victim. To me, this suggests that he is watching her suffer. If he speaks a few words to his first victims, I am sure that he has more to say to the latter two. He almost certainly asks them questions and, although we don't know, I suspect they are unlikely to be able to answer. The victim dies slowly, clearly in agony. Again, we do not know if he was there once or many times, but the fact that he posed the body on the fourth attack – on Bethany Miles – suggests to me that he returned to the victim throughout her incarceration.'

De Vries is nodding. Grace Bellingham is bringing together all the thoughts that have been unable to coalesce in his own mind.

'Bethany Miles is taken from a car park, with her child in the car, albeit asleep. That location at the garden centre, the nursery, is fraught with risk and danger. It tells me that he is becoming desperate, that once he has identified his next target, he is prepared to take ever-greater risks to obtain her.'

She pick up a tumbler of water, sips it, scowls. 'No ice.' She rises and moves to the kitchen. He hears her shaking the ice-box. When she returns, her water contains some slender shards. 'What happened to the weather while I was gone?'

'Getting hotter, but this year, I've never known anything like it.'

He watches her drink, studies the liquid as she swallows. He feels the slightest cooler breeze from the terrace, closes his eyes as it plays over his face.

'Bethany Miles reveals most – are you listening? – reveals most about his actions and completes a progression that indicates a mind which, though certainly predisposed to evil, for want of a better word, has suddenly been entirely released by the freedom of full-blown psychosis within his brain. Simply, unlike a normal human being, he sees nothing unusual, nothing wrong in what he does and, I think, he believes that he is providing a service.'

'What service?'

'The whispered comments, the rape – which, as you know, is nothing to do with sex and everything to do with power – the posing of the eyes and the howling mouth. Power, yes, but what this is really about is punishment.'

'For what reason?'

'We only have a little to go on. Hazel Calder and her husband chose to have children who were then, perhaps predictably, to suffer ill health and death at a young age.' She hesitates. 'There's one child still alive?' She takes a deep breath and lets it out very slowly, contemplating. 'Michelle Ricquarts? Did she mistreat her children? Is she shaming them by stripping? Or is leaving them every evening her crime? You need to find that out.'

'I appreciate this helps us to understand him better, but what do we know that helps us to catch him?'

'I'll precis because I know you don't really like "profiler's jargon". Is that what you called it?'

'Probably.'

'He is almost certainly white, between twenty-eight and forty-four, although I would say more likely towards the top end of that range. He is unmarried and lives either alone or with an elderly relative. There is another possibility, which I believe might fit this profile. It is possible that he has children of his own and that he is widowed or divorced. Normally, I would say that this is unlikely but, given his movements, and the fact that he almost certainly leaves the victims to do other things, it should be considered. A demanding job, perhaps.' She takes a deep breath. 'You've got me involved, and I don't know the answers and all the doubts are coming back. This is what I wanted to avoid.' She glances down at her notes once more, clears her throat. 'You can see the pattern of attacks on the map. I would think that Marie Garsten is an anomaly: something took him to Somerset West and a strong urge, probably a reaction to something he saw, made him choose her. The location where she was found did not require much prior knowledge – it was an abandoned building site – and, anyway, I think he was driven to kill her. So, his home location is likely to be within the parameters set by the three other attacks. Your people can work that out.'

She sips from her glass. 'And one more thing. As well as a home address, he may well have a second place he likes to spend time in. It could be an office, or a park, but more likely a den, somewhere hidden, where he can think and plan.'

'How do we find that?'

'Until you have a real suspect, you probably don't.'

De Vries closes his eyes. He feels the tension in his face, tries to un-grit his teeth. In every case he pursues, it is his impotence that eats at him, his inability to set the running, to be forced to wait, in servitude, for luck or, worse, for his prey to act again, in the hope that he will gather the one sliver of evidence which might lead him to the right person.

'I would not rate him as being in a professional level of employment,' she says, 'but something a little below that. He may own a small business, or be a manager of one. We know that he travels around the peninsula, but I suspect that he avoids interaction with groups of people, preferring individuals. This is a man who eschews being seen or socializing in a group, although he may have specific friends from whom he gains knowledge or experience, even help. What else? He drives, he is strong, although I doubt that he is physically especially strong. He plans, carefully.'

'And he will attack again?'

'What I have learned is that, however close to a pattern these psychopaths follow, the next one may surprise you, but, yes, he

175

will attack again and, when he has tortured and mutilated that victim, he will pick his next. Everything here suggests the classic pattern: he will kill and kill again until he is caught.'

De Vries stands up, walks out onto the terrace, stares up at the dark slopes, deep blue against a glowing indigo sky. Even here, in the bustling suburbia of Claremont, a cicada trills. From this terrace, he cannot see the City Bowl in its crab's embrace by the Mountain, but the yellow glow from it affords Devil's Peak a radiant halo.

He waits a moment, hoping that Grace Bellingham will join him, that perhaps he might put his arm around her shoulders. He turns, sees her bent over the table, her head resting on the highest stack of papers. He comes inside, touches her hair lightly with the palm of his hand, whispers goodnight.

The thermometer by De Vries's bed reads thirty-one degrees, despite his windows having been open all day, curtains drawn against the evening sun. He sits on his bed heavily, finds himself immersed in a mushroom cloud of fine dust. He coughs, stumbles to his feet and into his bathroom. He looks outside. Through the still, thin branches of the tree, he sees the tall, slender, beautiful black woman, lying almost flat on her mattress, the dog's paws on her belly, a mug of tea between her cupped hands. The television flickers, the tinny voices chatter. He feels shadows falling on him as the rectangular cubicle glimmers with bright pale-blue light.

On the leaves of the trees, on his burned-out lawn, on the yellowing shrubs and wilting flowers, he sees the dust: a landscape within hearing of a violent eruption. He plods back into the bedroom, pulls the sheet gently from his bed, and walks outside onto the sagging veranda, being careful to stay clear of the rotting balustrade, held up only by the giant tendril-like trunk of bougainvillaea. Holding his breath, he shakes the sheet gingerly, replaces it on his bed and lies atop it. Exhausted, he does not register the clay-like residue that has adhered to the sweat on the back of his hands and neck. His face is like a clay mask, pock-marked and old.

Cape Tribune

AL-QAEDA ATTACKS MOTHER CITY

Ministry of Justice spokespeople confirmed yesterday evening that the suspects behind the fatal bomb explosion in Long Street last week were allied with al-Qaeda West Africa. Despite no claim being made by the terrorist organization, Terrorist Squad officers have identified the remains of two men with known links to the terrorist cell, which has previously issued threats against what it regards as the decadent lifestyle of the so-called developed cities of South Africa.

ANC security sources said that since the Democratic Alliance took control of the Western Cape Province security provision has stagnated and that its citizens and tourists were now under direct threat.

'Under ANC governance, Cape Town experienced no serious external security threat in a dozen years, yet since the DA took over, the incidents in Cape Town have escalated to the extent that mass murder can be committed in the midst of the business and tourist areas of the city.'

The question all Capetonians must ask is this:

ARE WE SAFE TO ENJOY OUR CITY?

Cape Herald

AL-QAEDA IN CAPE TOWN

The Hawks, terrorist specialists and the SAPS have confirmed that the perpetrators of last week's Long Street bomb attack were allied to

Muslim extremist group al-Qaeda. The death toll now stands at 13, with more than 20 victims still in hospital, some in a serious condition, with doctors saying that a half-dozen more have less than a fifty per cent chance of surviving.

In the first press briefing of substance, Terrorist Squad officers say that they believe the two men, originally of Iraqi descent, left the radical al-Qaeda grouping, al-Mourabitoun, also known as al-Qaeda West Africa, as they felt that too little direct action was being planned, travelled down through the interior of Africa to Cape Town, where they planned and then executed with deadly force their suicide attack on the Mother City. Justice Department spokesmen claimed that analysts had been aware of the potential threat from al-Qaeda in southern Africa but that Democratic Alliance Party politicians had dismissed it as 'scare-mongering to damage the thriving economy of the Western Cape'.

How this attack will impact on tourism to Cape Town, both from within the country and from abroad, is yet to be understood, but DA administrators are now under scrutiny as to whether they have in place sufficient security to protect travellers to Cape Town.

New Cape Gazette

CITY ON FIRE

* Al-Qaeda strike at heart of Mother City – Muslim extremist link confirmed. 14 dead; many more 'not out of danger'.
* SAPS 'aware' but 'baffled' by serial killer stalking women with children. Two dead, two abducted. 'There may be others in the past and in the future.'
* Fires destroy forty dwellings. Three dead. Two parents and five children seriously injured. Police suspect arson.
* Students and unions demonstrate; marches close city streets. Heat claims one victim.
* Water restrictions now critical.

* DA administrators struggling to cope as tourists cancel visits and desert streets. Cape Town businesses threatened as city faces worst crisis of confidence since apartheid.

Sally Frazer swivels in her chair, rises to stand, faces the centre of the room, addresses De Vries.

'Before you ask, I don't know, and nor does anyone else, where Ali Jelani is.' She sits back down, beckons for De Vries to sit next to her. 'However, I did call both Mark Garsten and Luke Miles to ask them about their children and they both told me stories.'

'It's all about the children,' De Vries says, yawning, his hand reaching his mouth just as it is closing again.

'Yes, I think it is,' she says. 'Luke Miles told me that his son, Josh, had broken his leg when he was playing around the family car while Bethany Miles was driving. She was late collecting her daughter from an end-of-year event and, in effect, she had backed out of the driveway and driven over Josh when he was on the ground.'

De Vries raises his eyes to heaven.

'Some of us are good drivers,' Sally Frazer says. 'There was a crowd of people who gathered before the ambulance arrived. Apparently, some of them were pretty scathing about her.'

'What about Mark Garsten?'

'That was weird. He said that about ten days before she disappeared, she had come home from collecting the children from school, had pulled up at the traffic lights and the man in the car behind her got out and came to talk to her. There were people around and he was white, so she lowered her window. Apparently, he told her angrily that she should not be smoking in the car with children inside.'

'She give a description?'

'Not that the husband remembers, no,' Frazer says. 'He tried to help her dismiss it. He said that she was obviously pretty upset because she knew that he would be displeased to hear that she was smoking in the car, but she told him about it anyway. He said that she told him the man had been very threatening and it had unnerved her all the way home. She thought he might be following her, but she wasn't sure. Mark Garsten said that he went outside and checked the street, but he couldn't see anything.'

'This all ties in with what Dr Bellingham and I were discussing last night,' De Vries says. 'Yesterday evening.' He pauses, frowns, glances at his watch. 'It's seven forty-five a.m. Have you been home?'

'Briefly,' Frazer says. 'You said this is the moment that we have to stop him before he strikes again. When you say that, I can't sleep.'

He leans back in the cheap office chair, its front legs in the air, plastic back arching.

'Hazel Calder suffered from dwarfism, had three children, all affected. Two died in childhood. Michelle Ricquarts leaves her daughters alone while she goes out to strip – do we know anything else about them?'

Sally Frazer shakes her head, says: 'Marie Garsten smokes in the car with her children there and gets warned about it. By our man, you think? And Bethany Miles runs over her son's leg and breaks it.'

'Okay, let's go back a moment. Marie Garsten: where did this incident occur?'

'Just off Irene Avenue in Somerset West. I haven't spoken to Traffic yet, but even if there were cameras, it's been a month.'

'You ask the husband if she could describe the car?'

'I did, and he said she knew nothing about cars and didn't mention it.'

De Vries gets up, walks to the table where the squad-room

180

coffee jug sits next to the chipped, thick-rimmed crockery, flicks the empty glass container, turns back.

'We have a connection: children. Injured, deformed at birth, mistreated in some way. We know that he spends some time down towards Strand and Somerset West because he happened to see Marie Garsten and her children in their car. It's good, but how does it help us to catch him?'

Don February and Ben Thwala enter the squad-room in conversation, stopping when they see De Vries and Frazer at work.

'Any progress, sir?'

De Vries regards them. 'Thanks to Sally, some . . . Not enough.' He licks his lips. 'I'm going to make a quick call. When I come back, I want decent coffee for all of us, sweet things to eat, and the home address of Penelope van Reidel.' He opens his wallet, slaps an orange 200-rand note on the table. He looks up at Don and Ben Thwala. 'This is important police business, gentlemen. Get on it.'

Don February has icing sugar on his lips, making him resemble a minstrel from the New Year's Day parades, his eyes wide and shining. The strong coffee, pastries and doughnuts have imbued each of them with new energy.

'Security cameras on the private residences surrounding Rose's nursery: were they checked?'

Thwala swallows quickly. 'We asked, door-to-door, but private cameras usually do not retain footage.'

'What about those linked to a central computer, held by the security company?'

Thwala nods, still chewing. 'Sometimes, then, yes.'

'Just see what you can find.'

Don says: 'But we do not know who to look for or which road he would have taken.'

'No, but we know what car Bethany Miles was driving. He would have arrived a little before her or soon after. He couldn't afford to sit around in the car park attracting attention. More likely, he followed her. We might just pick up something . . .'

'It will be no more than flashes as they pass on the road. Most of the cameras only cover the gateways.'

'Don. This is what we have left. He's giving us nothing so we have to find it ourselves: a sliver, a glimpse. And you don't have to do it: this is why we second officers . . .'

Sally Frazer passes him a torn slip of paper. 'The Van Reidel address. Oranjezicht.'

De Vries tips back his head, taps the base of the little cardboard shot-cup of espresso, relishes the thickness of the residue as it hits his throat.

'Okay. I'm going to Oranjezicht. I've got a visitor coming. Don't engage with him. Put him in my office, offer him nothing, and tell him I'll be back soon. They'll call up from downstairs.'

Oranjezicht sits elevated above the City Bowl, adjoining the fashionable end of Kloof Street, bounded by the lower slopes of the Mountain. In Klipp Street, the fine Victorian villas remain as single dwellings, the old fruit trees contorted over century-old stucco walls. Even early in the morning, the sun seems to blaze almost horizontally over the tops of the skyscrapers, burning the wide roads and steep side-streets of the district. De Vries waits for two large domestic workers to wheeze their way up the pavement before opening his car door. Twelve Klipp Street is a soaring double-fronted villa, with dark stone steps leading to tall double doors, glazed with bevelled glass and ornate ironwork. He feels the sweat at his neck as he is merely climbing the staircase. In answer to the doorbell, a video monitor with speaker illuminates to his right and a strident male voice says: 'What do you want?'

De Vries holds up his ID. 'A word with Ms van Reidel.'

'You have an appointment?'

De Vries opens his mouth, but he hears her voice on the intercom.

'It's all right.'

Ahead of him, he sees a door open to a room off the long hallway. Penelope van Reidel dismisses a maid, who has appeared from the distance, with a flick of her wrist that is so much part of the lilting stride which propels her to the door. She swings it open.

'Colonel de Vries, before nine a.m.'

'We tried to contact you yesterday afternoon and yesterday evening . . .'

'Yesterday I was busy.'

'. . . but you did not respond.'

De Vries waits to be invited in, but she stands in the doorway, blankly mute, unmoving.

'Do you understand busy?'

'I'm busy, Ms van Reidel, trying to stop a man abduct, rape and then slowly kill another woman. I don't care about pleasantries, or playing games. I need to find Ali Jelani. It seems only you know her whereabouts.'

'I have no idea where Ali Jelani is.'

'She's providing you with copy.'

'It's filed electronically. She could do it from the other side of the world.'

'But she's not on the other side of the world. She's here in Cape Town, being fed information by a source with intimate knowledge of these crimes. Either that source is part of my team, in which case that officer is jeopardizing everything we are working

183

for, or the source has knowledge of the scenes or the perpetrator. Do you understand how dangerous that is for Ali Jelani?'

'She is a brave and determined young woman.'

De Vries moderates his voice. 'There is nothing admirable about withholding vital information from the police, especially if doing so results in the unnecessary death of another victim.'

She studies him silently, then stands aside, allowing him to step over the threshold into the cool hallway. She closes the door, passes him, and walks to the room from which she first appeared. De Vries hears her heels against the polished yellow-wood floor.

'Just wait there.' She pulls the door behind her. It moves soundlessly, heavy and protective. The deep click of its closure reverberates down the broad hall with its antique furniture and fresh flowers, glowing wooden ceiling, gleaming, immaculate paint-work. He hears the muffled sound of domestic travail from within, the roar of the city behind him no more than stifled exclamation. He waits in the silence, understanding the power-play, the su-periority of her position. His breathing is shallow, but calm, yet he can feel the blood in his arteries right down to his fingers.

He sees the brass handle turn, the door reopen.

'Ali Jelani will speak only if certain conditions are met.'

'You spoke to her?'

'I am to judge the sincerity of your undertaking.'

'You told me you didn't know where she is.'

'I don't. She is contactable. I have done that for you.'

'What conditions?'

'She wants to meet casually, in a public venue of her choosing, with a senior female detective, plain-clothed, who has discretion. She wants assurance that she will not be taken to a police station, or prevented from continuing her work.'

'Agreed.'

'Agreed? Just like that?'

'Yes.'

'And I should believe you?'

De Vries smiles thinly. 'I understood that you were to "judge the sincerity of my undertaking".'

The corner of her mouth twitches minutely.

'You are good at what you do. I discovered that. Appallingly flawed, probably scarred. Unreconstructed, hereditarily racist, numbingly misogynist . . .'

'You should hear about my faults.'

'But you're not funny. Not at all.' She studies him, their eye-line plumb. 'I have your word that Ali Jelani will be left unmolested, that you agree to her terms?'

'You do.'

She stands utterly still, regarding him, then slowly raises her left hand, passes him a heavy handwritten card.

'The woman you send, what name will she use?'

'Sally.'

'Sally it is, then.'

'Is that it?'

'You have the venue, the time. For now, my trust. That's it.'

'Thank you.'

'It's like obituaries for famous people. I have two alternative front pages for you, De Vries. Which gets printed is entirely in your hands now.'

He bows to her. 'Better a headline than an obituary.'

Mike Solarin hears the chanting from several streets away, feet stamping on the hot tarmac, drums and tins beaten, the hoarse, amp-boosted cry leading the chorus. The cacophony hangs in the dry, still air like brake-lights in a time-lapse night-time cityscape.

He turns the corner, is taken aback to register the numbers

outside the Jumu'a Mosque of Cape Town. A core of perhaps a hundred protesters wave flags and placards, sing, chant and echo shouted phrases. The signs are either blatantly anti-Islamic or accuse Muslims of appeasing extremism. Some complain of new mosque construction in Cape Town. Beyond and around this group stand another two hundred, bedraggled, on the periphery. He studies their faces, sees them mouthing words, taking photographs, occasionally nodding in assent.

Solarin stops in the shade, leans against the cool stone façade of an old building just off Grey's Pass in the very centre of Cape Town, watches three Metro cops stand at the foot of the wide pink steps leading to the plain wooden doors beneath the pillared façade of the dignified, modest building. Their expressions tell of fatigue from the heat, assault on their senses, alarm at the increasing number of protesters, at the growing volume of the chants. Two men start screaming hysterically, leading an elderly woman to the foot of the steps. Her cries and wails draw more women around her. Each begins to cry, to moan, to yowl in mourning.

Solarin pulls himself away from the wall, the crying grating down his spine as he takes a wide arc around the demonstration. In the distance, mingling with the human sirens, he hears police response vehicles approaching, fears for what might happen. At the corner of the street, he circles within his step, glancing back at the scene, walks on. Out of sight, he stops, peers around the corner of the grey monolithic building, looks back at the gathering. Where he had been standing, another figure now waits, observing the scene. He wipes his eyes with the back of his hand, replaces his dark glasses, focuses. Beyond the blindingly bright white sunlight, in the comparative darkness of the shade, Ray Black stands, watching the scene.

Solarin laughs to himself. The man wears dark glasses too, the details of his expression indiscernible. He cannot truly see this, but he half observes, half imagines, that Ray Black is smiling, satisfied, his arms crossed in front of him.

'Sergeant Frazer.' De Vries is moving fast into the squad-room. 'Delightful as you already look, please find yourself a casual summer dress, adorn yourself appropriately, and get ready to go out for lunch.'

Several team members look up. He reaches her desk, says quietly, 'You're meeting our elusive journalist at twelve. I'll brief you on the way.'

'Me?'

'It's a girl thing, apparently. Our ears only.' He glances around him. 'Let the tongues wag.'

She says: 'Mr Stephen Jessel. He arrived about ten minutes ago.' De Vries looks towards his corner office, can see only the back of Jessel, upright in one of the chairs that face his desk. 'He's a bit of a whiner.'

'I hope you ignored him.'

'I did, but it is hot in there.'

'He only has a few minutes more. That's where I spend the rest of my career.' De Vries leans towards her. 'I was serious about the dress.' He looks at his watch. 'I think we should go at eleven fifteen.'

He straightens up, considers putting on his jacket, thinks better of it, moves to his office. As he swings open the door, Stephen Jessel rises.

'Did you turn off the air-conditioning in here?'

'No, Mr Jessel. This is how we live.' He moves around his desk, hangs his jacket on the other guest chair and slumps in his seat. 'Take your jacket off. This is a very informal meeting.'

He thinks that Jessel is wearing the same shirt and tie as he had been on his first visit to the Special Crimes Unit. He observes Jessel's shirt is already damp with perspiration, sticking to his chest, revealing pale, clammy skin beneath the thin material.

'Please may we come to the point, Colonel? I don't have the luxury of spare time in my day. This meeting inevitably compromises the next and so on throughout my schedule.' He lowers his voice. 'If you wish to discuss the man we discussed at our last meeting, I need to be reassured that the same terms of confidentiality are in place.'

'Totally.'

'And, other than his Christian name, it would be better if specific details were not discussed at this time.' He glances behind himself, through the glass partition onto the squad-room. 'Is there a more private room?'

'I just want to know a few very simple things.'

Jessel turns back around to face De Vries, feels in his briefcase and produces a clipboard, which he places on his lap.

'Very well.'

'When we last spoke, you – and then subsequently Leigh himself – told me that he did not leave his house often, and when he did, it was usually with some of his friends. Is that right?'

'Yes.'

'I asked you how you knew when he went out and you told me that he simply informed you. Do you have no other method of checking his movements?'

Jessel shifts in the sticky chair. 'Leigh Finnemore is not imprisoned. He is both a free man and the subject of surveillance and monitoring. He has lived in Plumbago Lane for almost a decade and there has never once been a complaint about him. Nor have I ever had cause to criticize the actions he has taken. Therefore he is free to move around as he wishes, but I know – it is known – that he rarely ventures outside.'

'Does he have use of a car?'

'There is a car in the garage there, yes. A Volkswagen Beetle. An old one. To begin with, Leigh ignored it, but now he sometimes washes it in the garage. I helped him get it serviced and fit to drive. I hoped that it would allow him a little more freedom. He occasionally takes it for a circuit down Camps Bay Drive, along Beach Road, up to Kloof Nek and back again. He says he feels that is far enough and he is happy to come home. It probably takes less than fifteen minutes. That is how he is.'

'Does he ever take anyone with him?'

'Not that he tells me.'

'And do you check his mileage?'

Jessel frowns, then laughs. 'No. Why would I?'

'To monitor how far he has driven.'

'Perhaps that is something I should do, but I haven't. If I did find that he travelled further afield, it would bring me pleasure. It would represent more self-confidence and a chance that he might be releasing himself from what is, these days, almost self-imposed solitude.'

'So no one monitors where he goes, or with who, or when?'

Jessel sighs. 'Not empirically. I discuss with him how he feels, what he's done, what he would like to do.' He fastens his pen under the clip at the top of the board and leans over it towards De Vries. 'If these questions are because you still suspect him of some involvement in the incident at the other end of Plumbago Lane, then I merely repeat what I told you last time. I have not seen any indication of aggressive or violent tendencies in Leigh.'

'But just entirely hypothetically,' De Vries says casually, 'if Leigh Finnemore wanted to go out at night – for whatever reason – stay out for an hour or two and come home, no one would know?'

'He would inform me.'

'He *should* inform you.'

'I have no reason to think that Leigh is withholding from me.'

189

De Vries smiles. 'But the answer to my question is no?'

'Out of context, and with no understanding of the subject or his history, I accept that the answer to your meaningless question is no.'

'That's what I thought.'

'Was that that man Jessel? The one who authorized the section eighteen on . . . Leigh Finnemore?' Henrik du Toit gestures that De Vries should follow him.

'I was on my way to you anyway, sir.'

'I'm sure you were, Vaughn.' They walk up the staircase in silence. 'What was he doing here?'

De Vries closes Du Toit's office door behind him.

'I just wanted to clarify some information.'

'And did you?'

'I did. Jessel confirmed what I already suspected. Despite what he told us last time, the impression he tried to give, Finnemore isn't surveyed or monitored. He's looked in on occasionally. He has use of a car and can go out when he wants, without letting anyone know, day or night. Before you say anything, I know his neighbours say they've scarcely seen him, but I've been in that street several times now and, first of all, I haven't seen any of his neighbours – not one, not once – and second, if he is going out late at night, those people are all asleep in their back rooms, escaping the wind. They'd see nothing.'

'You're painting him as a suspect?'

'He is a suspect. How can anyone who has murdered before not be a suspect?'

'He has killed before, perhaps accidentally. There is a difference.'

'There is, if you believe all that psychological mumbo-jumbo.'

Du Toit holds up his hands, a gesture to which he frequently finds himself resorting when listening to De Vries.

190

'These crimes are all linked to children,' De Vries says, 'to the treatment of children. You read Grace Bellingham's profile, sir?'

'I have, and I'm worried that you're calling me "sir".'

'Leigh Finnemore fits that profile like the proverbial glove.'

'All right. Just wait. What about this journalist woman?'

'Ali Jelani. We're going to talk to her shortly. At least, Sergeant Frazer is, woman to woman.'

'You found her.'

'It required some persuasion . . .'

There is a silence.

Du Toit says: 'Aren't you going to ask? Aren't you curious?'

'About what?'

'How you can be on the front page of a newspaper drawing criticism of the SAPS, this department, our unit, and there has been no thunder from above?'

'I was revelling in not knowing the answer to that mystery.'

'I told General Thulani that you had persuaded Dr Bellingham to assist us — and that was a coup, that you were making excellent progress in sorting out what was happening, and that you were working fourteen-to-sixteen-hour days and deserved some down time.'

'I'm grateful for your confidence.'

'Is it misplaced?'

'Well, you should know by now, Henrik. It's a gamble.'

'This is the coolest I've been since my summons to the top floor.'

She looks at De Vries, smiles. 'Air-con was recharged when it was serviced, two weeks ago. Eats petrol but, hey, best part of my day is in here.'

Sally Frazer turns her VW Golf onto the slip road off Nelson Mandela Boulevard down to Salt River, draws up at the queue to turn onto Main Road.

'You know what we want from Jelani,' De Vries says. 'What she knows, how she knows it. And, while you're at it, why she's being so elusive. Tell her that you need to be able to reach her if she prints any more articles. Gain her confidence.'

'I'm still SAPS.'

De Vries glances across at her. Her hair, so resolutely tied in the office, is loose over the collar of a pale blue summer dress. Bare legs show.

'Hard to believe.'

She turns onto Main Road, which runs from town all the way down to Muizenberg. Here, in Salt River and Woodstock, it is lined with factory shops and warehouses, the old businesses, which still just about keep a foothold along the main drag, and, increasingly, artisan coffee bars, restaurants and galleries. Even so, the street is full of people, there is noisy trading from stalls and markets, taxi-vans honking, produce transported by horse and cart, on scooters, atop the heads of stoical women.

She takes the Railway circle and heads for Observatory, a suburb that absorbs poor, artistic, student and hipster, every age, colour and religion. Half a kilometre from the designated meeting place, De Vries tells her to stop. He squints past her to a bar on the opposite side of the road.

'It says it has Wi-Fi, air-con, food, drink. This is my field-office.' He gets out of the car, leans back in through the passenger door. 'You know where I am. I know where you are. Don't let her take you anywhere without calling me. This Françoise place is over Station Road, *ja*?'

Frazer nods. 'I know it, sir.'

He ducks out, raises his voice against a passing truck. 'Good luck.'

'François/Françoise' is a bar and café, excavated from the shell of an old industrial building just off the main road. Its windows are dark and heavily barred but, within, fairy lights sparkle, Chinese lanterns glow and, beyond, green-tinged daylight suggests a leafy courtyard or garden.

Sally Frazer has walked past its door before, late at night, glancing momentarily towards discordant music, seeing cigarette tips glow in a fog of nicotine; she remembers that, at night, it is a venue for local bands. She turns sideways to slide through the narrow navy-blue metal door, finds the interior soothingly cool and devoid of glare. A gleaming brass coffee machine hisses at the end of the long dark turquoise-tiled bar, behind which a huge mirror reflects the ceiling-high display of fancy bottles, plastic street-stall toys and ceramic figurines, vintage signs and framed maps.

She walks past sparsely filled tables towards a wide opening onto a leafy courtyard, shaded by fig trees. She examines a bed of cannabis plants, their huge leaves sieving the sunlight, dappling it onto the cobbled ground. A sign states: 'Male Sativa Plants: Like Their Human Equivalents, Providing Little of Consequence'. She scans the half-dozen café tables, moves back inside.

In an alcove to her left, she sees a small African woman, head bowed, studying her. Sally Frazer determines to put the intonation of recognition into her voice.

'Ali . . . I'm Sally.'

The woman stands. Frazer moves past Jelani's outstretched hand, holds her shoulders, kisses her lightly on both cheeks. Ali Jelani shrinks from her, retakes her seat. Her eyes dart from side to side, her breathing accelerates.

'Are you okay?' Frazer asks. Staccato nodding. 'You wanted it casual. I thought we'd look like friends.'

'I do not consider you people my friends.'

'You want a drink?'

'Coffee. Black. They'll come.'

Frazer leans back, taking in the obstructed view to the

courtyard, her line of sight down the length of the bar. She catches one half of her face in a painted café mirror. With her hair let down, she scarcely recognizes herself.

'This is very private here. We can talk.'

'Maybe . . .'

A girl, probably a UCT student working her vacation, attends their table. Frazer orders for both of them. Ali Jelani continues to shake, eyes down but wide, her small fingers clenched.

'What's the matter, Ali?'

She looks around once more. 'You do not understand. All my life I have been afraid, ever since I was a child.'

'Afraid of what?'

Ali Jelani sniffs. 'Being trodden on, being ignored, being banished, being used . . .'

'Can we talk about your writing?'

'No. You can hear me first. I say what I want to say.'

Two young black girls, arm in arm, their heads immaculate and gleaming, walk past into the courtyard. Both are talking on cellphones. Frazer watches Ali Jelani inspect them. Their coffee arrives. Jelani pulls her cup close to her, guards it with her hands.

'I come from Kenya. They call it a city, but it is only a town, called Eldoret. It is in the west. The Voortrekkers took it from my people in 1910, so I have come to take land here in South Africa, in the Cape.'

'All right . . .'

'Do you have any idea how hard it is for a girl to be educated where I come from? To study and learn? I did that. I volunteered and I wrote, and I gave the newspaper and magazine editors my work for nothing, and still they would not take it. Because I could not write as well as a man? No way . . .' She raises the cup to her lips, blows on the surface, sips gingerly. 'You have a husband?'

'Not yet.'

Ali Jelani laughs sadly. 'You have a choice! I was pregnant when I was seventeen, and though I begged him no, he made me pregnant again only a few months after my child was born. I gave him two girls and he wanted boys, so he left us and he told the town that I was cursed.'

Momentarily, she seems to have forgotten her fear. Her eyes never meet those of her interlocutor. They stare beyond her cup and saucer at the scratched wooden school desk that is their table, as if she is examining the markings in search of a lost story.

'So, despite my burden, I travel this continent to write and still it is hard for a woman, even when she is writing about women. I follow the African Union Mission to Somalia, spend six months volunteering in the Walalah Biylooley refugee camp, covering the struggle against female genital mutilation. I go to Ethiopia and Rwanda and Burundi. Last year, I travel to Syria to speak to the women who have been raped as an act of war, as a way for men to exert their strength, to impregnate women so that they might be damned for all their lives.'

Her voice is rising. The whites of her eyes seem to shine in the dim interior. Frazer raises her palms on the surface of the table.

Ali Jelani's nostrils flare, but she moderates her voice, leaning in towards her. 'No one would publish my work. Online only, in a country where the internet is still a rarity.'

'So you came here?'

'You are not listening to me. In your country, thirty-eight per cent of women have been raped. Men admit it, like it is a badge, a credit to them. Twenty-eight per cent of men admit it. Boast . . .'

'I know the figures, Ali,' Frazer says firmly. 'My colleagues and I deal with the aftermath of them every day. Believe me.'

'You know figures . . .' Ali Jelani sounds scornful, her thin fingers insect-like around the handle of her cup. She raises it, sips, sips again, says: 'You are not interested in what women must face here?'

Frazer speaks calmly: 'There is much to do, and many ways of achieving it. In our own ways, perhaps we are both achieving something. We must talk about your work for Penelope van Reidel at the *New Cape Gazette*.'

'That woman is whiter than alabaster. She has known nothing but wealth and privilege, but she is the first here, in the national press, to give me an opportunity. I grasp that opportunity. It is only a thin branch but I will make it bear fruit.'

'The stories about Hazel Calder and Michelle Ricquarts: how did you find them?'

'Work. Research. Labour.'

'But how?'

'I just told you.'

'Ms Jelani . . . Ali . . . These were two unpublished crimes in two different policing areas. We just need to understand how you made the connection between them, and then to Marie Garsten, who lived and was found fifty kilometres from here.'

'A good journalist has her sources.'

'You don't need to name your source but you can tell me: is it from the SAPS?' She lowers her voice on the final words as if speaking a taboo.

'It may be.'

'If you know something about who is committing these crimes, you must tell us.'

Jelani still stares downwards. Her eyes rise only to survey her surroundings, then lower again. Once they are beyond making any contact with Sally Frazer, she says:

'Do you know who is committing these crimes?'

'We are working very hard to find out. Why would you not speak to us?'

'There are many who want to silence me.'

Frazer turns towards the sound of voices. Four white women amble past them into the courtyard; two return and scrutinize the available tables indoors, then stand behind them, chattering, waiting for their friends to make a decision. She looks across the table at Ali Jelani. She cannot be more than thirty-five, perhaps younger, her small face fixed in its expression of toiling determination, jaw set, eyes constantly moving. Usually a person's face reveals as many secrets as words are spoken, but Frazer cannot see her eyes, or interpret veracity from her features, either frozen or animated, like a repeating tick.

The women move indoors towards the front of the bar.

'Who told you about the crime scene where Bethany Miles was found? You have to understand, whoever is giving you this information is either stealing from us – the police – compromising our investigation, breaking the law, or they have knowledge of the crimes because they were there.'

For the first time, Ali Jelani does not counter immediately, seeming to consider what is being said to her.

Frazer waits, then says: 'You must tell me. Whatever you think your source is giving you, whatever advantage you gain professionally, it is too high a price.'

Ali Jelani raises her head, speaking quietly and deliberately: 'There is always a price to be paid.'

Frazer leans towards her until their faces are almost touching. 'These women are stripped and bound and left alone in the dark without water for days. They are gagged and blindfolded, tortured and raped by a man who believes it is his right to punish them. He will not stop. Whoever is giving you your information must know more than we do. Help us.' She leans back, aware of her breath, of the heat in the alcove. She sees Ali Jelani's chest rise and fall; sees her struggle to wet the back of her throat; one hand gripping the index finger of the other. She waits until Jelani meets her eye. 'Whatever you think you can achieve with your writing, is any of that worth it if another woman is taken by a man, tortured and bound and murdered?'

197

Jelani looks down. Her small head seems to quiver.

'I write about African women, what they have to suffer.'

'You wouldn't help a white woman?'

'Don't lecture me on discrimination . . .' She trails off, the scorn in her voice desultory, her mind absorbed with other thoughts.

'Surely women must stand by women. What other chance do we have?'

Jelani shakes her head. 'You know nothing of the suffering of women on this continent.'

Frazer swallows her desire to argue, to fight her assertion, tells herself that she has only one role here. She drains her cup, looks around for a waitress.

Jelani reaches down to a small handbag woven from grass. She rights herself.

'You smoke?'

Frazer shakes her head.

'Please get me some cigarettes. Strong. They are behind the bar.'

Frazer stands, looks back at Ali Jelani, who has her bag on the table, a pen between her lips. She rounds the corner, asks the tall, smooth-skinned black guy behind the bar for cigarettes. As he turns back, smiling, she realizes that he is very beautiful, his face perfect, high cheekbones, broad eye sockets, his glowing complexion unblemished. She pays for the cigarettes, wonders whether he is the eponymous François, turns to their table, turns again, François/Françoise: perhaps he is both . . . She smiles to herself, glances back at her table. Ali Jelani is gone.

Frazer checks for Jelani's handbag, any sign that she might have slipped away to the bathroom, but there is nothing except a blank sheet of paper. She looks back down the length of the café, certain that Jelani did not pass behind her while she was at the bar. In the body language of her fellow customers, she takes in laughter and concentration, relaxation and boredom. She hurries to the lavatories, finds both sexes' facilities deserted, moves into the

198

courtyard, scans the tables. In the far corner, behind one of the beds of sterile cannabis plants, she sees a door with a release bar. A fire-exit sign is hidden by one of the leaves. She stares at the table closest to her. A woman looks up.

'She went through there.'

'Just now?'

'*Ja.* One minute ago, sure.'

She pushes down on the release bar, drops her own bag on the ground to stop the door snapping shut and locking her out, finds herself in a narrow backstreet. The service entrances to the shops beyond line the far side, garages, fire-escape ladders and waste bins the other. She sees no sign of human life in either direction. She feels nauseous and angry, made foolish by a simple ruse.

She pulls the fire door open, retrieves her bag, returns to their table, sits. She sees the waitress and calls for the bill.

'The lady I was with . . . Has she been here before? Have you seen her?'

The girl shakes her head, turns away.

Frazer sees the sheet of paper in the waitress's hand, realizes that there is faint writing on the reverse.

'That paper.' The waitress turns. 'Can I have it back?' She takes it from the girl, waits until she has gone before turning it over. A single line is written in a faint, spidery hand. She feels her chest ache, bile rise. She slaps a hundred-rand note on the table, slides it under the brass ashtray. She starts to stride towards the door, out into the light, into what she finds is a blinding, stupefying sun, stumbles on the cracked pavement as she begins to run towards her car.

'Let me in!'

He sees light flutter in the peephole. He turns to the two uni-formed officers with him.

'Wait by the lift until I'm inside.' He watches them go. 'I'm alone, Grace.'

The door to Grace Bellingham's apartment opens abruptly. He enters, does not see her, hears the door slam behind him. She stands with her back to it.

'You call me, you tell me to lock the doors and windows, not to answer the front door. What danger? What danger am I in?' He comes towards her, but her stare stops him mid-stride. 'I want to know exactly what the nature of this threat is.'

'Come and sit down.'

'No, Vaughn. You're in my home. You made me do this for you and now you just do what I ask, or I swear I'll make you regret it.'

He sees that she has been crying, cheeks tear-stained. He walks over to the seating area by the wide windows.

'We tracked down this journalist, Ali Jelani. She took the photograph of us at the bar the other night, wrote the article, all the articles in the last six weeks. According to my sergeant who met her . . .'

'Your sergeant?'

'She wanted a woman – she'd only speak with a woman. I sent Sally Frazer. She's part of my core team. She's good. She says that before Jelani escaped and disappeared—'

'She lost her? This sergeant who's good?'

'—she got the impression that not only was she very afraid, but that she had had contact with our attacker, or someone close to him. She thought that she was making a breakthrough, but Jelani demanded cigarettes and used that opportunity to get away through the fire escape.'

'Jesus.'

'It happens.'

'But the warning?'

'On a sheet of paper, left by Jelani.'

'Show me.'

'It's being examined by our people in town. Jelani told a story about her background, but we don't know if any of it is true.'

She walks towards him. 'What did it say, Vaughn?'

'Your name. That he wanted to take you.'

She closes her eyes, the breath flowing from her body. She doubles over, pulls herself back up to face him.

'That's not good enough. I need the exact words.' De Vries hesitates. 'For Christ's sake, just tell me.'

'"He wants to take G. Bellingham soon."'

'The pronoun, not the name?'

'Your name?'

'His name.'

De Vries frowns. 'Just "he".'

'If he were a third party, she might use a name to distinguish between the killer and her contact. She's been in communication with him.' She shakes her head. 'Jesus, she could be working for him. You need to find out if she's been threatened, coerced, if her family has . . .' She walks around him towards the sitting area, her breathing fast and erratic. He follows her. 'He wants to take me. You're sure he used the word "take"?'

'*She* used it. It was her handwritten note.'

She is panting. He tries again to come close to her.

'Stay away. Just stay away. I begged you not to involve me. I've been back one week and this happens. Because of you. Because whatever you think of yourself, about your life, you don't really like being on your own, do you? You don't like sleeping alone and you don't like working alone, so you have to involve someone else, and I told you I didn't want it to be me . . .' She swallows tears, her hand pushing her hair from falling over her face. 'You have no idea what I went through in Virginia. They used me to reach this man, this monster of a man, and I was tired and broken and since then I can't sleep, can't work, can't think, and I let you, you . . . You make me do this.'

'I'll pay for a ticket. Get a flight. There's bound to be a seat tonight. Go to London, Amsterdam, Berlin. Get away from here. When I catch him and it's safe, come back, and I swear I'll never ask you anything again.'

'No.'

'No?'

'You don't run from these people. You run and they have power over you for ever. They know you run, so they find ways to follow you even if they're incarcerated, even if they're dead. You never stop running.'

'When we have him, he won't hurt you. You said yourself, these people are loners.'

'I didn't say that, and you know nothing about these men.'

'Then help me catch him.'

Her eyes flare. He sees her run the three steps towards him. She balls her fists and thumps them into his chest. The first blow against his heart winds him, shocks him; he stumbles, but she keeps pummelling him, over and over again, on his back, his neck, his head. He backs away, but she follows him until his back hits the wall and he has nowhere else to go.

'Help you catch him?' She is shouting, voice distorted by rage. 'Be my bait?' He tries to look up at her, but she punches him again. 'Yes, that's what men think women should be. That's what those cunts in America did to me. That's what they wanted, so they used me to get it.'

'I'm sorry, Grace . . .'

'You're sorry. You can't control your team, you can't control your witnesses and you sure as hell can't control him.'

She stumbles to the utilitarian sofa, falls onto it. De Vries waits where he is. They are both breathless; he feels tightness in his chest, feels blackness descend on him. Even as he says the words, he knows he will not be believed.

'I can't undo this, but I can protect you.'

Her neck seems to give way, her head lolling onto the top of the backrest. She gasps to find a voice.

'Leave me alone.'

'I can't do that.'

She hauls her head up, sits forward, says quietly: 'I'm angry with you, but sure as hell I'm angrier with myself.' She punches the sofa. 'What have I become? I used to be strong.'

He moves across the room, kneels next to the sofa.

'I'm sorry, Grace.'

'Make me tea.'

'Tea?'

'Yes, a mug of tea. Two sugars. Then sit down over there while I think what to do. I need to think.'

He struggles up, moves to the front door, opens it. The two officers are by the lift as instructed. He beckons to them.

'Outside this door. Anyone approaches, draw your weapon.' He studies them. 'You understand that order?'

They confirm that they do. He closes the door, goes to the kitchen, turns back to her.

'Let me take you to my house. If he knows about you, he may know this address. The whole of upstairs can be locked down. I did it for Suzanne and the girls. No one can get in. You can rest.'

'Rest? You have no idea what this means.'

'It means I can look after you.'

She slumps lower into the sofa. 'It means I am already a prisoner.'

'Dr Bellingham has set up an office in my house. Three officers posted. She can lock herself in.'

Henrik du Toit seems to be staring at his mouth, watching the words emerge.

'If you are convinced that is the safest option.'

'I am.'

'I know how you feel about her, Vaughn. Are you certain you're making the right decisions for the right reasons?'

'As sure as I can be right now.'

'And this note? I've spoken to Sergeant Frazer. She says she felt she'd shifted this Jelani woman's view of what was happening, that the note is a genuine warning, based on what Jelani knows.'

'I think it is.'

'I want to ask you this: does Dr Bellingham fit the profile of the attacker's victims?'

'She's divorced, messily,' De Vries says. 'Her relationship with her children has been strained. Her biography is public knowledge online. Frazer's been researching what's in the public domain about her, says that in interviews Bellingham openly describes the effect of her work on her marriage, her family. If children are the link, there is reason to believe she could be targeted but, frankly, I think it's more likely that whoever the perpetrator is, he saw the picture of us in that *Cape Gazette* and thinks her involvement in the case makes her a target.'

'He thinks she can find him?'

'Possibly. And if the Jelani woman is working for the killer, even through a go-between, she could have given him Bellingham's history, her training and experience in the States.'

'Even if we believe that Jelani does have some form of contact with him,' Du Toit says, 'why would he tell her his target?'

'We don't know he didn't tell her who his previous two targets were.'

'Jelani had prior knowledge of his victims and told nobody?'

De Vries sighs. 'I don't know, sir. We know next to nothing

about Ali Jelani. The editor, Van Reidel, claims to know little about her. I think she started providing newsworthy copy and all scrutiny was abandoned in the name of a good story.'

'I hope you're wrong about that, Vaughn. It would be callous beyond belief.'

'I have long pondered the inhumanity of women towards women . . .'

'That's not funny. We need answers, and action, not attempts at glib wit.'

'We have two teams dedicated to working on this around the clock,' De Vries tells him, ignoring the criticism. 'I'll be briefing my team for the operation this evening.'

Du Toit shakes his head. 'Whatever it is had better work because I can tell you—'

'That you have had General Thulani and, no doubt, Pretoria on your back,' De Vries says wearily. 'Am I right?'

'You are. We're being scrutinized. As ever. I want every decision you make recorded and documented.'

'As ever.'

'How would he even know where Grace is now?'

'It's safest to assume that he does,' De Vries says. 'Or will.'

'And you think he'll risk trying to attack her?'

'Dr Bellingham's own profile suggests that he will take greater and greater risks. She knows these men, and she is afraid. That makes me afraid.'

'What makes you even think that this Jelani woman won't warn him?'

'Because if she is in contact with him or an informed third party, and she is as frightened as she claims, she won't risk letting him know that she has been speaking to us, let alone that she has shared his plans.'

'And we have no idea where Jelani is?'

'Not at the moment.'

'She's Kenyan?'

'She is not registered as a resident.'

Du Toit sits back. 'All right.'

'Have I answered all your questions, sir?'

He sighs. 'Frankly, Vaughn, I have no idea.'

As De Vries pulls off the street, waits while the gates slowly open inwards, he reflects that, in neighbouring houses, officers have taken up positions at various times in the past hours to monitor not only this road but the adjacent ones also. All vehicles and pedestrians will be photographed and recorded. The three officers left with Grace Bellingham have not shown themselves since originally taking their places. His entire team's presence is, he believes, concealed.

He edges into the driveway, parks to the side to provide a clear line of sight to his front door for the officers posted directly opposite. He gets out, takes four bags of shopping from the boot, walks to the entrance porch. The hard-wood door is heavy and solid, has protected him and his family for almost thirty years. He takes strength from it as he places his palm against the smooth surface and pushes it open. Inside, in the now unused formal dining room directly to the right of the entrance, an officer waits in the dimming evening light, pockmarked by the glimmering shadows of the branches of the two pepper trees. Until the front door is closed, De Vries does not acknowledge him. In the open-plan kitchen and living room, a second officer sits at the table, looking out on the scorched garden and half-empty pool.

De Vries sets the bags down in the kitchen, realizes that the space is airless and oppressive. The ceiling fan stopped weeks previously, still not mended.

'All well?'

'Yes, sir. No phone calls, no visitors. The builders left next door at seventeen fifteen. The couple you described on the balcony began moving their possessions inside and shut the sliding doors.'

'Good.'

'The school at the back there, sir? Dr Bellingham said she saw people in the grounds. We looked from the back windows and there were four men tending the cricket pitch. They left at . . .' he glances at the pad on the table '. . . sixteen forty.'

De Vries unlocks and opens the French windows onto the garden, looks up at the back wall of his property, to the tall eucalyptus trees on its far side, which line the boundary to the school playing fields. Not a leaf moves. It is silent. In the rectangle formed by his house and the perimeter wall, the last shards of sunlight reveal that the sultry air is thick with dust, filled with slow-moving, hovering insects. His throat tickles. He ducks back inside, runs the cold tap, pours himself water in his morning coffee mug. 'There'll be food soon. Only pies and pizzas. Has Dr Bellingham come downstairs?'

'No, sir. We took her a jug of water, later some ice from your freezer, and some tea.'

'If she comes down to eat, you can each take a few minutes' break. Otherwise, be alert for any sound or movement.'

The officer nods.

De Vries wants to shower, to change. His clothes stick to him and he can smell himself even amid the stale, acrid air. He turns away from the officer, leans over the kitchen sink, holding himself steady with tired arms, closes his eyes, sighs silently. He understands that there is only one good outcome from the night ahead: the capture of the killer. If nothing happens, his judgement will seem impaired, the threat to Grace Bellingham still active.

Yet he does not really believe that the man will come, struggles to reconcile Ali Jelani's motivation, both in the writing of her stories and in revealing the supposed nature of the threat. Until he understands that, he considers her an enigma of little use.

Mike Solarin reaches the café drenched with sweat, regretting that he has chosen to walk. Ever since the morning, he has been disturbed by the memory of Ray Black overseeing the demonstration outside the mosque, the unavoidable sensation that fear and loathing are fomenting in the city. He stands beneath the air-conditioning unit above the queue by the counter, feeling the perspiration thicken and cool on him, his head throbbing. As the temperature in the Cape rises, the mountain fires blaze, threatening property and life, so the atmosphere of dread intensifies, as if the skin of the city itself were alight, burning away, revealing the blood and bile within. He feels dizzy, nauseous, turns away to a table close to the back of the café, sits, tries to breathe slowly, deeply.

After a few minutes he feels better, sits up.. The door opens, and he waves, stands.

'Mike.'

They shake hands.

'Don.'

They smile. Neither is their birth name.

'I will get you coffee? A cool drink?'

'Shall we be very civilized?' Solarin says, affecting an English accent. 'Iced coffee?'

Don walks to the counter, orders two large iced coffees, pays at the till, returns to their table.

'You did not tell me that you were in town.'

'Posted here, attached to the Terrorist Squad. I was surprised myself. Think they drafted everybody in.'

'Quick work, Mike.'

Solarin frowns, glances around them. Jazz is playing quietly, a few other customers chatter or study laptops. None of the tables in their immediate vicinity is occupied.

'Maybe . . .'

Don February meets his eye. Solarin's expression seems blank, yet Don reads him.

'It is safe to talk here?'

'*Ja.* Better it is in public. Maybe I have a follower . . . You are my friend from university, from training. It is natural that you and me, we should meet up for a drink.'

The waitress brings them their coffees. They both admire her, both drink almost the entire contents of their glasses. They gesture to her for another round. Four pink tourists lumber in, loud and sweaty, rucksacks swinging against the counter, clipping the back of the head of a solitary newspaper reader. Don and Solarin talk about their lives in Cape Town and Pretoria, Don's wife, Solarin's now ex-girlfriend. More iced coffees arrive; the tourists take their drinks to go. The café reverts to its soothingly cool, low hum of recreational coffee-drinking.

'Imagine,' Solarin says quietly, 'if you were seconded to a team of officers investigating a major incident and, within a few hours of starting out, you are recalled because the matter is concluded, solved, and then you learn from a contact that the forensic evidence does not match up, that each element of the investigation is kept entirely separate from everyone but . . . I don't know who . . . someone. Imagine that you are on the road and it turns out that you have almost reached a location which might have been indicated by the forensic science and then, with your otherwise disinterested partner repeatedly, secretly, on his cellphone, you are recalled. How would you feel?'

'Like you feel,' Don says quietly.

'You are happy to be where you are. You maybe should keep your head down, but you think, Something is not right here, something which should not be left. A miscarriage of justice, a misappropriation of blame.'

'That is like my boss speaking.'

'Yes,' Solarin says quickly. 'That is what I thought. Colonel de Vries.'

'He is not doing so well just now. We have an investigation, which is . . . Well, you have seen the papers. It is not good.'

'I know. I hear what they say, but he has been effective in the past. You have confidence in him?'

'I do. It is tested, Mike, but I do.'

'Maybe I talk to him.'

Don smiles. 'I think he might see you as the next generation. But I do not know whether it is a good idea.'

'Why?'

'Because, you associate with him, it will not be good for you. I hear what people say. He is almost alone now. They think he is toxic.'

'But is that because he will not play political games? Because he wants the truth?'

'Partly, maybe . . .'

'That is how I want to be. That is how I am.'

'The politicians and the SAPS – they are so closely linked. You go against them, you may lose everything.'

'Maybe to win you have to risk everything.'

Don laughs. 'Oh, my God, Mike Solarin, the young black Vaughn de Vries.'

Solarin doesn't flinch. 'He has some time – in a week, even two – you call me. *Ja*, Don?'

'I will do that for you – but you just be careful, my friend. You may get what you want.'

Grace Bellingham comes downstairs to eat in the kitchen. She is quiet, drawn, her eyes nervous. She is not wearing make-up, her hair unbrushed. She wears a plain linen dress, pale against her tanned legs, which shine with perspiration. She does not make eye contact with the guards, does not acknowledge De Vries. Instead she walks to the French windows and stands at the threshold, her arms at forty-five degrees to her body, fingers wide. She catches no breeze. She lowers them, shoulders sagging, studies her surroundings. The walls of the garden are high, the gate down the side of the house to the street is locked and carries razor wire; the top of the wall by the neighbours' house is tipped with broken glass. When De Vries brings pies and a salad to the table, she sits at its end, granting her a view of both the internal entrance and the garden.

One officer eats on a tray, sitting in the adjoining living area. Another remains on the stairs, protecting the hallway, while the third showers, preparing for the long night ahead.

'Will you eat?'

She looks up at him.

'It passes the time.'

He sits with his back to the garden at right angles to her. He watches her slice the pie into four, place one slice on her plate and pull the salad towards her.

'What's your betting?' De Vries asks quietly. 'Will he come?'

'That rather depends on whether he has information, doesn't

211

it? On the one hand, does he know where I'm staying? On the other, has someone told him about this operation?'

'If the answers are yes, and no?'

'I don't believe that he would tell someone, even someone he believes he can control, who a victim would be. This is more likely a test of Jelani's loyalty than a genuine threat to me.'

'That's why you're calmer: you don't think this is real?'

She puts down her cutlery slowly. Everything she does has slowed. She says, deliberately:

'I am not calm. All I have to save me is my work. I have considered what he has done and what we know about him. My view is that he may want to scare me, perhaps dissuade me from aiding you. It wouldn't surprise me if something happens tonight to frighten me, but however great a risk he might be prepared to take, trying to abduct me defies logic, however desperate he may feel.'

'I hope he doesn't, but if he does, we are here.'

She smiles, picks up her knife and fork, positions a cherry tomato and a cube of feta cheese on the prongs.

'These men are cleverer than you think.'

De Vries's domestic worker winds the clock, but never adjusts it; its chimes are soothing but near worthless in providing a guide to time.

'What's that?'

He peers at his watch, back at Grace Bellingham. 'Twenty to one.'

They sit in the living area, an officer at the dining table, looking outside. He unlocks the double doors, hopes to feel coolness as he opens them wide. Air, a degree or two cooler than indoors, waits for him, intransigently refusing to drift in. Despite the small fan brought from De Vries's bedroom, the room is muggy, still; everyone is sweating. A cricket, probably in the bougainvillaea on the pergola outside, chirrups consistently, marking out the seconds, the minutes.

'Thank you for staying with me.'

'I'm not sleeping anyway.' He turns to her. 'But you should.'

Grace Bellingham twitches minutely. 'I won't, though.'

'It's hot. If I had time, I'd have worked on the pool . . . Not that we're allowed to refill them, with the drought restrictions. Anyway, you're safe enough here. You want anything?'

'Just water. Ice, if there's any.'

He pauses at the doorway, tilting his head to hear over the sound of the insects. He turns towards the kitchen, then back again, steps into the black garden, the outdoor lights inactive for the last two years. He turns to the officer at the table.

'Be on your guard.'

Grace Bellingham looks up. 'What's happening?'

He closes the doors, locks them. 'Probably nothing. Maybe an animal on the other side of the wall: a bird, squirrel. And there's smoke. Not braai. I'll get my torch.'

He goes into the hallway, calls upstairs:

'Be aware. I can smell smoke.'

De Vries fetches the torch from the hall table, returns to the kitchen, shines it around his garden. As the beam passes the back wall, it catches thick, billowing smoke. He refocuses his eyes, passes the beam over the area a second time. He is certain.

'Fire over the wall.' He turns to the officer. 'Get the fire crews out.' Then, to Grace Bellingham: 'This is it.'

Even as the officer calls, De Vries can see the fire now without a torch. The blaze is rising from the base of one of the eucalyptus trees, the fallen leaves and small branches piled up at their bases providing a natural accelerant. The dark smoke is orange-tinged

as it rises above the wall. He sees the lower branches of the neighbouring trees ignite; the flames rise high and straight into the
canopy. Through the narrow slits of window left open, he can hear
the cracking and crackling, see the oils in the bark of the branches
burst into flames. Tiny jets explode from them at right angles
against black sky.

He speed-dials. 'You see it?'

'*Ja*, sir. Fire crews summoned. Do you want me to arrange your
evacuation?' Don's voice is quiet and calm, unchanging.

'No. Not yet. That's what he wants. No one move. Maintain
positions. Just send an officer to the front gates of the school –
top of the road, fifty metres on the right. Whoever started that fire
has to get out.'

He disconnects, looks back at the scene outside his home.
Already the alarms on the neighbouring houses are sounding; at
a certain point in their tone, they clash, and the discord hurts his
ears. In front of him, four huge old trees are now ablaze, his garden brightly lit by the fast and almost constant flicker of flames,
their sickly yellow reflecting dully and slowly on the surface of
the thick green water of the pool. He can feel the heat even
through the glass. A falling branch hits the windows, sits shattered,
smouldering, on the pink brick paving around the pool. He is
afraid now that the inferno will take hold of his property.

He looks behind him. Grace Bellingham stands, pressed to the
back wall, seemingly mesmerized. He turns back, assesses the
likelihood of the fire catching hold of his house, feels overcome
by the smoke and dust and heat in the air. It is so still that the
flames rise vertically; even the sparks just carry higher and higher
into the sky. De Vries knows the danger of forest fires on the
Mountain is very real. He forces himself to relax; the grip on his
weapon loosened. Suddenly, there is a burst of shots, Grace
Bellingham screams, slides to the floor. He falls, weapon out in

front of him. In the garden nothing stirs but the tumbling, smoking boughs from the branches that overhang the pool. He hears the fire hiss as engulfed branches hit the surface, sees the steam rise from the mire. Over the wall that adjoins his neighbours' house, he sees the thatched roof on their pool house emitting thick dark smoke, the flash as it ignites, illuminating the garden and the room. The inferno fills his brain – flames blaze in his eyes even when they are turned inside, to the tiled floor of the living room. Finally, his mind processes the sound.

'Not gunshots.' He listens. In the distance, there are sirens. 'Not gunshots, Grace. Fireworks. Probably fireworks.'

He waits. Sirens. SAPS patrols.

'Grace?'

In his mind, the firestorm at the back of his house, panic and fear among his neighbours. At the front, chaos: residents, fire officers, uniforms, rubber-neckers. He does not know whether to take her out to the front, or remain where he is until they are either forced to evacuate or the scene is controlled.

'Grace?'

He looks around, sees her on the floor. He crawls to her.

'Are you okay?'

He hears her crying, sees her body shudder. 'Come here.'

He moves to her, takes her arm, pulls her to her knees. They crawl to the hallway, stand in the crook of the staircase.

'It's all right. The firemen are here. Fucking uniforms will be swarming all over the street. It's over. You said he'd try to frighten you, show you he knew where you were. He's done it.'

She is shaking, does not reject his arm around her shoulders, moves her hand into his.

Through the garden windows, he can see the flashing lights of a fire engine beyond the perimeter wall. The fire is high in the dwindling canopies now, burning itself out; the blackened skeletons of the eucalyptus trees glow and smoke. He sees water spray over his wall into his field of vision.

He pulls out his phone. 'Don. Keep everyone watching. He could come back. He could try something while people are on the street. Not likely, but let's keep this tight.'

'Yes, sir.'

'I'm staying here unless compelled to move.'

'Understood, sir.'

He rings off, feels Grace shaking under his arm. Her head is down, neck bent. There is no panic, no hysteria, but there is no fight left in her either; no energy, no life force. She feels limp and helpless. As the adrenalin, which has kept him alert, begins to diminish, he feels frustration and failure course through him. The killer came, and they didn't catch him, perhaps didn't even see him. The hall is haltingly floodlit by the flashing lights of the emergency services stationed outside his house; the armed officers still wait in his kitchen, his dining room, on the landing. Her hand feels cold, clammy. She has bent over so low that his arm no longer comforts her. He does not know what to do with his hands. He does not know what to do.

PART 3

De Vries sleeps fitfully, the smoke in his nostrils forcing him awake sporadically. He checks the garden from the upper-floor door to the veranda. In the bright dawn, beyond the wall, one fire engine waits silently, lights still flashing. The men are leaning against the vehicle, faces black – or blacker – holding cans of cold drinks.

He pads over the polished floorboards, listens at Grace Bellingham's door, thinks he hears her slow, consistent breathing. Just after eight a.m., the heat through his curtains drives him into his shower. Under a spray of feeble pressure, he lets the unheated water cool him, rinse off the thick sweat that, through the night, seems to have oozed, then dried, onto his body. His mind races through what he must do in the hours ahead, how he can look after Grace, re-energize the investigation, answer the accusations of aimlessness in his thinking. He dresses, knocks loudly on the guest-room door, trudges downstairs to the kitchen.

Outside, the water in his pool seems black from the charred debris on its surface. The paving is soaked from the hoses, the residue sludgy and grey. There are thin wisps of smoke or steam emanating from the thickest sections of the eucalyptus trunks. The air is heavy, dark with particulate, difficult to inhale without choking.

The doorbell rings. One of the three new guards calls, 'Brigadier du Toit, sir.'

De Vries hurries to his front door, opens it.

'Sir.'

Du Toit walks past him, through the hallway to the back of the house.

'Is this safe?'

'Safe enough. The fire crews are still around.'

'You didn't think to evacuate Dr Bellingham?'

'I did, and rejected the idea. The house remained the safest place for her to be. I think she has slept and I'll bring her into the office this morning.'

'Anyone see anything?'

'Not that they're saying, but we'll debrief. We have hours of surveillance to consider . . .'

'But no one beyond the perimeter wall there?' He nods outside.

'No. Since the wall is so high, I didn't post anyone that side. I felt he could not approach from that direction.'

'But he did.'

'He, or somebody else, nearly set the entire neighbourhood on fire, but there was no ingress from that point.'

'How is Dr Bellingham now? Does she feel safe?'

'I don't know. She wasn't convinced the threat to her was real.'

'Not real?' Du Toit gestures at the scalded garden.

'She felt, sir, that he was more likely to try to frighten her, possibly both of us. And he – or someone else – did.'

'And today?'

'Find Ali Jelani, work to identify the killer. He's clever. He's careful. But if that was him last night, he's taking greater risks, and that is how we'll catch him.'

Du Toit turns, paces the room. 'Your house all right?'

'Apparently. My neighbour's pool house burned down. The

guys out there confirmed last night that it was deliberate. The fire was started.'

Du Toit is looking into the kitchen, not at De Vries.

'I didn't tell you yesterday, wanted to keep you focused. They're thinking of sending a specialist unit from Pretoria.'

'How long do I have?'

'You're not surprised?'

'Not any more.'

'Perhaps today, possibly tomorrow. They're still working something up there, but they're keen to gain control, manage the press, take it from us.' Du Toit turns. 'You all right?'

'Yes.'

'No haughty indignation? No catalogue of justification?'

'I'll continue to strive to find this man,' De Vries says calmly. 'We have a profile, but we have virtually no evidence. I don't believe that anyone else, any other team, could have worked harder or more efficiently, but, sir, we will redouble our efforts.' Even as he says the words, he hears the weariness in his voice, questions how truly he believes his own defence.

Within thirty minutes of reaching Headquarters, De Vries has the back-up team, under the supervision of his unit's technical officer, Joey Morten, studying footage from two houses located on two different roads leading up to Rose's nursery. Despite it being more than ten days since Bethany Miles's abduction, both security companies are found to keep recordings for fourteen days and have released them. Neither camera is directed specifically at the streets, instead focused on monitoring who enters or exits the properties, but, with care, the cars passing the camera on the streets can be identified.

First, officers are charged with identifying Bethany Miles's metallic green Audi Q5. Then, working forwards from the sighting of the car, they must check for all vehicles that subsequently pass the two points in the direction of Rose's nursery until the time that the car, with the Miles' young daughter in the back, was discovered in the car park. Following this, others will track backwards, checking cars that arrived before Bethany Miles passed the point at which she was picked up on camera. All this information will be written up, allowing for comparisons with vehicles noted by the teams of officers around the scene last night.

Next, De Vries sends Ben Thwala and another officer to try to work out where the arsonist entered the school grounds the night before, and where a vehicle might have been parked.

Grace Bellingham descends to the basement to meet Harry Kleinman, with whom she had worked when she had been attached previously to the SAPS. They will, she claims, discuss the wounds found on the two murder victims, continue to search for clues in the killer's methodology.

Rejecting his suggestion to remain at home to rest, she had sat upright in the passenger seat on the way into the office, silent, staring forward blankly. He drove, uncertain whether to try to engage her in conversation or leave her. His own mind was so full, he stared ahead too, head spinning, his focus on the road faltering. As he turned from De Waal Drive to drop down into town, he caught the edge of a road island, jolting the car up at the back. His eyes opened wide, hands gripping the wheel.

'Sorry.'

She said nothing.

At nine forty a.m., De Vries receives a phone call that takes him out of his office and up to Vredehoek. This time, as he climbs the steps to Penelope van Reidel's grand villa, the front door is opened by a maid, dressed in black, with a frilly white apron. The editor stands in the hallway by the open door to her study.

'I am at a crucial stage of a murder investigation. This had better be significant information.'

'Significant, Colonel, and disturbing.' She ushers him into a grandiose book-lined room and invites him to sit down. She sits behind a broad antique desk.

'Ali Jelani told me that she was in danger,' she says, 'that she believed she was being followed. At her insistence, I agreed to call her every morning at eight. If she did not answer, I was to assume that she was in trouble. This morning, her phone is switched off.'

'Why didn't you tell me this before?'

'Because I left it to her to tell you. I assumed that she would explain this when you, or whoever you sent, met her.'

'You tried again?'

'Of course. I called the cellphone company; I have contacts and associations. They confirm that her phone is off. There's no signal registering.'

'When did you last speak to her?'

'She told me yesterday that she was working on another element of her story, that she would provide pictures.'

'What element?'

'She didn't specify. I understood, from what she said, it was a police operation.'

'Did she mention a name?'

'Dr Grace Bellingham.'

De Vries's stomach churns. An idea is already developing and, second by second, he believes it feels right.

'Where was Jelani last night?'

'I don't know.'

De Vries stares at her. 'Speculate.'

'On assignment?'

He gets up, walks slowly from her desk. He looks out to the panoramic view over the City Bowl, the skyscrapers silhouetted against the matt silver water in the Bay, the mountains of the peninsula on the horizon duck-egg blue against an even paler, cloudless shade. 'Ali Jelani may have been abducted by the killer.'

Van Reidel looks shocked. 'How can that be?'

'There was a police operation last night, which did concern Dr Bellingham, but she was not personally threatened.'

'So?'

'A fire was set . . .' He stops. 'You know this already?'

'About the operation? About the fire? Yes.'

'How?'

She smiles. 'I run a news organization. This is what we do.'

'Did you suspect that Ali Jelani had access to a contact close to the killer?'

'I assumed her information came from you, the SAPS.'

'Well, it didn't. We considered that she was either in direct contact with the killer or being used via a third party. Dr Bellingham speculated that he could have been testing Jelani by revealing Bellingham as a possible target. If that is the case, Ali Jelani failed her test spectacularly.'

'And now he has her?'

'Possibly.'

'That creates an entirely new angle . . .'

'New angle? For the story?'

'We helped you before. We can help you again.'

'Where did Ali Jelani say she would be last night?'

'You asked me that. I don't know.'

De Vries puts his hands on her desk, leans over it towards her. 'You said that she told you she would be submitting copy for your newspaper, including photographs. She told you the name, Grace Bellingham. Did she not tell you what her plan was?'

Penelope van Reidel shudders. Her strident, confident voice breaks minutely. 'She told me she expected something to happen last night, that she would be there. She would bring me the story.'

'She would be there?'

'Yes.'

'So you let her take that on alone?' De Vries asks.

'I had no choice. That's all she told me. I didn't know what she meant. She had worked alone before. She insisted on it. The story was hers. It remained her property until her copy was approved for the paper.'

'And it didn't really matter, did it, Ms van Reidel? Just so long as you got your story. Isn't that how it works?'

'Ali Jelani was not employed by this newspaper.'

'Why was that?' De Vries's voice rises. 'Was it so that if something happened to her you could deny responsibility for effective oversight?'

'No.'

'Or did you dangle the prospect of a full-time post in return for an explosive series of reports about this killer?'

'No.'

'Perhaps you suspected that she had contact with this man, and encouraged it, incentivized her to bring you everything. Was that how it worked?'

Now she sits back calmly, her hands on the armrests, her back straight.

'Ali Jelani,' she says quietly, 'came to me. I checked her story about the first two women: Hazel Calder and Michelle Ricquarts. Your SAPS press liaison officer confirmed that the information contained within the pieces was accurate. She made the connection. Her.'

'How long have you been calling to check on her?'

'Six weeks. Since she wrote the piece on Marie Garsten in Strand . . . She said then that she was worried she was being followed, possibly targeted. I suggested she contact the SAPS, but she dismissed the idea.'

'You obviously weren't very persuasive.'

'Jelani was a mystery. I took a punt on her because she seemed instinctively to have found something. You need people working for you who have a good nose, and an exhaustive mind. I have responsibility for scores of journalists.'

'But,' De Vries says, 'I bet she's the only one you called religiously every twenty-four hours, that you nurtured to bring you details, without questioning how she might be obtaining them. I guess it didn't matter. Everything and everyone is expendable, aren't they, in exchange for the story?' He stands. 'You live in a beautiful home, Ms van Reidel, but you're wading in shit. My shit. After a while, you're going to find you really don't like it. Keep calling Ali Jelani. You hear anything, anything at all, you tell me immediately.'

'What's happening?'

He is standing in a queue outside a coffee shop on Kloof Street, cellphone squashed against his right ear, his left forefinger pressed hard into his left. He wouldn't normally bother to wait, but this café serves the strongest, thickest coffee in Cape Town.

'Sergeant Thwala has located where someone could have entered the school grounds last night,' Don February says. 'A damaged area of the fence. He is going door-to-door asking about unfamiliar cars or persons in the area after midnight. The fire chief confirmed that petrol was used to start the fire, there was evidence of fireworks . . .'

'Hang on.' De Vries feels in his pocket for his wallet, his cell-phone jammed under his chin slowly slipping until he catches it, gets the cash, grasps the phone firmly in his hand. 'Go on.'

'He said that the fire would have taken hold instantly. There were piles of dry leaves and branches, which had been brushed up against the wall over several years by the ground staff.'

'All right. Cars around the nursery last week?'

'Still checking. They have to slow the recording almost to a stop before they can try to identify the vehicle make. Half the cars are white. Only Sergeant Morten seems to be able to identify specific makes and models.'

'You want coffee?'

'Yes.'

'I'll be back in ten minutes.' He faces the bored-looking barista. 'Two treble espressos.' He thinks what Don February drinks. 'And a cappuccino.'

Don February stands barely above him, even though De Vries is seated.

'Something is happening.' There is the slightest hint of excitement in Don's voice.

De Vries drops one empty espresso cup into a bin, passes him the cappuccino, flicks the lid off the second espresso, tips the contents down his throat.

'What?'

Don leads him across the squad-room towards Sally Frazer and Joey Morten.

'Ben Thwala called in to say that a couple in Killick Road, which is the other side of the playing fields, did see a car at around twelve thirty this morning when they arrived home after a party. A white Toyota Prius. The man remembers it because he

PAUL MENDELSON

says his children had been telling him that he must buy a hybrid car, like a Toyota Prius, and his wife had never seen one, so he pointed it out.'

'They see the driver?'

'No.'

De Vries shrugs. 'That could have been anybody.'

'Yes, but look at the picture here from the surveillance officers in the road that adjoins yours, sir.'

A black-and-white picture, obtained using a super low-light device, looking almost like an old-fashioned negative, is visible on the screen in front of them. The time code shows 00.55.

'Where is that?'

'Roma Grove. Parallel to your street. Outside numbers fourteen and sixteen.'

De Vries frowns. 'That's the top of the road by Rondebosch Common. There's a cut-through right there, between about sixteen and eighteen. You can walk through without going up to the main road. You get a plate?'

'Partial,' Joey Morten says. 'There are fewer than two hundred white Priuses in Greater Cape Town. We'll find it, but we're having problems with some of the computers.'

'Why?'

'I don't know. Possibly overheating.'

De Vries turns to Sally Frazer. 'Have you got the other team looking for a white Prius?'

She replies quietly, 'Usually it's better just to let them continue. You start mentioning a possible vehicle, people get careless with cars that aren't white, or don't look immediately like a Prius.'

De Vries addresses all of them:

'This could be a break. This could be our chance. Did no one see a woman on her own in my road last night? She could have been there one minute and gone the next.'

228

'Nothing in the surveillance reports. Are you asking about the journalist?'

'Ali Jelani is missing. Not answering her phone, despite arranging a specific time to be called. If she was there last night and so was our killer, she could have been taken.'

'Not Dr Bellingham?'

'Exactly.'

Don says quietly, 'Dr Bellingham is in your office, sir.'

De Vries looks up, sees that she is sitting in a chair with her back to the squad-room. He sees all his guests like this first – the backs of their heads.

'All right. Whatever it takes, let's identify this vehicle, see if we can link it again to other scenes.'

He turns towards his office, aware that, in his head, something has clicked, an understanding not yet quite appreciated, like a glimpse in peripheral vision. He enters his office, throws his jacket onto the adjoining chair. She turns around slowly, says:

'Ali Jelani is gone.'

'How did you know that?'

'She is?'

'She's missing, yes.'

'I thought more about last night. It was never about me. It was too ridiculous that he would tell anyone who he was going to take. I should have known. He manipulated Jelani and played me, and made fools of all of you. He wanted Jelani all along. He used her, then got her into the open – chasing the story, waiting for the picture – and, when the fire trucks and patrol cars arrived, and there were people on the street, all half asleep, shocked by the fire, fearing a conflagration that would consume their houses and possessions, he probably just walked up and took her.'

'We're tracing a suspicious car.'

229

She raises her eyebrows. 'I wasn't thinking straight. I'm sorry. I was selfish.'

'You were afraid.'

'Afraid of something that didn't exist. My perspective's shot. I told you, I'm spent, finished.'

'You're just tired.'

'I'm tired like you can't believe. I still missed the obvious.'

He looks out over the squad-room. 'You okay here? You want to go home?'

'I'll stay here. You go.' She indicates the sofa in the corner of his office. 'I may lie down.'

'Tell me when you want to eat.'

She doesn't answer. She gets up, sits on the sofa, lets her body fall onto the seat, adjusts a cushion under her head, curls her legs into herself.

He closes the door.

It strikes him as he hears the catch on the office door lock. He freezes. He hears the bustle of the squad-room, stares straight at the woodwork of the doorframe, sees nothing. He swallows, takes his phone, dials the number. It switches straight to voicemail. He pockets the phone, strides towards the other end of his floor. Through a missing blind, he sees Du Toit in his office, head over paperwork. He knocks, walks in; Du Toit has not moved his head.

'Henrik.'

'What?'

'I need your help.'

'That is your default position.' De Vries moves to his desk, thumps his hands on the surface. Du Toit raises his eyes. 'Good news?'

'Maybe yes, maybe no.'

Brigadier du Toit sits up, stretches his back, wipes his eyes. De Vries sees white residue at the corners of his mouth, wonders whether he has been asleep.

'What do you need?'

'The department that employs Stephen Jessel, controls the section eighteens and other restricted information. I need you to call them.'

'You need to speak to Leigh Finnemore?'

'No. I want you to ask them about Jessel, about his work record, where he operates and who his charges are.'

'Jessel?'

'We've identified a suspect car. Not confirmed yet, but around scenes. It's a Toyota Prius. I only know one person connected with this investigation who owns a white Toyota Prius. Stephen Jessel.'

Du Toit frowns. 'I don't understand. You think Finnemore has used this car?'

'No, Henrik. Forget Leigh Finnemore. I think that Stephen Jessel could be our man. He works with disturbed people who must be protected and from whom the public must be protected. He travels around. He has reason to be in different places at different times. We know for a fact that he has visited one of the sites in which a victim was found: Apostle Lodge. He admitted that he had driven to the house with Finnemore – to show him the neighbours on his street.' De Vries sees nothing resembling recognition or understanding in Du Toit's eyes. 'With respect, sir, can you call his department, find whoever is in charge and bring him here, along with Jessel's history and employment record? It needs to come from you, or even General Thulani. Immediately. Complete discretion, absolute secrecy. Jessel cannot be forewarned.'

Du Toit nods. 'If you're wrong?'

De Vries shrugs, exasperated. 'Then I'm wrong. For Christ's sake, sir. Ali Jelani is missing, presumed abducted. If that's the case, we have maybe two, three days to find her. That's if he doesn't take revenge on her betrayal immediately. Can you do this now?'

De Vries takes Don February and Sally Frazer aside.

'For the moment, us three only. I may be wrong.' He turns to Frazer. 'Find the licence plate for a Stephen Jessel. I don't know his home address, but it won't be far from town. See if it matches the partial you picked up from the surveillance.'

'Jessel is government?' Don asks.

'Government appointed. I don't know who runs his department. It doesn't matter.' He glances back at Frazer. 'He's the guy supervising our section eighteen, in Plumbago Lane. He owns a white Toyota Prius. Don, if it's a match, back-trace his home address and any other details on him. Keep it quiet just now.'

He stands up straight, watches the two officers move away to the relevant workstations. He sees Henrik du Toit stride towards him. Du Toit gestures to De Vries's office. He cuts him off.

'Dr Bellingham is resting, sir.'

They walk to the milky windows at the far side of the room.

'I spoke to the woman who runs the department. She says Jessel is on a sabbatical.'

'What?'

'You work ten years as a supervisor, you get a four-month sabbatical. He's taking it from the end of September this year until the end of January. She's biking over his papers.'

'September coincides with the first known attack – on Hazel Calder.' De Vries shakes his head. 'But why were we put through to him when we enquired about number one Plumbago Lane, Leigh Finnemore?'

'I asked that. It's a sabbatical, but it excludes section-eighteen charges. He remains on call for those. He has three. One went into hospital mid-September this year; attempted suicide. The other went back to Valkenburg Mental Hospital in August – at the request of Stephen Jessel.' De Vries nods. A pattern is forming, fitting the little information they have. 'The car?' Du Toit continues. 'You have any more on that?'

'We're doing it now. It's with February and Frazer only, until I'm sure.'

'We all met this Jessel. Did you sense anything in him?'

De Vries sighs. 'No, sir. I was more interested in his charge, a man who had killed before. I just found Jessel annoying, petty and obstructive.'

He sees Sally Frazer waving to him from the middle of the squad-room, reflects that any other officer would come over to him, but Frazer summons him. He smiles to himself, indicates to Du Toit to come with him. With Joey Morten and Ben Thwala, they form a group around one of the desks.

Frazer says: 'We have the final two digits of the registration plate. They match Stephen Jessel's car.'

'My God.'

She glances up at Du Toit, continues: 'We have a white Toyota Prius, only two digits of the registration mark identifiable, passing the camera on Southern Cross Road, just by the junction that leads to Rose's nursery. It is one minute, eleven seconds behind Bethany Miles in her Audi Q5.'

'Can you see who's driving?'

'No. It took Sergeant Morten here some time to confirm that it was a Prius and to unscramble the registration so that we got even that. It's the same final two digits.'

'They are unique to Stephen Jessel's Toyota Prius,' Morten says drily. 'It is enough to testify. But there's no detail. A good attorney could cast doubt over the enhancement technique I had to use.'

'To hell with the judges right now,' De Vries says. 'We have a rare car close to the scene of the fire, on the adjacent road to mine last night, and now following Bethany Miles. This is the car. We need to know who was driving it, but it's the car. How many vehicles were there between her and the Prius?'

'Two,' Morten says immediately. 'You'd need a wide tail down Southern Cross Drive. Long open straight.'

'Have you tried to reach Jessel?' Du Toit says.

'Straight to voicemail.' He turns to Don. 'You found his home address?'

'According to the records, he moved in August this year from a property near Milnerton to a place called "Two Feathers Estate".'

'Where the hell is that?'

'I am not certain, sir, but I think that it is one of the new developments off the N2 going into Somerset West.'

'Somerset West, Strand. He could have been house-hunting and found that abandoned building site . . .'

'And Michelle Ricquarts was taken to a shack on Milnerton Beach,' Frazer says.

'It's coming together,' De Vries says. 'Subject to consultation, sir, I think that we should consider releasing pictures of Stephen Jessel and Ali Jelani and hoping that someone, somewhere, has seen them.'

'Are we certain he has her?'

'Not certain, but it fits. Dr Bellingham reached the same conclusion that we did. Last night's fireworks, literally, were misdirection. He was there to take Jelani, not Bellingham.' He turns to Sally Frazer. 'You met Jelani, researched her background. Dig deeper. See what you can find, particularly what happened to her children. If we're right on the children connection, she will have done something to hers that provoked him.' He turns back to Du Toit. 'We need everything we have on Jessel.'

'I'll get back to his boss, see if we can't visit her or get her in. This is all good, but hold it here, between us, for one hour, see what else we can find. Then we'll make a decision on the press.'

'There isn't much,' Du Toit says. De Vries studies the man's collar, wet with sweat, top button fastened, tie tight at his neck, wonders if stoicism is implicit to his rank; reflects that, like him, Du Toit is old-school and that details matter. No wonder they are treated with suspicion by the new order. 'Either in the personnel files or from his boss: reliable, solitary, efficient. No one knew anything about his private life, but his boss thought he lived alone. The only real mystery is how he got appointed in the first place. In 2000, he was working pretty much as a low-grade office manager. Yet six months later, around the time of the transitional government, he was promoted to case officer. He's stayed there, moving up a couple of grades, ever since.'

'Nothing on his personal history?'

'No. His next of kin was noted as an aunt in London, UK. But there's nothing about his education, where – or even whether – he went to university, training, etc. It looks like a classic case of fraudulent assimilation. He simply became part of this semi-autonomous government department.'

'That's far from unique, especially around that time,' De Vries says. 'Records were being shredded, people were making their escape. It would have been easy for him to slip in and, once in, stay there . . . What about this sabbatical?'

'The woman is new there,' Du Toit says. 'She said she simply had no cause to look into Jessel. He was there, and his work was solid and reliable. In June last year, a few weeks after she was parachuted in, he approached her, explained that he had deferred his ten-year sabbatical and requested that he take it from late September onwards, since he was moving house. She told me he had leave owing over the years as well, and there was no reason to deny him.'

'His phone's still off. Warrant February is leading a team to his property on this new lifestyle estate, but I think we know he won't be there.'

'Where will he be?'

Du Toit's question hangs in the heavy, still air. They both turn to Grace Bellingham, who has sat silently in one of the two chairs against the side wall. She looks up at Du Toit.

'I'm not providing answers, Henrik.'

'It would be helpful if you could.'

She closes her eyes, a hand on her forehead.

'Suggestions?'

She sits up, wears a pat smile, says wearily: 'I suggest . . . that this man fits my profile pretty much exactly, except that he is a few years older than I would have anticipated. The fact that his next of kin is noted as an aunt in the UK suggests that his parents and siblings, if he had any, are either dead or not in contact with him. Obviously a broken home, a shattered upbringing are the first things you might consider when trying to find a motive for what seems to be a late-blossoming psychosis.'

'Thank you.'

'Furthermore, I suggest that this man is less likely to leave his victim this time, since he will want more value from the effort expended in capturing her. He will escalate his violent, sadistic behaviour towards her and, as a result, her life expectancy is shorter than those of his previous victims.' She stands up.

Du Toit rises also, followed by De Vries. 'Finally,' she says, her face blank, 'since I can't trust myself to function efficiently, I suggest that you don't rely on me to assist you any further.'

The Two Feathers Estate exists as an entity within a tall, double-layered steel fence. It is in its own territory amid the yellowed scrubland and burned-out grass of land reclaimed from the foothills of the low mountains that run alongside the southern coastal road. Cameras on poles taller than the fence watch the empty roads that meander around the half-built development.

The white render on the impressive gatehouse is already cracked, the surrounding landscaping dead or dying, the lawns yellow or brown, save for the emerald carpet outside a blindingly white show-home, flanked by poles bearing sagging flags.

Don February leads his three vehicles to Jessel's address, followed by two further security vehicles from the estate. The small rectangular house is on a close, each identical home facing others across a glorified roundabout. Only if you look high above the houses might you see hills or mountains, or nothing but empty blue sky above the distant coastline. Having surrounded the building, it is soon ascertained that no one is at home. The security team from the estate co-operate in opening the front door and disengaging the alarm. Don leads three officers inside.

He is struck first by the staleness of the air. Because of the demands of the alarm system, he is informed, no windows can be left open. The furniture is sparse and old-fashioned, positioned accurately and, where possible, symmetrically, as are items on shelves and counters. Everything is neat, but there is little of it. In the kitchen, the staleness becomes stench. He pulls open the waste bin, recoils. Flies rise, circling, unwilling to leave the gift of the black sack. He looks inside, withdraws packaging from a ready meal obtained from the supermarket, Pick and Pay; notes the date.

As he retraces his steps to the front door, he glances at three letters found in the mailbox, now bagged as evidence.

In the adjoining garage, there is no car, or any evidence that there has ever been one. Outside, in the backyard, there is no furniture, no braai, flowerbeds empty and dusty, a single staked tree in the right-hand corner, virtually leafless. The coastal breeze, which has travelled over industrial developments, local roads and the freeway, feels hotter than the ambient air. He takes out a cotton handkerchief, dabs his forehead.

He observes the search of the upstairs bedrooms, speaks further to the security personnel on site, rings the doorbell on the adjoining properties, but there is no answer. He asks several questions of the man calling himself the head of security, then leads his team out of the close, past other geometric arrangements of characterless houses, around the circle with the faltering borehole fountain, through the security gates back onto the local road, which leads to the N2 freeway into town.

De Vries stares at the foam bulb on the microphone stand; if he focuses on that, he can imagine there is no crowd of journalists, no brass watching him.

'We now want to speak with this man, Stephen Robert Jessel, whose home address is: number seventy-two Two Feathers Estate, Old Mansion Road, on the outskirts of Somerset West. We believe that he can help us in the search for the missing woman, Ali Jelani, a Kenyan journalist working freelance for the *New Cape Gazette*, who disappeared yesterday evening and who we believe may have been abducted by the same man responsible for two attacks and two murders on women in the Cape Town area over the past few months.'

De Vries looks at the expectant group of journalists, the two television cameras, two black men standing together at the back of the room, wearing un-creased suits and dry, fresh shirts.

'The contact details and photographs are in your packets. Please ensure that the numbers and email addresses are clearly displayed and transcribed correctly.'

As he sits down, voices are raised, hands waved. The press liaison officer, who stands to the side of the table behind which are seated De Vries, Henrik du Toit and Don February, points at the front row, calls out a name.

De Vries bows his head. He dislikes press conferences and public appeals, the reading of statements about, inevitably, an incomplete investigation but, most of all, he dreads the same questions from the same journalists, to which both he and they know he cannot give a straight answer. Instead, the clumsy verbal dance begins until they tire of its droning and repetitive rhythm. It is a pointless, depressing game, in an acidly humid, overcrowded room, late in the evening of a long, wearisome day.

He stands up, nods at Du Toit, walks from the room, hears the cacophony increase. He goes towards the small private custody area at the rear of the building, steps outside, lights the cigarette he has been palming for the previous minutes. It is damp, but he draws strongly, swallowing the thick, dark smoke.

'Don't do that.'

De Vries follows Henrik du Toit to his office, one weary dog trailing another.

'Close the door.' Du Toit sits. 'You can't do that, Vaughn. You can't just walk away. Don't sit down. Just stand there and listen. You made a breakthrough. There's a chance you've found our man, but I've told you before, you have to disseminate that success to the public. You have to reassure them that we have everything under control. You walk off like that, refuse to answer questions, what impression does it give?'

'That we're busy?'

'Did you see those two at the back? Pretoria. I told you they're watching us.' De Vries sighs. 'I know you don't care, Vaughn, but sometimes there are duties to be performed.'

'My duty is to catch Stephen Jessel and to find Ali Jelani. I can't do that if I'm wasting time with those people.'

'You may need those people to find Jessel. Warrant February tells me that he may not have been back to his home address for close on a week. We have no idea where he might have taken this woman, and, although it may be a novelty for car-buffs, this Toyota Prius just looks like any other white wedge on the roads, so the chances of anyone seeing it, let alone Jessel or Jelani, must be very small.'

De Vries nods. 'The public won't find them. I will.'

Du Toit sees assurance in De Vries's face, finds it fleetingly comforting.

'Why is Dr Bellingham so morose? She must realize that she is no longer a target for this man.'

'Dr Bellingham is tired, sir. Tired to the core. She has dealt with evil as a daily routine for twenty years and she has had enough. Although I'm not there quite yet, I sympathize.'

Du Toit shakes his head. 'None of us finds this work easy. Isn't that why we're here, fighting to try to bring these people down, with the experience we have? Because, frankly, we believe that others can't.'

'I wonder how long we'll keep thinking that.'

'For as long as we win, Vaughn. That's how long.'

De Vries snorts. 'Win? Have we ever done that? If we have, it's never felt like winning. Not once.'

None of the windows in the headquarters building opens. All are sealed to preserve the coolness occasionally granted by the air-conditioning system. De Vries has had the window behind his desk illicitly unsealed; he holds his hand out of the open window in his office, cigarette burning five storeys above the darkening downtown streets. Sally Frazer and Don February sip cool drinks, eat take-away sushi and sandwiches respectively.

'Nothing?'

'Not much,' Frazer says. 'The usual characters, a few Prius sightings, which we can try to follow up, but nothing on Jessel or Jelani.'

'What hurts,' De Vries says, 'is that we had them both. Jessel was here in my office and I didn't see it. I used to think that when I had a man in front of me I knew. Not any more. You were this close to Jelani. Now they're both gone.'

Frazer swallows, puts a folder on her lap.

'I have more on Jessel. He's forty-eight, only child, grew up in the Northern Suburbs. Lived in the Cape all his life. No record of education, matric or university. No criminal record. He has a bank account, which is in credit and always has been. He inherited the family home, used part of that money to buy this new property in Two Feathers Estate. Never been in debt.' She flips pages. 'Now it gets interesting.' She looks over to Don February, who is eating slowly, listening to her; De Vries is half out of the window. 'Can you hear me, sir?'

'Where did Dr Bellingham go?'

Don February covers his full mouth, says: 'She took a cab, sir. I went down with her, but she insisted. Said she was going home.'

De Vries ducks back inside. 'Sorry, Sally.' He unscrews a two-litre bottle of still water, sloshes some down his throat, spills it on his shirt, sits heavily. He revolves his wrist to restart her report.

'Stephen Jessel's father was involved in a hit-and-run in 2004. He died in hospital five months later. The driver and car were never identified. Jessel's mother was alive until two years ago. In 2006, she was attacked in an underground car park in the early evening. She had hydrochloric acid thrown in her face. She lost the sight in both eyes, and suffered extensive scarring. There were no witnesses, no apparent motive. Her handbag was untouched.'

'No one thought about him? Stephen Jessel?'

'Bellville handled the investigation. I read the precis of the docket. Stephen Jessel was questioned, but was eliminated early on. He claimed that he was at work at the time of the attack, supervising one of his charges. His alibi was a respected doctor and a patient at Valkenburg Mental Hospital.'

'That place . . .'

'It gets interesting, sir. The patient who signed the witness statement is Leigh Finnemore.'

'Finnemore provided an alibi for Jessel in 2006?'

'Yes, and there is, as they say, more. The name of the doctor was Johannes Dyk.'

De Vries feels acid in his chest, his mouth dry.

'I knew that man. You remember, Don? Dyk was dying, but seven years earlier he had been advising the SAPS on the child-abduction case. He knew what had happened to those boys. He misled us, covered for a paedophile ring.' He grabs the water bottle again, tips it, gulps.

'Jessel's mother was hospitalized,' Frazer continues. 'Apparently her son visited her a few times early on, then wasn't seen again. I spoke to someone who remembers his mother. They contacted him through work when his mother became terminally ill but no one remembers him coming to see her.'

De Vries switches on his old Anglepoise lamp. Outside, the sun has passed behind the Mountain and dusk has set in over the CBD. Already, in the street below, multicoloured lights are spilling from bars onto the dry, dusty pavements, strains of music drifting in the rising exhaust fumes past the open window.

'This isn't about children,' De Vries says. 'It's about parents. If Jessel was behind his parents' accidents then that was the beginning. Whatever they did to him, he got his revenge. It's what he's doing now, how he's choosing his victims.'

'I looked into Ali Jelani,' Don says, wiping his mouth with his handkerchief. 'She told Sally at their meeting that in Kenya she had two daughters and then her husband or partner left her. I cannot confirm this, but I did find an online article written by her last year where she describes leaving her children with friends and travelling to Syria. She said that she had planned to go for two weeks but had ended up staying for three months. She said that she felt bad leaving her children, who were seven and nine at the time, but when she saw the Syrian children she thought, My kids are lucky, they must just get on with it.'

'That sounds the kind of thing Stephen Jessel doesn't like.'

'Contacting Jelani online would have been easy,' Frazer says. 'Even though she was afraid, the information she was getting was too good. And when she learned that Dr Bellingham was the next target, she must have felt safe.'

De Vries sighs. 'Wherever he's taken her, he will have planned for it as carefully as he entrapped Jelani. We need to check for properties under the control of this section-eighteen department, an old family country home . . . I don't know. The places he chose previously were planned but, ultimately, opportunistic.' He frowns. 'He's moved into that estate. Check whether he looked at other properties in the area, whether there are unfinished developments, deserted buildings on land purchased by developers . . .' He flicks his wrist, but his watch is stuck to his skin. He twists it with his other hand. 'We all need to get some rest. Longest day of the year tomorrow. We're going to need every minute of it.'

'Why are you here?'

De Vries stands, again, in the dim, nylon-carpeted corridor, feeling the static electricity crackle around his shoes.

'I care about you, Grace. I need to know you're okay.'

The door opens. She is in her underwear, a wine glass in her right hand.

'Don't even think about it. This is extreme action in the face of an extreme climate.'

'What happened to the air-con?'

She walks away unsteadily towards the open doors to her balcony, points at a printed sheet on the kitchen table.

'System's overloading. One room at any time only. I'm cooling the bedroom.' He follows her onto the balcony. She is lying on a recliner, as if sunbathing in the gloom. He looks down over the railing, over the yellow-lit suburbs, back up to the view of the dark Mountain, Devil's Peak hiding the moon. Compared to the heat of her apartment, there is a little coolness in the night air, but no breeze. Days now without wind, without cloud: unheard of in Cape Town.

'Your profile was right. We discovered more about Jessel.'

'I'm not interested. I don't want to know. How I felt two nights ago, it reminded me of why I came home, why it's over for me. I can't hack it, and I don't want to.' She bends her head back to look at him. 'Don't you see them, Vaughn, when you close your eyes? Their ugly bloody-lipped mouths spewing all those lies, distortions . . . words to try to seduce you to their view of the world, to their sick, revolting, torturous, murderous desires.' She stares at him, studying his eyes, then relaxes her head again. 'I don't think you do, do you? I think you just fall asleep and wake up. They're not inside you.'

'No, they're not. I have the victims in my head. I have to represent them. I don't care about anyone else. If I can't, or I don't serve them well, that's who I see, and they judge me.'

She nods. 'I knew we were alike. Maybe not the same, but alike.'

'All the lights of the city, on the Cape Flats . . .' he looks up over the balcony '. . . the moon, the stars. That's what people look at: the brightness. We only see the dark. That's what we do. That's where we have to look . . .'

She empties her glass. 'The bottle's in the fridge. Fill me up and help yourself. In that order.'

He drops his jacket on the sofa, fills her glass and empties the bottle into a tumbler. There is barely ten centimetres.

'You want me to go get more?'

She reaches up, takes the glass, sips. 'There's red in the cupboard, but you're not staying.'

He pulls over the chair, sits next to her. She stares out at the night sky, glowing yellow from the streetlights around the other apartment blocks, turning black, the stars above them faint. He turns to study her. Her underwear is black and minimalist. Her head nods in time to some unknown rhythm. In the distance, he hears jazz, but it is not that to which her limbs minutely dance.

'Am I allowed to ask you one question?'

She shuts her eyes. 'That's your Colonel de Vries voice. Do you ever stop? If I say you can sleep with me tonight, lie in my fridge of a bedroom, will you just stop for one minute?' De Vries looks away from her. 'It's a serious offer. Fuck me and shut up, or ask me and leave? What do you want, Vaughn? What do you really want?'

'Grace Bellingham believes that, if Ali Jelani represents his ultimate prize, Jessel will have somewhere ready for her, and that place will have a special, long-held meaning for him. We need to look back at his family history, find somewhere he used to go when he was happy – or where he escaped to when he was unhappy – before whatever went wrong with his parents happened. Old hotels, holiday cottages. We have to go back in time . . .'

'I thought,' Sally Frazer says, 'Dr Bellingham had removed herself from this investigation.'

De Vries glances away, feigning a yawn. 'We did a deal.' His cellphone rings. He looks at the display. There is no name, but it is a number he recognizes.

The Grand Daddy Hotel on Long Street is more chic than shabby, a bohemian boutique hotel, beloved by tourists and locals with a liking for the unusual. Inside, bar, restaurant and lounge are all theatrically decorated, burnished with copper, murals on the walls, wood panelling. Each bedroom is different, with contemporary South African artwork, interior design and craft on display. On its roof terrace, you can stay in sparkling bare aluminium Airstream trailers, each interior curated by a South Africa design maven. There are flowerbeds, pot plants and trees. Under canopies on a raised deck at its centre is the Pink Flamingo Rooftop Cinema, complete with vintage popcorn machine, rugs, a bar, picnic hampers. On Monday nights, guests and visitors settle down at dusk, watching the flickering screen until all is dark around them.

De Vries is hot and out of breath just from jogging the short

painted staircase, which leads up to the roof. The heat seems to
seep down it to meet him on the small landing, like a wave. The
terrace, already baking in the mid-morning sun, appears deserted
but for one member of staff at the rear, tidying chairs. He slowly
rounds the first of the trailers, the sun's reflection momentarily
blinding him. His eyes water. He blinks. Beyond the potted shrubs,
by the wall and low railing overlooking Long Street, he sees the
back of a straw-hatted figure. He approaches slowly, squinting.
The figure turns.

'You were quick.'

De Vries stops, says quietly, 'You're an important man.'

Stephen Jessel smiles. 'It seems I am.'

'Why did you want to meet here?'

'It seemed a sensible rendezvous, convenient for whatever decision you make.'

De Vries stands still, just sheltered from the dazzling white light
by the edge of one of the canopies protecting the seats in the
cinema. Jessel is in the sunshine. He wears the same jacket,
the same tie – possibly, De Vries thinks, the same shirt – as when
they had met twice previously.

'What decision is there to make?'

'Whether to take me a few hundred metres across town – I'm
sure you have officers on the stairs back there, maybe on the
street – interrogate me, put me in a cell or let me leave this fine
establishment, walk up the street, perhaps buy a cold drink,
wander away.'

'Where is Ali Jelani?'

'Indeed, where is she?'

'I would like to talk with you, Stephen, but isn't it a little hot
up here?'

'I like the sunshine . . . And I brought a hat.' He raises it, forms
the same blank smile, replaces it, relaxes his mouth.

From below, there is a steady background hum of traffic, taxi-vans honking; occasionally music sails up on the urban thermals. Yet atop this building, in the stock-still air, there is a different measure of peace. De Vries tries to make his voice calm, yet, even to him, it sounds strident.

'What do you want?'

'Nothing.'

'Nothing?'

'It would have been easier just to carry on with my life peace-fully, but you made that rather difficult, didn't you? What was I to do? My face on the television, in all the newspapers. Obviously it was logical to meet you . . .'

De Vries finds Jessel's casual self-confidence annoying, wishes he could step forward, place handcuffs around the thin, hairy wrists, drag him down the stairs. He knows, that with Ali Jelani's life at stake, he cannot; realizes that were Jessel to climb the low wall and railing, he could be over the side before he could reach him. He has seen men jump before and, no matter what he thinks of them, for weeks afterwards, he cannot banish the sensation of falling. Nights are punctuated with jolting awake from vertiginous dreams, the feeling of vomit rising as blood drains from his head.

'I'd stay there, Colonel,' Jessel tells him. 'You're in the shade, and your current proximity feels about right. Don't you think?'

'Did you attack Marie Garsten and Bethany Miles?'

'If I had need of an attorney, he would tell me not to com-ment, but you seem to think that I did.'

'And Hazel Calder and Michelle Ricquarts?'

'Those poor women, whose names were, until I promoted them, unremarkable and unmemorable, suddenly flow off your tongue, like they're celebrities. I hope they're celebrated for what they truly are.'

'What is that?'

'At best, thoughtless, ignorant and cruel. More likely, each con-sidered their circumstances carefully and chose to abuse.'

De Vries observes Jessel's stillness and composure, arms by his sides, the yawning concrete crevasse of Long Street ten storeys down behind him and, then, almost out of focus in De Vries's field of vision, the charmless façades of the office buildings on the other side of the street. Jessel seems to control not only this roof garden but the space around him, stretching into the blue sky, as far as the vertical sliver of Table Mountain just visible at the top of the street.

'The decision I must make?' De Vries says, trying to keep his voice even, to veil his impatience at being forced to agree to Jessel's arrangements. 'Why would I let you walk away?'

A broad smile now, reflected in his eyes.

'Ali Jelani has written a long and heartfelt article about the women I have made celebrated. It describes their abusive be-haviour and how, in our thoughtless, uncaring society, such offences are tolerated and appeased, even when we are directly witness to them . . . People seem to believe they have a right to be parents, to breed at will. Some wish to buy themselves providers and carers for their old age, or they believe society expects it of them. Others want company in the house, or per-haps their religion tells them they cannot prevent the birth of one conceived through casual pleasure. Their abilities and suitability are not assessed. They are never checked. A woman produces a child so she – and usually the man – can do whatever she chooses with it.' He stares at De Vries. 'This article will be published or Ali Jelani will die. The article explains that if I am allowed to walk away, I will reveal where she is held. If I am incarcerated, she will die. The article states that it is your choice, De Vries. You decide whether she lives or dies. And I'm sure that there will be many voices to help you, many opinions in the media, on television, online. The whole country, perhaps the world, will join you in your dilemma.'

'What have you done to her?'

'Hidden her.'

'Deprived her of food, water?'

'Deprived, yes. There is also a pharmaceutical contribution, which ensures a consistent and inevitable deterioration. I prefer certainty.'

'What is it?'

'You keep asking questions, but there is only one question worth answering, and that is in your gift.'

'Why torture her? Why not publish her article and let her go?'

'You're doing it again, De Vries. The fact is, truth is revealed in the hours leading to death. A person is both physically and mentally weakened, but the lifeblood of hope spurs them to a remarkable candour, a sudden self-awareness wholly lacking hitherto.'

'So you torture them?'

Jessel frowns. 'I prepare them for revelation.'

In the distance, De Vries hears a helicopter. Beyond Jessel, he sees blue lights rising up the cream concrete sides of the office buildings.

'You can't walk away now, Mr Jessel. Perhaps later. I will have to discuss the terms of your deal with my superiors. But now . . .'

The thumping of the helicopter rotors grows closer. Suddenly its shadow darts across the terrace, its steel abdomen rising above the adjoining office block, its side emblazoned with SAPS markings. The canopies begin to sway, their concrete bases tipping. Chairs fall from the raised deck, plants bow and wave – even the trailers wobble. Jessel holds his hat, ducks his head. The helicopter passes them, the sun streaming through the blades, flickering on the curved mirrored trailers, like blinding interference. It rises and banks over the adjacent buildings.

Jessel shouts: 'You understand my terms?' De Vries nods, steps towards him. 'No cuffs. Take my arm and lead me, but no cuffs. Not here. Not on the street.'

De Vries grabs him, pulls him in shuffling steps around the obstructions towards the exit to the terrace, the engine noise reverberating in his head, the floor vibrating, his eyes watering, projecting white shadows on the inside of his eyelids, like an old monochrome movie, one frame at a time, with each long, gritty blink.

Sally Frazer says: 'Jessel's father was a pharmacist in Kenilworth where they lived. I have an address, but I'm not sure it's still there. I think that's where the new development is. I'm checking.'

De Vries turns away from Sally Frazer's desk, moves across the room.

'Anything come up on CCTV showing Jessel's car?'

Don February shakes his head. 'Most of the freeway cameras are just speed traps. I checked and no Toyota Prius has been captured in the last week.'

De Vries sees Henrik du Toit entering the squad-room. Du Toit catches his eye, heads for De Vries's office.

'Close the door.'

De Vries waits while Du Toit chooses to sit in a visitor's chair, then moves around the desk to take his own seat.

'The good news is that Pretoria are pleased. Obviously, they concur with General Thulani that there is to be no deal, but I think we knew that, didn't we?'

'That gives us, maybe, forty-eight hours to find Ali Jelani, assuming she's still alive. If you remember, Grace Bellingham suggested that he would be even more violent than the previous attacks.'

'You're not going to talk to him?'

'At some point, yes,' De Vries says. 'He can wait. First, he's enjoying being the centre of attention far too much so it may disturb him to be ignored. Second, he believes that Jelani is a bargaining chip, so he won't tell us where she is unless he's released, and, finally, we have better things to do.'

'You have to find Jelani,' Du Toit says. 'What other better things are there?'

'The article he claims Jelani wrote. We don't yet know to which newspapers he's offered it. Maybe all of them, but I'd bet pretty good money that the *New Cape Gazette* is top of his list, since Jelani has, to all intents and purposes, been writing for it.'

'I agree, but how should we be involved?'

'You don't want to try to stop them printing it?'

'We don't want them to print, but we won't ask. We can't be seen to be trying to influence what newspapers do or don't write.'

De Vries snorts. 'So, what is the point of our press conference, then?'

'To impart information to be disseminated to the public.'

'But it's what we want to tell them. It's not the truth. How is that not influencing what the press do and don't print?'

'Don't be naive, Vaughn. The press won't know what the truth is, or was, until later, and by then the story has moved on. If we were to ask this *New Cape Gazette* not to publish, and they told their readers, what would that look like?'

'I'm too naive to understand the distinction, sir. I'll take your word for it.'

'Whatever happens, it's bad. There's nothing good about it. You said he told you that you would be named?'

'It would be my decision, he said, whether Ali Jelani lives or dies.'

'Well, it isn't.'

De Vries laughs. 'No, sir.'

'Stephen Jessel will decide, and if he's psychotic, as Dr Bellingham predicted, then he will decide to let her die. Unless you can find her, of course.'

'Back to me. I understand.'

'So, your first action now?'

'Get in Penelope van Reidel. Find out what she really knows, whether she has this article.'

'Perhaps . . .' Du Toit twitches. 'Perhaps go to see her. It might be advisable to keep the press, and her especially, on side.'

'So, we pander to the fourth estate. I understand entirely, sir.'

'You don't, Vaughn. You never have. But, fortunately, I do. So, be guided.'

'Can I get on now?'

He stands, looks down at Du Toit, passes him as he lets himself out of his office.

'There can be no deal.'

They look at De Vries, awaiting more, but he says nothing.

'Can he not be made to believe that there is a deal and then, once he has revealed the whereabouts of the hostage, we can recapture him?'

De Vries turns to Ben Thwala.

'No.'

'Why not? I mean, in theory, sir?'

'Because the SAPS can't be seen to agree to this man's terms. Can you imagine how it would look if the TV cameras followed him walking out of here? We would have no guarantee that he would keep up his end of the bargain, or that we could catch him again. He may have planned some ingenious escape. So, the brass are right. He stays here and what happens to Jelani is down to us.'

Sally Frazer says: 'It was a house in Kenilworth. The family lived there for seventeen years, from when Stephen Jessel was three until he was twenty.'

'Where did they go then?'

'The parents went to a flat in Kenilworth, close by. There's no record of whether Stephen ever lived with them there, and I can't find anything about him at all between the ages of about nineteen and thirty, when he first started working the Section Designation Department, as a clerk.'

'No country house, weekend home?'

'No. I can't really tell, but there's no evidence to suggest that they were well off.'

'Relatives?'

'None that I can find. Not even the aunt in the UK who is noted as his next of kin. The address doesn't exist. The father was an only child, and I can't find birth records for the mother.'

De Vries turns to the circle of officers.

'If he's picked a random location, we're at the mercy of a witness, and he's proven very good at not being noticed. Dr Bellingham believes he'll have picked somewhere special for this victim. Special to him. He feels increased animosity towards her, not only because of her perceived abandonment of her children but because she betrayed him personally when he tested her.'

'We keep looking,' Frazer says.

'Don, talk to Brigadier du Toit about broadcasting an appeal for witnesses, but keep me out of it . . . And did you turn anything up at Jessel's house?'

'Nothing to suggest another location he has shown interest in. No, sir.'

'Right. Stick a couple of officers on the CCTV cameras. We spotted him last time. We might do again.' He turns back to his office, stops, calls to Don. 'I need to find the *New Cape Gazette* editor, Van Reidel. Find out where she is.'

'I have the article.'

Penelope van Reidel sits upright but relaxed at her desk in front of the stained-glass panel. De Vries notices that when he slouches in the chair opposite her a golden halo appears directly above her head; he assumes this has been designed.

'How was it delivered?'

'By email . . . and, before you ask, I've already had my IT team try to find out where it came from, but they say it's been tampered with just sufficiently to make it untraceable.'

'My people might be able to do more. I assume you're prepared to forward it in its entirety to us?'

'Perhaps.'

'Ms van Reidel . . .'

She holds up her hands. 'It was made very clear in the message that accompanied the article that it was not to be released or shown to anyone before the edition tomorrow morning.'

'I'm not interested in what a psychopath specifies, or in breaking some sadistic embargo. I want the material to study for clues. What you choose to do with it is entirely up to you.'

'Nonetheless . . .'

'Stephen Jessel is in a cell, but Ali Jelani is probably lying somewhere, bound to a chair, deprived of water and injected with a drug that will kill her if we do not find her. Even you, surely, cannot prioritize your front page over the life of a woman, one whose work you desired, encouraged and paid for?'

'Even I? Is that what you think of me?'

255

'That wasn't personal. It comes with your position. And I don't have time for feigned self-pity or, indeed, obtaining a court order, but if you won't co-operate with me, I will waste my time and that of my officers in getting a judge to sanction it – perhaps that is a detail your rival titles will wish to advertise – and then I will take the article and analyse the means by which it was sent to you, because that may prove vital to saving Ali Jelani's life.'

'You can take a breath now, Colonel.' She reaches inside her desk, pulls open a wide drawer, takes out a wide double-page layout and places it on her desk. 'This is the draft layout, which you may take with you. Leave the address you want my people to send the email to.'

De Vries stands, slaps a card on her desk. 'Good.'

'We have co-operated with you throughout.'

'Have you thought that, by printing the article this man has sent you, you are co-operating with him, rather than us?'

'He makes it clear that, if we do not print, Ali Jelani will die.'

'His hostage will die anyway if we don't find her, because he has no intention of telling us where she is, whatever anybody does or doesn't do. However, we have a free press in our new country, so you can do whatever you would like to do.'

'Indeed . . .' She stands also, proffers her hand across the broad desk. 'Colonel, when you read the article and you reach the part that concerns you, I want you to remember it wasn't personal. It comes with your position.'

The email is studied by Joey Morten and another officer expert in online activity. It has been sent using an encrypted private email address, unregistered and almost impossible to trace.

'Anyone can set up and use this type of account,' Morten says. 'I have one. Feels safer when you're sending any kind of private information. This one bounces it around a bit before forwarding it so that you can't identify where it came from.'

'Could the company?'

He looks at Sally Frazer. 'In theory, they must keep records of all data they carry, but in practice they won't co-operate because it would undermine their business. Probably take you years going through the courts.'

'Could we try asking them?'

Morten smiles. 'Sure, send them an email.'

'So I'm clear for the boss: we don't know when or where this was sent from, and we can't find out?'

'*Ja*. Definitely not within the timescale.'

'Can you run a cryptology program, or something like that?'

Morten and the other officer look at one another.

'What is that?'

'Something that looks for a message in the text. Is it possible that Jelani has given us a clue?'

Morten scratches his head hard. 'Sergeant Frazer, you've been watching way too much TV.'

'It could be worse, sir.'

De Vries looks up at Don February, then back down at the article layout, which has been blown up and is now spread across two desks.

'"I sat in front of Colonel de Vries and looked him in the eye and he knew nothing,"' De Vries reads. '"I met him a second time and then a third, and he was blind." It goes on. "Until I set my puppet journalist to work, the SAPS did not know there was any connection between the crimes. I had to tell them. They knew nothing. This is what you pay your taxes for. Ali Jelani was questioned by a female officer. They sat facing each other at a café, and when Jelani told her what I had instructed her to say, she disappeared while the officer's back was turned."'

'The public will understand that these are his words. A murderer.'

'But they're true, Don. We had him and we had Jelani.'

'We did not know . . .'

'It doesn't matter. People will read what he claims about the women, about the victims.' He points at the spread. A photograph of each victim is displayed above the paragraphs describing the alleged treatment of their children. 'Apparently, Michelle Ricquarts's daughter wrote online that she wanted to become a stripper also. That's probably what triggered Jessel.'

Sally Frazer walks towards them.

De Vries swings around to her, expectant. 'Anything?'

'No, sir.'

General Thulani's office is verging on tepid, yet feels cool to Du Toit and De Vries. The man himself, tie off, his jacket on the back of his chair, is sweating, as are two fully uniformed senior officers from Central Division.

'I do not need to tell you,' Thulani begins, 'that when this article is published, there will be a firestorm. Expect the radio, the television, the worldwide web: all will be alight with indignation. We will be advised this and told the other. I have already instructed the brigadier here,' he indicates the man sitting on the far right of the semicircle in front of his desk, 'that his officers must expect reaction from the public. They must be prepared. And all of this on top of the explosion last week . . .'

'Long Street is fully reopened. We know who the perpetrators were. Terrorists.'

Thulani looks down at the brigadier.

'It may be open, but there are boarded-up businesses, closed bars and restaurants, damage to the buildings. The scarring tells the story and that is why the tourists are not so much in town. We hear that our city has more visitors than ever this year, and then there are these two events. It will only be bad news. Cape Town will be the centre of attention for all the wrong reasons.' He leans forward, pours himself a glass of water from a carafe, drinks half of it. Ice clinks. 'We are not here to reflect on the negative, gentlemen.' He turns to Du Toit. 'What can Central – and the other divisions – do to assist you?'

'We need witnesses. We need to find Jessel's white Toyota Prius, but, in all probability, it's hidden. Above all, we need a sighting, at some point, of Jessel in his car.'

One of the uniformed officers says: 'Can we ask all residents to make a check of garages, cellars, empty buildings?'

Thulani's heavy eyes fall on him.

'That can have undesirable side-effects. People's privacy is invaded, trespass is sanctioned. You risk their injury in trying to gain access to such buildings. And, as we have seen before, if you involve the public with more than their eyes, they all think they are police officers. It is the beginning of vigilantism.'

'We cannot even be certain that she is held within Greater Cape Town. He's operated before in the Strand and Somerset West areas, and he recently moved from Kenilworth to a new estate there. We've alerted the Somerset West teams.'

'You have nothing else?'

They all look to Du Toit, who resists the temptation to turn to De Vries.

'We have no definite information as to where he might have taken the hostage. His former and current address have been checked. Most pressingly, we believe that we have thirty-six hours, at most, to find her.'

'Why that timescale?'

Now, Du Toit does involve De Vries.

'Assuming that he treats her like his previous two victims, she'll have no water or food. He claims he uses a drug to speed up the effects of dehydration until vital organs fail. We don't know, but it would explain why the pathologists cannot pinpoint an exact reason for expiration.'

'This is very bad,' Thulani says.

'We have Jessel,' Du Toit says. 'We will question him this evening, but it is hard to imagine what will persuade him to give up where he has taken Ali Jelani.'

Thulani takes a black silk handkerchief from his trouser pocket, dabs his upper lip.

'We have no carrot and no stick. That is how we have to police in the twenty-first century.'

Du Toit glances to his left without moving his head; De Vries says nothing.

De Vries works in the squad-room with his team, studying every-thing that was found in Jessel's Somerset West home. Ben Thwala takes officers to the Kenilworth-Wynberg borders to visit Jessel's previous home and speak to the neighbours. De Vries wants to interview Jessel, but knows he will do better to wait: Jessel will give him nothing unless he has something to give him in return, even if it is one piece of information he is not expecting them to know. When the fans are directed away from them to stop papers being blown away, the heat settles in the open rectangle of the squad-room, the smell of body odour increases, pages stick to fingers, and the work rate slows. Don February buys every officer an ice cream; they all sit licking and sucking them for five minutes, in silence, breathing heavily . . .

The air smells of woodsmoke. Fire on the Mountain, maybe close, maybe many kilometres away. Looking up between Lion's Head and Signal Hill, the air is hazy-white, the Mountain about to turn from sun-bleached rock and grasses to deep purple shade as the sun sets on the Camps Bay side.

The squad-room on the opposite side of the building is deserted, dark and calm. Ahead, De Vries sees Du Toit's corner office, light showing through the heavy blinds with which he protects himself. He knows that, like him, Du Toit will work late, hoping that the volume of research eventually produces a break-through. As he approaches, he hears a second voice. He knocks, is called in, enters.

She does not turn her head, but he recognizes her immediately. 'Sir . . . Dr Bellingham.'

Du Toit waits for De Vries to sit.

'Dr Bellingham has come in at my personal request. She will not involve herself with the case further, or be present when Jessel is interviewed. It would not be appropriate for anyone else to know that she is making a contribution. Am I clear?'

'Yes.' He turns to Bellingham. 'Is Henrik on the same deal as me?'

'Deal?' Du Toit says.

'There's a reason,' she says sourly, 'that Vaughn is not renowned for his sense of humour,'

Du Toit frowns at her; De Vries smiles to himself.

'We were about to begin,' Du Toit continues.

'In fact, you had already asked me an important question: am I surprised by Jessel turning himself in?' She sits up. 'On the face of it, yes, since it seems likely that he could have made his escape if he had chosen to do so. However, he may have felt that escape was now impossible and that he could create as much publicity as possible for what he sees as his crusade by taking the action that he has.'

'Do you think he believes that we might release him?'

'With most psychopaths at this point in the offending cycle, I would say that their brains have become . . . focused, and that that focus is constantly narrowing: a corridor down which their next victim lies and which they must travel, making all preparations necessary, in order to get there. This, clearly, is something different.'

'He intends to let her die?' De Vries asks.

She turns to him. 'Possibly. Without becoming more involved than I am prepared to be, I can't say. It's conceivable that he'll reveal her whereabouts to demonstrate his mercy, to humiliate you and the SAPS, but, equally likely, he may already have killed her.'

'How likely is that?' Du Toit says.

'Guessing, trying to answer Vaughn's question without sufficient knowledge, I would say that ten per cent of the time he will save her, ten per cent of the time she's already dead. The most likely scenario is that he will refuse to give up the information and blame you for her death.'

'But he must know that, whatever he does, he'll never see the light of day again?'

'He may not see it that way, but I agree. Unless he has something else planned, his position is hopeless. For that reason, you can offer him nothing, so we all know how the scene will play out.'

'Unless we find her.'

'Unless you find her, yes.'

Du Toit has been sitting very still, very upright. His eyes meet De Vries's.

De Vries says, quietly, painfully: 'We don't have anything.'

She nods. 'He has demonstrated skill throughout his spree. He has taken increasing risk, but it has been weighed reasonably, interference has been judged effectively. I think it's most unlikely that you'll discover her whereabouts either from him in interview or through an error he has made.'

'I asked Dr Bellingham to consider any information that might guide us to where Ali Jelani could be being held.' Du Toit looks over to her expectantly.

Grace Bellingham sighs. 'There's not much here to go on. He's meticulous, intelligent, more reasoned than I would expect, but, despite all his cries that this is a crusade to highlight injustices he sees as having been meted out to undeserving children, this ultimately comes down to him. What happened in Stephen Jessel's life that might cause him to act the way he has?' She leans forward into the breeze afforded by the free-standing fan Du Toit has installed in his office. 'Sorry, but it's stifling.' She reaches for the small bottle of mineral water on the desk in front of her, gulps half of it, replaces it.

'Jessel's actions with his victims suggest the following. He binds them. This is for control, but it also suggests that he may also have been bound, or his movement restricted. It may not be as literal as that. He may simply have felt trapped – as most children do if they are abused. He either wants to, or actually does, rape them. This is control and power also, but it is likely to represent a sexual crisis in his own life. It's probably, but not definitely, from childhood and, with the history of his parents and their . . . how shall we say? . . . unexplained accidents, it seems that his first actions may have been revenge.'

'For what?' Du Toit says.

'For whatever event or set of events triggered this extreme distortion of the brain.'

'But why women? Did his mother abuse him?'

263

'Possibly. It would seem both parents may have been involved. However, I do have one theory. It revolves around the blinding of Bethany Miles. He knew that she would die – he may even have been present at her death – so why gouge out her eyes, and then pose them? There doesn't have to be a reason, of course. Profilers and psychiatrists waste many hours trying to decipher the meaning of every action and, sometimes, these actions have no meaning. They can be a deliberate attempt to mislead. They may be a hyper-sadistic act made on the spur of the moment when they are drunk with bloodlust. However, here, I wonder if Stephen Jessel is making a point about these women not watching, or watching over, their children.'

'Abuse leads to abuse,' De Vries says blankly. 'We see that repeatedly. I almost feel as if rationalizing the cause diminishes the act. Jessel committed evil crimes and we are lucky to have him behind bars.'

Bellingham turns to him. 'Your first point is banal but sadly true. I disagree with you entirely on your second point but commend you for describing his crimes as evil rather than the man himself.'

'I watch every word I say.'

'That,' Grace Bellingham says, 'will make a pleasant change.'

'Because describing sadistic, evil, ruthless killers as anything other than victims upsets too many liberals.'

'Thank you, then, for managing one sentence,' she says disagreeably.

'Do we,' Du Toit says loudly, 'have a basic theory as to what might inspire Jessel to his behaviour?'

'I think so,' Bellingham says, looking at Du Toit, angling her body away from De Vries. 'As I stated before, I think he had been using Ali Jelani as an unwitting ally for several weeks, and whether or not he planted the information about the supposed attack on me intentionally to test her or whether he did it because he assumed some trust or even understanding between them, Jelani betrayed him immediately. From the article, he had clearly followed her, knew her whereabouts, knew that she stayed within the sight of friends as much as possible. His plan to entrap her was complex, either by coincidence or design, and that suggests that, as a victim, she is important to him. Especially now, since it is her abduction that has led us to catch him.'

She leans forward, tips the water bottle into her mouth, drains it. 'He will almost certainly already have prepared a place for his next victim, whether he ever intended it to be me or not. It will be personal. It will link to his abuse or his escape from abuse. The family home, the home of family friends or relatives, a country home, perhaps even a guesthouse or rental. This goes back to the beginning.'

'He moved house a month ago,' De Vries says. 'We searched it. I've gone through everything myself this afternoon and there's nothing.'

'What about his previous house?'

'Thwala went there with a search team. They even tried some house-to-house. Just the usual. Quiet neighbour, kept to himself. No trouble, no music, no parties. No friends, as far as they could discover.'

'It's too recent anyway,' Grace Bellingham says. 'This all happened a long time ago.'

'So why now?'

'There is usually a catalyst or a trigger. These can be huge events, or so tiny as almost to be unnoticeable.'

'What is the difference,' Du Toit says, 'between a catalyst and a trigger?'

'You're right, Henrik. It's semantics. For me, a trigger is usually an event that occurs within the brain, stimulated by an act or event that releases powerful memories and, with those, many profound emotions. These flood the brain and begin the narrowing process I described earlier. Again, for my own personal use, a catalyst is most often a person – although on one occasion it was a dog – who stimulates a sudden anger, either because they have suffered in a similar way, or because something they say or do simply clicks inside the other party and their route forward suddenly becomes clear. Sometimes this can be suicide, or attempted suicide. More often, it is revenge.'

'Is it worth reviewing his parents' accidents?' Du Toit says.

'In as much as I suspect that he had a hand in them, yes. In terms of discovering the whereabouts of Ali Jelani, no. They can wait.'

'What should I say or ask Jessel that might get him to make a mistake, or reveal where Jelani is?'

She turns to De Vries. 'In truth, in twenty-four hours, nothing. I spend months talking to these men, every day. You can ask him about his childhood, but I doubt that he'll engage with you. Although he appears doomed, he'll think that he holds all the cards, that he has power over life and death. That is what people with his state of mind crave.'

'Who should I take in with me? A male officer? A woman?'

'Definitely not a female officer. It is against women he harbours such resentment and anger. Face him on your own. Do not provoke him, threaten him, be sarcastic. In fact, just turn the usual De Vries right off. Listen to what he says. Seem lightly impressed, respect his craft, get him to tell his story. Just possibly, he will say something that helps you to pinpoint where the first abuse occurred. That could, conceivably, lead you to his hostage.'

'You won't come in with me?'

'Vaughn, Dr Bellingham made this quite clear . . .'

'No,' she says, turning to him. 'I've told you repeatedly. You need to understand the difference between determination and wanton blindness. I am spent. I can't do it, and I won't. I warned you that there is a price to be paid for dealing with men like Jessel. You are closer to the edge than you think.'

'I will do whatever I have to do to try to save Ali Jelani. That's all I can think about.'

'That,' Grace Bellingham says quietly, 'is exactly the point. Stephen Jessel will know that, and he will use it against you.'

'Stephen Jessel is in a cell, or shackled in my interview room. He won't be using anything against me.'

'You didn't believe me the first time I told you so I'll say it again,' she says intently, a forced calmness in her voice. 'These men influence, manipulate and attack from the grave, from inside prison, from within a sealed room. Ali Jelani may not be the only one still in danger.'

'Why are you both still here?' De Vries looks at the two tired officers, faces sallow in the fluorescent lights

'I'm not going home.' Sally Frazer says. 'Don is staying here too. We probably have less than a day.'

'We are thinking, sir,' Don says, 'unless you want one of us beside you, we would sit in the observation room, hear what Jessel has to say. If he references anybody or any location, we can immediately follow it up.'

'Good. I'll keep it short. If he won't talk, we'll leave him.'

'When will you begin?'

De Vries puts on his jacket. 'Now.'

The corridors are silent, the light dim and insipid, the air unmoving. He finds himself slowing as he reaches the custody desk, still uncertain what he will say or do. He nods to the custody officer, who opens the door to the interview room. He approaches the table behind which Stephen Jessel sits, upright but relaxed. He places plastic cups of water on the table, takes his seat.

Jessel stares at the cups. 'Why has yours got ice?'

De Vries silently swaps the cups over.

Jessel smiles. 'You doctored the one with ice?'

De Vries picks up the cup with ice, drinks from it, replaces it in front of Jessel.

'The cup is dirty now.'

'Take your choice, Mr Jessel. Ice, or no ice. They're both cold.'

Jessel reaches forward. 'It would be easier if I didn't have these cuffs on my wrists.'

'The protocol is to cuff you behind your back. I requested that you were cuffed in front of you so that you would be more comfortable. You can drink quite easily.'

Jessel picks up the cup, twists it, lifts it to his lips.

'This discussion is being recorded. Please confirm that you've refused to request an attorney or accept the offer of one being made available.'

'I have.'

De Vries mutters the verbal description of the interview, the personnel, the time. He looks up.

'Where is Ali Jelani? Everyone will know her story, why she was punished. You gain nothing by letting her die.'

'It is very hot in this room.'

'It is the same throughout the building.'

Jessel smiles. 'Ali Jelani? I suppose you are somewhat . . . pressed for time.'

'Do you disagree with my analysis?'

'I neither agree nor disagree. What time is it now? Did you say five past nine? Ali Jelani thinks she is strong, but I think she will be dead by morning.'

De Vries shivers. 'Did you trust her? Did she betray you agreeing to talk to us?'

'I have never trusted anyone since I was eight years old.'

'Why is that?'

'I'm sure that Dr Bellingham will already have speculated. Perhaps you have just come from a meeting with her. She probably told you what to ask and what to say. Am I right?' He stares at De Vries. 'I think I am.'

'I'm only interested in what you have to say, Mr Jessel. I don't listen to speculation.'

'She told you to humour me, appear interested in what I have to say, even if it doesn't help you in your quest?'

'I just want to know why. Why you would do what you've done, what you are continuing to do.'

'That isn't true. You just want me to tell you where the woman is.'

'I do want that. I also want to understand why you are doing this.'

'Why? You believe that I will spend the rest of my life in prison . . .'

De Vries takes a sip of his water.

'What happens in our childhood affects the rest of our lives. What happened to you?'

Jessel sighs. 'For my eighth birthday, my father bought me a Hornby H0/00-gauge model railway.' He is leaning back, speaking quietly. It sounds like a recitation. 'It was a two-track layout, complete with signals and control for up to four locomotives. The stations and streets and houses and shops each had tiny lights inside them. In the dark, the trains could travel through the night. We set it up together in the cellar of our house. It was my place. The place where my father and I could play together. When I was nine years old, my mother brought hot chocolate and cookies to us as a surprise. She saw what my father, her husband, was doing to me. I remember looking up at her. I was ashamed but I was also glad she could see, that it would stop. I understood from the look on her face that what was being done to me was wrong. I knew that. I could feel it, and what she told me by her look was that I was right. I hoped that the police would come and take my father away, that I would be left with her only. And, then, what happened? Nothing. She never spoke of it again, never returned to the cellar. When I was fourteen years old, I refused my father. He threatened me, but I threatened him more. It ended there for him. It ended there for her . . .'

He looks blankly at De Vries. 'I failed at school, had few friends, left home when I was sixteen. I worked in a hostel, and I lived there. No one hurt me. I got a job with the Section Designation Department. I knew that I would find people like myself there. When I listened to the case officers talk about them, I could hear the disdain in their voices, the mistrust, the visceral hatred. When the blacks took over from the whites, I made myself a case officer. Senior officers had left and they needed people to look after the mess. They wanted to believe I was who I said I was. They needed me, to supervise the damaged, dangerous few. And I met them.'

'Why did you attack Hazel Calder?'

'Didn't Dr Bellingham tell you not to interrupt me?'

'No.'

Jessel studies him, continues: 'The time had come.'

'To attack these women?'

'To sacrifice myself for the victims who have no one to represent them.'

De Vries frowns. Jessel's justification is as his own.

'Did you kill your parents?'

'They were unpunished.'

'That doesn't answer my question.'

'Words can be used to mean anything. What is the difference between yes and no?'

'The other women. Why did you take them? Why did you make them suffer?'

'Punishment.'

'For what purpose?'

Jessel bridles. His voice sounds petulant.

'What is the purpose of punishment? It is a deterrent. To warn others who might be tempted to err. I not only punished the guilty, I warned the rest of them. Naturally it must be well advertised. And I found two more women, guilty themselves, who would help me. It required no effort on my part. They begged me to let them help me. A newspaper editor starting a new title, in search of the exclusive, the story that would define her paper, and an ambitious Kenyan journalist, whose greed for success blinded her to all rationality and judgement—'

'Where is she? Where is Ali Jelani?'

Jessel slowly raises his wrists, places them on the table in front of him, meets De Vries's questioning stare.

'Waiting in the corridor of death.'

'Tell us where she is.'

'Release me. The bargain is simple. The public will not understand why you let her die. They will reason that, once she is safe, I can be recaptured.'

'So why offer us a deal you know we cannot accept?'

'So that you can fail.'

'No one cares about me. You claim to care for children, but you will make Ali Jelani's children motherless. How is that good for them?'

'She abandoned them. They will scarcely notice her passing.'

'You're wrong. Your father abused you and your mother

271

betrayed you, but the women you are taking are trying to be good parents. We all make mistakes.'

Jessel leans back, says quietly: 'You do.'

'What mistake, in your opinion, am I making now?'

'You will see.'

De Vries's tongue plays with his teeth. He feels time passing, cannot believe that anything is being gained by giving Jessel an audience.

'Time passes for all of us. For Ali Jelani. For you. For the guilty. Only when I no longer had to struggle for my own survival did I think about what I wanted to achieve. I read the papers, read the stories about women who harm their children, who abuse or abandon them. And then, just as I was about to begin, I read online about a woman called Ali Jelani. A woman who, in her desire to succeed for herself, left her two young children with people she'd barely known a month. It was perfect: she could be both accessory in – and victim of – my work.

'I told her I would attack Dr Bellingham and I waited to see what she would do with the information. Mrs Jelani was so frightened that she was being followed, when she looked around she could not even see the obvious. When she met a female police officer whom I recognized from my visit here last week, I knew that she had chosen her path. I followed her to your home street, decided to frighten you and Dr Bellingham a little and cause a distraction. Then, while you were all busy with the fire, I stopped just where she was waiting – where I had seen her hide herself so that she could record and photograph my capture – and took her. No one even heard her call out. Fire engines and police cars are like that – they provide perfect cover.' He leans forward. 'How is Dr Bellingham? Did she think that I had come to fetch her?'

'You could have set fire to the entire city.'

Jessel shrugs.

'You can be merciful. You can release Jelani.'

'You can release me.'

De Vries stands, the sound of his chair pushed back against the concrete floor jarring, shocking.

'There's nothing more to say.'

Don February and Sally Frazer are not in the observation suite. He walks to the squad-room, realizing that his clothes are soaked with sweat. A feverish shiver passes through his body. He thinks of Grace Bellingham and her warnings about the cost of inter-action with people such as Jessel. He feels diminished by his interview; feels weaker.

Three junior officers are still at work. Frazer and Don stand together in front of a trestle table, on which numerous larger documents and printouts are spread.

Sally Frazer turns to De Vries.

'His home was where the abuse took place, which he left as soon as he could. That's where Dr Bellingham said we should look, so that's what we're doing.'

'It's a building site.'

'It's a development. Completed in phases. Two are finished. I think the land where Stephen Jessel's house was located is part of that finished phase.'

'You think there's another building there? On that site?'

'I think he may have bought there. I rechecked what passed through his bank accounts. He paid three million for his Somerset West house, but we checked, and it cost two point three five.'

'Two Feathers in Somerset West and the Kenilworth develop-ment are projects of the same developers/estate agent,' Don says.

'So that's how he could hide the money?'

'It's a reasonable theory,' Sally Frazer says.

'We managed to get a plan of the new apartments,' Don says. 'I called a friend of mine who works in the Planning Department and he had the plans at home on his laptop.'

'I wonder what else he brings home from work.'

Don turns to De Vries. 'It was a work laptop . . . He emailed the plans for the original layout of dwellings, and the new development. We have tried comparing the two to pinpoint where Jessel's former home would have been, but it is not clear. Sally has asked Joey Morten to adjust the scale and superimpose one over the other. He is working now at home.'

De Vries feels charged as if, before they fail, he has one concrete chance.

'We need to go now. You'll stay here and co-ordinate, Sally? Don, come on. We can be guided once we're there.'

The pre-Christmas roads are quiet at ten p.m., but the journey still takes longer than De Vries anticipates because of an accident on Hospital Bend travelling towards the Southern Suburbs. He is uncertain how to get there the quickest, but settles for the local roads, driving along Camp Ground, past Palmyra Junction and towards what used to be called Lansdowne Road, but which is now called after an imam whose name he cannot remember.

Kenilworth is a sprawling suburb. Higher up on the hill was, and largely remains, smart: grand villas and mansions on large plots. Lower down, by the racecourse, the houses in the suburban streets are modest, many being redeveloped into apartments. Eventually finding Doncaster Road, then McKinley Road, De Vries slows to search for the show-home and sales office. Many of the nearby streetlights are out, the roads and pavements quiet. Following painted hoardings around the vast site, they finally stumble upon gates and, beyond, the show-home and sales office.

Don gets out of the car, peers through the gates. He turns to the keypad and intercom, presses a button low down.

'No one is answering.'

De Vries calls Sally Frazer, is told that the overnight caretaker is a Mr Chalbri. He will assist them, and as soon as she can identify the likely property, she will call back.

After less than thirty seconds the ornate iron gates part, and they drive in. The development is partly a building site, partly completed apartments. The road is covered with red mud, spilled gravel and sand. They stop by the show-home and site office, which are both dark. A plastic snowman stands incongruously on the healthy lawn, glowing greyly. They get out into the still heat, which smells of hot concrete and diesel fumes. Above them, two massive cranes stand sentinel, red lights at their apex slowly flashing in time. Two apartment blocks stand at right angles to one another; maybe one in ten windows is showing light. The place seems eerily deserted.

Around the corner, a dirty Chevrolet Spark appears, drives fast and stops hard. A small Indian man hurries out towards them. 'Colonel de Vries?'

They hold up their ID.

'Mr Chalbri?'

'Yes, yes. I speak to your lady colleague. She asks about a particular address, back from when there where big old houses here, but she does not know what it is yet.'

'Are there residents here?' De Vries asks.

'Yes. Maybe about thirty apartments in Lake View and Furlong Rise.'

'Do you know them? Can you get names?'

'I know most, yes. There is not security as such, you see. I am here to help residents and receive deliveries out of hours. The security men are over on the other side, guarding the tools and machines.'

'A single man,' De Vries says. 'Stephen Jessel.'

Mr Chalbri shakes his head. 'No, I do not know that name. Of course, I do not know everybody.'

'A white Toyota Prius?'

'Oh, yes, I have read about this. The man who takes the women?' He furrows his brow. 'You think he is here? His car? A white Prius. No . . . Maybe. There are white cars.'

De Vries looks around at the empty, muddy side-roads.

'Where do people keep them?'

'All underground car parking.'

'Take us there.'

'To where? The car park? Yes, please, but which block?'

De Vries looks at Don, who has his ear pushed against his cellphone.

'Sally says she thinks the Southerly block is positioned over where Armour Road used to be, where the Jessel family lived.'

'The Southerly block,' De Vries barks, turning on the spot, trying to decipher his position.

'Furlong Rise, over there.' Chalbri points to the further block, on ground raised slightly above where they are standing. 'You want to drive?'

De Vries is already walking. They follow him. Don stumbles as he continues to listen to Sally Frazer. He hangs up, trots to catch the other two.

'Sergeant Frazer says that when the plans are overlaid, there is no single apartment which occupies the land on which the Jessel family home lived. All the apartments are built at a different orientation.'

De Vries frowns. Inside, he feels that this grey, miserable place hides Ali Jelani.

Furlong Rise is squat, wider than it is tall, each front-facing apartment sharing long, curved balconies. De Vries wonders what they must see. Perhaps a glimpse of racecourse, more likely the warehouses and shopping malls, and probably the freeway. The building seems to grow in volume as they draw close. De Vries stops, waits for Chalbri to reach him.

'Is there a basement?'

'The car park only.'

'First floor, then.' He turns to Don. 'Can Frazer at least tell us which end it could be?'

'Eastern end.'

Chalbri points to the left-hand side of the building. Few windows are lit. They have still seen no other human beings.

'Is it always this quiet?'

'At night, yes. In the day, there are men on construction and people still making fixes to these blocks too. Next year, all these apartments will be full.'

De Vries looks up at what constitutes the first floor of apartments, sitting only three metres above ground level. He hesitates, rubs the sweat from the front of his neck in the V between his thumb and forefinger. The location feels right, but the apartments he is scrutinizing do not.

'We're looking for a cellar. A basement.' His voice sounds loud and strident in the still, concrete night.

Chalbri jumps. 'Yes. I do not know. You want to see the car park?'

De Vries starts walking. 'Yes. We need to look underground. Can we get in?'

'I have the key-card.' Chalbri overtakes him, hurries to the ramp, pushes the key card against a sensor and watches the barrier rise. Together, they trot down the ramp into complete darkness. Chalbri switches on a torch, which hangs on a string from a trouser belt loop. 'When the car enters,' he says, 'the lights come on. That is what should happen.'

De Vries looks round, sees that Don has a torch also.

'He could have left it here. The Prius. Safe as anywhere.'

They proceed to where the parking spaces start. There are maybe a dozen cars; none is a Toyota Prius. At the far end of the parking area, there is a dimly illuminated lift lobby behind sheet glass. They approach it. De Vries pulls the torch from Don, shines it either side of the lobby.

'What are those doors there?'

'Service rooms only. Plant rooms.'

'We can see inside those?'

'Yes,' Chalbri says, 'but there is no one inside. I check them all and relock them when I take over at seven p.m.'

'Are you sure?'

'Yes, sir. Every night, it is my first duty. In both buildings.'

'No other rooms down here?'

Chalbri is fiddling with the loaded key-chain.

'Maybe this way . . .' He enters the lift lobby and takes the door on the far right. 'This is the corridor to the stairs and the main starboard lobby.'

The corridor is lit only by grey LEDs. De Vries is already depressed by the soulless building. The working day would begin and end here, in the car park, in the narrow grey corridor. They reach a right-angled turn to the left. Chalbri stands by two sets of doors on his right.

'There are these rooms.'

'What are they?'

'I do not know, but I think that they are servants' quarters for the two big double-size apartments above. There may be stairs into the upper floor.'

De Vries knocks loudly on one door, then the next.

'Is anyone there?'

'I do not think so. The two big apartments are not lived in yet.'

De Vries looks down at Chalbri.

'Open them.'

'Open these doors? I do not know whether I can.' He looks down at the keys, squinting in the low light. 'In theory, I am supposed to have every key here.' De Vries feels a sudden pulse of adrenalin. Everything feels right: direct and uninterrupted access from the car park, an underground room. He looks at Chalbri sorting through what must be more than a hundred keys.

'This seems close,' Don says. 'And, if these are storage rooms, it would explain why Jessel apparently only paid half a million for it.'

'I know.' De Vries's hands are sweating, palms clammy.

Chalbri approaches the nearer door.

'Let me try this. The tag says . . . No.'

He fumbles again. Don can feel the frustration in De Vries's posture. The lights in the corridor extinguish. Chalbri stands rigid. Don illuminates the bunch of keys, and Chalbri continues search-ing, says:

'The lights go off when there is no movement. Make movement.'

De Vries takes a few steps backwards and forwards in the dark. He raises his arms and waves. The lights stay off. De Vries walks towards the sparkling bundle of keys. Chalbri places a key in the lock. All hear it turn.

'Stay here, sir,' De Vries says.

He takes Don's torch, pushes open the door. The movement of the light switches has no effect. The narrow corridor opens out to a small, low-ceilinged bedsit. The two doors off the corridor open up to bathroom and, on the other side, the biggest room in the dwelling, the kitchen. De Vries enters each room, scans the floor, checks for further doors or cupboards, sees nothing but unfinished work, cheap fitted cupboards and basic furniture. He turns, retraces his steps.

'The other door?'

'I have the key,' Chalbri says, holding it up in the beam of his torch.

'This is closer to the road,' Don says, studying his cellphone. 'The Jessel home was on the road, on Armour Road.'

De Vries pushes ahead through the door, finds the same layout. This time the light switches produce wall lights in the corridor. He paces down it towards the bedsitting room, finds it empty; the bathroom – there is a shower curtain and two bottles of shower gel and shampoo; towels, a bathmat. He slams the door, opens the next to the kitchen. The lights come on and, on top of an island preparation table, he sees her. De Vries struggles to form words, his throat constricted.

'Here. Don, ambulance. Tell Chalbri not to come in.'

The body is spot-lit from the ceiling by a cluster of three halogen lights. She is naked, tied to the surface on her back. A huge kitchen knife sticks out of the surface where it has been stuck between her legs, the blade facing her flesh. There is blood between her legs, oozing off her face. Against the white-tiled floor, white Formica worktop, the white walls, the blood stands out so brightly, crudely scarlet. He walks towards her, concentrating on not gagging. He sees her face, one eye staring, the other socket empty and rust brown. He leans over her, gently prods her arm. It twitches.

'She's alive. Ambulance. Get Chalbri to open the gates, direct them here. Hurry.'

He looks back down at Ali Jelani. Her open eye blinks and flutters. He jumps back, then returns to the work surface, tries to dislodge the embedded knife but cannot. He whispers to her not to move, searches the kitchen for a knife, pats his pockets, finds his small school pocket knife, pulls out a blade, starts to saw through the first black cable tie. As he releases her arm; shaking, she brings it down by her side. He sees her left eye focus on him.

He says quietly, his voice breaking: 'Ali Jelani. You're safe.'

Tears form in her eye.

At the lift doors, Du Toit is waiting.

'What took you so long? They told me you'd come back ten minutes ago.'

'Do you mean to say congratulations, sir? Don and Sally Frazer brought it together. They deserve the credit.'

'Well done, Vaughn. Now what are you doing?' He waits until De Vries meets his eye.

'I'm talking to Jessel.'

De Vries starts to move away towards his squad-room. Du Toit follows.

Sally Frazer hurries to him. 'Is she all right?'

'The paramedic said her pulse was strong enough, but she's very weak. I'll visit the hospital later or first thing.'

'Colonel.' De Vries turns to Du Toit, who addresses Frazer: 'Take a couple of minutes somewhere else, please, Sergeant.' He watches her go, turns to De Vries.

'Leave Jessel alone.'

'I'm going to tell him we found her, that she's alive.'

'Why?'

'Because I want to. Jelani had her right eye gouged out. She must have bled for hours, left alone to die. Can you imagine that?'

281

'It serves no purpose.'

'It serves my purpose. Ali Jelani's right eye wasn't in the room.'

'Vaughn, stop it. You've beaten him. You picked up a serial assault-and-murder case late and there has been no other fatality. Take the win.'

'I am. I'm taking my prize. It'll be recorded. I won't compromise anything.'

Du Toit shakes his head. 'It won't feel like a prize in the morning.'

Jessel sits as he did before but, this time, his arms are behind his chair. De Vries walks to his own chair, undertakes the identification process, starts the interview. He looks up at Jessel, who speaks before him.

'You found her?'

De Vries twitches, says: 'We found her and she's alive. We found her at your old house, in the cellar. You were abused so you chose to abuse, terrorize, torture, murder others. You're out of here in the morning, and you can spend your time in Pollsmoor working out what sob story you're going to tell in court. If you make it there . . .'

'I can see that you are very pleased with yourself, Colonel de Vries.' Jessel is sitting forward now, the blank smile in place. 'Before you send me away, be certain you don't need me. Would be a shame to have to turn out again to fetch me.'

De Vries stands. 'No one wants you. Nobody needs you.' He leans towards Jessel. 'You took out Ali Jelani's eye. What did you do with it?'

'That is something neither she nor you will ever know . . . But it is with me always.'

Jessel smiles broadly. De Vries recoils from him, his smile, his breath, the image that, in De Vries's exhausted, blasted brain, he has conjured.

He pours again, fills the paper cups half full.

'I have a driver I can call,' Du Toit says. 'Don't drive home.'

'I never drive when I'm drunk, sir.'

'You said you'd go to the hospital. Leave it. She's not going anywhere and they won't tell you much anyway . . . I called Grace . . . Dr Bellingham. Phone's off. She helped us, Vaughn. She focused us on Jessel's past, where the first abuse occurred.'

'She did.'

'Was there . . . is there a problem between the two of you?'

'She offered me a Faustian deal, except this one had two options, both bad.'

'Well, it was worth it, this deal.'

'If you say so.'

They drink in silence, in the gloom, letting the lightest of night-time breezes drift through the open window, stir the heat with whirlpools of tepidity. Only when the sound of a roaring, swearing drunk in the street below reaches them does De Vries say: 'He sounds like I feel . . .'

'You think about it,' Du Toit says. 'He's taken five women, subdued them. He doesn't look capable.'

'You'd be surprised where the strength comes from to commit evil. I've seen it before.'

'I was thinking about Jessel when he came here regarding Leigh Finnemore, our section eighteen. You didn't like him from the start.'

'No.'

'He'll probably end up at Valkenburg.'

'Prison for life,' De Vries says. 'I don't care if he's sick. Don't care if he was abused, don't care if he claims he's lost his mind. He's capable of thought and, whatever he or they say, he knew what he was doing, and he knew that it was wrong. He admitted it. "I sacrifice myself for the victims." That's what he said. He wouldn't think that if he didn't know he was doing wrong. He gave himself away. So, no, I don't want him to receive help, don't want him to be able to tell his story. The death penalty increasingly seems appealing.'

'But it doesn't work, Vaughn.'

'Justice moves too slowly. There are too many opinions, too many apologists.' De Vries is banging his fist on the desk, but it makes little noise. 'Too many people afraid of infringing these people's human rights. It's black and white: guilty or not guilty, according to the evidence. You're guilty, you're gone.'

'Gone?'

'While we wait, while we obey the rules, they pass us, they overwhelm us. We have to deal with the consequences. You talked about winning, Henrik. Is that winning?'

They hear the sound of a vacuum cleaner, swing around, see a cleaner entering the squad-room. They watch him straighten up, take a long piece of lavatory paper from his trouser pockets, ball it, wipe his brow.

He dozes fitfully at his dining table. He has contemplated bed but, even with all the windows open onto the upper balcony, his room is hot, the air motionless. Downstairs is tangibly cooler and it keeps him there. The entire house smells of smoke, lodged in the curtains and carpets, cushions and sofas. He has dutifully drunk a pint glass of water, but still decides to open another bottle of red wine. Occasionally he loses consciousness while holding his glass, jolts awake, fearful that his wine has spilled. Each time his head bows, his chin hits his chest, he sees them: Hazel Calder, pulling her legs apart for him; Michelle Ricquarts scrabbling to escape the wooden beach-shack; Marie Garsten, grey like the raw concrete of the building-site cellar, raped and left to die . . . Half conscious, he is holding his breath. He splutters, but does not wake . . . Bethany Miles in the dark, damp emptiness of Apostle Lodge. He sees her black concave eyes, ants forming psychedelic patterns reflected and distorted on the chrome frame to which she is bound, her mouth twisted to a scream. He sees the metal bird on the roof, hears it cry. He sees the blank windows of the building, the blank eyes of Bethany Miles, the single eye of Ali Jelani, crying.

He wakes, mouth dry, neck sore. He sits up, slowly moves his open hand towards the glass, folds his fingers gently around the goblet, brings it to his mouth.

Dawn wakes him; treble-tinny music from outside stirs him. He lifts his head, opens gritty eyes, realizes that it must be the black couple who guard next door, out on the balcony. He wonders whether they woke him or whether for him now sleep is transitory. He is tired, but not hung-over. He is too drunk to be that. He views his charred, scarred garden, half-empty pool with its scalded wood and black ash surface, sees for the first time a distorted white plastic garden chair, melted by the fire. A gallery in Bree Street, he thinks, would pay for that. He showers while the coffee machine heats up. He makes two strong cups, downs them, fills his flask with two more measures and doubles the volume with brandy.

As he walks outside, he hears the music louder. He walks around the side of his house and looks up, seeing the balcony from the diagonal. The tall girl is dancing to music from, he thinks, the cellphone she has in her hand. She sways, she smiles, she raises her arms above her head. He turns away, envious that her joy can, seemingly, be accessed so easily, begrudging the joy itself.

He drives carefully to the hospital, fumbling in vain for his dark glasses, the morning sun burning his eyes, making them water. He feels wretched, dehydrated.

There is a disturbance in the waiting room, a physical fight. He is too tired to intervene, walks towards the wards. The only information he gleans is that Ali Jelani is out of danger. There are no doctors, no consultants to talk to him, only nurses, just as tired as he, but sober. It is enough.

He walks into the quiet car park, twists his wrist. It is seven ten a.m. He calls Grace Bellingham. Her phone is off. He sits at what he knows to be slow traffic lights from the hospital side-road onto Main Road. His head droops, although his breathing is fast. Grace Bellingham had told Henrik du Toit to call her anytime if there was news, yet her phone is off. He shivers, presses down on the accelerator, drifts left through the still red lights, speeds into the queue of traffic.

Her apartment is silent. He rings the bell, knocks repeatedly, calls through the letter box. A neighbour appears at his door to complain. De Vries badges him, avoids speaking, knowing that the words will not yet flow fluently. He doorsteps the building caretaker, demands that he gain access to Dr Bellingham's flat as a matter of life and death. He brooks no resistance, takes the spare key, sets off back to her floor, unlocks the door. Immediately, he hears the alarm bleeping a countdown. He stares at the keypad, realizes he does not know the disarming code. He turns away, strides into the living room, checks the bathroom, utility room and bedroom. Her bed is made. As he hurries to the exit, the alarm sounds. He feels his ears burn, slams the door, trots to the lift. In the entrance lobby, he meets the caretaker, slaps the keys into his cupped hands, leaves him amid the cacophony and inevitable dispute that will follow, runs to his car. His heart is beating hard. He feels pain in his left side, bile rising. He swallows it, starts the car, guns it away from the apartment block.

'Close the door.' Du Toit rises, walks around De Vries, shuts it. 'You're drunk, Vaughn. I thought we had an arrangement, an agreement—'

'I went to her flat. She's not there. No phone. She wanted to be informed what was happening.'

'Dr Bellingham could have gone anywhere.'

'She said she was going home. She's not there, the bed's made.'

'She may have wanted to sleep undisturbed and then, this morning, left early.'

'Listen to me,' De Vries says, sitting forward awkwardly in his chair. 'I've been drinking – and you started that last night, remember – and I haven't slept, but don't tell me what I know and don't know. Grace Bellingham hasn't been in her flat for at least twenty-four hours. I can smell that, Henrik. That's what I do. I detect.'

'So, what are you suggesting?'

'She's been taken.'

'Taken? Jessel has been in custody since we last saw Grace Bellingham.'

'Last night, when you told me not to, and I spoke to him, he said: "Be sure that you don't need me before you send me away." He said it like he knew I'd want to talk to him again. This is what Grace told me: these men can control things from within a cell.'

287

Du Toit sits back. 'I don't believe it. There'll be a simple explanation. She went to stay with a friend and her phone ran out of battery.'

'She claims she has no friends.'

'You claim that too. You take a comment like that with a pinch of salt.'

'Stop it. Stop trying to divert me. I'm telling you. She is missing. She could have been taken, and Jessel as much as warned me.'

'Very well. Send someone else over to her place to check it out. Get February or Frazer to pass the info on to Central and the other divisions. You need to sober up, get yourself together.'

'I'm perfectly together. This is what Jessel meant. I have to speak to him again. He'll offer us the same deal.'

'And we'll refuse it.'

'And we'll refuse it, but this time we have no clue, no idea where she might be, even who has taken her. And, if she's gone, we owe it to her. I talked her into this, to be involved, so I owe her.'

'Just be professional. Don't speak to Jessel. Do you hear me? Not yet. Not until I've thought.'

De Vries rocks in the chair, his eyes half closed.

'If it isn't him, we have no idea where she might be.'

Du Toit walks around his desk, puts his hand on De Vries's shoulder.

'We don't even know that she's gone.'

The face of a bear stares up at him from the surface of his cappuccino. Mike Solarin turns the cup to show Gugu KwaDukuza. She smiles, sips her red Grapetiser.

The Pretoria weather is hot but not stifling, still but breathable. There is drought here too, but it is well behind that being endured by the Cape. The city's trees, parks and green spaces still seem lush and refreshing. In the Magnolia Dell Park in Pretoria, families are picnicking, children play sports, dogs chase each other.

In the distance, Mike Solarin sees him. He nods at Gugu, stands, steps off the deck, and walks away from Huckleberry's Café. The man seems many years older now than when he had known him only ten previously, his short curly hair white. He holds a child's hand. She seems to pull him, like a tug a tanker, slowly trying to build up momentum. Nassor Mbwana was his mentor, a man who survived the Struggle, then took his place as a public figure within the SAPS, not for personal enrichment but for his country. He, Solarin believes, is the role model for this country, not the likes of Zuma or Malema. The older man sees Solarin, waves with his free hand.

'Mike . . . How are you, my friend?'

'Well, sir. Well.'

'This is Amara.'

Solarin puts his hand on the back of the child's head gently, but she does not look up, still tugs Mbwana's arm.

'We have an appointment with ice cream.'

Solarin falls into step with the old man and the child.

'I am sorry, sir, to disturb your time with your granddaughter.'

'That is all right. There is only so much to be said about ice cream. You are well? You are not in trouble?'

'No, sir. I merely wish to ask for your advice.'

'Well, that is what a mentor should offer.' He looks down at the child, sighs. 'But, first, there is a more pressing matter I must deal with.'

De Vries sits in his office, mind racing, his body still but for the jogging of his right leg. He has already sipped, then swigged, at his flask. He waits for Don February to return from Grace

Bellingham's flat; for Du Toit to talk to Joey Morten about tracing cellphones; for Sally Frazer to try to trace Bellingham's departure from their building the previous evening.

By eleven a.m., her now untraceable phone is still switched off. Grace Bellingham is recorded leaving the building at 21.47 hours the previous evening, walking to the right, and around the corner where, for several months, none of the CCTV cameras has been operational.

'No one saw Dr Bellingham last night at her apartment,' Don tells them, 'but she had only just moved in, and most other residents had not met her. It does not seem that she was there recently. We found her passport and some jewellery, as well as US dollars in cash.'

'Why didn't we drive her home?'

Du Toit turns to De Vries. 'I offered. She wanted to leave discreetly. Not round the back in a police vehicle.'

'You could have sent someone round the front looking like a cab.'

'I could, Colonel, but that was not what Dr Bellingham requested.' Du Toit's voice is tight. 'All right, we don't know that she is missing but we must accept that it is a possibility.' He looks at Don February. 'You've sent out alerts?'

'Yes, sir.'

Du Toit looks warily towards De Vries, considers not asking the question.

'What are you going to do?'

'Well, sir, if you've had time to think, talk with Jessel.'

'Is there really any point?'

'Probably not, but, by accident, he helped us to find Jelani. If Dr Bellingham is missing – if she has been taken – then Jessel knows. It will have been his plan. Maybe he will just gloat and

290

grandstand, but maybe he will say something again to help us. I think I'm in the perfect state to act the stool pigeon.'

'Regrettably,' Du Toit says, 'I agree.'

They sit at the table on the edge of the deck with Gugu KwaDukuza, looking out across the park to where Amara is sitting cross-legged on the crisp, coarse grass, contentedly licking her ice cream. Solarin has spoken, documenting everything he has discovered during his part in the investigation and the evidence collected from other sources. He pauses only when a dog runs between their ankles, tail slapping their calves. Mbwana kicks it away. KwaDukuza explains her evidence, and Solarin concludes. Nassor Mbwana listens attentively, frown growing increasingly deep, until his broadly spaced eyebrows almost meet. When Solarin finishes, Mbwana sniffs, draws his hands together on the table, interlocking his fingers.

'Who have you spoken to of this?'

'Just you, sir.'

He nods. 'That, at least, is good.' He looks around him, glances down to Amara, who is stroking a Jack Russell terrier. 'Now that you have made lieutenant, Mike, you have to understand that men,' he looks across to KwaDukuza, 'and women, who are high up in public bodies in South Africa, have a wider responsibility than merely low-ranking officers serving in the SAPS, the Hawks, wherever it might be. Decisions must sometimes be made for reasons that, to be fair, the ordinary man in the street may not appreciate. You understand?'

'For what reason has it been decided that clear, coherent evidence should be ignored?'

Nassor Mbwana raises his hand. 'No, no, no. Do not say that. You have suspicions and doubts. There are unanswered questions,

but there is no conspiracy here. The withholding and compart-
mentalizing of information is for national security. It is so that
those lowly workers seeking answers within their sphere are not
provided with the entire picture. So that leaks may be contained
and identified from the scope of the material released. This is all
entirely natural . . .'

'But if the media pass on falsehoods . . .'

'The media will take anything and twist it.'

'But this is what we are telling them.'

'This is what is thought best to tell them.'

'I do not think—'

'That is right,' Mbwana interrupts, his quiet, steady voice rising.
'You should not think. Your duty is to adapt to your new role, to
dedicate yourself, and to be as good as you can be. Do not be distracted by politics or with challenging how things are done. You
are too young yet to do that.' He takes a sip of tea, leans back,
relaxes. 'They waited until I was sixty-three before they moved
me to the very top floor, shared their secrets. They knew that then,
only then, I was ready.'

'And are they secrets worth keeping?'

Mbwana's lips twitch. 'They are mainly very silly. But how a
country is run, how it protects and controls its citizens. This is all
complicated but, for society to flourish, it must be done.'

'So you do not think that I should speak to Colonel Juiles?'

'No. Definitely not. Leave it. Learn. Do not approach anyone.
I have known you some years, Mike, since you first came to us. I
don't want to have to repeat this conversation to anybody. I would
not want any harm to come to you.'

'Harm?' Gugu KwaDukuza says unexpectedly, loudly. 'What
harm, and from who?'

'Harm only to Mike's career,' Mbwana says smoothly.

'Is that what you meant?'

'There is danger, miss, in challenging that which you do not understand.'

'There is danger,' Solarin says firmly, 'in staying silent.'

'Trust me, Mike. One danger is greater than the other.'

KwaDukuza says: 'You talk of harm and danger . . .'

Solarin puts his hand on Gugu's arm, gives her a reassuring glance.

Mbwana is waving to Amara.

'I must go.' He stands, and Solarin and KwaDukuza mirror him. He turns to Solarin. 'Know your place in the scheme of things, and all will be well.' He bids both of them goodbye, walks slowly to the edge of the deck, steps down onto the grass. His hand is grabbed; the slow, uneven procession begins.

'He is not the gentle old man he pretends to be,' KwaDukuza says.

'No.' He looks down at her. She is breathing hard. He sits.

'I think he was threatening you, maybe us . . .'

'That was a very gentle piece of advice, Gugu. Nassor Mbwana documented the abuses of the police force during the Struggle and, afterwards, he became one of the new SAPS himself to see that the abuses of the past were not repeated in the new South Africa. He has had many fights, and he is still standing.'

'Maybe because he represses what he does not want to hear. He was telling you to be quiet, Mike. Telling you to shut up about what we know, or harm will come to you.'

'I think that it was more career advice.'

She pouts, says: 'You think what you think, and I will think what I think. It is time to forget what we know . . . What we think we know . . .'

Solarin wonders whether some have the capacity for that: to forget, to clear their minds and begin again, unknowing, innocent. For him, what is known cannot be unknown. He looks at her face, set and drawn, smiles, offers her his hand. She either does not see it, or affects not to. He feels a barrier materialize between them. He withdraws his hand slowly, places it by his side, hanging free.

'You see, I was right,' Jessel says quietly. 'Fortunate I'm still here.'

De Vries has one glass of water in front of him. He leans forward, yawns broadly in front of Jessel.

'Sleepless nights, Colonel de Vries? More missing women? And drinking too . . . You're in a bit of a mess . . .'

'You say what you want to say,' De Vries says. 'Then the van will take you.'

'The van will take me and you will never see Dr Bellingham again.'

'I found Ali Jelani.'

Jessel laughs. 'You found Jelani because I told you where to find her. A child could have heard what I said and found Jelani. I hope you haven't taken credit for that.'

De Vries sips the water. 'Is that it?'

'Release me, or Bellingham dies. When she has expired, another woman will be taken. Maybe someone close to you, someone you value enough to make a deal. How far will I have to go?'

'About thirty kilometres to Pollsmoor,' De Vries says blankly. 'From there, I don't know the exact distance to Hell.'

Jessel shakes his head. 'You take me to that place, to Pollsmoor, and Bellingham dies instantly.'

De Vries stares at him through heavy dark eyes, scarcely open. For the first time, he senses a tiny quiver of stress in Jessel's voice, a momentary tension in the corner of his left eye.

'Not my decision,' he says. 'Procedure. The only way it could be stopped would be under extraordinary circumstances.'

'What might those be?'

'A current and revealing interview, in which the senior officer felt that crucial information in an investigation was imminent.'

'What information?'

'You know what information.'

Jessel opens his mouth, hesitates. 'I have no information for you.'

De Vries gets up. Twice Jessel has revealed minute indications that he is no longer in control, that he is beholden to whoever has taken Grace Bellingham. He watches him led away, realizes that he has just bet the life of the hostage on his reading of his prisoner.

Number one Plumbago Lane is surrounded by bleached grass, almost white. The shrubs are, in early summer, autumnal. The hottest afternoon sun blasts the houses in The Glen and those on the slopes of the Twelve Apostles down to Camps Bay. As he walks along the paving stones to the front door, he can feel the heat through the soles of his shoes. He rings once and, after a minute, a second time. Through the closed door, a deep voice says:

'We don't answer the door to strangers. You must make an appointment.'

'Colonel de Vries, Special Crimes. We have authority to speak with Mr Finnemore.'

A hesitation, then: 'I haven't received such authority.'

'His department released information to us and granted us access to Leigh Finnemore.'

The door opens. A broad Afrikaans man stands in the gap.

'Keep your voice down. This property and its inhabitant are subject to a section-eighteen order.'

'I'm aware of that. Let me in, please.'

295

The man stands firm, the door held by thick, strong fingers on big hands, studies him.

'You're the man who arrested Stephen Jessel, *ja*? He's discredited, hey? You need new authorization from the department head.'

'What's your name?'

'Rolf Viljoen.'

'Mr Viljoen,' De Vries's voice is low now. 'We have a situation where another woman may be at risk. Leigh Finnemore could have been one of the last people to see Stephen Jessel. They knew each other for a long time. I need to talk to him now.'

'I have to follow procedure. Just contact my boss, get the go-ahead and he's all yours.'

De Vries feels his teeth grind, hears the noise in his head. He closes his mouth, aware that his breath must stink.

'How long have you known Finnemore?'

'We rotate section eighteens sometimes. Gives us a new angle, check we're not missing anything. I know Leigh pretty well over the years.'

'You seen any tendency to violence?'

Viljoen shakes his head. De Vries glances at his watch, lets his shoulders fall.

'Rolf, the clock is ticking for me, maybe another hostage too. Give me five minutes now with him – you can be there – then I'll go get the permission.'

Rolf Viljoen's eyes dart from side to side. He frowns deeply. '*Ja*. You can come in.'

De Vries strides past Viljoen through to the kitchen. The back windows are open and he hears running water, steps out through the doors, sees Leigh Finnemore, naked but for a pair of black underpants, showering himself with the hosepipe. He turns to Viljoen.

'There's a level-three water-saving order in place. No hosepipes. Or are your clients exempt?'

'They are not clients and, yes, my department is exempt.'

Viljoen steps forward and reaches down to the tap on the back wall of the house, slowly turns it until the flow ceases.

Finnemore walks towards them, his long pale body freckled and glistening with water. He stands up close to De Vries, smiles broadly at him, smirks.

'Best way to cool off.'

'Safer than swimming . . .'

Finnemore frowns, tilts his head.

De Vries watches the water from his eyelashes, his nose, fall to the ground.

'Dry off. I want to talk to you.'

'Do you want tea?' The same smiling, slightly detached tone.

'No.'

Viljoen passes Finnemore a towel. He rubs his hair hard, making it stick out. He takes off his wet pants, drops them on the paving, walks into the kitchen and pulls on a T-shirt and shorts.

'What do you want to ask Leigh?' Viljoen says.

De Vries waits until Finnemore has sat at the table, then sits opposite him.

'Did you go out last night, Mr Finnemore?'

'No.'

'Not at all?'

'Not at all.'

'I can vouch for that,' Viljoen says. 'At least, between six and ten p.m. I was here.'

'Did you like Stephen Jessel?' He stares at Finnemore, sees almost no change to his blank countenance.

'He was strict with me, but fair. He explained what I had done,

297

what I needed to do, how I should try to make an independent life for myself.'

'Was he ever violent towards you?'

'Never.'

'Did he ever talk to you about violence? Against women, perhaps?'

'Colonel . . .' Viljoen's deep voice obscures Finnemore's denial, but De Vries scrutinizes him, watches the lips form the negative, sees the eyes freeze momentarily. 'I do not think that this is appropriate.'

De Vries nods gently, but his stare does not leave Finnemore. 'When did you last see Stephen?'

Leigh Finnemore's eyes redden.

'I don't understand. I don't know what you want. I liked Stephen and now he is evil. He has hurt women. I'm right, aren't I?' He looks up at Viljoen. 'I don't understand. I don't know what you want.'

'Enough now.' Viljoen puts his arm in front of De Vries, between him and Finnemore. 'I think you must do what we discussed.'

'And I will, Mr Viljoen. But it's a simple question. Just one simple question, for our inquiry. When did Leigh last see Steve Jessel?'

Finnemore sits rigidly. De Vries can see his breathing as his narrow chest rises and falls within the taut, still damp T-shirt. He senses a tension between Finnemore and Viljoen, waits silently. A long time passes before Viljoen says:

'This is why we have rules. You must go.'

De Vries rises, glances at both of them, walks towards the front door.

Viljoen unlocks it, opens it wide.

'You have to be careful with these people, Colonel. They are disturbed, disoriented, delicate.'

'He has a strange affliction indeed,' De Vries says. 'The inability to answer a simple question.'

He turns downhill at the junction, free-wheels the twisted road towards Camps Bay. At the traffic lights, he drifts right, meets the afternoon traffic on the main drag, white sand and cold blue sea beyond palm trees to his left, greasy, frenetic bars, restaurants, cafés and shops to his right. He pulls into a no-waiting zone, displays a parking badge on the dashboard, opens his door. The car horn startles him. He feels pins and needles in the palms of his hands, his throat dry. He closes his eyes, takes a breath, checks his mirror, waits until there is a gap in the traffic, pushes the door open again with his foot and struggles out. He crosses the road to the Indian restaurant, the quietest and coolest venue on the strip, walks deep into the room, into the dark, away from a few late diners on the pavement. He has sat down before a waiter has even approached him.

'Two tall lagers, lamb madras, pilau rice.'

'For two?'

'For me. Make it quick.'

He picks up his cellphone, speed-dials Don February. There is no news of Grace Bellingham, no evidence as to her whereabouts. Stephen Jessel has arrived at Pollsmoor Prison without any contact with the outside world. That will be denied him until further notice. He can hear from Don's voice that he is floundering, that there is nothing to go on, no leads, no clues. He hangs up, stares outside through, from where he sits, merely a wide-screen slit, sees the solid flow of tourists, the taxi-vans, the cars, the blue haze of pollution before the trunks of the palms, a sliver of sandy whiteness and blue water as high as the ceiling.

He looks for staff, waves at a waiter, then sees his beers

approach. He takes the first glass from the waiter's hand, downs half of it. He feels the cold envelop his mouth, his throat, the channel through the middle of him; he senses the tightness in his head ease, the thumping at his temples lessen.

He sits back, wonders about Leigh Finnemore, the alibi provided by Viljoen. The longer he contemplates, the more suspicious he is of Finnemore. He calls Don back.

'All known friends, associates, acquaintances of Stephen Jessel. Has he had contact with Pollsmoor Prison before? Did he visit anyone?' He hangs up, dials Du Toit's cellphone.

'I need authorization on Leigh Finnemore again. I spoke with him, but there's a new guy, Rolf Viljoen. He says we need to speak to his boss.'

'Why do we need to speak to Finnemore?'

'Sir, we do. Trust me. Finnemore knew Jessel better than anyone, probably spent the most time with him. I want to talk to him, maybe bring him in.' He hears nothing. 'Sir?'

'I'll make the call. Stay away from him until we have the permission.'

He hangs up, sits back from the scalding plate that is manhandled in front of him, smells the food arrive. He is almost too charged to eat. Almost.

De Vries spends the afternoon waiting to be brought information. When none materializes, he dozes, his stomach heavy and swollen. Henrik du Toit calls him to his office, tells him that the Section Designation office is prevaricating over providing access to Finnemore. He walks back to his office in a daze, his head subsumed with fear for Grace Bellingham, with guilt, with self-pity. By six p.m., most of the officers have left. Sally Frazer comes to his office to inform him that she needs to go home. He looks at her drawn face, stiff neck, wonders why anyone chooses to do this job. He follows her out, bustles all remaining officers home, suddenly craving solitude. When the squad-room is empty, he stands in the middle, his domain, finds himself emotional and drained, his hands by his sides, his head bowed. He stays there, as if underneath a shower, letting the responsibilities he has miscarried rain down on him.

'Are you all right? Sir?'

He seems to wake up, sway, steady himself, his hand on an arm clothed in coarse fabric.

'You should sit. Do you need water?'

Don leads him to a chair by one of the workstations. He struggles to open his eyes, feels a plastic cup between his fingers. He lifts it, sips.

'Tired.'

'You have worked too long, sir. You must sleep.'

He looks up, confirms that it is Don February standing over him.

'Don't let Du Toit see me like this.' He holds up a hand dismissively. 'Been drinking. So hot. Beer just seemed better than water.'

'I will be here for another one hour,' Don tells him. 'Then I must go or there will be big trouble from my wife. She will call you again.'

'We don't want that.'

'We have an invitation to dinner with neighbours she has been . . . What does she call it? Like a gardener?' He smiles broadly. 'Cultivating . . . for two years now. This is a big moment, socially. That is what she tells me.'

'Go,' De Vries says.

'I will stay with you just now.'

Don sits down at his desk, his back to De Vries.

'I have been looking at Leigh Finnemore, as you asked. It is not easy to find his history before the incident when he was ten years old.' Don types efficiently at the keyboard, uncertain if De Vries has heard him. 'I requested to have access to the beta-test site they are establishing with births, deaths, marriages all being recorded, transferred online. I think that they will keep it restricted, but maybe allow the public to access parts of it.' He scrolls through pages. 'I have this just now.' He stops, spins on his chair, sees De Vries bent over the desk, his breathing shallow, wheezing. Don gets up, walks over to him, leans down, checks his breathing. It is steady. De Vries exudes a musty, sour smell of alcohol from his clothes, his skin, his breath. Don recoils, turns back to his desk. A list of results for the search fills the screen. He runs his eye down the records, finds what he wants, clicks on the name.

After dark, De Vries sleepwalks to his office, falls onto the old sofa, which sits against the side wall, grabs a cushion and fashions it into a pillow. His dreams are filled with strident voices summoning him, hands pulling at his clothes, jostling him into a chair before a wide table, pushing him upstairs into the dock, separated by glass from the courtroom. One by one, they face him: his accusers. Failed responsibility, squandered opportunity, betrayed promises. Though weak, he stands tall, his dignity keeping him upright. He accepts each charge, feels the weight on him increase, feels the pressure grow.

He sees each of the victims of Stephen Jessel, each of their agonies, but Grace Bellingham's face is superimposed on each of their bodies: stunted and gnarled, sallow and rough, dusty and swollen, a disfigured face on a body encased in ants, like a bee swarm or a torso dipped in tar.

He wakes sobbing, scrabbling at the sofa, at his clothes. His wrists are raw; he realizes he must have been scratching them in his sleep.

His window is open. He can feel a breeze for the first time in days. Holding onto the chairs, he edges around his desk, sits heavily in his own seat, pulls it towards the window and breathes in deeply. His hair is matted to his forehead; there is blood on his cuffs from his wrists, yet he feels better. As consciousness returns, he feels an energy inside him, low but pervasive, which keeps his head aloft his neck, his brain running once more. He looks around his office, sees a fluorescent yellow square of paper on the floor by the sofa. He stands, feels his head spin, shuffles across his room to retrieve it. It is written in Don February's hand, presumably stuck somewhere, perhaps on himself, before he left for the evening. He squints at it, fumbles back to his chair, turns on the old Anglepoise lamp.

Finnemore mother (Julie/Julia) family name = Stahle
Architect in 1971 of Apostle Lodge = Anke Stahle – famous in Germany in
1980s. Related?
Servers down. Will check later. Don

He stares at it, his mind operating on some form of low-power mode. He stands, gingerly this time, exits his office and crosses the deserted squad-room to the water-cooler. It dispenses cold water to him, and he drinks three plastic cups before taking a fourth back to his office. It is eleven p.m. He has slept for almost four-and-a-half hours. His cellphone rings.

'It is Don.'

'Sorry, Don. Was out of it. This note . . .'

'I am calling to tell you . . . I left the dinner for a few minutes . . . because the internet was down in the office. Anke Stahle, who designed Apostle Lodge, lived there with her family for eight years. That is how her daughter, Julie, met her future husband, who lived at the other end of the street, across Camps Bay Road, at number one Plumbago Lane.'

'What?'

'Anke Stahle gave her daughter Apostle Lodge, maybe sold it to her, around the time she got married. Leigh Finnemore grew up in that house. That is where he killed his sister.'

De Vries's mind races. 'Why didn't we know?'

'Jessel must have removed it from the files and did not tell us.'

'Because he was protecting Finnemore.'

'Maybe, yes.'

'But it implicates him. That's where Jessel took Bethany Miles . . .' He feels a sudden stabbing pain in his chest, as if a knife is being driven into him. He gasps. 'I have to go.' He stabs at his phone, sees it drop onto the desk, spin. He doubles over in his chair, fighting for breath. He feels the pain dissipate, a fever run up through his ankles, to his groin, his stomach, his head. Dizziness envelops him, drenches him in sweat, leaves him. He looks up carefully, reaches for his water, sips, then gulps it down. Suddenly he knows . . . thinks he knows. He stumbles to his feet, snatches at his keys, half falls from his office.

At the top of Kloof Nek Road, he looks in his rear-view mirror, sees the city illuminated behind him, the moon on the horizon. As he crosses over the pass and drives down the other side, he feels a portentous shadow fall over him. The moon disappears from sight as he approaches the turning to Plumbago Lane. On the steep downhill road, he brakes, realizing that he is travelling too fast. He almost overshoots the left turn, his tyres screeching on the still-hot tarmac. He straightens his car, drops almost to a crawl, free-wheels towards the end of the street.

Beyond the gaping fall down to the garage area, Apostle Lodge is dark. The windows reflect only dull pinpricks of light from neighbouring houses, slivers of headlights from cars as they take the sharp turn right above them on Camps Bay Road. The bird cowl is still, silhouetted black against the indigo sky. He gets out of the car; crickets whine, cicadas chirp. He loves these noises but, here, they bear down on him. He cannot hear the cars on the road, or the music he suspects is drifting uphill from the Camps Bay strip. Then, to his left, up against the face of the Mountain, he hears the elongated, anguished cry of a bird of prey. It stirs him from his stupor.

He grabs the torch from the glove compartment, finds that it works, puts on the pair of winter gloves which are part of his kit kept in the boot. He approaches the raised walkway, traverses it gingerly, tacking from railing to railing, allowing the beam of the torch to light his way. The overhanging trees and sunken position of the house make it very dark, but also slightly cooler. It is quiet too: he is aware only of his own strained breathing. Ahead of him, police tape dangles from one side of the railing. He steps over it, tests the front door, finds it locked and unyielding. He moves along to the left of the building, around to the side door. Here, the insect noise is amplified, coming from the overgrown, dried-out gorge behind him. He checks both in and under the flowerpot where the keys had been left for Jessel to bring in Bethany Miles, but they have gone, correctly collected and sealed in evidence. Moving on to the back garden, he leans over a window and peers in as he did before. He braces himself for the shock of someone knocking on the window from inside but, this time, the house remains silent. He steps back, walks carefully down the crispy lawn until he is thirty metres from the house, looks back up. At the top of the Mountain, the cable-car station is dark, the light breeze smells of woodsmoke, perhaps from mountain fires a

305

hundred kilometres away, the crickets in the dry riverbed to his right fill his ears with a cacophony of alien sound.

From the dying flowerbed, he pulls out a piece of rock the size of a tennis ball, stretches his fingers inside the gloves, assesses his strength, braces himself and marches up to the house. He angles his head away, swings at the window with the rock in his hand. The glass cracks, but holds. He turns again, and this time the impact bursts a hole in the thick dark pane. He pulls at the glass, levering it out of its frame, dropping the triangles onto the path outside. When he has cleared the base of the window, he leans in, scanning the perimeter of the full-width room with his torch, finds it empty. He hauls his leg over the frame, raises the other and jumps down. Apart from the chrome floor lamp, the furniture has been taken away. There are two dark patches of blood from where the chaise longue had stood, but the ants are gone. There are flies, but he cannot hear their buzzing over the interference of the night-time insects outside.

The house feels strange to him again, just as it did the night they found Bethany Miles, but he does not attempt to switch on the flickering fluorescent lights. It is cool, yet his face burns. He checks the back door from the inside, finds the anteroom door locked, with no key apparent. He retraces his steps to the entry corridor, occasionally startled by his own shadow distorted against the textured concrete walls. He climbs the stairs to the bedrooms, finds each empty, the air stale and old. In one of the bathrooms, he idly shines his torch into the toilet bowl and finds larvae hatching in water stained red with the blood of some creature brought to the birth site to provide food.

He turns back, descends the stairs, aware that he is clutching the banister rail to steady himself. He feels weak, propelled only by adrenalin and the sudden conviction he had felt back at his office when he had been overcome by the pain and emerged with new insight.

The front door is locked also but he turns the two heavy handles and hears the locks snap open. He leaves the door unlocked, turns right onto the staircase down to the garage. The steps are bare concrete and this part of the house is the coolest. At the bottom, he reaches the metal door that he believes opens out into the garage. He tries to slide the two heavy bolts, which lock the door from the inside, but they do not move. He puts the torch down by his feet, shining at the base of the door, leans against it, tries the bolt again. This time the bar shifts across. He pauses; listens. He repeats the process with the upper bolt. This time, he hears it. He grabs the handle and twists. It moves, but the door is locked also by a key. He puts his ear to the door. When he hears nothing, he thumps the metal, calls out. It is so faint that he might only be imagining it, but he believes that he hears a cry.

There is nothing else on the stairs, no sign of the key. He turns. Above him, he sees a shadowy beam of light pass in front of the door to the stairs. The shock chokes him. His hands, already sweating inside the gloves, seem weak, scarcely able to hold the torch. He extinguishes the beam, freezes, tries to control his frightened, uneven breathing. In the silence he hears not so much footsteps, for, on the concrete floor, there are none but the sounds of human movement. The door to the stairs moves slowly, as if held firmly by a hand. In the utter blackness, he slowly reaches for his weapon, realizes that, in gloves, he will be unable to hold it: his finger will not fit the trigger cage. He moderates his breath, slides the glove from his right hand, lets it fall, almost silently, to the floor. Above him, the door has been left ajar, the light, which he believes is from another torch, seems more distant, though still present.

He takes the first step upwards, feels the weakness in his legs, his energy dissipated by the fear that holds him in its vice. Here,

307

there is no banister rail, no support. He holds his torch in his left hand, though he thinks he will be unable to illuminate it, his weapon in his bare right hand. He leans against the wall in the dark, pushing himself, hand on knee, up each individual hurdle. As he reaches the top, the light through the door intensifies. He senses rather than hears someone approach. The torch slips from his grasp, lands on the concrete with a metallic crack. He pushes his weight against the wall, steadies himself, now with both hands on his weapon, releases the safety.

The door above him opens. His voice box produces no warning, but for a strangled groan, his mouth gaping. The torch beam blinds him. He catches only the silhouette of the heavy figure before the door is slammed. He hears the lock turning. He launches himself up the final steps, beats on the wooden door, shouts, at first hoarsely, then more clearly.

'Open the door. It's De Vries. Colonel de Vries, SAPS.'

He bangs on the door again, listens, watches for the light in the sliver of opening beneath the plane of the door. Suddenly he sees the torch beam, brilliant and glaring on the floor under the door. The voice, loud and coarse, startles him.

'Who are you?'

'Colonel Vaughn de Vries. Open up.'

'You're armed?'

'Open the fucking door! Who is this?'

'Marten Cloete.'

'Open it!'

The lock is fumbled, the door swings open. De Vries does not lower his weapon, but stumbles over the threshold, pressing Cloete back down the corridor towards the front door.

'Drop the bat. Drop it.'

Cloete looks down at the baseball bat in his left hand, seems confused, lets it fall. It clatters on the hard floor.

'What are you doing here?' De Vries can hear the fear in his own voice.

'The window. I heard someone breaking the window round the back. Was it you?'

De Vries nods. '*Ja.* Why are you inside? Why didn't you call the cops?'

Cloete shrugs. 'I live next door. I keep an eye on things.'

'How did you get in?'

With his chin, Cloete points back inside the living area. 'Through the window.'

De Vries studies him. He scarcely trusts himself right now, but he recognizes a simple candour in the man, believes his story, believes his innocence.

'I need your help.'

'Sure.' Cloete lowers his hands.

'You have a crowbar? Something we can open a metal door with?'

'Why do you want—'

'Do you have it? Can you help? I'm not going to tell you why. Can you help?'

Cloete nods. '*Ja.* You want me to go get—'

'Yes. The front door is open. Go now.'

Cloete turns, trots the length of the hallway to the front door, lets himself out.

De Vries breathes fully for the first time in minutes, oxygen flooding his lungs. He wipes his face with his sleeve, fumbles his cellphone from his trouser pocket. Wet, shaking fingers scroll down the contact list. He rejects Don February, who lives twelve, fifteen kilometres away. He calls Ben Thwala, hears a sleepy voice trying to sound awake, alert.

'The keys to Apostle Lodge. Where are they?'

'Evidence, at HQ, sir.'

'I need them. All of them. Sorry to wake you, but I need them now. I may have found Bellingham.'

'You are there?'

'Yes. Now.'

'I can take my bike. ETA HQ maybe fifteen minutes, you in twenty-five.'

'Good. Be careful. All the keys. The garage remote. Everything.'

He hangs up.

He hears Cloete on the walkway, a grinding against the metal railing.

'Tony Vermeulen is out there now, watching me.'

'Forget him. Bring that down here.'

He flicks the switch at the top of the stairs, but no light comes on. He descends the staircase feeling his muscles burn, retrieves his torch, lights the door. When they are at the bottom, he holds up his hand.

'Wait.'

He presses his ear against the door once more but, with both of them breathing heavily, he cannot hear anything.

He reaches for the crowbar, realizes that Cloete probably has more strength than him, indicates the lock.

'Don't think it'll work, but try. I may have the key coming, I don't know.'

'You think there's someone in there?'

'Ja.'

'Is this the garage?'

'Ja. The other side.'

'Can you not open the garage?'

'No. Maybe. I don't know. Try the lock, Marten. Do it.'

He shines the torch at the lock, watches the big man try to insert the claw of the crowbar, sees that there is nowhere for it to find purchase. After a few moments, Cloete shakes his head.

310

'We tried. You need the key, man.'

De Vries gestures for him to go back up. He wants to call out, call to Grace Bellingham. His doubt stops him. He climbs the stairs once more.

'Go outside. We'll try the garage door. You think there's an override?'

He indicates that Cloete should take the lead, out of the front door, across the walkway, onto the street. Ahead of him, he sees Tony Vermeulen looking down at them.

'Get back in your house.'

'What's happening?'

'Get back in your house, sir. That's an order.'

The issuing of instruction calms him: the familiar reassures. He watches the man turn, amble slowly back, turning to study them. De Vries turns, bends his knees, begins to descend the steep track, leaning back into the gradient. At the bottom of the slope, in the parking area, he shines his torch around the heavy ridged-metal shutter to the garage. There is no sign of a handle or wheel. He tries to lever the door up, but it is locked down firmly. He pounds on the door with his fists, puts his ear to it, hears nothing.

'SAPS. Is anybody there?'

He hears that his voice lacks conviction. The call is half-hearted. He listens again, then stands straight, almost backs into Cloete. 'Okay, Marten, thanks for your help. You can go back home now.'

'No, it's fine, man. I can stay.'

He looks at Cloete, fears another pointless, stubborn verbal battle.

'We'll go up top and wait for my officer. You can't enter the house with us. May be a crime scene – you'll contaminate it.'

They clamber back up the gradient. De Vries walks as far as Cloete's low front wall, sits, pulls out his cigarettes.

'Were you here when the German family lived here, the previous owners?'

311

'*Ja.* They arrived thinking they had found Paradise, but it didn't last for them.'

'Why?'

'The wife hated the house. Said it felt haunted. There's some kind of protection on it. They couldn't change it. Spent a fortune on it and then it didn't feel like theirs, you know? I don't like it, man, I tell you, living next to it all this time. Something not right there.'

'And before the German family?'

'It was empty a long time. When we moved here, there was no one there.'

'You know about its history?'

Cloete shrugs. 'No.'

De Vries checks himself, aware that he might be about to break the confidentiality of the section–eighteen order regarding Leigh Finnemore.

'Architect was famous. German. Made a name for herself.'

Cloete seems uninterested. De Vries angles his body away from him, draws deeply on his cigarette. When he exhales, the smoke stays in front of him, unmoving. Under his open collar, he is sweating. His clothes adhere to him. His heart beats fast in his ribcage; he is aware of every pulsation. He takes a deep breath, wonders whether, when he listened at the inner door, he really did hear a cry, a moan.

Time passes slowly. Cloete stays silent. Tony Vermeulen appears at his porch sporadically, staring at them. A few other lights illuminate in other houses; curtains move; shutters inch open.

He hears the powerful motorbike decelerating down Camps Bay Drive, brake, turn into the street. Ben Thwala jumps off, retrieves packages from the sleek, glossy box at the back.

'Sorry to disturb your night, Ben.'

Thwala looks surprised at the use of his first name, follows De

Vries down the slope to the parking area, rips open the package, which contains the remote control, depresses the button. The door rises lazily, emitting the ear-splitting metallic screech. By the time it locks into place on the ceiling of the large garage, De Vries has scanned the empty room, heart sinking, doubting himself. He feels the energy inside him dissipate.

'I don't understand. I heard something through that door.'

He moves inside, flicks the light switch, but nothing happens, approaches the metal door at the back. It, too, is bolted top and bottom.

'There's no key for here?'

'I tried during the search. Tried every key here. None of them fitted. Back of the door is at the bottom of the stairs inside.'

De Vries steps away, frowns. He studies the ceiling of the garage, paces back to the door.

'Wait here a minute. Double-check the keys.'

He trudges back up the driveway, passes Marten Cloete, who is looking down on them silently, crosses the walkway and pauses at the front door. He leans over the railing, assessing the relative position of the garage door to the front door, counts the paces back to the internal staircase, descends. It strikes him then that the bolts in the garage seem redundant. You might have bolts on the inside to prevent anybody accessing the house from the garage – although the lock seems to do a convincing job already – but why would you have them in the garage? The paces from the front door to the stairs, minus the distance he travels as he descends, do not match the depth of the garage. He bangs again on the door with his fists, presses his ear against metal. In the utter silence of the house, in the dim stairwell, he is certain he hears a stifled cry, a muffled, high-pitched moan.

He trots up the stairs, his pelvis aching, legs weak, back outside. 'Give me your crowbar.'

Cloete hands it to him, wanders away. In the garage, Thwala has each set of keys laid out on the floor, testing them in turn.

'You heard me bang on the door?'

Thwala says: '*Ja*. In the distance. You were banging this door?'

'I don't think so. I think there's a space in there. This door isn't the back of the one inside. It's another door. There's a room in there, and I heard noises . . . The bolts: they don't make sense unless you want to make sure that both these doors can't be opened from the inside.' He hands Thwala the crowbar. 'We tried this inside. Try it here.' He points at the door. 'There's a ridge. You might be able to get it in.'

Ben Thwala struggles to find purchase, finds that it grips halfway up the side of the door, but the structure does not move.

'Try this.'

They turn, find Marten Cloete standing at the entrance to the garage with a sledgehammer.

'You can hit it with this. I brought metal-cutters too.'

De Vries walks over to him, receives the tools.

'Thanks. But you have to go back up. It's the rules. Wait at the top.'

Cloete turns reluctantly, trudges back up the slope. De Vries hands Thwala the sledgehammer, drops the metal-cutters, takes hold of the crowbar, still jammed in the frame.

'Just make sure you hit it and not me.'

Thwala lines it up, hits the crowbar. De Vries's fists jump off the handle. He shakes them. The crowbar stays in position. Thwala swings at it, hits full-on. The door buckles and swells slightly around the lock. Thwala hits it a further four times before the door cracks open, swings back hard on itself, hits the back wall of the garage.

De Vries retrieves the illuminated torch from the floor, points it into the dark gap ahead. He lights up perhaps four metres of

314

empty space, enters, shines the beam to his right, onto a wooden door. He turns the handle, finds it locked.

'Get this open.'

Thwala returns with the crowbar. He inserts it into the wooden frame, jerks at it a couple of times until the wood splinters, hardware drops to the floor, the door opens. De Vries pulls it back, shines the torch into the area.

Ahead is a blank breeze-block wall. To the right, he sees Grace Bellingham.

'Jesus.'

He steps over to her, seeing, but blind to, her nakedness, withdraws the gag stuffed into her mouth, touches her face. She jumps, whimpers.

'Bring those cutters.'

He takes off his shirt, ties it around her torso. He looks up at the manacles around her wrists, holding her arms above her head. He looks down at her bound ankles. His heart is racing.

Ben Thwala comes in, focuses on the manacles, lines up the metal-cutters in the beam shone by De Vries.

'Be careful of her wrists.'

Thwala guides the jaws around the metal, checks that they will not cut into her flesh, edges his hands down to the furthest points of the arms, strains to pull them towards each other. The metal snaps. Grace Bellingham screams.

'You're all right. We'll have you out of here.' He stares into her eyes, both still in their sockets, sees blankness, as if she has shut herself down against the agony and terror.

Thwala moves to the other side, checks the position before breaking open the manacle. Bellingham's arms fall. She breaks at the waist, slumps into De Vries's arms. He holds her there, the torch squeezed downwards to light her ankles. The room is pitch black but for the partially obscured torch beam. It is cool, but smells of urine and concrete dust. He thinks, Blood, perhaps vermin. He hears the metal snap on the first, then the second ankle binding. His head throbs, mind spinning. When she is free, he takes her weight, waits for Thwala, and begins to half lift, half drag her from the tiny room, through the metal door, into the garage. De Vries takes back his shirt and ties it around her waist; Thwala pulls off his T-shirt and they manhandle it over her head, over her body. They take her up again, begin to walk outside, slowly climb the incline. As they reach the top, he sees a group of residents watching them from the street.

'Get back. I need sheets, blankets, water.'

They reach road level, stumble towards De Vries's car. He passes her to Thwala, unlocks the vehicle, opens the back door. They gently fit her into the seat. She leans backwards, panting now, but she does not keel over, her palms on the seat either side of her, like push-bike stabilizers.

'Water. Bring some cold water.'

The people stand away from them. De Vries leans against the side of his car, energy exhausted, hears Ben Thwala calling for an ambulance, for back-up. Water and a rug arrive, are left. De Vries hands her the big glass of water, holds it underneath for her as she shakily brings it to her lips, begins to drink.

When she has finished and lowers the glass, she opens her eyes, straining for each breath.

'Did he make you take anything? Inject anything? Grace, this is important.'

She shakes her head, mouths: 'No.'

'Did you see him?'

'No.' She forms the word, it struggles from her. 'He was strong.' He reaches for her hand. She pulls it away. He asks:

'When did he take you?'

'Leaving you last night. Hit from behind.'

He kneels on the ground, leans inside the car. 'You're safe.'

'No.' She turns her head to face him, her eyes struggling to focus, each word separate, certain: 'I will never be safe.'

She turns away, stares ahead. He watches her tears fall, from two clenched eyes, her face distorted and convulsed with fear, with horror, with relief.

PART 4

'It's not open to debate.'

Henrik du Toit stands by De Vries's bed, glances out of the window across the road to the yellow parkland.

'Pretoria have sent someone in.'

'To close it down.'

'To handle the press, more than anything. They'll second our people, play it by the book, run through the motions and, if it falls in their lap, they'll catch him.'

'Is that good enough?'

Du Toit looks down at De Vries.

'It is if they say so, and they do. So let it go.'

'Let it go? I hate that hippie shit.'

Du Toit sits by the raised bed, picks at the grapes on De Vries's bedside table.

'Two weeks, Vaughn. You're exhausted, dehydrated, stressed. You don't even know yet if it's more serious. You leave here, sit at home, rest. After that you're back here for more tests on your heart, and only when the consultant gives me the all-clear do you come back. Be clear: that is how it's going to happen.'

'Someone, probably Leigh Finnemore, took Grace Bellingham and would have killed her. If it is him – whoever it is – they'll do it again.'

Du Toit holds up his hands. 'Calm down. Everyone on your team understands that. They'll be working with the officers from Pretoria. Forensics are all over that Apostle Lodge.'

'Finnemore. Search Finnemore's house. Someone has the key to those metal doors, to that cellar. Find them in his house and you have him. He lived there. It's his old house. That's why Jessel used it for Bethany Miles, why he used it for Grace . . .'

'He didn't use it. Someone else did.'

De Vries snorts. 'Believe me. He used it.'

'Warrant February has already suggested searching for those keys. We got clearance yesterday and the teams will take the place apart. You have to relax.'

De Vries grimaces as he tries to get more upright in the bed. 'Hard to relax when you're angry.'

'So stop being angry. It must wear you down.'

'Stop? Henrik, when I left the army, I thought about South Africa and all that was wrong with it and it made me angry, and I thought it's no use just being angry, I have to do something. That's why I joined the police. That's what keeps me doing what I do. Sometimes maybe it's right to be angry.'

'You saved two women's lives.'

'Two women.' He sounds exasperated. 'You talk about winning. You are surrounded by a million stinging ants and you tread on a few. Is that winning? That's what my life is, standing up for people after it's too late, making no difference.'

'It's something. Try to be more positive. Be nicer to people.'

'I don't like people.'

Du Toit sighs. 'Perhaps there's a course for it.'

'You already sent me to Interpersonal Dispute Resolution.'

'Did I?'

'I went twice, got sick of their shit and told them to fuck off.'

Du Toit smiles, stands. 'You're obviously feeling better. Grace

Bellingham was discharged this morning. Did they tell you?' De Vries shakes his head. 'She's leaving Cape Town, maybe the country. Didn't say when or where, but you can't blame her.'

'I blame myself.'

Du Toit walks to the door. 'I'll be checking on you, so don't leave your house. I may call in to see you if there are developments.'

'When do I get out of here?'

'The doctor said soon. Be patient. It's for your own good.'

'Why is it when people say that it's always because something bad is about to happen?'

The newspapers are dominated by the drought, the heat, and the fires that are sweeping across the Overberg, down onto the Cape Flats, towards Cape Town. The Mountain has been burning too, helicopters towing huge rubber sacks of water flying in and out of the Newlands Forest station.

By the fourth day at home, Christmas Eve, he is bored and frustrated. Henrik du Toit visits, bringing a hamper of healthy food with him; even the Christmas pudding is devoid of alcohol. De Vries tops up his glass with one hand, while pushing the empty bottle by his chair under it.

'Are you supposed to be drinking?'

'I think they said one bottle of good white wine per day.'

'A glass, perhaps . . .'

He shrugs. 'A glass, a bottle . . .'

'I don't know how you operate at all with what you drink.'

'It's *how* I operate, Henrik. It's fuel.'

'It's killing you.'

'Only a little faster than nature.'

'Someone been keeping you updated?'

'Don February's called me a couple of times. Remarkably, I'm actually doing what you told me.'

'If I believed you,' Du Toit says, '*that* would be remarkable.'

De Vries turns to him, attentive, smiling. 'Please tell me, sir, how is Pretoria's investigation progressing?'

Du Toit rolls his eyes. 'They spent three full days in Finnemore's house. No keys, no incriminating evidence whatsoever. They looked at his computer, searched every cupboard, took down panelling, partially dismantled the kitchen. Nothing. Apparently Finnemore has been placed in care over Christmas. He's depressed and suicidal.'

'I doubt that.'

'No matter what you think of him, he's clear for now. I spoke to the psychiatrist assigned to him. She says it's a classic reaction to the betrayal of trust by Stephen Jessel.'

'Textbook.'

'What?' Du Toit frowns.

'Textbook. Like the books on his shelves.'

'I know you don't think Leigh Finnemore is a victim, but he's shown no sign of causing anyone harm for the last twenty years. Instead, he's just a naive, repressed young man.'

De Vries stretches out on the sofa, his arms behind his head. 'That's what he wants us to believe.'

Du Toit shakes his head. 'Why?'

'Why? Because he was in and out of Valkenburg Mental Hospital at a time when we know, for a fact, that there were dangerous people there supposedly treating disturbed patients, and he associated with Stephen Jessel for twenty years. You think one killer doesn't recognize another?'

'Stephen Jessel deceived a lot people. I imagine Leigh Finnemore wasn't much of a challenge.'

De Vries smiles sourly. 'You always think the best of people,

Henrik. Isn't that very disappointing? Jessel said to me – out loud in interview – he went to that department, made himself a case officer because he wanted to meet disturbed people. People like him. He wanted to meet the child killers, the parent murderers, the sadists and perverts. And Finnemore is one of them, I'm telling you.'

'You can tell me all you like. There's no evidence. Believe me, your team tried.'

'Rolf Viljoen.'

'What about him?'

'You meet him?'

'No. Warrant February interviewed him, but he checks out, seems pretty normal.'

'I'll tell you what I've told Don. Anybody who comes into contact with Finnemore, watch them.'

'You've no business telling Warrant February anything. You're not involved . . .' He turns to De Vries. 'What are you doing tomorrow?'

'Tomorrow?'

'Christmas Day.'

'Is it?' He laughs without smiling, stares past Du Toit into his bleached front garden. 'Maybe talk with my daughters. Otherwise, it's always been just another day.'

'You want to come to us? We're staying in town because, with Pretoria here, I can't go anywhere.'

'No . . . Thanks . . . Alone . . . That's what I like.'

On Boxing Day, he wakes to hear a drill in the house next door. He has no idea what time it is, but he resents the disturbance. He swings out of bed, peers from the window towards the building site next to him. He can see nothing but a tiny stream of dust escaping from the narrow opening in the sliding doors. He watches the dust form a trail in the air, drifting towards him. He coughs.

At noon, Don February arrives. The pepper trees in the front garden are yellowing, their branches heavy with dusty pink fruit. The bougainvillaea flowers are brown and falling, the garden yellow, russet, unattended, coated with a fine layer of snowy dust. He finds De Vries sitting on his front stoep, a wine bottle in a Pyrex bowl of ice at his side, a book on his lap.

'I thought you might want some company,' he says. 'Just for an hour. I am on a short leash. My wife's family are staying.'

'You glad to escape?'

'A little, maybe.'

'Wine?'

'No, thank you.' Don sits on a wicker chair at right angles to him. 'I want to ask you something.'

De Vries rubs his eyes, folds over the page early in the book, places it on the tiled floor under his chair.

'First time I've been asked anything for a week. As long as it's not how I am. That's a *kak* question.'

'You remember my friend from university, Mike Solarin?'

'Yeah, the Nigerian guy . . .'

'Half Nigerian, yes. He was promoted and moved to the Major Crimes Unit out of Pretoria. He was appointed to the investigation into the bomb in Long Street.'

'The al-Qaeda attack?'

'Yes, and no. Mike and a colleague of his in Forensics found evidence that does not match that conclusion.'

'They report it?'

'That is what I am telling you. They were very careful. They took it to an officer who they felt they could trust. They said that when they told him, he was afraid, instructed them not to continue. To go bury the evidence, get on with their other work. They were shocked, but they did as he said.'

'Probably wise, up there in Pretoria.'

'I have talked about you with Mike before. What I am here asking you, sir, is, will you meet with him?'

De Vries takes a deep breath. 'What good would that do?'

'I do not know, but I think that you might have similar ideas . . . and you did say that you were very bored.'

De Vries smiles. Don has developed a habit of retaining everything he hears and using the same words against witnesses and suspects, a technique people find discomfiting.

'Where is he?'

'In Pretoria. He says that he will fly down tomorrow if you agree.'

'I hate this time of year. You're supposed to have been happy and you realize that you haven't been and now you have to prepare to be happy again for New Year and this time you know you won't be – and when that's over, you're back at work, poorer and sadder and no wiser.' He looks at Don, who sits calmly, seemingly oblivious to his diatribe. 'Okay, Don. Why not? Tell him yes.'

Even before De Vries knocks on the door, he discerns that the apartment is empty. Each year that passes, he realizes that he knows more of what he will see behind a closed door. He waits, listens. Then he retraces his steps to the lift. When the doors open, the caretaker puts his hand over them to stop them closing.

'I saw you come in. She left last week.' He looks inquisitively at De Vries's unyielding face. 'You wanted Dr Bellingham?'

'Did she say where she was going?'

He shakes his head. 'Her belongings were taken by a storage company. The yellow and blue lorries.'

'I'm going down.'

'Get in. I only came up because I recognized you.' He stands away from the door, punches the button for the ground floor, lets De Vries step inside. The lift descends silently. The caretaker waits for De Vries to exit first.

'Hang on.' The caretaker pulls an envelope from his pocket and, without leaving the car, he stretches to hand it over. The doors close.

De Vries examines the envelope, his name and rank written in block capitals. The envelope has, he believes, been opened and resealed. He rips it open and withdraws a half-sheet of paper, handwritten.

> *You could have made a different decision.*
> *You could have spared me.*
> *I scratched his head. I guarded my hand. These are for you.*
> *I won't testify. I won't come back. But, you will know.*
>
> *Grace*

He frowns, fumbles the inside of the crumpled paper. A small plastic packet falls to the ground. He picks it up, holds it to the light. It contains two hairs, a tiny quantity of dust, perhaps skin. He recalls Grace Bellingham in the back of his car, sitting with her hands on the seat, fingers held above the velour, refusing to hold his hand. He uncrumples the envelope, replaces the packet, stuffs it into his pocket, walks away. An old wound aches.

'You shouldn't believe everything you hear about me.'

'I don't, sir.'

De Vries smiles sourly. 'It's much worse.'

328

Mike Solarin laughs. His chuckle echoes from the cool tiled floor of the stoep. 'Maybe that's why I'm here.'

'Why are you here, Lieutenant?'

The late-afternoon sun burns them even through the branches of the bougainvillaea. The dappled light forces Solarin to keep on his dark glasses against the blinding pinprick beams. De Vries squints, slumps or rises in his chair to keep them from his face.

'What has Don February told you?'

'What does that matter?' De Vries says. 'You tell me.'

'He says I can trust you.'

'You can only trust me if I trust you. I don't know that yet.'

Solarin raises the can of lager.

'Thanks for this.'

De Vries nods, takes a sip of red wine.

'All right, kept short. Ask what you want later. Hawks, Terrorism Squad, media, the people: we are all told the Long Street bomb was the work of two disenchanted former al-Mourabitoun members, Iraqis. Suicide mission. The investigation is subdivided, each element kept separate from the next. Regular teams are suddenly replaced by new people. Only those at the very top get to see the full picture. But there's a problem. The timing and placement of the explosion seem suboptimal. One forensic team finds evidence of a receiver-detonator, another that the explosive is old South African Army ordnance, yet another that there was residue from grapes, a variety almost unique to a particular area between Oudtshoorn – where the lorry was stolen – and Cape Town. I'm sent there, then withdrawn before reaching it, just two hours after the grapes evidence is submitted. The officer I'm put with is in contact with our CO – I think tipping him off about our location. Then I see him again. He's either following me or overseeing a demonstration, which turns violent, outside the Jumu'a Mosque a few days later. I'm silenced by my CO, Colonel Brent Juiles. Then another old friend, a man from the time of the Struggle, I consider a mentor of mine: he basically threatens me to back off. Back in Pretoria, I'm put in charge of some data-retrieval shit, an office manager's job, but many weeks' work . . .'

He trails off, wonders whether, even with all his doubts spoken aloud, he is imagining something which is not there. He looks up at De Vries.

'Is that it, Lieutenant?'

'It?'

'*Ja*. Is that your case?'

Solarin feels a shiver of doubt, of fear, course down his back. He says quietly: 'Something is not right.'

De Vries leans forward, pours himself another full glass, replaces the bottle carefully on the tiled floor beneath the table, drinks slowly.

'Take off your glasses.'

'Sir?'

'Take off your glasses, Lieutenant.' Solarin pulls them away from his face, folds their arms, lays them on the table. 'Now, be clear with me. You have travelled, from Pretoria, to tell me this collection of almost random information, which, according to you, amounts to what? Suspicion?'

'Any one of them,' Solarin says. 'Any one alone would be reason to check the conclusion of the investigation, due diligence. Together, they pose too many unanswered questions for me to be able to ignore.' He sits forward, his voice rising, counting off his statements on his fingers. 'No one I know has seen evidence of these so-called al-Qaeda men; no one has acknowledged the detonating device; no one has identified where these men obtained their explosives and, if they did, who might then be working with them. Nothing is explained.'

De Vries is watching him, seemingly relaxed, cradling his wine glass on top of his stomach.

'So?'

'So,' Solarin says forcefully, 'so this could be anything. This could be a cover-up from the very top. When I am involved in a case, I do not finish until I am satisfied. I do not stop until I believe I have uncovered the truth. I do not care – because I believe that we don't have the luxury of caring – what happens to me, to my career. I want to do my job.' De Vries laughs. 'What? You think this is funny? You think I came here all this way for you to laugh at me?' De Vries laughs again. Solarin stands up. 'What?'

'Lieutenant, you are doomed to suffer a lonely career under intense scrutiny, mistrust, discrimination, mistreatment and danger to you and those around you.'

'You think I am wrong? You think I am some conspiracy theorist who belongs not in the SAPS but writing some crazy online blog read by no one? Yes? You will not help me?'

De Vries puts his glass on the table, gestures for Solarin to sit, leans towards him, his voice low and deliberate.

'I think you are right. I think you should be in the SAPS and, yes, I will definitely help you.'

The traffic is heavy only as far as the turn onto the N2, then increasingly lighter going against the earliest commuters, past the airport towards Somerset West and Sir Lowry's Pass, across the Overberg, out along the south coast of South Africa. De Vries sits back in the reclined seat, his eyes closed. When he is awake, he is aware of the velocity of the vehicle, the kilometres passing, the steady hum of a sophisticated modern car running at 120 k.p.h. or more.

When they pull into a garage, he gets out to stretch, walk off

331

his fatigue, buy cool drinks, two hard-boiled eggs, two hot pies from the kiosk. Solarin pulls the car into some shaded parking, and they eat and drink with the doors open.

'Sorry. I don't sleep so well at night. Other times, no problem. Just not at night.'

'It's fine.'

'You want me to drive now?'

'Up to you. It's an easy car. You thought about what we will do?'

'I'm waiting for a call from a colleague of mine. He's going to find out what he can about the guys who cover Wingerdedorp. It'll be someone from Calitzdorp, but we won't get involved there.'

'Seems like less a town and more a main street with a bar, a shop and a few houses. Otherwise it's just the farms and vineyards.'

'But we don't know that it's right, what we're looking for?'

'No, but it is where almost all the Souzão vines in South Africa are planted. That makes it a strong favourite.'

De Vries nods. 'Let's keep going.'

They pass Mossel Bay, then the N2 becomes the Garden Route, travelling through the thin layer of lush and fertile ground between the mountain ranges and the Indian Ocean. The vistas broaden: the sky expands to fill their entire field of vision. The coastline comes into view, kilometre after kilometre of white sand lapped by light blue water, narrow lines of surf and turquoise swells waving gently landwards. The cabin is cool and quiet. De Vries admires Solarin's ability to sit with him in silence.

By noon, they have reached George. They stop again for petrol and a break, swap seats, and set off again for Oudtshoorn, aware from the digital readout of the temperature rising just short of forty degrees centigrade. Inland, the road is lined by endless fields of yellowing grass within wire fences, containing the country's greatest concentration of ostriches. The birds stand, bewildered, beneath rows of eucalyptus trees, looking out over their plateaus of dying grassland.

They drive through Oudtshoorn without stopping, turn onto the R62, the end of the route Solarin never got to travel on his previous expedition. They both understand that this is the way the stolen lorry will have travelled – if they are correct – on its way to Calitzdorp, then off the main road along dust tracks to Wingerdedorp. There are few places where it could have been witnessed other than by the oncoming traffic, and for them the twisting, scenic road would have been distraction enough.

Calitzdorp is little more than fifty kilometres from Oudtshoorn. The frequency of farm stalls and country cafés increases as they near the bustling country town, the proud sign boasting that it is the 'Port Capital of South Africa'. On the main street, two large coaches disgorge tourists to browse the quaint cafés, shops and copper-spired, verdigris-steepled Dutch Reformed Church.

'You been here before?'

De Vries laughs. '*Ja*. Ex-wife and I drove the R62 with our daughters, all the way. They were five and six, something like that. Children, winding roads, long journey. Both sick in the car. We spent the night here. You?'

'Never got that far.'

De Vries accelerates.

'Let's find out what they didn't want you to see . . .'

After detours, they find the road out to Wingerdedorp. Within half a kilometre, the tarmac runs out and the cabin is filled with the rattle of spitting grit from the dusty country tracks hitting the underside of the car. Behind them, a slow wake of dust drifts across the fields and an occasional vineyard, settles on the parched ochre ground. The road turns back on itself, runs parallel to the mountains in the distance, then turns towards them. Their way is now bordered on both sides by vineyards, lines of bright green amid broad swathes of deep red soil, diminishing into a simmering, shimmering heat haze.

Wingerdedorp is no more than a collection of buildings either side of the gravel road, ending in a nicely proportioned Cape Dutch house, which, before the hamlet was established, would have been a farmhouse. There are, on either side of the road, narrow tracks leading to discreetly signposted vineyards and estates. In a paddock to the left of the farmhouse, a single horse stands patiently under an ancient oak, flies buzzing its face, tail flicking.

'This is the town,' De Vries says. 'And that is its one horse.'

Solarin smiles.

'What do you want to do?'

'There's a bar, an inn, back there. You saw it? Die Druiwetros. That's pretty feeble: the bunch of grapes. These places are usually the centre of everything. I'm going to make my presence felt.'

'I can take the car?' Solarin asks.

'Yes.'

'There are workers' cottages back there. I can ask about the lorry. Whether there have been strangers in town . . .' He laughs at the cliché. 'What they've seen. Maybe they will talk to me.'

De Vries nods. 'You'll come back to the bar? There doesn't seem to be anywhere else to get a drink, something to eat. I'll stay there.'

He turns and drives back up the road, stopping outside Die Druiwetros. De Vries gets out of the car, feels the heat envelop him in what seems to be a scalding vacuum. Solarin swaps into the driver's seat.

'Good luck.'

De Vries watches the car move away, watches the dust drift

between the small dwellings, out into the fields and vineyards. There is one other car parked close to the bar. Otherwise, there is no one on the street, no sound of music or talking or machinery. He can almost hear the sun scalding the roofs, the trees, the grit on the track popping.

He steps towards the dark-green-painted wooden door, pushes it open, finds himself in a dark but cosy bar. At the back, a similar door opens onto a bare yard, shaded by vines, under which sit some assorted wooden chairs and rickety tables. One table is occupied by an elderly couple. They sit staring downwards, uncommunicative.

'*Welkom. Wat kan ek vir jou doen?*'

The man is deeply tanned, white beard and short white hair contrasting starkly with his lined skin. He stands behind his little bar, his smile strained. De Vries returns the greeting in Afrikaans, asks for a cold beer.

'What brings you to our *plaasdorpie?*'

'Police business.'

De Vries watches the man's hand quiver on the little tap above the trickling beer.

'*Ja?* Nothing happens in Wingerdedorp. Maybe one day I forget to change the barrel and there is no cold beer, and then I might get trouble, but the guys soon decide that brandy and Cokes are as good at the start of the evening as at the end.' He chuckles uneasily.

'I'm thinking more about visitors,' De Vries says calmly, watching the man place the beer on the bar. He picks up his glass, drinks half of it, nods. 'That's good.'

'It is good, isn't it?'

De Vries looks down at him. 'Visitors?'

'A few. Folks who love port. They go to Calitzdorp. They taste some wine. Then, maybe someone tells them, "This is mainly for

335

show. You want to visit the specialist farms. Drive twenty minutes to Wingerdedorp. There you can taste the wine we keep for ourselves . . .'" He gestures to the shelf of crudely labelled bottles behind him.

'You have rooms? If I want to stay a night?'

The barman frowns. 'Maybe, *ja*. You want tonight?'

'Maybe.'

De Vries drains his glass, gestures for a refill. The man places it under the tap, concentrates overly hard on the simple procedure.

'My name's De Vries. You the owner here?'

The man nods gravely, does not look up, murmurs, 'Japie van Rooyen.'

De Vries says nothing until the glass appears above the counter and is placed in front of him.

'Ten, twelve days before Christmas . . . Maybe thirteenth, fourteenth, fifteenth December. You see an old white lorry in town? Maybe going to one of the farms?'

'Lorries come and go all the time.'

'This isn't harvest time, Japie. An early nineties Nissan, with a white trailer?'

Van Rooyen's eyes dart up towards De Vries, then down again. He pouts, shakes his head.

De Vries forces himself to sound casual: 'The farmers: they come down here for a drink?'

'*Ja* . . . Most nights.'

'Good. What time?'

'Early. Maybe five p.m.'

'I can talk to them then.' He stares at Van Rooyen. 'I think you know what lorry I'm talking about. Driven by strangers. You know where it went?'

The bar is silent; the couple outside say nothing. There is no wind, no noise from the street, and even if there were, it would not penetrate the thick stone walls and heavy wooden doors. If there are birds and insects in the air, none stirs, all are quiet.

'Better not say . . .'

De Vries leans over the counter. 'Better to say, Japie. You don't want trouble. I don't want trouble. Tell me.'

The old man shakes his head. De Vries thinks he looks paralysed, afraid of him, this stranger in his bar.

'All right . . . You serve food here?'

'*Ja*. Pies, cheese, sandwiches.'

'I'll come back in an hour. You'll have sandwiches and pies for two of us, *ja?*'

Van Rooyen nods.

The main street is still deserted. De Vries finds a spot under a low, wind-blown tree, where he can sit on a rock wall and watch in both directions. He checks his phone, but there is no signal. He feels light-headed but refreshed. The heat is intense and claustrophobic, but he wants to be on the street where he can be seen. In the first half-hour that he waits, he sees not a single person, nor any vehicle. A thin brown dog walks determinedly down the length of the road, glancing at De Vries without breaking stride. At the Cape Dutch house at the end, it jumps the low white wall and disappears.

As the white vehicle emerges from the heat haze, he assumes that it is Solarin, but the engine noise is wrong. The white bakkie trundles past, the passenger staring at him. It turns onto a farm track at the end, but De Vries hears it stop, its engine idling just out of sight. Minutes elapse and then it reappears. This time, as it passes, from under hooded eyes he sees the passenger lean across the cabin, point his cellphone at him, presumably taking a photograph. The bakkie accelerates and disappears beyond the village.

De Vries smiles. Small-town inhabitants, suspicious of a stranger in town. Japie van Rooyen has silently, unknowingly, confirmed to him that they are in the right place. Now he will wait.

It is ten minutes more before Solarin appears in the Mercedes. De Vries is soaked with sweat, gasping for liquid once more. Solarin lowers the passenger window.

'You okay?'

'*Ja.* Come in and have a drink, something to eat.'

'Just now. You want to get in first?' He leans over and opens the passenger door. De Vries feels the cool air hit him as he sits down. Solarin passes him an unopened bottle of local mineral water. 'Got it from the camp kiosk. It's cool, not cold.'

De Vries tips it, drinks half without swallowing, almost chokes himself.

At the far end of the street, Solarin parks beneath an ancient eucalyptus tree, leaves the engine running to power the air-conditioning.

'They were here,' Solarin says.

De Vries turns to him. 'Who were here?'

'The lorry, two vans, strange cars. I went into the little township out there. Mainly domestics, handymen, a few farm workers. No electricity, no sanitation, just borehole water and that's it. No one wanted to talk, but I found an old woman, lived there last sixty years. Says she sleeps during the day and lives in the night. Cooler that way. Rest of the township thinks she's mad. Two in the morning, two weeks ago, she was washing outside. Suddenly she could see lights over at the Snyman farm.'

'Snyman?'

'Rudi Snyman. He owns the farm that backs onto the mountains. She wasn't sure it was at the farm itself but nearby, maybe at the mountainside. Said she could hear engine noise. People, she said, a group of people. Don't know whether we can believe everything, but she seemed genuine, and certain of what she saw. Then there was a lorry – couldn't say that it was ours, but like that – and two vans, went past on the track about four thirty a.m., before dawn.'

'The landlord of that bar.' De Vries says quietly. 'He knew what I was asking. Frightened, though. Think he called up his friends. Car came by, men inside fancied me, took a picture.' He laughs.

'That good?'

'*Ja*, that's good. News travels fast in a place like this. I want to see who comes out of hiding, who watches us, who threatens us . . .'

'Talk about threat: this woman said she was too old to be afraid, but on the way out, two of these guys get out of the car after the lorry and vans have gone by, come into the township, armed, brace this woman, push their guns into her body, anyone else awake, told them not to speak to anybody, that their lives depended on it.'

'Islamic terrorists?'

'No,' Mike Solarin says. 'Chinese.'

Their late lunch is simple but good: cheese and thick slices of white bread with creamy butter, two thick slices of meat pie with strongly flavoured meat jelly between the filling and the pastry. Solarin drinks one beer, then Coke; De Vries two more beers. The couple who had sat in the yard are gone. Van Rooyen serves them their drinks and a coloured girl brings their plates of food. Once again, the room is silent.

'You think they will come?' Solarin's voice is almost a whisper.

'They'll come, or we'll go. One way or the other.' De Vries chews a large mouthful of pie. When he has almost swallowed it, he says, 'You have any signal on your cell?'

Solarin produces it, glances at the display, shakes his head.

De Vries says, very quietly: 'You carrying your weapon?'

Solarin nods. 'The boot is locked. I checked the alarm when the car was delivered.'

'We may not have time to reach the big guns. Course, we may not need them. Just keep your ears open. They know the silence better than us.'

'You don't want to go to this Snyman farm?'

'Your lady friend ever see Chinese here before?'

Solarin laughs. 'Never. She said she only thought they were Chinese because she had been looking at old copies of *National Geographic*, and that's what they looked like.'

'So Snyman isn't who we really want. I'm waiting for the Chinaman.' He puts down his cutlery, wipes his mouth with the napkin, places it on the plate. Solarin looks up at him. De Vries meets his eye, says nothing. In the silence, they hear a phone somewhere in the building. It is answered on the first ring.

By six thirty p.m., two couples – one white, one coloured – have come into the bar. They all sit outside in the shaded yard. They seem local, take no notice of De Vries and Solarin.

They hear the phone again inside the building. A few moments later, Japie van Rooyen ambles over to them.

'Colonel de Vries? There's a phone call for you.'

A development is what he wanted, but this is unexpected.

'Who could know I was here?'

'You can come through to the hallway.' De Vries rises and follows Van Rooyen. 'You didn't tell me if you wanted a room . . . two rooms, tonight.'

'Depends.' He picks up the receiver. He has no idea who might be calling him. '*Ja?*'

'This is Colonel Wertner . . .' After the silence of the country-side, the quietly spoken Van Rooyen, the head of Internal Investigations' voice sounds even more aggressive and grating than it does in the city. 'Where are you?'

De Vries swallows, chokes a laugh. 'Evidently you know where I am, Wertner. What do you want?'

'You are to leave Wingerdedorp and return to Cape Town now. Bring Lieutenant Solarin with you. This order comes directly from Pretoria.'

'I bet it does . . .'

'Failure to comply will result in immediate suspension, and a full disciplinary inquiry. Make that clear also to Solarin.'

De Vries's mind whirs. Contact from his own department had not entered his mind; that someone in the SAPS might be involved was only just within his sphere of probability.

'Who in Pretoria?'

'Don't ask questions. Just comply with the order.'

'Listen, Wertner,' De Vries says, struggling to retain at least a spoken composure. 'Tell me what you know because, one way or another, this is going to have repercussions. Where in Pretoria does this come from?'

'That is not of concern to you.'

He takes a very deep breath, says quietly, slowly: 'It is of concern to me and, I promise you, it will be of concern to you.'

'Don't threaten me.'

De Vries faces the corner of the bar, pushes the receiver hard against his face, feels the slime on his skin, the throbbing in his temples. 'I'm not threatening you, you cunt. I'm deciding whether you're part of this or just some pig-stupid messenger. Where in Pretoria?'

He hears a faint hiss, distant machination, wonders whether it is the landline stretching across hundreds of kilometres of country-side, or Wertner's brain.

'Justice Ministry.'

'Thank you.'

'That changes nothing, De Vries. Get back here. Start now.'

'Do you know what I'm doing, Wertner?'

'No, and I don't want to. I've been authorized to make this one hundred per cent clear to you. It is a direct order and, if disobeyed, will result in the end of your career. Are you clear?'

'Quite clear.'

'Call me when you reach Cape Town, whatever the time. I will relay that information to Pretoria.' De Vries says nothing. 'Are you there, De Vries?'

'I'm just thinking . . .'

'Don't think. Obey. You know that at this moment I technically outrank you. Obey me, obey the ministry, obey Pretoria.'

De Vries lets his breath out very slowly, silently, says:

'Tell them we're on our way.'

They leave Die Druiwetros noisily, thank Japie van Rooyen vociferously, explain that they have been recalled, walk to their car. De Vries drives to the end of the main road, glances at the gates to the Snyman farm, turns and drives on, windows open, a radio talk show blaring amid a roar of interference.

Once they are past even the small rural township, De Vries turns off the radio, seals the windows. Even now, as the sun falls, the heat is stifling. He drives as far as Calitzdorp, where they stop at the garage, have the tank filled. Then De Vries drives to a quiet, tree-lined side-street, parks in a dark bay overhung with low branches. He opens the windows, switches off the engine.

'We have to decide what to do.'

They have already discussed the phone call, De Vries em-
phasizing the seriousness of the threat against them.

'I'm not going back until we know,' Solarin states.

'That's easy to say,' De Vries says, 'but you have to understand:
this isn't an idle threat. You have a chance to make a difference in
the SAPS. We have to decide if this is a battle worth fighting,
worth risking what we have now.'

'You said Wertner is Internal Investigations. Why didn't your
boss call?'

'Director du Toit is old school. If they involved him, he'd cause
trouble subtly and for a long time. General Thulani doesn't much
like being used as a go-between. I don't think either of them
knows what this is, or whoever this is in Pretoria is aware they
wouldn't touch it. That's why they went to Wertner.'

'He frighten you?'

'He frightens me for you. Me, I'm too old to worry about
threats like that. It happens often now. This is the second time
someone in Pretoria has taken exception to what I'm doing. If
people tell me not to ask questions, it just makes me want to ask
them even more.'

'I am not going back to Cape Town,' Solarin says. 'Not empty-
handed a second time. If the Justice Ministry don't want us to
investigate, they're covering something up.' He pauses. 'They're
covering up the murder of fourteen innocent people, an attack on
the Mother City. How, why, would they do that?'

'I don't know. But I'm telling you, if that is what they're doing,
they won't leave us alone. Someone from Wingerdedorp has a
direct contact with Pretoria. That worries me.'

'So we go in hard.'

De Vries laughs, his face deeply set in concentration. 'Maybe . . .'

'If it's what we think it is,' Solarin says quietly, 'if we break it,
do it now, right now, no one can act against us.'

Dusk is settling on the town. Their shaded parking space is now dark, the trees obscuring the feeble streetlight and the moon. De Vries starts the engine.

'Problem, Lieutenant, is that in this country, the whistleblower still gets shot.'

They drive through Calitzdorp, coloured light bulbs on strings outside bars, glowing fluorescent-tube-lit signs promising the best ostrich and port wine, out onto the dark R62. Three kilometres from town, De Vries pulls over, extinguishes his headlights and waits. He watches in the rear-view mirror as Solarin stares ahead. Not one car passes them in the next three or four minutes.

'I turn here,' De Vries says, 'or I drive on?'

'No decision. Let's go.'

De Vries turns to study him. Solarin is the same age as Don February, but he seems younger, fitter, his skin darker, unblemished. Yet, in his expression, De Vries sees determination, fire, which he knows that once he possessed. He questions whether his own hunger for righteousness is waning: deep in his stomach, he feels that they should return to Cape Town. He narrows his eyes, squints at his country around him, fading in the dusk. If he drives home now, his heart may as well fail. He turns his head back to face the road ahead, relishes that Solarin says nothing, does not question him in these moments of silence.

From the sensation of blood coursing through his fingers, the adrenalin slowly adulterating his system, he knows that he has decided, knows that he will turn and drive to Wingerdedorp. He glances again at Solarin, his features set, waiting. He wonders whether there will ever be a time when he drives back to Cape Town, back home, or whether this is his life, to disobey, to challenge, to make his own path whatever the dangers.

He nods to himself, checks his mirrors, turns the wheel and crosses the main road onto the dirt track, which, according to their map, doubles back and rejoins the road to Wingerdedorp. He extinguishes even his side lights, drives at maybe 40 k.p.h., solely by the light of the expanded moon, which sits at forty-five degrees in the dark sky above the surrounding mountains. To their right, the Milky Way is spattered across the blackness. It seems that Wingerdedorp is located between the light of the stars and the beam of the moon, nestled in the blackness. For the first time that day, the cabin seems cool, although the car's glass is still warm.

By a stand of eucalyptus trees, he pulls the car over, exits the vehicle, opens the boot, covering the light with a plastic bag. He and Solarin unroll a hessian sheet to reveal a shotgun and a small, short, automatic machine gun. Solarin picks the latter, rests it in his arm, tests the catches.

'You ready to use that thing?' De Vries says.

Solarin turns to him, sees his face slick with sweat, grey in the moonlight.

'No point carrying if you're not.'

They get into the car, pull back onto the track, drive in silence until they meet the main gravel road. De Vries is about to turn towards the village when he sees headlights approaching. He backs away from the junction, and they wait. The bakkie does not slow, or seem to see them, as it roars by. He brings the car to the turn, makes it, begins to drive back towards Wingerdedorp.

There is no way to approach the drive to the Snyman farm without traversing the main street. Four of the six streetlights are out, illumination from the few houses that front onto the street is veiled by curtains, only a half-dozen cars and bakkies are parked outside Die Druiwetros. They drive slowly past the inn, on towards the Cape Dutch farmhouse at the end of the street. It, at least, is resolutely dark. De Vries turns right, stops at the gate. Solarin jumps out, finds no padlock, opens it, watches the car through it and re-latches it, before returning to the vehicle. The moon is now partially obscured by the mountains, and driving without lights has become more hazardous.

After two or three kilometres, they see dim light to the left of the road, pull up. Solarin produces a small pair of binoculars, struggles to find the lights amid the vast expanse of grey mountain and black sky, then takes time to fine-tune the focus and let his eyes adjust to the view.

'It's a squatter camp or settlement. Maybe half a dozen dwellings. Probably more than shacks. Small houses. *Ja* . . .'

'Farmworkers?'

'I'm guessing so, but . . .'

'But what?'

'Seems strange.' He lowers the binoculars.

'Why strange?' De Vries asks.

'Looks like new houses. Small, concrete. Electricity, TV, phonelines. Just seems out of place.'

'You want to go see?'

Solarin hesitates.

'Or we push on to this Snyman farm?'

'*Ja.*'

He pulls back onto the dry track, which has become more sand than gravel now, the wheels fighting for grip. A kilometre on, as they round the corner, ahead they see the main farmhouse. De Vries lowers his window, drives forward at a slow pace.

'Don't think they can see us . . . Don't think they can hear us.' He winds the window back up.

'Unless someone's told them we're coming.'

'Hopefully,' De Vries says, 'someone's told them we've gone home.'

The road begins to run more directly towards the mountains now, the moonlight obscured. It is so black, De Vries can no longer see his way, feels compelled to switch on his sidelights to proceed.

When they are three hundred metres from the farmhouse, the track widens into a lay-by containing two large piles of gravel, stacks of wooden crates. De Vries does a three-point turn, faces the car the way they have come, stops under a shrubby tree, turns off the engine.

They say nothing, get out, check their weapons and begin to walk fast, side by side, up the track towards the farmhouse, which is built in traditional Cape Dutch style, single-storey, with a long, low stoep running the broad width of the front, pink stone steps leading up to dark green double wooden doors, vines covering built-in pergolas over the stoep, dark wood-framed windows showing a dim light within. The crickets and cicadas are loud, but there is no breeze, no sound of voices or music or dogs.

When they are about fifty metres from the house, two strong Rhodesian ridgebacks appear, ears cocked, noses raised. They stand like stone ornaments at the foot of the stairs to the front door. The two men freeze. Solarin swivels his eyes towards De Vries. De Vries nods slowly, lays down the shotgun, begins to walk towards the house. Solarin sinks to the ground.

'Anybody at home?'

De Vries hears his own voice, dislikes the anxiety he hears in his call. The dogs snarl – a deep, low growl, their taut bodies soundboxes projecting the warning. De Vries's gaze is fixed on them, but they remain where they are. He slows his pace.

'Rudi Snyman?'

347

He sees a curtain move in the window to the right of the main doors. He takes one pace forward, waits, then another.

Suddenly the double doors open; harsh white light floods the steps. The dogs turn, rise, speed to the feet of the three men who walk out of the building. The first is short, squat; two taller men holding shotguns flank him.

'Who is this? What do you want?'

De Vries walks briskly towards them, ignoring the weapons. 'Rudi Snyman?'

'Stop where you are. This is private property.' His voice is high and nasal, thick with Afrikaans accent.

'*Ek kom net om met jou te praat,*' De Vries says – I have come only to speak with you.

The small man walks towards him, squinting in the dark to make out his face. The men behind him have raised their weapons, pointing at De Vries.

'I am Rudi Snyman,' the small man says, stopping a few metres from him. 'And I know who you are.'

'*Ja?*'

'You were ordered to go home, Colonel.'

'What were you ordered to do, Mr Snyman?'

Snyman's eyes flare. 'I am not ordered to do anything. This is my land, my property, and you will turn around and leave now.'

'I only want to talk.'

'I do not want to talk.'

'Where are the weapons?'

'My men are holding the weapons we have on the farm. They will not hesitate to use them if you refuse to stop trespassing.'

De Vries tries to interpret his response, reads it as an admission that there are, or were, other weapons, unacknowledged.

'Maybe call the SAPS. Have me thrown off your land, Mr Snyman.'

The small man steps towards him, his men following, their eyes trained down the barrels of the shotguns.

'I have authorization to take whatever action I want to protect my farm. From the *kaffirs*, from the Democratic fucking Alliance, from people like you.'

De Vries can feel his heart pounding, feels it shudder, the heat surround him, hemming him in, a straitjacket. He breathes, believes that, on the surface, he appears calm . . .

He raises his hands, steps forward. The men behind Snyman seem to focus on their prey, prepare to fire.

'You only have to speak with me.'

As the last word leaves his mouth, he sees Snyman's gaze change, his little head nod on the tanned, lizard-like neck. His men bound forward; a barrel is swung. He tries to duck, but it catches him above the right eye. He feels something in his head crack, pain stream into his right eye, feels himself falling. His ears are bombarded, subsumed by a deafening rattle. His torso meets the dusty ground, the side of his head hitting the red earth hard, eyes closed. Instinctively, he brings his hands to his head, covers his ears from what now sounds like screaming animals.

He forces his eyes open, sees blood in huge droplets atop the sandy grains of dirt spatter and disintegrate. He strains to push his head up, watches one of the armed men crumpling, wailing as he clutches his kneecap, his shotgun falling, barrel bouncing on the hard earth. He pulls his head up further, sees the look of terror on the other guard, gun lowered, then hears another burst of fire, and the same horrific screaming as he falls on top of his gun. He registers Snyman standing frozen, his mouth open, eyes bulging, lungs empty of breath. He hears shouted instruction from behind him, senses boots stamping across the undergrowth. He ducks his head, breathes, his lips thick with sand and dust and blood. He tests his body, feels movement in his arms and legs, the shock

349

beginning to dissipate. He pushes all his weight onto his palms, flat against the hot soil, heaves himself up. Boots pass his head, hands reach down to pick up the two shotguns. He is on his knees now.

'Take them.'

He looks up at Solarin, sees his face taut, eyes wide, radiating utter focus. He struggles to his feet, using one of the guns as a crutch. Solarin passes him his stubby machine gun, pulls out his handgun. He pushes Snyman backwards, the little man struggling to keep upright. At the steps to the house, he falls, landing on the pink concrete, screaming and chattering, begging for mercy, all confidence sucked out of him, like a vacuum suddenly broken, his small hands curled and shaking in front of him. Solarin puts one foot on the step above him, leans down close over him, his weapon pressed into Snyman's face.

'Who came here? What did they take?'

Snyman's eyes bulge, the sound of whimpering and yowling from his men filling the silent, dark, sweltering air. He shakes his head fast, terrified.

'I'll kill your men, then I'll kill you. Tell me.'

'Can't.'

'You can.' He withdraws the barrel of the gun, then repositions it, harder, into the side of his head. 'Do it.'

'Two bakkies. Chinese. Guy called himself . . .' he struggles to find the words, to form the sounds '. . . Liu Xiang.'

'What did he want?'

'The cave.'

'What cave?'

'Didn't know. Cave in the mountain.'

Solarin pulls him up, the gun still pressed into him.

'Show me.'

Snyman is fighting for breath. 'Over there. Five, six Ks . . .'

'Then we'll take your car.'

Solarin looks around, studies De Vries. 'You all right, sir?' De Vries nods heavily, tries to ignore the blood on the ground, the crying of the two men still prostrate, convulsing. 'Can you check them for weapons, cellphones?'

De Vries feels light-headed, disoriented, the scene almost imagined. He stumbles to the first of the men, begins to check him over, recoils from the quantity of blood, retrieves a cellphone. Solarin pulls Snyman towards the bakkie parked to the side of the house. De Vries frisks the other man, awkwardly extracts a knife from the back pocket of his jeans, a cellphone from the front. Both men are quiet now, breathing heavily, pressing their hands against their spewing wounds. He pulls himself up, staggers across the dirt towards the bakkie where Solarin and Snyman wait, Solarin in the driver's seat, his weapon pointed at Snyman in the back. De Vries gets in next to Snyman, produces his own pistol.

'Guide us. Don't fuck us about.'

Solarin faces front, starts the vehicle, pulls away, turns onto the track Snyman has indicated.

'Tell us about these men.'

'They came in the middle of the night. The dogs heard them. We went out here and they were there . . .'

'Who?'

'The Chinese. There was a stand-off. I didn't know what was there. Still don't. Said they had stuff kept there from years back. There were seven, eight of them. They wanted access to the cave so we did a deal. That's all this is: a deal.'

'What deal?'

'Money. Secrecy. I promised them. They said if anyone found out, I'd be finished.'

'They were right.'

Snyman turns to De Vries, his little face white, quivering. His mouth moves, but nothing more emanates. There is silence as the car cuts between the end of the rows of vines and the scrubby outland of the farm, moving closer to the mountain outcrops that protrude into the land.

Snyman stares continually at De Vries, his eyes swivelling to register the car's position, then back onto the muzzle of the pistol so close to his face.

'There.' Snyman points with a finger in his lap. 'Up there.'

Solarin pulls the bakkie over, climbs out of the vehicle, looks up at the rock face, fewer than fifty metres away, gestures for Snyman to get out.

'You lead the way.'

De Vries gets out of the car gingerly, sees vines to their left, vine cuttings, dried-out grape bunches on the track where they are parked. Solarin pushes Snyman, who hobbles to a well-trodden but narrow, sandy path between spiky shrubs and low, almost leaf-less trees. The moonlight is dim now, occluded by the rock face, but Solarin has his torch lit, its beam leading the way along the path. Within two minutes, using steps constructed with rocks set into the ground, they have climbed towards the edge of the mountain, and Solarin can see the gaping mouth to the cave.

'What was there?'

'I don't know . . .' The words scarcely leave his lips. He coughs, chokes, swallows. 'Weapons, maybe. Explosives. I didn't know it was there. Owned this place forty years, never been here, but they knew, the Chinese.'

Standing by the face of the low mountain, the rock seems to exude heat, a strong smell of animal urine.

'What's there now?'

Snyman shakes his head, quivers. 'Don't know . . . Nothing . . . Baboons . . .'

'We're going in.'

Solarin meets De Vries's eye. De Vries nods slowly.

They enter the open overhang of the cave, the heat still not dissipating. From above, they hear a loud plaintive barking. It drags the breath from De Vries, makes his heart thump.

'Baboon.' Solarin says. 'Probably territorial. Unlikely to be any inside.'

The cave narrows at its back. A stained wooden door lies smashed and broken, pushed aside. De Vries sees animal scratches on its surface, deep and wide. Solarin points the torch ahead of him, pushes Snyman through the low, narrow opening. Inside the chamber, the smell of urine is replaced by an artificial, chemical smell of old ordnance, human sweat, the air still heavy, still hot, despite the location within the mountain. The room opens up to the right, the jagged wall lined with rusting metal staging and shelving. Solarin pushes Snyman against the far wall, instructs him not to move. Then he starts to examine the detritus remaining on the shelves: some paper wrappings, metal bindings, disintegrating boxes of ammunition.

He turns to Snyman, his voice strident, reverberating around the cave. 'What was here?'

Snyman cowers, shakes his head. 'Never came inside.'

'Yes you did – or you saw what they took.'

'Weapons . . . Maybe weapons.'

'I think I know what this is,' De Vries says. 'Secret stores, all over the country. National Party-sanctioned, maybe even supplied, for the Afrikaners, all through apartheid times. Allowed for local vigilantes in case of trouble. Plenty haven't been found or decommissioned.'

Solarin gathers what he can find, places it in the ammunition box that is least damaged. He shines the beam on the ground, finds ammunition there, a stick of some kind of old explosive propped up in the far corner. He reaches forward to retrieve it, then withdraws his hand, stands upright. He holds the torch in one hand, photographs it with the other. Then he turns and, illuminating the chamber as best he can, he photographs the entire space.

De Vries waits by the entrance to the chamber, his gun still pointing at Snyman's torso, his senses slowly returning to normal, alert to what is happening within and also to what might be approaching outside.

Solarin pockets his cellphone, gathers the box under his arm, moves to the exit, stops in front of Snyman.

'They go anywhere else?'

Snyman shakes his head.

Solarin studies him, the torch beam making the little man's face seem very white and wrinkled.

'We're done.'

He makes for the exit to the chamber.

De Vries bars his way. 'Not yet. I'm not done with this man.' He hands Solarin his pistol, approaches Snyman. 'Who did you call?'

'Call?'

De Vries feels the frustration well inside him, as if his patience has utterly deserted him. He shouts in Snyman's face: 'Japie van Rooyen called you. You sent men to see who I was and then you called someone. Who was it?'

'A number I was told to call . . . if anyone came asking questions . . .'

'Give it to me.'

'On my cellphone.' Snyman pats his pockets. 'I don't have it. It must have fallen out.'

De Vries grabs him, feels his pockets, finds the slim phone, pulls it out and waves it in his face.

'You're a pathetic little shit, Snyman. You, the people on this phone, these Chinese. It's finished. The whole thing is done.'

He grabs the man's damp shirt, pulls it towards him, then pushes him back against the wall. He slides down the edge, ends up sitting, doubled over.

De Vries turns to Solarin. 'Now we're done.'

They turn, leaving the man in the dark. De Vries picks up the damaged wooden door – it is lighter than he expected – and pulls it across the opening.

Solarin takes a short heavy branch, props it against the door, smiles at De Vries grimly. They turn. Both start. Ahead of them, just outside the cave, is a huge baboon. It paces a few metres in each direction, turning its huge muscular body back and forth, its eyes never leaving them. De Vries and Solarin back up towards the cave wall. Solarin lowers the torch, reaches for his handgun.

'Don't shoot it,' De Vries says urgently. Solarin turns to him, frowning. 'Just don't. Fire to the side. It'll run.'

Ahead, the baboon is stationary, its thick arms bent, head low and facing them. Its eyes are fixed on them, its focus seemingly on the weapon. De Vries sees Solarin's hand shake as he squeezes the trigger. They slowly turn their faces away. Solarin fires. The explosion reverberates around the cave, shattering their ears. When they look up, the baboon is gone but, in the distance, they can hear barking, the sound of branches breaking, heavy bodies crashing through undergrowth, dislodged rocks tumbling, as the rest of the troop escape the noise.

The two men approach the mouth of the cave gingerly, looking from side to side, but there is no sign of animal life. They trek down the pathway to the bakkie. Solarin hands De Vries the box of evidence, starts the vehicle, begins to retrace their journey back towards the farmhouse.

'You know where you're going?'

'No.'

De Vries laughs, shouting above the noise of the straining engine.

'Why did you tell me not to shoot the animal?' Solarin asks.

'Seen baboon carcasses hanging up outside farms to frighten away the troop. Most horrific sight ever. Still have nightmares about it.'

Solarin shakes his head. 'You have many demons, Colonel.'

De Vries finds himself nodding, uncertain whether it is concurrence or just the motion of the vehicle on the rutted track. He squeezes his eyes shut, rubs them, feels the grit in their corners. He thinks aloud, murmurs:

'The Chinese take the arms, load up a lorry, blow it up in Long Street. Why?' Solarin shakes his head. 'Then the Justice Ministry does some deal with a slimy fucker like Snyman so nobody finds out. Stops your investigation, threatens us with our careers. What the fuck is happening?'

He gasps, suddenly aware that his body is aching, ears ringing. Now that the adrenalin is dwindling, the pain above his right eye is penetrating his skull. He touches the bloodied bruise, cries out as the bakkie jolts over a deep rut and his head hits the hard ceiling. Solarin does not let up speed, powering on towards the farmhouse, which appears, still dimly illuminated, to their right. As they turn towards their hire car, Solarin says: 'The men . . . They've gone. Get your gun.'

De Vries fumbles for his weapon, checks it, keeps it in his right hand as Solarin brakes hard next to the Mercedes. They transfer their weapons, the evidence they have found, into the boot.

'Where did they go?'

Solarin points to drag marks leading towards the steps to the house.

'Got themselves inside, probably managed to call for help. We need to go.' He turns back to the Mercedes. 'You happy I drive?' De Vries nods, takes the passenger seat. 'Keep a lookout. If they have associates, they may be waiting for us along the road, or in

356

Wingerdedorp. We have to get this out to other people or it's worth nothing. What we say is worth nothing.'

He starts the engine. They feel the cabin fill, first with warm air, then a cool breeze, becoming cold. The solid car surges effortlessly ahead along the gravel road towards the village. Halfway back, they see the beam of a torch at the roadside.

'Open your window,' De Vries says. 'Keep down.'

De Vries primes his handgun, points it past Solarin towards the right-hand side of the road. By the time they reach the point where they saw the light, it is dark. Solarin accelerates, De Vries focuses on any movement from the roadside, sees nothing. The car speeds by, jumping and jolting over the rough surface.

'Lookout maybe,' Solarin says.

'Could be. What are we doing about the gate?'

'Don't know. Felt solid. No way round it. Don't think we can ram it.'

They are approaching the short, straight section of road that leads to the gate and, beyond, to the end of the main street of Wingerdedorp. Solarin brakes hard.

'I need my weapon.' He reaches into the back of the car, retrieves his handgun. 'You think I need the automatic?'

'Let's just move.'

They drive on, see the gates, approach slowly. There are no lights, no apparent movement. Solarin lets the car idle, opens his window, leans out of the car, his gun primed. De Vries opens his door, jumps out, runs to the gate, opens the latch, hauls the gate open, stumbles back to the car, slams the door.

'Nothing. Let's go.'

Solarin pulls forward slowly, his headlights picking out the end of the main street, across the front of the old farmhouse, to the gate marking the boundary of another wine estate.

The collision is so sudden neither has time to register the unlit

357

bakkie accelerate into the driver's side of their vehicle, the door bow, airbags explode. Solarin cries out, the windscreen cracks, then shatters, car skidding sideways towards the ditch at the side of the road. Solarin screams, grabs the wheel, angles it to the right, punches the accelerator. The car jolts away, swerves, skids, glass nuggets flying across the dashboard in a blast of hot night air. The Mercedes jerks across the road, Solarin fighting for control. De Vries grabs at deflating airbag material, pulls it away, shoves it out of his window.

'You all right?'

'*Ja.*' Solarin's answer is strangled, his jaw tight, teeth gritted.

De Vries looks behind them. A pair of full-beam headlights blinds him. He shouts above the sound of the road, the straining engine, the vehicle behind them.

'We got tyres?'

'Dunno.'

The rear windscreen suddenly shatters. The deafening explosion of the shots hits their throbbing ears only afterwards. Both duck, too late, instinct controlling their limbs. Solarin puts his weight onto his right foot, and the car accelerates still more, weaving up the main road, past the inn, out into the darkness of the Little Karoo. Behind, the lights still blind them, the vehicle maybe a hundred metres back, getting closer, yet shrouded in the thick dust. The speed of their vehicle seems visceral and alarmingly existent, the hot wind sucking the moisture from their mouths, from their eyes, slapping their faces through the open windscreen, the noise of the engine strident, the tyres spitting gravel and dust, popping and screeching.

As the road begins to turn and bend, the car seems to drift dangerously around the corners.

'Slow, Mike . . .'

He lets up on the accelerator, but the lights behind them catch them up until they can, once again, hear the older, louder engine thundering close behind them.

'Jesus. Back offside tyre . . . I'm losing control . . .'

De Vries stares at Solarin, sees his face contorted, fighting pain, knows that he will soon fail.

'Drive smoothly as you can.'

He lowers his window, checks that it is locked, leans out, turning away from the blast of night air. He can see nothing behind him, but for the headlights through the dust. His body is shaken about, seat belt around his shoulder, then around his neck. He feels pressure on his chest and ribs, fights the desire to fall back inside the vehicle and tend his wounds. He aims above and between the lights, fires off two rounds. The car behind brakes, the lights retreat.

'Breathing space, Mike. Keep going . . .'

Solarin does not reply. De Vries sees the headlights approaching again, regains his position, closes his left eye, fires four more shots, thinks that he hears glass breaking, knows immediately that the beams no longer follow them, but have veered off diagonally. Suddenly, there is nothing behind them but the dust and darkness illuminated red by the tail lights of their car. He pulls himself back inside the cabin, feels the car slow suddenly, looks across at Solarin, his body slumped over the wheel. He grabs the wheel, pulls the handbrake half on, grapples to punch his own foot between Solarin's legs, on the brake. The car swerves, leaves the road, thuds over a ditch. He stamps on the brake pedal once more, and the vehicle jolts to a stop.

De Vries pulls the handbrake full on, peers behind them through the broken rear window, clambers out of the car, around to the driver's side, releases Solarin's belt and pulls him clear of the cabin. Solarin screams. De Vries lays him on the ground. His body is heavy, slick with sweat, his breathing deep and laboured.

He murmurs something. De Vries bends down to his face, tilts his ear towards him.

'Ribs.'

He stands up, looks around them once more, sees nothing, hears nothing. If their pursuers went off the road, they must be a kilometre back. He squats down again.

'We can't wait here. Can you walk?'

Solarin tries to struggle to his feet, but seems unable to gain balance.

'We can't stay here. I'm going to lift you, help you around the car, get you inside. If we can get to Calitzdorp, we should be okay.' He leans down, grabs Solarin under his arms and pulls. The animal moan fills the silent night air, passes over the hidden vines into the distance. When he finally lowers him into the passenger seat, positions his legs in the footwell, he is exhausted, Solarin whimpering.

He surveys each of the wheels, finds three of the tyres intact, the fourth low but, he hopes, still usable. The bodywork and glass are a wreck, but the engine still runs smoothly. Before he squeezes back inside, he looks up at the sky, the Milky Way directly above him now, the blackness almost white.

The room is as he remembers it: oversized, high ceilinged, previously ornate, now Spartan. In the far corner, the broad desk sits at a diagonal. The man behind it seems small, insignificant.

'I hope, for the sake of your career, no one else knows about our meeting.'

The voice is a quiet tenor, clear and precise.

'No one.'

'How is your friend, John Marantz?'

Marantz is a former British security-services officer, whose wife and daughter were kidnapped and murdered. He exiled himself to Cape Town and drank his way through five years of mourning with De Vries. Marantz had introduced him to this invisible man, with his contacts and encyclopedic knowledge of his country's workings.

'Don't see him so often now. He's rediscovered women.'

'If it keeps him out of trouble . . .'

Eric Basson raises his head, stands, shakes De Vries's hand. His own is strong; it determines every element of the greeting. He gestures for De Vries to sit.

'Your message was entirely predictable but, I confess, I had not expected it.'

'I have something for you.'

'Of course you do, and you want something from me.' Basson smiles. 'I understand our transaction, Colonel. Indeed, I have been speculating what it is that you might offer me.'

De Vries sits back, observes Basson across his desk. He has met him twice previously, when Basson's knowledge and contacts helped him to solve a complex political case and, arguably, save his life. He describes himself, De Vries remembers, as 'a conduit to the past' – an apartheid-era fixer for the then government, now working in some capacity both for, and as an observer of, the new administration.

'The Long Street bomb.'

Basson smiles. 'Ah, yes . . . Not your investigation. You, I assumed, were busy with Stephen Jessel.'

'I still am. That isn't over yet.'

'No?'

'No.'

'That is interesting. What do you wish to tell me?'

De Vries has questioned before whether Basson is a man with whom he should work, knows that he is already in debt to him, a man likely to demand repayment.

'Couple of weeks ago, on a farm near a tiny village called Wingerdedorp, twenty kilometres from Calitzdorp, a cache of old weapons and ordnance was taken by a group of Chinese men. Forensic evidence places the lorry that exploded in Long Street at that farm. The owner, who agreed some deal with them, told me that the leader's name was Liu Xiang . . .' He looks up at Basson. 'Why are you smiling? You know this man?'

Basson is nodding, the smile turning his thin lips minutely upwards.

'That explains much.'

'Who is Liu Xiang?'

Basson shrugs. 'Nobody knows. It is a very common name in China. A Van der Merwe, John Smith, John Doe. In fact, there may be more than one man operating under that name. Like the blacks in the past, that's the problem we're having with the Chinese just now: our eye isn't adjusted yet to distinguish between them.'

'But you've encountered that name before?'

'I have, and I will tell you about it – and it will interest you, but first, I will tell you what I did already know.' He sits up. De Vries recognizes the relish this man takes in his knowledge. 'Whatever happened in Long Street, it was not caused by the men the authorities and media claimed. Akram Ibrahim Jabouri, allegedly one of the suicide bombers, died in prison five weeks ago from, my source informs me, a combination of interrogation techniques and suicide. Abdu-Allah Baravan was arrested secretly over eight months ago and was being held in the Northern Cape. To my knowledge, he is still there. So I, and a few others well informed, we knew that what was being advertised was false. Your explanation makes perfect sense.'

'Why?'

'Because the moment I realized that this event was not what it purported to be, I suspected the influence of a particular

362

individual, allied with the Justice Ministry and the SAPS, yet independent of oversight. A man working officially in some capacity, but unofficially in another role, to the benefit of the current administration.'

'The ANC?'

'For one small but influential element of the government, yes.'

'This man I dealt with before, Major Mabena. He instigated a state-sponsored killing for purely political ends . . .' He thinks back to a previous murder case where a potential donor to an opposition party was killed to stop her bankrolling a new political party. De Vries traced the action to Mabena, yet the controlling SAPS forces in Pretoria blocked any attempt to detain him.

'Colonel Mabena now. A man well liked in certain circles.'

'He organized the attack?'

'From what you tell me, from what I already knew, that seems likely. Liu Xiang is his man.' Basson adjusts his position. 'Let me make it clear to you, Colonel, since I believe your work has a tendency to make you insular. In the last two decades, the ANC and the Chinese have worked extensively together throughout our country. Deals, resulting in much mutual enrichment, have been signed. Our future, inexorably linked to China, has been planned in minute detail. All that might derail such all-consuming concepts is the loss of power by the ANC. They are losing control of municipal and local government, not just here in Cape Town but right along the south coast, even in Eastern Transvaal – which should be a heartland of ANC support. The Democratic Alliance is proving capable here, and Julius Malema's EFF may yet wrest control elsewhere. The government may do anything to try to keep control. Half a century of unwavering support from their people and, now, after twenty-two years of corruption, incompetence and in-fighting, their people are turning against them. So the ANC is striving to discredit the Democratic Alliance in provincial government: the removal of direct international flights to Cape Town by the state airline and others, a media war, the instigation of rioting and disorder and now, perhaps, the claim that Cape Town itself is unsafe . . . It's crude.'

'Fourteen dead, twenty still in hospital, for what?' De Vries stops himself, moderates his voice. 'Political capital? I wouldn't call that crude. I'd call it . . . despotic.'

'I try to keep emotion out of these matters.'

'Maybe you shouldn't. Maybe you should be angry.'

Eric Basson takes slow, shallow breaths. 'I've spent my entire life angry, Colonel de Vries. Just like you. Look at us now. All we can do is work. Our change is incremental, but it will be there.'

'You don't even seem surprised.'

'Conspiracy theorists believe that what they tell you is remarkable because of the magnitude of the deception. But what they describe is not amazing at all. Government agencies across the world engage in operations more incredible than the most imaginative conspiracy theorist can comprehend.' Basson narrows his eyes, sits back in his chair. 'I hope you have not come expecting me to disseminate this information?'

'No, but you might suggest how we can use it to eradicate Mabena and anyone who has ever used him.'

'You can't. Or you shouldn't. Expose what you know, but step back into the shadows. You're not a political animal, nor should you be. Stay anonymous, fighting for what you believe, out of the limelight.'

'Lately the light does not agree with me.'

'Then you and I have one more thing in common.'

'And how do I expose this story?'

Basson chuckles disbelievingly. 'Surely? Surely you have considered this.'

'I got back to Cape Town yesterday.' He touches his face. 'Think you can see it was a rough journey. Colleague of mine is worse off . . .' he chuckles, holding his ribs '. . . but at least we're doing better than the opposition.'

'But you have a slight problem with your own people?'

De Vries stares at him. 'A slight problem . . . I'm hiding. The SAPS want to arrest me and my colleague, probably for treason. Does that term still exist in our constitution?'

'Then let me assist you. I understand you have made some recent contacts in the newspaper world. Perhaps a new title, seeking exposure, would be interested in the story. And I think such a story could make a newspaper.'

'Or break it.'

'That option should not, perhaps, feature in your pitch. But, then, I am sure that you can think of an appropriately pioneering journalist, one who has recently found herself in the public eye, who might pursue it?'

'How do you know what you know?'

'Information has been my life, Colonel. I obtain it however I see fit, and use it to forward the cause I currently endorse.'

'An information mercenary?'

'If you will. Such a stance staves off disillusionment. For you, for your loyalty, what do you get? No matter how hard you fight, no matter how many battles you win, the war is already lost.'

'I don't believe that.'

'Of course not . . . But that doesn't alter the outcome.'

'The information on the Islamists. You have proof? I can use that?'

'I will think of a way that allows its use, that the evidence can be brought to you, or to your choice of journalist.'

'I may be in prison. I can rely on you?'

'You may.' Basson studies him. 'For a man kneeling on the gallows, you seem strangely unafraid.'

'Sanguine? Is that the word? If I cannot change the country I inhabit, maybe I should go . . .'

'Idealists in South Africa have to wait a long time. I don't see you as a patient man.'

'I'm not an idealist. I just believe in right and wrong. My definition.'

Basson smiles again. 'Stay away from politics, then. Stick to homicide. So much cleaner.' He stands, proffers his hand. De Vries takes it, meets his eye. 'I will do whatever I can to assist you in the coming time.'

'Thank you.'

'But don't forget,' Eric Basson says lightly, 'I *will* call on you one day.'

'That's something I never forget.'

De Vries walks away from the desk, many steps across the expansive, empty room, never turns back.

He sits at his long, empty kitchen table, stares down its length to his dark, scalded, vanishing garden. Everywhere he looks now in Cape Town, he sees plants and trees dying around him. Lawns are yellow or brown, pavements smell of urine, tarmac melts and distorts.

He rips the foil with the tip of the corkscrew, stabs the cork, twists and pulls. He hopes that Mike Solarin has done as he advised: disappeared for a few weeks, perhaps even gone home. He pours, stares down at the deep red wine. In the past weeks, he has been in too many confined spaces holding terrible secrets. He wants to rise and open his French windows to release himself from his cell, but he lacks the energy even to get up. There is a flash in his brain: he sees muzzles of guns, dark and hollow, pointed at his face; he sees Ali Jelani's bloody, empty eye socket, hears the tiny, helpless moan of life that startled him. He looks over to the darkened living area, puts the glass to his lips, drinks.

His doorbell rings. He studies the video answerphone, pushes the remote to open his gates, struggles up, hears the clock strike midnight as he walks towards his front door.

Henrik du Toit stands hunched as the door swings open. He pushes past De Vries, closes the door behind him.

'What have you done, Vaughn?'

De Vries feels dizzy, wide awake, but viciously tired.

'My duty.'

'No,' Du Toit snaps, spinning to face him. 'That you haven't. I told you: you want to survive, you obey orders, you toe the line, you keep your head down. What is it with you?'

De Vries walks past him, through the darkness, into his kitchen. 'I won't even tell you, Henrik. Then, if it all goes to shit, nothing will stick to you. You've trusted me before . . .' He leans unsteadily over the table, supporting himself with one hand, using the other to pour more wine.

'I told you to stay at home.'

De Vries shrugs. 'I did. I tidied the garden, cleaned the pool . . .'

'I came here. You'd paid a gardener to do it. I spoke to him. He told me. Why can't you let anything go?'

'Because that's what everybody else does. Someone has to take a stand.'

'Then let that someone not be you.'

'What have the Pretorian guard discovered about Grace Bellingham's abduction?'

Du Toit shakes his head. 'Not much. They interviewed Stephen Jessel in Pollsmoor. He was looking pretty beaten up – literally. Not at all co-operative.'

De Vries wonders when he will reveal Bellingham's unusable but possibly revealing sample. Potentially, it is collateral.

'They spoken to Leigh Finnemore?'

'I doubt they've been permitted to. He was taken away from his home while the searches were undertaken. Why are you obsessed with him?'

'Because everybody thinks he's a victim. They won't see what he really is. He links Apostle Lodge, Stephen Jessel, sadistic slow murder, probably with vengeance at its core.'

'Why couldn't you just have stayed at home?'

'Can't rest when I know something's wrong.'

'I can't protect you,' Du Toit says. 'Not this time. There's a nationwide warrant out for your arrest, and another officer's, a Hawks man, for God's sake, Solarin.'

'Then get out. Leave. You don't know where I am.'

'But they do,' Du Toit says. 'They'll come here.'

'Maybe.'

'What will you do?'

'Finish what I started.'

'Meaning?'

He straightens, rocks slightly, puts his hand on Du Toit's shoulder.

'To you, Henrik, there is no meaning.'

In his dreams, De Vries's mind replays his encounter with Stephen Jessel on the rooftop above Long Street. At some point, his form changes, like an image in a heat haze, a mirage, and he is then a short Chinese man holding an old-fashioned, oversized mobile phone. He bargains with De Vries, who rejects him, and then he pushes a button on the keypad and, below them, a little further up Long Street, a white lorry explodes, buildings shudder, glass shatters. Human screams and mechanical sirens mingle. De Vries feels sick, feels lost, feels responsible.

Rolf Viljoen stands at his threshold, barring any entry to Leigh Finnemore's house. De Vries steps from the scorching stone steps back onto the burned-out lawn.

'You can't keep coming here without an appointment. You will expose Leigh and that will be in direct contravention of the section-eighteen order.'

'Listen to me,' De Vries says, his stare fixed on the man. 'I have authorization from your office, complied with fully. I'm not asking for permission to interview a witness or a suspect. They make themselves available to me, or I arrest them.'

'You can't arrest a section eighteen.'

'Watch me. And watch yourself, Mr Viljoen, because I will arrest you for obstruction of a police investigation. You are here. Leigh Finnemore, I assume, is here. That is all I require.'

'But you didn't know I was present.'

'I do now.'

De Vries's head feels full and heavy, his stomach empty yet swollen. He wonders if he can retain his self-control. The sun on the back of his neck burns his skin; he has never experienced heat like this in Cape Town. He has lain in too long, too late; coffee has proven ineffectual. He looks around him; knows he has little time.

'Get out of my way, sir. Fetch Mr Finnemore and arrange for him to be interviewed by me. Do this now or I will take you both to my headquarters. You will both be charged, and you will both be imprisoned.'

Viljoen ponders, but accedes, standing aside. De Vries trots through to the back room, finds Leigh Finnemore sitting at the

369

kitchen table. This time, there is no smile of greeting. He stares silently at De Vries who pulls a chair from under the table, sits facing Finnemore. He points to the end of the table.

'You sit there, Mr Viljoen.'

He produces two sealed packets from his pocket, puts on latex gloves, extracts, from the first one, a Perspex tube containing a cotton bud-like element, stands and moves towards Viljoen.

'Open your mouth, please, sir.'

Viljoen slides his chair back. 'What are you doing?'

'Procedure. We didn't take a DNA sample last time. We need it for the records.' Viljoen stands, stumbles backwards. De Vries looks at him, catches him glance at Finnemore. 'What's the problem, sir?'

'You. I work for Section Designation . . .'

'You could be the president, sir. We can still take DNA.'

'Not,' Finnemore says quietly, 'without an attorney.'

De Vries turns to Finnemore. The man's voice is different, strident and assured. Finnemore looks back at him, his eyes staring to the top left of the room, smiles nervously, giggles.

'What did you say, sir?'

Finnemore swallows, then sings, to a tune like a nursery rhyme, 'Not without an attorney . . .' Speaking normally. 'That's what Stephen told me.' The singing again: 'Not without an attorney.'

De Vries smiles at him sourly. 'Stephen isn't here but, if you prefer, we can all go down to the station, spend a bit of time there. I may have to put you in some cells as we're very busy but we'll probably get to you in a few hours, perhaps tomorrow . . .'

He studies Viljoen, observes his eye meet Finnemore's once more. Rolf Viljoen steps around his chair, sits down, opens his mouth. De Vries takes the sample, seals the tube and writes on it. Then he opens the second packet, proffers the bud at Finnemore, who stares at the tip as it approaches him, his eyes dark. He lets De Vries wipe the bud against the walls of his mouth. When De Vries removes it, Finnemore looks up at him, smiles mischievously. The tube is sealed, the label marked, the items replaced in his pocket.

'That was simple after all,' De Vries says, sitting back down. Neither man responds. Each seems uneasy.

'Is that it?'

He turns to Viljoen, stares at his eyes.

'No, sir. I told you. I've come to speak with your charge. I asked Leigh whether he'd ever been inside Apostle Lodge – the house at the other end of the street. Have *you* ever been inside that house?'

Viljoen's expression is set, but his breathing stalls. 'No.'

'Never?'

'No . . .' The single syllable struggles to escape from the held breath.

De Vries still stares at him, waits, watches his eyes, the pulse in his neck, the movement of his fingers interlocked with one another on the surface of the table. The silence intensifies. Viljoen's jaw locks tight.

'What do you want to ask me?' Finnemore says, his voice back to being light and musical, tone naive.

De Vries smiles, turns slowly to face him.

'You told me you had never been inside Apostle Lodge. But that isn't true, is it, Leigh?'

Finnemore regards him from his straight-backed height.

'You asked me whether I had been inside since I moved here. I told you no. That is the truth.'

'Your long-term memory isn't so bad after all.'

Finnemore sits rigid, static, says nothing.

'Your grandmother designed that house and built it. The start of a successful architectural career. You lived in Apostle Lodge as a child. You killed your sister in that house. When you came back to live here in Plumbago Lane, you told me that you and Stephen Jessel, a confessed multiple killer, went to see the house. What did you tell him about what went on in there?'

Finnemore does not move. De Vries looks over to Rolf Viljoen. 'Did you know that Mr Finnemore lived in Apostle Lodge, sir?'

Viljoen seems confused: he frowns, shakes his head.

De Vries smiles at him. 'I think you did.' He turns back to Leigh Finnemore. 'So, sir, you lived at Apostle Lodge, and when I came here to talk to you about another murder in that house, you said nothing. Why was that?'

'All my life,' Finnemore says quietly, 'for as long as I can remember, I have tried to forget what happened. Tried to understand why I did something I would never do. I'm ill. I know I'm ill, but I'm trying to get better . . .'

'That obviously works, usually?'

'What?'

'That story. Beautifully delivered, by the way. A little over-rehearsed, perhaps . . .' De Vries leans towards him over the table. 'But I didn't believe you when I first met you, and I don't believe you now.'

Finnemore remains sitting straight, his hands in his lap, his shoulders relaxed.

'What do you mean?'

'You knew exactly what you were doing twenty years ago, and you've parlayed this child-like act of yours into a very comfortable way of living, haven't you? And the man you spent so much time with, Stephen Jessel, he turns out to be a murderer too.'

He glances at Viljoen, but he sits dumbly, perplexed.

'He must have relished the idea of killing in the same house as you, Mr Finnemore. Did you discuss it? Did he consult you?'

Leigh Finnemore slowly brings his right hand up from his lap, scratches his right eyebrow, lowers his arm again. His eyes seem milky, dead. He looks in De Vries's direction, unfocused, silent.

'The keys to the doors of the anteroom between the garage and the internal staircase. No one ever found those. You had them, of course. Who did you give them to?'

Finnemore blinks languidly, his light eyelashes falling and rising almost in slow motion, his head still, breathing slow. It is as if he is falling into a trance. Rolf Viljoen gets up, moves to Finnemore, sits next to him, begins to rub his back and shoulders, starts whispering, then talking quietly, reassuring him, encouraging him to wake up, to move, to breathe. He glances at De Vries.

'You see what you've done? There's a reason this man needs protecting. He's vulnerable. You bully him, you can put him back months, years.' He raises his voice. 'This will be in my report, Colonel de Vries.'

De Vries rises, looks down at them both, certain now.

'And you, Mr Viljoen, will be in mine.'

'There are men here,' Don February says, 'looking for you.'

De Vries sighs. 'Tell them you called me, told me to come in. Don't say you haven't. They can check your cellphone.'

'You will be all right, sir?'

'Either yes, Don, or no.'

In the background, he can hear the bustle of his headquarters building: phones, fast footsteps on stone or marble, echoing. The signal seems to fade, then return strongly.

'What do I do?'

'What you always do when this happens. Keep your head down, stay in contact if it's safe. You got the package for Steve Ulton?'

'The envelope?'

'Ja.'

373

'Dr Ulton has it now.'

'I told him, so I'll tell you. Just you. Not anyone else. It's DNA from Dr Bellingham's assailant. She scratched his head, I think. Took it, preserved it. Useless in evidence now, but it could point the way.'

'You have a suspect?'

'Two. Leigh Finnemore, the section-eighteen guy at the other end of the road, and his new supervisor, Rolf Viljoen.'

'We combed that house for three days.'

'It won't be like that. Finnemore finds these men, controls them. When I get back, I'll find a way.'

'You are going somewhere?'

'Yes, Don, that's inevitable.'

'We could have met at Ben's Diner again,' Danie Malgas states. 'Had a decent piece of meat.'

De Vries laughs. The car's engine is idling, the air-conditioning fan stuttering, cabin hot and ripe. The backstreet is empty, sandy, blasted by the sun.

'Danie. You know how it is. Sometimes you don't want to be seen with someone.'

'I know,' Malgas says. 'That's why my wife always wants to do it in the dark.'

De Vries hands him the envelope.

'Hang on to it. If I don't come back, and you want to risk your pension, open it, come help me out.'

Malgas takes the fat envelope sombrely.

'What is it?'

'Just an account, evidence, of what's been going on. Someone pretty powerful in Pretoria is going to take me down. I need to know my friends have this, that they'll use it if I'm in trouble.'

'You know I will.'

'It could be just one guy and a room full of senior blind eyes. They may let him operate only while he's doing what they want him to – unofficially. If so, we may have enough to take him down, expose what this is . . .'

'What is?'

'You may never need to know. Or it could be an entire department with orders from the very top. In that case, I may just disappear.'

'Maybe that's what you should do, man. Disappear.'

'Maybe,' De Vries says, 'but that's not how I operate. Besides, I'm still working on our case.'

'A second killer?'

'Yes. And, if I'm right, a man who first killed when he was ten, who is now enabling others to kill also. Never been caught, always thought a victim.'

'Everybody is a victim now,' Malgas says.

'That's what we have to do: distinguish between the villain and the victim. Something not very fashionable.'

'Never been a problem for me.'

'Nor me,' De Vries says. 'Just everybody else.'

He sits in his car, his back aching, neck stiff. A feeling of resignation is overcoming the adrenalin that has driven him for the last forty-eight hours. He knows how quickly the depression will settle, the boredom begin to eat into him. To live for control and then to relinquish it. He shakes his head. He knows there is no other way. The back of his shirt is soaked, his groin damp, feet wrinkled, as if he has fallen asleep in the bath. He realizes that to leave his vehicle, even to buy a coffee, is to risk his liberty, but acknowledges that moment is approaching now. He closes his eyes

375

against the bustling pavements, the busy streets, the corridor of buildings bearing down on him, seemingly converging at the horizon, trapping him, as he surely will be.

He runs through what he has done. The *New Cape Gazette*, Penelope van Reidel's surprise; Ali Jelani's weak, pitifully grateful interest. His envelopes of evidence, his reports, co-signed by Mike Solarin, the pictures, the hearsay from Eric Basson, which, if unsupported, will weaken their case, possibly fatally, all have been distributed to those whom he trusts, those whom he hopes will publish and opine and investigate. He has established safety protocols if they fail, or withdraw or recant, but even these, he fears, could be overcome.

Above all, he regrets that he still does not know whose DNA Grace Bellingham has trapped, although he suspects it will be that of Rolf Viljoen. All this time Leigh Finnemore has been present at the periphery of his vision. Finnemore knew Stephen Jessel for twenty years, perhaps Rolf Viljoen less well for half that time. He just cannot clarify who influences whom.

He glances at his watch, wonders where Mike Solarin is now. He hopes that he is among a multitude of anonymous others, unseen. To have him free provides hope that, if all else fails, there is one who can fight.

He looks up through his windscreen, then back in his mirror. He can see a group of suited men jogging up the hill towards him. He swings out of the car, stretches his shoulders, slams the door and locks the vehicle. Then he strides into the middle of Long Street, looking down at the newly laid tarmac, until he is standing in what would have been the epicentre of the explosion. Cars hoot, brake, cut each other up to avoid him, but he knows that he will not have to wait long. Already he can see two cars he recognizes as likely being unmarked SAPS cars. The men are less than one hundred metres from him, panting and sweating.

He glances around, sees two photographers on the left-hand pavement; on the balcony on the opposite side of the road, a video camera is pointed towards him. He turns to look back down the road, realizes that the cars have stopped moving, that he is suddenly alone in the street, cars beginning to back up down the hill as far as he can see. The heat on his neck is intense. The men in front of him spread out across the road, their handguns pointed at him. He raises his hands. A black car brakes behind them and the broad, bald skull of David Wertner emerges. He strides towards him, between the armed officers, the satisfied smile bursting from his pug-like features.

'I'm not even going to say it, De Vries.'

'Why not? You've waited a long time for this moment.'

Wertner leans forward, grabs De Vries's arm, turns it behind him, grabs the other wrist and cuffs him.

'You lived a charmed life, but it's over now. For good. You're on the next plane to Pretoria.'

De Vries opens his mouth, but decides that the man is not worth his breath. He walks, unresisting, with Wertner, towards the car. Two other officers flank him. He does not look at the passers-by, stationary now on the pavement, or his fellow officers, their heads turning to watch a senior officer taken down. As he turns to get into the rear of the vehicle, he resists just for a moment, looks up at the tip of the Mountain above the seemingly infinite point at the end of the street. The cable car is almost at the summit. The sun catches its revolving cabin, a ray of perfect white intensity shooting down Long Street, illuminating it for a split second, blinding him as his head is pushed inside the darkness.

EPILOGUE

Leigh Finnemore ties a bandanna over his hair, fastens the helmet. He looks at himself in the mirror: tall, slim, black Lycra, anonymous. He picks up the light sports bike, exits from the side door. He freewheels down the side of the house and onto the street. Within seconds, he is at the junction with Camps Bay Drive. He turns, drops down to the cross street below, which runs parallel with Plumbago Lane, speeds silently to the end, through a gap in the thicket of low trees. He dismounts, lays down his bike under an overhang of rock, begins to climb along and up the side of the rocky channel, which, in winter, carries water off the Mountain. The moon will be gone soon, but he does not need the light.

It takes him less than five minutes to reach his vantage point. He takes off his helmet and bandanna, sits at the place he has known his entire life. The rock allows him to take a seat and lean back, his head resting on a stone pillow. Above him, the only house visible is Apostle Lodge. It stands dark against the even deeper darkness of the Mountain. The insects squeal and buzz; the stars move in their apparent crescent around him. Time evaporates and envelops him. He never feels that he sleeps here, yet hours will pass. Perhaps, a meditation.

This night, the bird cowl twists slowly, gratingly, in the light breeze from the sea, an anguished cry, inanimate yet alive. He looks up at the Twelve Apostles, their peaks haloed by the dying moonlight, their troughs filled with spilling, perfectly white cloud.

His breathing calms. He turns back to Apostle Lodge. The view of his old home both frightens and reassures him. He thinks of his old bedroom, the cupboard that was his den, his exploration into the gorge beyond the garden, the feeling of freedom, of isolation, of control. Here, he made his decision to kill, planned how he would drown the girl; how it would be afterwards. But his life has become something more than he could have dreamed. The persona forced upon him protects and indemnifies him, allows him to take revenge unsuspected, influence and recruit, manipulate and control. He comprehends his power and the potential it bestows. He smiles to himself: it sits lightly on his shoulders.

ACKNOWLEDGEMENTS

I would like to thank Krystyna Green and Martin Fletcher, who have guided me and identified the means to hone my work into the finished product. My gratitude goes to Hazel Orme for her diligence in identifying imagined words, grammar and meanings – and for persuading me to correct them. I would also like to thank Rebecca Sheppard for patiently attending to my desire to lay out text in an unconventional way, and proof-readers who have spotted continuity irregularities and outright nonsense. Finally, thank you to my much-cherished friends in Cape Town, who contributed ideas, comments, Afrikaans expressions and much local richness that might otherwise have eluded me, and to the composers of numerous disparate and un-noted web pages at which I have glanced and from which I have been inspired.

Season

of

Spells

SYLVIA HUNTER

Allison & Busby Limited
12 Fitzroy Mews
London W1T 6DW
allisonandbusby.com

First published in 2016.
This edition published in Great Britain by Allison & Busby in 2017.
This paperback edition published by Allison & Busby in 2017.

A CIP catalogue record for this book is available from
the British Library.

10 9 8 7 6 5 4 3 2 1

ISBN 978-0-7490-2049-1

Typeset in 10.5/15.5 pt Adobe Garamond Pro by
Allison & Busby Ltd.

The paper used for this Allison & Busby publication
has been produced from trees that have been legally sourced
from well-managed and credibly certified forests.

Printed and bound by
CPI Group (UK) Ltd, Croydon, CR0 4YY

The Kingdoms of Britain, Eire & Alba

Kingdom of Alba

Din Edin

Kingdom of Eire

Duiblinn

England

Cymru

Oxford

Cardiff

London

Portsmouth

Bournemouth

La Manche

Kernow

Truru

Rosko

Caen

Normandie

Roazhon

Maine

Kerandraon

Douarnenez

Breizh

Angers

The Duchies

Legend

Kingdom of Britain

Province of Britain

Capital City ⊙

Principal City •

Maps by Cortney Skinner

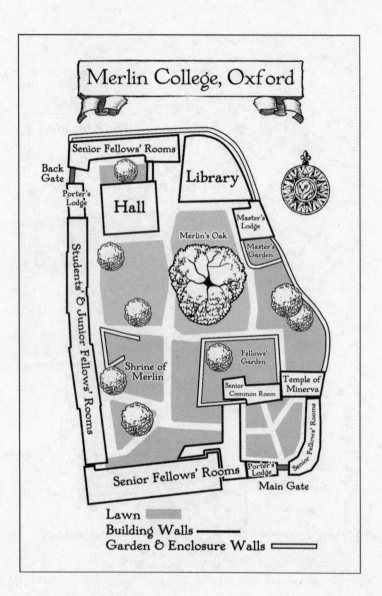

Merlin College, Oxford

Senior Fellows' Rooms

Back Gate

Porter's Lodge

Hall

Library

Master's Lodge

Master's Garden

Merlin's Oak

Students' & Junior Fellows' Rooms

Shrine of Merlin

Fellows' Garden

Senior Common Room

Temple of Minerva

Senior Fellows' Rooms

Senior Fellows' Rooms

Porter's Lodge

Main Gate

Lawn

Building Walls

Garden & Enclosure Walls

PART ONE

Din Edin to London

CHAPTER I

In Which Sophie and Gray Depart on a Journey, and Gwendolen Loses a Wager

'Well, Magistra?' said Gray.

The small flock of new graduates broke apart, smiling and laughing, and Sophie Marshall emerged from it to look up at her husband. He was beaming all over his kind, honest face, and when she stepped towards him, holding out her hand for him to shake by way of congratulation – for they had not met since before the day's long ceremonials – he laughed aloud and swept her into a fierce, albeit chaste, embrace.

Sophie's friends hooted and applauded.

'Where next?' Gray said, when Sophie had her feet under her once more. 'Have you some grand festivity to attend, Magistra, to which I may escort you?'

Sophie tilted her head, laughing up at him, and – trusting to the confusion of motion and noise that surrounded them – said, 'I had hoped that a handsome Doctor of Practical Magick might give me his arm as far as Quarry Close. And after that . . .'

Astonishing, she thought, with an inward grin, that being nearly six years married, she still could make him blush.

'Sophie!' cried a voice behind her. 'Gray!'

Sophie turned on her heel to find her friends (and Gray's colleagues) Mór MacRury, Rory MacCrimmon, and Sorcha MacAngus, together with Lucia MacNeill – it was she who had been calling them – elbowing their way through the crowd.

A new round of back-slapping and embracing ensued, after which Mór said brightly, 'We shall see you both at the bonfire this evening, I hope?'

Sophie and Gray exchanged a lingering glance; Sophie, for her part, was calculating the hours remaining until dusk, and finding the number sufficient.

'Of course,' she said, turning a general smile upon her friends. 'We should not dream of missing it.'

Then she caught Gray's right hand in her left, and they began making their farewells.

The succeeding fortnight was lost to a mad welter of preparations for departure. In May, Lucia MacNeill – heiress to the chieftain's seat of Alba, and, if all unfolded as planned, soon to be Sophie's sister-in-law – was to journey to London to meet her future husband and the rest of Britain's royal family. Gray and Sophie, in her capacity as Princess Royal, were to travel south as part of Lucia's retinue, and there remain until after her marriage to Prince Roland, so that Sophie might serve her friend as guide and interpreter of London society.

It was not, in truth, a prospect which Sophie greatly relished; not only was she, in her own estimation, very ill-equipped to be anyone's guide to that circle of society in which Lucia MacNeill must be expected to move, but the task must bring her into prolonged and frequent contact with her stepmother, Queen Edwina, a circumstance unlikely to occasion joy to either. Lucia *was* her friend, however, and might very well have need of a sympathetic ear in the course of her sojourn in Britain. And of course she wished very much to see her sister Joanna, and Gray's sister Jenny, and Jenny's growing family.

The Marshalls' immediate plans, in any case, had thus been determined for them; but it remained to decide – or, perhaps, to discover – what they were to do with themselves thereafter. Were they to return to Din Edin and their work at the University, or even a permanent home in Alba? To Oxford, in hopes that a second sojourn there might be more successful than the first? To London, or to the house in Breizh which had belonged to Sophie's stepfather, Appius Callender, and now was Gray's? All these possibilities had been the subject of six months' intermittent and inconclusive debate.

The packing-up of their small house in Quarry Close, therefore – their home, and a very happy one but for the dramatic disruptions of their first spring in Din Edin, for the past three years – had something of the character of a magistrate's court, each object in it being interrogated as to its possible fate, should any of a variety of futures come to pass.

'Gray,' said Sophie one morning, for example, 'I have found that three-volume work on botanical magicks by Niall MacNeill, which you spoke of returning to Lachlan Ruadh MacDougall. Shall I set them aside for him?'

Gray, on hands and knees with his head and shoulders inside a cupboard, sat back on his heels, thrust one dusty hand through his equally dusty hair, and said, 'Yes – no – I must just read once more through the chapter on Niall MacNeill's experiments with wild celery; he claims to have used it to prevent a rival of his from executing a shape-shift, and Rory and I have been meaning to put his method to the test—'

11

'Absolutely not!' Sophie exclaimed, hugging the books to her chest and taking a step backwards. 'Of all the absurdly dangerous—'

She closed her eyes briefly – counted ten in Latin, then in Gaelic – invented a compromise which might put off the real decision to another day. 'If I copy out the chapter for you, in my very best hand,' she said, 'so that you may have the necessary information to hand when next you and Rory find yourselves at leisure to conduct hazardous experiments, may I then return the books to Lachlan MacDougall?'

Gray sneezed; Sophie extracted her handkerchief from her sleeve and handed it to him.

'Very well,' he said, when he had finished with the handkerchief. 'I thank you, *cariad*.'

'You may thank me,' said Sophie firmly, 'by finishing with that cupboard, and making a start upon the one under the stairs; and by remembering that we shall be living out of our trunks and valises for the foreseeable future, and must consider their contents accordingly.'

She reflected a little guiltily on the contents of her own trunks, and went upstairs to agonise once more over the ratio of commonplace books to gowns and bonnets.

Their methods, in other words, were not conducive to either speed or efficiency, and Donella MacHutcheon, the daily woman who had had the care and feeding of Sophie and Gray since their arrival in Din Edin, exclaimed in despair at their manner of going on. When the day of departure arrived, however, it found the Marshalls' affairs sufficiently in order that they might oversee the strapping-up of their trunks and ascend into Lucia MacNeill's carriage with a reasonably clear conscience – though still with no clear notion of what, beyond the journey itself, their future might hold.

* * *

12

Lucia MacNeill studied her friends as they settled themselves, side by side, on the opposite *banc* of the carriage. Sophie was rather pink in the face, and Gray patting the pockets of his coat as though searching for something, or (perhaps more likely) reassuring himself that he had not left some item of importance behind. They looked, in fact, nearly as unsettled and anxious as Lucia felt – not at all a reassuring beginning.

Lucia clasped her gloved hands tightly together and looked out of the window at the narrow row-houses of Quarry Close, crowded together like herring in a barrel. She tried to imagine the Sophie who lived here – who so matter-of-factly presided over her creaky dining-table and cramped kitchen, who existed in a perpetual semi-disorder of half-read books and half-finished essays and ongoing academic debates – as the Princess Edith Augusta Sophia, only daughter of Henry of Britain; and, as usual, failed.

The carriage quickly left Quarry Close behind, and soon enough was joined by its companions: the equipage carrying Lucia's cousin Sìleas Barra MacNeill and her husband, Oscar MacConnachie, envoy to the British Court; and Lucia's personal squadron of her father's household guard, mounted and travelling as outriders, together with Sophie's guardsmen. Not all of Lucia's guardsmen were, in fact, men; she expected some degree of trouble on that score, but had determined that she must begin as she meant to go on, which was not by compromising either her troops' esprit de corps (a pretty phrase *en français* which she had learnt from Gray Marshall) or her own safety for the sake of her betrothed husband's sensibilities. Compromises there must be, of course, but if he was to be her consort, he must take some things in stride.

Despite the crowds assembled to see Lucia off, which impeded the progress of their convoy to a quite extraordinary degree, they had nearly left Din Edin behind by the time Sophie said, in an uncharacteristically hesitant tone, 'You shall not be away so very long, after all.'

Lucia turned from the window. 'I beg your pardon?'

Sophie's brow was crumpled in concern. 'You have been looking out at Din Edin as though you half expected never to see it again,' she said. 'But if all goes well, you shall be coming back in a few months' time, with Roland; and if it does not . . .'

If it does not, I shall be coming back very soon indeed, with my tail between my legs like a dog who has lost her sheep.

But there was no need to give voice to such a melancholic thought.

'Yes,' said Lucia instead, attempting cheerfulness. 'Very true. Now, I shall be your guide to the country round about, so long as we are in Alba; but once we are over the Wall, you must return the favour, and tell me all about everything we see, so that I shall not be entirely ignorant when we reach London.'

'Not that necklace,' said Joanna.

'Why not?' said Gwendolen. Though her tone demanded justifications, her fingers were already reaching for the clasp.

'Why not?' echoed Joanna's niece Agatha, watching them dress for Lady Lisle's ball from her perch on the end of Joanna's bed.

'It spoils the line of the décolleté, just there,' said Joanna, pointing. She turned back to her dressing-table and rummaged in her jewel-case, finally laying hands on what she wanted: a twisted string of round beads, smooth amethyst and faceted violet glass, and the matching set of ear-drops, a gift from Jenny for her fifteenth birthday.

'Sit down,' she said, turning again. 'You are entirely too tall.'

Gwendolen smirked and folded herself gracefully into Joanna's abandoned chair.

In this way, Joanna's face appeared directly above hers in the dressing-glass as Joanna fastened the amethysts about her slim throat and adjusted their set on her collar-bones, and side by side when Joanna bent, out of Agatha's line of sight, to kiss the curve of Gwendolen's left ear.

'Perfect,' Joanna pronounced, straightening up again with both hands resting on Gwendolen's shoulders.

As Gwendolen reached for the ear-drops, their eyes met in the mirror – cheeks flushed, eyes shining – and they shared a secret, promising grin.

'Aunty Gwen!' said Agatha. 'Do you suppose Mr Trenoweth will ask you for the first two dances?'

Gwendolen's smile went rather fixed. 'I suppose he may, duckling,' she said. 'He must ask someone, presumably, though I do not know why he should ask me in particular.'

She turned her head this way and that, examining the effect of the ivory rosebuds in her dark hair.

'Oh, but *I* know why!' Agatha crowed. She had got her feet under her, and scrambled up to stand on the bed's low footboard, clinging to the bedpost with one arm – imagining, Joanna knew, that she was a sailor standing lookout up aloft. 'Mr Trenoweth's sister is Lady Lewes, and she came to call upon Mama once, and said that she hoped he might ask you to marry him! . . . But I do not know what Mama said about it,' she added, now sounding rather cross, 'because Rozena found me and made me come out from under the sofa, and so I did not hear any more.'

Joanna (who knew exactly what Jenny had said, and to whom, and why) stifled a chuckle at Agatha's disgruntled tone; but her mirth died away as, out of the corner of her eye, she caught a glimpse of Gwendolen's face.

'I think I hear Rozena calling you, Captain Agatha,' she said. 'Run away now, and we shall be sure to come and see you before we go.'

Agatha clambered down the end of the bed with what she fondly imagined to be a nautical cry and slipped out of the room, closing the door firmly behind her.

When the sound of her running footsteps had faded, Joanna caught Gwendolen's hands in hers, turned her away from the looking-glass, and peered up into her eyes. 'None of that,' she said firmly. 'We have had all of this out before, and you know that Jenny is with us and not against us.'

Gwendolen briefly squeezed her eyes tight shut, then opened them again and sighed. 'Yes,' she said. 'I do know it, Jo.'

'And Mr Trenoweth has not been making a nuisance of himself?' Joanna said.

Another sigh. 'No, not particularly. He is a perfectly unobjectionable young man, you know, now that he has set his matrimonial sights elsewhere.'

'I am glad to hear it,' said Joanna. 'Now, before we go downstairs—'

The words began what had become a sort of ritual between them, for occasions of this kind, when they should both be spending most of the evening dancing with other people. Gwendolen continued it by casting an approving eye over the tiny pink roses in Joanna's hair, her garnet earrings, her new gown of rose-pink satin, the silver buckles decorating her dancing-slippers; Joanna returned her glance for glance, enjoying the blush that spread prettily over Gwendolen's sharp cheekbones as she grew conscious of being admired.

Joanna tipped her face up towards her friend's, and for just a moment lost herself in the press of Gwen's lips upon her own – so familiar now, yet always half unexpected, always astonishing. Her hands found Gwen's hips, her waist; crept up her spine to press her closer.

'You look very lovely,' said Gwendolen, drawing back at last, too soon.

'And so do you,' said Joanna. 'As you know very well.'

Gwendolen, being taller, held out her arm – bent at the elbow, as a gentleman does for a lady – and when Joanna tucked her hand under it, pressed it close against her ribs. 'Shall we go, Miss Callender?' she asked.

'Certainly, Miss Pryce,' said Joanna, matching her light, untroubled tone; and, moving as regally as either of them knew how, they swept out of her bedroom, along the corridor, and up the stairs to the nursery, to bid farewell to Captain Agatha as promised.

Joanna was afterwards to look back on the beginning of that summer as a sort of idyll – no different on the surface from the years that preceded it, but bathed in a rosy glow of affection, freed (to some degree, at any rate) from the shadow of their shared but always unspoken anxiety by Jenny's explicit promise to entertain no offers of marriage for either of them, no matter how apparently eligible. Less than a month before Lucia MacNeill's anticipated arrival in London to make the acquaintance of her betrothed, the ladies of the royal household were consumed with preparations, and the Kergabet ladies with them; but though the endless talking-over of tedious minutiae sometimes frustrated and bored Joanna and Gwendolen almost past bearing, they had only to meet one another's eyes, and the tedium gave way to relief and occasional jubilation.

All too soon, however, a hired carriage deposited Mrs Edmond Marshall in Grosvenor Square to disturb the peace of its occupants. Ostensibly her purpose was to be of use to her daughter – presently expecting her third child – but Joanna rather suspected her of a desire to *make* use of Jenny, or at any rate of Jenny's connexions. Or perhaps, if one were being charitable, Mrs Marshall might simply (in common with half the kingdom, to judge by the influx of persons into London at present) have been possessed of a desire to gawk at Lucia MacNeill of Alba.

At any rate, there was nothing to be done but to make Jenny's mama welcome, and to keep her – so far as possible – from fretting Jenny into a state of misery. It was a task in which Joanna was grateful, this time, to have Gwendolen's assistance.

'I tell you,' she said, low, as they stood on the steps of Lord Kergabet's house, watching two footmen assist their visitor's descent from her equipage, 'Mrs Marshall the elder is the most tiresome woman I have met in the whole of my life.'

'Oh, come, Jo!' said Gwendolen, grinning behind one hand. 'Did you not travel the whole way to Din Edin with Lady MacConnachie, and live to fight another day?'

Eight days later, Joanna and Gwendolen sat pressed close together on the window-seat in Joanna's bedroom, listening to the rain.

'I did not think anything could be more tiresome than a long journey with Lady MacConnachie,' said Gwen, after a moment, 'but now that I have spent fully a se'nnight in the same house with Lady Kergabet's mama, I must admit that you were quite right.'

She reached for her reticule, rummaged in it briefly, and handed over two silver coins.

Joanna took them from her with a triumphant grin; but her conscience smote her, and, sighing, she handed them back and folded Gwen's fingers gently around them.

'I ought not to have taken your wager,' she said. 'I knew how it would be, for she stayed here a month entire when Agatha was born, and drove Jenny nearly to distraction; she was not nearly so horrid when you met her here before, being so pleased to have a grandson at last. It would not be fair of me to take your coin.'

'Well, then, I ought not to have wagered!' said Gwen, laughing. 'We cannot be everlastingly going back on our word to one another, Jo, only because one of us occasionally makes an idiotic bet; and I assure you that I should not let you off if our positions were reversed.'

Joanna considered this. Then a thought struck her, and – feeling greatly daring, for it was full day, though pouring with rain, and this window plainly visible from the square below – she said, 'Very well; I decline to accept your coin, but you may pay your wager in kisses instead.'

Gwen gave her a long, stern look, then drew the curtains and did so.

CHAPTER II

In Which Mrs Edmond Marshall
Is Inexplicable, and Sophie
Conceives an Idea

Sophie and Gray parted from Lucia at their last halt before reaching London, she to travel in Oscar MacConnachie's carriage to the Royal Palace, and they to continue to Lord Kergabet's house in Grosvenor Square. Lucia had been brought up from infancy in the knowledge that she might one day be named her father's heir, and was as well versed in the concealment of private trepidation as anyone of Sophie's acquaintance; whether her composure were real or assumed, therefore, was almost impossible to determine, but Sophie knew very well that she herself, in Lucia's place, would have been quaking in her sturdy calfskin boots.

'Do you suppose . . .' she began, peering through the window of their carriage as the other receded into the distance – then, changing tacks, 'It will all go off very smoothly, I am sure. Oscar MacConnachie knows what he is about.'

Gray chuckled – showing, Sophie could not help thinking, rather less care than he ought for the well-being of their friend – and said, 'I notice you do not say the same of Sìleas Barra MacNeill.'

Sophie waved this away impatiently. 'Of course I do not,' she said. 'Nobody *could*, you know – though she is all very well in her own sphere, of course, and she is Lucia's cousin, which Lucia may find comforting. I hope it may be so, at all events.' She grimaced, keeping her face turned away from Gray's so that he should not see it. 'I should not have been averse to having Cousin Maëlle to protect me, when first I went to stay with *my* mother-in-law.'

Gray's chuckle this time was low and rather bitter. 'Nor I,' he said. 'You do remember, I hope, *cariad*, that we may well be staying with her on this occasion also, in a manner of speaking.'

'I remember,' Sophie sighed. 'Of course I remember. But at any rate we shall be in Jenny's house; it is not quite the same as actually living under your parents' roof.'

They spoke thereafter of anything and everything but the Marshalls of Glascoombe, and spent a good deal of time pointing out to one another scenes and landmarks which they had had no sight of since their last visit to London – on the occasion of Prince Edward's wedding, nearly two years past. As an attempt to take their minds off the coming ordeal, it was (at least in Sophie's case) an abject failure. But at any rate, she reflected, they should not waste this last precious sliver of private conversation in dredging up past hurts and irritations.

The household which assembled to greet them had been translated from the house in Carrington-street to a much larger and more imposing one in Grosvenor Square, more befitting the dignity of Lord Kergabet's present position on His Majesty's Privy Council; and not only Joanna and Gwendolen Pryce but also Gray's mother joined Jenny, her children, and their nursery-maid in the silver-papered hall where Treveur and his minions were attempting to divest the newcomers of their travelling-cloaks and hats.

Jenny had written to warn them that she expected a maternal

visitation at some point during the summer; his mother's presence, therefore, did not startle Gray – until she approached him, beaming, and put up her face to be kissed.

'Mama,' he said, nonplussed. He kissed her cheek, and when he unbent his neck again was further startled to see her turning to greet Sophie with even greater effusiveness.

Over their heads, Gray met Jenny's eyes, as full of bafflement as his own thoughts. Sophie and his mother had avoided coming to blows during their first and only sojourn in the same house, but only just, and according to Jenny and Joanna, Mrs Marshall the elder habitually referred to Sophie as *that girl* and had more than once dropped dark hints about love-spells. What could possibly be behind this sudden change of heart, if such it was? Gray knew not whether he ought to feel wary or relieved, and instead of indulging himself in either, turned his attention to his niece and nephew, and submitted to being climbed upon, as though he had been a tree.

'Your mama seems friendlier,' said Sophie, meaning, *She appears to detest me less than formerly.* She tugged at the bedclothes; Gray grumbled good-naturedly but ceded her a further hand's breadth of coverlet. 'Perhaps time – or absence – has reconciled her to your unfortunate choice of bride.'

Gray, tucked up behind her, shifted slightly so as to kiss the top of her left ear. 'I hope she may be sincere, *cariad*, for your sake,' he said – meaning, she suspected, *I hope she may be sincere, but I should be surprised to find her so.* Or perhaps this was only the effect of her own deep caution with respect to her mother-in-law.

'And she mentioned to me after dinner,' Sophie went on, 'that your brother Alan went up to Oxford in the autumn, at last, and is reading alchymy at Plato College! Does not that sound as

22

though he were turning out rather better than you feared?'

'It does,' said Gray. 'For which I thank all the gods, for I have not the least idea to which of them thanks may be owed in this case. Now, why should she have told you that, I wonder?'

'Gray.' Sophie's attempt at a reproachful tone ran afoul of a strong urge to laugh, and Gray kissed her ear again, and drew her closer. She wriggled round to face him, laid a hand on his cheek, and said seriously, 'If your mama is inclined to be conciliating, love, I do not mean to look a gift horse in the mouth.'

'Of course you do not,' said Gray, with a fond smile just visible in the cool glow of the magelights they had called to light them to bed. 'And may it so continue.'

Sophie drew breath to ask him what he meant; he tilted his head and kissed her, however, and she forgot her question entirely.

The Marshalls of Din Edin were not by nature early risers, but the arrival at their door of morning tea, heralded as of old by Daisy's quiet knock – together with a suite of morning noises quite different from those of Quarry Close, or of a country inn-yard – brought them down to breakfast at an hour which even Jenny, surely, could not consider excessively late.

Mrs Marshall, it appeared, was yet abed, and though neither was so ill-judged as to say anything about it, Sophie did not think she was imagining the look of relief that crossed Gray's face, mirroring her own feelings, upon finding his mother absent from the breakfast-table.

The conversation was at first general and perfectly ordinary, but partook of an ease and candour which had been altogether absent from the dinner-table on the previous afternoon. Mr Fowler soon afterwards appeared, and by degrees the conversation took a more political turn: first to a dispatch from one of Lord Kergabet's agents in the Duchies, which reported that the local lord was recruiting foot-soldiers on behalf of some unknown person improbably styled Imperator Gallia, or Emperor of Gaul, which occasioned much discussion and not a little scoffing; and then, by way of the Marshalls' impressions of Lucia's state of mind when last seen, to the Kergabet household's latest news of Roland.

'Prince Roland,' said Miss Pryce unexpectedly, 'hopes that Lucia MacNeill's conversation may be more lively than her letters.'

'Does he,' said Sophie, frowning. What could this signify?

Mrs Marshall's arrival in the breakfast-room necessitated a change of subject – which (fortunately or unfortunately) she herself provided, by turning to Sophie with an expectant expression and announcing, 'You must tell us all about Din Edin, and the Alban princess.'

Lord Kergabet and Mr Fowler exchanged a look, and rapidly though very civilly took their leave.

'Graham is a most unsatisfactory correspondent,' Mrs Marshall continued, oblivious. 'Though I suppose there cannot be very much to relate, when all of one's time is spent amongst piles of dusty books! Now that you are come back, however, I hope you may be able to persuade him to put them aside, and go out into society from time to time, so as to make the best of your visit.'

'Mama,' said Jenny, in a tone of gentle reproof which Mrs Marshall entirely ignored.

Gray said nothing. Sophie swallowed her outrage, reminding herself that her mother-in-law, for sound political reasons, did not and could not know the true tale of their first year in Din Edin, nor understand how near she had come to losing her second son for good and all.

'I believe, ma'am,' she said, when she felt able once more to speak without fatally offending her listener, 'we may expect to enjoy a good deal more society during Lucia MacNeill's visit than ever in our lives before; and I assure you,' she added with a smile, 'that I shall be more than satisfied to return to my dusty books at the end of it.'

She had meant it as a rebuff, if a gentle one; Mrs Marshall, however, seemed not to hear it as such, for she said, 'Tell me, my dear, is it true that the Alban princess walks about Din Edin unescorted, and plays at being a student?'

Gray's head rose sharply, his eyes narrowing. 'Lucia MacNeill does not play at anything she does, Mama,' he said. 'She is not a student at present, but she is certainly a scholar – a very fine one, indeed, and every bit as clever as Sophie.' This, Sophie knew, was among the highest compliments of which Gray was capable. 'It is quite as usual in Alba for clever young ladies to take up University places, as for clever young men to do so.'

'Which is just as it ought to be, *I* think,' said Joanna stoutly, and Miss Pryce, after a cautious glance at Jenny, said, 'I quite agree.'

'And she does not walk about Din Edin unescorted,' said Sophie, before any of them could go on, or Mrs Marshall present some retort. 'She has guardsmen lurking in the shadows, always, just as I have.'

'Have you, indeed?' Mrs Marshall looked about the breakfast-room (quite empty of royal guardsmen), her eyebrows pointedly raised. 'They must be past masters of concealment, I conclude?'

'Of course I can have no possible need of a bodyguard in Jenny's house, ma'am,' said Sophie. *If I swallow any more outrage, I shall have a dreadful bellyache.*

By now every eye had turned to see how Jenny would bear her mother's insult to her hospitality; Mrs Marshall seemed to recognise at last exactly what she had said, and how it was likely to be understood. Flustered and wrong-footed, she tittered – a

25

startling sound from a woman of her age and dignity – and in an entirely transparent attempt to turn the conversation said, 'Genevieve, my love, you are eating no more than a sparrow! I hope you are not unwell? In your condition—'

'No, Mama,' said Jenny patiently; 'I am quite well; I was down to breakfast an hour ago and have eaten all I can hold, I assure you.'

After a further quarter-hour of limping conversation, consisting mostly in ingratiating questions from Mrs Marshall, and in less and less patient answers on the part of everybody else, Joanna and Miss Pryce (who had increasingly been exchanging covert looks of amusement and exasperation) excused themselves from the breakfast-table and went away. Mrs Marshall frowned after them; Sophie, on the contrary, rather wondered at their not having fled sooner.

As always during visits to London, and irrespective of her role as shepherd or chaperone to Lucia MacNeill, one of Sophie's tasks was to mend fences with her father.

She therefore found herself occupying an idle hour in the library of the Royal Palace, in the interval before the family dinner, so called, to which she (but not Gray) had been summoned; and it was here that she found it – tucked almost invisibly between two quarto volumes, its leather binding faded and its endpapers badly foxed. *A Dove amongst the Peacocks,* the title-page read; *Being the Tale of the Founding of Lady Morgan College, Oxon.*

She had forgot until this moment the astonishment, the fascination, with which she had pored over this volume, when first she discovered it amongst her mother's books; the wondering, bubbling joy, to learn that such a place – a college for the education of women, founded by a clever Cymric heiress hundreds of years ago – existed, and to imagine that she might one day aspire to a place there;

the falling of her heart when Mama told her, her eyes soft with regret, that in fact it had closed its doors two centuries before.

This copy of the book bore a variety of scuff-marks and several illegible annotations in ink, but no cataloguer's mark or number; very possibly, no one but Sophie knew of its existence here.

'Gray,' she said, 'see what I have found—'

Then she recalled that Gray was not here, was at this moment no doubt eating his dinner in Grosvenor Square, and scowled ferociously at the bookcase before her.

She laughed at herself, if a little crossly – *I am justly served, for thinking Gray impossibly absent-minded!* – and sat down to examine her find.

The volume was more or less as she remembered it, insofar as she remembered it at all – which was odd, considered rationally; in general she had an excellent memory for books, yet the contents of this one seemed to have slipped sidewise from her mind whilst her attention was elsewhere. The frontispiece, an engraved view of the College buildings with the central dome of Minerva's shrine, caught her gaze, familiar-strange – like and not like the buildings themselves, glimpsed behind the ivy-covered outer wall on the far bank of the Cherwell in Sophie's Oxford days, always at the periphery of her attention, never reaching its centre.

She had first seen that derelict dome, those overgrown walls, from the window of a hired carriage on a rainy autumn day. The sight had gripped her with a sorrow so profound as to steal her breath – the memory of it, lost till now, returned in force, and she let the book fall on the table, struggling to draw breath around the sudden tightness in her chest.

And she had had another thought – had wished, had *yearned* to restore that dead place to vivid life – and Joanna had said—

'Mother Goddess,' Sophie breathed, as the vice-grip on her lungs began to ebb.

—Joanna had said, *Perhaps you may do so, when you are a princess again.*

'How could I have forgot such a thing?' she spoke aloud now, only for the reassurance of hearing her own voice – which, to her immense relief, sounded absolutely as usual. 'How could I live two years in Oxford, and never once—'

She stopped, arrested open-mouthed by another vivid recollection: an evening stroll over the Cherwell bridge, the fragrant Midsummer-tide twilight, her hand tucked through Gray's elbow, faint splashing and young men's voices singing and calling to one another from below, and the dome of Minerva catching the light of the setting sun, and Gray's voice, thoughtful: 'What a place it must have been, in its day!'

And again the press of sorrow and loss, the yearning to see the gate flung open and the halls and quads filled with scholars once more.

There is a pattern here, Sophie thought. *There is, there must be – but, by the gods, I cannot see its shape.*

Now that the idea had caught hold of her once more, however, it was easy to succumb to its persuasion. There had been a college for women in Oxford once; why should there not be again? Sophie's namesake and distant quasi forebear, the Princess Edith Augusta, had been one of its patrons, as well as a student there; why should Sophie not fill the same role?

The Princess Edith, it was true, in her capacity as co-Regent for her brother Edward, had had access to powers and resources which Sophie had not; true, too, that to assume the mantle of patronage in respect of a living, thriving institution was one thing, and to rebuild it from what might well be literal rubble, entirely another. *But if it could be done . . . If* I *might be the one to do it . . .*

The steward's knock upon the library door startled her out of her thoughts, and half out of her seat; but by the time it was followed by the man himself, she had regained some of her composure.

'If you would be so good as to join Her Majesty in the small reception room, ma'am,' he said, with a nicely judged bow.

'Of course,' said Sophie.

She tucked the book into her reticule – no one would miss it, she reasoned, and she should return it upon a subsequent visit, of which there were bound to be many – and followed him out of the room, making notes in her mind as to the possible means of proceeding.

Point the first: search the remainder of the Palace library for further published works.

Point the second: gain entry to the Archives, and find whether any unpublished documents exist which might shed light upon the problem.

Point the third—

Point the third: how did I come to forget something so very much worth remembering . . . ?

But now, at this moment, there were her father and her brother Ned to be reassured as to her well-being, and Delphine's shy raptures over the child she was expecting; young Harry to be regaled with tales of life in Alba, and Roland to be talked out of his nerves; and Queen Edwina – with her seemingly unbreakable habit of addressing Sophie as 'Edith' – to be borne with cheerfully.

But when next I have leisure for my own pursuits . . .

CHAPTER III

In Which Lucia Meets Her Match

On the morning of her third day in London, Lucia MacNeill, daughter of Donald MacNeill, holder of a graduate degree in practical magick and heiress to the chieftain's seat of Alba, stood in her borrowed bedchamber – truly alone for almost the first time since leaving Din Edin – and gazed disconsolately at her reflection in a tall cheval-glass.

She could not fault her appearance; her unruly curls were smoothed and tamed into a knot low on her neck, and her simply but exquisitely cut sea-green gown made the most of her slim figure and of the colour of her eyes. She looked, in short, as much like a suitable successor to her father as she was ever like to do. She adopted a grave expression, suitable for affairs of state – then turned away abruptly, hands clenched and lips pressed tight together, when it threatened to dissolve into either giggles or tears.

The last leg of Lucia's journey to London had been made in the sole company of her cousin Sìleas Barra MacNeill and Sìleas's husband, Oscar MacConnachie, to whom – thanks to the latter's status as Donald MacNeill's envoy to the British Court – had fallen the duty of introducing Lucia therein. Sìleas was a kindly and motherly companion, for whose presence Lucia (who had lost her own mother at the age of ten) was duly grateful; she was also, alas, a rather tedious one, for her mind ran solidly in a very few tracks and could not be jolted out of them. And she was at present waiting just outside the door, and very likely fretting over Lucia's odd behaviour.

'You are the heiress to the chieftain's seat of Alba,' Lucia said aloud, sternly, as she turned back to the glass. She stood straighter. 'Confirmed by the clan chieftains in full council, with the blessings of Brìghde and of the Cailleach. If the prospect of ruling a kingdom does not alarm you, why should you so dread meeting your mother-in-law?'

Dread it she did, but there was nothing to be gained by delaying the inevitable. Lucia smoothed her hands down her skirts one last time and went out to meet her fate.

Queen Edwina, it transpired, could scarcely have appeared less frightening: a small, plump, smiling woman, blue-eyed and golden-haired, who rose to welcome Lucia with every appearance of genuine pleasure at her arrival. She addressed Sìleas Barra MacNeill as *Lady MacConnachie*, which Lucia recognised after a heartbeat's frozen confusion as the appropriate British form of address for Oscar MacConnachie's wife.

A lovingly polished welcome-cup – bright gold on its inner surface, and finely etched without, prominently bearing the Tudor rose – stood ready to hand, half filled with a deep red wine. The Queen took up the cup; drank deeply from it, holding Lucia's gaze; and, passing it into Lucia's hand, spoke the blessing in formal Latin: 'My welcome to this house, Lucia MacNeill of Alba, and to this kingdom.'

Lucia accepted the cup. 'I thank you for this welcome,' she

replied, in the same tongue. 'May the gods smile on you, on this house and on this kingdom, and all who dwell here.'

The wine was much too sweet for her taste, but she did not like to appear less than enthusiastic (or, worse, to seem suspicious), and so drank deeply nonetheless.

The formal ritual thus accomplished, Queen Edwina rose a-tiptoe to kiss Lucia on both cheeks, and bestowed upon her a beaming smile that creased her bright eyes nearly shut.

Lucia's English and Français were not so fluent as she might have wished, her lessons with Sophie Marshall having dwindled in frequency as she grew increasingly occupied with her father's affairs; but she rallied herself to return this unexpected gesture, making her best and most grateful curtsey to the Queen and saying hesitantly in English, 'I am so very glad to make your acquaintance at last, Your Majesty.'

Queen Edwina smiled even more widely and clapped her small white hands in childlike delight – reminding Lucia inescapably of Sophie, though otherwise the two could not have been more unlike. 'How clever you are, my dear! However do you contrive to speak so naturally, when you must have learnt from books?'

'Oh! I did not learn from books,' said Lucia; 'Sophie taught me.'

'Of course.' The Queen's welcoming smile grew a little fixed, and her warm voice a little cooler. 'Yes, I understood you to be already acquainted with the Princess Edith.'

Rattled, Lucia cast a pleading glance at her cousin: *I have put my foot in some rabbit-hole, but which?* Sìleas, however, either did not or chose not to understand her difficulty.

In any event their private audience was at an end, it seemed, for a liveried servant now opened a door opposite the one through which Lucia had entered the room, admitting a veritable parade of ladies. Lucia at first set about learning all their faces, but gave up the attempt when a familiar face and form leapt out at her from the mass of strangers, and Sophie's voice cried, 'Lucia MacNeill! Come here at once, and let me see you.'

'Sophie!' said Lucia, delighted and relieved, as Sophie (contradicting her own instructions) ran forward to embrace her, as eagerly as though they had been parted for months instead of days. At once she regretted it – ought she not to have said *Your Royal Highness*? – and cast a glance over Sophie's shoulder to see how this relatively intimate greeting might have been received.

Queen Edwina, indeed, wore a slightly pinched expression; whatever had been Lucia's earlier transgression, it appeared she had now compounded it.

'Never mind,' said Sophie, speaking in Gaelic, and very low, into Lucia's ear. 'It is only that she does not like me, because I am my mother's daughter; I did warn you, you know. I shall endeavour to prevent my unfortunate shadow from falling too heavily upon you.'

Before Lucia could express either protest or acquiescence, Sophie was returning her to the care of Queen Edwina, with a graceful curtsey and a pretty, altogether un-Sophie-like apology for stealing her away.

The rest of the introductions went rather better. Sophie's uncharacteristic deference to her stepmother continued, though Lucia strongly suspected her of storing up sharp remarks for some later, more private conversation. Lucia made the acquaintance of Prince Edward's pretty, diffident young wife, and if the Princess Delphine was no longer quite so blushing and bashful as Sophie had once described her, she certainly did not accord with Lucia's notion of a future Queen. On the other hand, she was very evidently doing her part to ensure the continuance of the royal line.

Next came Lady Lisle, who seemed genuinely delighted to make Lucia's acquaintance and genuinely to have nothing else to say for herself; Lady Kergabet, wife of King Henry's chief advisor and, Lucia recalled just in time to avoid abject humiliation, already familiar to her as Sophie's much-admired sister-in-law Jenny; Madame de Courcy, with whose husband – the British envoy to Alba – Lucia had already a long and sometimes very surprising acquaintance; the elderly Lady Craven, and the humblingly elegant Madame de Mayenne, and at least a dozen more. Lucia smiled at them all, and thanked them for their kind welcome, and tried not to feel as though all of them but Sophie were studying her like some exotic insect under glass.

Was it her imagination that beneath the warm, sometimes almost effusive welcomes there lurked a note of anxious apprehension?

She was not to be introduced to Prince Roland himself until the following day, a proceeding which seemed less idiotic now than when Sìleas had explained it to her this morning. By tomorrow, one might hope – with this first ordeal behind her – she should have had a proper night's sleep, and a long talk with Sophie, and should have got her feet under her once more.

The next afternoon, Sophie and Joanna stood side by side, a little apart from Jenny and Delphine, and watched Roland advance towards Lucia MacNeill. Lucia herself was accompanied only by her cousins, Sìleas Barra MacNeill and Oscar MacConnachie, and appeared to Sophie to be regretting the women-at-arms of her personal guard, whom she had left behind in her temporary quarters in the Queen's wing of the Royal Palace. She was entirely calm and composed, her hands steady, her red-gold hair impeccably dressed, and smiling in welcome; but to Sophie the composure seemed just slightly too stiff, the smile just slightly too symmetrical.

Roland, on the other hand, looked so straightforwardly nervous that Sophie felt quite sorry for him.

'Lady Lucia,' said the Queen, 'allow me to present His Royal Highness, Prince Roland Edric Augustus.'

Roland made an elegant leg, spoiling his performance very slightly by glancing up at Sophie and Joanna as he raised his head, and by going pink in the face. It made him look rather younger than his seventeen years – which was a pity, as he already seemed so young beside his poised and elegant betrothed.

'Roland: Lady Lucia MacNeill, heiress to the chieftain's seat of Alba.'

Lucia's deep curtsey was flawless – to Sophie's secret relief, for Lucia had practised it on her endlessly, first in the sitting-room of the house in Quarry Close, and more lately behind closed and guarded doors in her Palace quarters, persisting long after Sophie's assurances that she had mastered it. ('It is not that I am afraid of doing it wrongly,' she had explained; 'I am afraid of forgetting where I am, and putting out my hand instead, as I should do at home.' Sophie could not deny that this was a risk, having done the same thing herself half a dozen times at least.)

Smiling benignantly upon her son and his betrothed, the Queen collected the rest of the party and withdrew, so that the Prince and his bride-to-be might converse in relative privacy.

Everyone with whom Lucia was at all acquainted retreated to the far end of the Queen's elegant sitting-room, leaving her alone with Prince Roland and a silent, impassive pair of Royal Guardsmen;

and Lucia, accustomed to debating learned mages and giving orders to her father's generals, could think of absolutely nothing to say. She forced herself to stop staring down at her folded hands, to raise her head and meet Roland's gaze with a smile; and at once was glad that she had done so, for he seemed equally ill at ease.

'Y-you are very like your portrait,' said Roland at last, producing a nervous half smile. His pleasant tenor voice was slightly husky, by nature or by circumstance it was impossible to say. Did he sing as beautifully as his sister?

'Am I? You are not much like yours,' Lucia said, startled by this last thought into perhaps too much honesty. 'I suppose you have grown up since then.'

Roland's pink cheeks grew pinker. 'I have grown nearly four inches,' he conceded. His hands gripped the knees of his fine buckskin breeches. Like his mother, he spoke in Latin; had he yet made any efforts towards learning Gaelic, or must Lucia begin at the beginning? Ought she to try out her English or her Français? Or might that make the conversation more awkward, rather than less?

It was maddening to know herself capable of mustering and leading an armed expedition to a distant corner of her own kingdom, of understanding Alban law and administering justice as her father's deputy, and yet freeze in agonised indecision over such a trivial question.

'Have you been out riding?' she enquired at last, still in Latin. 'You are dressed for it, I think?'

He looked down at the buckskins, at his tall polished boots, as though surprised to see them. 'I-I-I meant to go out later in the day,' he said. 'Before dinner. You are fond of riding, are you not, Lady Lucia?'

'Lucia, please,' she said, laughing a little, for Roland had been so addressing her for some time in his letters. 'I am, yes. I have had no opportunity since arriving in London, but I hope I shall do so; Joanna Callender tells me that she and her friend Gwendolen Pryce are in the habit of riding in the park every morning before breakfast – I am not perfectly sure which park she meant – and perhaps I may be able to join them on some of those excursions.'

'Miss Callender is a thorough horsewoman,' Roland said. 'Though I wish she would not insist on riding astride.'

'Whyever not?' said Lucia, baffled.

Roland blinked at her. 'Why, because – because it is not proper for a lady,' he said.

When in Rome, Lucia reminded herself, and smiled. 'In Britain, perhaps,' she said mildly, 'but in Alba I assure you it is accounted entirely proper.'

'Ah – I – of course,' Roland said, his cheeks flushing up once more. 'I meant no offence! I have been endeavouring to learn your customs, as you know; but Oscar MacConnachie is not much interested in riding, and Lady MacConnachie still less.'

'Sìleas Barra MacNeill is no horsewoman at all,' she acknowledged, and noted with approval that though Roland had referred to her cousin in the British manner, he was not confused by Lucia's using her Alban name.

A second long pause followed, in which Lucia cudgelled her brains in search of something to say. She had once hoped that they might become sufficiently acquainted through the exchange of letters as to make this meeting more reunion than halting introduction; but her correspondence with Roland had begun very formally and continued stilted and awkward, and she had concluded that if friendship and intimacy were ever to grow between them, it could not be by that means.

37

But this alliance was for the good of Alba; her father and she, with their most trusted advisors, had debated for more than a year how best to play their hand – *her* hand – and had their choice not already paid off handsomely, in the bride-gifts which had helped save her people from starvation? In the friendship between Sophie and herself which had, quite literally, helped to heal Alba's ills?

And no matter how fraught and fragile their kinship, surely no brother of Sophie's could be entirely uncongenial?

Perhaps Roland too had been thinking of Sophie, for just as the excruciating silence was threatening to stretch past breaking, he said, 'Sophie has been trying to make me promise to study at the University, when – when I come to Din Edin.'

Lucia concealed a rueful smile at this evidence that he had as much difficulty as herself in speaking aloud the words *when we are married*.

'You do not much like the notion, I collect?'

Roland's full lips quirked. 'I am not stupid,' he said – Lucia thought frantically back over her words; had she suggested that she thought him so? – 'but I am no scholar. I do not see how anyone should choose a stack of dusty books telling how mages took their tea in my great-grandfather's time, over a fast gallop through the deer-park on a fine day.'

Then his cheeks grew pink again, and his bright blue gaze slid away from hers, as he grew conscious of the oblique insult in his words.

'You are a man after my brother's heart,' said Lucia, entirely without thought; 'I predict that the two of you will get on famously.'

'I hope we shall be good friends,' Roland said, and now he smiled shyly, 'as I have been with my own brothers.' After a moment he added, in what seemed a corresponding burst of honesty, 'Mostly.'

The recognition struck Lucia, all unwelcome: it was not Sophie, at all, whom Roland put her in mind of, but her own fourteen-year-old brother, Duncan.

'I am sure you shall,' she said, returning the smile to cover her unease. 'And I hope you may change your opinion of the University, when once you have made its acquaintance. If dusty books are not so much to your taste, perhaps you may follow in Sophie's footsteps in the School of Practical Magick. The University is a famous place for making friends, you know.'

Roland looked thoughtful. 'I suppose it must be,' he said slowly; and then, in a confiding rush, 'My brother Harry is wild to study magick at Merlin College, when he is old enough. I wish he may persuade my father to let him go; but it is not at all the done thing, you see, as it is in Alba. Jo – Miss Callender went to school when she was younger, in Kemper, and she is forever telling Harry stories of her escapades. I am sure that most of them are her own invention, but,' he concluded, rather wistful, 'I think perhaps I should have liked to go to school with a crowd of other boys – besides my brothers, that is.'

A brief but painful sympathy gripped Lucia, for the little boy Roland had once been – though considering that little boy's doting mama, his panoply of playthings and carefully vetted tutors, the small army of servants undoubtedly devoted to his needs and wishes, made her sympathy recede somewhat. Nevertheless—

'Miss Callender is a good friend of yours, I suppose?' she said, before the strong temptation to say, *We shall not let our children be lonely, as you were*, could quite overcome her better judgement.

'Yes,' said Roland. 'That is – she is Sophie's sister, and a sort of assistant to Sieur Germain de Kergabet – oh, but you will know all of that already, for you met Miss Callender in Din Edin, did you not? – and of course you will have heard how all of us first became acquainted—'

'I have not, in fact,' said Lucia, taking pity on him, 'but I hope you may tell me of it, another time?' For Sophie never would consent to tell her that tale, and Lucia continued desperately curious. 'Oh! And I have brought you something.'

Roland's eyes brightened, like – alas, yes, *exactly* like – Duncan's on being offered some treat.

Lucia opened her reticule, extracted the small, flat parcel, carefully wrapped in fine linen dyed scarlet, and handed it across to Roland; their fingertips brushed, for just a moment, and he ducked his head. *We shall never make a diplomat of you at this rate, Your Royal Highness.*

He turned the parcel about in his hands – strong hands, with a horseman's calluses; Lucia spied a scraped knuckle on the right hand, and a spot of ink on the left – before carefully tugging on one end of the bow-knot. The wrapping fell away, and Roland studied the slim codex thus revealed, whose title, stamped in gold leaf upon the front board, he perhaps did not recognise as meaning *Poems of the Inner Isles.*

'You are fond of poetry, I know,' said Lucia, abruptly shy. 'It occurred to me that you might wish to become better acquainted with some of the poetry of Alba. And,' she added, 'that verses might make your study of Gaelic a less onerous task. I . . . I have not much patience for poetry myself; I enlisted the aid of my cousin Ciaran Barra MacNeill, who is my father's serjeant-at-arms and a great collector of poems, to guide my choice.'

Roland drew one index finger along the book's spine. 'I thank you,' he said, looking up at Lucia, 'very much indeed. This is a most thoughtful gift, Lady – that is, Lucia. I . . . May I hope for your assistance in translating it?'

He looked as doubtful, hopeful, and off-balance as she felt, and, perversely, Lucia took heart from the knowledge that they both were equally at sea.

'I should like that very much,' she said.

They smiled at one another, faces half-turned; the silence now seemed more hopeful than otherwise. Before either of them could make any further overture, however, Queen Edwina came bustling back again to observe their progress, and to exclaim at and fuss over Lucia's gift in a manner which made Roland blush furiously and Lucia wish she had left the accursèd book in Din Edin, and the moment dissolved once more into awkward, limping conversation.

'I understand that Lucia MacNeill has invited you to take tea with her in her rooms?' said Queen Edwina.

'Yes, ma'am,' said Sophie.

The Queen nodded. 'You may do so,' she said, as though Sophie had been asking her permission, or seeking her approval. 'And then, of course, you must speak with Roland; and afterwards—'

'Am I to be a go-between, then?' said Sophie, daring to interrupt. 'Or a spy? I must tell you, ma'am, that I have no great liking for either notion.'

Her stepmother regarded her steadily. 'Roland admires you,' she said (she did not add, *the gods alone know why*, though Sophie could hear the sentiment hovering unspoken), 'and Lucia MacNeill, I am told, considers you an intimate friend; hence His Majesty's request that you act as a guide and companion to her whilst she remains in London. All that your father and I ask of you, Edith, is that you refrain from encouraging either of them to . . . to seek out objections.'

'Sophie,' said Sophie firmly.

41

Queen Edwina blinked. 'I beg your pardon?'

'My name is Sophie, ma'am. Not Edith.'

'Your name is Edith Augusta Sophia,' said Queen Edwina, in a tone which suggested she was exercising patience in speaking to a small child, or a simpleton.

'So it is,' Sophie acknowledged, 'but *I* am Sophie.' It seemed a foolish thing to insist upon – but if so, surely the Queen's own insistence upon *Edith* was no better?

Queen Edwina frowned; before she could reply, however, Sophie drew a steadying breath and said, 'I should like us to be friends, ma'am, so far as circumstances permit. And my friends have always called me Sophie.'

It was a gamble; and, like many another such, it failed.

'You must not think me ungrateful for the care and affection you have bestowed upon my sons,' said the Queen, 'but surely you cannot imagine that anything resembling true friendship can subsist between us.' Her small, soft hands – entirely free of calluses and ink-stains – smoothed down her figured muslin skirts; then she raised her eyes again to Sophie's face and, perhaps misinterpreting her expression, added in a kinder tone, 'You need not fear that I wish you any ill, Edith.'

With some effort, Sophie refrained from wincing. *She has no power over you that you do not grant her yourself.* 'No, ma'am,' she said.

'Your father may rely on you, then, I trust, to carry out his wishes with respect to Roland and Lucia MacNeill?'

Sophie hesitated before replying, uneasy in the extreme. But if she had only to avoid *encouraging* either of them to object to the other . . .

'Yes, ma'am,' she said at last.

The Queen gave a brisk nod of satisfaction. 'You may go,' she said, gracious in victory; and Sophie, after a nonplussed moment, made her escape.

Lucia MacNeill received her with a quite astonishing enthusiasm, considering that they had last met less than a fortnight since. Having sent one of her attendants to procure the makings of tea, she then banished them all to the sitting-room and poured tea for Sophie in her bedchamber – an awkward makeshift, certainly, but no more so than many an impromptu meal they had shared in Din Edin, in the years since their bizarre joint venture on the Ross of Mull had made Lucia an intimate of the Marshalls' tiny house in Quarry Close, and Sophie a regular visitor to Castle Hill.

'May I ask you a question, Sophie?' she said.

'Of course,' said Sophie, accepting her cup of tea.

Lucia poured for herself; looked down at the delicate cup and saucer in her hands, then up at Sophie; and at last said, 'Tell me truly, what is there between Roland and your sister Joanna?'

Sophie, astonished, paused with her teacup halfway between saucer and lips. 'They were the best of friends, once,' she said, 'though there was some coolness on Roland's part, I understand, when he learnt of her part in arranging his betrothal – behind his back, as he saw it.'

'Hmm,' said Lucia. 'Yes, perhaps that may explain . . .'

They sipped their tea, both frowning in thought.

An old and half-forgotten notion occurred to Sophie – oblique complaints, a letter impatiently tossed aside – and she added, 'I have a theory that at one time Roland fancied himself in love with Joanna, a fancy in which she of course could not encourage him.'

'Oh!' Lucia's fine arched brows rose, and her lips twisted in a rueful little grimace. 'Yes, certainly your sister must have found such advances most unwelcome.'

'It is only a theory of mine, as I said,' said Sophie, wishing that she had not said anything at all. 'I may be quite wrong – though it does account for several remarks of Roland's, and one or two of Joanna's, which at the time I could not at all make out. But even if it was not all my own fancy, Lucia, it was years ago.'

'Indeed,' said Lucia. 'But in any case, it is not as though Joanna were on the hunt for a husband.'

Sophie blinked. It was true that Joanna seemed remarkably uninterested in marriage, matchmaking, and young men generally, though the Kergabets' extensive acquaintance must include – at least from the pragmatic and determinedly unsentimental perspective which Joanna appeared to have adopted for herself – many very eligible candidates. Sophie had not much expected her sister to fall desperately in love, but it seemed reasonable to suppose that she should prefer an establishment of her own to a perpetual dependence upon one or other of her relations; and, Joanna's personal fortunes being what they were, a good marriage was undoubtedly the best means of achieving that goal. But then, Joanna had political ambitions, which very few potential husbands were likely to encourage; and besides—

'She is very young to be thinking of marriage,' said Sophie.

'She is older than Roland,' Lucia pointed out, 'who certainly is *very* young to be anyone's husband, but no one else seems much inclined to object on that account. And *you* had been married nearly two years at her age, by my reckoning.'

'I had,' said Sophie, frowning at *no one else* as much as at the remarks that had followed it, 'and you know my thoughts upon that subject.'

'In any case, that is not what I meant,' said Lucia. Sipping her tea, she regarded Sophie sidelong, as though attempting to gauge the effect of her words in advance of speaking them. 'I meant – well – Gwendolen Pryce, you know.'

'What of her?' said Sophie.

Her thorough bafflement must have shown in her face, for Lucia's eyes widened and she said, sounding almost dismayed, 'Oh! Sophie, you cannot mean – do you tell me that you did not *know*?'

'Lucia MacNeill.' Sophie deposited her teacup very precisely on the corner of Lucia's dressing-table and clasped her hands together in her lap. 'You are my dear friend, and very nearly my sister, and I am enormously fond of you; but if you do not cease talking in riddles—'

Lucia had the grace to look abashed, and hastily said, 'Your sister, I believe, is not seeking the companionship of a husband because she has already a companion who suits her better.'

In itself, this did not much clarify things; but in the context of Lucia's previous remarks upon the subject of Gwendolen Pryce . . .

'Oh,' said Sophie, feeling thoroughly at sea. 'I . . . I had not considered that possibility.'

It had not escaped her notice, of course, that amongst the ladies of her father's court there were some whose eyes alighted with appreciation and affection not upon any gentleman, but upon one another; and, for that matter, Mór MacRury, one of her closest female friends in Din Edin – and once Lucia's tutor – shared with a lady lecturer in Astronomy both her lodgings and a companionship which looked to Sophie very like a happy marriage.

The notion of Joanna's being likewise companioned had never crossed her mind. But the moment she began to consider it, the fragments of observation fell into place – the constant presence of *Gwendolen says* in Joanna's letters; the small half smiles, the chaste but affectionate touches to shoulder or elbow; the tone-deaf

Joanna's apparent pleasure in sitting by the pianoforte whilst Miss Pryce played and sang; the two dark heads bent close together over a book – and she said, 'I am a fool.'

'Sophie?' said Lucia, hesitant now. 'You are not . . . distressed by this news?'

Sophie looked up sharply. 'No!' she said. 'That is . . . yes; if there is indeed so strong an attachment between my sister and her friend, I am very much distressed that Joanna should not have trusted me with the knowledge of it. But as to the nature of that attachment: no, certainly not.'

'No,' Lucia repeated. 'No, of course you would not be, in that way. But, Sophie, I should not have said anything about it to you, had I for a moment suspected that you did not know already.'

No, Sophie reflected: Lucia, so much more the diplomat than herself, would have refrained from even such delicate hinting as she had first engaged in, had she not supposed Sophie already in the secret.

'You must not blame yourself,' she said. 'I cannot think how I failed to see it. And I understand, of course, why Joanna and Miss Pryce should wish to be discreet; but I cannot understand – but never mind, Lucia! What else did you and Roland talk of, then?'

'Of riding, a little,' said Lucia. 'And poetry, and Gaelic, and—' She stopped abruptly, and for whatever she had been about to say substituted, 'this and that.' A small, sardonic smile, then: 'I fear I shall be forced to cultivate a taste for romantical poetry, or your brother will have nothing to do with me.'

'Roland is perhaps too much inclined to be romantical,' said Sophie, 'but he is not a fool – though I cannot deny that he is a very young man, with some of the follies thereof. And now you

46

are here, and have begun to be properly acquainted, I am sure he cannot fail to appreciate his good fortune.'

Lucia smiled tightly and sipped her tea. 'I do wish,' she said, returning cup to saucer, 'that your younger brother did not remind me quite so much of my own.'

Sophie winced. 'Lucia . . .'

'Will you make me a promise, Sophie?' Lucia set down her teacup altogether and gazed earnestly into Sophie's eyes.

'Of course,' said Sophie at once.

Lucia's eyes narrowed in something like amusement, and it occurred to Sophie belatedly that perhaps she ought to set more hedges round her promises to foreign heiresses, allies or not.

'I know you have been appointed my keeper and nursemaid,' said Lucia, 'and if I must have some such person, I am grateful that it should be you. But, as you are my friend, Sophie, will you promise to tell me the truth, always? Even when it may be unpalatable or inconvenient?'

'Of course,' Sophie repeated. So little for Lucia to ask of her, after all. 'Yes, of course.' She held out her right hand, Alban-fashion, and Lucia clasped it; and after a long moment's thought she said, 'I swear upon the blood we have mingled and the magick we have shared, to give you the truth as I understand it, so long as I shall live and remember.'

There was nothing particularly arcane about such an oath; but nonetheless Sophie felt something shiver through her, like a distant echo of that long-ago sharing of magick. By Lucia's pensive, grave expression, she had felt it too.

'Thank you,' she said solemnly, and waited a long moment before releasing Sophie's hand.

* * *

47

Sophie had no particular wish to speak to Roland at once; her head was spinning with new facts and with evidence dramatically realigned, and she wanted nothing so much as a quiet hour to put her thoughts in order. But Queen Edwina had made it very clear that a conversation with Roland was expected of her; and as between Roland and his mother, the choice was evident. Sophie, accordingly, went looking for her brother.

She found him wandering about in the shrubbery and persuaded him to sit with her upon a bench in the rose-garden. Taking a leaf from Joanna's book, she did not attempt subtlety but asked him outright: 'What think you of Lucia MacNeill, now that you have seen her for yourself?'

Roland looked down at his feet – rotated his left ankle, broken last summer in a fall from the saddle – rose from the bench, tugged a wilted rose off its stem, and began pulling it to pieces.

'I do not understand her,' he said at last, his tone skirting the line between forlorn and merely petulant. 'We have been corresponding for the best part of two years, and now we have met at last, and still I know next to nothing of her heart. She is always wanting to talk of some book or other – of politics, or magick, or of tactics and strategy – what sort of young lady prefers talk of politics to talk of love?'

'The sort, I imagine,' said Sophie dryly, 'who has been brought up to rule a kingdom.'

She rose to her feet, approached her brother (a little warily, for he was now grown taller than herself), and, gently removing the abused rose-leaves from his fingers, drew him back to sit with her once more upon the stone bench.

'Ned was brought up to rule a kingdom,' he said mulishly, 'and it has not prevented him from making sheep's eyes at Delphine whenever they are in the same room together, or from sitting in the garden with her, reading minstrel-tales aloud.'

Sophie refrained from pointing out that this speech had a strong flavour of Joanna Callender about it.

'I am sorry that Lucia should not have made a better first impression,' she said.

'That is not what I said,' Roland protested. The petulant tone was quite gone, and he looked genuinely astonished and not a little dismayed. 'Not at all. Only . . . Sophie, I had not the least notion what to say to her! It was bad enough when we were a kingdom apart, and writing letters to one another – I had time then to read the difficult passages over, and study how I might reply—'

'You mean, I suppose,' said Sophie, 'that you do not feel sufficiently clever to carry on an ordinary conversation with an educated woman, and that you fear being accounted her inferior – no – you fear that you will *not* be accounted her superior?'

Roland stared at her a long moment, before at last one corner of his mouth quirked – their father to the life – and he said, 'I take your point, Magistra.'

Sophie kissed his cheek and patted him on the shoulder, in her best elder-sisterly manner – which Ned, Roland, and Harry seemed able to take seriously, though Joanna (who knew her much better) never had.

'I am sure you will manage it,' she said.

CHAPTER IV

In Which Sophie Attempts
a Reconciliation

'Horns of Herne!' said Joanna, at breakfast some days later, looking up from a letter which had been waiting by her plate when she and Miss Pryce came in from their morning ride.

'Language, Jo!' said Miss Pryce. It was no very loverlike speech, to be sure; but Sophie, who had been watching Joanna and her friend closely since her conversation with Lucia, recognised the same half-exasperated, half-affectionate tone in which she herself occasionally spoke to Gray. *How in Hades did I never see it before?*

Hoping for some reply from the Oxford friends to whom she had dispatched requests to investigate their personal or College libraries and map-rooms for materials relating to the history of Lady Morgan College, Sophie herself had again been disappointed – which only increased her interest in everyone else's correspondence. She craned her neck to see the direction on Joanna's letter, and her eyebrows flew up as she recognised the hand. 'From Amelia?' she said, astonished; a letter to either herself or Joanna from their elder sister, still resident in the house in Breizh where all of them had grown up, was a rarity indeed. 'Truly this is a day of wonders and portents! What does she say?'

'That she and Lady Maëlle are coming to London,' said Joanna, still in the same tone of astonished dismay; and – continuing over Sophie's involuntary *What!* – 'at once. And it is worse even than that, because the letter was mis-sent to Carrington-street, and is nearly a fortnight old.'

Jenny sat up straighter, winced, and laid one hand on her belly, just now beginning to round out. 'We ought to have expected it, I dare say,' she said. 'Half the kingdom is coming to London at present, the better to catch a glimpse of Lucia MacNeill.'

'This must have been a very hasty decision, however,' said Sophie, frowning, 'unless, I suppose, other letters have also gone astray.'

And that was odd, too; in fact, the more she considered this odd turn of events, the odder it grew. Amelia was not, it was true, the most faithful of correspondents, but it was not like her to forget Joanna's direction altogether.

'Does she give an address in London?' Jenny enquired, in a tone which tried very hard to be neutral, and nearly succeeded.

Joanna returned her attention to Amelia's letter, and presently said, 'Yes.'

Jenny's covert expression of relief was erased almost at once by Joanna's reading out the address in question, which proved to be that of an hotel almost equally unsuited to Lady Maëlle's elevated station and to her limited means.

'I shall have to invite them to stay, of course,' she said. 'Apart from anything else, I should never live down the stain on my reputation otherwise. But, Vesta preserve us! Where am I to put them? The South Room and the Lilac Room are not likely to be finished for another month, and the plasterers have left the Rose Room in such a state . . . !'

Joanna, Miss Pryce, and Sophie – the only other occupants of the breakfast-room at present – exchanged a look.

'If Gwen and I were to share her room, Jenny,' said Joanna after a moment, 'you might give mine to Lady Maëlle, as it is the largest, and the Little North Room to Amelia.'

'That is generous of you,' said Jenny – looking, however, not at Joanna but at Miss Pryce. 'What say you, my dear?'

Miss Pryce met Jenny's gaze steadily. 'Certainly,' she said. 'I have not the least objection. Indeed, I should be happy to offer my room in place of Joanna's, but, as she says, hers is the larger.'

'That will appeal to Lady Maëlle's sense of her own consequence,' Sophie agreed. *Jenny does not know, of course*, she thought, bemused by the entire exchange. *Or . . . does she?*

'I think, however,' said Jenny, acknowledging Sophie's remark with a brief, mischievous glint of her hazel eyes, 'I shall pander a little to your sister's consequence, also, by shifting Mr Fowler into the Little North Room, and giving her the Kingfisher.'

She nodded decisively, then rose from her chair and sailed out of the room, presumably to send an invitation to Lady Maëlle de Morbihan and Miss Amelia Callender in care of Bracquart's Hotel.

Not for three days after the belated arrival of Miss Callender's letter, and the swift dispatch of Jenny's invitation, was any further word of the travellers from Breizh received in Grosvenor Square. It came in the form of a note – written, in Lady Maëlle's small, austere hand, on ivory-coloured writing-paper engraved with the elegant *B* of Bracquart's Hotel – which, upon being opened and read, caused Jenny to press her lips together and close her eyes.

Gray could not help rather wishing that Sophie's imperious cousin might persist in maintaining her independence, for the sake of poor Jenny's nerves. On the other hand, Joanna had regaled him and Sophie (over tea in the nursery, on the nursery-maid's half-day) with the tale of Lady Maëlle's last encounter with his mother, and he could not entirely suppress a competing wish to see what might happen this time.

Jenny's next invitation seemingly produced a change of heart, and on the following afternoon Lord Kergabet's carriage was dispatched to retrieve the two ladies from their temporary lodgings and bring them to Grosvenor Square.

The household, or most of it (Mrs Marshall having sniffed about *country manners* and resolutely kept her seat in the morning-room), assembled on the front steps to greet the newcomers. Standing close beside Gray, her hand gripping his behind the curtain of her skirts and his coat-tails, Sophie fairly hummed with anxious anticipation – and, as Gaël Roche opened the door of the carriage and unfolded the steps, with the thrum of sympathetic magick through the bond that connected her to Gray.

Lady Maëlle, he saw, was still as stout and straight-backed as ever, if rather more grey; the young servant who descended from the barouche box, where she had been conducting an animated conversation in Brezhoneg with Gaël, he recognised as the erstwhile Callender Hall housemaid Katell, now presumably acting in the capacity of lady's maid. Miss Callender, on the other hand, Gray should scarcely have known out of context, for the plump rose-and-golden prettiness he remembered, the tendency to look down her nose at all the world, had bloomed into a true and quiet beauty.

'Amelia!' Sophie exclaimed. 'How well you look!'

Miss Callender's composure cracked very slightly, Gray fancied, at the unfeigned enthusiasm in her stepsister's voice; but it was for a moment only. 'Your Royal Highness,' she said, making a graceful curtsey.

Sophie, hands outstretched in glad greeting, faltered and went very still. 'Amelia,' she repeated, in a doubtful tone, 'what—'

Miss Callender was spared from any immediate necessity of explaining herself, however, by Lady Maëlle's holding out her arms to Sophie, and by Sophie's flinging herself joyfully into them.

Gray said, 'How do you do, Miss Callender?'

Her lovely damask-rose face flushed a little, and she looked down, smoothing her skirts with hands grown suddenly restive. 'I am well, I thank you, Mr Marshall,' she said. 'And . . . and yourself?'

'Gray, what are you about?' said Sophie, laughing. 'Come and make your bow to Cousin Maëlle.'

He turned to them, meaning to do so, but Lady Maëlle forestalled him by approaching with both hands outstretched to clasp his own. 'How do you do, my dear?' she said, smiling so warmly and maternally at him that he blinked in surprise and almost stammered his answering 'Very well indeed; and yourself?'

'I am glad to hear it,' said Lady Maëlle, smiling. 'I fear your wife is a most frustrating correspondent; her letters tell me all about the books she is reading, and the price of butter and eggs in Din Edin, and nothing whatsoever about herself. And Joanna is grown shockingly neglectful, since she became such fast friends with this Miss Pryce of hers – Miss Pryce will be that tall, dark girl, I suppose—?'

'Yes,' said Gray. This sunny, confiding iteration of Lady Maëlle had begun to unnerve him rather, and he was not sorry when a summons from Jenny recalled them both to the duties of welcomes and introductions.

For the most part, the moves of the dance were not difficult to predict: Miss Callender and Miss Pryce, all complaisant smiles to one another's faces, could be seen eyeing each other sidelong whilst each was conversing with somebody else; Joanna and her eldest sister executed a cautious embrace, each looking as though she were remembering every cutting remark she had ever made to the other. Katell was quickly swept up by the laughing Breizhek grooms, and as quickly rescued from their attentions by Mrs Treveur, who sent Gaël and Loïc away to their work with fond exasperation.

Sophie, having been so thoroughly rebuffed, made no further attempt at conversation with her stepsister, and instead tucked her arm through her cousin's and bent her head to speak rapidly and unceasingly in her ear, pausing only to permit the occasional small gust of laughter.

As they passed into the house – and now at last Gray understood his mother's refusal to leave the morning-room, for of course she should have had to cede precedence not only to Jenny but also to Lady Maëlle – Miss Callender lingered a little, looking up at the grand facade of Jenny's house with an expression curiously both wistful and disapproving.

'After you, Miss Callender,' said Gray, for he could not leave her standing in the street alone (even so salubrious a street as the west side of Grosvenor Square). She started a little, turned her head so that her bonnet-brim hid her face, and preceded him obligingly enough up the steps and through the front door.

'I should not have known Amelia again,' Gray confessed, as Sophie and he were dressing for dinner, 'had I seen her in some other place.'

Sophie looked at him with narrowed eyes, her head upon one side. 'She is much prettier than she used to be,' she said. 'But she has forgot how to smile.'

'Yes,' said Gray, 'but that is not what I meant, exactly; she was never much given to smiling at me in any case. No; the difference is . . . Well, perhaps it is only that she has grown older, while we were not by to see it.'

'Well! If that is so, we must hope she has grown wiser, also,' said Sophie darkly, 'and will not fall prey to unscrupulous persons.'

'What sort of—' Gray began, but Sophie flapped one hand at him.

'It is an old tale,' she said, 'and I shall not tell it to you whilst we are under the same roof with Amelia; that, I think, she could not forgive me, Princess Royal or no, and I should not blame her.'

Amelia, it appeared, had taken up music again. When the ladies removed to the drawing-room after dinner, she eyed the pianoforte with eager interest – poorly concealed – and upon Jenny's sitting down upon a sofa, drew near and asked in a low voice whether she might be permitted the use of it; and when, permission granted, she sat down to play, her performance was recognisably much better than Sophie's remembrance of it.

Sophie too, insofar as the other demands upon her time permitted, had been renewing her acquaintance with Jenny's pianoforte, so different from the scuffed and battered (though always meticulously tuned) third-hand instrument that had graced the tiny front room of the house in Quarry Close. Might Amelia's renewed interest in this once-shared pursuit open the way to some manner of reconciliation?

Certainly Sophie's efforts in that direction thus far had not enjoyed much success. Enquiries after the health of tenant farmers and half-remembered neighbours in Breizh had been answered in a reproving tone which reminded Sophie, more pointedly than mere words could have done, that she might at any time have come to see them for herself, and had not. Offers of excursions to see the sights of London were politely but firmly declined, and attempts by either party to interest the other in her pet topic – in Sophie's case, her new-found (or renewed) fascination with Lady Morgan College and its history; in Amelia's, the London season – tended to disintegrate with alarming rapidity into childish squabbling.

On one warm, close evening, astonishingly free of engagements and scented with the roses Mrs Treveur had set in silver bowls all over the house, Sophie extracted from her music-case the collection of (mostly Alban) songs which she had learnt and painstakingly transcribed during her years in Din Edin, and, turning to Gray, said, 'What song shall we have tonight, love?'

'"Fear a' Bhàta",' said Gray at once.

'Are you sure?' Sophie cast a doubtful glance at Lady Maëlle, at Amelia. But Gray nodded, and, reasoning that, of all those present, only they two had enough Gaelic to appreciate the melancholy import of the lyrics, she shook out her fingers, arranged her music on the rack, and began to play – and, for the first time since coming back to London, to sing.

She scrupulously suppressed the magick that tried to weave itself into her song; nevertheless, by the final verse, Amelia had laid down her fancy-work and drifted close to the pianoforte, studying the hand-notated music over Sophie's shoulder.

'You sing so beautifully,' she said, low, when Sophie lifted her fingers from the keys, and – astonishingly – settled herself on the bench beside Sophie, so close that their elbows touched. 'I had forgot how you used to sing, when we were small. Until you stopped.'

With enormous effort, Sophie contrived not to gape at her. 'I never stopped,' she said, after a long moment. 'I sang to Joanna, always. But out in the park, and in the fields, because the Professor forbade it. Or had you forgot that, also?'

Amelia flinched – pressed her lips together – turned away. Then she stood abruptly, retreated to the sofa, and seated herself a careful distance from Joanna and Miss Pryce, who had their heads bent together over a book, and took no notice of her.

Sophie's stomach churned with a sickly stew of guilt and grief and half-forgotten anger, and she could not think how to apologise.

They met again the next morning across the breakfast-table, and Sophie put down her knife and fork and took her courage in both hands.

'Amelia,' she said.

Amelia looked up.

'I am sorry,' said Sophie. 'For what I said to you last night.' She tamped down her reflexive annoyance at Amelia's expression of surprise. 'It is not your fault that the Professor so detested the cuckoo in his nest, and encouraged you to detest me likewise. And when you paid me a compliment, I ought not to have thrown it back in your face.'

Amelia blinked, and for what seemed a very long time said nothing.

At last she looked down at her plate, then up again at Sophie, and said, 'I was always so very jealous of you.'

'Of *me*?' said Sophie, incredulous. 'Because I was not permitted to go to school, or to read the books I wished to read, or to—'

58

'Because Mama loved you so.' Amelia's words cut across hers like ice cracking. 'You, and no one else in the world – certainly not her *other* daughters.' She laughed; her laughter sounded as though it hurt her. 'Of course I see now why she could not love *me*. I ought to have known, even then.'

Tears stung Sophie's eyes. *What has become of the world, that I should have cause to weep for Amelia?*

'It was not because you were not hers,' she said, and swallowed against the lump in her throat. 'It was nothing to do with you, at all – with either of you.'

'Do you think I did not know it?' Amelia demanded, in a sort of harsh half whisper. 'Papa and she were entirely unsuited to one another, and ought never to have married; and she could not love either of us, because we were his children.'

Unsuited. Sophie hesitated in an agony of doubt: to tell Amelia, or not to tell her, that her beloved papa had repeatedly forced himself on Sophie's mother? *Mother Goddess, did he do the same to Amelia's mother? No, surely not.* But the thought niggled, and Sophie could not bring herself to inflict it upon Amelia.

'Mama may not have loved you or Jo as she loved me,' she said at last, 'but she loved you well enough to take thought for your safety, and seek to spare you pain.'

'I do not see how,' said Amelia, frowning; too late, Sophie recalled that Amelia did not know the truth of her stepmother's death – had never read, in Queen Laora's last letter to her beloved cousin, the words, *I weep to think of my girls left in his power.*

It was not an explanation which could be given in a quarter-hour's time, over breakfast; and, indeed, Sophie had not the least idea where to begin, nor whether she had any right to tell her mother's secrets.

'You may ask Cousin Maëlle, if you doubt me,' she said instead. 'She knew Mama far longer and better than I.'

Amelia was tearing a bread-roll into tiny pieces, and resolutely not raising her eyes from her busily working hands. Sophie watched this process to its natural conclusion – the sight was oddly hypnotic – as she collected her thoughts.

'We were none of us very well served by our childhood, I think,' she said at last. 'But it does not follow that we must carry our hurts like stored-up treasures all our lives. We were good friends, once, Amelia, as well as sisters; might we not try to be friends again?'

Or, at the least, to lay down our arms and cease to be sworn enemies?

'We might have gone on being friends, if you had not turned Joanna against me,' said Amelia – not accusingly, but as though stating a settled fact; and before Sophie could draw breath to object, 'And driven off every suitor I ever had, for now I do not suppose I am likely to have any more; and if you had not the power to turn me out of my own home—'

'Catharine Amelia Callender.'

Amelia's litany of accusations cut off abruptly, giving way to a silent, furious glare.

Sophie swallowed hard. *If that is how she sees things, I wonder that she should have been willing to come within a hundred miles of me.*

'You may believe whatever you wish about Joanna,' she said, 'and I freely confess that I once kept watch whilst she put half a dozen frogs in Walter Mandeville's bed, because by that time we both of us knew better than to attempt to tell you of his improper advances to the housemaids.'

She overrode Amelia's squeak of outrage, for she had one last thing to say: 'But I have never had any intention of turning you out of that house, Amelia, and never shall have; you may think what you like of me, but you must never think *that*. You shall always have a home there, if you wish it.'

Then, not waiting to see or hear Amelia's reaction to this, Sophie pushed back her chair from the table, stood, and left the room, abandoning her unfinished breakfast; the sight of it made her stomach churn.

She strode blindly along this corridor, down that staircase, and when at length she came back to full awareness of her surroundings, she found herself in the small park at the centre of the square, standing before a stone bench not unlike the one on which she had sat with Gray and Jenny, long ago, when her life was just beginning to unravel. The sun was shining, and the scents of chamomile and clover, box and elm and chestnut, rose up around her like a blessing – as though Hegemone, goddess of plants and growing things, had led her here to soothe away her irritation of spirits.

Sophie shook her head and chuckled wanly. What a notion! Yet the warm sun and the scents of green things growing were already beginning to loosen the knot of old guilt and new hurt that had gathered beneath her ribs, so that she felt able to breathe again, and even perhaps to think.

Lady Maëlle found her there, nearly an hour later, still wrestling with her conscience.

'Your mama loved gardens,' she said, settling herself beside Sophie on the sun-warmed bench, 'even your stepfather's gardens, for all that she grew to loathe the man himself. A garden is its own creature, you know; we may say to ourselves, *This belongs to me*, but in truth a garden belongs only to itself, and to the gods.'

'I always loved the Professor's gardens, also,' Sophie admitted. 'They seemed quite a different world from the house itself. And they were always full of beautiful things – even in winter – and of hiding-places.'

'Indeed,' said Lady Maëlle, with a small, enigmatic smile. 'And what makes you hide amongst the oak and the ash and the bonny ivy-tree today, *ma petite*?'

For the oak, and the ash, and the bonny ivy-tree / They flourish at home in my own country, Sophie's mind supplied, catching at the quotation and fleshing out the melody of the Border-country song. She waved it away impatiently.

'Amelia,' she said, looking down at her feet. 'All of my attempts to make friends with her seem to run aground in the same way. Now she has accused me of turning Joanna against her – she believes I mean to turn her out to starve—'

Lady Maëlle startled her anew by curling one arm about her and drawing Sophie's head down to rest against her shoulder. 'You must give her time,' she said, shifting into Brezhoneg, 'and a little space to think.'

'Time?' Sophie demanded. She sat up straight. 'Space? She has scarce set eyes on me these past five years!'

'Perhaps,' Lady Maëlle said gently, 'you might consider the matter from Amelia's point of view. Suppose that rather than having been hurt yet again by a stepfather who had long and openly resented your existence, by the use he attempted to make of you, you had been betrayed by the father whom you loved wholeheartedly, believing yourself beloved in return.'

'Oh,' said Sophie, in a very small voice. Of course she had

believed herself to be considering Amelia's feelings – why else offer her the use of the house which she so loved? – but evidently to much less purpose than she had supposed.

'And suppose further,' Lady Maëlle went on, 'that rather than emerging from your trials possessed of a powerful magickal talent, a doting husband and devoted friends, a royal title, and an unlooked-for opportunity to attain the education you have long dreamt of, you had found yourself branded the child of a traitor, almost friendless and without prospects, through no fault of your own—'

'If I could give the house and the gardens and all of it to Amelia and Joanna, I should have done it long ago, and gladly!' Sophie interrupted, unable to keep silent any longer. 'I did not ask to be given it – Gray did not ask – but he consented to it, only because we should then be able to offer them a home there! . . . And you, of course, ma'am,' she added.

Lady Maëlle inclined her head with a wry smile. 'And I thank you both for that kindness,' she said. 'But I am well accustomed to depending upon the hospitality of others; and you must consider, too, that I left Callender Hall a servant, and returned to it as myself. Your sister Amelia was its mistress once; to expect gratitude for your generosity in making her a perpetual guest in the house which she expected that she – or at any rate her husband – should one day inherit, was perhaps unreasonable.'

'I have never asked for Amelia's gratitude, either,' said Sophie tightly, 'or anyone else's. She is perfectly free to consider herself mistress of, of *that house,* if she likes—'

'But she is not mistress of it, truly, nor ever shall be,' said Lady Maëlle, gently, 'though she loves every room of it, whilst you cannot bear even to speak its name. And Amelia knows it, if you do not.'

'What is it you wish me to *do*, Cousin Maëlle?' Sophie's demand sounded, to her own ears, mortifyingly like an infant's pleading.

'Think on it, child,' said Lady Maëlle.

Then she kissed Sophie's unresisting cheek and took herself away.

CHAPTER V

In Which Amelia Is Inscrutable, and Lucia Hears a Tale

'Jenny,' said Sophie hesitantly – this conversation had seemed much more advisable in the abstract, turned over and over in the back of her mind whilst the most of her attention was occupied with Amelia, than it did now, in the flesh – 'has either Joanna or Miss Pryce any thought of marrying, do you suppose?'

Jenny, blessedly calm, looked up from the letter she was composing, put down her pen, and gave Sophie a measuring look.

'I should not think so,' she said at last; and after another long moment, 'Why do you ask?'

'Joanna is my sister,' said Sophie – not unreasonably, she felt.

'But Miss Pryce is not,' said Jenny. 'For that matter, Joanna's being your sister is a perfectly sound reason for asking *her* what plans she may have for the future, but it is no reason at all to ask *me.'*

There followed a long and increasingly uncomfortable silence, which Jenny made no move to assist Sophie in breaking; and at length Sophie said, 'I only – they are both of them handsome and clever, and if they have not much fortune between them, they have at least the great advantage of your patronage; I expected them both to be besieged with suitors, and yet it is no such thing. And,' she added, 'as Jo is a ward of the Crown until she marries, I should have expected her to be looking about her in search of some independence, if for no other reason.'

'Sophie,' said Jenny firmly, 'if I believed Joanna's life to be in jeopardy, I should not hesitate to divulge any confidence of hers which might assist in saving it. As things stand, however, I can only repeat that whatever questions you may have about your sister's plans, you must ask her yourself.'

'Yes, of course,' said Sophie, in a chastened tone, and bent her head to her sewing.

All the same, she reflected, *I have my answer: Jenny knows something about Jo and Miss Pryce, which she considers none of my affair.*

She was not altogether pleased to have so provoked Jenny, for whom she felt enormous affection and esteem; but short of asking Joanna outright, *Does Jenny know?*, this had seemed the best means of mapping out the territory.

In any case, Joanna and Miss Pryce – allowing for the dampening presence of Mrs Edmond Marshall – seemed well contented; Amelia, on the other hand, did not.

'Amelia is hiding something,' Sophie announced, almost before the door had closed behind her.

They had been in London only a fortnight, and already Gray was growing weary of the daily tensions of living in Jenny's house not only with Sophie, Joanna, and Miss Callender, but with his mother and all the various persons whom she had also contrived to antagonise, and beginning to think longingly of Din Edin – of Oxford – even, almost, of Glascoombe in

Kernow, which at least offered one set the less of familial grudges to navigate.

Had Sophie not been bound to her shepherding of Lucia MacNeill more or less by royal command, he should have been urging an end to the visit several days since; he had even, for the first time, begun to consider begging the hospitality of the Royal Palace – though, knowing Sophie's opinion upon that subject, he had not yet dared mention it to her.

'Oh?' he said now, turning. 'Why do you say so?'

Sophie seated herself at the dressing-table and began pulling the pins from her hair. 'She had a letter this morning at breakfast,' she said, 'which must have given her some sort of shock, for she turned very pale; do you not recall Cousin Maëlle's asking her whether she was quite well?'

'Vaguely,' said Gray, from within the folds of the shirt which he was pulling off over his head. 'I confess that your sister Amelia was occupying very little of my attention at the time, as Mr Fowler was telling me—'

There was a brisk knock upon the door; Gray hastily struggled back into his shirt as Sophie called, '*Quo vadis?*'

The door-handle turned, the door opened a few inches, and Joanna's face peered round its edge. 'May I come in?' she enquired – rather belatedly, in Gray's view.

'Come in or go away, as you like,' said Sophie, 'but in either case, do shut the door, Jo.'

Joanna opened the door, stepped through it, and closed it again behind her; Sophie dropped the last hairpin on the table-top and took up her hairbrush.

'Let me,' said Gray. She half turned towards him, holding out the brush; he took it from her, but, out of sight of Joanna, indulged himself by running his free hand through the silky mass of her hair before setting to work.

Joanna folded herself into the armchair onto which Gray had recently flung his coat, tucking up her bare feet beneath the hem of her dressing-gown.

'Sophie,' she said, 'what ails Amelia, do you suppose?'

'I have been asking myself the same question,' said Sophie. She repeated the tale of the letter for the benefit of Joanna, who had come in too late from her morning's ride to see its arrival for herself, and concluded: 'She would not say what was in the letter, nor who had sent it. And I cannot blame her – she is not a child, and her correspondence is her own business! – but there was something in her face, and her voice – I do not know Amelia so well now as I once did, but I should have sworn that she was truly frightened.'

Gray's hands stilled. 'Frightened,' he repeated. 'Now, what could frighten the indomitable Miss Callender?'

'Gray,' said Sophie severely, meeting his gaze in the glass with her eyebrows drawn together. 'I am entirely serious; I beg you will not make fun.'

'I was not making fun,' he protested, startled. 'Why should you think so?'

Sophie twisted round to look at him straight on; from the armchair, Joanna regarded him with a deeply sceptical expression.

'Truly,' he said. 'Have I never told you how much your sister alarmed me, when first I came to Breizh? The proud and elegant Miss Callender, undisputed mistress of all she surveyed, very evidently finding fault with my very existence, and liable to report my least misdeed to the Professor at once! I was never so much relieved as when she determined me to be of no consequence, and ceased to pay me any attention.'

As he spoke, an expression of disbelief had spread over Sophie's face; now she rose to her feet and hopped nimbly up to stand upon the seat of her chair, so as to lay her hands on Gray's shoulders and smile down at him – a small, rueful smile. He wrapped one arm about her to steady her.

'I was eaten up with jealousy,' Sophie said, after a moment – very softly, for his ears alone – 'though I do not think I understood it at the time. All the young men I had ever met paid court to Amelia, you see, and I had never begrudged her their attentions; but for some reason I could not bear that you should be like them.'

'"For some reason", aye,' Gray agreed solemnly. 'I see. Come down from there, my green-eyed goose.

'Now,' he said, when Sophie had resumed her seat, and he his brushing, 'my question stands: who, or what, might she be frightened of? I do not suppose you chanced to catch a glimpse of the letter, or of its direction?'

'I did not,' Sophie admitted. 'We were placed across from each other, as you may recall' – Gray had no particular recollection of anyone's placement at the breakfast-table, apart from his own, but did not like to say so – 'but I did see the envelope for just a moment, and it bore no frank.'

'An express?' said Gray, surprised. He had finished brushing out Sophie's hair, and was braiding it into a long plait. How his brothers would jeer at him! And how comfortable to discover that he no longer cared what either of them thought. 'Or delivered by hand?'

'I have not the least idea,' said Sophie, 'though we should have heard an express arrive, I think, as the breakfast-room overlooks the square.'

Gray considered this. 'It does not seem very likely that Amelia should take any of us into her confidence,' he said, tying off the plait, 'but surely if something were very much amiss, she would confide in Lady Maëlle? Or,' he added more confidently, 'Lady Maëlle would find it out.'

'That is what *I* should do,' said Joanna – not, perhaps, an entirely accurate assessment – 'but only the gods know how Amelia may proceed.'

'What I cannot understand,' said Sophie, 'is why they should be here at all. Amelia has never once set foot in London since the Professor's trial, to my certain knowledge; no one could suppose that she had any wish to see me, or to see you, Jo – so why, then, should she choose to come here *now*, when you and I are both to spend all the summer in Town, as we have never done since that year?'

'Half the kingdom has come to London to see Lucia MacNeill,' said Gray, not unreasonably. 'Might not Lady Maëlle have wished to do the same, and brought your sister along with her?'

'Oh, but it was Amelia's notion to come,' said Joanna. 'Katell told me – she was a whole fortnight persuading Cousin Maëlle to make the journey.'

'Was she, indeed?' Sophie pounced on this admission. 'But why on *earth* . . . What did Katell say, exactly?'

'I hardly know,' said Joanna, which was not precisely true. 'It was a perfectly ordinary conversation, Sophie, not an interrogation. She said . . .' She tilted her head back and closed her eyes briefly, casting her mind back. She could not, *would* not repeat everything Katell had told her. 'Amelia complained of the utter lack of eligible young men in the neighbourhood of Cal—of your house,' she said at last, 'or so Katell told me, and said that if she were not to die a miserable spinster, living on sufferance in someone else's home—'

Gray winced, and Sophie said (speaking under her breath, but not so inaudibly as she perhaps supposed), 'How *dare* she!'

'—she must have a season in London, as she ought to have had when she was my age, so that she might have some opportunity of marrying, even if she cannot hope to marry well.'

'I must say,' said Gray, with a thoughtful frown, 'that does not seem a likely tactic to succeed with Lady Maëlle.'

'Oh! No, it did not succeed at all,' said Joanna. 'I only mention it because it shows that Amelia cannot have been thinking clearly; she knows Cousin Maëlle as well as either of us – better now, perhaps – and she may not be exceptionally clever, but she is not *stupid*. No; she persuaded her, according to Katell, by other means entirely – appeals to her better nature, and reasoned arguments, and on at least one occasion, tears. But—'

She paused, biting back the words, *But I have seen Amelia set her cap at many a young man, and this . . . is something else entirely.*

'I do not pretend to any expertise in the matter,' said Gray, slow and thoughtful, 'but it seems me that if your sister is come here in order to hunt for a husband, she is going about it in a very odd manner indeed.'

Sophie hummed, not quite in agreement, and frowned at her reflection in the mirror. 'I *do* think something is amiss,' she said; and after a moment, more cheerfully, 'but I do not suppose much harm can come to Amelia, whilst she is living in this house.'

The following morning, however, when Miss Callender appeared in the breakfast-room (of which Gray and Sophie had hitherto been in sole possession), looking pale and shadow-eyed and strung tight with some unspecified anxiety, Sophie startled all three of them by exclaiming, 'Amelia, what is the matter? My dear, you look very ill – is there nothing we can do to help you?'

Miss Callender looked properly gobsmacked and, for just a moment, as though she were considering telling Sophie her troubles. But the moment passed, and she gathered her considerable dignity tight about her and said, 'I did not sleep well; I believe I have a little cold. It is nothing of consequence.'

Then she sat down at the table, helped herself to scones and apricot jam, and rang for a fresh pot of tea.

A tense near-silence prevailed in the breakfast-room until Treveur came in with the tea, at which point Sophie, still looking rather shaken, excused herself and fled.

Gray took a deep breath. 'Miss Callender,' he said, and then – for they were close kin now, in a way – amended, 'Amelia, if ever Sophie or I may be of any help—'

'You are very kind,' she said evenly. 'I assure you, there is not the slightest need.'

She took a last sip from her cup, replaced it silently and precisely in its saucer, and rose from the table. 'Good morning, Mr Marshall,' she said, and left the breakfast-room.

Kindly but comprehensively rebuffed – the rebuff entirely expected, the kindness an unprecedented gift – Gray finished his breakfast in thoughtful silence.

Sophie is quite right: something is much amiss here.

The Princess Delphine was fond of walking in the gardens of the Royal Palace, and Prince Edward equally fond of indulging his wife. As, not for the first time, Lucia, Sophie, Roland, and Joanna all agreed that they had rather be out of doors than not, the excursion diffidently proposed by Delphine quickly became a general enterprise.

This afternoon their path took them through the inner gardens, towards the main fountain and the slope down towards the river, where, not twenty feet from the steep-cut bank, could be seen a large, oddly-shaped green . . . thing.

'What is that?' enquired Lucia, pointing – not only because she was curious, but because a silence had fallen, and if she could not think of anything to say she could at any rate provoke one of her companions to do so.

'The maze!' said Joanna. 'Has no one told you of it, Lucia?'

No one had; whilst Edward and Delphine fell gradually farther and farther behind them, therefore, Joanna and Roland (with occasional interjections from Sophie) regaled Lucia with the somewhat baroque history of the Palace maze.

It had been commissioned, Joanna explained, by Roland and Sophie's distant ancestor, the seventh King Henry, and designed by an ancestor of Madame de Courcy, wife of the British ambassador in Din Edin.

'He was raised to the peerage for his pains,' said Joanna, 'but was later executed because one of Henry the Great's mistresses lost herself in it.'

'What became of her?' asked Lucia. It must have been something dire – though had not Henry the Great famously had several of his numerous wives beheaded? 'Did she . . . starve to death, or—'

'No,' said Joanna thoughtfully, 'though that would make a far better tale.'

Roland stifled a snort of laughter behind his hand, and strode off to hurry Edward and Delphine along.

Sophie, however, frowned at her sister and said, 'Jo, how can you?' in a tone of genuine reproach.

'She did not starve to death,' said Joanna to Lucia, ignoring both of them, 'but she wandered for some hours before she was missed, well after the sun went down; and when one of the gardeners found her and brought her out, she was raving of disembodied voices whispering in her ears, cold hands clutching at her in the darkness, wailing and sobbing from thin air.'

Sophie shivered.

'Shades?' said Lucia doubtfully. 'Or someone playing a very unpleasant joke?'

'It might have been either, for all I know of the circumstances,' said Joanna, shrugging, 'or something else entirely. Some drug or poison, perhaps, which induced hallucinations. No one has ever discovered what, exactly, befell her in the maze, but she continued persuaded that the maze was haunted by the shades of those who had perished in it – which, so far as I know, no one ever has. She refused to remain any longer at court, and in the end – after Madame de Courcy's ancestor was beheaded over the affair – the King arranged a marriage for her, and she retired to a life of utter obscurity on her husband's country estate. She lived to a ripe old age, but never recanted her tale.'

They pondered this in silence, accompanied by the gentle plashing of the fountain.

'A pity she did not know a finding-spell to bring her safely back to the fountain,' said Lucia at last.

'It would not have helped her,' said Sophie. 'The maze is not only yew-trees; it is woven through with spells to dampen findings and summonings. Like an interdiction, you know, but more specific. It is one of the tasks of the Court mages to maintain the spells. Though, I suppose,' she added thoughtfully, 'it may not always have been so. I wonder – were the dampening-spells worked on the seedling trees, to grow with them, or were they added later? Perhaps the maze was not thought difficult enough without them? Do you suppose . . .'

'You must both have walked the maze, I suppose?' said Lucia, in an attempt to reel in Sophie's wandering attention. 'Perhaps you might show me the route.'

'I have walked it many times,' said Joanna, 'and—' She broke off abruptly, and began again with, 'But Sophie and I are expected in Grosvenor Square this evening, and I fear we have already overstayed our time.'

Sophie, glancing up to gauge the angle of the sun, seemed about to object; Joanna trod on her toes, however, and she subsided. Lucia pretended not to have seen any of this.

'In any case,' Joanna continued cheerfully, 'Roland knows the maze better than either of us.'

Lucia eyed Roland, who appeared to have given up his brother and sister-in-law as a lost cause and was making his way back towards the fountain, and turned this notion over in her mind. Joanna was transparently throwing them together; but was it because she believed Roland might welcome such an excursion, or simply from a sense of her duty to promote this match?

Less thinking, Lucia MacNeill, and more acting in your own interests.

'I shall ask him,' she said.

She carefully did not look at Sophie, for she was remembering their conversation of a few days past, during one of Queen Edwina's soirées.

'How does Roland go on in his Gaelic lessons?' Sophie had inquired.

'Very well indeed,' said Lucia, 'when—' She caught back the words *when he can be bothered about them*, and instead said, 'when he can find the time to study.'

Sophie had not been at all taken in. 'He is young yet,' she had said quietly, slipping into Gaelic.

And Lucia, gritting her teeth: 'That is very plain.'

'Lucia, Roland admires you, and thinks you very clever and rather formidable. He is half afraid to speak to you on any serious subject, lest he say something which will lower your opinion of him beyond repair—'

'Sophie.' Lucia closed her eyes. 'Tell me truly, is Roland in love with someone else?'

'Why should you suppose such a thing?'

'You made me a promise, Sophie,' said Lucia, as gently as she could manage. If what she suspected were indeed so, she must find some way of conveying to him – without giving offence – that so long as he upheld his end of their bargain, he might do as he liked besides; but all depended on accurate intelligence.

'So I did; and I have no notion of breaking it. You suppose me deeper in my brother's confidences than I have ever been. I believe . . .' Sophie paused, gazing at nothing in particular, before continuing: 'I believe he had persuaded himself in love with . . . with some idea of you, constructed from your portrait and perhaps your letters, and from his own imagination—'

'And I am nothing like the Lucia MacNeill of Roland's imagination,' said Lucia. 'Well, I am sorry to disappoint him, but, for the matter of that, it was never my intention to promise myself to a man who prefers poetry to statecraft.'

Sophie turned back to her. 'Do you mean to cry off, then?'

'"Cry off"?' Lucia repeated the English phrase – she

recognised the words, but what did they mean together?

'Put an end to your betrothal,' said Sophie, reverting to Gaelic; and, while Lucia was still gaping at her, 'I know you are empowered to do so, irrespective of your father's wishes; even had I not known it before, I received separate lectures on the subject from my father, my stepmother, and Joanna, all of whom apparently feared that I might encourage you to seek happiness elsewhere.'

'Sophie, what has *happiness* to do with it?' Of course, one had rather be happy than not, all else being equal; but could even so romantical a person as Sophie have so profoundly mistaken Lucia's point?

Now it was Sophie's turn to gape, though almost at once she smoothed her face into stillness. 'It is all I wish for either of you,' she said, low. 'For any of those I love.'

Lucia had drawn a deep breath, then – released it – squared her shoulders. They could have only a few more stolen moments in this quiet corner, before they were winkled out and borne off to be displayed to Her Majesty's guests.

'I did not mention this because I resent Roland's affection for any other person,' she said. 'I do not wish him unhappy – or myself, either – but, Sophie, you must know that my father and yours, in agreeing to this match, were not acting to secure any one individual's happiness but in the best interests of their kingdoms, of their people. Our people. To throw such considerations away—'

Sophie, when well and in control of her magick, was more adept at keeping her feelings from showing on her face than anyone else Lucia had ever met, her own famously unflappable father included. To one who knew her well, however, that inscrutable expression was itself a signal of danger ahead: Sophie would not trouble to conceal her state of mind so thoroughly unless there were something of great import to conceal.

They had eyed each other for a long, fraught moment, until Lucia's own words came back to her and she understood what she had just said, and to whom.

'I am my father's heir, Sophie,' she said, very gently, 'and this marriage was my own idea as much as his. My case is not at all the same as your mother's, or yours.'

Sophie's expression had relaxed slightly, so that she looked merely cautious, rather than frozen like a fox caught by lantern-light. 'I . . . No, I suppose not,' she conceded, and the topic had mercifully been dropped.

Now, fetching out a smile for Roland as he came within speaking distance, Lucia felt uncomfortably under scrutiny – if Sophie and Joanna meant to go back to Grosvenor Square, why could they not go at once?

'Our thanks for a charming afternoon,' said Joanna, winking impishly at Lucia. She clasped Lucia's hand and stretched on tiptoe to press a sisterly kiss to Roland's cheek; then, almost before Sophie had made her own farewells, took her sister by the hand and towed her away across the lawn.

PART TWO

London

CHAPTER VI

In Which Lucia and Roland
Make a Discovery

Edward and Delphine were nearly within earshot now, at last; they appeared to be gazing lovingly into one another's eyes and no doubt were cooing endearments, a performance which Lucia did not greatly care to witness yet again. She looked at Roland, and back at the maze.

Her curiosity had been pricked by the others' tales; the sun was growing warm, and the maze would provide some shade; and as between exploring a maze and watching Edward and Delphine make sheep's eyes at one another . . .

'You must have walked the maze many times, I suppose?' she said, striking out towards it, though without quickening her pace.

'Of course,' said Roland.

He smiled at her, suddenly, briefly; so unexpected was it that she could not help grinning back.

'Once,' he said, 'Ned and Harry and I so lost ourselves in it that by the time the undergardeners found us and brought us out, we had missed our dinner. We had never seen Nurse so cross – I suppose she must have been frightened out of her wits, not only of our coming to real harm, but of the consequences to herself – and she forbade us to step even one foot into the maze. Of course after *that*, we could not rest until we had conquered it.'

'Of course not,' Lucia agreed. Roland darted his eyes at her, dubious: did he suspect her of making sport of him? 'I quite understand the necessity,' she said. 'My cousin Morag MacNeill and I once climbed to the top of Arthur's Seat on a moonless night, only to prove her elder brother wrong, for he said that we should be too frightened to do it.'

'And were you?' said Roland.

She had his ear now, plainly, for good or ill.

'Quite terrified,' she said cheerfully. 'Either one of us alone, I dare say, could not have got past the castle gate in broad daylight. We egged each other on, however, and when the sun rose, there we were, asleep like puppies in the lee of a boulder on the top of the hill. We had meant to go back straight away, you see, so that we should not be missed, but from Castle Hill to the top of Arthur's Seat is a very long walk for a child of ten; and there comes a point, it appears, when exhaustion overcomes terror, even in the dead of night.'

Roland produced an admiring whistle, then cleared his throat self-consciously.

'And you?' said Lucia. They were standing very near the entrance to the maze now, and much better that he should be thinking of his own past deeds – or misdeeds – than of hers. 'What came of your clandestine explorations?'

A fleeting grin; another sideways glance. 'Ned's tutor set him the tale of Theseus and the Labyrinth,' said Roland. 'I rather suspect him of doing it on purpose. And we begged a ball of twine from the kitchens—'

'Oh!' exclaimed Lucia, who had been studying her Ovid, at Sophie's instigation. 'The Minotaur, and Ariadne and her thread!'

'Yes, exactly,' said Roland.

Lucia studied his profile; he was smiling now, truly – the deep, slow-blooming smile that dimpled his cheeks and narrowed his eyes to gleaming slits, fringed by honey-gold lashes. He was rather appealing, in point of fact, when he smiled.

'Harry and I were all for rolling up the twine again on our way out,' he said, 'once we had found the centre at last, and could prove we had been there. But Ned had thought it through – Ned is not so quick a thinker as some, you know, but there is not a more methodical fellow in the kingdom, I am sure! – and he said, "If we do that, we may not be able to find our way in the next time."'

'That is so,' said Lucia, interested by this view of Edward-as-strategist. She glanced up; Edward and Delphine would hear them in a moment, always supposing they had any attention to spare from one another.

'So instead,' Roland continued, oblivious, 'he made us go over and over the path until we knew it cold, and leave signs which no one else would recognise – just in case; and *then* we rolled up the twine and gave it back to the kitchen-maids. Some of the signs are there still.'

That was encouragement, surely?

'Will you show me?' said Lucia. 'That is, if you are not sworn to secrecy.'

Roland blinked – glanced again over his shoulder at his brother and sister-in-law, still some yards away – looked at Lucia.

Then he turned on his heel, cupped his hands around his mouth, and called, 'Ned! Delphine!'

They raised their heads; Edward shaded his eyes with his free hand and quickened his pace.

'We are going into the maze,' said Roland, when they drew near enough for speech: not a question but a firm statement of fact.

Prince Edward's eyes lit – a tiny spark, but a spark

nonetheless – and he said, 'I have not been into the maze for . . . it must be years! Delphine, we must go with them; you shall like it of all things, I am sure.'

Delphine did not look as though she expected to like it; she pressed closer to Edward's side and in a small voice said, 'Is it not . . . Are there not unquiet shades within? Ought we to disturb them?'

'That is only a tale, Delphine,' Roland scoffed. So dismissive was his tone that Lucia, though she agreed with him entirely and found Delphine rather trying at the best of times, winced a little; Edward's glare could have melted steel.

'You need not go in if you do not like it,' said Edward, kindly (no one, thought Lucia, would guess that he was only a year Delphine's elder), 'but there is no truth in those tales that the maze is haunted, I promise you. And Roland and I know the way very well; we shall not lose ourselves.'

'I . . . I had really rather not,' said Delphine. Was she actually shivering? 'Ned, I am a little cold; may we not go indoors now?'

Roland and Lucia, for the moment utterly in sympathy with one another, exchanged a look of disbelief: was Delphine sickening for something, that she should feel a chill in the sun-warmed, almost breezeless Palace gardens?

Edward looked anxiously down at his wife, and up at his brother. 'Of course,' he said, but doubt edged his tone. 'But, Roland, it does not seem to me proper that you and Lady Lucia should be wandering the maze unaccompanied. Perhaps you may put off your excursion for another day.'

Lucia, who had been studying Delphine, did not at once appreciate Edward's objection; when its implication dawned, she rolled her eyes (which made him wince) and said, 'Edward, I give you my word of honour that we shall behave with the utmost propriety.'

'Indeed, Ned,' Roland added, though Lucia remarked that he took care not to look at her, 'you ought not to judge others by your own habits. Good morning, Delphine; I hope you may soon be quite recovered.'

And with courtly ceremony he turned aside, neatly snubbing his elder brother, and bowed Lucia ahead of him into the maze.

The yew hedges that made up the walls of the maze were carefully pruned and shaped to prevent them growing together overhead, but so high were the walls that the moment of entering the maze felt to Lucia like passing from broad day into twilight. She paused to look about her, trying whether she could guess which was the correct turning to take or spot the first of the signs left by Roland and his brothers.

'I yield,' she said at last, finding that she could do neither. 'I am in your hands, my lord; lead on!'

She spoke half in jest – an appeal both to Roland's self-consequence and to the sly, mischievous sense of humour which she could nearly always see lurking beneath his armour of princely dignity – and was delighted to see him take up her small challenge.

'There,' he said, and stepped across the path to thrust one hand into the hedge straight ahead of him – a blank wall facing the entrance, which curved away on either side.

Lucia stepped up beside him.

Feeling about inside the hedge, Roland frowned, then rose a-tiptoe to explore farther up; and at last said, 'Ha! Yes, here we are. The hedge has grown up more than I expected, since I last sought out the marks – I do not need them for myself, you know. We cut them near to the ground, so that Harry should be able to find them.'

He smiled fondly, shaking his head, and Lucia's mouth curved in a fond smile of her own: Harry topped both his elder brothers by half a head now, and she liked Roland the better for not resenting it.

'Had we better cut the marks anew, lower down?' she said. 'For . . . for Ned's children to discover, one day?'

Roland turned from the hedge (his hand still buried in the foliage, his arm still stretched above his head) and in the dimness his eyes glinted at her. 'Ned's children must find their own way into the maze,' he said. 'It will do them good. But we shall cut the marks again for their own sake,' he added, his teasing tone gone abruptly sober, 'in memory of the boys we were, and to make our own memories for—' He looked away from her.

'For our own children,' said Lucia quietly, touching his free hand, soft and quick, with her fingers.

Roland's boot-heels came down again with a quiet *thump*, and he dropped his arm and turned fully to face her. 'Lucia,' he said, low. He reached for her hands, and she let him take them, hoping against hope that he should not be intending to descend once more into poetry.

And he did not; but what he did say was very nearly as bad: 'Lucia, tell me – can you – shall you ever be able to love me?'

Lucia shut her eyes briefly to keep from rolling them. 'I like you very much, by times,' she said honestly. *When you do not insist on speaking to me of love, and reading romantical poetry at me.* 'Many a happy marriage has been built on less solid foundations. Can we not let that suffice for the moment?'

Roland sighed, plainly disappointed. He did not drop her hands, however, or turn and stalk away in high dudgeon; Lucia therefore considered her plea to have met with some success.

'Will you show me your marks?' she said, after a moment, tilting her head up towards the hedge-wall.

Roland nodded, and let go of one of her hands in order to guide the other. She, too, had to stretch up onto her toes, but her searching fingers soon found what they sought beneath the foliage: a scar in the curved surface of the yew-bark, smooth where the shingled outer layer had been stripped away, in the shape of the letter *W*.

'Because we first turn west?' she asked, coming back down to her heels.

'Yes, exactly,' said Roland. 'Now . . .'

He rummaged in his coat pockets and brought out an elaborately adorned pocket-knife.

'Oh!' said Lucia.

Roland – in the act of crouching down to look for a suitable space of bark near to the ground – looked up at her with his brows drawn together in bafflement. 'What is it?' he said.

'I expected magick,' she explained, half apologetic and fearing lest he should take offence. 'I had forgotten, I suppose, how young you and your brothers were, at the time of this adventure.'

'We were very young,' said Roland, slowly and thoughtfully, 'but I own I had not considered the possibility, even now. I blame my tutors,' he added, his wry grin flashing momentarily, 'for they have been telling me since first I learnt to call light that relying too far upon one's magick carries as much danger as failing to learn to control it. But now that I do think upon it – if the marks were made by magick, one could find them by magick, is that not so?'

Lucia, crouching down beside him, nodded. 'Whether that confers a benefit or a disadvantage depends, I suppose, upon your purposes,' she said. 'One could make a mark which can *only* be found by magick, but if one were minded to use magick to defeat a maze, there are easier ways of doing so.'

Roland chuckled. 'I was for having Ned use a finding-spell to bring us to the centre,' he admitted. 'I should have used one myself, had I been capable of it at the time. Ned would have no part of it, however – it would be cheating, he said, and would prove nothing but that he could work a finding, which everyone knew already – and of course he was quite right. We learnt afterwards,' he added, just as Lucia was about to repeat Sophie's remarks upon the nature of the maze, 'that the whole of the thing is spelled against finding- and summoning-spells. I am glad we did not know it at the time, however, for it was a comfort to Harry to think that should we lose ourselves after all, there was only Ned's favourite finding-spell between us and rescue.'

A comfort to Harry, indeed, thought Lucia, with an inward smile.

'One of my tutors was a scout in my father's guard,' she said, 'and had been a forester in his youth, before he became a guardsman.' She reached into the hedge at elbow height and felt about for a trunk or a large branch to suit her purpose. 'It was his doing that Morag MacNeill and I were able to carry out our hare-brained scheme, though I never told anyone so, for fear he might be punished for encouraging me in reckless behaviour, which he had never done. He taught me—'

The pads of her fingers brushed over a smooth, broad curve where the outer bark had sloughed off itself, and she curved her palm over it and let it rest there.

'These trees are not like the trees I knew as a child,' she said. 'They are tame trees' – Roland raised his eyebrows; Lucia ignored him – 'and belong to the world of men as much as to their own. But perhaps they may still remember their ancestors . . .'

She reached inwards for her magick – the power she had been born with, twined together with that of Clan MacNeill and of Alba itself, invested in her as her father's heir – and with the scarlet-and-gold thread of it in her hand, reached outwards to find the spirit of the tree under her palm. For a long moment, nothing stirred; but at last she felt (saw, heard: to describe in the language of the physical senses the sensations of using magick was an enterprise that continually defeated her) the thread of sweet green light that was the yew-tree's pulsing lifeblood, faint and distant and tasting of iron as well as of leaf-mould and wood, and gently tangled her magick into it.

But the tree was not *her* tree – the ground from which it grew was not her ground, and her own was far away.

Lucia let the magick go and drew her hand away, surprised to find that she was breathing hard and perspiration beading on her forehead.

'It is not my tree,' she said, answering Roland's worried expression. 'It will not mark itself for me, as the trees of Alba would do.'

Roland studied her – studied the yew-hedge – laid his hand alongside hers against the smooth under-bark.

Acting on instinct above all (though later she would see the parallels with events in an ancient yew-grove on the Ross of Mull), Lucia caught his other hand in hers and sent another tendril of her magick questing cautiously towards his.

'Mother Goddess!' said Roland, low and reverent. 'I did not know – is it always – *Oh.*'

And now, under their two hands, drawn out by the calling of Roland's magick to the tree's, the mark took shape, rising out of the bark – embossed upon it, rather than incised into it, but otherwise echoing the original in every particular.

Roland blinked hard, shaking his head like a dog coming in out of the rain. When he turned to Lucia, his eyes were alight with something like awe.

'It called to me,' he said wonderingly. 'The tree – or all of the trees – it called to me. Not – it – it *knew* me. How can such a thing be?'

He had turned away from her again, and was running his fingertips over the raised *W*, peering through the branches. He raised his other hand and almost absently muttered, '*Adeste luces*'; a globe of magelight, no larger than a gooseberry, bobbed into existence in the air above his palm, then floated into the yew-hedge.

'It is exactly like,' he said. 'And yet the tree made it – or I thought it did.'

Now he sat back on his heels, frowning at Lucia. 'This is an astonishing thing,' he said, 'yet you do not seem even mildly surprised. Does none of this' – he waved a hand, and the magelight described a drunken tumble inside the hedge – 'seem at all out of the ordinary to you?'

Lucia shrugged. 'If I am astonished at anything,' she said, 'it is – well – your astonishment. Though of course there are Albans aplenty who know nothing of such magicks, and understand still less. Not every father would have his child taught by a man who speaks to the trees.'

She smiled – a peace-offering of sorts – and climbed to her feet. Roland returned the smile, but when Lucia extended a hand to him to pull him to his feet, his eyebrows rose in astonishment and instead of taking it, he scrambled upright and offered her his arm.

I have put my foot wrong again, thought Lucia, a little despairingly, as she allowed Roland to tuck her hand up under his elbow. *I suppose I ought not to have implied that I am as strong as he is.*

But all the same, Roland had looked at her with wonder in his eyes – had smiled at her – was guiding her through the maze now, with his hand warm over hers, and pointing out each turning where a mark might be renewed – was talking of magick, and of gardens and labyrinths, and not of poetry or of love – and all of this, despite her repeated missteps, felt like the beginnings of victory.

'The way is not so difficult, you see,' said Roland, pausing at what must be the final turning.

They had been a long time in the maze, through stopping so often to renew the little Princes' way-finding marks; the sun, sinking towards the western horizon, had dipped below the barrier of the high yew-hedges, making the path through the maze dimmer than ever. It might have been gloomy, but Lucia did not find it so; the trees knew Roland, welcomed him, as the woods of Alba had always known and welcomed her, if more sedately, and if they did not yet know her, she could imagine the possibility of their coming to do so.

She had chosen her guide well, though for what undoubtedly were, from the trees' point of view, entirely the wrong reasons.

They rounded the last turning, and the high, close hedge-walls fell away.

'*Cailleach mór!*' breathed Lucia, staring around her.

'It is something to see, indeed,' said Roland; and if he sounded very slightly smug, who could blame him?

They stood in a great three-sided clearing, carpeted with chamomile, clover, and creeping thyme, so that every step smelt of sunshine. In its centre stood a weathered sundial, whose brass gnomon was green with age, and whose foot seemed to grow up from amongst the thyme-stems like a great stone toadstool. In each corner was ensconced a small, well-tended shrine, and along each wall a low stone bench grown over with thyme, and over the whole fell a profound and listening silence. The air was so still that Lucia almost hesitated to breathe, for fear of disturbing it – yet bright and alive with expectation.

'Hegemone,' Roland murmured, gesturing to the buxom figure atop the nearest shrine, whose feet, like the sundial's, were hidden by vines twining about her legs and up her uplifted arms. 'She who watches over growing things. Apollo and Diana, sun and moon.' Two figures: a man who held a harp, a woman with a bow. *Your goddesses may be handy with a sword or a bow; but your women, almost never. Why is that, I wonder?*

'And Minerva,' said Roland, nodding at the last shrine.

Lucia peered at it across the clearing – or was it a grove? – and slipping her arm out of Roland's, took a few hesitant steps towards it, skirting the sundial.

'That is an owl,' she said last. 'An owl who sits upon a helmet, and holds a sword in his claws.'

'Yes,' said Roland. 'Minerva's sacred bird – her sword – her helm.' He paused, looking from Lucia to the owl-shrine and back again, and at last said doubtfully, 'You will not like to make an offering, I suppose. I shall do so, however, if you have no objection?'

'Objection?' said Lucia, bewildered. 'What objection could I possibly have to your making offerings to your own gods in your own garden?'

'Well,' said Roland. He looked at his boots. 'They are not your gods, I know; and I have heard that in Alba, the gods of Britain are . . . not well regarded.'

Lucia sighed. 'Alba resisted the great legions of Rome,' she said, 'when Britain did not; there are still far too many Albans who cannot, or will not, regard their gods with anything but suspicion.' This was something of an understatement, as Roland must be aware. 'It is not all the gods of Britain whom such persons so resent, you understand, but only those who are also gods of Rome. But in any case, Roland, I should never ask you to disavow your gods! No matter how much an altar to Minerva or Apollo in the Castle may irritate the priests of the Cailleach.'

She paused, turning this notion over in her mind, and added, 'In fact, now I think on it, I believe that may be rather an advantage than otherwise.'

Roland looked up at last, brows furrowed, to gauge whether this were a serious suggestion; and before Lucia knew what had happened, they were laughing together.

Roland began searching his pockets. The much smaller pockets of Lucia's worked muslin gown producing nothing of interest, she hunted through her reticule and at length extracted a long blue-black feather which she had picked up in the course of their walk; a copper ring in the shape of two snakes, a gift from Sìleas which, however, fit none of Lucia's fingers; and a linen handkerchief embroidered with the lion of Alba.

'Will any of these do?' she enquired diffidently, holding out her hands to Roland. 'Or I suppose chamomile-flowers, or clover—'

'One of the secrets of the maze,' said Roland, 'is that any offering you make here, you must bring in with you from the outside. I had not the least notion of going into the maze today, however, and so—'

He had been rummaging in an inner pocket of his coat, and now withdrew from it a folded paper. This he unfolded, and read through with an expression of chagrin growing upon his face. 'No,' he said – to himself rather than to her, Lucia judged – and tucked it away again.

Eventually he discovered a pen in one pocket and a silver coin in another, which he appeared to consider satisfactory. 'But may I have the crow's feather?' he said, and smiled at Lucia when she gave it to him.

Roland knelt at the shrine of Apollo and Diana, and laid the silver coin upon the tiny altar before the twin figures of the gods. His prayer was silent, or at any rate was spoken too softly to be intelligible; Lucia was glad of it, though she could not entirely suppress a flicker of curiosity. At the end of it, however, he bowed to the altar and spoke aloud the same formula she had by now heard used more than once in more public forms of worship: '*Do ut des.*'

I give, that you may give in return.

The pen was offered to Minerva ('It was made from an owl's feather,' Roland explained; 'Sophie's pens are all made so, and she brought some as a gift for Harry'), and the crow's feather to Hegemone. Having finished this third offering, Roland rose to his feet and said, 'Shall we rest here a little? These benches are more comfortable to sit on than they look, I promise you.'

Lucia let him steer her towards the bench that separated Minerva's shrine from that of Apollo and Diana, and perched on one end of it whilst Roland settled himself on the other, his knees angled towards her own. The bench was not a long one, and they were closer together than Lucia had been prepared for, though not perhaps so close as Roland had meant.

'It is very beautiful,' she said. 'Is it true, the tale of the old King's mistress who heard the shades of dead men and women howling for vengeance, and had to be sent away?'

Roland's eyebrows shot up, and he let out a bark of incredulous laughter. 'You must not believe every tale Joanna Callender tells you,' he said.

'Is it not true then?'

'It is certainly true that she left court,' said Roland. 'There are records of the King's gifts of property and so on in the Archives, or so I am given to understand. And that Henry the Great had the fellow who designed the maze – he must have been an old man by then, if the walls were grown high enough to lose oneself in! – beheaded. Henry the Great was always beheading people, however,' he added, with a glinting smile which made him look, for just an instant, like a fair-haired, blue-eyed Sophie, though they resembled one another so little in any other respect. 'It need not mean that any of the rest is true. I have certainly never seen or heard anything of the kind, nor has anyone else, that I know of.'

Lucia hummed thoughtfully. As between Roland and Joanna, which was the more likely to have the true tale? Roland, who had lived all his life at court, had certainly the better opportunity to gather information; but he seemed to catch at facts and rumours haphazardly as they floated by him, whereas Joanna went after them like a hunting-dog on the scent.

'It has occurred to me,' she said, 'that perhaps it was the trees she heard, without knowing it.'

Roland's eyes widened. 'Indeed,' he said. 'I had not thought of that.'

They sat in silence a long moment – a more comfortable silence than was usual between them, for which Lucia was briefly grateful; until it occurred to her that the rustling of leaves all about her had no breeze to go with it.

'The trees,' she said, very softly. 'The trees are speaking to us – to you, I mean. What do they say?'

Roland, who had been looking about him (in search of a breeze to explain the noise?), turned to her wide-eyed. 'I have not the least idea,' he said.

Lucia considered, her eyes closed, her ears pricked to catch at the least possibility of meaning in the sounds about them.

Put out your hand, she was about to say, when upon opening her eyes she saw that Roland had already thought it; on his feet again, he had stepped close to the nearest hedge-wall and was reaching in. Lucia, forgetting entirely her resolution to conduct herself in a manner becoming a lady of King Henry's court, drew her knees up to her chest, braced her boot-heels on the edge of the bench, and, wrapping her arms about her shins, settled down with her chin upon one knee to observe him.

The moment dragged on, and the shadows lengthened; above the hedge-walls there appeared the upper edges of a flame-and-crimson sunset, and its alchymy turned Roland's fair hair to burnished gold.

Roland stood with both hands in the hedge, one foot braced behind him and his head tilted in rapt attention. He ought to have looked absurd in such an attitude; in fact, however (thought Lucia to herself), he might have been one of his kingdom's several mischievous gods, caught in the act of emerging from the trees to tempt some unsuspecting mortal maiden.

It was a disconcerting thought – but not, in the circumstances, unwelcome. She turned it over in her mind – tried to imagine kissing him, as she had kissed several of the cousins who had been her childhood playmates, and found the notion not altogether unappealing – but all too soon was brought up short by a vivid impression of Roland's resemblance to her brother, Duncan.

At last – just as Lucia was growing truly anxious, and weighing

the consequences of making some attempt to gain his attention –
Roland let out a shuddering sigh, and pulled his hands out of the
foliage to scrub them through his hair.

Lucia scrambled to her feet as he turned away from the
hedge, still gripping fistfuls of curls on either side of his head. He
raised his head and found himself face-to-face with Lucia across
the stone bench; though she had scarcely altered her position
since first sitting down, he seemed genuinely astonished by her
presence.

He was swaying on his feet; alarmed, she darted forward and
caught him by both elbows.

'Sit down,' she said, keeping her tone level, 'and tell me what
you heard.'

Roland resisted briefly, but his body, it seemed, conceded
what his mind would not, and before long his knees folded him
obediently into a seat on the bench.

He turned his face to hers, and – an unprecedented intimacy –
brought one hand up to cup her cheek. 'Lucia,' he said, and smiled
dreamily.

Lucia blinked. Her cheek was warm where he had touched it;
the same hand, his left, came down to rest over hers in her lap, and
reflexively she turned her hand over to clasp his, palm to palm.

'The trees,' she prompted again, to cover her confusion but also
because she was desperately curious. 'What did they say to you?'

'I did not understand above half of it,' said Roland, still in that
alarmingly dreamy tone. 'But they are not so tame as you think.'

His hand in Lucia's trembled. It was all the warning she had
before his eyes rolled up and he tumbled sideways off the bench,
dead to the world.

* * *

For the space of four heartbeats Lucia sat frozen in shock. But not for nothing had Ceana MacGregor trained her, and Donald MacNeill chosen her as his heir; by the time the fifth battered at her ribs and thudded in her ears, she was up and moving.

'Magick shock,' she said aloud in Gaelic, as she knelt at Roland's shoulder and felt for a pulse at his throat. Yes, there it was – quicker by half than it ought to be, as her own certainly was, but strong and steady. 'You are badly magick-shocked, Roland, and what am I to do for you?' She gently straightened his limbs, turned him onto his left side so that he should not choke to death if he should happen to be sick, and, lacking anything that might serve as a pillow, settled his head in her lap.

'We are at the centre of this maze, and I have got nothing to feed you or to warm you with, and how are we to get out again, with you in such a state? And what were you thinking, to be doing . . . whatever it is you have been doing?' Her left hand was in his hair, Lucia discovered; it was very soft. 'Has no one taught you to know your limits? To say true, Highness, I have met half-grown children with more sense. Though of course I have also met your sister, Sophie, who, as you may know, thinks nothing of—'

Roland stirred and muttered something unintelligible.

'Roland,' said Lucia, more gently, carding her fingers through the tumbled curls, and craning her neck in an effort to see his face properly without jostling him; and, shifting into Latin, 'Roland, can you hear me?'

By way of reply, he groaned softly and curled forward a little, as though he were attempting to roll himself into a ball like a hedgehog but could not quite manage it.

'Are you hurt anywhere?' Lucia enquired.

Roland managed a sort of negatory hum.

'Has anything of this kind ever happened to you before?'

'Nnnn.' His shoulders shifted as he planted one hand flat on the creeping thyme and attempted to lever himself upright.

'Lie down, if you please,' said Lucia with some asperity; and, in response to his inarticulate noise of protest, 'I have been magick-shocked before, Roland, if you have not, and I had rather you did not fall over again before we have had time to determine what we ought to do.'

He subsided at last, and rolled his head so as to peer up at her. His face was ashen, his eyes nearly all pupil. Had he struck his head in falling? He blinked slowly – attempting, Lucia supposed, to bring her into focus – and the shade of a smile passed across his face, sweet and sad.

Lucia laid one hand along his cheek and was taken aback by the fierce tenderness that briefly swamped her thoughts when he turned minutely into her touch – just as Duncan had, as a motherless small boy, ten years and more ago, and yet . . . altogether not.

'Is there some way of summoning help from here?' she said. 'A signal of some kind, in case of emergencies?'

'Mmm,' said Roland. His eyelids drooped, then rose again, revealing pupils still blown wide. 'Signal, yes. Shan't use it . . . I sh'd never live it down.'

'Roland, we must have help of some sort to make our way out,' said Lucia, patiently. 'You are in no condition to walk so far, and as we had not the foresight to bring a picnic supper into the maze with us, there is not much to be done for you until we *are* out, except rest; there is nothing to eat here, but thyme-leaves and chamomile flowers, neither of which is much to the purpose. And I am not of a size to carry you, even if I were quite sure of the way, which I regret to say that I am not.'

Roland frowned. 'But . . . marks,' he said. 'On the trees, marks.'

Would he remember, later, the things he had done and said in this misfortunate hour? Lucia rather hoped not, for the sake of his pride. She had never seen magick shock manifest in precisely this way – had she not known better, she might have supposed Roland deep in his cups – but then, it took some people oddly.

'You marked the way, yes,' she agreed, 'but the marks are not easily found, if one does not know where to look, and I do not know where to look so well as you do.'

Roland was struggling to sit up again, and this time Lucia, conceding the battle in hopes of winning the day, helped him to do so. He leant heavily upon her supporting arms, and did not resist when she tightened them about his waist and shoulders.

They sat thus, Roland folded awkwardly into Lucia's encircling arms, as the sun sank below the horizon and the stars began to prick the dark fabric of the sky.

The principal means of treating a person suffering from magick shock was to keep him warm, feed him well – preferably on cold meat, hard cheese, and strong tea with plenty of milk and honey – and put him to bed to sleep off its effects. Lucia had, as she had told Roland, been the sufferer herself on more than one occasion, as she grew towards mastering her talent, and she did not for a moment believe that Roland had never before been affected likewise. More importantly, however, so often had she been called upon to cope with the consequences of someone else's magickal miscalculations, that the necessary steps were by now a matter of instinct. To know – to *feel* – what was needed, and to be prevented by circumstance from providing it, made her twitch with frustration. No food was to be had; she dared not call fire, for nothing here could be spared to burn; and though the day had been so warm, night was coming on and a chill mist creeping in from off the river.

Had she only had her mother's knife with her, and a flame or some spirits with which to clean it, she might, in this extremity, have attempted the spell which, as a mage of Clan MacNeill, she had been taught on her sixteenth birthday – a sharing of magick through the sharing of blood; she had used this spell only twice in her life, but as it had ultimately saved not only several persons' lives but also her father's kingdom, she felt reasonably confident in its efficacy. But the knife, in its sheath embroidered with scarlet lions rampant, was tucked away safely in a locked dispatch-box in her bedroom, and thus was no good to anyone.

After this, thought Lucia bitterly, *I shall carry it with me everywhere, whatever Father may say about it.*

What she could provide (and it was little enough) was light, and the warmth of her own body in the gathering chill, and a firm encouragement to rest; and these she was engaged in supplying – her back pressed painfully against one end of the stone bench, both arms wound tight about Roland's rib cage, and his head heavy on her shoulder – when a distinctly human set of noises caught her ear, and resolved themselves into footfalls, a haphazard rustling of leaves, and someone calling, 'Prince Roland! Lady Lucia!'

CHAPTER VII

In Which the Crown Prince Effects a Rescue

Roland reacted to the sounds of his rescuers only with a groan of weary irritation. Lucia, on the contrary, would have leapt to her feet with cries of joy, had she not been restrained by the limp weight of Roland's body in her arms.

Instead she laid her hands over his ears, drew in a deep breath, and bellowed, 'Here! We are here, by the shrine of Hegemone.'

The footfalls accelerated, and after a moment a small crowd of persons – nearly all of them Royal Guardsmen – tumbled out into the central clearing. At the head of the column was Prince Edward; pink-faced with exertion, he paused with hands on knees to catch his breath and look about him. Upon catching sight of Lucia and Roland, he straightened at once and said sharply, 'What ails him? Is he hurt?'

'He is magick-shocked,' said Lucia, 'and I had nothing to feed him, else we should have been out of the maze again by now, I expect. I suppose you have not brought us anything to eat?'

Edward had crossed the clearing now, and was crouched on his heels beside Lucia, peering into his brother's tallow-pale face. 'Magick-shocked?' he echoed, raising his eyes to Lucia's. 'How comes this?'

'It is a long tale,' said Lucia, 'and not a simple one, and I should be happy to tell it to you, Edward, at some other time; but at present—'

'At present, we have more pressing concerns,' Edward agreed. He laid his palm against Roland's forehead, then his cheek; lifted one eyelid, and frowned at whatever he saw beneath it. Then he was on his feet again, organising his small troop.

The trees were rustling anew, more frantically than before, though there was still no breeze to speak of; but Edward seemed not to remark it.

Lucia was grateful for his sensible, practical approach to the present predicament, however.

'What is the hour?' she enquired. It was very nearly full night now, which at this time of the year made it late indeed; they must have been missed hours ago, surely, and what in the world had everyone supposed them to be doing all this while?

'I have not the least idea,' said Edward, absently. He stretched out an expectant hand to one of the guardsmen. 'Reynolds, your flask, if you please – no, not *that* one – the brandy.'

Reynolds hesitated, frozen in the act of unshipping his *cantine*; Edward's expression grew thunderous. 'Mars and Mithras!' he hissed. 'Now, man, at once, and a plague upon your scruples.'

Reynolds fished a smaller flask out of a pocket and presented it to Edward with a muttered *My lord*. To Lucia's surprise, Edward turned at once to pass it into her hand.

Lucia was not at all convinced of the wisdom of applying neat spirits to a case of magick shock, but Roland had now six strong men to help extricate him from the consequences of his folly, which must soon put him in the way of receiving proper care; meanwhile, a sip or two of brandy could not greatly harm him.

It did not greatly help him, either, she judged, when she had trickled a little of the brandy between his lips; he sputtered a little, and opened his eyes only briefly before subsiding once more into near insensibility.

'Before all else,' said Lucia, looking up at Edward, 'we must get him indoors and well wrapped up. It is fortunate that the night is not colder, but—'

'Hughes – Gagnon – with me,' said Edward, turning away.

Lucia forbore to comment: Edward might be as rude as he liked to her, she decided, so long as he was helping her to help Roland.

Hughes and Gagnon – who proved to be the two largest of the small troop of guardsmen – stepped smartly forward and made a carrying-chair of their clasped arms, into which Edward (disdaining the assistance which Lucia tried to offer him) lifted his brother. Roland's head lolled against Gagnon's broad shoulder; his eyes opened again and focused for a moment on Lucia's magelight, floating now just above her head.

'*Fove quod est frigidum*,' he said distinctly – *warm what is chilled*; it was a quotation from something she had heard before, and heard in an accent very like Roland's, but she could not for the moment call the source to mind – then closed his eyes and slumped once more against Gagnon.

'Yes, Roland,' said Lucia, noting with annoyance the hint of a catch in her voice. *Well, Roland is not the only one who is feeling the chill.* 'We certainly shall.'

She stepped in front of Hughes to take Roland's hand in hers; it was like touching a tree-branch covered in ice. 'Your coat,' she said sharply to Edward. 'At once.'

He was peeling it off already, and as quickly helped her to drape it about Roland's broader shoulders and tuck it round his frigid hands.

'Now, let us go from here at once,' said Lucia, 'if not sooner.'

Edward led them out of the maze, as he had led his search party into it, and Lucia was surprised to find that the journey took very little time.

'I assure you, Lady Lucia,' said Prince Edward, a little stiffly, as they strode across the lawn towards the Palace, 'that my guardsmen are all entirely discreet; you need not fear that any breath of impropriety will—'

'What impropriety can you be talking of?' Lucia demanded, indignant. She did not care if the others heard her. 'Your brother was suffering from magick shock, and as I had not the means at hand to provide any other curative, I did the only thing I could do, which was to keep him warm. I do not see what impropriety could possibly attach to any action of mine – or of Roland's, either,' she added.

'Nonetheless—'

'Nonetheless, what?' Lucia's patience, already worn thin by lack of food and by the evening's events, was rapidly shredding. 'If I did not know better, Edward Tudor, I should suspect you of believing that I ought to have let your brother freeze to death for the sake of your precious *propriety*.'

To his credit, Edward looked honestly appalled at this suggestion. 'Of course not,' he said, in quite a different tone. 'No, never that.'

'Well, then,' said Lucia. Relenting in the face of his evident dismay, she patted his arm in a sisterly manner and said kindly, 'I should be quite as frantic and irrational as you were, if such a thing were to befall my small brother. Fortunately, however, Duncan is not so much given to outrageous escapades as I was at his age.'

Edward looked at her sideways, eyebrows raised.

'Come now, brother dear,' said Lucia, attempting a rallying tone. 'Did you imagine that my father chose me as his heir for my biddable temper and my lack of adventurous spirit?'

Edward looked, in fact, as though he had never thought of asking such a question in the whole course of his life – and perhaps, thought Lucia, he never had.

After all, poor Edward had been heir to his father's kingdom from the moment of his birth, whether he liked it or not.

Whatever else it might be, King Henry's palace was well supplied with talented healers and with very good cooks, both of them, it seemed, ready to hand at a moment's notice. Almost before the rescue-party had reached the staircase that would take them up to Roland's rooms, a plump little man in healer's robes was trundling down to meet them, issuing orders to his apprentice for conveyance to the kitchens.

Lucia answered the healer's questions – his name, she contrived to learn, was Henri Vauquelin – as best she could as they all went up the stairs and along the corridors, and in this way crossed the threshold of Roland's rooms with the rest.

Whilst the healer and his apprentice were peeling Roland out of his damp clothing and tucking him up in bed, Lucia busied herself in the adjoining sitting-room, tidying into neat symmetrical stacks the books scattered on the table and plumping the cushions on the silk-upholstered settees and the one heavy, slightly battered armchair which, she judged, was Roland's favourite seat. She would not be ruled by the threat of idle talk, but nor was she eager to court it by lurking in Roland's bedroom whilst he was being undressed.

When the apprentice healer emerged with an armful of

discarded clothing, however, she straightened from her by now fruitlessly repetitive cushion-plumping and, with a nod to him, passed back through the doorway, equally without fanfare and without the slightest attempt at subterfuge.

Look as though you believe in your right to be where you are, her father had once told her, *and the great majority of persons will never think to question you.*

But Queen Edwina and Prince Edward, it seemed, did not live by this maxim, for the former looked outraged, while the latter came forward at once to intercept her.

'You must be very tired,' he said – kindly, but firmly. 'Let me ring for someone to escort you to your own rooms—'

'I had much rather stay here,' said Lucia. 'I should not be easy in my mind otherwise, not knowing how Roland does.'

'Your devotion to Roland's well-being does you credit, my dear,' said the Queen. 'You must see, however, that it would be quite improper.'

Lucia did not say, *Roland and I were alone in the maze for hours; what can it matter now?* She did not ask what acts of impropriety Edward or his mother imagined might take place between Roland and herself whilst he lay half dead from magick shock; she did not say, *If you truly believe me capable of taking advantage of a man in such a condition, I wonder that you should have allowed me within ten leagues of your blue-eyed boy.*

Instead, for Roland's sake (for in truth she was growing very fond of him, if not in precisely the way he wished her to be) and for the sake of avoiding a diplomatic incident, she swallowed back all of these thoughts, produced an innocent and complaisant smile, and said, 'I shall do very well here, I assure you. Surely there can be no impropriety in a young lady's watching by her betrothed husband's sick-bed, in full view of two healers and a pair of guardsmen?'

'That is not the point,' said Edward – but almost absently, as he glanced aside at Henri Vauquelin, who presently was clasping Roland's wrist and frowning.

Whatever other faults she might find with Edward, Lucia did not doubt that he loved his brothers. He was, she judged, eager to conclude the present debate so that he might return to personally superintending Roland's care.

Surreptitiously, Lucia planted her feet, lest the aforesaid guardsmen be called upon to remove her bodily; they were larger and stronger than herself, but she should at least not do their work for them. All the same, she rather wondered at her own vehemence. Her growing fondness notwithstanding, until now it had never for a moment occurred to her to resist being parted from Roland – *Am I a child, holding tight to my doll only because the nursery-maid threatens to take it away?*

'My dear Lucia,' Queen Edwina began, 'I must insist—'

'Lady Lucia,' said Henri Vauquelin, cutting across her with the calm self-confidence of a man whose calling places him, when he so chooses, above the whims of mere monarchs. 'Prince Roland is asking for you.'

'I beg you will excuse me, Your Majesty,' said Lucia. She did not wait to observe Queen Edwina's reaction to this new development; whatever it might be, she should not let it dictate her conduct.

Henri Vauquelin ushered Lucia back to Roland's bedside, where his apprentice eagerly surrendered to her his seat on a hard chair, together with a jug of beef tea, a porcelain cup, and a spoon.

'He must take some nourishment, ma'am,' said the healer, murmuring in Lucia's ear. 'It may be more welcome from your hand.'

Lucia folded herself into the chair and accepted the jug

and spoon almost absently, her attention all on Roland.

Truly he looked shockingly ill, even for a man suffering from magick shock; with the alarming exception of some of Cormac MacAlpine's victims – kidnapped, beaten, and held under interdiction – Lucia had rarely seen such ashen skin on a living person. The sight of him, waxen-faced amidst the white pillows and midnight-blue coverlet, wedged open a door in her mind which for the most part she succeeded in keeping locked up tight, and for a moment she was ten years old again, attending upon her mother's deathbed, at once desperately sad and secretly, guiltily eager for some respite from the melancholic miasma which had enveloped the whole of Castle Hill for nearly a year, spurring her to escapades such as that illicit ascent of Arthur's Seat only to escape it.

But it was a moment only, for she had many years' experience in setting her shoulder to that door and shutting away what lay behind it.

'Roland,' she said, keeping her voice low and (with some effort) even. His wheat-gold lashes fluttered; she set down the jug on the floor by her feet, dropped the cup and spoon upon the coverlet, and bent towards Roland to take his hand in hers. His fingers felt chilly against her palm, but not so much like a row of icicles as previously. *That is one good sign, at any rate.*

She squeezed his hand gently and repeated his name – once – twice – until his eyes fluttered open once more and, after an agonising moment of wandering, found her face.

'Lucia,' he said, a croaking mutter somehow flavoured with deep relief – why? Where had he feared she might go?

'Yes,' she said, smiling down at him – letting her own relief show plainly on her face. 'Here I am. How do you, my dear?'

'I . . .' Roland closed his eyes, wet his lips, opened his eyes again.

'We were in the maze,' he said. 'The . . . the trees were . . . singing?'

Lucia swallowed her astonishment. 'Were they indeed?' she said mildly. 'You must tell me all about it at some other time, when you are better.'

Roland frowned at this, as she had suspected he might. 'Better, how? Were we set upon by . . . Has the maze its own angry Minotaur, now?'

'You are badly magick-shocked,' Lucia explained. With her free hand she smoothed the fall of fair hair back from his forehead. 'We were foolish not to bring along a picnic supper, as it turns out, for I could do nothing for you until your brother came in search of us with a band of guardsmen.'

Roland blinked up at her, his eyes wide and very blue in his too-pale face. 'Lucia, I—'

'You have yet had nothing to eat,' said Lucia, forestalling him. Freeing her hand, she bent to retrieve her jug and took up the abandoned cup. 'I ought not to have kept you talking all this time, when you might have been eating.' She poured a little of the broth into the cup – not too much, lest Roland's hands (or her own) tremble enough to spill it; he would, she was quite certain, resent the indignity of being fed with a spoon. 'Will you drink a little of this beef tea, to begin with? Or, if there is something else you had rather, I am sure—'

Wordlessly, Roland reached for the cup. Lucia handed off the jug to Henri Vauquelin, standing quietly at her elbow, and – for she was herself very hungry, and so tired that her limbs seemed cast in lead – did not try to intervene when his apprentice stepped forward at her other side to help Roland sit up and rearrange the pillows at his back.

'What you did was very well done, Lady Lucia,' said Henri

Vauquelin. His voice, she thought, was rather louder than necessary; to whom was he speaking, really? 'Prince Roland was fortunate in his choice of companions.'

'It was fortunate that the night was so mild,' Lucia replied, 'and that Prince Edward came seeking us so soon.'

No one had yet asked either of them, she observed with a strangely detached curiosity, what in the world Roland had been doing to bring this affliction on himself. *That, I suppose, is a conversation for some less eventful hour.*

Henri Vauquelin bent closer and, under the pretext of taking Roland's pulse, said quietly, 'Your bride understates her value, Highness. You, I trust, will not be tempted to do the same.'

Roland swallowed the remainder of his cupful of beef tea, and, resting the cup amongst the bedclothes by his hip, said solemnly, 'You may be sure that I shall not, sir.'

His voice still much resembled the creaking of a rusted gate-hinge; yet somehow the tone and the words had the character of a vow.

There was a commotion from the direction of Roland's sitting-room; Lucia looked up sharply, irrationally fearing that Queen Edwina might have sent for some even larger and more threatening guardsmen to take her away.

But Roland's mother and brother hovered in the doorway as before, and the only addition to their vigil was—

'Father,' said Roland, in an odd tone compounded of astonishment and trepidation. His hand caught at Lucia's fingers and held fast.

Henry of Britain swept past his wife and eldest son and strode across the room to stand at the foot of Roland's bed.

Henri Vauquelin and his apprentice bowed respectfully; Lucia made to rise from her chair to do the same, but Roland tightened

111

his grip on her hand, and she fell back into her seat with a small huff. 'Your pardon, Your Majesty,' she said instead.

He nodded at her, vaguely, and reached down to grip Roland's right foot through the coverlet – an intimate and oddly endearing gesture, at which Lucia caught herself smiling fondly. *Henry Tudor is not so very grand, after all, when his wee boy is ill in bed*, she thought.

His Majesty did not speak to Roland, however, but to the healer, in the clipped tones of a serjeant-major: 'Tell me. Leave nothing out.'

'Prince Roland is suffering from magick shock, Your Majesty,' said Henri Vauquelin, 'compounded by a prolonged period of exposure, without food or drink, prior to his rescue. Thanks to the Lady Lucia's quick thinking, however, the consequences are not so dire as they might have been, and His Royal Highness will live to fight another day.'

The King now turned his full attention to Lucia, who was moved by the weight of his intent, measuring gaze to say, 'I assure you, sir, that I did only what anyone would have.'

'Nonetheless, Lucia MacNeill,' said King Henry, so nakedly sincere that his face was difficult to look at, 'we are in your debt.'

'I beg you will not think of it, Your Majesty,' said Lucia.

At Henri Vauquelin's insistence, Lucia was included in the small conclave assembled in Roland's sitting-room, whilst Queen Edwina took her place at his bedside. This seemed to Lucia not altogether as it should be; the Queen appeared well enough contented with her lot, however, and as Lucia had certainly no desire to be shut out of the discussion, she pressed Roland's hand, bent quickly to drop a kiss on the top of his head, and followed Henri Vauquelin out of the room.

The door having been shut behind them, the conference was brief and pointed: Roland was to keep his bed; to be fed on plain, nourishing foods; to be kept warm; to be prevented from any premature experiments in the use of magick, no matter how apparently benign.

'And above all, in cases of this kind,' Henri Vauquelin concluded sternly, 'it is vital that the patient not be upset, or subjected to the least nervous strain. Such as, for example' – and here his eyes settled pointedly on Prince Edward – 'may result from disputes as to which members of the household are to be permitted to bear him company during his convalescence.'

'As you say, sir,' said Edward, looking at his boots.

'As Lady Lucia's company appears to be of material benefit,' the healer continued, 'she is to be given the freedom of his rooms until such time as he is fit to leave them as well as whatever accommodation and assistance she may require. Do I make myself clear, Highness?'

'Entirely clear, sir,' said Edward.

'Very good,' said Henri Vauquelin. 'Now, as to yourself, Lady Lucia: when had you last anything to eat?'

Lucia blinked, considering this question. 'I . . . I cannot now recall,' she admitted at last. 'Certainly I made a very good breakfast—'

'Something will be sent up for you from the kitchens,' said the King, before anyone else could say anything at all. 'At once. Whatever you care to name.'

'To be perfectly frank, sir,' said Lucia, 'I should be heartily glad of breadcrusts and apple-cores at present, so they were plentiful and not actually mouldering. Whatever the kitchen may see fit to send up, I assure you, shall be eaten in its entirety and without complaint.'

King Henry appeared to be considering this carefully.

'In that case,' said Edward after a moment, with a cautious glance at his father, 'I shall order everything that Roland likes best to eat, in case something may tempt him also.'

'An admirably parsimonious solution,' said Lucia. In truth it was an effort of will by now merely to stay on her feet. She turned to Henri Vauquelin. 'May I return to Roland, now?' she asked. 'If you have no further need of me at present?'

'Certainly, certainly.' The healer ran a shrewd eye from Lucia's toes to the top of her head and back. 'In fact, I should advise you to go and sit down as soon as ever you may, my dear, before you fall down.'

'I thank you, sir, very much,' said Lucia. She bowed to the King, and to Edward – no more than a brief inclining of her head, so real was the danger of losing her balance and sending them all sprawling to the floor – then turned away.

As she approached the threshold she heard Henri Vauquelin say, in a low, considering tone, 'That, sir, is a very competent young woman.'

Brìghde's tears! I should certainly hope so, said Donald MacNeill's voice, indignant, in her mind's ear. Lucia smiled to herself as she set her hand to the door-handle, and leant her shoulder harder against that other door from which, now more than ever, her memories of her mother's last illness threatened to cast their poisoned caltrops under her feet.

CHAPTER VIII

In Which Lucia Faces the Consequences

As Lucia had good cause to know, an ordinary case of magick shock, promptly and properly treated, need occasion no more serious alarm than an ordinary cold in the head. But a cold in the head can, in particular circumstances, hold the seeds of a more dangerous illness of the lungs; what worse consequences might follow from the exacerbation of magick shock by like circumstances, such as hours spent out of doors, lying on the ground, with no protection from the evening chill, from the river mist?

It was not this question only, however, which disturbed Lucia's sleep.

Two hours since, her guard captain, Ceana MacGregor, had arrived at the door of Roland's rooms, demanding entrance. Lucia had eaten (rather haphazardly) a little of nearly every dish sent up from the kitchens at Edward's instructions; thus fortified, and with Henri Vauquelin's support, she had faced down Queen Edwina's attempt to insist upon her going away to sleep in her own rooms, and at last prevailed; and now, therefore, having left strict instructions with Ceana MacGregor and with Marcus Cattermole, the apprentice healer whose name she had at last succeeded in discovering, that she was to be told *at once* if Roland should wake and ask for her – no matter the hour or the circumstances – had allowed herself to be tucked up for the night, under several layers of blankets, upon the chaise longue in Roland's vast dressing-room.

She had seldom felt so deeply tired, and ought by rights to be dead asleep. In fact, however, she had arrived at that in-between place where exhaustion dragged irresistibly at her eyelids whilst nervous tension kept her thoughts running in circles at breakneck speed. And the thought which most often, and most sharply, surfaced from the maelstrom was this: *If I had not encouraged him, had not given him the notion of listening to the trees in the maze, then he should never have been in such danger.*

When from time to time she achieved a fitful doze, such thoughts followed her into her dreams, so that she stood again with Roland in the centre of the maze, urging him on to new and deeper explorations of the magick of the place, overriding his caution, his doubts, his murmurs of protest – all of them entirely uncharacteristic of the real Roland, and thus, as some half-waking part of Lucia's mind knew perfectly well, not Roland's at all but her own – until the trees drew him in entire, and yew-bark began to grow over his terrified face.

It was rather a relief to her than otherwise, therefore, when in the dark before dawn Ceana padded into Roland's dressing-room, laid a gentle hand upon her shoulder, and murmured in Gaelic, 'Wake up now, and come with me.'

Lucia sat up, heavy-eyed and blinking, her heart hammering in her throat, and found she could summon no words in which to reply. Instead she wrapped herself in the dressing-gown which Ceana held out for her – Roland's, perhaps, but certainly not Lucia's own – and followed her out into Roland's bedroom.

The room was full of light – candlelight, warm and flickering – and in the midst of it Roland was sitting up in bed, staring at something which only he could see, and muttering rapidly under his breath words which Lucia, from this distance, could not distinguish.

Marcus Cattermole, standing on the far side of the bed, caught Lucia's eye and beckoned her nearer. She stepped forward, her hands clasping her elbows.

'Roland,' she said softly as she approached – once, then again. Did he wake or sleep? Impossible to say: his eyes were open, lips and tongue forming words of some sort; but, on the other hand, he seemed altogether oblivious to his surroundings – seemed not to see any of the several persons haunting his bedchamber, nor to hear Lucia speaking his name . . .

She was near enough now to hear him speaking – muttering, rather – and the more she listened, the more she began to incline towards the view that he was dreaming: though she did not speak such a number of languages as, for example, Sophie or her husband, Lucia was quite capable of recognising many tongues in which she could not express herself to much purpose – and this was none of those.

Or, rather, it was all of them, and more besides: odd unrelated words in more than half a dozen languages – Latin and Greek, English and Français, Brezhoneg and Gaelic and Cymric, and others Lucia could not be sure of – thrown together like crazy-paving and yielding no sense whatsoever. Was Roland attempting some sort of magickal working? It was a troubling thought, in the circumstances, yet it seemed to Lucia that a man who could not string together enough words in one language to form a sentence – coherent or otherwise – was apt to be equally incapable of the concentration necessary for magework.

What, perhaps more importantly, did Roland *believe* himself to be doing, at this moment?

'Roland,' said Lucia, more loudly.

When once more he failed to react in any way, she glanced at Marcus Cattermole, then drew a fortifying breath, let go of her own left elbow, and laid her right hand across Roland's shoulder-blade.

At her touch, Roland came instantly full awake, turning on her and grasping her wrist with a speed and strength of which she should not, a moment ago, have believed him capable. His eyes, wide and wild in the candlelight, caught her gaze and held it.

She winced as the bones of her wrist ground together. Roland observed it – she saw his eyes widen further, his face go still – and his grip relaxed as quickly as it had closed a moment since.

'Lucia,' he said. He sounded as breathless as though he had been running. 'Lucia, what do you here?'

Have we not had this conversation once already? Lucia marshalled her swirling thoughts and spoke as calmly as she was able: 'You are suffering from magick shock,' she said, 'and must stay abed for the present. Henri Vauquelin wishes me to bear you company whilst you are recovering, and your mama has kindly given me leave to stay.'

Roland's face had gone wary. *I have said the wrong thing once again*, thought Lucia, *but what?*

'Monsieur Vauquelin wishes,' Roland repeated. He turned his head a little. Just enough.

Now, too late, Lucia saw her error very clearly. 'I cannot speak for Henri Vauquelin, of course,' she said, and with her free hand reached for Roland's; though his fingers did not return the pressure of her own, nor did he make any attempt to extricate them. 'But if I may venture a guess, his advice was based on his observations of both your behaviour and of my own.'

Roland's gaze swung slowly back to Lucia's face, his brows furrowed in puzzlement. *Again, with smaller words. And may what I am about to say never come to Queen Edwina's ears.* She bent nearer, lowered her voice, and said, 'Henri Vauquelin gave orders that I should stay because you and I both wished it, but Edward and your mama thought it improper.'

What reaction she had expected to this revelation, Lucia could not have said precisely; in light of recent events, however, she had certainly *not* expected Roland's wide, sunny smile – the smile of a child, or of a man who has drunk more than he ought – or that he should regard her with sweet, trustful eyes and say, 'I am glad of it.'

Keeping hold of Roland's hand, Lucia settled herself gingerly upon the edge of the bed. 'Will you lie down again now, and go back to sleep?' she suggested.

Roland looked away again, apparently to study the fall of the coverlet over his knees. 'I had rather not,' he said, very low.

'Bad dreams?' said Lucia, in the same tone. When he did not reply, she added, 'I should not wonder at it. Mine have been very bad indeed.'

'Is there any more of the gooseberry tart?' said Roland, too brightly. He turned his face so as to avoid meeting her eyes. 'Or the duck? I am very hungry.'

This was so transparently an attempt to evade her question that Lucia rather wondered at Roland's trying it on. Nonetheless, if he were offering to eat, she should not be the one to stand in his way.

'I shall go and see,' she said, therefore, and made to rise from her perch on the edge of the bed. But Roland's grip on her hand tightened, vice-like, and raw panic flared in his eyes for just a moment before he pressed his lips together and reasserted his will over his feelings.

'Perhaps Marcus Cattermole may go instead,' said Lucia. She

directed at that gentleman a hopeful smile and a small apologetic shrug of her shoulders.

'Of course,' he said, and went away to investigate the remaining contents of the covered trays on the sitting-room sideboard.

Snatching at this moment of almost-privacy, Lucia turned her attention back to Roland. He had loosened his grip on her, but without altogether letting go; his outward composure plainly concealed deep disquiet. This was Roland's first serious encounter with magick shock, she reminded herself, and if he were feeling rather fragile, therefore, it was not to be wondered at. But why should his anxiety take this particular form?

'You are afraid of my abandoning you to your fate,' she said, leaning closer than Queen Edwina would at all condone. 'Though what fate, I have no notion. You need not be, Roland, truly.'

Roland ducked his head. 'Not . . . not of your going,' he said. 'Not that.'

'What, then?' said Lucia, mystified. She waited a long moment for some reply – verbal or otherwise – and when none was forthcoming, at last said, 'Roland, will you not tell me—'

Booted footsteps heralded the return of Marcus Cattermole, carrying a dinner-plate on an invalid's tray. 'I regret that the gooseberry tart was all ate up, Your Highness,' he said, depositing the tray across Roland's knees, 'but there are some of these marchpane-cakes and nearly all the Cheshire cheese, and I have brought you the last of the scones and clotted cream and raspberries.'

'I thank you,' said Roland, reaching for the cheese with his free hand.

Over his bent head, Marcus Cattermole gave Lucia a look which clearly said, *There is more to this matter than we yet comprehend, my lady, and you and I both know it.* Then he withdrew himself to an armchair in the far corner of the room, took up a thick octavo codex which had been resting splayed open upon the arm, and settled down to read, as nonchalantly as though he had been in his own sitting-room.

Lucia cast him a grateful nod which, being bent over his book, he did not see, and resolved to thank him later for his discretion and tact – though she did not doubt that if he felt it needful, he should not hesitate to report all her doings and Roland's to Henri Vauquelin. Then she settled herself more securely on the edge of Roland's bed, at an angle convenient to the tea-tray, and with her free hand secured a scone.

'Roland,' she said, 'may I have the use of my other hand? I should like some clotted cream and raspberries with this scone.'

Roland looked up at her, his face all open, guileless surprise. Lucia waggled her fingers as best she could; he looked down again, this time at their clasped hands, and said softly, 'I – I am sorry – I did not mean—'

He opened his hand, and Lucia – moving slowly and carefully – retrieved hers, deposited her scone on the edge of the tray, and reached for the pot of clotted cream.

'There is something amiss,' she said, keeping her voice calm and even and her eyes on the movements of her hands: splitting the scone, spooning up the cream. 'Something beyond mere magick shock, as though that were not enough to be going on with. I should not for the world attempt to force a confidence – and least of all from you – but . . . if you should feel yourself in want of a confidante, Roland, you need look no farther.'

She chanced a look up – briefly, under her lashes – and saw that Roland was chewing thoughtfully on a marchpane-cake, the other half of which he held poised before his lips. He caught her gaze, swallowed, and, lowering his hand, said, 'You had bad dreams, you said. Tonight.'

Lucia nodded.

'You . . . you are not prone to them, in general?' said Roland diffidently. 'Some people are, I know, though I am not.'

Your sister Sophie, for example, thought Lucia.

'In general, not at all,' she said, truthfully enough. 'But my dreams were very bad tonight, when I contrived to sleep at all. Roland—'

'I hope you have not been too uncomfortable in the dressing-room,' said Roland, a little of his erstwhile solicitude creeping into his tone.

'Not at all,' said Lucia, rather less truthfully; then, pressing on, 'I slept the better for knowing myself within call if you should wake.'

Better being a relative term: she had not slept so poorly in many years, but in her own rooms in the Queen's wing of the Palace, she was quite certain, she could not have slept at all.

'I . . . I thank you,' said Roland. He sounded almost shy. 'Was Mama very angry?'

'Your mama, and Edward too, must care for our reputations,' said Lucia, 'as we neither of us take much notice of them ourselves. It is a trying duty, I have no doubt.'

Was that the shade of a smile curving his lips? *Good.*

But the smile, if such it was, was there and gone in a breath, and Roland was saying earnestly, 'I wish you will not antagonise her, Lucia.'

'I have no wish to do so,' said Lucia. Despite herself, her tone was rather chilly. It was not that she begrudged her husband his mother's affection – and the Queen had been very kind to her, Sophie notwithstanding, until their confrontation over Lucia's right to watch at Roland's bedside. *Perhaps someday I may be equally defensive, though I hope I shall not have cause.* 'But—'

'No, no,' said Roland, gesturing with a half-eaten scone like a boy half his age. 'That is not – no. I love my mother,' he said, ducking his head as though half regretting this admission, 'you must never think otherwise, but . . . but I see how she treats Sophie, and . . . and I had rather that you and she were friends.'

Lucia nodded, mollified. 'Her Majesty has made me very welcome,' she said.

For some time, unspeaking, they picked desultorily at the remnants of their impromptu picnic, the quiet punctuated at regular intervals by the *shiff* of turning pages from Marcus Cattermole's corner – a salutary reminder that they were not, in fact, alone.

'Roland,' said Lucia at last, a little hesitant but also desperately curious. 'Roland, what do you remember of last evening? Of the time we spent in the centre of the maze?'

Roland tilted his head thoughtfully, then straightened it again with a wince, rubbing at the side of his neck. 'Almost nothing,' he said. 'Though . . . more now than when first I woke and found myself here. But' – and here his brow furrowed and his voice took on an edge of frustration – 'I cannot make *sense* of the things I remember.'

Marcus Cattermole coughed quietly; Roland turned briefly to look at him before continuing in a much lower tone: 'I am not mad – am I? – to think that you told me to listen to the trees?'

'I did tell you so,' said Lucia, 'and I rather wish that I had not, as events transpired. But it seemed to me that they wished very much to speak to you, and I thought such vehemence must have some reason behind it. Do you . . .' She hesitated. 'Do you remember anything at all of what they told you?'

Roland screwed up his face in thought. After a moment he said, 'When you say *told* . . .'

Lucia inclined her head expectantly; she had not the least idea what he might be about to say, which only made her the more impatient for him to say it. For some time, however, Roland toyed absently with the spoon from the clotted-cream pot, covertly watched the apparently oblivious Marcus Cattermole, tilted his head back to look at the ceiling, and in general did everything but answer her question.

At last, when she had nearly given up hope of obtaining any sort of reply, he looked her full in the face and said, 'When the trees in Alba speak to you, as you have told me they do, *how* do they speak?'

Lucia looked back, nonplussed. '*Speak* is a metaphor,' she said. *Brìghde's tears! Is he so much discomfited because he expected* words?

Roland's expression – indeed, his whole bearing – slumped in what looked very like relief. 'Thank all the gods!' he said, loudly enough that Marcus Cattermole glanced up from his book, though only for a moment; then, lowering his voice again and gripping Lucia's hands, 'I suspected myself of going mad.'

'I am no healer,' said Lucia, cautiously, 'to judge *mens sana,* but you do not seem to me particularly inclined to madness.'

She was rewarded with a small, wry smile, and by Roland's letting go of her hands to help himself to the last marchpane-cake.

'My Latin is at fault, perhaps,' she continued, whilst he was still chewing. 'I am fluent enough for most purposes, but this is a magick I learnt in Gaelic, and have never spoken of in any other tongue; perhaps I might—'

'Lucia,' said Roland, touching her hand once more – a gentle, almost hesitant touch, worlds away from his earlier frantic clutching. 'Lucia, *tapadh leat*. Truly, if you had not been with me, had not been so quick-witted, I—'

His use of Gaelic to thank her made her smile, but that he should be thanking her at all—

'No,' she said. She was shaking her head, she found, without having intended it. 'No, I cannot – Roland, had I not encouraged you, not' – she held up a hand to forestall the protests presaged by Roland's gathering frown – 'not *pushed* you to explore a magick with which you had no experience whatsoever, you should not have needed anyone's quick wits.'

'I am not a *child*,' said Roland. He folded his arms across the placket of his nightshirt and frowned more deeply, unfortunately reinforcing the very picture he was attempting to disclaim. 'I am entirely capable of resisting the temptation to experiment, when I choose to do so. You are not to blame for my having chosen otherwise in this case.'

But I am older than you, and have been better taught, Lucia thought, *and plainly I know many things which you do not*. She had also had considerable training in diplomacy, however, and for this reason among others spoke none of these thoughts aloud.

'You are generous to say so,' she said instead.

Roland rolled his eyes, which – more even than the colour returning to his face, and the lively glint to his eyes – reassured her of his eventual recovery. 'Shall we strike a bargain?' he said, smiling cheerfully enough, and offering her his right hand in the Alban manner. 'If I undertake not to thank you for saving my life, will you undertake in return not to blame yourself for its having been necessary?'

Lucia could not help returning the smile. 'Agreed,' she said, and clasped his hand. 'But,' she added, when Roland had gone back to chasing an errant raspberry about the rim of his plate with the clotted-cream spoon, 'you have not answered my question: what can you remember?'

He looked up sharply, spoon poised above the plate. 'You were there,' he said, 'and were not . . . incapacitated, as I was, by my stupidity.' His Royal Highness entirely now, he waved off her protest. 'Your recollection of events, I am sure, must be perfectly clear. What use to you can my vague, confused impressions be?'

'You heard the trees,' said Lucia, simply, 'and I did not.'

Roland studied her, unspeaking, for a long moment.

'And it means so much to you,' he said at last, 'to know the thoughts of the trees?'

Put in such a way, it did seem an eccentric taste. 'It is as I told you,' said Lucia; 'the trees seemed afire to speak to you, and why should that be, unless they had something to say?'

She had meant to stop there – to speak the rational portion of the truth, that is, and not the untidy, sentimental whole of it – but the rest tumbled out of her mouth before she could stop it. 'And – you will think me very foolish, I suspect' – looking down at her hands tensely pleating the fabric of the unfamiliar dressing-gown – 'but I am a stranger in your kingdom, and I suppose I hoped your trees might speak to me of home. I – I hoped, too,' she added, hurrying over the words lest she lose her nerve to speak them at all, 'that you might feel more at home in Alba, if you knew something of the ways of trees.'

Roland was silent so long that Lucia grew apprehensive and chanced a sidelong look up at him – then, seeing his expression, raised her head to look him full in the face.

'I am sorry,' she began. 'I did not mean—'

But Roland caught her hands and shook his head at her, as if too overcome to speak, and her words trailed away into abashed silence.

'A day or two ago, Lucia MacNeill of Alba,' said Roland after a moment, 'I should have said you had not a poetickal breath in your body; you cannot wonder that I should be . . . a little surprised by your saying such things. I have written a deal of poetry myself, I fear, and you may believe me when I tell you that I should have retired from the field in triumph on the strength of such words as yours.'

Lucia, who had not at all intended poetry, and indeed rather regretted the degree of sentimental nostalgia to which she had given way, could not at all think how to reply to this.

'I,' she said, and stopped.

But Roland, for a wonder, seemed to comprehend what she had not said. 'You need not be the heiress of Alba every moment of every day,' he said softly, tracing the tip of one forefinger in a slow circle on the back of her hand. 'There is no shame in leaving a little space to be Lucia MacNeill, from time to time.'

From time to time, Roland of Britain, you are a very wise young man.

She smiled at him, and whatever he perceived in her expression seemed almost to light him from within, so luminous was his answering smile.

After some moments (or possibly hours) spent in the exchange of smiles, with Marcus Cattermole's softly turning pages for accompaniment, Roland said – very low, and in halting Gaelic – 'I do not know at all that I understand the trees; but I believe they tell me, *told* me, that they see an enemy – of mine? Of my father's? Of their own? I cannot tell – and warn . . . *warned* me to beware.'

Lucia sat very still for a long moment, considering this.

'Has your father many enemies?' she enquired after a moment, still in Gaelic. 'Have you?'

'I . . . My father . . .' Roland's voice faltered, then fell still. After a moment, however, he lifted his chin and began again, this time in Latin: 'I do not like to speak of it before you, but I trust you will excuse it, in the circumstances—'

With some effort, Lucia refrained from rolling her eyes. 'You surely cannot suppose me ignorant of the factions in my own kingdom which continue to oppose this alliance?' she said levelly, in the same tongue. 'The objectors are fewer now, and less belligerent – it is not popular to denounce Britain and all its works, as it was before your sister showed herself a hero on Alba's behalf – but some remain. I do not think, however, that any of them could have followed me here without being discovered.

'Though,' she added, 'I shall consult with Ceana MacGregor and Oscar MacConnachie in the morning, and see what may be done to investigate the possibility.'

Roland nodded. 'I thank you,' he said, 'for covering that angle of the matter, and I trust we shall find that there is nothing in it. Closer to home, however – you know, I expect, that some years ago Sophie was among those responsible for foiling a conspiracy upon my father's life?'

Lucia, who had not, rocked back in astonishment; then considered of whom they were speaking, and with a rueful chuckle said, 'I ought not to be surprised at it, upon reflection. This I suppose is part of the tale of the Lost Princess, which everyone in Alba is wild to hear, and which Sophie will never consent to tell any of us?'

'I do not know what tales may be told in Alba,' said Roland, a little stiffly, 'but should you wish to hear a true account of the matter from one who was there, I am quite ready to oblige you.'

There was a rustling from the corner; glancing up, Lucia saw that Marcus Cattermole had abandoned his book, at least for the moment, and was observing them with some interest. When his gaze crossed Lucia's flat stare, however, he blinked self-consciously and said, 'If you have no objection, m'lord, my lady, I should be the better for stretching my legs.'

'No objection whatever,' said Lucia.

He rose from his chair, laying aside his codex, and made for the door; Roland watched him out of the room with narrowed eyes.

Lucia settled back in her chair – her own legs were rather in need of stretching – and said, 'Well?'

'Er,' said Roland. 'What *has* Sophie told you?'

'Very little,' said Lucia. 'I know that her mother ran away with her when she was only a baby, because she objected to the terms of the marriage your father had contracted for her; and that she reappeared very suddenly some years ago, but was rarely seen at Court. All of which I knew before ever I met Sophie, and certainly before I discovered who she is.'

'Hmm. Yes.' Roland cleared his throat – ducked his head – smoothed his fingers fussily along the coverlet. 'It was Samhain-night six – five? – years ago, at the Royal Ball. There is always an enormous masqued ball for Samhain, you see. Sophie was there with Lord Kergabet's party – he was not a member of the Privy Council then, indeed I am sure my father had never laid eyes on him since he was first presented at Court – because she and Gray and Joanna had discovered a plot to poison my father.'

Lucia nodded, wide-eyed; news of such a plot had reached her own father's court in Din Edin, though shorn of details – including, it appeared, Sophie's involvement in the affair – within a month of its failure.

'I can be certain only of what I saw and heard myself, you understand,' said Roland; 'the rest is hearsay, more or less. In any case, the poison was in the libation to the gods, from which the King must drink before pouring the rest out onto the altar. It was Joanna's father who poisoned the wine, and my uncle Edric – Mama's twin brother – helped him do it, though it was not either of them who first had the idea.' Roland's face screwed up in disgust. '*That* honour goes to Viscount Carteret, who was then my father's chief advisor; it seems he fancied himself a kingmaker, and meant to promote himself from advisor to King Henry to regent to King Edward before the opportunity passed him by. And he might well have succeeded, too,' he added, 'if he had kept his conspiracy at Court – there was one of the Royal Healers in the plot, as well as Uncle Edric – and not brought Appius Callender and his students into it, in order to get at a better class of poison. And at Sophie, of course.'

'Whatever did he want with Sophie?' said Lucia. 'That is – I should have suspected him of wishing to put *her* on the throne, but . . .'

'An alliance with Iberia,' said Roland. 'Again. He did not think Sophie was truly the Lost Princess, but he meant to marry her off to some Iberian princeling all the same, for if he could not tell one half-Breizhek girl from another, nor could they.'

'Ah,' said Lucia. It had not occurred to her, for some reason, that this danger might have resurfaced; it was no wonder that the subject of royal marriages made Sophie twitch.

'If they *had* believed Callender to be telling the truth,' Roland went on, thoughtfully, 'perhaps Carteret and his co-conspirators might have taken better precautions. Or perhaps not – who can tell? In any event, they did not, and Sophie and her friends used her mother's magick to move about the Palace unnoticed, and my grandmother's magick – you have heard Sophie sing, I suppose? – to stop my father from drinking the poisoned wine.'

'Brighde's tears!' Lucia breathed.

'Only, none of it was quite enough to stop him from doing what he thought was his duty to the kingdom, by completing the Samhain-night offerings; so she made herself look like her mama, and *that* so shocked him that he dropped the wine-cup, and no one was poisoned after all. There was a deal of fighting after that, and my father ordered all of them arrested, for he was in no state to understand which of them were traitors and which heroes, and there was a trial the next day. Ned and Harry and I saw nearly the whole of it, because Mama would go bursting in to plead for Uncle Edric's life, and spit at Sophie, and we could not stop her.

'They ought all to have been executed for treason, but only Carteret was, in the end; the rest are shut up in the Tower of London still.'

Roland's voice was growing hoarse, and his eyelids beginning to droop; Lucia was therefore not altogether sorry to hear the door open wider, and see Marcus Cattermole slinking back in.

'Well,' she said briskly, 'you ought to sleep again now, if you can. Shall I just—'

She reached for the topmost pillow – meaning to rearrange them so that Roland might recline in more comfort – but halted mid gesture, startled, at his abrupt, involuntary '*No!*'

'Your Highness—' Marcus Cattermole started forward.

Roland ignored him utterly; Lucia flung up a hand – a gesture unconsciously copied from Ceana MacGregor – and their minder subsided, though Lucia could feel the wary tension radiating from him like some overambitious warming-spell.

'I shall stay here beside you,' she said – quietly, as though she had been speaking to a frightened child. 'As long as you like.'

To her own ears the words, the tone, sounded unbearably condescending; at any other time, she should have expected Roland to scoff at them, and blamed him not at all. But it seemed the lingering effects of magick shock, or of the nightmares of which he refused to speak – or, perhaps, of some other hidden hurt which

Lucia could not imagine – still held sway, for instead his stricken expression smoothed out into relief, and he loosed his renewed grip on the sleeve of her borrowed dressing-gown and settled back into his nest of pillows.

'Do you,' he said, so low that Lucia was forced to lean close in order to hear him. 'Do you—Sophie knows a spell, for sleep without dreams; I do not suppose you . . .'

Lucia shook her head in genuine regret. 'I am sorry,' she said, folding Roland's left hand into her own. 'I do know one or two other sleeping-spells, however, and perhaps that may answer?'

'Perhaps,' Roland agreed.

'Close your eyes, then,' said Lucia, and when he had done so, she laid her right hand across his brow, gathered her magick, and began to weave her spell.

'Lady Lucia,' said Marcus Cattermole in a warning tone, as he recognised what she was about.

Lucia looked up just long enough to stare him down, not pausing in her working; then returned her full attention to Roland, whose pulse and breathing were slowing at last into true sleep.

The spell concluded, she gently disentangled their hands and, greatly daring, bent to kiss his brow, then settled herself in her chair by the bedside and composed herself to snatch what rest she might.

CHAPTER IX

In Which Sophie Seeks Reinforcements

'I have a thing to tell you,' said Sophie, erupting into Lucia's sitting-room with her arms full of codices and a quite unaccountable grin spread across her face, 'which I hope may cheer you a little, now that Roland is going on so well. May I?'

Lucia had spent nearly every waking moment with Roland since their adventure in the maze, and was now too exhausted even to speak; she waved a hand at her friend – *Proceed, then* – without much enthusiasm. How could Sophie, who had made the journey from Grosvenor Square to sit with her brother for some hours nearly every day, and had to all appearances worried for him as zealously as his own mother, be so full of sparkling energy now?

Sophie closed the door behind her, surveyed the available seats, and settled herself at one end of the canary-striped sofa. She deposited her stack of codices upon an occasional table, and laid across her knees a leather portfolio tied up with red tapes, which she at once occupied herself in opening.

At last she extracted something from within – a sheet of parchment, it appeared, not large, which had until recently been rolled, for upon being released from the flattening portfolio it at once began to curl inwards from both sides.

Lucia sat up a very little, cautiously interested despite herself.

Sophie leant forward and spread the . . . parchment, yes, it was certainly parchment, across the low table that separated the sofa from Lucia's armchair, and weighted its corners with objects extracted from her reticule: a lump of blue sealing-wax, two copper coins, a heavy silver ring set with some sort of black stone.

Grudgingly, Lucia sat up straight, the better to see the thing on the table-top. It was . . . Was it a map? No: a bird's-eye view of – of a castle?

'Not a castle,' said Sophie. She grinned, and Lucia could not help smiling back at her. 'A college.'

Lucia blinked.

'Lady Morgan College,' Sophie elaborated, touching delicately with one finger the title scroll spread out across the top of the page. 'Established in the reign of King Henry the Fifth, and abandoned at the time of the Princesses Regent, two centuries ago or thereabouts. I disinterred this from a mislabelled pigeonhole in the Palace Archives; I know almost nothing about its provenance, however, as it does not seem to have been included in the archivist's catalogue.'

She looked up at Lucia, bafflingly expectant.

'Abandoned, why?' said Lucia, seizing upon one of the several puzzles presented to her, more or less at random.

'No one knows,' said Sophie. She had begun to exude an air of suppressed excitement, which Lucia could not at all understand, but to which she could not help responding. 'So far as I have been able to discover. Of course, there are a great many books I have not yet read – I have not been long about this business as yet – which may perhaps contain some clue.'

Lucia glanced at the small tower of books on the table.

'And you have brought me some of them?' she hazarded.

'Oh! No, not at all,' said Sophie. 'That is, yes; I have already read all of those, but you must read them, also, if you are to help me with my project.' She reached for the topmost codex, and handed them one by one to Lucia, who had just time to read their titles as they went by: *An Historie of Lady Morgane College, Oxford. Lady Morganne: A Life, Written by Her Nephew. The Oxford Colleges and Their Patrons. The Lives of the Princesses Regent. A Woman of Substance: The Extraordinary Life of Lady Morgan of Clwyd. A Man of Oxford: Being the Memoirs and Recollections of Arthur Claudius Antony de Coucy, Mag. D.—*

'Your project?' Lucia just succeeded in catching the books now attempting to slide off her lap in both directions, and attempted to herd them into a stack once more. 'What project is that? I do wish you might learn to begin at the beginning, Sophie.'

Sophie paused, still with a book in either hand. 'Oh,' she said, and her mouth twisted, a small self-deprecating smile. 'The beginning. Well—'

There followed a long, thoughtful silence, during which Lucia (familiar by now with Sophie's tendency to drift, and content for the moment to let her do so) examined the codex on the top of the pile, which proved to have been published in the reign of Sophie's grandfather. Arthur Claudius Antony de Coucy, Mag. D., she had concluded by the second folio, had been a dull and self-important fellow almost on the order of Xanthus Marinus, and she rather wondered that Sophie should have persevered through four hundred and forty-eight pages of his recollections.

At last Sophie said, 'The beginning is not at all to the purpose. The *end* is, that I think it is time someone brought Lady Morgan College back to life.'

This extraordinary statement was delivered with the same sunny smile and matter-of-fact confidence with which the Sophie of Quarry Close, tucking a stray curl behind her ear with inky fingers, might have said, *I mean to walk up to Arthur's Seat tomorrow; should you like to join me?*

This was, Lucia reminded herself, the woman who had set off across a foreign kingdom, alone but for two other young women who did not even speak the local language, to rescue her kidnapped husband from a would-be mage-king – and, against all expectation, succeeded in rescuing not only said husband but half a dozen other prisoners and, indeed, the kingdom itself. A woman, in fact, who made a habit of rescuing entire kingdoms. Resurrecting an abandoned college might well seem a mere rainy-day amusement by comparison.

'And that someone is you, I suppose?' she said, nevertheless. 'You mean to wave your hand, and say, "Let it be so," and there is an end to the matter?'

'Of course not,' said Sophie scornfully. 'I am not such a ninny. Nearly every don in every Oxford college will detest the very notion. My stepmother will tell my father that I am only jealous of Roland, or perhaps of Ned, and attempting to draw attention to myself, and will insist on his ordering me to desist. Joanna will fault my atrocious timing – you were quite right, Lucia, by the by, about Joanna—'

Lucia blinked, confused by this non sequitur; after a moment the mystery resolved itself, and she said quietly, 'Ah,' but Sophie's monologue had run on without her, like a boulder rolling downhill: '—and Jenny and Kergabet will ask me whether the matter might not better wait for a less tumultuous season, and Ned will attempt to reason with me, and say that I need not suppose that all young ladies are as mad for scholarship as myself. And,' she added, folding her hands around one knee, 'my mother-in-law will shake her head and tell Gray very sweetly and sorrowfully that this is what comes of marrying in haste, and without due regard to the views of one's family.'

'Indeed,' said Lucia. She was relieved by Sophie's apparent return to sober reason – though pondering, too, the significance of Gray's absence, and Roland's, from the list of objectors to her scheme.

Her relief and her pondering were alike short-lived, however, for at once Sophie smiled widely and said, 'And that is exactly why I need your help.'

'There is one thing I cannot understand,' said Lucia to Sophie, when next they met, looking up from *An Historie of Lady Morgane College, Oxford*. 'That is, there are many such things in this affair, but one chiefly: why, if – someone – were so determined to see the College closed once and for all, should they have left its buildings standing empty?'

Sophie grinned at her, very much in the manner of a tutor expressing pride in a student's perspicacity. 'Exactly,' she said. 'I have been wondering why the buildings were abandoned, when they might have been used by some other college – there has been at least one new-built since Lady Morgan College was closed – or even knocked down so that the land and the materials might be put to some other use.'

'Indeed,' said Lucia, thoughtful.

'I thought,' said Sophie, absently summoning her teacup and balancing it on her knee, 'that someone must know why things fell out as they did. I had great hopes of a book called *The Rise and Fall of Lady Morgan College*, which was written within a generation of the College's closing – most of the others, as you see' – a careless gesture, here, that nearly sent the teacup flying – 'are concerned with its founding, or with its foundress, and go no further than its period of flourishing – but I could find only one copy, and that had been badly damaged in some sort of flood.'

'An odd coincidence,' Lucia remarked. It did not sound to her like anything of the kind.

'You are no believer in coincidence, I know,' said Sophie, 'but I have no evidence, at present, that any mechanism was at work beyond ordinary negligence and ill fortune. At any rate, I have written to a few friends in Oxford, to beg their assistance in locating more books – beginning with any further copies of the damaged one – but have not had any reply. Besides, it is the Long Vacation, of course, and only the Fellows among them are at all likely to be in college at present.'

'But is it not an odd thing,' Lucia persisted, 'that you should be the first in – two centuries, is it? – to ask these questions? If I were a student in Oxford, I should be quite unable to let such a mystery rest, I think; and do not thousands of people see the College before their eyes every day? The dome of the Temple of Minerva, at least, is visible from quite far off, I believe you said. Did you never attempt to explore the place, in your time at Merlin?'

'Shrine, not temple,' said Sophie absently. Her expression folded up into a thoughtful frown. 'I believe I did mean to do so,' she said, slow and considering, 'but always I had other demands upon my time – or it was the wrong season, or the wrong time of day, or—' She broke off, staring at Lucia in some strange compound of excitement and chagrin. 'I am a fool,' she said. 'I am twelve kinds of fool, Lucia!'

She began a frantic search through the scattered volumes and manuscripts, muttering to herself the while in a hodgepodge of languages, as the fancy took her. Lucia toed off her ridiculous kid slippers, tucked up her feet, and prepared to wait out the fit of investigatory madness.

She had not long to wait, as it proved. No more than a quarter-hour had passed, by Lucia's judgement, when Sophie laid down the last codex she had picked up, flung up her hands, and threw herself into an armchair with a frustrated huffing sigh, for all the world like a five-and-a-half-foot child balked of its desire for sweetmeats.

'You did not find what you were seeking, then?' said Lucia, cautiously.

Sophie blinked at her for a moment, blank-faced, as though she were not altogether certain who had spoken or why; then her gaze sharpened, her face twitched back into life, and she said, 'On the contrary; I have found exactly what I expected to find. Which is to say, nothing at all.' She pitched forward suddenly, dropping her face into her hands, and between her fingers said miserably, 'Oh, Lucia, how could I have been so *stupid*!'

It was not a question, exactly, and Lucia could think of no very useful reply. 'I suppose,' she said after a moment, still feeling her way with great caution, 'that you have had a change of mind on the subject of coincidence?'

'You suppose rightly,' said Sophie, and raised her head. 'I spent two years at Merlin, Lucia, and of course I was not *idle* – I saw my tutor every other day, because I was afraid of falling behind the other students, you know, and I attended as many lectures as I could, and read everything I could lay my hands on – but that I should not even have time to *think*, to *speculate*, after—'

Again she broke off abruptly, this time to stare vaguely off into the middle distance. When she spoke again, her tone was softer, reminiscing. 'When I first saw Oxford – my very first glimpses of it, through the rain, on the day we arrived from Breizh – there was the dome of the shrine, in the midst of those derelict buildings, across the Cherwell, and I felt I had seen it before. And I had, of course; there was a drawing of Lady Morgan College in a book of my mother's. I had read of it more than once, and had pondered what it might mean, that such a College had existed once, and that it existed no longer – what it might have meant for *me*, for such a place to exist in the world, even if I could never come near it.'

Lucia felt that a window had been opened to her, briefly, on the blank untalked-of years of Sophie's childhood, and was half afraid to speak lest she break the spell. What must it have been like for that younger Sophie, to know herself cut off from the dearest ambition of her heart? For all the other young women like her – like Lucia, like Mór MacRury, like poor duped Catriona MacCrimmon – who had not had the good fortune to discover themselves to be princesses, with royal fathers willing to reshape the world (or some small corner of it) on their behalf?

'I should imagine you must have done,' she said.

'But between times, somehow,' said Sophie, ignoring Lucia's interjection, 'it slipped my mind. And till that day when I saw the dome, I had forgot all about it.'

Lucia frowned.

'And when first I saw what remains of Lady Morgan College, I felt . . .' Sophie clasped her hands tight together, squeezed her eyes shut, tilted her face up towards the ceiling. 'I felt such sorrow as I had never felt before, nor have felt since – and I have had some cause for sorrow, now and again.'

Lucia nodded.

'But – you will understand, I hope, what I mean – it was not *my* sorrow. Or not mine only. It so overwhelmed me then, I think, because . . . because it was so much larger than myself. I did not understand it at the time, of course. I did not understand anything to speak of, then; everything was strange and wrong and, and simply impossible, and that seemed no different from any of the rest, I suppose. And there was no time, of course. But later—'

She paused, and looked earnestly at Lucia.

'Later, when I did have time, when I was there within reach, *I did nothing*. And not only did nothing, but scarcely thought of it at all.'

'Sophie, you had other—'

'You are not *listening*,' said Sophie, abruptly vehement; Lucia blinked. 'As I did not listen when I ought to have done. It called out to me for help – I heard that call, when no one else did – and then I ceased to hear it; it simply . . . slipped my mind, as though it were no great matter. Do you not *see*, Lucia, what this must mean?'

Lucia did not, and said so. 'And I hope you will not take offence,' she added, 'when I say that I fear you may be reasoning in advance of the evidence.'

Sophie scowled at her; then, unexpectedly, chuckled. 'That is entirely possible,' she conceded. 'But it is also possible – is it not? – for a spell to exist which could produce such an effect.'

'Do you know of any such spell?' enquired Lucia, who did not. 'Spells of concealment, certainly; but what manner of spell could prevent you from *thinking* of a thing which you are perfectly able to *see*?'

'I have not the least idea,' said Sophie. 'But, indeed, if my magick can protect me from the notice of other people – can persuade them that I am not worthy of remark, that the person they see is of no interest to them – then why should not a similar effect be possible on a larger scale?'

Lucia considered this. As a theory, it was not implausible; all manner of things might exist in the world, without one particular person's knowing of them. 'But the books,' she said, waving a hand at them.

Sophie frowned. 'What of them?' she said – not dismissive, but enquiring.

'What I mean is – well, that they exist at all, surely, is evidence that the College is worthy of remark?'

'No,' said Sophie positively. 'Not at all; only evidence that its *history* is worthy of remark. *That* is what I could not find, you see: none of these authors has anything whatsoever to say about why the College was closed, or what became of it thereafter – though some of them at least must have been there to see it – and until just lately, Lucia, *I had never wondered why that should be so.* Does that not suggest to you some manner of magick at work?'

Lucia nodded slowly; it was difficult, indeed, to imagine any other explanation. Except—

'But why now, in that case?' she said.

Once more Sophie rummaged about amongst the codices, and extracted a battered volume upon whose front board was stamped the title *A Dove amongst the Peacocks.*

'This,' she said. 'My mother's book – that is, another copy – which I found by chance in my father's library, not long before you and Sìleas Barra MacNeill arrived in London. If it *was* chance,' she added darkly. 'Finding it made me remember; and I have kept it by me since, so I have gone on remembering. It has taken me all the time since to lay hands on these others, for apart from that plan, they are not in the catalogues, and none of the archivists knew of their being here.'

Lucia examined the book's flyleaf, upon which was written,

very small, the single name *Julia*, then turned to the title page. This repeated the title, and below elaborated, *Being the Tale of the Founding of Lady Morgan College, Oxon.* The author, it appeared, was one Charlotte Octavia Boucicault, D. Phil.; the date, more than two hundred years past.

'Well,' she said at last. 'You may leave the other books, and I shall undertake to read them.'

Sophie beamed at her.

'But,' said Lucia, 'I hope very much that you have got a better plan this time than haring off alone, without telling anyone where you are going, and hoping for the best.'

'Well! As to the *where*,' said Sophie, taking this rebuke in good part, 'of course we must go to Oxford; but not yet. I am sorry to say it, but we shall have no chance at all of doing anything – even so much as making the journey, though it is not more than sixty miles – unless I can persuade my father that nothing dreadful will come of it.'

Lucia looked from Sophie to the codex in her hands, and back again.

'Sophie,' she said slowly, reluctantly (for, as Sophie had correctly deduced, she was no less eager than her friend to escape the Royal Palace), 'how can you be sure that it will not?'

'I suppose,' said Sophie, 'it depends upon what you mean by *something dreadful*.'

CHAPTER X

In Which Lord Kergabet Receives a Letter

Amelia, with Lady Maëlle for chaperon, was gone to a ball given by Madame de l'Aigle in honour of her daughter, with whom Amelia had been at school; Mrs Marshall (who had not been invited) had complained of a sick headache, and, declining all offers of assistance, shut herself up in her room.

The rare dinner *en famille* – more or less – which resulted from this conjunction of circumstances was a relief to Joanna, who had felt for some time as though she walked on eggshells and would be penalised by the Fates for breaking any. The relief, she fancied, was more general also; the family in Grosvenor Square, and Gray and Sophie, had been let into the secret of Roland's alarming brush with magick shock, and of the cryptic warning he claimed to have received from the trees in the King's maze, and to their vivid anxiety for Roland's welfare had been added the strain of keeping these secrets, and the details of Sophie's recent visits to her brother, from their guests.

The conversation over the soup and the fish course, unsurprisingly, had been continually circling back to these subjects: was it, *could* it be, true that Roland – that anyone – was capable of communicating with trees? And, if so, how much store ought to be set by a warning received in such a way?

'This business of talking to trees,' said Mr Fowler, in a *now let us be sensible* tone which at once put Joanna's back up, 'seems altogether too fanciful to me.'

'Roland may be rather fanciful, I grant you,' said Sophie (something of an understatement, in Joanna's view), 'but Lucia MacNeill tells the same tale, and Lucia is no more fanciful than you are, Mr Fowler. It is not impossible, I suppose, that they should both be victims of the same illusion-spell, or some such thing, but—'

'But if both Roland and Lucia can be preyed upon by a mage powerful enough to craft such an illusion, on the very doorstep of the Royal Palace, then the enemy is at the gates indeed,' said Joanna, and Kergabet and Mr Fowler nodded in rueful agreement.

Treveur and Daisy came in with the joint of beef and its companions, and discussion of unexpectedly communicative topiary was suspended until their departure.

'I fear Lucia has put the cat among the pigeons rather,' said Sophie, when the door had closed behind Treveur. Rather than expanding upon this cryptic remark, however, she fell silent, and began tracing one finger round and round the rim of her wine glass to make it sing.

Joanna's mouth was full, but Gwendolen prompted, 'How so?'

'Your pardon?' Sophie blinked at her for a moment, then seemed to catch up the dropped thread of her thoughts. 'Oh! Why, because she would insist on sitting up with Roland all night, not only at first – which might have been excused, in light of the circumstances – but for several nights afterwards. Her Majesty said nothing to me about it, of course – or about anything else, for that matter – but Edward begged me to intercede, for the sake of propriety; as though I should do anything of the kind!'

'Her Majesty would do better to thank her for saving Roland's life, in my opinion, than to fret over the proprieties,' said Jenny, with unusual asperity; and, observing the raised eyebrows around the table at this departure from her usual staunch support of Queen Edwina in all matters not related to her fragile detente with Sophie, she continued, 'Well, and where should you be now, all of you, if *I* were inclined to set propriety above—'

'Above rearranging all of our lives for our own good?' said Gray, lifting his glass to his sister with a small smile. 'Where indeed.'

He looked at Sophie, seated across the table between Joanna and Mr Fowler, and the smile grew tender, crinkling up his hazel eyes. Joanna hastily looked away; but this did not at all answer, for now her gaze crossed Gwendolen's, and she found her own face rearranging itself likewise.

'I have had a letter from Roland,' said Sophie unexpectedly. 'He is feeling quite himself again, he says, and I think – reading between the lines, you know – is growing very impatient with being treated as an invalid. And Lucia has told him of our scheme for Lady Morgan College, and my notion of beginning by exploring what remains of it, and he is eager to assist in the enterprise – or so he says – and volunteers his help in whatever capacity I may deem most useful.'

'Does he, indeed,' said Sieur Germain, thoughtful.

'He is only trying to impress Lucia MacNeill,' Joanna scoffed. The notion of Roland as a champion of scholarship was too ludicrous for words, and as a champion of scholarship for *women*—

Sophie smiled. 'Gift horses, Jo,' she said mildly. 'What of it, if so? At any rate,' she continued, 'I have engaged to go with Lucia tomorrow to call upon Madame de Courcy in Half-moon-street, to tell her of our plans; Jo, Miss Pryce, I wondered whether you might wish to come with us, as Mademoiselle de Courcy is such a particular friend of yours?'

'Why Madame de Courcy, love?' said Gray, looking up from the plate of roast beef and greens which he had been systematically demolishing. 'I did not know that you were at all acquainted with her.'

'Because,' said Joanna, before Sophie could reply, 'Madame de Courcy is clever and well read, and has travelled to Eire and Alba, and to Flanders; and because she has three clever and well-read daughters, who would like nothing better than to be afforded the same opportunity as their brothers.'

'I wonder that Courcy does not arrange for them to study in Din Edin, then,' said Gray. 'As he has a home for them there already.'

Joanna had often wondered the same; Agathe was very young, of course, to be sent to live with her papa in a foreign city, but surely Mathilde and Héloïse, nineteen and seventeen respectively, might perfectly well have gone – with one of their brothers for escort, perhaps.

'If you were a mother of young daughters,' said Jenny, resting one hand (perhaps unconsciously) upon her middle, 'should you rather send them sixty miles to Oxford for their education, or four hundred miles and over the border to Alba?'

'Ah,' said Gray. 'Yes, that is a point, indeed.'

He went back to his dinner, staring vaguely at a spot of sauce upon the tablecloth.

'I should be delighted to come with you,' said Joanna to Sophie – who smiled at her, but rather absently – 'if Lord Kergabet has no objection. Gwen, shall you—'

There was a commotion below – rapid hoofbeats on the cobbles, and a hammering at the front door – and Joanna was out of her seat, in the act of darting to the window to peer down into the square, when the door of the dining-room opened to admit Treveur and a breathless courier in the royal livery, bearing a letter for Kergabet. Joanna quietly resumed her seat, and anxious glances passed up and down the table; such arrivals were not uncommon in the household of His Majesty's chief counsellor, and could not be assumed always to signal a crisis, but given present circumstances in the royal household . . .

Kergabet broke the seal at once and began to read; as he read, the colour drained from his face, and Joanna felt chill tendrils of fear creeping over her skin.

'My love,' said Jenny (by which Joanna knew her to be badly rattled), 'what news? It is not – there is not some worse news of Prince Roland?'

Kergabet laid the letter carefully down beside his plate; when he looked up, his gaze fixed upon Joanna. 'Your father and his cronies, Miss Callender,' he said, 'have escaped from the Tower, and are now at large.'

'*Oh*,' said Sophie faintly. From Gwendolen's place at the table came a sound like a stifled yelp; from Mr Fowler's and Gray's, almost simultaneously, low exclamations assuredly not suited to a lady's dinner-table. Joanna slowly unclenched her fingers from her fork and knife, slowly laid these instruments down upon her plate.

'I do not see how they could have done,' she said, distantly surprised that her voice did not tremble, much. 'They were held under lock and key, and within strong wards – were they not?'

'They were,' said Kergabet grimly. He pushed back his chair and rose to his feet, the letter still in his hand. 'Your pardon, my dear,' he said, addressing Jenny, 'but I must go and see His Majesty at once' – then, turning, 'Fowler, with me.'

Mr Fowler scrambled out of his own seat, leaving his dinner half eaten.

'The rest of you—' Sieur Germain broke off sharply, perhaps recognising that he was, after all, standing in a Grosvenor Square dining-room and not in the barracks-yard of the palace Guard, and resumed in a more moderate tone, 'Jenny, my dear, I trust it goes without saying that your mama need not as yet be burdened with this news.'

'Sir,' said Joanna, making to rise also.

Kergabet turned in the doorway and looked at her; she seemed to feel the weight of his regard, pressing her back into her seat, though that was surely fancy – perhaps, she thought, the shocking news had turned her brain.

'I am sorry, Joanna,' he said. Sincerity rang in his words – and regret and apprehension with them – and Joanna sat up straight in surprise at his form of address. 'Your involvement in their capture is likely to make you a target of revenge, if it is revenge they seek, and I should be criminally careless to expose you more than necessary.'

Joanna drew breath to protest that she did not at all regard any such danger, and had survived worse dangers in the past, but Kergabet forestalled her: 'Were circumstances otherwise,' he said, 'I should of course wish your assistance; but as things stand, you cannot be seen to be involved in this affair. You are too canny a judge of politics to suppose otherwise.'

A dozen arguments sprang to Joanna's mind – the foremost of which, unhelpfully, was, *I shall go mad if you leave me in the dark!* – but sober reason told her that Kergabet was right; any hint of her knowing more than she ought about her father's affairs must be damaging to more than herself. Deflated, she sank back into her chair, leaning her elbows heedlessly upon the table, and watched Kergabet and Mr Fowler out of the dining-room.

A long speechless moment ensued, in which Joanna could feel everyone else at the table watching her and pondering what to say.

What are you afraid of? she asked herself, furious to discover that her hands were trembling and tears stinging her nose. The answer came to her in a heart-stuttering flash: *Whoever or whatever is more powerful than the guards, the locks, and the wards on the Tower of London.*

'I beg you will excuse me, Jenny,' she managed to say, carefully aligning her knife and fork. 'I have rather lost my appetite.'

She rose from the table in her turn, and stalked out of the room, her gaze fixed in the middle distance so as not to risk seeing anxiety, concern, mistrust – worst of all, *pity* – in their faces.

By the time Gwendolen's hesitant knock (their private signal, six knocks divided into groups of two) sounded at what was presently their shared bedroom door, nearly an hour later, Joanna had had her brief, furious cry, composed herself, stonily ignored the anxious enquiries of Lady Maëlle and Sophie, written out a passionate defence of her right to participate in the manhunt for her father, read it over, torn it into tiny pieces, burnt it to ash in the basin on the washstand, and sat down at Gwendolen's desk to devise a new stratagem – an enterprise in which, thus far, she was signally failing.

'Come in,' she said, squaring her shoulders and turning to face the door.

The door opened slowly, and Gwendolen's narrow face peered round the edge of it, brow furrowed, as though she were uncertain of her welcome in her own bedroom.

'Come *in*,' Joanna repeated. 'And shut the door behind you.' After a moment she added, belatedly, 'Please.'

Gwendolen did so, but having closed the door, leant her back against it rather than crossing to the desk. Joanna had drawn the curtains, shutting out what daylight remained, and that side of the room was dark, out of range of the small lamp which cast its pool of candlelight upon the desk; Gwendolen held out one hand, her lips moved briefly, and a pale globe of magelight drifted upwards from her palm to hover near the ceiling. She stood still a moment more, muttering something under her breath, audible now but incomprehensible: a warding-spell, presumably, against eavesdroppers. Useful skills, both, which Joanna rather envied, though Gwendolen was apt to deprecate her own talent as small and insignificant.

'Are you . . . Are you well, Jo?' she said at last.

Joanna scowled. 'I am perfectly well,' she snapped, hating Gwendolen's diffident tone, hating her father and his misguided ambitions, hating her own weakness in the face of this crisis. *As though* my feelings *were of greater importance than the danger to the kingdom!*

'You don't look it,' said Gwendolen, stepping away from the door.

The unaccustomed diffidence had entirely vanished from her voice, and Joanna exhaled relief. She turned back to the desk, folded her arms upon its polished surface, and buried her face in the crook of her left elbow.

Footsteps approached; Gwendolen's hands settled on her shoulders. 'I know how little you like to be left out of things, Jo,' she said. 'I should not much like it, either, but . . . but I cannot quarrel with Lord Kergabet's reasoning.'

Joanna groaned. 'Nor can I quarrel with it,' she said miserably. 'If I could, I should have done so at once. I do not doubt he has arrived at the logical and rational conclusion, but that does not make me like it any better.'

'Well.' Gwen's thumbs skimmed across Joanna's shoulder-blades. 'You shall soon have thought of a scheme, I expect; you always do. And then we shall—'

We?

Joanna raised her head and half turned to look up at her friend. 'This is not a matter for larking about, Gwen,' she said earnestly, 'like Sophie's Oxford project. I should not care for the risk, if it were only to myself, but these men have killed before – not in battle, nor in their own defence, but by poisoning in cold blood – and if it were not for Sophie and the rest, they should have been regicides as well as murderers. I cannot allow you—'

She stopped, abashed by the scowl gathering on Gwendolen's face.

'And what was Cormac MacAlpine, then, if not a murderer and would-be regicide?' Gwendolen demanded, taking a step backwards and folding her arms. 'If *that* was not too much risk, why is this? For you ran towards that danger willingly enough, and made no objection to my running with you.'

'That was different,' Joanna began, indignant, but she could take her protest no further, unable to articulate in what, exactly, the difference consisted.

Cormac MacAlpine had kidnapped Gray – last in a string of captives whose ill fortune it was to be foreigners in Alba, and possessed of powerful magick – with the twin aims of using Gray's power and of ensnaring Sophie for the same purpose; which was, as Gwendolen rightly noted, to sweep Clan MacNeill from the throne of Alba and install himself in Donald MacNeill's stead. He had also, it later transpired, been wooing Sophie's friend Catriona MacCrimmon, whose family harboured some ancient connexion to Clan MacAlpine on the distaff side, with a view to establishing a new MacAlpine dynasty; though, to Catriona MacCrimmon's credit, she had not known the half of the means to MacAlpine's ends, and had behaved with great courage in defying him, once she began to learn the truth. MacAlpine's ultimate threat had been to the throne of Alba – indeed, as it proved, to the kingdom itself – but Joanna, in determining upon her course of action, had been motivated purely by the threat he represented to Gray and, through Gray, to Sophie.

What, then, was different here? Deprived of their head, the traitor Lord Carteret – beheaded upon Tower Hill in the wake of the conspiracy's revelation, as they should all have been, had not King Henry indulged his fit of clemency (*And look what that coin has bought us now, Your Majesty!*) – what threat did her father and his co-conspirators presently represent, and to whom? Of Appius Callender himself she knew enough – or thought she did – to draw some conclusions: he had long been prone to petty score-settling, seldom averse to cheating as necessary to win his small contests of power, always ready to take offence and to put the worst possible complexion upon any word or action of anybody else. Imprisonment had undoubtedly changed him, for how could it not? But still Joanna had no doubt that if left to itself, his mind would turn at once to revenge – and Joanna's own part in bringing about his downfall paled into insignificance beside those of Sophie and Gray, and of Lady Maëlle, and of Kergabet and even Jenny (who had twice had him thrown out of her house).

But as for Gwendolen Pryce . . .

'You are safe enough from my father's attempts at retribution, I believe,' she said at last, 'so long as he does not know what you are to me.'

Gwendolen's arms remained folded, however, and her fine dark brows drew closer together. 'And what am I, then?' she enquired, in what Joanna recognised as a dangerously level tone. 'Am I your pretty, innocent little bride, to be protected from the great perilous world at all costs? A swooning damsel for you to rescue and carry off on your prancing steed?'

The idea was so preposterous – aside from the obvious, Gwen was two years older than herself, and nearly a head taller – that Joanna nearly laughed aloud; but it was clear to her even in her present disconcerted state that this would be an enormous tactical error.

'No,' she said instead. 'No, of course not. Gwen, I—'

'We have made one another no vows, Jo,' Gwendolen continued, cutting across her, 'but surely you understand that were it in my power, I should pledge myself to you before the whole of Britain, by any vow you chose.'

'Yes,' said Joanna, weakly. 'Of course I know that.' She swallowed past the lump in her throat, and went on: 'And *you* understand, I hope, that I feel just the same.'

Gwendolen's expression softened a little. 'I have sometimes suspected it,' she said gravely.

'Then you understand why—'

'Jo.' Gwen dropped to her knees at Joanna's feet, clasped Joanna's hands in hers, and looked earnestly up into her face. 'Suppose that I were the one in danger – should you wish me to spare you the knowledge of it? To refrain from doing all I could to combat that danger, from a desire to shield you alone?'

Put in those terms, the notion seemed not only foolish but repugnant.

Gwendolen had not done, however: 'And you have not forgot, I hope, that if any one of us had set off alone on that mad sortie to the Ross of Mull, all of those poor fellows locked up in Castle MacAlpine should now be dead, or worse, and very likely all of us with them.

'In any case,' she concluded, 'did you not hear what Sieur Germain said to you?'

Joanna cast her mind back – ran over his words – and after a long moment said, '*Gwen!* Oh, Gwen, how clever you are!'

Gwendolen grinned, and Joanna tugged at her hands until she knelt up far enough to be soundly kissed.

For Kergabet had not said *you must not be involved in this affair*, but *you cannot be seen to be involved.*

It was not until the small hours of the morning that Joanna's busy brain cast up to her, like fortuitous flotsam upon the shingle of her conscious mind, the question of Amelia.

Amelia, whose behaviour Sophie had called peculiar – who had received at least two mysterious letters – whose motives for coming to London (as related by Katell) had seemed so suspect.

These questions had been superseded entirely, in Joanna's mind and no doubt in Sophie's, by the escapades of Roland and Lucia, and now by the potential disaster of the prisoners' escape. Now, however – if it were not merely the effect of a wakeful night, the sort of notion which daylight reveals to be utterly crackbrained – it occurred to Joanna to ask herself whether the three mysteries might not be connected. And if that were so . . .

Beside her, just visible in the faint glow of the banked fire,

Gwendolen slept quietly, curled on her side with one hand tucked beneath her pillow and the other just grazing the corner of Joanna's; the bed they presently shared was not a large one. Joanna gripped Gwendolen's shoulder and gently shook it, murmuring her name.

Gwendolen stirred – frowned – opened her eyes at last, her eyelids heavy, and in a voice blurred with sleep said, 'Jo? Is all well?'

'No,' said Joanna. 'I need—'

Gwendolen's eyes opened wide; she sat up straight, as though stung into motion, and reached for Joanna, taking her by both shoulders and peering earnestly into her face. 'What is it?' she demanded. 'Are you ill? Is someone—'

'No one is ill,' said Joanna firmly. 'But I have had an idea – about my father, and Roland's trees, and Amelia.'

Gwendolen favoured her with a sort of exasperated half laugh, flopped back down onto her pillow, and briefly pressed the heels of her hands to her eyes.

'An idea,' she said, through an enormous yawn.

'Yes,' said Joanna. She propped herself on one elbow. 'Does it not seem an odd coincidence that Amelia should be so very eager to come to London, and should be receiving mysterious letters and behaving so much unlike herself, at just the same time when her father has inexplicably contrived to escape what ought to have been the securest captivity?'

Gwendolen, somewhat to Joanna's disappointment, did not seem particularly astonished by this notion. 'It does,' she said, 'seem a very odd coincidence indeed.'

Then she stretched her long arms above her head, produced another enormous yawn, and said, 'For the gods' sake go back to sleep, Jo. This will all keep for the morning.'

She lay down again, curled up with her back to Joanna, and closed her eyes.

Joanna glared down at her, at the pale shape of her shoulder in the firelight, the dark stripe of her plaited hair. But no better soporific existed than the sound of Gwen's deep, even breathing so near at hand, and at last, in spite of herself, Joanna tucked herself against the curve of her friend's back, and drifted once more into sleep.

Sophie and Gray woke very early the next morning, and arrived in the breakfast-room almost before the breakfast itself – though not before Joanna and Miss Pryce, whom they found respectively demolishing a plate of brioches and yawning over a cup of tea.

'Amelia knows something,' said Joanna at once, and à propos of nothing whatsoever, the moment they crossed the threshold.

'Amelia presumably knows all manner of things,' said Sophie, bemused. Whatever choleric or melancholic humour had led Joanna to flee the dining-room and shut herself up in Miss Pryce's room all yesterday evening, in the wake of Sieur Germain's revelation, had now, it seemed, passed off. 'What—'

'About *Father*,' said Joanna, lowering her voice and leaning across the table. 'Those letters – her insistence upon coming to London *now*, for no good reason – the very odd way she has been going on, since arriving here—'

'Jo,' said Gray, regarding her gravely over the rim of his teacup, 'you understand, do you not, that you are accusing your sister of high treason?'

Miss Pryce blanched.

'No, no,' Joanna said impatiently, 'it is no such thing. I am only accusing her of doing whatever Father tells her; I do not suppose she had the least notion what any of it meant.'

'And what is it you suppose her to have done?' said Sophie. She had spent a miserably wakeful night, and dreamt of horrors when at last she slept; she did not feel capable at present of any degree of reason – but, after all, it was she who had first supposed that Amelia might be hiding something. *Only, I did not imagine anything so dangerous. Or so very, very foolish.*

Joanna made an impatient gesture. 'I have not the least idea,' she said. 'That is, not yet. Nothing particularly dreadful, I should imagine; passing along messages she did not understand to persons of whom she knows nothing, very likely, or arranging for the purchase of items whose purpose she could not divine. Truly, Sophie, you must not suppose that I am seeking revenge upon Amelia, or anything of the kind; I am only thinking of whether she may be able to tell us anything to the purpose.'

Gray nudged Sophie's cup of tea towards her hand; she looked at it, shuddered at the thought of drinking it, and looked away again. 'Has she heard the news, do you suppose?' she said.

'Surely not,' said Miss Pryce. 'Unless Madame de l'Aigle is curiously well informed. We can scarcely be said to have heard it ourselves, and Lord Kergabet was surely the first of His Majesty's court to be told.'

'Amongst the first, at any rate,' said Joanna. 'I agree with Gwen, however: Amelia cannot possibly have heard of it yet.'

She glanced towards the door and went as still as a cornered mouse; Sophie followed her gaze, and saw at once what was amiss.

'Heard of what?' said Amelia.

CHAPTER XI

In Which Joanna Takes Steps

'*Miss Callender!*' *said* Gwendolen, too cheerfully. 'I did not think to see you so early today. You must tell us all about Mademoiselle de l'Aigle's ball.'

Amelia frowned very slightly at Gwendolen and – to no one's surprise – ignored her question entirely. 'What is it I have not heard of?' she said, looking steadily at Joanna.

For a long moment Joanna studied her in turn. Framed in the doorway with one delicate hand on the door-handle, Amelia looked beautiful and fragile, her cheeks a little paler than usual, her blue eyes wide.

We are to say nothing to Mrs Marshall; Kergabet was very clear upon that point. But surely he did not mean us to keep Amelia in the dark also? And, besides, if what I suspect of her is so . . .

'I should sit down, if I were you, Amelia,' said Sophie. She patted the back of the chair beside her own; Amelia's frown deepened, and instead she took the seat by Gwendolen's, nearest the door which she had quietly closed behind her. Sophie, apparently taking no offence at this snub, poured out a cup of tea for Amelia and handed it across the table, where it was roundly ignored.

'Joanna,' said Amelia expectantly.

Joanna swallowed; this was more difficult, when it came to the point, than she had had any reason to expect. 'A messenger brought word from the Palace,' she said at last, 'whilst you were out, that the Professor and the others have escaped from the Tower of London.'

'The professor? Which prof—oh, Mother Goddess!' It was as well that Amelia had taken Sophie's advice, however ungraciously, for her pale face grew nearly green and she groped for her teacup with a shaking hand. 'Father? You mean that Father has—? Joanna, how – when—'

Sophie was up out of her seat and going round the table. Amelia saw her approach and turned from it; Gwendolen met her with a gentle hand on her wrist and a soothing murmur of words, whilst contriving also to meet Joanna's eye and nod minutely: *Go on, then.*

Sophie retreated, biting her lip.

'I know nothing more than I have just told you,' said Joanna. Beneath the table, she clenched her fingers in the folds of her gown. 'Had you no warning of this, Amelia, truly?'

Amelia's head snapped up. 'Of course not,' she said, in a passably persuasive tone of outraged astonishment. 'How should I have done?'

'No one blames you.' Sophie's voice was gentle and kind, as though she were soothing a spooked horse. 'If you will only tell us – or tell Lord Kergabet, or Jenny – what you know, what the Professor wrote to you, or bid you do, then I am sure no blame can attach to you for fulfilling the demands of filial obedience.'

'I'm sure I have not the least idea what you mean, Sophia.' Amelia's chin lifted in the old familiar way, the better to look down her elegant straight nose; she shook off Gwendolen's hand on her arm and folded her hands on the tablecloth.

'We know about the letters, Amelia,' said Sophie, still speaking in that gently coaxing tone.

'Which letters, pray?'

Joanna opened her mouth, impatient to have the thing over, but closed it again without speaking when Gwendolen caught her eye and, with another minute shake of her head, warned her off.

'I think you know very well which letters,' said Gray. Like Sophie's, his voice was calm and gentle, his expression kind; but beneath the placid surface something darker lurked, which made Joanna very glad that her brother-in-law's level gaze was not presently directed towards herself. Gwendolen blinked at him in surprise; Sophie made a small abortive gesture, as though she considered attempting to restrain him, but held herself back. She was muttering something to herself, too low for Joanna to hear.

Amelia, however, had either more nerve or less perception than her sisters (or, perhaps, both), for she appeared able to confront him without quailing. 'You may think what you please,' she said. 'It is no business of mine.'

'I think,' said Gray pleasantly, taking a sip of tea, 'that whatever your father and his cronies are about may pose a significant danger to the kingdom – to His Majesty personally – to Sophie and Joanna, and to my sister and her family – and I should not like to believe you, Amelia, so lost to compassion as to protect a quintet of convicted traitors at the cost of your own sisters' safety – to say nothing of your duty to your king.'

He paused for another, more leisurely sip, his gaze steady on Amelia's increasingly tension-taut face. The expectant pause stretched out; Joanna dug her close-trimmed fingernails into the palms of her hands, consumed with the effort of restraining her questions, her impatience, her peremptory demands.

'I have done no wrong to anyone,' said Amelia at last. She was composed, her voice steady, but her hands, too, were clasped so tightly that her knuckles showed bone-white through the skin.

'No one has said so,' said Gray – still calm, still perfectly reasonable. 'But your father and his co-conspirators have done a considerable number of wrongs to a considerable number of persons, and we have all of us a duty to do whatever we may to prevent their continuing to tread the same path.'

'My father—'

'Your father,' said Joanna, furious and unable any longer to bite her tongue, 'has poisoned a man in cold blood, for his own gain, and conspired in an attempt to repeat that achievement on a larger scale. Your father ought by rights to have been beheaded as a traitor. Your father—'

'He is *your* father as well as mine, Joanna Callender!' Amelia cried. She was out of her seat in a trice and leaning towards Joanna, both hands flat upon the table.

Joanna sprang to her feet, almost without intending it, and mirrored her posture, distantly annoyed at being still half a head shorter. 'To my everlasting regret, he is,' she replied; and, surprising herself by the honest laughter that bubbled up from her chest, she continued, 'That is, he was; I find I am disinclined to acknowledge him. Do you know, Amelia, I begin to believe that it was my gift from the gods to be wanted by neither of my parents, loved by neither, so that I might be free to steer my ship to a better harbour, amongst people whose good opinion does not depend upon my parentage, or my sex, or the circumstances of' – she faltered momentarily, then amended – 'of my birth.'

A shocked and ringing silence followed this outburst – Joanna was as deeply shocked at having spoken such thoughts aloud, as any of the others could possibly be to hear them – whilst the two sisters stared at one another across Lady Kergabet's breakfast-table.

This time it was Amelia who broke the stalemate; drawing herself up tall, arms folded, she said, 'It was not Papa's fault, any of it; it was *hers*.' She turned to Sophie. 'Your precious mama's. We should have gone on quite happily, the two of us, if—'

'You cannot possibly know what might have been,' said Sophie, with a surprising lack of heat. 'You were not above three years old when they were married; you knew no more than I did that we were not sisters born.'

Joanna, distracted from her own concerns, looked from one of them to the other with narrowed eyes; this exchange had all the earmarks of a debate continuing after some earlier interruption.

'In any case, Amelia,' said Gray, 'no one supposes that the original notion was your father's; the priests of Apollo Coelispex established at the time that he was recruited into an established conspiracy by Lord Merton, at the instigation of the late Viscount Carteret, because he was a mage of Merlin College and could help them to an appropriately subtle poison for their purposes.'

'But—' Amelia's befuddled expression reminded Joanna that she had not been present whilst the rest of them (together with the conspirators) were examined by the truth-seeing priests; impossible to say what she might know, or believe, about the events leading up to her father's arrest and imprisonment. 'But it was *her* they wanted, as bait for the King.'

'Is that what the Professor told you?' said Joanna. 'It was not the whole truth, if so. And I do not suppose he happened to mention that he had promised you in marriage to one of his students – he had not yet made up his mind which of them to favour – in return for their assistance with his part of the scheme?'

Amelia blinked at her, the very picture of maidenly outrage. 'Mr Taylor had nothing to do with any of it!' she exclaimed. 'Nor dear Mr Woodville, either. And I shall never believe such a thing of Papa; the very notion is ludicrous.'

Gray and Sophie and Joanna exchanged a look of grim surmise. Gwendolen looked on in patient bafflement, trusting presumably that Joanna would enlighten her at some less frantic moment.

'That was not the verdict of the priests of Apollo Coelispex,' said Gray, reasonably, after a moment.

'Then, evidently,' Amelia retorted, speaking with great precision as though she feared what might spill out if she relaxed her vigilance for a moment, 'the priests were mistaken.'

'Amelia, the priests of Apollo Coelispex are truth-seers,' said Joanna. 'His Majesty called upon them precisely for the purpose of ensuring that there should be no mistake in the verdict.'

'But Mr Taylor was not present to be examined!' Amelia protested.

'All of his confederates were questioned, however,' said Gray, 'as were your sisters and I. Of course I cannot say precisely what testimony was given by any other person, but I *can* state categorically that one of Apollo's chosen heard me tell of Woodville's part, and Taylor's, in procuring . . .' He paused, glanced uncertainly at Sophie, then continued: 'in procuring, through highly suspect means, a key ingredient of the poison, at Professor Callender's direction; and that Apollo Coelispex judged my account a true one.'

Amelia's mouth was set in a hard line, and she gazed steadily at a point somewhere between Gray's arm and Joanna's shoulder.

'I am sorry to further tarnish your image of your father,' said Gray at last, more gently. 'But is it not better that we should see the world as it is?'

'I beg you will excuse me,' said Amelia, stiff and formal, to no one in particular. Still meeting no one's eye, she rose from her seat (Gray rose also, as though by reflex), turned away from the table, and set her hand to the door-handle.

It rattled, but would not turn. Gray sank back into his chair. Was it he who had tampered with the door? Or Sophie?

Amelia turned back, strung tight with fury – Joanna flinched away from her venomous expression – and apparently quite free of any such doubt. 'How dare you!' She pointed a shaking forefinger at Sophie. 'Let me out.'

Sophie flinched also, but when she spoke, her voice was steady. 'This is not some petty quarrel over a doll or the seat nearest the fire on a chilly evening, Amelia,' she said. 'I *dare*, as you put it, because you have information which may be material to the welfare of the kingdom—'

'As though you cared two pins for the kingdom!' Amelia's cheeks were flushed, two bright spots in her pale furious face, and her blue eyes burnt. 'As though you cared two pins for anyone but your precious self! How could I have thought you truly wished for peace between us? It was this you wanted all the time, of course it was. It is not enough that you should have taken my father from me – my home – every prospect of a good marriage – now you mean to take even this—'

Even this? Even what? What in Hades is she talking of? Joanna tried to catch Gwendolen's eye, but Gwendolen had no attention to spare for her at present; like the rest of them, she was riveted by Amelia. *Amelia could not hold us more in thrall if she were working some dire magick upon us.*

165

'—and I tell you plainly, *Your Highness*, I shall not let you do it.'

They regarded one another for a long moment – Amelia stiff and bristling and furious, glaring for all she was worth; Sophie visibly labouring to maintain her calm facade, and only just managing it – and Joanna began genuinely to fear that words had now been spoken which could never be called back. If she did not love Amelia as she loved Sophie – indeed, Amelia had more often been a burr under her saddle than not – once upon a time Amelia had stitched clothes and bonnets for Joanna's dolls, had acceded to her pleas for yet another game of hunt-the-slipper, had held her close and said nothing when, on that first long and difficult night at school, Joanna had slipped out of her own bed, crept about in the dark, and clambered up into her sister's.

'Sophie,' said Joanna quietly, 'let her go.'

Sophie turned to her, mouth opening on some protest or denial. Joanna raised a hand to forestall it and, carefully rising from her chair, edged round the table to Sophie. She felt Amelia's eyes on her, burning; and Gwen's, full of anxious care.

'Truly,' she said, standing a-tiptoe to murmur in Sophie's ear, 'there is no victory to be had here. Whatever she knows – if indeed she knows anything at all, and is not again an ignorant victim of others' machinations – you are only making her the more determined never to tell you.'

Sophie sighed, a soft and almost silent exhalation, and her eyes closed briefly. 'I know it,' she said, very low. 'I—'

Whatever she had been meaning to say, however, she evidently thought better of it.

Joanna clasped Sophie's shoulder – whether to comfort or to restrain, even she herself was not altogether sure. Sophie, at any rate, made no attempt at escape. At length she drew in a breath, let it out, and raised her head to look squarely at Amelia.

'I have never had any wish to hurt you,' she said, 'though I do not suppose you will believe me when I say so. But, Amelia—' She paused; Amelia stood straighter, if that were possible, and glared harder. 'If you insist on protecting your father – on protecting men whom the gods themselves have declared guilty of treason and deliberate murder – that is for you to decide; but we shall none of us help you do it.'

Then she snapped her fingers.

Amelia did not deign to reply, but turned so quickly back to the breakfast-room door that her skirts swirled out behind her. The door-handle turned smoothly under her hand, and half a moment later the door closed behind her with a decisive *snick*.

Sophie sank into the nearest chair, staring after Amelia; the others, warily, stared at Sophie.

At last, with a soft rustle of skirts, Gwendolen straightened in her chair and leant her elbows upon the table. 'Ought I to go after her, do you think?' she said.

'To what purpose?' said Sophie dully.

Gwendolen deflated.

Joanna frowned down at the top of Sophie's head. 'Later, perhaps,' she said, smoothing out the frown with some effort, so as to direct an encouraging half smile at Gwen. 'It is a good notion, but not just now, I think.'

Unless she was much mistaken, Amelia had been mere moments from giving way to angry tears, and woe betide anyone who might happen to witness them.

Sophie flung herself up out of her seat and paced two rapid circuits of the breakfast-room.

'*Cariad*, we cannot even be certain that Amelia knows anything to the purpose,' said Gray, catching her hands as she rounded a corner of the table.

'And we cannot be sure that she does not,' Sophie retorted.

'But in any case,' said Joanna, restraining her impatience with some difficulty, 'there is nothing to be done about the matter now.'

Sieur Germain de Kergabet was not seen again in Grosvenor Square for several days, or at any rate not in daylight. On the third evening he at last reappeared – grim-faced and pale with fatigue, with Mr Fowler, arms full of dossiers, drooping in his wake – well after dinner, and though Sophie and Joanna darted downstairs as soon as they heard the front door opening, Jenny was there before them, bundling her husband off to, in her words, *sleep until the sun is up again*. Sophie, Gray, Joanna, and Miss Pryce had thus to contain their impatient questioning – and, worse, to entertain Jenny's mama – for the remainder of the evening.

This they managed well enough for the first half-hour, as Amelia had a great deal to say of the milliners' shops she and her friend Mademoiselle de l'Aigle had visited in the course of the day, and of Mademoiselle de l'Aigle's brother who had escorted them. Amelia, it appeared, was keeping the ill news to herself, and the recent acrimony was not to be acknowledged outside the closed circle of its participants – for which small kindnesses, after several days' stony silence, Sophie was grateful. But Gray's mother (whatever Sophie might privately think of her from time to time) was neither stupid nor inattentive, and it was not long before, despite the others' best efforts, Mrs Marshall turned to her elder son and said, 'Whatever has Genevieve been doing upstairs all this time? I hope Lord Kergabet is not unwell? Perhaps I may be of some help?'

Gray shot Sophie a look of pure panic, and Joanna began to

talk, very brightly and rather too fast, about a fine pair of grey carriage-horses she and Miss Pryce had lately had sight of, almost the equal of Jenny's; to which conversational breeze Miss Pryce trimmed her sails willingly enough, but which failed signally to engage its target.

Whilst this stratagem of Joanna's was going forward, Sophie was wrestling with her conscience, which spoke to her in the gruff baritone of Dougal MacAngus, lecturer in magickal ethics at the University in Din Edin: was it, or was it not, a permissible breach of principle to use her magick to distract her mother-in-law's attention from a matter which they had been expressly instructed not to discuss with her?

A pleading glance from Miss Pryce decided her. 'Miss Pryce,' she said, rising from her chair and drifting over to the pianoforte, 'Amelia, may I impose upon either of you to turn my pages, or perhaps to indulge me in a duet?'

Miss Pryce sprang up from the sofa as quickly as though she had sat upon a hatpin. 'I should be most happy, Mrs Marshall,' she said, and, bending close to Sophie's ear with one hand on her shoulder, 'A lullaby, perhaps? Or something like it?'

'You are very quick, Miss Pryce,' said Sophie, low, and began riffling through her collection of songs in search of the Cymric song which she had so often heard Miss Pryce sing to Agatha and Yvon in the course of this sojourn in Grosvenor Square, and had entertained herself one rainy afternoon by setting down and harmonising.

'Oh, but you must wait for Genevieve!' said Mrs Marshall. 'Whatever can be taking such a time? Graham, do you not think I ought—'

'Let me?' said Miss Pryce quietly, when after some searching the necessary page had yet to come to Sophie's hand, and Sophie yielded up her seat at the pianoforte.

Whilst Mrs Marshall went on talking of Jenny, in fretful counterpoint with Gray's unpractised attempts to soothe or divert her, Miss Pryce settled herself on the piano-stool, flexed her long fingers, and setting them upon the keys, produced an experimental series of chords. Then she looked up at Sophie over her shoulder, and at Sophie's tiny nod, turned back to the instrument and began to play and sing:

Huna blentyn, ar fy mynwes,
Clyd a chynnes ydyw hon . . .

Miss Pryce had a very pretty voice, though not a strong one; it shook a very little with the force of her anxiety. Having seen her, as Sophie had done, with her dark hair shorn to boyish curls, dressed in clothes borrowed from one of Kergabet's grooms, matter-of-factly plotting the theft of an Alban publican's draught horses in the service of a sub rosa rescue mission on the Ross of Mull, such anxiety seemed out of character; but, after all, there came a point in that sort of undertaking after which nothing seemed altogether real, and one could only fight one's way forward, for there was no way back – none of which was necessarily useful preparation for Mrs Edmond Marshall.

For Miss Pryce as for Sophie herself, however, singing appeared calming to the nerves, for as she settled into the burden (*Ni chaiff dim amharu'th gyntun/ Ni wna undyn â thi gam . . .*) the clear mezzo-soprano was steady and sure – and, better still, Gray, Amelia, and Joanna (did Joanna know how clear the longing showed upon her face?) had all turned attentively to listen, depriving Mrs Marshall of her audience.

Sophie laid a steadying hand upon Miss Pryce's shoulder and felt her way into a descant upon the melody. She did not have the words by heart as Miss Pryce did – it was for this reason as much as any other that she had been attempting to find her notated copy – and so resorted to improvised and vaguely Cymric-sounding nonsense; Miss Pryce's shoulders twitched briefly under her hand, in censure or amusement.

Once, long ago, the magick Sophie had inherited from her grandmother by way of her father had flowed out along with her voice without conscious thought, without effort – in fact, altogether without her knowledge, inflicting her cheerful or melancholic or pensive humours upon everyone within earshot. For some years now, however, she had been labouring at the task of bringing it under her conscious control, and acutely mindful of her capacity to do harm by this means; the result was that she had now to find her way into the magick, as well as the music that would carry it forth.

She ought to have chosen some other song, of course – one whose words and melody she knew as she knew the lineaments of her sister's face, or of Gray's – so that she might sing by instinct alone, and devote all her conscious thought to the magick. *But, however, le mal est fait*, she told herself, and, satisfied that she should at least not disgrace herself, sank down into the awareness of her *magia musicae*, surveyed the metaphorical gates with which she had learnt to keep it in check, and began unlocking them one by one.

By the time Sophie and Miss Pryce had sung once through the latter's lullaby and once through 'Llywn On' (the more effective as a spell-song, because Sophie knew it so much better, though it was by no means a lullaby), Gray was yawning enormously, and everyone else appeared to be fast asleep. Miss Pryce turned on the piano-stool, stifling a yawn of her own, and said, quietly astonished, 'Well!'

Sophie crossed the room to perch on the arm of Gray's chair, winding her arms unselfconsciously about his neck (there was no one to see but Miss Pryce, and she, Sophie knew, had seen much worse).

'I ought to feel guilty,' she muttered into the hair above his ear, 'but I confess I cannot quite manage it.'

'Nonsense,' said Gray bracingly. 'Desperate times, desperate measures . . .'

He yawned so widely that his jaw produced a tiny, ominous creaking sound, then scrubbed his free hand through his hair. Sophie leant more fully into his embrace, closed her eyes, and sighed.

It might have been some hours later, or perhaps only a few moments, that she was startled awake by Jenny's voice, exhaustion mingled with sardonic amusement, enquiring, 'And what have we here?'

Sophie sprang up – she had somehow slid down from the chair-arm into Gray's lap, as though her former position had not been humiliating enough – so quickly and carelessly that her shoulder caught Gray under the chin and her elbow jabbed him in the ribs.

'Oof,' he said sleepily, rubbing at his jaw. He blinked up at Sophie, then at Jenny, who stood just inside the drawing-room door, wearing an unseasonably woolly shawl and a bemused expression, and at last said, 'Well?'

'Oh, no,' said Jenny. 'None of that, if you please. You may ask your questions in the morning.'

'Jenny?'

They all three turned at the sound of Joanna's sleep-roughened voice. Joanna and Amelia had dozed off on the blue sofa, one heeling over to port and the other to starboard; Joanna, rousing herself, looked for a moment more like a badger dressed for dinner than like a well-brought-up young lady.

Miss Pryce, at the piano, rubbed one eye and suppressed a yawn. 'What's the hour?' she said.

'I have not the least idea,' said Jenny, 'except that it is past time for all of you to be abed, my wayward goslings. Sophie, what on the gods' green earth have you done to my mother?'

'I—'

'What we shall have to do again before long,' said Gray, 'if we are not to speak to her of what is in all of our minds. I am out of practice in withstanding maternal interrogation, Jenny, and your disappearing upstairs for the whole of an evening was bound to raise Mama's suspicions—'

'There was no help for it,' said Jenny. She cast an anxious look in the direction of her mother; Sophie followed her gaze but found Mrs Marshall still asleep in Jenny's chair, very gently snoring. 'He was half dead with fatigue – and Mr Fowler no better – and he would never rest if I did not *make* him.' Another glance at Mrs Marshall – a furrowing of brows – and then she said, 'Have you thought what you shall say to them, when they wake?'

'There was no help for this, either,' said Gray firmly.

'I do not think I meant your mama to fall asleep, exactly,' said Sophie. Her conscience was prodding her with renewed force now, and she was regretting having yielded to the impulse to end the conversation by any means necessary. 'Only to stop asking questions which none of us dared answer, and threatening with

173

every other breath to charge up the stairs to your assistance.'

'Mother Goddess!' Jenny breathed, her face going rather pale. 'I thank you, in that case, from the bottom of my heart; though I should rather like to ask Lady Maëlle—' An anxious, questing glance about the room. 'Where is Lady Maëlle?'

Joanna and Sophie exchanged a look: Jenny was distraught indeed, if her ordinarily perfect recall of all her guests' comings and goings had been disrupted to this extent. 'She is gone to stay with Lady Karaez,' Sophie reminded her, 'to assist with her lying-in.'

'Yes,' said Jenny, nodding. 'Yes, of course. How stupid of me to forget!' She put up a hand to her head – the movement a near-twin to Gray's habitual gesture, but stymied by the arrangement of her hair – then pressed the other to her eyes.

'Jenny,' said Sophie, approaching her with some caution to lay a hand on her arm. 'Jenny, when had you last a proper night's sleep?'

Jenny's hands came down from her face; she clasped them together, then visibly loosened her grip. 'I have been rather anxious,' she conceded.

'Of course you have,' said Joanna, 'playing hostess to half the kingdom whilst your husband is off doing the gods know what in pursuit of a band of—' She shut her mouth with a snap; swallowed; and after a moment continued, 'Go along to bed, Jenny, I beg. Gwen and I shall be hospitable in your stead; and perhaps things may look better in the morning.'

Or better yet, the afternoon.

Jenny protested, but plainly her heart was not in it, and before long they had succeeded in sending her away to bed, with Gray's arm to help her up the stairs. Sophie, Joanna, and Miss Pryce looked at one another, then studied the two sleepers; at last Sophie said, 'Miss Pryce, come back with me to the pianoforte; Jo, sit down again . . . Where were you? Ah!' Joanna had found her place at one end of the blue sofa and was arranging herself, somewhat implausibly, as though reading the book of philosophical treatises which Gray had left behind on a nearby occasional table. 'Yes, that will do splendidly.'

Sophie sat down at the pianoforte, struck up a rollicking melody in triple time, and poured a judicious measure of magick into a wholly illusory feeling of cheerful energy as she began to sing: '*O, whistle and I'll come to ye, my lad!*'

It was a deliberately provocative choice – a song of the Borders, such as Mrs Edmond Marshall most disparaged, and of unabashed female flirtation, which (by her lights) was worse – and Sophie's magick, or the song itself, or both, soon had the desired effect: first Amelia, then Mrs Marshall, started and snuffled awake, and neither seemed at all reluctant to believe that they had only nodded off briefly, when Joanna told them so.

CHAPTER XII

In Which Sieur Germain
Calls a Council of War

Early the following morning Sieur Germain quietly gathered his forces – in the persons of Joanna, Miss Pryce, Sophie, Gray, and Mr Fowler – in the library. To Sophie's secret relief, both her brother-in-law and his secretary looked much the better for their night's sleep: grimly resolute, rather than merely grim.

They seated themselves along the sides of the long reading-table, upon which the morning sun cast blocks of light through the eastward windowpanes. At the head of the table, Sieur Germain cleared his throat.

'This is highly irregular,' he began, 'and I must tell you that I am acting against the wishes of several senior members of His Majesty's Privy Council; but in my view all of you have, for your own reasons, a vital interest in the question at hand, and a right to fuller information than His Majesty may as yet see fit to make public.'

How exactly this assessment applied to Miss Pryce – and not to Amelia – Sophie was not certain; but perhaps, in Kergabet's estimation, Miss Pryce had earned her right to be in all the family secrets by her extraordinary bravery and resourcefulness on the

Ross of Mull, and if that were the case, Sophie could not disagree.

'The prisoners have now been at large most of a se'nnight,' Kergabet continued, 'and as yet we know very little more of their methods or whereabouts than we did on the day of their escape. A general search of vessels departing England, Cymru, and Kernow has been ordered, as well as a search of all conveyances departing London, and descriptions of all the prisoners have been circulated to the Watch Captains of every city and town large enough to possess such a thing.'

Sophie nodded.

'And, of course, as well as such practical measures Lord de Vaucourt and his colleagues have undertaken various scryings and finding-spells – also, I regret to say, to no avail.'

'Perhaps Sophie and I may be of some assistance in that endeavour,' said Gray. Ignoring the wary frown which instantly creased his brother-in-law's face, he continued, 'A colleague of ours in Din Edin was kind enough to teach us some very useful variants on the standard finding-spell, which may be used to extend the spell's range or to continue it over a period of several days.'

Joanna muttered something under her breath to Miss Pryce, presumably in reaction to this statement, which Sophie chose to ignore.

'I thank you,' said Sieur Germain. 'I shall convey your offer to Vaucourt this morning.' He had ceased frowning – in fact, he looked rather pleased – and no wonder: here was a means by which they could be useful, but quite without drawing danger upon themselves or the rest of the household. 'In the meantime, however, I must ask that you bear in mind the danger which these men may pose to the three of you particularly' – he looked gravely at Sophie, Joanna, and Gray in turn – 'and continue to refrain, so far as is possible, from advertising your presence in London.'

'That horse has long left the stable, I fear,' said Joanna.

'I must confess,' said Sophie, attempting to convey the same sentiment with more dignity, 'that I do not see how our presence can possibly be concealed. Joanna is known to the whole of London society, it seems to me, and this past se'nnight excepted, I have been seen with Lucia MacNeill at every gathering of note since I arrived.'

Her brother-in-law gave her a grim little smile. 'Nevertheless,' he said.

Sophie could see his point – she was not a fool – but after such freedom of movement as she had enjoyed in Din Edin, under the eyes of watchers so discreet that she need not remark their presence unless she wished it, the prospect of continuing in what amounted to house arrest held even less appeal than formerly.

'Sophie,' said Joanna, with a small incredulous laugh, 'surely *you* are not objecting to be told not to draw attention to yourself?'

Sophie frowned at her but was forced to concede that this was, in fact, an absurd position for her to take.

'I will undertake to conduct myself with all possible discretion,' she said primly, therefore, and Sieur Germain nodded, apparently satisfied.

'And it need not even be said, I hope,' he continued, now addressing Joanna and Miss Pryce, 'that there can be no question of anyone's riding in the park unescorted, at dawn or at any other time, until this business has been . . . satisfactorily concluded.'

Joanna and her friend, who ought surely to have predicted this, looked briefly outraged; before either could protest, however, Kergabet quelled them with a look.

'There is another complication, however,' said Sophie to

her brother-in-law. Briefly she recounted the substance of their tumultuous conversation with Amelia, emphasising her own conviction and Joanna's that Amelia was concealing something connected to her father's escape.

'A complication, indeed,' Sieur Germain sighed. He rested his forehead briefly on one fist – for just a moment revealing the weight of the cares that pressed upon his broad shoulders – then met Sophie's gaze with a return of his earlier calm resolve.

'I should not expect that Amelia will talk of this to anyone,' said Sophie, 'but – begging your pardon, sir – Mrs Marshall is not a fool; this is not a secret that can be kept for very long, not within this house.'

What she wished very much to say, but – being a guest in Kergabet's house – did not quite dare, was that Mrs Marshall had as much right as any of the rest of them to know what was afoot, if only so that she might take herself off home and out of the way of events.

Sieur Germain acknowledged her words with a curt nod. 'We had hoped, of course,' he said, 'for the expeditious recovery of the prisoners, so that the public need not be alarmed unnecessarily.'

Sophie did not need Joanna's sotto voce gloss to interpret this as *So that this disaster might the more easily be hushed up.*

'Regrettably, however . . .'

'Yes,' said Gray. 'We shall of course be guided by you, sir, but I must agree with Sophie: this news is not likely to improve with age.'

'I shall speak with your mother this evening,' said Kergabet. Had they, in fact, persuaded him of something? Or had he been intending such a conversation in any case?

'I am glad to hear it,' said Gray.

'Lucia MacNeill has already been told what is afoot, however, I hope?' said Sophie. 'I have kept my promise, sir, and said nothing in any of my letters; but Lucia must think it odd that my visits should cease so abruptly.'

'Lucia MacNeill is in the secret, yes,' said Kergabet, and – astonishingly – smiled. 'Oscar MacConnachie had also to be informed, of course, and Lady MacConnachie was all for retreating post-haste to Din Edin, but Lucia MacNeill would not hear of it. "If Sophie Marshall did not flee Din Edin after seeing her father and brother stoned to death in effigy," she said, "why in Brìghde's name should you suppose me willing to flee London now?" She is her father's daughter, certainly,' he concluded in an approving tone.

'I suppose Roland will be feeling very smug,' said Joanna; and, in response to Sophie's questioning look (for this remark seemed to her an utter non sequitur, and in rather poor taste besides), 'His conversation with the yew-trees, you know – the trees warned him of an enemy, he said, and an enemy we surely have.'

'You consider Roland and Lucia's account reliable, then,' said Gray. 'That there was such a message, and that it did indeed come – somehow – from the yew-trees in the maze.'

His tone was not sceptical, exactly – a man who had spent what amounted to whole months of his life in the body of an owl, after all, had not much luxury to scoff at other people's odd tales – but on the other hand, he had not seen all that Sophie had on that mad midnight escapade in Cormac MacAlpine's sacred grove.

Fowler looked up, alert to the possibility of an ally.

'It is all alike to me,' said Joanna frankly. 'It does not seem very plausible, I grant you, but, as Sophie says, Lucia MacNeill is not given to flights of fancy. And,' she added, 'I have seen a great many even less plausible things, Gray, since first you came to stay with us in Breizh.'

'As have I,' said Kergabet, with a small and rueful smile.

And that, thought Sophie, was certainly true, whatever else might or might not be so.

'I do not doubt Roland and Lucia's account,' she said, 'not at all; but what I cannot understand is how those yew-trees should come to have knowledge – let alone foreknowledge – of the prisoners' escape.'

'One does ask oneself that question,' said Gray dryly. 'Among others.'

'We ought to hope with all our might that this is indeed the danger the trees warned Roland of,' said Miss Pryce. The rest of the table turned to look at her. 'Because,' she continued, her quiet voice steady in the face of their collective scrutiny, 'if it is not, then there is some other enemy in the offing, of whom we know nothing at all.'

On this sobering thought their council broke up, Sieur Germain and Mr Fowler to yet another conference with Vaucourt and his staff, and the others to occupy themselves as best they could, without either stirring out of doors or drawing attention to themselves by any sort of unaccustomed conduct.

The letter was postmarked from Oxford, sealed with the owl-and-oak-tree device of Merlin College, and was directed in a crabbed and tiny hand. This hand was not that of Master Alcuin, who had last written to report that, alas, no copy of *The Rise and Fall of Lady Morgan College* was to be found in the libraries of Merlin, Marlowe, Plato, or King's; nor that of Gareth Evans-Hughes, Fellow of Merlin and friend of the Marshalls, with a further report on the contents of the map-room in the Merlin College library. Had one of them, perhaps, recruited some colleague to the cause? Unlikely, but not altogether impossible.

'What is that?' said Joanna, as Sophie studied it.

'I have not the least idea.'

She broke the seal and unfolded the letter.

To Her Royal Highness, the Princess Edith Augusta Sophia, greetings, the salutation ran – not, in Sophie's experience, a promising beginning. She sighed, and read on:

> *It has come to our attention that a movement is presently afoot to re-establish at Oxford, on an equal footing with Colleges hitherto established and presently operating by Royal Charter, a College for female students, on the site of that institution lately known as Lady Morgan College.*

Now, how had the letter-writers, whoever they were, discovered this fact? What they spoke of as a *movement* was in fact Sophie herself and whatever friends and relations she was capable of collecting to assist her; should she succeed in obtaining her father's sanction for the project, of course, the case would at once be altogether different, but at present she could not expect His Majesty even to attend to such a request, let alone throw his patronage behind it.

You *are the patron*, she reminded herself – it was a difficult thing to remember, always. *If you can only sway Father to the cause, you shall have the royal coffers – or some fraction of them, at any rate! – at your disposal, and the wherewithal to engage whatever tradesmen, artisans, and workmen may be required.*

But not whilst the King's attention – and very soon, no doubt, the kingdom's – was riveted upon the matter of the escaped traitors.

You may perhaps be unaware, Your Royal Highness, the letter continued, *of the many learned treatises which demonstrate the female mind to be ill-suited for higher learning. A list is therefore appended of several such treatises which may be suitable, and of which copies are known to be held in His Majesty's library.*

'Some very kind Oxford dons,' said Sophie to Joanna, looking up from the letter, 'have undertaken to explain to me why I ought not to worry my pretty head over the question of Lady Morgan College.'

Joanna snorted into her cup of tea: in view of her present state of tight-strung anxiety, a pleasing phenomenon for which Sophie silently thanked her Oxonian correspondents. She read out to Joanna the beginning of the letter, and continued:

Far be it from us to disparage the innate aptitudes and talents of the female sex, which, from the earliest times, has excelled in its proper sphere, that is, in the management of a household and family; of a shop or other concern; of children, as a governess or schoolmistress; or of any number of similarly practical transactions; all, in their way, as essential to the common good as the labours of any farmer, soldier, merchant, or scholar.

Nor do we deny that there may exist the occasional woman capable of those precise, well-regulated, and thorough habits of thought which alone permit the productive study of the complex, inaccessible, or arcane; that is to say, our stock in trade at Merlin or any other Oxford College. Generally speaking, however, young ladies can derive no benefit from being shut

183

away in College libraries and reading-rooms for years upon years; nor does any net benefit to society accrue from their having been thus incarcerated.

'Incarcerated!' Joanna snorted.

'You know how fond scholars are of metaphor, Jo,' said Sophie mildly, and read on:

We urge you, ma'am, not to judge the inclinations and capabilities of young ladies generally by your own exceptional experience, and, instead, to consider as a model your sister-in-law Lady Kergabet, who is admired throughout the kingdom for her hospitality and her capable management of her illustrious husband's household and estate, and not for any attempt, successful or otherwise, to ape the accomplishments of her father, her brothers, or her husband.

'*Ape!*' Joanna exclaimed. 'Of all the unspeakable—'

'Do be quiet, Jo,' said Miss Pryce, unexpectedly, from her corner. Joanna turned sharply to glare at her over the back of the sofa, but to no avail: 'The more often you interject with righteous protests, love, the longer we shall be in getting to the end.'

Joanna's spine stiffened; Miss Pryce's face drained of colour, and her knitting-needles fell still. Then Joanna turned, her mouth already opening on some excuse, some explanation – even, perhaps, denial.

Sophie held up both hands to forestall her and, before she could speak, said, 'You need not hide from me.'

For a long moment they stared at her, wary and still as

rabbits surprised by a flash of magelight. Then Miss Pryce nodded slowly, her eyes darting from Sophie's face to the back of Joanna's head. 'I thank you,' she said, low; and then, more firmly, 'Come here, Jo.'

The words themselves scarcely mattered, for Sophie easily recognised her tone: whatever she might say would always have meant, *I thank you for your kindness, but I have not the least intention of discussing this matter with you, either now or at any other time.* She nodded, acknowledging the tone rather than the words.

Joanna rose to her feet – obedient to her friend's wishes, Sophie observed with a wry smile, as she had never noticeably been to anyone else's – and retreated to perch on the arm of Miss Pryce's chair.

'There,' said Miss Pryce, smiling at Sophie and laying down her knitting to take Joanna's left hand in her right. 'I shall pinch her if she threatens to interrupt again.'

Joanna, predictably, emitted a squeak of outrage; Miss Pryce gave her hand a gentle squeeze, however, and she subsided.

Sophie ducked her head and cleared her throat to cover the grin she could not quite suppress. Fortunately for her composure – though less fortunately for her good humour – this returned her attention to the letter in her hands, and she sighed, cleared her throat once more and resumed:

> *While not wishing to disparage your own scholarly accomplishments, ma'am, we urge you to heed the wisdom of experience, which confirms that man's sphere is not woman's, and that Dame Fortune does not smile on those who flout this truth; and to take counsel of your elders, and seek some other means of exercising what appears to us to be commendable*

philanthropic fervour: the endowment of an infirmary or lying-in hospital suggests itself, for example, or the foundation of an infant school . . .

The names of the signatories occupied nearly a full closely written page: a dozen Fellows of Merlin College, five from Marlowe College, eight from Plato, half a dozen from Shakespeare, four from King's, two from Bairstow. No College Master was among them, but this might mean only that the Masters – who served at the King's pleasure, though chosen by the Fellows – did not wish to antagonise her father. At least five among the Merlin Fellows she had personally annoyed by attending their lectures, first openly and then, having been asked to leave when they deemed the subject matter unsuitable for female eyes and ears, in a suit of clothes borrowed from one of Gray's friends; if only she had been more skilled at disguise, in those early days . . . !

'I wonder,' Sophie mused, 'what the learned Fellows of Oxford think of Lucia MacNeill.'

'*I* wonder what they think of *you*,' said Joanna, with a little snort of derisive laughter. 'It is perfectly evident that not one of them knows the least thing about you; you are the most determinedly contrary person I have ever met, and if I wished to persuade you to do something which you were not perfectly certain of, that is precisely the sort of letter I should write.'

'You are discounting yourself, I suppose,' said Sophie, amused.

'I beg your pardon?'

'From the category of the determinedly contrary persons, I mean. I shall not attempt to deny that I dislike being lectured and condescended to; but that *you* of all people should call *me* contrary . . . !'

Joanna, wisely, did not attempt to argue the point; over her head, Miss Pryce gave Sophie a small, sardonic smile.

'In any case,' said Sophie, 'I fear that the very kind intervention of the learned Fellows is unlikely to produce the outcome they expect.'

CHAPTER XIII

In Which Sophie and Gray Endeavour to Be Helpful

Somewhat to Sophie's surprise, Sieur Germain's promise to offer her aid and Gray's to Lord de Vaucourt bore fruit within two days, in the form of a brief and exceedingly correct note – delivered to Grosvenor Square by a confidential courier – which formally requested the participation of Doctor Marshall in the search for the escaped traitors. *His Majesty's carriage*, Lord de Vaucourt wrote, *shall call for you and Her Royal Highness in Grosvenor Square at the second hour after noon.*

It was not the most promising of beginnings; still, the relief which Sophie felt at this news of swift reprieve from her present quasi captivity, and from her mother-in-law and Amelia, made her feel almost ashamed of herself. In preparation for this excursion, and to relieve these very mixed feelings, she busied herself in making a mental list of potentially useful spells and in packing up a selection of relevant sources.

'They must be desperate indeed,' observed Joanna, when apprised of this development; 'ordinarily, Vaucourt develops a twitch and a case of hives at the mere mention of your name.'

Sophie frowned, both at her flippant words and at the sardonic tone in which they had been uttered – though it was true, too, that Lord Vaucourt's letter did not mention her name even once. 'I know that you do not underestimate the gravity of the circumstances, Jo,' she said. 'How can you make light of such a thing?'

'Because,' said Joanna, folding her arms defensively across her chest, 'if one does not sometimes make light of grave circumstances, one is apt to fall into despair, and may never succeed in climbing out again.'

Had that been a reference to Sophie's own behaviour, in the dark days after Gray's disappearance from Din Edin? *No, surely Joanna would not be so cruel.*

But the thought lingered, nevertheless.

Joanna tossed her dark head, handed back to Sophie her summons from the Royal Palace, and retreated to the sofa, where she astonished her sister still further by taking up a work-basket, extracting from it what looked very like a half-constructed baby's bonnet, and settling down virtuously to her work. There being nothing more to be done in response to Lord de Vaucourt's note until the promised conveyance should arrive, Sophie sighed, fetched out her own work-basket from behind Jenny's armchair, and joined her.

They sat in uneasy silence for some time, punctuated occasionally by Joanna's bitten-off exclamations of annoyance with her needle (from which the thread had escaped), her thimble (which had let the point of the needle through), and the (apparently insufficient) pins securing the bonnet's brim to its gathered crown. At last Sophie – after many sidelong glances at her sister's deepening scowl – cast up her eyes, laid down her own embroidery in her lap, and said, 'Give me that, Jo.'

Joanna looked up. 'What? Why?'

'Because,' said Sophie patiently, 'I can see that you have got into some sort of difficulty, and I should like to help you out of it. May I?'

She held out her hands, and Joanna, with visible reluctance, surrendered the bonnet. Sophie examined it, assessing the damage: the gathers had gone askew, crowded together on one side and pulled almost straight on the other. Painstakingly, she picked out two dozen small, slightly uneven stitches, wound up the thread, and set it aside.

'Pincushion,' she said.

No pincushion appeared in her outstretched hand; looking up, she found Joanna regarding her with arms folded and jaw mulishly set.

'Please,' said Sophie, repressing the urge to ask, *Do you know how very much you resemble a sulky child?*

Joanna clearly did know it; without another word, she looked out the pincushion and handed it over, and watched attentively as Sophie unpinned the two halves of the bonnet, redistributed the gathers, and set about pinning them together again.

'There, do you see?' Sophie said. 'If you first pin the middle and both ends, and then quarter each half, like this, you will not have so much trouble.'

'Yes, I see,' said Joanna.

Sophie looked up abruptly at her tone. 'You need not take it so much to heart, Jo,' she said. 'There is more to life than sewing baby's bonnets.'

'It is not *that*,' said Joanna, scathingly.

'What, then?' Sophie handed over the bonnet, now properly pinned.

Joanna took it, retrieved and rethreaded her needle, and began her work all over. Concealing a sigh, Sophie took up her own work again, and silence reigned once more until all at once Joanna's bent head came up sharply and she exclaimed, 'How can you bear to sit here, *sewing*, when out there somewhere—'

'Because,' said Sophie, precariously calm, 'if one does not sometimes sit quietly at home, in the company of people one loves, one is in danger of losing the courage to go forth and do unpleasant things in defence of those people. As I think you know very well.'

It was Joanna, after all, and not she, who had begun today's impromptu sewing-circle.

The soft *click-swish* of the door-handle turning made them both look up. The door opened, and framed in the doorway stood Gwendolen Pryce. She was slightly out of breath and had very much the air of one hastening to deliver a message; whatever the message might be, however, it was lost for the moment, for no sooner had her gaze alighted on Joanna's face than her own went wide-eyed with anxiety, and she came quickly into the drawing-room, exclaiming, 'Jo, whatever is the matter?'

'Nothing,' said Joanna, so unconvincingly that Sophie was not at all surprised when Miss Pryce frowned at her and replied, 'If you cannot tell a better lie than that, Joanna Callender, you had much better tell the truth and have done.'

Joanna looked down at her work and set another slow, careful stitch.

'Joanna and I,' said Sophie, 'have been discussing the nature of patience under trying circumstances.'

Miss Pryce turned to her with an expression compounded of surprise and an unexpected comprehension, but said only, 'Have you, indeed.'

Joanna had by now, it appeared, composed herself sufficiently to meet her friend's eyes. 'We have,' she said, 'and I shall tell you all about it in a moment, but you have not run pell-mell up two flights of stairs only to—'

'Oh!' said Miss Pryce, visibly chagrined. She turned to Sophie. 'Mrs Marshall, there is a very grand carriage outside, with the royal arms and two footmen up behind. Do you know where I might find Mr Marshall? You both are wanted, it appears.'

Sophie, startled, dropped her work on the sofa, crossed the room, and peered out of the window in an attempt to gauge the angle of the sun, then down into the street. Sure enough, a carriage bearing the arms of Britain – the lions of England, Normandie, and Maine; the Cymric dragon; the ermines of Breizh and the choughs of Kernow – waited before Lord Kergabet's front door. 'Maître de Vaucourt is before his time, surely,' she muttered to herself – but no matter. It was not as though she were reluctant to begin.

Vaucourt seemed not to share his colleague's opinion that Sophie and Gray ought to be keeping a low profile; surely there could be no more conspicuous means of travel than that carriage, with its plainly visible royal arms, its coach- and footmen in the royal livery, and its four glossy chestnut horses.

'Gray is in the library, I expect,' she said, returning to the sofa and tucking her work away, 'hiding from his mother. I shall go and fetch him. I thank you, Miss Pryce. I shall see you both . . .' When? She had not the least notion. '. . . later.'

Her thoughts already on the task ahead, she went away to look for her husband.

They were alone in the carriage for the duration of the journey, for, the coachman and footmen aside, Maître de Vaucourt had sent no one to escort them – which meant either that he trusted them to need no minder, or that none of his associates could be spared for the purpose. For some time neither spoke; Gray had brought with him a thick dossier from which protruded untidily a variety of pages closely covered in various hands, including his own, and was engaged in perusing it, occasionally muttering to himself under his breath, whilst Sophie looked out of the window, enjoying the brief and necessarily finite absence of other company.

Then the carriage, travelling at speed, took a particularly sharp corner and threw her and Gray against the fortunately well-padded off-side wall, scattering Gray's papers over both *bancs* and the floor.

'Horns of Herne!' said Gray, exasperated. He righted himself and began to gather them up again.

'Do you know,' said Sophie, laughing as she collected the pages which had flown in her direction, 'I believe this may be the first time we have been alone together by daylight since leaving Din Edin.'

Gray blinked at her in apparent bewilderment.

'What have you been thinking of, then?' She glanced through the papers in her hands. 'Cameron's mapped finding, first of all, of course; but I do not suppose Maître de Vaucourt has a spelled map like Rory MacCrimmon's . . .'

'Very likely not,' said Gray, 'if the spell is truly an Alban one, but Alasdair Cameron's having invented it there does not preclude some other mage's doing the same somewhere in Britain. Besides,' he added, producing something which, though not quite the cheerful grin he seemed to have intended, was nonetheless a very welcome change from the grim tension of the past several days, 'other applications exist for a spelled map of that nature, besides Cameron's mapped finding, and I dare say that His Majesty's generals have thought of most of them.'

Sophie handed over her stack of papers; Gray shuffled them back into some sequence known only to himself and lost himself in them once more for the remainder of the journey. For some time Sophie watched him fondly, till at length her gaze drifted to the city passing by without – the people going about their business, happy in their ignorance of whatever person or power had intervened to set free her stepfather and his co-conspirators, and of the purposes (whatever they might be) behind that act.

Circumventing the walls and the locks, the guards and the wards, cannot have been easy, she reflected, *and therefore it must have been worth a good deal of trouble to someone.* Thus much was perfectly evident; but to whom, and why, it was frustratingly difficult to imagine.

'Your Royal Highness,' said Master Lord de Vaucourt stiffly, bowing, when His Majesty's major-domo had ushered them into his workroom. Having thus disposed of Sophie, he turned to Gray: 'Doctor Marshall. I thank you for accepting my invitation.'

An invitation, was it? thought Gray, with some amusement. *A peremptory summons, I should have said.*

'We could scarcely do otherwise, my lord,' he said pleasantly, 'having volunteered our assistance to begin with. You have work for us to do, I conclude?'

Vaucourt cleared his throat, and looking away, gestured them towards the long worktable in the centre of the room. Gray and Sophie exchanged glances, but took two of the offered chairs at the near end of the table. Sophie deposited on the table before her what looked very like a particularly capacious netted work-bag, at which Vaucourt silently curled his lip, and began tugging off her dove-grey kid gloves.

'We thought,' said Sophie, before he could continue, 'that we might discuss the possibility of using Cameron's mapped finding, or something like it, worked in a relay to extend the range of the spell.'

Gray maintained what he hoped was an expression of detached scholarly interest, but inwardly he felt fiercely proud of her, calmly setting out a sensible course of action before a man at least twice her age, whom they both knew to disapprove of her on principle.

Vaucourt, it transpired, had never heard of Alasdair Cameron's mapped finding, but, the nature of this working having been explained, opined that what was wanted was in fact Larbalastier's Spell of Location, and that the requisite set of maps were to be found in the Palace Archives.

'But, however,' he said, 'of course it has already been tried, without success; either the traitors are protected by wards or shielding-spells, or they are beyond the reach of any finding-spell.'

Or both, added Gray to himself, thinking of his own incarceration, in an interdicted cell in a remote part of Alba. 'Hence,' he said aloud, 'Magistra Marshall's suggestion that we employ a relay.'

He caught Vaucourt's twitch of irritation at the use of *Magistra*, but fortunately Sophie did not.

'A relay,' Vaucourt repeated, surprised and sceptical. 'You refer, I suppose, to the collective working of spells of concealment, or of shielding-spells, as practised by military mages?'

Gray could scarcely fault Vaucourt's ignorance of other uses of relays, having himself been entirely unaware that any such working existed until after his Alban friends had employed one in rescuing him from Cormac MacAlpine. 'I have never seen a finding worked using a relay myself,' he said. 'Magistra, perhaps you might describe your experience?'

Sophie reached into her work-bag – which in fact Gray knew to be filled largely with books – and extracted a codex, bound in once-fine but now rather battered bottle-green leather. Setting aside the bag, she opened the book and riffled through its pages until she found the one she wanted, then turned it about and slid it across the table to Lord Vaucourt.

'This is the fullest and clearest explanation I know of the use of relays in finding-spells,' she said. 'I have taken part in several experiments on a small scale, but on the occasion of which my husband speaks – which was, I believe, an experiment on a larger scale, rather than a practised manoeuvre – I was a witness only.'

'Even in Alba, I suppose,' said Vaucourt, not looking up from *On Findings and Summonings: Revised and Expanded, with Illustrations of Specialist Uses Thereof*, 'such a major working must be considered outside the female sphere.'

Presumably he had not remarked the words stamped on the book's front board, below the title:

by Morag Ruadh MacQuarie, Mag. D.
revised and expanded by Rory MacCrimmon, Mag. D.,
and Sophia Marshall, Mag. B.

Sophie caught Gray's eye and, out of Vaucourt's sight, rolled her eyes at him.

'In fact,' she said evenly, 'if memory serves, at least half the mages present were women. I was not among them only because, as it happened, I was too ill to do more than look on.'

Now Vaucourt did look up, frowning. 'You understand, of course, ma'am, that there can be no question of—'

The workroom door opened once more, this time to admit

Lord Kergabet and Mr Fowler, and Vaucourt desisted from his argument – wisely, in Gray's view – to greet the new arrivals.

'I suppose,' said Sieur Germain, 'there is no use as yet in enquiring after your progress?'

'An interesting suggestion has been made,' Vaucourt conceded, 'as to the possibility of working a finding-spell collectively, in the same manner as, for example, a regimental shielding-spell.' His eyes narrowed thoughtfully, and when he spoke again there was a suggestion of satisfaction in his voice, quite at odds with the words themselves: 'The notion is not without promise, in theory; but in practice, of course, it is quite impossible.'

'And why should it be impossible?' Sophie demanded.

'Indeed,' said Kergabet, 'why should it? Ordinarily, of course, I should defer to you on any question of magick, Vaucourt, but as my brother- and sister-in-law have considerable practical experience in these matters, I have made it a rule never to dismiss their suggestions untried.'

An expression of raw dislike flashed over Vaucourt's face – there and gone in an instant – as Kergabet and Fowler, uninvited, seated themselves at the table, Kergabet to Sophie's left and Fowler to Gray's right.

'Firstly,' he said, 'the necessary range is too great, even for a collective working; these men may have travelled many hundreds of miles by this time, in any direction.'

'In that case, we must expand the relay, so as to further extend the range,' said Gray. He was struggling to keep his temper, for they should get nowhere at all by shouting. 'More to the point—'

'And, secondly,' Vaucourt continued, cutting across him until Gray gave up in disgust, 'even were it possible to locate them by means of a collective working – which is by no means certain, for in addition to the matter of distance, there is, as Doctor Marshall may remember, every likelihood of their being protected by wards or shields – the nature of a finding is such that—'

'As Master Vaucourt may remember,' Gray broke in, seeing that Sophie's equanimity had begun to fray about the edges, 'the suggestion made was that we employ Cameron's mapped finding – or, as it may be, Larbalastier's Spell of Location – which, of course, does not require that the finding-spell be maintained until spell-worker and target are brought together. You have said, I believe, sir, that an attempt has already been made using the Larbalastier spell?'

'Several attempts, in fact,' said Vaucourt, in an icy tone. 'None of them at all successful.'

'But those attempts did not make use of a re—I beg your pardon, of a collective working,' said Sophie, 'and therefore—'

'Ma'am,' said Vaucourt tightly. 'Far be it from me to disparage your . . . particular talents, but a collective working is a delicate and difficult undertaking, in which each participant must implicitly trust and rely upon all the rest, and a chain which can never be stronger than its weakest link. I cannot reasonably require any of my colleagues or assistants to embark upon so delicate and difficult a project, knowing that its success and their own safety depend on the skill and competence of a woman.'

It was not surprising, exactly; but—

'I confess, Master Vaucourt,' said Sophie (Gray saw, but hoped that Vaucourt might not, how near she was to losing her composure), 'that I do not altogether understand why you should have accepted our offer of assistance, if, as it now appears, you believe we can be of no help to you.'

Vaucourt smiled at her – a tight little smile with no mirth

and no friendliness in it. 'Having spent so little time at court, Your Highness,' he said, 'you may perhaps not recognise the importance of diplomacy.'

Gray, who had not the least idea what might be meant by this remark, looked across the table at his brother-in-law, and upon his face beheld an expression of outrage which made him blink in surprise.

'Do I understand, sir,' said Kergabet, 'that two of the most powerful mages in Britain have freely offered their help in resolving the present crisis, and you are intending to *refuse* it?'

'Certainly not,' Vaucourt replied, bristling. 'I should welcome Doctor Marshall's assistance.'

On Gray's other side, Mr Fowler exhaled a sharp *huh!* and muttered under his breath, 'You will wish you had not said that, m'lord.'

Gray himself, his mind frozen in outrage, looked across the table at his brother-in-law, at Sophie.

Kergabet wore a predictably indignant expression, but Sophie – Sophie, who ought to have been incensed at this open, unequivocal insult – met Gray's eyes with a small, resigned grimace.

I had rather swim the Thames in the dead of winter than make common cause with this man, thought Gray, furious. *And yet . . . if any opportunity offers for me to hasten the recapture of Callender and the rest, how can I possibly justify refusing it?*

'Of the pair of us, Maître Vaucourt,' he said, 'I am neither the more powerful, nor the more versatile.'

Vaucourt's expression was utterly baffling: why in Hades should Vaucourt *pity* him?

'Be that as it may, Doctor Marshall,' he said, 'you are the more . . . suitable.'

'The more congruent with your own prejudices, in other words,' said Gray.

'Gray.' Sophie's arm stretched across the table, and her fingers folded over his; magick shivered through their joined hands. 'This is more important than either of us, and certainly more important than my wounded self-regard.'

She spoke deprecatingly – as though this last were a frivolous jest – and her face was perfectly expressionless. Vaucourt actually chuckled, causing Mr Fowler (who knew Sophie rather better) to shake his head despairingly.

Gray turned his hand palm upwards and clasped Sophie's, briefly but firmly. 'As you say, Magistra,' he said, and, turning to Vaucourt, 'I am at your disposal, sir.'

Vaucourt nodded – acknowledgement without thanks – and at once made Gray regret his decision by saying to Sophie, 'If you will excuse us, ma'am . . . ?'

'Certainly.' Sophie let go Gray's hand, rose gracefully from her seat, gathered her books (all but Morag Ruadh MacQuarie's treatise on findings and summonings, which still lay splayed under Vaucourt's hand; Gray made a mental note to retrieve it later), and made for the door, swinging wide around Vaucourt's chair.

Vaucourt summoned two of his assistants, whom Gray vaguely recognised as Merlin men some two or three years younger than himself, and dispatched one to retrieve the maps from the Archives, and the other to gather the rest of the Court mages for another attempt at a finding-spell.

CHAPTER XIV

In Which Joanna and Gwendolen Disobey Orders

Kergabet had not, in so many words, made any promise to keep Joanna abreast of the progress of his investigation. In the course of that first fortnight, however – whether because he considered himself to have made such a promise or because he genuinely wished to hear her views – he contrived to convey some piece of news to her almost every evening, and listened with every appearance of keen interest to her reciprocal news, when from time to time she had any to convey.

Yet though he told her what he could, it was little enough: that the prisoners had contrived to escape without alerting their guards, without visible damage to the premises, and entirely without trace of any sort; that they had left no possessions behind them which might be used in scrying to discover their intentions or their present whereabouts; that the guards did not appear to have been drugged, but a scry-mage in His Majesty's service opined that they might well have been bespelled. The investigation into their disappearance – headed jointly, though not very harmoniously, by Kergabet and by His Majesty's chief mage, Lord de Vaucourt – had as yet discovered nothing of more substance than this, and Joanna felt Kergabet's frustration almost as a physical force whenever they spoke of it. No doubt he was equally aware of the singing tension that gripped her almost always now, compounded of impatience with the slow pace of progress, frustration at her own powerlessness to help, and simple anger at her father. Though of course she was not so arrogant as to suppose that his actions had anything to do with her, or with Amelia – Sophie, or at any rate Sophie's central role in delivering him up to Maître de Vaucourt and the priests of Apollo Coelispex, being a different matter altogether.

Of Sophie and Gray's attempt to assist in the search for the escaped prisoners, Kergabet would say only that things had not fallen out as he himself had hoped, and neither Sophie nor Gray would say anything at all – though their air of suppressed fury, since returning from that initial conference with Vaucourt, and the habit they had developed of fleeing to the library every morning after breakfast and employing Sophie's concealing magick to discourage anyone but Kergabet from remarking their presence there, disinclined Joanna to question them on the subject in any case. They had quarrelled with Vaucourt, Joanna concluded – or Sophie had – and were now pursuing some investigatory avenue of their own, without his knowledge or consent. She wished them joy of it, despite her bitter irritation at being excluded from their counsels.

In her heart of hearts, too, relief flashed guiltily whenever the library door closed behind Sophie, for it meant at least that she was safe at home, and not running off into the gods knew what peril.

Sophie and Gray are not helpless, she reminded herself sternly, beginning to unpick a whole row of stitches which she had set wrongly whilst brooding over the problem of Professor Callender and his friends.

But they were just as capable three years ago, when they first went north into Alba, and much good it did them then!

'They are both still alive and well, are they not?' said Gwendolen.

Joanna started violently, knocking the knuckles of her right hand against the arm of the sofa. Had she been thinking aloud, then? It seemed so. *Thank all the gods that Mrs Marshall and Jenny are out paying calls!*

Gwendolen tucked her crewel-work away in her work-basket, then left her chair to kneel at Joanna's feet.

'Jo,' she said quietly, 'you must not fret yourself to death over this business. You have not been sleeping well – have you? Is it the nightmares again? There are shadows under your eyes, and your hands are shaking.'

Joanna, appalled, looked down at her hands – lying idle in her lap now, for she had dropped her latest attempt at fancy-work in her astonishment at being addressed – and saw that it was quite true.

'I am half sick with being penned up in this house,' she admitted.

By Kergabet's decree, the morning rides which had been their settled habit remained suspended; and thus this morning, once again, they sat quietly stitching in the morning-room rather than galloping through the park. Though Joanna thought this precaution ridiculous, for Jenny's sake she had not argued the point, but she was beginning to feel that she should soon go mad if she were not released from this prison – even so large and comfortable as it was.

'And not you only,' said Gwendolen, pulling a face. She sat back on her heels, and after a moment said – as though changing the subject – 'What news from Prince Roland and Lucia MacNeill?'

Joanna sighed. 'None to speak of,' she said. 'I suspect Her Majesty of keeping them under house arrest, for safety's sake – and I confess I cannot blame her.'

'If I were in their shoes,' said Gwendolen, 'I should take ship for Din Edin as soon as I might, and stay there until the . . . the prisoners are back in the Tower, or better yet at the end of a rope.'

Joanna blinked at her, and she scowled, defiant: 'You think me bloodthirsty, I suppose?'

'Not at all,' said Joanna frankly. 'I could not understand at the time what His Majesty was about in commuting the traitors' sentence to imprisonment, and the present circumstances certainly have not changed my opinion on that point.'

Gwendolen's scowl had shifted into an expression of puzzled speculation. She retrieved Joanna's abandoned fancy-work from its scatter across the carpet, stacked the coiled skeins of silk in a tidy heap atop the folded muslin, and placed it squarely across Joanna's lap, then rose to her feet (too neatly by half, for a person with such long legs, thought Joanna in irrational annoyance), turned, and settled herself beside Joanna on the sofa, pressed close against her side.

'But your father,' she began. 'Do you not think—'

'Gwen, you cannot suppose that after all this time – after *everything* – I should still be sentimental about my father?'

Dropping her gaze to her own hands clasped in her lap, Gwendolen said softly, 'I hope you do not think the less of me, because I cannot help feeling sentimental about mine?'

Joanna, shocked out of her indignation, reached for Gwendolen's hands and covered them with her own. 'When your father has been convicted of treason, murder, and attempted regicide,' she said, 'when he has laid a fatal trap for some friend of yours, and without regard to the possibility of its killing you instead, then I shall wonder at your regretting him.'

Raising her eyes, Gwendolen turned her hands palm upwards, the better to wrap her fingers about Joanna's, and produced a grim smile.

Joanna swallowed hard, increasingly aware that this conversation was too fraught, skirted too close to violent emotion, to be conducted in broad day, in Jenny's morning-room, where anyone might interrupt it. She searched for words – some sardonic remark, inflected with gentle humour, which would turn Gwen's grim smile true – but found none; and, not for the first time, she cursed whatever god's whim made her so tongue-tied in the presence of the person with whom she most longed to be eloquent.

The fateful day began in a perfectly ordinary manner: with Joanna and Gwendolen saddling their horses in the stable mews just after waving off Gaël's attempt to do it for them. Trailed by Gaël and Loïc, they rode to the park at a sedate walk – conspicuous only in being two young women riding astride in a Mayfair street – and once through the gates, paused side by side to survey the bridle-path.

In fact, it was no ordinary morning, being the first since the escape of the prisoners from the Tower upon which Joanna and Gwendolen had once more been permitted their daily ride – and then only under escort.

The prospects seemed good: the path was dry and almost deserted, and the sky as clear as it ever was in London. Joanna – feeling half out of her mind with joy simply at being out of doors again – turned her head to look at Gwendolen; Gwendolen met her gaze with a sly grin and, with a minute pressure of her calves and an almost imperceptible twitch of her hands on the reins, urged her chestnut mare, Elain, into motion.

Joanna and Kelvez were only a breath behind her. They walked, then trotted, then cantered past several startled gentlemen ambling along the bridle-path, and at last – when they had outstripped the

205

last of these, as well as their own indignant escort – leant forward and urged their mounts into a gallop.

Kelvez and Elain had been stablemates two years and more and had each other's measure; their own hearts were in the race as surely as their riders', and they flew down the straight leg of the bridle-path neck and neck. At the last moment Joanna urged, 'Just a little farther, lovely!' and they drew ahead by the length of Kelvez's glossy head, just in time to pass under the pair of bay-trees, arching together over the path, that marked their usual finishing line.

They slowed, laughing breathlessly, and rounded the curve at a jogging trot – just as if all were quite as usual, with no vague and ill-formed threat hanging over London like the sword of Damocles.

'I told you I should break your streak, Gwen,' Joanna crowed. As she was turning in her saddle to grin at Gwendolen, a strange young man – wild-eyed, his hair and clothing all anyhow, as though he had slept the night in the wood – came crashing through a weeping beech and onto the path just ahead of them.

He clutched at Elain's bridle, causing her to snort and back and attempt to rear; had Gwendolen been a less skilful horsewoman, Joanna thought, she should certainly have been thrown, and this reckless, idiotic stranger kicked half to death. Kelvez, almost equally agitated, sidled her hooves and tossed her head, and Joanna had both hands full in calming her.

'Which of you is Miss Callender's sister?' the stranger demanded. 'Where is she? I must speak with her.'

Joanna looked up, startled, and very nearly said, *I am*, before prudence and common sense prevailed. 'Unhand my friend's bridle, sir,' she said instead, infusing her voice with the spirit of Mrs Edmond Marshall – chosen as the least obliging person of her acquaintance. 'What do you mean by assaulting us in this manner?'

He let go of the bridle, allowing Gwendolen to back Elain away from him, and lurched towards Joanna. He must truly have been sleeping rough, she thought, as he drew nearer, and not only last night: his clothing had been good once, and being now extremely dirty and growing ragged, looked all the worse for the contrast; his hair was lank and long untrimmed, his face long unshaven and its bones too prominent beneath the skin. He smelt not only of unwashed male body (which was bad enough) but of rank fear – to the horses' more sensitive noses, the smell must be like the fumes of Tartarus – and his eyes—

Joanna could not bear to look at his eyes.

He lunged for her bridle, but Kelvez was having none of it. She snorted and whinnied and made to rear, her ears flattened in warning; whilst Joanna fought to keep her seat, bending forward along the mare's neck to avoid pulling at her mouth, the stranger staggered backwards out of the range of her hooves, with abject terror stamped upon his face.

'Jo!' Gwendolen's voice was firm and insistent. 'Jo, are you or are you not in charge of that horse?'

It was not, perhaps, the approach any reputable trainer of horses would have taken, but it put Joanna very strongly in mind of Morvan, her father's large, patient coachman and stableman-in-chief, who had taught her nearly everything she knew about horses. She had always suspected Morvan of concealing some vast, horse-related magickal talent, for when he spoke, horses stilled and gentled. If so, Gwendolen, she thought, had some of that talent too.

Whether or not there was any magick in Gwen's words, however, her voice cut through Joanna's incipient panic, reminding her that much worse things were possible than falling off a horse.

Ignoring the madman on the bridle-path, therefore, Joanna

settled her weight deep in her saddle and stirrups and turned Kelvez's head just enough that, off balance, the mare came down onto all four feet again. Then, seizing the moment whilst she could, she straightened her spine, dug in her heels, and said firmly, '*Walk on.*'

Kelvez sidled uncertainly; but when Joanna once more urged her forward, she seemed to decide to take what was fast becoming the path of least resistance: around the mad stranger and towards Gwendolen and Elain.

Close to, Gwendolen looked a great deal more frightened than she had sounded; Joanna reached for her arm and squeezed it, murmuring, 'Will you trust me?'

'Of course,' said Gwendolen reflexively. Joanna turned away before the doubt already glimmering in her eyes could become a full-fledged objection.

She swung her right leg over to the mare's near side and slid smoothly down to stand on the path. 'Stay here,' she said, handing her reins to Gwendolen and surreptitiously squeezing her gloved hand, 'in case a diversion is called for.'

Then she squared her shoulders, lifted her chin, and turned back to face the madman who was seeking Amelia.

He stood still as she slowly approached him – tensed for flight, like a hare or a deer – and, when she halted just out of arm's reach, visibly restrained himself from clutching at her to prevent her from escaping.

'Who are you?' Joanna said. 'Where are you come from, and what in Hades do you want with Amelia?' *And what*, she added to herself, *do you imagine that Amelia might want with you?* She attempted to imagine an encounter between this man – terror-struck and filthy – and her fastidious sister, and could conjure no version of it which did not end with Amelia's recoiling in disgust and fleeing the scene.

'You do know her, then,' said the man. 'She told me that you often ride here in the mornings, so I have been waiting—she is in London? You must bring her – I must speak with her—'

Joanna folded her arms and glared. 'I shall do nothing of the kind,' she said. 'Do you imagine me to be in the habit of delivering up my friends to the clutches of wild men who assault inoffensive young women in public parks?'

Joanna's glare – she had modelled it on Lady Maëlle's – was well known to make grown men quail, and this one was no exception; but, quailing, he nonetheless stood his ground.

'You must,' he insisted. 'I beg of you—'

'If your business is so very urgent, then, you will not object to give me your name.'

The stranger stared at her for what seemed an age, biting his lip and worrying his hands.

'My name is Henry Taylor,' he conceded at last, and Joanna's unease congealed into horrified disbelief.

'Then where are all the rest of you?' she demanded. 'Six men escaped the Tower and vanished; where are the other five?'

'I shall tell all I know,' said Taylor (if so he was indeed), 'in return for His Majesty's protection. But I must see Am—Miss Callender.'

'If you are playing tricks,' said Joanna, lowering her voice to a furious half whisper, 'if any harm comes to anyone of my acquaintance by your doing, I shall make sure that you live long enough to bitterly regret it.'

Taylor held up his hands in surrender. 'I have no wish to harm anyone,' he said. 'Quite the opposite. That is why I must see Miss Callender, and at once. You need not be afraid; if you are Miss

Joanna Callender, then your brother-in-law is Marshall of Merlin College, and I am an old friend of his.'

'You are nothing of the kind!' Joanna exclaimed, outraged. 'You were a tool for my father and the rest of that ill-met company, and hoodwinked Gray into becoming another such. If that is your notion of friendship, Mr Taylor, I think I may safely say that we are none of us eager to call you friend.'

'I do not see that Marshall has done so badly out of it,' said Taylor. He no longer sounded at all mad, to Joanna's relief, but did sound rather like a sulky child.

Joanna did not attempt to argue the point, for it was true that had not Gray been so stupid as to lend himself to Taylor's midnight errand on behalf of his tutor, he should not now have been Sophie's husband, nor the owner of the estate in Breizh which had belonged to several generations of Callenders. *But that is down to our making the best of things*, she reminded herself, *and not to any generous impulse of Mr Taylor's.*

'Tell me what it is you want with Amelia,' she said, though she had a sinking feeling that she knew it already, 'and I shall convey the message. I make no promises as to what she may choose to do with the information.'

It could do no harm to convey a message, she reasoned – whereas the longer she stood here arguing, the greater the risk of irreparable harm to her reputation, and to her protectors', from someone's happening upon this conversation and spreading the tale all over London. If agreeing to carry his message would induce him to go away . . .

And it was not impossible that whatever information he possessed, supposing that he could be induced to part with it, might be genuinely valuable.

'You must bring your sister here,' said Taylor. 'Or see that she comes here. Tomorrow, at the same hour – or, if not tomorrow, the day after. She will not be permitted to come alone, I must suppose; let her bring Marshall with her, if needs be, but no one else.'

'You are very demanding for a man in your position,' said Joanna. Was this some manner of trap? If so, to what purpose? 'Why should either my sister or Mr Marshall agree to such a demand? For that matter, why should I not summon the Watch this moment, and have you taken in charge?'

Under the layers of grime, Taylor's face blanched, but again he stood his ground: 'Because I have information of value, which I shall be disinclined to share if I am arrested and thrown back into prison.'

'Very well; you wish to surrender on your own terms,' said Joanna. That was logical enough. 'Then why not take advantage of your present audience to convey your information directly to His Majesty's ear?'

Taylor first looked baffled, and then – to her astonishment, considering their relative situations – his lip curled, and he said, in a condescending tone with which Joanna was tediously familiar, 'What – you – and your friend?' He waved a dismissive hand at Gwendolen; out of his line of sight, she returned a very rude gesture borrowed from Gaël. 'I hardly think that would answer.'

Joanna repressed a strong impulse to pull off one of her boots and clout him with it. 'As you like,' she said, with her most unladylike shrug. 'I have promised to convey your message; I have made no promises as to the result. If indeed your intent is to turn King's evidence, I expect we shall meet again before very long. Good morning, Mr Taylor.'

And so saying, she turned on her heel and strode away towards

Gwendolen and the horses – and the approaching rumble of hooves which presumably heralded Lord Kergabet's grooms.

If her heart was pounding in her throat, there was no need for anyone – and Henry Taylor most particularly – to know it.

Smarting from the tongue-lashing they had received from Gaël and Loïc, Joanna and Gwendolen stopped only long enough to see to their horses before banging through the area door, through the kitchen, and up the servants' staircase. At last they burst pink-faced and out of breath into the breakfast-parlour, where the rest of the Grosvenor Square family, together with Lady Maëlle, were sitting over their meal.

Six faces turned towards the sound of the door, their expressions variously astonished, indignant, and bewildered; six pairs of eyes, beholding the two young ladies in their dishevelled riding-clothes, widened in alarm. Joanna spared a prayer of thanks to Morpheus, god of dreams, that the rest of Jenny's guests were not yet come down to breakfast; she was in no state to put up a front of unruffled calm for Mrs Edmond Marshall.

'Joanna! Gwendolen!' Jenny exclaimed, starting up from her chair with an awkward lurch. 'Whatever is the matter?'

'Henry Taylor,' said Joanna, breathless. 'In the park. Hiding.' She turned to her brother-in-law: 'Gray, he said—'

'You rode straight away to summon the City Watch, I hope and trust,' said Sieur Germain. His tone suggested considerably more hope than trust. 'Rather than engaging in conversation with a convicted traitor and dangerous fugitive from His Majesty's justice.'

Gwendolen's right hand found Joanna's left, concealed behind their skirts, and Joanna pressed her fingers gently in reassurance.

Even after all this time, it seemed, Gwen did not entirely trust that some transgression of hers would not inspire Kergabet or Jenny to pack her off back to Papa and the objectionable Stepmama in Clwyd.

'I did consider fetching out the Watch,' said Joanna, truthfully enough, 'but he did not seem to intend us any harm; he is only very stupid about horses.'

Sophie frowned; before she could speak, however, Joanna ploughed onward: 'We are both perfectly well, and the horses likewise, and there has been no harm done to anyone, so there is no need to discuss it. The *point* is that this Mr Taylor says that he must speak privately with Amelia – he would not say why, though I fear it is not difficult to guess – and that he has information of some kind, connected with the conspirators' escape, which he will consent to reveal in exchange for His Majesty's protection and, of course, this meeting with Amelia. I tried to gain some hint as to the nature of this information, but he insists upon speaking of it to you, Gray, and no one else – and only if he is permitted to see Amelia.'

Gray looked deeply baffled. 'Why on the gods' green earth should Henry Taylor wish to confide in me?' he said.

'He called himself your friend,' said Joanna. Gray snorted. 'Which does not accord very well with what we know of him, but perhaps imprisonment has worked some magick upon his heart and mind – or perhaps he has quarrelled with the rest of them, and now finds himself in want of allies. By the look of him, he has not had very good luck since he left his prison.'

'Or perhaps it is a trap of some sort,' said Jenny. 'Whatever is afoot, Jo, I do not like it at all.'

'It may be a trap, of course,' Joanna conceded. 'I have considered the possibility, Jenny, I assure you. I do not know what he hopes to catch in it, however, besides poor Amelia.'

'A mage, one presumes,' said Kergabet. 'Or mages. It would not be the first time.'

Sophie went very pale, and reached for Gray's hand across the tablecloth.

'If it is a trap,' said Joanna, aiming for a calmly reassuring tone, 'it is a very clumsy one.'

'In any case, half of them are mages themselves,' said Gray. 'Unless our information on the subject is very much out of date. And if Henry Taylor expects me to come to his aid, or considers me likely to believe anything he says—'

'And this information which he claims to have?' said Joanna. 'What of that? He must know *something* – perhaps not where the others are now, but at any rate where they have been, and how they contrived to escape.'

'Not to mention who helped them,' Gwendolen put in. When Mr Fowler gave her an astonished look, she said, 'Well, it is perfectly evident that someone must have done!'

So it was indeed, in Joanna's view, though Sieur Germain and his investigators had been at considerable pains to keep their conclusions on this point from reaching the public ear, lest they inflame the rumours of conspiracy already circulating.

'I am perfectly ready to speak with him,' said Gray, 'if Sieur Germain has no objection. But as to Amelia's being exposed to such a risk—'

'*I* have an objection!' Sophie exclaimed, leaping to her feet. Gray twisted round in his seat to look up at her. 'I have *numerous* objections – quite apart from Amelia's going, which of course is perfectly impossible. To begin with—'

214

'But if I might speed the others' recapture,' Gray said, almost too softly for Joanna's ears to catch. He had caught Sophie's hands – curled into fists at her sides – and engulfed them both in his larger ones, clasped close to his lips. 'You would not have me shirk that task, love, surely?'

Looking away in some discomfiture, Joanna met Gwendolen's eye across the table, and knew at once that she, too, had been unable to continue watching Sophie and Gray.

'No,' said Sophie, with a small, defeated sigh. Joanna heard the rustle of her gown as she resumed her seat, and looked back along the table to see her prop her elbows upon the tablecloth and bury her face in her hands. Her voice, when next she spoke, was muffled: 'No, of course I would not.'

Gray's hand was on Sophie's shoulder, but his gaze was steady on his brother-in-law's face. He did not see, therefore, the moment when Sophie raised her head from her hands, nor the terrifying light in her dark eyes.

Oh, gods and priestesses. She has had an idea, and I fear we shall all of us regret it.

'What say you, my lord?' said Gray.

Sieur Germain, grim-faced, replied, 'Such a summons seems to me highly likely to indicate a trap. I cannot forbid you, of course; but I should strongly counsel you not to go alone.'

'He need not be alone,' said Sophie. Straightening away from Gray's hand on her shoulder, she unfolded herself from her chair, turned to face her husband and brother-in-law, and closed her eyes.

'Sophie—'

The transformation took only a moment – so skilled was Sophie now, so thoroughly in control of her magick, that the intervening stages were scarcely visible to Joanna's eye – and by the time her eyes

215

opened once more, one sister had vanished and the other appeared.

'He need not be alone,' Sophie repeated, in perfect mimicry of Amelia's voice, and smiling Amelia's slightly superior smile, 'for Miss Callender can go with him.'

The silence which greeted this pronouncement was so thick that Joanna's ears fairly rang with it.

'That is a perfectly idiotic notion.' It was Gwendolen who spoke at last; all of them turned to look at her, and she coloured a little but did not look away. 'Begging your pardon, Mrs Marshall. If, as you suppose, these men have set a trap to catch mages, why in Hades should you wish to deliver up two mages instead of one?'

Sophie looked down Amelia's nose at Gwendolen, so entirely Amelia that Joanna shivered. 'You seem, Miss Pryce,' she said, in Amelia's most icily condescending tone, 'to be labouring under a misapprehension. I have no notion of delivering up anything to anyone, and myself and Mr Marshall to Henry Taylor, I assure you, least of all.'

'Nevertheless, Sophie' – Jenny had now found her voice, it appeared – 'I must agree with Gwendolen. I do not see what advantage—'

The faux Amelia shook her head briskly, in the manner of a hound with water in its ears, and abruptly was Sophie again. 'Have you *met* my sister Amelia, Jenny?' she demanded, laughter warring with exasperation in her voice. 'The advantage is that whatever they may expect of Amelia, they shall not be expecting *me*.'

'Has it occurred to anyone,' said Joanna, 'to ask Amelia's opinion?'

To judge by the looks that were turned in her direction, this suggestion was quite as shocking as Sophie's had been.

'After all,' she continued, pressing her advantage, 'she is not a child; she is six and twenty, or nearly, and surely knows her own mind. Perhaps she may know what this Mr Taylor is about; perhaps he may be willing to tell her things which—'

'Six and twenty or not,' said Lady Maëlle, 'and child or not, Amelia remains a ward of the Crown so long as she is unmarried – as do you, Joanna, you may recall. And, as the duly appointed representative thereof, in respect of your sister, I have every right to decide what is, and is not, in her best interests to be told.'

Joanna and Sophie exchanged a look.

'And do you not think, *Mrs Wallis*,' said the latter pointedly, 'that enough harm has been done already in this family by the keeping of secrets?'

Lady Maëlle winced – just visibly – at the use of her quondam alias and, when Jenny said firmly, 'I quite agree,' acquiesced gracefully enough to Amelia's being consulted.

'Gwendolen,' said Jenny, when this largely silent skirmish had been won, 'will you run up to Miss Callender's room, please, and ask her to come down and speak to us in the morning-room?'

'Yes, ma'am,' said Gwendolen at once, and, with a single enigmatic glance over her shoulder at Joanna, hastened out into the corridor.

'Miss Pryce has been a very long time in fetching Amelia,' said Sophie, worrying at the edge of the fichu which she had taken out of her work-basket for the purpose of hemming it. 'Ought one of us to—'

'*No*,' said Joanna firmly. 'Of all of us, Gwen is the least likely to irritate her simply by existing; we can do no good by—'

She broke off, following Jenny's startled gaze.

Gwendolen stood in the doorway, one hand gripping the

jamb; she was out of breath, as though she had been running, yet her face was pale.

'Miss Callender is not in her room,' she said. 'Nor anywhere else in the house, so far as I can discover. Her bed looks as though it had not been slept in, and Mr Treveur says that her boots were not put out to be cleaned, though I am quite sure I saw them last night when I put out Joanna's and mine, and she has left the small drawer of the dressing-table ajar – the drawer where I used to keep my coin-purse, when that dressing-table was in my bedroom in Carrington-street – and I opened it and found a stray copper coin that had rolled to the back' – here Gwendolen held up her other hand and opened it palm up to show the coin's dull coppery gleam – 'but otherwise it was quite empty. And—'

'Enough,' said Lady Maëlle, so sharply that Joanna started in her seat. 'Has any of you seen Amelia this morning? Joanna?'

Joanna shook her head numbly, and one by one the others did the same.

'She went up to bed very early yesterday evening,' said Jenny, her voice slow and heavy. 'Do you not recall?' Joanna, her heart sinking, did. 'She had a sick headache, she said, and I did not doubt her, for she did look ill – I had begun to remark it at dinner. I remember I asked her whether I had not better send you up to her, Lady Maëlle; but she said no, she was going to sleep straight away, and should be quite well in the morning—'

'You ought to have told me,' said Lady Maëlle. Joanna flinched from the furious anger in her voice.

The expressions breaking across their faces, as severally they arrived at the conclusion that, in fact, no one had seen Amelia since the previous afternoon, exactly echoed the sick panic which clutched at Joanna's heart and roiled nauseatingly through her belly.

'I can see now that I ought,' said Jenny – her voice perfectly calm, though her face was waxen and her hands clenched tightly on the arms of her chair. 'But at the time—'

Lady Maëlle drew breath to speak again; Joanna, hoping to forestall her, said, 'Has she had any more mysterious letters? Had she any yesterday?'

Treveur and Madame Joliveau were summoned. No, said Treveur, there had been no letters for Miss Callender by the morning post yesterday, nor the evening post either. However, yesterday being the first of the month, he had been occupied all the afternoon, together with Madame Joliveau and Lady Kergabet, in the settling of the household bills; he was not prepared to swear, therefore, that no letter or message could have entered the house by any other means. Indeed, they agreed, there had been a quantity of messengers, couriers, and so on coming to the door at all hours, since this dreadful business of Dim'zell Joanna's father (here he nodded at Joanna, an apology for having drawn this connexion), and though all the staff of course had strict instructions to let none of these persons past the front door . . .

'I thank you both,' said Jenny at last, and sent them away to question the housemaids, the parlourmaids, the footmen, and (on the subject of Miss Callender's boots) the boot-boy, George – if possible, without exciting their curiosity.

Joanna thought again of horses and stable doors, and rather fancied that Jenny and Kergabet were thinking the same, but there must be some effort made, at least to delay – for surely they could not prevent it altogether – the moment when Amelia's sudden departure should become fodder for the sort of talk which all were desirous to avoid.

Meanwhile Sophie and Gray had been muttering together in a corner of the morning-room – in their case, an almost infallible sign of magickal doings. Upon the departure of Madame Joliveau and Mr Treveur, they emerged from this conference to resume their seats upon Jenny's new green-and-gold-striped sofa; their faces were grave, and they held hands quite openly (Gray's huge left hand altogether eclipsing Sophie's right), as though they could not quite bear to let go.

'That was a finding-spell, I presume,' said Kergabet. He glanced out of the window, repressed a sigh, and looked at Mr Fowler, who said, 'I shall go and see about the carriage, sir.'

Of course, thought Joanna, very belatedly; they ought to have been about their business long since, and should have been, if not for Henry Taylor, if not for Amelia.

'It was,' said Gray, as the door was closing behind Mr Fowler. 'Either Miss Callender is not within eighty miles of this house, or she is in the company of someone capable of working an extremely strong warding-spell, and of recognising the wisdom of doing so.'

'This Henry Taylor,' said Jenny at once; 'could he do so, do you think?'

Gray's russet-gold-brown eyebrows drew together in a doubtful frown. 'I should not have said so,' he said, 'particularly in light of the description of him which we had this morning – exhaustion and starvation do not tend to strengthen one's reserves of magick. On the other hand . . .'

His voice trailed off, and for a long moment he said nothing but stared vaguely in the general direction of the window, from which were visible the tops of the trees in the square.

'On the other hand?' Sophie prompted patiently.

Gray turned away from the window, blinked several times, and said, 'On the other hand, I have not set eyes on Henry Taylor for the best part of seven years, and even then, we were not friends; I have no reason to suppose my impression of his capabilities at all accurate, and of course no means of knowing what else he may have contrived to learn since last we met.'

'Nonetheless,' said Sophie, 'if, as we believe, Amelia left the house yesterday evening after the rest of us went up to bed – the evidence of the boots, you know – I think the most likely explanation is that she has already got more than eighty miles from London, rather than—'

'Why eighty miles, Sophie?' said Joanna.

'I am drawing a logical inference,' said Sophie primly. 'After the . . . the business in Alba, we recruited all of our colleagues to experiment with finding-spells, so that if anything of the sort should ever occur again . . .' She swallowed, cleared her throat, and continued: 'My range is fifty miles, and Gray's, thirty; ergo, working together, we ought to be able to manage eighty at the least.'

'Mrs Marshall,' said Gwendolen, sitting up very straight, like a pointer which has caught a scent, 'what if – I wonder – the spell you sang, in Din Edin – might that—'

Joanna stared at her, bemused; this inarticulate jumble of words was quite unlike Gwendolen's usual mode of expressing herself. But she knew very well what sort of spell was meant, and it seemed that Sophie did also, for she said at once, 'I am quite prepared to try it; but you know, I think, that on the occasion you speak of, I had had . . . considerable assistance from Lucia MacNeill—'

'Well, as to that,' said Joanna, 'surely Lucia MacNeill would have no objection—'

'*You* may be sure of it, but *I* am not,' Sophie retorted. 'But in any case, Jo, the effect would not be at all the same, because now we are not in Alba.'

Joanna and Gwendolen sat back in disappointment; Lady Maëlle, whose outrage appeared to have subsided to an impotent simmer, said bleakly, 'I apologise for my intemperate words, Lady Kergabet. The blame is mine; I have known that child since the age of three, and ought to have seen that she was scheming.'

The door opened. 'The carriage, sir,' said Mr Fowler.

CHAPTER XV

In Which Sophie and Joanna Conduct an Uncomfortable Interview

'*No, ma'am,*' *said* Katell positively. 'And if I did,' she added, with a defiant glance at Lady Maëlle, 'I shouldn't tell anyone.'

She does know something *about it, at any rate*, thought Sophie. She exchanged with Joanna a look of grim surmise.

'Katell, no one wishes Amelia any ill,' she said. 'She and I have . . . we have not always seen things just alike, as you know, but you surely cannot think that I should take this occasion to crow over her mistakes?'

Katell looked away uncomfortably but said nothing.

'But if she is gone off alone, Katell,' Sophie persisted, 'anything at all might befall her – she does not know London as Miss Joanna does, or Miss Pryce – she has no magick to protect her, nor any other sort of protection either – and with the Professor abroad in the world somewhere, plotting the gods alone know what—'

They ought not to have brought Lady Maëlle with them, she decided. It had seemed a wise precaution, a reassurance to Katell; but it appeared that Katell's habit of shielding Joanna from the

Professor's temper had transmuted itself into a determination to keep Amelia's secrets from her guardian.

'Cousin Maëlle,' said Sophie – dubious of success but determined to make the attempt – 'I have just remembered that J—that Lady Kergabet wished very much to consult you upon, er, upon a matter of midwifery. I do apologise – I cannot think how I came to forget—'

Lady Maëlle, of course, was not taken in for a moment, but Lady Maëlle had not in any case been the target of Sophie's gambit. Her dark eyes narrowed – *I see what you are about, Sophie Marshall* – but she nodded briskly and, saying only, 'We must hope there is no great harm done,' took herself off, very likely to listen outside the library door.

Within the library there followed several further attempts at reasoning Katell into cooperation, which she resisted as steadfastly as before – until at last Joanna's unwonted patience came to a jarring end, and she interrupted Sophie's latest *Please, Katell,* by saying sharply, 'Katell, I wish you will tell us whatever it is you know about Amelia; but if you will not, it does not much signify, for Lady Kergabet has only to scry something of hers, and then we shall know all of it.'

In several respects, as Joanna must know, this last was not precisely true; Katell, however, could only just call light, and to Sophie's knowledge had never seen a scry-mage working close to. Sophie was not much surprised, therefore, to see her defiance begin to waver before Joanna's decidedly unsubtle threat.

The sisters exchanged a meaning look, and by unspoken consent sat back in their chairs and regarded Katell (standing before them with her hands twisted into her apron, her honest face growing pink) in silence. Like both of them before her –

for this patient, expectant silence was a weapon which Jenny had deployed against Sophie more than once, and Joanna, in all probability, dozens of times – Katell could bear it only so long.

'It is not fair!' she burst out at last, all furious indignation.

Sophie's ears pricked; she leant forward, clasping her hands between her knees. 'What is not fair?'

Katell paused a long moment – the pause, and Katell's expression, spoke to Sophie of calculation, though that might be only the effect of her own guilty conscience – but at length said, 'That you should be so very cross with Miss Amelia, only for doing what you did yourself.' Misreading Sophie's expression of dismay, she hastily added, 'Begging your pardon, Miss Sophie.'

'Mr Henry Taylor, I presume?' said Joanna with a sigh.

Abandoning her wary study of Sophie, Katell rounded on Joanna. 'And what of it?' she demanded. 'Why should not Miss Amelia run away to be married to a handsome Oxford man, the same as her sister?'

'I did no such thing!' Sophie protested.

Joanna and Katell looked at her, briefly united in disbelief.

'It is quite true,' said Sophie, with some spirit, 'and Miss Joanna knows it as well as I do, Katell, whatever anyone else may say. Mr Marshall and I did *not* run away to be married; we ran away for a different reason entirely, and it so fell out that we were married along the way.'

Joanna hid a most unladylike snort of derisive laughter behind her hand; Sophie glared at her, and she left her seat and began to pace about the room.

'In any case,' said Sophie, returning her attention to Katell, 'Mr Taylor is not an Oxford man, handsome or otherwise; he is a convicted traitor. A man who took part in a plot to poison the King.'

This, it seemed, Amelia had not confided to her accomplice; Katell's brown eyes widened in alarm, and she swallowed hard before saying, 'I am sure that can't be right, Miss Sophie. Or' – her voice grew more confident as she evolved an alternative theory – 'if it *is*, I'm sure Miss Amelia can't have known of it.'

'She did know of it, Katell,' said Sophie gently; 'I know she did, for we spoke of the matter very lately. But I believe she thinks better of Mr Taylor and his friends – and of the Professor, too – than they deserve.'

Behind Katell, Joanna rolled her eyes; this time Sophie could not glare at her without Katell's seeing it, and so she confined herself to a brief crimping of her lips. 'But whatever Miss Amelia may believe of them, Katell, they are *not* good men, and I do not believe she is safe in their company.'

Katell bit her lip and twisted her apron in her hands as though it had been a floor-cloth which wanted wringing out.

'I am sure Miss Amelia would never go away with a young man unless she intended marriage,' said Sophie, pressing her advantage, 'but what Miss Amelia intended and what Mr Taylor means to do may not be the same, you see.' Despite herself, she heard her voice go pleading, felt Joanna's gaze sharp on her face – wondering at her tone, or suspecting her of prevarication? 'Amelia and I have not always been very kind to one another, but if she should come to harm, harm that I might have prevented—'

'She had letters from him,' Katell burst out. She sounded near to weeping – and no wonder, if she was betraying a promise of secrecy. Truly, thought Sophie, it was cruel of Amelia to have put her in such a position. 'He promised to marry her, and to take her where her father is, and that he and the Professor have powerful friends, and will be great men there.'

'Where?' Joanna demanded.

Katell burst into tears, and flung herself at Sophie. 'I don't know,' she sobbed into Sophie's shoulder. 'She never told me that. I don't know.'

Did she know herself? Had she any idea what she was about? Oh, Amelia . . .

And whilst all of us were brangling over whether she ought to be permitted to speak with him, in a public park and in Gray's company, for a quarter-hour, she must already have been planning to elope with him!

But if that were so, then why—

Katell interrupted this promising train of thought by clutching at Sophie's shoulder-blades and sobbing, 'I gave her my word, and now look!'

'All right, Katell,' said Sophie, holding her tight. 'All right. I am sorry that we should have made you break your word. You did right to tell us, I promise you.'

Over Katell's heaving shoulders, Sophie caught Joanna's gaze and held it. *We shall have to ask Jenny to scry Amelia's things in any case.*

To Joanna's surprise, Lady Maëlle was not lurking in the corridor listening at the door, and, indeed, was nowhere to be found. Having given Katell over to the care of Mrs Treveur, the acerbic but kind-hearted Breizhek matron who ruled over Jenny's kitchen, Joanna and Sophie went in search of Jenny. In the morning-room they found Mrs Marshall at work on a vast and complex piece of petit-point, and in the library, Gray, surrounded by stacks of books and poring over an enormous codex – but no Jenny.

They ran her to earth at last in the nursery, nearly at the top of

227

the house, where she was ensconced in a rocking-chair with Yvon curled in her lap and Agatha hanging perilously over the chair-back. All three were listening raptly to Gwendolen, who sat cross-legged on the nursery carpet with a book open in her lap. '*Au bout d'une quinzaine d'ans,*' she read, '*le Roi et la Reine étant allés à une de leurs maisons de plaisance, il arriva que la jeune Princesse courait un jour partout dans le Château, et montant de chambre en chambre . . .*'

Sophie coughed.

Gwendolen looked up sharply. 'What is the matter?' she said.

'Aunty Jo!' said Yvon, pointing with a chubby finger. 'Story!'

Agatha dropped to her feet, ran forward, and caught Joanna and Sophie by the hands. 'Come! Sit down!' she said. 'Aunty Gwen, tell us what happens next to the beautiful Princess!'

Gwendolen glanced up at Joanna as if seeking permission to continue; Joanna nodded minutely, and silently shaped the word *Later.* Gwendolen returned the nod, bent her head to the book, and took up her interrupted tale.

Sophie meanwhile had allowed herself to be towed half across the nursery and deposited on the cushioned window-seat. Rather than joining her, however, Joanna paused by Jenny's chair and, bending close to her ear, murmured, 'It is as we suspected, and possibly worse.'

Jenny's wide hazel eyes fell closed, and her arms about Yvon tightened briefly. 'What had Katell to say?' she said, low.

'A farrago of lies, I strongly suspect,' said Joanna; 'but not her own lies, and, unless I miss my guess, not even my sister's.' In a rapid undertone, wary of Yvon's listening ears, she sketched the purport of Katell's confession. 'But what she did not know – or, at any rate, would not admit to knowing, and by then I believe she had abandoned concealment – is *where.* I hope, therefore—'

'Yes,' said Jenny. 'Bring me something of hers – come to my room, when you have dressed for dinner – and I shall do what I can.'

Joanna blinked, nonplussed. She and Sophie had marshalled their arguments, arming themselves to overcome Jenny's scruples on the subject of scrying Amelia's abandoned possessions without her consent – but here was the skirmish won for them, without a sword drawn.

'I thank you,' she said at last, and, after gently ruffling Yvon's tow-coloured curls, turned away to settle beside Gwendolen on the carpet.

Under cover of their muddled skirts, Gwendolen's free hand found Joanna's and held tight.

'Dougal MacAngus would have my head,' muttered Sophie, sifting through the contents of Amelia's dressing-table drawers, very little of which recognisably belonged to Amelia. Of course even Dougal MacAngus would make an exception in the case of a missing person – but *was* Amelia missing, in that sense, or had she merely made a choice with which her family and friends vehemently disagreed?

Joanna's face appeared around the door of the wardrobe, into which her head and upper body had vanished some time before. 'I beg your pardon?' she said.

'Never mind.' Sophie waved a hand vaguely about the scene of their various transgressions – of the laws of hospitality, of their sister's privacy, of (though as yet only in prospect) the tenets of magickal ethics – and returned to her rummaging.

The results thus far were not encouraging; as well as making a nearly clean sweep of her fungible assets, Amelia appeared to have taken away with her – or otherwise disposed of – all of her jewellery, her brushes and hairpins, her dancing-slippers—

'Aha!' Joanna emerged fully from the wardrobe, and thrust towards Sophie a battered reticule, embroidered with pink and red carnations and closed by a wide ribbon of dull green. Loose threads spilt from the edges of a rent in one side.

Sophie regarded it doubtfully. It was difficult to imagine Amelia as the owner of such a bedraggled object, but had it belonged to Miss Pryce, whose bedroom this ordinarily was, Joanna could not have mistaken it.

'The carnations,' said Joanna, impatient, waggling the limp satin. '*I shall never forget you.* Amelia's friend Claudine Harcourt made this for her when she left school, and Amelia made her one very like it.'

'I shall take your word for it,' said Sophie. 'Have you that copper coin from the back of the drawer . . . ?'

Joanna extracted the coin (or, at any rate, *a* coin) from the folds of her sash and held it up.

They knocked diffidently upon the door of Jenny's room; as Joanna pushed open the door, Jenny turned from her dressing-table, smoothing her skirts over her knees with anxious hands.

'What have you found?' she said.

Joanna produced the carnation reticule and handed it over.

Jenny's eyebrows rose in doubt – exactly as Sophie's had done, not a quarter-hour since – and Joanna, anxious and impatient, bit back a sharp reply. 'It is Amelia's own, I promise you,' she said instead; as a further thought occurred, she added, 'Indeed, I rather wonder that she should have left it behind.'

'She must have packed up her things in a great hurry,' said Sophie.

Jenny flattened the worn and shredded silk across her lap and studied it thoughtfully. 'A gift from a dear friend, perhaps?' she said.

'Yes, exactly,' said Joanna.

'Perhaps,' said Sophie, 'we may find Amelia by seeking out Mademoiselle Harcourt?'

Joanna sighed. 'Perhaps we might,' she said, 'but that Claudine Harcourt – Madame Deschamps she was by then – died four years ago.' Sophie flinched. 'Thrown from a horse, by Cousin Maëlle's account – it was not Amelia who told me of it, of course.'

'Be quiet, please, both of you,' said Jenny, not unkindly.

Sophie reached for Joanna's hand – to still the anxious fidgeting of her own, Joanna suspected – and they sat side by side, unspeaking, whilst Jenny prepared her scrying-spell.

There was not much to see, and they had in any case seen all of it before. Jenny cupped Amelia's abandoned reticule in both hands, closed her eyes and steadied her breathing, and murmured the words of her spell – as obscure to Joanna now as they had been when first she heard them, all those years ago, applied to a ring of keys which Sophie had stolen from the pocket of the Professor's coat.

On this occasion the process seemed to go on for a very long time. Joanna leant up close to Sophie and breathed in her ear, 'What is happening? Is all well, do you suppose?'

As she drew back, Sophie turned to her with a small, unhappy frown creasing her brow. 'Scrying is a closed book to me, Jo,' she said quietly. 'I have not the least idea. I *do* know that a scry-mage must never be interrupted midspell.'

Meaning, in fact, *Hush, Jo.*

Joanna pressed her lips together and called on Lady Juno to grant her patience.

When at last Jenny raised her head and opened her eyes, her expression was surprisingly calm.

'Well?' said Sophie.

Jenny sighed. 'I cannot decide whether this object was well or poorly chosen for the purpose,' she said. 'It was in your sister's possession for more than a decade and strongly associated with her, but it is so thickly wrapped about with aetheric echoes that to find those we are seeking would, I think, be no easy feat for any scry-mage – even one far more skilled than I.'

'Jenny—'

Jenny held up a hand, and Sophie subsided, quivering.

'Fortunately, I am better acquainted with Miss Callender than a more skilled stranger could possibly be, and fortunately, too, the echoes we need are amongst the most recent, though not the strongest, which made my task easier than it might otherwise have been.' She looked down again at the lovingly worked carnations. Where, Joanna wondered, was this interminable lecture leading? 'Less fortunately, your sister's feelings of guilt at leaving behind this last relic of her girlhood friend have created such a strong echo as nearly to obscure those associated with her plans.'

'*Jenny*,' said Sophie, a pleading note creeping into her voice, 'you know I should have no objection, in the ordinary way, to a lecture on the art of scrying, but in this case—'

'I am coming to the point, Sophie, I assure you,' said Jenny. 'From what I have been able to see – and it is little enough, as I have tried to explain – Miss Callender's thoughts, at the time when last she handled this reticule, were on the subject of Mr Henry Taylor—'

'That, at least, is no surprise,' said Sophie, with a grim little nod. 'There is no use in my going to the park as Amelia to meet him, then, I suppose.'

'It would surprise you very much, if you had *seen* him,' said

Joanna. Try as she might, she could not make the pieces fit. 'Truly, Sophie, I cannot imagine a man less likely to appeal to Amelia!'

'No doubt he will have found some way of making himself presentable,' said Sophie, waving an impatient hand. 'He is an educated mage, after all – and, by Gray's account, a dab hand at persuading people to do things they ought not. Jenny, what else has Amelia been thinking of?'

'Of Mr Taylor, as I have said,' said Jenny patiently, 'and of her father, and she seems to have been anticipating a journey across the Manche, to Trouville-sur-Mer or perhaps Honfleur. I must stress,' she added, reading their eagerness to start after this scent at once, 'that I cannot say what she *has* done, or where she has gone – only what she thought of doing, or meant to do. And of course it is not unlikely that Trouville-sur-Mer and Honfleur are only two of a long list of possible destinations on the Normand coast, which she happened to remember.'

'But,' said Sophie, 'but, Jenny, when you scried my stepfather's key-ring – over and over, you remember! – you learnt things from it which – what I mean is, *why* cannot you see anything of what Amelia is doing, or thinking, or feeling now?'

'I shall try again, naturally,' said Jenny. 'I shall try every day, if there seems any possibility of its being a useful undertaking. But, as we are speaking of that former example, do you not recall my saying that it was difficult to discover anything of use, because your step-father was so angry with you that I could see almost nothing else?'

Sophie nodded slowly. 'Yes,' she said after a moment. 'I see.'

Joanna let go Sophie's hand, felt about in the folds of her own sash, and after a moment succeeded in retrieving the forgotten copper coin. 'There is this,' she said, holding it out to Jenny. 'We thought the other must be the better source, because it had been hers so long, but . . .'

Jenny folded her long fingers – slender even now, though that would change in the months to come – around the not-quite-circle of dull copper; first one hand, then the other. 'Hmm,' she said, apparently to herself. Then once again she closed her eyes and sank into her scrying, lips moving silently through the words of her spell.

Her face grew pale, first by slow degrees, then all at once.

Joanna and Sophie exchanged anxious glances. Belatedly Joanna asked herself whether Jenny ought to have undertaken this task twice in such close succession (could not this second attempt, at least, have waited till after dinner?) – whether the first attempt had not been too draining in itself, without a second's being added to it – whether they were asking too much of her, and whether the consequence might be magick shock, or . . . something worse.

'But we must not interrupt,' said Sophie. Her face crimped unhappily; she shifted in her seat, and Joanna saw that she was actually sitting on her hands.

Jenny opened her eyes with a small, startled gasp; the copper coin fell from her hand, slid down the slope of her skirts, and rolled across the carpet until it ran against the toe of Sophie's shoe.

'Well,' said Jenny faintly, as Sophie bent to retrieve it. 'Well, certainly I did not expect *that*.'

Sophie laid the coin gingerly atop a nearby occasional table. 'Jo,' she said, 'will you go to the kitchen, please, and fetch back, er, some of Mrs Treveur's beef tea?'

As this irritatingly transparent attempt to get her out of the way – for what purpose, she could only speculate – was also more efficient than ringing for one of the servants to convey a message to Mrs Treveur, Joanna picked up her skirts and dashed down the servants' staircase to the kitchen, though not before glaring briefly at Sophie.

Persuading Mrs Treveur that there was no need to send for a healer (or for Lady Maëlle) took as much time as fetching out and warming the beef tea; when at last Joanna regained Jenny's room, she found a fire dancing in the grate and Jenny and Sophie perched side by side on the chaise longue, heads bent together as though studying something. A fluffy woollen shawl was incongruously wrapped about Jenny's elegant gown of mulberry-coloured silk. Moving closer with her heavy tray, Joanna discovered the object of their study: Amelia's forgotten copper coin, dull and beginning to go green, lay in Sophie's open palm, and beside it another, bright-new, of more or less the same size and shape.

'What has that coin to tell us, that the other had not?' she inquired.

She set down the covered tray upon the hearth, then handed the cup and spoon up to Jenny, who grimaced at the smell but, at Joanna's severe look, meekly set to.

'There is something very odd about this coin, Jenny says,' said Sophie, holding up the two for Joanna's inspection, 'so we thought to compare it to an ordinary one, and look!'

Joanna looked.

The new coin was indeed perfectly ordinary: on the obverse, a head in profile, recognisable as that of His Majesty the King, and the legend *HENRICUS XII REX*; on the reverse, a stylised sandal of Mercury within a laurel-wreath, and the previous year's date.

The other had been frequently clipped and was half grown over with verdigris, but closer examination revealed that it was not, as first Gwendolen and then Joanna and Sophie had supposed, otherwise an ordinary product of His Majesty's mint. The profile on the obverse was not King Henry's, nor his father's or grandfather's; the lettering round the rim was half clipped away, but Joanna could just make out *ANS* along the right-hand edge, and *FRA* along the left. On the reverse, what at first appeared to be a bundle of sticks resolved itself, when held at a particular angle to the light, into a fleur-de-lys.

'That is not so very strange, is it?' she said, after a thoughtful moment. 'This coin is a long way from home, certainly; but if it was Amelia's, then it came here by way of Breizh, and coin from the Duchies crosses into Breizh and Maine and Normandie often enough in the course of trade, when relations are good.'

She studied Jenny's troubled expression, relieved to see that at any rate her face was no longer the colour of a tallow-candle.

'There is something else, I collect,' she said. 'What is it?'

Jenny swallowed another spoonful of beef tea, then set the half-empty vessel aside and folded her hands upon her knee. 'The coin was Amelia's, in fact,' she said, 'but only very lately; she did not acquire it in the course of some ordinary transaction, but received it – received an entire purse of coin from the same source, not only copper but silver and gold – by the hand of a stranger, with instructions for its conveyance to some third person.'

'But *who*?' Joanna demanded.

'Had I been able to identify either of these mysterious persons,' said Jenny mildly, 'I should already have told you so. I was not.'

'And who made the coin?' said Joanna, in a more moderate tone – there was certainly nothing to be gained from antagonising Jenny. 'Or ordered it made? And where?'

Jenny shook her head. 'It was not made in Britain,' she said, 'but that much we knew already. The reverse is a fleur-de-lys; one or other of the Duchies seems indicated, as you have remarked yourself. More than that, at present, I cannot say.'

From below came the bright peal of the dinner-bell.

'Do you feel well enough to come down with us, Jenny?' said Sophie, laying a hand over Jenny's, still clasped upon her knee. 'You are still a little pale, I think – Jo, do you not think so?'

'I am perfectly well,' said Jenny firmly, before Joanna could make any reply; rising from her seat, she put off her shawl and went to the mirror to scrutinise her hair. This done, she turned back to them, hands on hips, and added, 'Come along!'

Joanna and Sophie followed her obediently out of the room. If Joanna chanced to remark that Jenny's gait was a trifle more measured than ordinarily, or that she kept a firmer hold of the bannister when descending the stairs, she was not so foolish as to mention it aloud.

CHAPTER XVI

In Which Gray Receives a Commission

There were guests for dinner, whom it had been too late to put off: Sir Herbert and Lady Beaumont, their eldest son, and their daughter, upon whom Mrs Marshall had matrimonial designs on behalf of her son Alan; for after the first, shocked reaction to Kergabet's news of the escaped prisoners, Mrs Marshall had quickly returned her attention to her chief aim in coming to London. Miss Beaumont was a perfectly inoffensive young lady – indeed, thought Sophie, she was very pretty, with her tawny-gold hair, finely sculpted features, and warm smile – and perfectly friendly to Mrs Marshall; the enthusiasm which the latter (and possibly also Lady Beaumont) supposed that young lady to possess for the absent Alan, however, appeared entirely her own invention.

Nevertheless Jenny had, at her mother's request, invited Miss Beaumont and her parents not only to eat dinner but also to spend the evening in Grosvenor Square. The evening party was to include more than a dozen further guests, among them – and here Sophie anticipated considerable chagrin on her mother-in-law's part – three unmarried young men, all of them personable, reasonably intelligent, and of larger fortune than Alan Marshall, as well as Madame de Courcy and her two eldest daughters.

Jenny had also intervened – or, rather, had outmanoeuvred her mother's intervention – in the seating arrangements, so that Miss Beaumont was seated to Sieur Germain's left, with Gray on her other side, and as far as possible from Mrs Marshall.

No one mentioned Amelia. Lady Maëlle, Sophie discovered, had invented an invitation from a cousin to an extended house-party at the fictional cousin's husband's estate in Kent, received by Amelia in the course of the previous se'nnight and taken up yesterday afternoon. Being who and what she was, she had succeeded in persuading Mrs Marshall to swallow this unlikely tale as though it were entirely plausible, first, that Amelia should have been in possession of a cousin with an estate in Kent and said nothing of it to anyone, and, second, that she should have abandoned London for the country when the London season was yet in full swing. And now, though Sophie knew her to be furious with Amelia, furious with herself, and half sick with fear that something far worse than an ill-considered elopement might have befallen her ward, she was calmly eating quail *en croûte* and discussing the relative merits of two different breeds of sheep with Sir Herbert Beaumont.

Where Lady Maëlle had been since leaving Sophie and Joanna alone with Katell, Sophie had not the least idea. There had been no opportunity before dinner to convey to her what Katell had confessed, or what Jenny's scrying had discovered, and Sophie itched with the desire to do so – to, if she were honest with herself, lay the whole of it before her erstwhile guardian like a child bringing her small woes to her mama.

Instead, however, she gathered her wandering wits, turned to the young man at her side, and in as ordinary a tone as she could manage said, 'Have you been long in London, Mr Trenoweth?'

Mr Trenoweth smiled winningly. 'A twelvemonth only,' he said.

'And how do you find it?'

'I find it very well supplied with beauty,' said Mr Trenoweth. 'And with dancing, and spritely conversation. I am very fond of dancing,' he added.

As Sophie was also very fond of dancing, this topic served them well for some time.

'I hope Miss Callender may be enjoying herself in Kent,' said Mr Trenoweth at length.

This remark rather startled Sophie, both by its unexpected consonance with her own thoughts and because she had not known Amelia and Mr Trenoweth to be at all acquainted with one another. When she did not at once reply, Mr Trenoweth frowned at her and said in quite a different tone, 'Mrs Marshall, are you quite well? You are very pale.'

Sophie drew her mother's magick about her, imagining it as a veil – so finely woven as to be nearly invisible, yet obscuring the truth of her feelings from her face – and said, 'Perfectly well, I thank you. I hope the same. I am not acquainted with these cousins, but my sister seems to have been pleased by the invitation.'

She had learnt from Joanna, though not without many a painful moment of revelation, the trick of telling plausible lies: only the word *cousins* was genuinely untrue.

'You are acquainted with the Mesdemoiselles de Courcy, however, are you not?' said Mr Trenoweth. His tone was light, almost offhand, but his expression betrayed his interest.

'A little, yes,' she said. 'The eldest is a great friend of my sister Joanna and of Miss Pryce.'

'They are known in London society to be *clever* and *bookish*,' said Mr Trenoweth. 'One does not altogether know what to make of such remarks.'

'Indeed?' Sophie raised her eyebrows. 'Speaking for myself, I think I should begin by considering their source.'

A sudden, startling grin flashed over his face, there and gone in a moment. 'That is the interesting thing, you see,' he said, sinking his voice to a confidential murmur. 'I have heard my sister call them so, and Miss Callender – Miss Joanna, that is – do so also; yet they do not appear to mean at all the same thing by the words.'

'I see,' said Sophie, who thought she did. 'If I may contribute my pinch of salt to the soup-pot' – this was an expression adopted from Donella MacHutcheon – 'I am not so well acquainted with the ladies in question as either Jenny or Joanna, but what I do know of them, I like very much. Mademoiselle de Courcy, I believe, is a great student of politics and of history, and I have heard my sister say that Mademoiselle Héloïse – she is talented, you know, which her sisters are not – takes a considerable interest in alchymy.'

'Does she, indeed,' said Mr Trenoweth, thoughtfully. 'And, if I may ask – I fear it is a great impertinence! – what think you of Miss Beaumont?'

Startled, Sophie glanced down the table at her, and found her smiling up at Sieur Germain. Too far away to distinguish their words, Sophie nonetheless thought she recognised her brother-in-law's expression as akin to the look of kindly but slightly weary patience he so often wore when conversing with Mrs Edmond Marshall.

'I think,' she said after a moment, choosing her words carefully, 'that Miss Beaumont is a kind, sweet, biddable young lady, who has not had much encouragement to think for herself.'

Mr Trenoweth followed her gaze, his thoughtful frown deepening. 'Hmm,' he said.

Then the table turned with the next course, and Sophie left Mr Trenoweth to the care of Jenny and talked determinedly of nature-poetry, Latin and Gaelic and English, to Mr Fowler, until the end of the meal.

'A word, if you please, Marshall,' said Sieur Germain quietly, drawing Gray aside with a hand on his shoulder.

'Sir?' Gray followed obediently, and not so quickly as to draw attention; when they had reached the secluded corner behind Miss Pryce's harp, he asked, 'Have you had news of the prisoners?'

'Yes,' said Sieur Germain, 'and no. There have been reports, of course, almost since the moment their escape became public knowledge – sightings of them in every hole and corner of the kingdom, and it is a task for Hercules himself to discover which of them may be true ones, if any. But our business together is something else entirely.'

Gray turned so as to continue looking at him whilst also keeping the rest of the party in his line of sight.

'As you know,' Sieur Germain continued, 'I have – or, rather, His Majesty has – agents in cities and towns across the Duchies, all of whom send in ciphered dispatches as best they may; their reports do not always arrive regularly, or in the intended sequence, and at times rumour is reported as fact, and only later corrected. When first one of our men in Touraine reported that local men were being recruited to serve a man calling himself Imperator Gallia, as you may perhaps remember, we all thought it as likely to be a practical joke as not—'

Gray nodded; he did remember, and could not deny that

the notion still struck him as unlikely to the point of absurdity.

'Yet this same man – or, rather, the same title, whether or not the same man is meant – has been mentioned in no fewer than half a dozen other agents' dispatches since, which of course is not proof but does suggest that there exists something worth investigating.

'Moreover, dispatches from our border garrisons in Breizh, in Maine, and in Normandie have lately reported that some large force is massing beyond the Loire, and another in the Comté de Blois and northward, on the borders of Maine and Normandie. The arms of Blois have been sighted, and of Anjou, Poitou, Touraine, and Acquitaine, among others—'

'Together?' said Gray, astonished.

Though no great follower of politics, and still less of military campaigns, he was at any rate aware that the Comté de Blois and the Comté de Poitou had been making attempts these seventy years and more to wrest the territory of Anjou – which, with the Comté de Touraine and the British province of Maine, lay between their own – from the Duc d'Acquitaine, each claiming a right, on behalf of their respective liege-lords, to defend it from the depredations of the other, and from the no longer particularly credible threat of British reconquest. Even had one of them prevailed at last, what could have induced the others suddenly to make common cause?

'Indeed,' his brother-in-law said dryly. 'You will thus perhaps understand the Privy Council's . . . curiosity.'

'Certainly,' said Gray, 'but—'

'Now, all of this is very curious, of course; but more lately my colleagues and I have ceased to be intrigued, and begun to be alarmed, for the reports we have been accustomed to receive have grown more infrequent, and for the last fortnight have ceased altogether. And that, Marshall, is where you come in.'

'I beg your pardon, sir,' said Gray, equally baffled and alarmed, 'but I do not see . . .'

'Do you not?' Sieur Germain chuckled, but quite without humour. 'Miss Joanna warned me to expect as much, I admit.' Whilst Gray was digesting this rather extraordinary remark, he continued, 'I wish to send you as my eyes and ears to Ivry, on the River Eure, where we have a cavalry regiment garrisoned and, as it seems, a large mixed force from several of the Duchies encamped opposite, lest we be tempted to cross the river, one supposes. And, from Ivry, where the trail leads you – without stirring up further hostilities, that is, for we have enough to be going on with at present without making, or provoking, an outright declaration of war.

'What has become of our agents in the Duchies? Can all of them have been captured? Killed? Suborned? How, and by whom? Who is it that calls himself Emperor of Gaul – if such a person exists indeed – and what is he about? And,' he added, 'it will not have escaped your notice that according to your sister's scrying, the absent Miss Callender was bound in the same general direction when she departed this house – or, at any rate, believed herself to be so.'

Gray discovered that he was gaping, and shut his mouth with a snap. 'I,' he began, and stopped. 'Do not misunderstand me; I am eager to be of service, as I have said – and also to ensure Miss Callender's safety; but I confess I do not altogether see why I should be more suited for *this* service than another. There must be . . . officers – agents – men trained to such work, and familiar with the territory—'

'Indeed,' said Sieur Germain once more, 'but none whom I, and the redoubtable Lady Maëlle, can trust as we both trust you.'

Gray swallowed against an incipient stammer. 'I thank you,' he managed, 'very much indeed. Both of you. May I ask, however—'

'Certainly you may.'

'Do I reason correctly, from your talk of trust and the lack thereof, that you also have reason to suspect the existence of . . . sympathisers . . . within Britain's own ranks?'

'It is not impossible,' said Kergabet gravely, 'though at present I have no specific suspicions of the kind. You hesitate,' he added – Gray's ears burnt in embarrassment – 'yet I know you do not lack for courage. You have reservations as to some aspect of the business; explain them to me.'

'I hesitate,' said Gray, 'because I cannot imagine what qualifications – beyond my loyalty to my kingdom, and your trust in me – I might possibly possess for a reconnaissance mission on the borders of the Duchies, with daring rescue to follow.'

Kergabet's eyebrows rose. 'Can you not?' he enquired. 'You have been trained in defensive magicks; you have seen battle, of a sort; you are an educated man, and a student of languages as well as a powerful mage; you have survived several months' imprisonment and' – a delicate pause; then – '*mistreatment* at the hands of a most unscrupulous enemy, and even when rescue seemed most remote, did not agree to his demands. Can you truly imagine no reason for my choice?'

Gray blinked.

'By that account,' he said slowly, 'I should seem the best man for the post.' He did not add that the said account did not sound to him at all like a description of himself.

'Indeed,' said Sieur Germain, with a small chuckle behind his hand.

A more urgent thought occurred to Gray, 'You are aware, I

am sure, of what befell Sophie, whilst I was imprisoned in Alba?'

Kergabet sobered abruptly. 'Certainly I am,' he said.

'Then you will understand . . .' Gray hesitated. But Kergabet *would* understand, if any man could. 'You will understand that I should prefer to have Sophie with me, as a partner in this undertaking.'

'Graham,' said Kergabet. Having made this startling beginning, he paused, folded his arms, and regarded Gray long and thoughtfully before speaking again. 'I am well enough acquainted with your character, I believe, to feel certain that you should never have made this suggestion, even to me, unless in your considered opinion the danger to her were less – or at least no greater – in accompanying you than in remaining here.'

'That is so, sir,' said Gray gratefully.

'That being said, however,' his brother-in-law continued, 'it is not I who must be convinced, you understand, but the Princess's father; and I tell you frankly that the odds of your succeeding in that endeavour are infinitesimally small.'

Gray nodded, disappointed but unsurprised. His Majesty – who knew Gray so little, and Sophie scarcely more – would not see, as Kergabet had done, the extent to which Gray's request grew from a concern for Sophie's . . . not *safety*, for to attempt to keep Sophie safe was akin to clipping the wings of an osprey and keeping it in a cage, but her happiness and well-being. He would understand it, rather, as reflecting selfishness on Gray's part, or headstrong foolishness on Sophie's.

Yet the thought of once more subjecting Sophie to the distresses of a separation – of doing so willingly and deliberately – and, almost worse, the prospect of breaking the news to her of his departure on an adventure in which she could take no part, and of which he could tell her almost nothing . . .

On the other hand, was it likely that he should be knocked on the head, taken captive, and held under interdiction, as he had been in Alba? The former, he conceded, was not out of the realm of possibility, though he hoped he should not be so caught off his guard a second time; but that an army on the move should have any means to hold a mage under interdiction – no, surely not.

So far, so reassuring; unfortunately, Gray could not help following out this line of reasoning to its logical conclusion: *Far safer and easier to execute him on the spot.*

He swallowed. 'I doubt not you are right, sir.'

'Are you *mad*?'

'*Cariad*—'

Gray shut his mouth abruptly as Sophie whirled to face him across the expanse of their bedroom, more nearly afraid of her than he had ever been before. The gods knew that he had witnessed more than one display of fury, of outrage, of self-destructive anguish – had been caught up in the destructive wash of her magick, had suffered for it, though never so painfully as Sophie herself – but never till this moment had that fury, that outrage, that anguish, with all the force of their shared magick behind it, been directed squarely and consciously at *him*.

He had not expected her to be *pleased* by Kergabet's proposal to send him alone to the Normand border, or with his own inclination to accept it – naturally not. After all, however, she had encouraged him to work with Lord de Vaucourt, despite the latter's making it insultingly clear that her own assistance was not wanted; she had conceded, if reluctantly, to his meeting with Henry Taylor, before Amelia's flight rendered the subject moot. Had he not had some justification for supposing that she might be similarly understanding in this case?

Sophie's face was starkly pale, save the twin scarlet patches of her cheeks; her eyes, darkened from warm brown to the black of water under river-ice, sparked dangerously, and her hands clenched ivory-knuckled in the folds of her sea-green gown.

'I had rather go with you than alone, love,' Gray said. She glared at him, dashed furious tears from her eyes with one trembling hand, but appeared to be letting him speak. 'Can you doubt it? I had a thousand times rather have you with me, for my own sake; and for yours, I had rather – I had *always* rather – you had useful work to do than be mewed up in idleness, waiting. But can you not see – it is as you told me, when Vaucourt would not accept your help, though he so badly needed it – this is a matter of more import than either of us.'

To his vast (if secret) relief, Sophie appeared to be listening.

'Kergabet has not much liking for the notion of sending you into what may soon become a field of battle,' Gray continued, 'but if the choice were his alone, I believe he should agree to it, for he knows both of us well enough to . . . to *believe* what we may be capable of, if he cannot altogether understand it. But, Sophie, it is not Kergabet who must be persuaded, and certainly not I; and I cannot blame him for wishing to set things in motion at once, rather than spending' – he had nearly, disastrously, said *wasting* – 'the gods know how much time in attempting to persuade your father.'

'*I* could persuade him,' said Sophie darkly. 'As I persuaded your mama to leave off her badgering, not so long ago—'

'But you would not,' said Gray, attempting to keep his tone both gentle and implacable. 'Not in such a case. And, besides, love, that is a method for the moment only; you should not be out of his sight for a quarter of an hour before he had all of London in an uproar, searching for you to bring you back to him, when instead—'

'When instead we ought all to be seeking the Professor et al., yes,' said Sophie.

The righteous fury had all gone out of her now, and left her resigned and sadly diminished. Gray – near tears himself, to his shame, for he liked leaving her no more than she liked his going – held out his arms, and Sophie crept into them.

'You will come back to me,' she said, her voice muffled by the fabric of his coat. 'You will come back safe, and not ... not ...' What words was she repressing, behind that swallowed sob? 'Promise me.'

'Of course, love.' Gray bent to kiss the top of Sophie's ear. *And if by some mischance I am too long about it for your liking, I expect you shall turn up again to rescue me.*

CHAPTER XVII

In Which Sophie Loses an Argument

Sophie saw Gray off just after sunrise – with solemn, quiet dignity, their true farewells having been made in the privacy of their bedroom, in the course of the night just past – and, having watched the anonymous hired carriage round the turning of Grosvenor Square and out of sight, turned back towards the house and climbed the steps with leaden feet. At the top of the steps she paused for a long moment, breathing slowly and carefully, and drew the veil of her concealing magick over herself from head to toes. *I am carved from marble, like the statues of Ceres and Proserpina in the square. I am clothed in armour as wise Minerva, and no barbed word can pierce it.*

Then she pushed open the door.

Breakfast was a painful ordeal, and Sophie escaped Mrs Marshall's volubility, Sieur Germain's silent remorse, and the cautious, quiet compassion of everyone else, as soon as she decently could, wishing all the while that she had thought to ask for her breakfast on a tray in her room.

Having retreated thither, however, she found it still worse, strewn with Gray's possessions – those not needed for his journey rooted out of their proper places and not yet tidied away – but firmly and indefinitely bereft of Gray himself; having indulged in a brief, useless, and infuriating fit of weeping, she smoothed away the evidence of her distress, tidied her hair, put on her best hat, and went downstairs to request conveyance to the Royal Palace.

Sophie had never before sought an audience with the King of her own volition, without prior invitation, and the process proved frustratingly lengthy – a just punishment, Sophie reflected, for her frequent reluctance to visit her father. *After all, he is the King of Britain; he has more pressing matters to attend to than a visit without portfolio from a wayward child.*

Or had he, on the contrary, deduced the purpose of her visit, and did he seek to avoid discussing it?

In any event, after being twice told that His Majesty was occupied with urgent business, and on a third visit kicking her heels in the rose-garden for well over an hour, she was at last summoned by a steward and conducted to His Majesty's study.

'Sophia!' King Henry rose from behind his desk and came forward to kiss her. 'You are well my dear, I hope?'

'Father,' she said, attempting a smile. 'I am well enough; and yourself?'

'As you say,' he replied, drawing her with him to sit on a lion-footed sofa at the far end of the room from the desk. 'Well enough.'

They spoke for some time – a little awkwardly, perhaps, but no more so than was usual for the two of them – of matters of mutual interest; the health and well-being of the Grosvenor Square family and of Queen Edwina and her sons having been duly canvassed, His Majesty revealed that the King's Own Cavalry Regiment, in which Prince Edward held a captain's commission, was preparing for active duty in Normandie, and wished to know how, in Sophie's opinion, matters stood between Prince Roland and Lucia MacNeill – which forced Sophie to admit to herself, if not to him, that she had no longer the least idea.

At last she could bear the weight of her unspoken purpose no longer, and without further preamble said, 'Do not you think, Father, that I have a duty to assist in the search for my sister?'

King Henry raised his fine-drawn white brows. 'Your sister?' he said.

'Stepsister, then,' said Sophie impatiently. 'We were brought up together, in the same house, the same family, such as it was; my mother was the only one Amelia ever knew, for her own died when Amelia was no more than a baby. We believed ourselves sisters for seventeen years; and I am capable of many things, Father, but not of overcoming an attachment seventeen years in the making.'

A year ago, three years ago, indeed, she should not have believed herself capable of such a speech; for some time before the sudden and irreversible disruption of their lives, Amelia and she had antagonised one another as, perhaps, only sisters can, when the comradeship of childhood has been curdled by jealousy and resentments only too clearly understood. But now Amelia was missing, very likely in dire trouble, and whatever Sophie's feelings towards her might be in the ordinary way, it was impossible to imagine abandoning her to her fate.

'And Lord Kergabet has sent Gray to Normandie to look for her,' she continued, rising from the sofa and turning to face her father. 'Not that only, of course, but partly that.' She had been wrong, she saw by his expression of surprise, to suppose that he had guessed her reason for wishing to see him; had he thought that Gray should for a moment consider not telling her where he was going, and why? 'I am only asking to be permitted to follow him there, and help in whatever way I am able.'

'It is quite impossible for you to go to Normandie, my dear,' said His Majesty. To his credit, he spoke regretfully, but a reluctant denial was a denial nevertheless, and brooked no protest.

Sophie drew breath, nevertheless, and made one. 'On the contrary, Father,' she said, 'it is quite impossible for me to remain here without my husband. You have not forgotten, I hope, what befell the last time Gray and I were separated by hundreds of miles?'

Gray, had he been present, might have pointed out (as he had pointed out to her during one of the quietly stormy conversations that preceded his departure) that unless the separation were a long one, and as he was not likely to be imprisoned under interdiction in the course of this journey, the likelihood of those consequences' being repeated was small. He might very well have been swayed, too, by the King's perfectly sensible assertions as to the dangers to which she would be exposed, so near the contested borders.

He was not present, however, being at that moment somewhere between London and the military garrison at Ivry, on the River Eure, and Sophie therefore felt entirely free to make use of whatever weapons might best serve her purpose.

'Sophia, a cavalry regiment is no place for a woman—'

'Have none of the officers wives, or daughters?' Sophie persisted. She turned on her heel and began to pace, lest the nervous energy engendered by this conversation spill out in some less acceptable manner.

She knew, and her father must also be well aware, that armies attracted camp-followers – the wives and sisters and daughters of the common soldiers, who in return for a half share of the daily ration did the cooking and washing for their own men and many others besides – and that therefore it was entirely likely that the Ivry garrison had already plenty of female inhabitants. *It is no place for a* gentlewoman, *I suppose he means.*

Rather than giving voice to any of these unhelpful thoughts, she said, 'Women serve in Donald MacNeill's household guard. Ceana MacGregor – Lucia's guard captain – was the finest archer of her clan when she was my age.'

Her father raised his eyebrows.

'I may not be capable of drawing a bow or swinging a sword,' said Sophie, in answer to his unspoken question, halting and folding her arms, 'but a mage-officer trained me in defensive and offensive magicks. I am not helpless, Father, I assure you!'

The King sighed. 'It is not that I think you helpless, my dear,' he said. 'Only that I do not wish to fling you headlong into danger, to no good purpose.'

'But you are sending Ned,' said Sophie quietly.

Ned will be King of Britain one day, he might have replied, *and her defence is part of his duty*; or, *Ned has been trained in arms, and in defensive magicks, since he was a child.* He might even have circled back to his original argument, by pointing out that Ned was a man, and she a woman, and the battlefield was not her place.

Sophie was prepared to rebut any or all of these answers: she was the Princess Royal and owed a duty to her kingdom as much as Ned did; she had seen real combat (if on a small scale), as he had not. Instead, however, her father looked at her with every one of his years writ clearly on his face, with the weariness of ages in his blue eyes (so like her brothers'; so different from her own), and said, 'I have lost you once, Sophia. I could not bear to lose you a second time, knowing so well what I had lost.'

Oh, Ned, thought Sophie, adding this to her mental list of things which she knew but must never reveal to any of her brothers.

'Papa,' she said – she had never called him so before, but the word was out before she could think better of it – 'you cannot protect me by packing me in goose-down and locking me up in a strongbox until the trouble is over! When you opened the box again, Gray and I should both be withered away, as we nearly were when he was Cormac MacAlpine's prisoner in Alba, and all your precautions wasted.'

She drew nearer to him, and dared to lay a hand upon his arm; he was looking down at her with such intensity, and wearing such a stricken expression, that she scarcely knew how to meet his gaze.

'You do not love me any the less, I think,' she continued, nevertheless, 'because I am not so biddable as I might be, or so eager to please.'

As she had hoped, this drew a wry smile and a fond, if rueful, chuckle. 'No, indeed,' the King conceded.

'And I swear by the Lady Diana,' said Sophie, taking her courage in both hands, 'by fleet-footed Mercury and Ceres of the hearth, that I can be of far more use to you – to the kingdom – in the field than I could possibly be at home. Only send me where my husband is, Father, and you shall see what we may accomplish together.'

It was not an idle promise; though each of them might be powerful alone, the rite of marriage *confarreatio* had linked their magicks so that together, working in concert, they were capable of quite remarkable things. Reminding His Majesty of the grave dangers of their connexion had perhaps begun to sap his determination to keep her here – out of one sort of danger, but bearing steadily towards the other; slowly, if distance were the only thing separating them, but with terrifying rapidity if things were to go ill with Gray, as they had in Alba – and Sophie hoped that this recollection of its power might complete that work.

Truly, however, she had always felt at sea in her dealings with her father – this near-stranger who knew at once so much of her and so very, very little – and the present conversation was no different.

King Henry, as Sophie had remarked before, knew the value of patient silence in unsettling his opponent. He deployed this weapon now, watching her calmly as she struggled to keep silence also; and before long she broke.

'I shall run away after him if I must,' she said, recklessly honest. 'I had rather not – I had very much rather not – I do know the duty I owe to you, Father, though you may not think it – but I shall not let any harm come to Gray on my account.'

'I do not doubt it,' said her father, disconcertingly calm. *Does he suppose I do not mean what I say?*

'A-and if I am forced to run away,' Sophie went on, 'I shall be all alone, or as good as; I cannot ask anyone else to follow me against your wishes—'

'Sophia!' The King held up a hand, and Sophie's impassioned argument fell away into silence. Again he let the silence stretch, until at last he said 'It was foolish of me, of course, to suppose that you might have grown less reckless with age, or less single-minded. May I propose a compromise?'

His raised brows, the slight tilt of his chin, made clear that the question was not pro forma; if Sophie wished to know in what this compromise consisted, she must say so.

And do I so wish? She could not decide.

But if a path existed which did not require her either to submit

256

to an indefinite separation or to defy her father outright and embark on a solitary flight across the kingdom, did she not owe it to Gray, and to herself, to seek it out?

'You may,' she said, folding her hands together to still their anxious fidgeting.

'Should you begin to experience any . . . symptoms which you recognise as connected with Mr Marshall's absence,' said His Majesty, 'or should you have reasonable grounds to suppose him likewise affected, you will inform me at once, so that I may arrange for his swift return; and in the meantime you will abide by my decisions on this question, and will give me your word not to attempt to follow him.'

Sophie pressed her hands together more tightly, and said nothing.

'However,' the King went on, 'I shall not insist on your kicking your heels at Court; so long as you are adequately guarded, I shall make no objection to your travelling a little way – to Oxford, for example – should you have some project in view, which I believe you have. You should have less leisure to fret and borrow trouble, I think, if your mind were better occupied.'

'You mean, I collect,' said Sophie, 'that in exchange for my agreeing to stay quietly in England whilst Gray is risking his life in Normandie, I shall be indulged in my – what was it those learned Fellows called it? – my *philanthropic fervour*, with respect to Lady Morgan College? Are you certain, sir, that you wish to extend your hand into that particular hornets' nest at present?'

Her father winced, just perceptibly, at her tone. And truly, thought Sophie, was his approval of this venture of hers not precisely what she had been hoping for, when she read the profoundly irritating letter from which she had just been quoting?

To do the thing openly and properly, with His Majesty's backing, and the resources to match her ambitions for the place, and a royal writ to fling in the teeth of those Fellows who thought it their right (nay, their calling) to thwart her?

But the price he asks . . .

She forced herself to consider the matter rationally. If only she could ask someone's advice – Gray's, of course, for preference, but then, if Gray were here, she should not have been in this equivocal position to begin with. Jenny or Lucia or Mór MacRury, Sophie was certain, would give her intelligent and sensible counsel; even Joanna could at least have offered another perspective on the matter, though Joanna's own decisions were as apt to be impetuous as soberly considered.

Well, then: if Gray were here, or Jenny or Lucia or any of them, how might they advise me in this case?

'May I,' she said, looking up at her father, 'may I have a little time to consider?'

'Certainly, my dear,' he said. He patted her shoulder – an awkward and diffident but oddly comforting gesture – and returned to his writing-desk, where he took up the topmost of a stack of dispatches and bent his gaze to it, effectively leaving her alone with her thoughts.

Sophie resumed her pacing, to and fro before the broad window, and began attempting to trammel the said thoughts into some sort of order.

First, then, the truth: her insistence on following Gray to Ivry was half anxiety (for Gray and, yes, for herself) as to the consequences of a separation, and half resentment at being mewed up in London, at loose ends and quite useless, whilst Gray and Ned and Sieur Germain and even, in her own small way, Joanna

258

were doing their part against the twin threats of the Duchies and the escaped conspirators, and for the rescue of Amelia. No very noble motive, that – and undoubtedly His Majesty knew it.

A further truth: her motives for seeking the rebirth of Lady Morgan College were no less complicated, and perhaps no more likely to withstand scrutiny. Of course she wished – quite unselfishly, if she did not mistake her own feelings – that young women of scholarly bent should have the same opportunity as their brothers for useful and challenging study, without having to beg for a place at the University in Din Edin, an expedient to which very few of their fathers were likely to agree in any case. But, too, she smelt a mystery clinging round the walls of Lady Morgan College, and burnt to puzzle it out. Why had it, after centuries of modest but respected scholarship, having educated thousands of students – including several daughters of dukes and even kings – and easily holding its own with the newer men's colleges, having attracted the personal patronage of the Princesses Regent in the reign of Edward VI, suddenly been closed? And not simply closed, but very nearly erased from history?

Lady Morgan had not been the first Oxford college to close its doors; Bairstow, for instance, stood on the erstwhile site of another college, nearly as old as Merlin, and (according to the Museum of the History of Magick) set up explicitly as a rival to it. Beaufort College had opened with great fanfare under the patronage of the Duke of Somerset, and for nearly three hundred years had been a great success, even luring some notable Fellows away from Merlin; but before it reached its fourth century, it had begun to lose its Fellows, its students, and its reputation to its elder rival, and at last faded into obscurity, until its land had been purchased and its buildings improved and expanded, under the patronage of the

Duke and Duchess of Grafton, into the present Bairstow College.

The whole of this history, with many additional minutiae which Sophie had not troubled to commit to memory, was documented in dozens of histories of Oxford, of magick in Britain, and of Beaufort and Bairstow Colleges, readily available in the library of this last as well as in those of Merlin College and of the Museum of the History of Magick. To judge by the extant recorded history of Lady Morgan College, on the other hand – as Lucia MacNeill had astutely remarked – the whole of it might as well have been plucked up from the bank of the Cherwell by a curious god or goddess and never seen again.

Except that the residents of Oxford, town and gown alike, saw it every day, half buried in rust and rubble and ivy, but unmistakably present – a corpse at the feast, so to speak.

Who owned the College buildings, and the land on which they stood, now that the College itself was no more? Why did no one seem to know, or even to wonder, and why had no one ever attempted (so far as Sophie had been able to discover) to make any other use of it? What, in the name of Clio, of Minerva, made all the histories stop short of the end of the tale?

Confess, Magistra Marshall: you fancy yourself a solver of mysteries, and worse than that, you fancy yourself cleverer than all those historians, than all the tens of thousands of Oxonians who have failed to solve the mystery since the Princess Edith Augusta's day.

If that is not hubris, my name is not Sophie Marshall.

Whatever her reasons – selfish or great-hearted, noble or altogether the reverse – certain it was that restoring Lady Morgan College to its former state was an aim dear to Sophie's heart. With the overt approval, if not the true patronage, of the King himself, that aim would become an attainable one; or, at the least, more attainable than formerly. A college, after all, is not only bricks and mortar, window-glass and furniture, pens and paper and books, but the people to use them – the Fellows, the tutors and lecturers, the students. Though sober reason told her that there had been clever, curious young women like herself in Lady Morgan's time and thereafter, and would be again, who would leap at the chance to study as eagerly as she had, what of all the fathers, the brothers, the husbands like Appius Callender, like Edmond and George Marshall, whom they should have to persuade to allow them that chance? And where should Sophie find the tutors and lecturers to teach them, when so many of the Fellows of other colleges had gone out of their way to express their disapprobation of the very notion?

There was, in other words, an uphill battle before her, in which even royal backing was no guarantee of victory.

Nevertheless, it was also true that were her father not making her this offer as a distraction, as a bribe to keep her feet safely (as he believed) on English soil and away from the armies of the Duchies – had there, in other words, not been far more urgent and important work for her to do, if only she were permitted to do it – she should not have hesitated even a moment before accepting it.

Am I truly considering cutting off my nose to spite my face?

She was wearing a path in the carpet of her father's study, Sophie found; she forced herself to stillness – swallowed hard – looked down at her clasped hands.

No.

'If I am to accept your terms,' she said at last, 'I must have your sworn word – your oath on . . . on the bones of my mother – that should Gray find himself in need of rescue – which the gods forbid! – there will be no delays, no arguments—'

'I am prepared to give my sworn word in the matter of a rescue mission,' her father said, holding up a hand to stem the mounting tirade, 'provided that it is understood that any such mission shall be undertaken by persons of suitable training and experience.'

Not, in other words, Sophie translated, *by yourself and your sister.* In fact, however – had he only been willing to acknowledge it – no person living could be better suited to this task than herself.

'Yes,' she said. 'That is understood, of course.'

In any case, we must pray that it does not come to that. Gray should not be wandering about Normandie alone, after all, but in the company of a regiment of soldiers; he was perfectly well able to look after himself, and, after the near-catastrophe in Alba, would be on his guard against . . . what? *There is the rub, indeed; he cannot know what awaits him there, and nor can any of us.*

'Then . . .' She hesitated, swallowing back what she feared might become bitter regrets; on no account would her father agree to her following Gray to Ivry, and it was futile to wish it, but remaining in England nevertheless felt like an abandonment. 'Then, yes, Father, I agree.'

Lucia was playing at chess with Roland – they were more or less evenly matched, being both apt to open with great caution and to grow increasingly reckless as the game progressed – when a discreet knock upon the half-open door of her sitting-room, where Ceana MacGregor and Conall Barra MacNeill stood guard, heralded the arrival of Sophie Marshall.

She looked altogether wretched, and Lucia was half out of her seat, crying, 'Sophie! Whatever is the matter?' when Sophie's eye fell on Roland, turning towards her in alarm. Before Lucia's astonished eyes, Sophie's ashen cheeks warmed to a healthier colour, the reddening of recent tears faded from her eyes, and something almost like a smile curved her lips.

'You will never guess,' she said, in a voice, again, almost entirely like her own. 'My father has given me leave to mount an expedition to Oxford, and I am come to ask you – both of you, though I did not know that I should find Roland here – to be of the party.'

Roland, not surprisingly, was looking from Lucia to Sophie and back again, wearing a frankly baffled expression. During his convalescence – or at any rate until her stepfather's escape from imprisonment had prompted her brother-in-law to confine her to the house – Sophie had been a regular visitor, and Lucia had believed the pair of them to be developing something approaching mutual confidence. It seemed, however, that Sophie was not prepared to allow her brother to witness her present distress, or to know its cause.

'Of course we should be delighted!' said Lucia.

'Yes, of course,' Roland agreed, ready enough despite his evident puzzlement; getting into the spirit of the thing, he said, 'When does this expedition of yours set forth?'

'I . . . I hardly know,' said Sophie. She reached for the high back of Roland's chair, which was nearest, misjudged the distance, and swayed on her feet.

Lucia's heart plummeted into her boots; Roland leapt up, knocking the chessboard askew and half the chessmen onto the floor, and each of them caught one of Sophie's elbows to guide her into the seat he had vacated.

'Roland,' said Lucia sharply, 'fetch your sister a cup of tea – put a great deal of honey in it, if you please – and whatever cakes may be left from the tea-tray—'

She desisted – he was already up and moving, pouring honey

263

into her own empty teacup with one hand and sweeping a dozen uneaten cakes and petits fours onto a clean plate with the other – and dropped to her knees beside Sophie.

'What is it?' she demanded, low. She spoke in Gaelic; it would not prevent Roland from understanding, but it would at any rate slow him down. 'Something is very much amiss; if I did not know better, I should say—'

'Kergabet has sent Gray to Normandie,' said Sophie miserably, in the same tongue. 'To spy for him – he believes there may be traitors in the ranks of my father's army – and to look for my sister Amelia, who has run away with one of my stepfather's henchmen, or so we have concluded. And,' she added in quite a different tone, sitting up straighter and scrubbing one forearm roughly across her eyes, 'I ought not to have told you any of that, so you will forget all of it straight away, if you please.'

Roland appeared at Lucia's shoulder with the cup of heavily sweetened tea and the plate of cakes; Lucia took them from him with a smile of thanks, set the plate upon the abandoned chessboard, and thrust the teacup into Sophie's hands.

'Drink this,' she said firmly, reverting to Latin, 'and when you are feeling more yourself, you shall tell us all about it.'

PART THREE

Oxford and Ivry

CHAPTER XVIII

In Which Gray Occasions
Some Surprise

It was a little past noon on a blazing-blue Marday when a Normand farmer's cart – driven by the farmer's stocky, tow-headed fifteen-year-old son, whose conversation through the whole of their slow, bone-rattling journey had, despite Gray's efforts, consisted entirely in variations on the two themes of *When I am old enough to go as a soldier* . . . and *If my father knew what my sister Ginette has been at with that Breizhek corporal* . . . – deposited Gray before a beflagged and imposing tent in the military encampment east of the city of Ivry. Having assisted in disentangling his passenger's belongings from the cured hams and rounds of cheese which constituted the remainder of his cargo, and tucking away with a broad grin the coins Gray dropped into his hand, the boy vaulted back up onto the driving-seat, took up the reins, and clucked his father's patient draught horses into motion.

'*Au revoir, monsieur!*' he called cheerfully over his shoulder as the cart trundled away.

The large young men standing sentry outside the tent eyed Gray with disfavour. Gray, however, had stared down, if not *many* a greater man, at any rate more than one; and, though not so broad in the beam as these fellows, he was half a head taller than either. 'I am to report to Colonel Dubois,' he said, drawing himself up very straight. 'My name is Marshall; I have letters for him from London.'

The sentries' expressions of distrust were altered not at all by this explanation, but the left-hand one did unbend so far as to say, 'Wait here, sir, and I'll enquire.'

He turned on one heel and vanished into the tent. His fellow contrived somehow to stare straight ahead whilst nevertheless visibly keeping Gray under his eye. The effect was rather unnerving; were they trained up to it, Gray wondered, or were men chosen for this duty because they possessed a natural gift for silent, stolid intimidation?

Surprisingly quickly, the vanished sentry reappeared, holding open the tent-flap and gesturing Gray within.

Colonel Dubois, at first blush, answered Gray's every expectation of the archetypal regimental commander; standing tall and straight behind his desk to receive his visitor, he possessed a cragged and weathered face bisected on the vertical by a nose as crooked as Gray's own – perhaps for the same reason – and on the horizontal by pale sharp eyes which swept over Gray's person in a single assessing glance. Only in one particular did he deviate from the Platonic ideal: he had evidently been working in his shirt-sleeves, for his regimental coat hung by its shoulders from the back of his chair.

'You have letters for me?' he said, holding out one hand.

'Yes, sir,' said Gray. Outside the Colonel's tent, he had stood to attention in a conscious attempt to intimidate the suspicious sentry; here, before the man himself, he found himself doing so quite involuntarily. He handed over Kergabet's letter of introduction, and with it the file of documents, tied up in red tapes, which until this morning had lain concealed beneath the lining of his trunk.

Colonel Dubois set aside the dossier and, following a minute examination of Kergabet's seal, broke open the letter. Gray watched him reading it, noting that he wore his chestnut-coloured hair longer than was the fashion in England, drawn back tightly and clubbed at the nape of his neck, and that it was liberally, but unevenly, streaked with grey; that three fingers of his left hand bore unmistakable evidence of having been broken and then poorly set, without benefit of a healer (talented or otherwise); and that there depended from his waistcoat pocket, on a sturdy leather thong, a soldier's talisman in silver, stamped with the emblem of Mars on one face and of Mithras on the other.

At length Colonel Dubois looked up. 'Have you never thought, yourself, Mr Marshall,' he said, 'of accepting a commission?'

Gray blinked. 'There was some thought at one time, indeed, of my going into His Majesty's service,' he said, carefully eliding the ownership of these thoughts, 'but in the end I proved better fitted for a scholar than an officer.'

'A pity, that,' said Colonel Dubois. 'There is a great demand for men of your particular talents.'

'My talents, sir?' Gray enquired, puzzled. What in Hades was in that letter of Kergabet's? 'Er – you mean a facility with languages, I suppose?'

'Languages?' The Colonel's eyebrows inched up his forehead like chestnut-furred caterpillars. 'No, of course not. Mr Marshall, Lord Kergabet gives me to understand that you are a shape-shifter – is it not so?'

Oh. 'Yes, sir; it is certainly true. I did not – that is, I was not aware of Lord Kergabet's having mentioned the matter to you.'

'And, if I may enquire, your other form is . . . ?'

Gray blinked again. 'An owl, sir,' he said. 'A Great Grey. It is native to—'

'A night-scout, by Mithras!' Colonel Dubois exclaimed. 'Yes, a great pity that you should be wasted in a library carrel.'

Rather than pursue this line of conversation, however, he reached for the file Gray had brought him, untied the tapes, and began reading through the topmost of the papers within, whilst Gray stood silently pondering what the next move in the game might be, and studying with interest the interior of the first military command-post he had ever seen. It was, in its way, not unlike the rooms of many a Fellow, lecturer, or student of his acquaintance – spartan in appearance, filled with the tools and detritus of an all-consuming profession – but meticulously well ordered. The interior was lit by a magelight lantern suspended from the tent's central peak; that it was magelight was apparent from its steady, silent glow and the lack of heat or smoke, but its colour was strange, a warm yellow rather than the usual cool blue-white.

'The quartermaster uses coloured glass in the lanterns,' said Colonel Dubois. Gray started slightly – had his host been reading his thoughts? – but, of course, he must still have been gazing at the ceiling, puzzling over the lantern, when the Colonel looked up from his reading. 'To guard against night-blindness. Now: to business.'

He took up a brass bell from one corner of his folding desk and rang a brisk peal upon it; this summoned a slight young man, wearing a lieutenant's coat and a patch over his left eye, who gave his commanding officer a smart salute and Gray a respectful bow.

'Mr Morvand,' he said, 'Mr Marshall is seconded to Captain Tremblay's company for the present, and may wish to go out with the scouting-party at dusk. He is to be billeted with the night-scouts. Kindly escort him there, and then to the Captain, wherever he may be at present. And see that he has a bed, and so on.'

'Sir,' said Mr Morvand. He turned to Gray and enquired, 'Have you much kit with you, Mr Marshall? Er, much baggage, that is?'

'That may depend on your definition, I suppose,' said Gray doubtfully. 'My things are outside, I believe – we unloaded them before the fellow with the cart went on to see the quartermaster—'

Colonel Dubois cleared his throat in very audible impatience, and Gray exerted himself to overcome his dithering: 'There is not more than I can carry, at any rate,' he said, and, to the Colonel, 'I thank you, sir.'

The Colonel grunted a vague dismissal, already absorbed once more in Lord Kergabet's dispatches and entirely oblivious to Lieutenant Morvand's parting salute.

They collected Gray's possessions – a small brass-bound trunk and a pair of valises – from the hard-packed ground before the Colonel's tent. The trunk, containing books and other magickal impedimenta, Gray had carefully packed himself; the valises containing clothing, brushes, shaving kit, and other necessities of travel had been packed for him in great haste by Sophie with help from Daisy, as Gray had been almost on the point of climbing into his brother-in-law's carriage for the journey to Brighton without them. Morvand, having attempted to lift the trunk, was glad to cede it to Gray and carry the valises; the attempt left him red-faced not, Gray judged, from physical exertion but from a sense of his own inadequacy.

'You have lately seen battle?' said Gray, to distract him.

'Not battle, exactly,' said Morvand, ducking his head. 'A

skirmish, involving weapons and magework, which both sides afterwards regretted. Near Klison, on the Sèvre.'

Now that they were out in the open, crossing the central square of the encampment (and drawing not a few curious stares), Gray saw that in addition to whatever injury might be concealed beneath the eye-patch, his companion walked with a pronounced limp, and he slowed his own long stride to compensate.

'You were wounded there?'

'I was.' Mr Morvand shrugged, as best he could manage with a valise under either arm. 'Lord Mithras smiled upon me; some others were not so fortunate. The healers did their best with what remained; I am of less use in the field now, but the Colonel knew my father, and has been kind enough to give me useful employment as his aide-de-camp.'

Gray caught back, just in time, the words *I am sure you are very useful to him*, which (though true) must have been unbearably condescending.

'These night-scouts,' he said instead, 'what sort of men are they?'

'They are men of Breizh, as I am,' said Mr Morvand, rather stiffly – as though his name and his manner of speech had not declared as much already. He turned his head minutely to glance up at Gray, then turned his one eye back to the way ahead. The camp – like Colonel Dubois' tent – was excruciatingly tidy, the tents arrayed in precise rows, the cookfires distributed with mathematical exactitude. Over all of it drifted the smells of smoke and, faintly, of horses.

'My wife is Breizhek-born,' said Gray, slipping easily from Français into Brezhoneg. He watched his companion sidelong, in his turn, as he added, 'That country breeds brave spirits, in my experience.'

Mr Morvand's shoulders straightened minutely, and his chin lifted a little. *Did he truly think I should think the less of him, only because he is a man of Breizh?*

'Mr Ollivier and Mr Lécuyer,' said Mr Morvand, 'are perhaps rather reckless than brave. Though not so reckless as the day-scouts, for at least they make their sorties under cover of darkness. Ollivier is a barn-owl, and Lécuyer – some other sort of owl, a brown one, but I cannot say which.'

So that is what the Colonel meant by his cryptic remarks about owls.

'They are shape-shifters, then?' Gray enquired. 'Are all the scouts . . . ?'

Mr Morvand waited some moments for an end to this question before supplying his own: 'Are all of them shape-shifters, do you mean, sir? Or owls?'

Gray himself was not perfectly sure which he had meant. 'Shape-shifters,' he decided. 'How many are there here in your camp?'

'Four scouts to each company, sir,' said Mr Morvand promptly, 'and we have only four companies of the regiment here at present.'

'*Sixteen* shape-shifters!' Gray could not imagine such a thing; he had not met more than three others in the whole course of his life.

'Oh, no, sir,' said Morvand, and produced the first genuine smile Gray had seen from him. 'Sixteen scouts all told; only those in Captain Tremblay's company are all shape-shifters, however, and very few of the rest. Most of the mage-officers are in Captain Tremblay's company, you see, because—oh, I beg your pardon, sir.'

He halted abruptly, turned on his heel – valises and all – and led Gray back twenty paces or so, to a tent which was exactly like all the others, but for a pair of scarred and pitted fence-posts driven into the ground before the door.

Morvand deposited the valises at his feet and rapped sharply with his knuckles against the nearer of the two posts, calling in Latin, 'Hallo the scouts!'

There was a long pause; Gray shifted the heavy trunk in his arms, pondered putting it down, and decided that he had rather not be required to pick it up again. Then the tent-flaps parted, and a stocky young man with a head of auburn curls and a most unmilitary two-days' beard stumbled halfway out into the sunshine, rubbing one eye with the heel of his free hand. He was very evidently off-duty, clad only in linen drawers and a shirt with neck and cuffs unlaced and gaping.

'Mr Marshall, may I present Mage-Lieutenant Arzhur Lécuyer of this regiment; Mr Lécuyer, Mr Graham Marshall of, er, London.'

Mr Lécuyer sketched a gesture vaguely reminiscent of a salute; Gray, who had not the least notion of the proper protocol for a civilian greeting an officer so thoroughly out of uniform, made him rather a stiff bow in return.

'The Colonel's compliments, Mr Lécuyer,' said Morvand, saluting somewhat less smartly than before, 'and Mr Marshall is to be billeted with you and Mr Ollivier for the present, and to join you on duty tonight if he so desires. I am to see his kit stowed away and then take him to see Captain Tremblay. The quartermaster's boys will be round with a bed and so on presently.'

What, Gray wondered, was comprised in the phrase *and so on*?

Lieutenant Lécuyer blinked up at him, then turned back to Morvand, his eyes narrowing. 'Billeted with us, why?' he said, switching into Brezhoneg. 'What does he mean, "join us on duty"?'

'I believe,' said Gray in the same tongue, concealing a smile, 'the Colonel feels that we may prove birds of a feather.'

Mr Lécuyer gaped at him a moment.

'You speak Brezhoneg,' he said.

'As I have just been telling Mr Morvand,' said Gray, allowing the smile now, 'my wife was born in Breizh. I am from Kernow myself; the tongues are not dissimilar. For example—'

The tent-flap opened again, and another stubbled, bleary-eyed face appeared, twisted into an expression of irritation beneath an uneven fringe of dark hair.

'Ah, Mr Ollivier,' said Morvand, who appeared to be enjoying himself.

The introductions were repeated – this time in Brezhoneg; Mr Ollivier emerged from behind the tent-flap, revealing himself to be half a foot taller than his fellow officer and clad only in his uniform breeches, but did not cease to look annoyed.

'What is it to do with us?' he asked Morvand.

Morvand shrugged – this conversation, thought Gray, was growing less martial by the moment – and said, '*You* may have a burning wish to go aboard your commanding officer, but I have not. The Colonel wishes him billeted with you. I expect he has good reason.'

Lécuyer, who had begun to look more alert, narrowed his eyes at Gray. 'What did you mean, "birds of a feather"?' he said.

With Morvand's help Gray bestowed his gear in a corner of Ollivier and Lécuyer's tent – less slatternly in appearance than its occupants' own persons might have suggested, it reminded Gray very strongly of a certain species of undergraduates' rooms at Merlin – and shifted the two camp beds to make room for a third. Gray eyed the dimensions of these and repressed a sigh; like the cots aboard the *Asp* and many a bed in the posting-inns where he had lately been sleeping, they were at least a foot shorter than himself. Then, with a brisk *Kenavo deoc'h! – Until we meet again* – Morvand left the two lieutenants to their own devices, and conducted Gray to the presence of their Captain.

Mage-Captain Tremblay was a lean, dark man of perhaps five-and-thirty, upon whose face life and military service had scored deep lines as well as a single long, thin scar from temple to cheek. Impeccably and immaculately clad, not a hair out of alignment, he was difficult to imagine as the immediate superior of Lécuyer and Ollivier.

Seated behind his camp desk, he frowned at Morvand through the entirety of the Colonel's compliments and the forms of introduction, then frowned at Gray, and at last said dismissively, 'I cannot spare any of my men to nursemaid a civilian attaché.'

Gray counted ten, in Greek, before replying, 'I have not the least intention of disrupting your operations, Captain; my charge is to observe the movements of forces in the Duchies on behalf of Lord Kergabet in London, not to interfere in any way with yours. Colonel Dubois has suggested that I might join your night-scouts on this evening's patrol – that is, if you have no objection?'

The frown deepened. 'Has he, indeed,' said Captain Tremblay. His voice was a deep, irritable rumble. 'And why in Hades should he do that, hmm?'

Gray glanced aside at Mr Morvand, whose rigid, wooden-faced stillness suggested either suppressed terror or suppressed mirth. *The mages are nearly all in Captain Tremblay's company*, he had said, and then had begun some sort of explanation which had never been concluded. The most logical conclusion, however, was simply that His Majesty's army considered it wisest to place mage-officers under the command of one who understood their ways – not to speak of their tricks.

'I should never presume to speak for Colonel Dubois,' he said, 'but I expect, sir, that I have been seconded to your company, and to your night-scouts in particular, because my particular talents are well matched with theirs.'

Captain Tremblay, he observed detachedly during the silence that followed, had a face very like an osprey's.

Then the Captain produced a short, sharp bark of laughter, brought his palm down flat upon his thigh, and said, 'An owl-mage, by Jove! I should never have guessed it.'

'Nevertheless, sir,' said Gray mildly.

'Sit,' said Captain Tremblay, waving one hand at a battered camp-stool in the corner. Gray fetched it out, set it before the desk, and, rather doubtfully, folded himself on to it.

'Off with you, Mr Morvand,' the captain continued. 'My duty to the Colonel, that is, and I shall see Mr Marshall safely returned to his quarters.'

'Sir,' said Morvand, who had been lurking near the door. He produced another of his sharply executed salutes for his superior officer, bowed politely to Gray, and took himself off.

The moment the tent-flap fell behind him, Captain Tremblay tugged at his immaculate neck-cloth, exhaled a gusty sigh, shrugged out of his coat, and relaxed into his chair as though his strings had been cut.

'Le Floc'h!' he called, and in Brezhoneg continued, 'Have we any of that claret left?'

A dark-haired young man – very young indeed, and also in his shirt-sleeves – emerged from what Gray now saw must be an interior room of the captain's tent. 'Sir?' he said, in the same language. 'Yes, we have, Unc—er, Captain. Will I fetch it?'

Out of the newcomer's line of sight, Captain Tremblay rolled his eyes. 'Yes, Mr Le Floc'h. The bottle, and two glasses, if you please.' He turned to Gray, and, reverting to Français, said quietly, 'My sister's boy. All manner of talent, alas, and very little in the way of either wits or common sense. I have undertaken for her sake to give him a profession and keep him out of trouble.'

'Are we,' said Gray carefully, 'speaking in Français so that your nephew should not comprehend us, or because you suppose me not to understand you when you speak to him in Brezhoneg?'

Captain Tremblay's languid gaze abruptly sharpened. '*Brezhoneg a ouzit?*' he demanded – the third man today to ask Gray this question – rocking forward across his desk. 'How comes this?'

Shifting into Brezhoneg and leaning his elbows on Captain Tremblay's desk, Gray explained, also for the third time today.

'There is some . . . ill feeling, I believe,' he concluded cautiously, 'between the Breizhek officers and the rest – or perhaps one side or the other is imagining it – but certainly Mr Morvand seemed very concerned that I should not think him or his countrymen disloyal, and I do not see why that should be unless some such accusation has been lately made . . .'

Tremblay cleared his throat, looked over Gray's shoulder, and met his eyes with visible reluctance.

'Tales have been spread,' he conceded at last. 'No one will own to beginning them – or to repeating them, for the matter of that – yet still, of course, they spread. Somehow the armies of the Duchies have lately developed an ability to take our forces by surprise, and we appear to have lost our talent for doing likewise. To the military mind, this combination of circumstances inevitably suggests that the enemy has been receiving information on our movements.'

'Yes,' said Gray, frowning thoughtfully. 'Even to *my* mind,

Captain, that seems a likely explanation, and it is certainly one that has occurred to more than one mind at Court.'

Captain Tremblay gave a quiet snort of laughter. 'Indeed,' he said. 'And so, of course, the Breizhek troops are suspect—'

He broke off abruptly as Mr Le Floc'h returned with a half-empty bottle of claret and two glasses. The young man made to pour out the wine, but his uncle waved him off – kindly enough – with an order to *see to the horses and the tack*, and when he had retreated, poured it out himself.

'Your very good health, Mr Marshall,' he said, raising his glass.

'And yours, sir,' Gray replied.

After a moment, picking up the dropped thread of their earlier exchange, he said, 'I do not entirely see, however – forgive me – why the premise *The enemy appears to have some means of knowing what we are about* should lead inevitably to the conclusion *The Breizhek troops are guilty of treating with the enemy*. The threat to all three provinces is equally great, surely; why should any of them be more amenable to treason than the others?'

Captain Tremblay drained his glass in one long draught and chuckled ruefully as he refilled it. 'You are not a student of politics, I conclude,' he said; and without waiting for Gray to reply, continued, 'The Duke of Breizh was granted the right to levy his own troops only five years since; hundreds of Breizhek officers resigned their commissions in other regiments in order to take up commissions in those newly levied by the Duke, and their loyalties have been suspect ever since.'

Gray considered this, already mentally composing the beginnings of a report to Lord Kergabet. 'But you did not,' he said slowly, 'nor any of the Breizhek officers whose acquaintance I have made thus far today. That is—' He paused, wondering whether he had misunderstood – 'that is, Colonel Dubois' regiment is not a Breizhek one?'

'It is not,' said Captain Tremblay. 'But the Colonel is Breizhek-born himself – though of a Mainois father, like myself – and an honourable man, if tediously attached to military pomp and ceremony.' He took another large swallow of wine. 'Those who departed their Normand or Mainois or English regiments are suspected of serving Breizh above Britain,' he said, 'whilst those of us who remain are suspected of harbouring divided loyalties, and of informing against our fellows – the ordinary sort of regimental rivalries, boiled up with political in-fighting into a most unpleasant ragout. It is the most natural thing in the world, therefore, that when any disloyalty is suspected, we should be at the head of the queue.'

Gray sighed.

Today, for the first time since embarking on this absurd journey, circumstances – Morvand's wary sideways look, and finding himself one flying shape-shifter among many, and the half-clothed Ollivier and Lécuyer in their dishevelled sleeping quarters, and now *this*, which he ought to have anticipated – made him grateful that Sophie was hundreds of miles away.

'Now!' Tremblay exclaimed after a moment, cheerful once more, 'You wish to fly out with the night-scouts, do you? What is it you are hoping to observe?'

Ollivier and Lécuyer stripped to their skins quickly and without ceremony – like undergraduates at the public baths – baring with no trace of self-consciousness whipcord-muscled limbs and torsos marked with a bewildering variety of small scars. Their talk and laughter never flagged, and Gray, encouraged, followed their example – only to falter in the sudden, shocked silence that engulfed the magelight-lit campaign-tent when, for a moment, he turned his back to his companions to fold away the shirt he had just pulled off over his head.

'What made those marks, my lord?' Ollivier enquired, after a long moment. 'Er . . . if I may ask?'

'A man with a horsewhip,' said Gray shortly, 'in a dungeon in Alba.' *Not that it is any affair of yours.* 'Shall we get on with this business?'

He turned back to face them, concealing for the moment the almost mathematically parallel rows of scar tissue that striped his back and shoulders, which repeated applications of healing magick had blurred and softened but could not erase. They were gaping at him, just as he had feared they might; yet it was not pity or disgust he saw in their faces, but . . . something else altogether.

'You are soldiers, both of you,' he said, not troubling to hide his impatience. 'You must have seen such marks before – or worse things.'

Lécuyer swallowed hard and gave a sharp nod; his right arm twitched, as though he were restraining himself from offering a salute.

'Colonel Dubois will send a runner with the signal,' he said, 'very soon now.'

Gray nodded. 'I should like, if it does not inconvenience you,' he said, 'to observe the process – I am a scholar, you know, and I have not many opportunities to—'

'Oh, look all you like, my lord,' said Ollivier, cheerfully enough. He glanced at Lécuyer, who shrugged.

They crouched on the dusty floor of the tent, balancing on the balls of their feet and the tips of their fingers. Ollivier closed his eyes and spoke his shifting-spell almost inaudibly, his lips pressed close together and moving as little as possible; Lécuyer drew his arms forward to encircle his shins, then bowed his forehead to his bent-up knees, hiding his face entirely. Whereas Gray's own transformation tended to happen slowly – those desperate, panicked shifts in the dead of an Oxford night and in the woods on the Ross of Mull excepted – His Majesty's scouts took no more time to put on their talons, wings, and feathers than to strip off their clothes; before Gray had even begun to guess at their choice of spells, there stood before him, blinking their round dark eyes in the lamplight and stepping delicately away from foot to foot, a pale-faced barn owl and a large brown-and-tawny eagle owl.

'Well,' said Gray.

He stepped out of his own drawers – much easier to do it now than later – and crouched down in his turn, feeling each small lump and pebble against the soles of his feet, then tilted forward until most of his weight rested on his toes.

This working no longer required much conscious thought; once summoned, his magick flowed easily into the channels of his owl-shape, and muscles and sinews followed in its wake. His bones were lighter already, primaries springing through the skin of his arms, his bare toes splaying into talons.

Owl-shaped, Gray remained taller than his companions – though less so than before – which Lécuyer, the eagle owl, clearly found irksome. Gray spread his wings cautiously, conscious of the number of things he might possibly dislodge or damage; Lécuyer spread his own, slightly longer, in answer. Ollivier, the barn owl, bobbed his head and hooted in avian laughter.

Perhaps fortunately, the dark head and broad shoulders of the Colonel's runner leant in through the tent-flap before the conversation could proceed any further. 'Ready to be off, are we, gentlemen? The sun is well down.'

He threw open the tent-flap, revealing himself to be wearing a lance-corporal's uniform and a falconer's heavy leather gauntlets, and crouched down to lift first Lécuyer, then Ollivier, onto his wrists. Then, for a long moment, he frowned at Gray, who tilted his head and stared back. At last an idea seemed to occur to him; he shifted the eagle owl from his left wrist to his right – the barn owl ruffled his feathers indignantly, but finally shuffled a little way up his arm to make room – then extended his left arm towards Gray.

'I am Lance-Corporal Kerambrun, my lord,' he said. 'If you will permit me . . . ?'

It was not a graceful process, and Gray's temper was not improved by the knowledge that Ollivier and Lécuyer, as well as having seen the evidence of his experiences in the bowels of Castle MacAlpine, were watching him hop and flap about to keep his balance. Gray's weight was evidently less than Kerambrun had expected, which occasioned some shifting of the passengers. At length, however, Lance-Corporal Kerambrun straightened up and emerged from the scouts' tent, with an owl on either wrist and a third clinging to his shoulder, and strode eastward through the twilit camp.

CHAPTER XIX

In Which the Princess Royal
Mounts an Expedition

'And what on earth has he told his mother?' said Lucia, incredulous, when Sophie had finished her tale. She had risen from the floor and resumed her seat on the far side of the small table which held the abandoned chessboard, and was leaning forward, her elbows resting on her knees, in rapt attention.

Sophie peered at her over the rim of her teacup, clasped tightly in both hands; the tea was almost too sweet to drink, but the heat seeping through the porcelain warmed her chilled fingers. 'That, I expect,' she said, 'he has left to Lord Kergabet.'

'I certainly should do, in his place,' said Roland unexpectedly, and with some feeling.

Sophie and Lucia looked up at him in surprise.

'Well,' he said, his cheeks going rather pink. 'Mothers can be rather . . . excitable—' Then, recollecting perhaps that both of his companions had lost their mothers before the age of ten, he muttered, 'Never mind,' and turned away to make a noisy pretence of tidying the tea-things on the sideboard.

'In any case,' said Sophie, 'it is entirely possible that Gray's mama will be pleased as much as alarmed; his father planned a military career for him, you see, and went so far as to purchase him a mage-lieutenant's commission, when he was nineteen. It was because Gray refused to leave Merlin College and take it up that Edmond Marshall disinherited him.'

Roland had not ceased to rattle the teacups, but Sophie fancied she could see his attentive listening in the set of his shoulders.

'I mean no disparagement of your husband, Sophie,' said Lucia, whose russet-gold eyebrows had flown up at the words *mage-lieutenant's commission*, 'but truly it is difficult to imagine a worse notion.'

Sophie laughed – a shaky, ragged-edged thing, but laughter nevertheless. 'Quite so,' she said; 'still, I must suppose that Kergabet knows what he is about. This must go no further,' she admonished. 'I ought not even to have told the two of you, but it beggars belief that either of you should—' She swallowed, and against her better judgement took a large swallow of too-sweet tea.

'Of course we shall neither of us say anything to anyone, Sophie,' said Lucia. Her tone suggested that she was suppressing further comment on the general theme of *What do you take me for?*

'Certainly not,' said Roland indignantly; after another moment, in a more diffident tone, he added, 'May we help you plan your expedition to Oxford, then?'

If Sophie's heart was no longer entirely in her Oxford scheme – if, in fact, a considerable proportion of it was in Normandie with Gray – it seemed her friends were prepared to embrace it wholeheartedly. Watching as they set aside their misgivings, and the many other demands upon their time, to assist her in planning and undertaking the initial exploratory visit to Oxford, Sophie strongly suspected that the interest and assistance of Kergabet,

Jenny, and Mr Fowler, at any rate, was owing not to any personal enthusiasm for the scheme but to a wish that Joanna should be got out of the way of the search for her father, and that Sophie should be diverted from pining over Gray's absence.

In light of the last such occasion, she reflected, it was not an idle worry.

Lucia's reasons for participating in the scheme she judged to be two parts genuine enthusiasm and one part longing to escape the Royal Palace; Roland's, almost entirely a wish to please Lucia. As for Joanna and Miss Pryce . . .

But there again, when have I ever been able to discover what either of them is thinking?

Whatever might be the motivations of the participants, their eager energy made quick work of the planning, and she was duly grateful.

That Mr Goff and Mr Tredinnick, her faithful shadows since first she and Gray set up housekeeping in Oxford years ago, should be of the party, was taken as read; His Majesty, however, had insisted upon the addition of a further half-dozen guardsmen under their joint command – despite Sophie's protests that this could only serve to make them conspicuous – and Lucia MacNeill's guard captain, not to be outdone, had volunteered herself and her troop as escort.

Lucia had rolled her eyes at this – Ceana MacGregor, Sophie had learnt early on, had known Lucia from birth and had been captain of her personal guard for the past decade, and the two were accustomed to take quite astonishing liberties with one another. Ceana MacGregor, however, had folded her arms and said, 'Either we all of us go to Oxford, Lucia MacNeill, or none of us goes, least of all yourself,' which pronouncement caused Lucia to throw up her hands in exasperation and give in.

The party which eventually departed Grosvenor Square for Oxford, therefore, comprised one prince, four ladies, and sufficient men- and women-at-arms to have cowed any but the most enterprising assailant.

Having taken possession of the entire first floor of the Dragon and Lion for the accommodation of her retinue, being the only respectable hostelry in Oxford presently able to offer hospitality to such a large party, Sophie left the other ladies to their unpacking and, in the sole company of Mr Tredinnick, set off on foot up the High-street towards the Broad, and Merlin College.

The Porter manning Merlin's gate was unfamiliar to her and showed no sign of knowing who she was. Quite prepared for this eventuality, Sophie nodded to Mr Tredinnick, who stepped forward and said affably, 'We are come to see Doctor Evans-Hughes; is he in college at present?'

The Porter narrowed his pale-blue eyes at them but conceded grudgingly that Doctor Evans-Hughes was indeed in his rooms. 'Is 'e expecting you?' he enquired.

'No,' said Tredinnick; 'that is, not today in particular. Mrs Marshall' – nodding at Sophie – 'has been in correspondence with him, however, and forewarned him of our coming.'

This was true, assuming that Sophie's latest letter, posted two days since, had been opened and read. In any case, if Gareth had not been here, Master Alcuin certainly should be, and could be counted upon to welcome them in.

The Porter looked askance at this, but, having informed Mr Tredinnick that *female visitors* were not permitted to wander the College grounds unescorted, sent one of his minions to enquire whether Doctor Evans-Hughes were willing to come down to the

Porter's Lodge to speak with them. Sophie and her companion loitered comfortably upon the pavement, observing the sparse late-summer foot traffic along the Broad and looking up at the walls of Merlin. Not so long ago, she had been – and Mr Tredinnick had pretended to be – a student there, and it surprised her to find that she did not much regret giving it up.

Gareth Evans-Hughes arrived on the heels of the Porter's boy – as rumpled as ever and rather rounder, pink-faced and out of breath – and upon beholding Sophie, shocked all present by nearly bowling her over in the enthusiasm of his greeting.

'Sophie Marshall, as I live and breathe!' he exclaimed, standing back with his hands on her shoulders. He continued, rather less accurately, 'How well you look! I did not look for you until tomorrow at the earliest. But let us not stand talking in the street; come in, come in!'

Ignoring the Porter's scandalised glare, he ushered them through the gate, signed the Porter's book on their behalf, and led them across the Quad to his staircase.

It being the Long Vac, Merlin was very sparsely populated, and they passed no more than half a dozen persons, Senior Fellows mostly, along their way. Sophie nonetheless took the precaution of making herself inconspicuous; there was no benefit to be gained from attracting attention to herself, or to Gareth either.

Having ushered them into his sitting-room – less altered even than himself, with the same creaking armchairs, the same shelves of odd and miscellaneous artefacts, the same haphazard stacks of books as when Sophie had last seen it – Evans-Hughes turned to Sophie and said, 'Wards, I think?'

'Indeed,' she said, and at once reached for her magick to work the strongest warding-spell she knew.

'Now,' said Gareth briskly, when she had finished, reaching behind a bronze knotwork buckle and a badger's skull to retrieve his welcome-cup, 'who is your friend, Sophie, and where in Hades has your husband gone off to?'

Sophie introduced Mr Tredinnick and Gareth to one another, put off the latter's second query with the promise of a fuller explanation *later*, and gratefully accepted his welcome, though the wine he poured into the small, battered copper goblet was so sweet that she had to restrain a grimace. Gareth himself was not so nice – upon tasting it, he had screwed up his face, swallowed hard, and said, 'The wine steward will have his little joke' – but what a host might permit himself to say about his own hospitality, a guest ought not.

They all sat down, Sophie and Mr Tredinnick arrayed before Gareth as though they had been his students come to read him their essays; Gareth leant forward with elbows on knees, clasping his hands before him, and said, 'I have found something in the Merlin Library, Sophie, that I think you shall like; but before I fetch it, will you – *can* you – tell me what you are about? And – if the, er, circumstances permit – why Marshall is not come with you? That is,' he added, hastily and quite needlessly, 'there is no reason on earth why you should not both do just as you please, of course! It is only that I am accustomed to your being inseparable.'

Sophie sighed. She was as sure of Gareth Evans-Hughes as she could be of anyone – else she should not have involved him in her scheme to begin with – but too many people were already in the secret of Gray's whereabouts.

'Gray is on an errand for his brother-in-law,' she said instead, 'which is as much as anyone may be told about it; and I am here to break into Lady Morgan College' – she could not help smiling at her two companions' identical expressions of shock at this turn of phrase – 'and poke about in its library – hence my request.' She leant forward in turn. 'You did find something, you said? May I see it?'

Gareth's face, which had creased unhappily at her refusal to elaborate on Gray's circumstances or whereabouts, broke into a smile, and he sprang up from his seat to rummage about in a desk drawer.

'Here we are,' he said at last, turning back to her, and handed over a long roll of parchment, yellow with age and beginning to crumble at the edges, tied up near each end with incongruously bright-new blue tapes. He looked about him, frowning a little. 'Let me just . . .'

'Er, perhaps this table, sir?' said Mr Tredinnick.

'Yes! Yes, that will do very nicely.'

Gareth hurried the scattered notes and documents into an untidy stack and removed it to the top of his desk; Sophie, having untied the tapes, slowly and carefully unrolled the parchment onto the table-top thus exposed, anchoring each side with the tips of her gloved fingers. Although rerolled smoothly, it showed irregular creases, as though having been rolled once, it had then been sat upon for some time.

Above and below her fingertips, the corners curled persistently inwards, but Sophie scarcely remarked it; she was staring, transfixed, at the centre of the parchment, on which was drawn, in a firm meticulous hand, a detailed plan labelled *Lady Morgan College, Oxon.*

'Gareth!' she said, looking up. 'Wherever did you find this?'

'Rolled up and forgotten at the back of a map-drawer,' he said, 'where it had been squashed flat for the gods know how long; I am

surprised that it did not fall into bits the moment I touched it.'
He was moving about the room, gathering . . . what? 'None of the
librarians or archivists knew it was there, or even that it existed – or
at any rate none of them would admit to knowing – nor what it was;
how in Hades did *you* know that I should find it?'

'It was a bow drawn at a venture entirely, I admit,' said Sophie
frankly. 'That is, I know that Lady Morgan College exists – or
did exist – and I supposed that plans must have been drawn of it;
and several of the books I have found on the subject mention the
existence of such a plan.'

Gareth came back to stand beside her at the table, and now she
saw what he had been about. Carefully he lined the edges of the
spread-out plan with a series of small objects – the skull of some
small creature, about the size of Sophie's palm; a miniature brass
lamp; an ancient-looking stoppered bottle of smoky-blue glass;
a paper-knife with a handle in the shape of a porpoise; and so
onward – to prevent its curling up again.

'And having found a view of the place forgotten and uncatalogued
in a pigeonhole in the Palace Archives,' she continued, while this
proceeding was going forward, 'it seemed to me that Merlin's
Archives, being older, might also possess uncatalogued documents
of which no one knew anything. Of course,' she added, 'we should
have staged our invasion in any event, but now we shall be better
able to plan our campaign.'

She bent her head again, tapped one index finger on the blank
space labelled *Great Quadrangle* (like Merlin's, a quadrangle in
name but not in shape), traced the footpaths that crossed and
intersected it. *Library*, she read, arching across the outline of an
oblong structure. *Refectory. Undergraduate Rooms. Portress's Lodge.*
And – yes, there! In the upper left-hand corner, just where memory

291

suggested it ought to be – a small, perfect circle with a square portico, adorned with a tiny drawing of an owl and, inscribed across a decorative scroll, the words *Shrine of Minerva Sophia.*

'The dome,' she said, more than half to herself. 'The green dome.'

'Ma'am?' said Mr Tredinnick, politely baffled.

Sophie blinked away the memory-vision of the compact copper-green dome, dimmed by mist and rain, rising above weed-grown walls and empty windows. 'This,' she said, pointing, 'is a shrine to Minerva as Sophia, personification of wisdom. My namesake, or one of them – the one my mother chose for me.' She paused, swallowed hard, and continued: 'More importantly for present purposes, it is visible from the near bank of the Cherwell, and appears on the plan exactly where I expected to see it, which means, I hope, that the plan can be trusted to reflect the thing itself. Now, I wonder, has the draughtsman recorded the date . . . ?'

Three dark heads bent over the plan, searching – Gareth with a magnifying glass unearthed from the chaos of his desk; it was Mr Tredinnick, however, who at length exclaimed, 'There!' extending a sturdy forefinger towards a stylised representation of a tree, seen from above, in the lower right-hand corner.

'By Jove! You have sharp eyes, Tredinnick,' said Gareth, in a tone of admiration quite untainted by envy or resentment. He held the glass over the little tree-top, and the three of them leant still closer – their heads nearly touching – to peer through it at the minuscule letters twined into the stylised branches.

'*Edwina Antonia Calixta fecit,*' Sophie read aloud; the feminine name surprised her but, upon consideration, ought not to have done. '*Anno xii Henricus VIII.*' She paused, eyes closed, to wrestle with the mental arithmetic. The Princess Julia had been born in the tenth year of her father's long reign, and Prince Edward in the twenty-eighth . . . King Edward had succeeded to the throne at the age of nine, and the College – so far as she had been able to determine – had been closed in the second or possibly the third decade of his reign . . .

'This was made within fifty years of the College's closing,' she said at last. 'More or less. Of course a great deal may change in fifty years, but – this is a marvellous find, Gareth, truly.'

She grinned at him, and his round plain face lit up with his answering smile.

The smile quickly faltered, however, as his gaze returned to the plan of Lady Morgan College. 'Sophie,' he said, slow and careful, 'are the rumours true? That you mean to . . . to sponsor a college for women, as Lady Morgan did?'

Sophie studied his expression – troubled; hopeful? – for some time before replying, 'If I can manage it, yes.'

'There is a good deal of . . . of feeling against it,' said Gareth. 'At Merlin particularly, but in the other Colleges also.'

'The august Fellows have made their views very clear to me, never fear,' said Sophie dryly. Where was this leading?

'Sophie, why did you not tell me?' The question did not surprise her particularly, but the *tone*—

'Why do you suppose? My father is not indulging me in this scheme from any real interest in its success, but only because—well, never mind exactly why, but to keep me *out* of something else entirely; there is every chance that this will all end in some costly and humiliating mess. Can you suppose that I wish to bring my friends into such a mess with me, who must go on living and working at Merlin when I have run back to Din Edin with my tail between my legs?'

Mr Tredinnick, whose presence Sophie (from long habit) had

momentarily forgotten, laughed aloud. Sophie turned to glare at him; subsiding to a chuckle, he said, 'Begging your pardon, ma'am, but if you were at all disposed to run *away* from trouble, I should soon find myself out of work.'

Gareth, infuriatingly, joined in Tredinnick's laughter, and Sophie glared harder at both of them, to little avail. Exasperated, she turned away and stared resolutely out of the window.

'If you have quite finished,' she said coolly, after a moment. They caught her tone and subsided, and Sophie turned away from the window again to address her friend. 'I may take it, I collect, that – in principle, at any rate – you are rather in favour of my scheme than otherwise?'

'Certainly I am,' said Gareth. His soft tenor voice held a trace of indignation, and the Cymric tilt that marked his speech in Latin, ordinarily almost too subtle to hear, had become very pronounced. '. . . but, there, I had forgotten that you are not acquainted with any of my sisters.' The bright grin resurfaced momentarily, though now with a wry edge. 'If you had been – and my sister Angharad particularly – you could not doubt it for even a moment.'

It was always a clever sister, Sophie reflected – half jubilant, half rueful – to make a man think twice about this matter; never, it seemed, any sense that the generality of women might benefit from, or might have any right to enjoy, the privileges which their brothers serenely accepted as their right. *Gift horses*, she reminded herself sternly, not for the first time.

'I am very glad to hear it,' she said, taking care that none of this inward argumentation should show on her face or in her voice. 'And when – if – when matters have progressed a little – if it seems likely that—'

She paused, looking at her hands. The investigation into

Merlin's Archives, though it had yielded such unexpectedly useful results, had been only half the reason for this visit – the more or less official, the openly acknowledged half. They were now come to the other, of which Mr Tredinnick was very likely to disapprove – and not without reason. *Can I afford to trust Gareth with this secret? On the other hand, how should I account for myself before the gods, if I did not use all the resources at my disposal?*

'I have another favour to ask of you,' she said at last, making up her mind.

Mr Tredinnick straightened his shoulders and frowned. 'Mrs Marshall—'

It was not often that Sophie made use of her rank to cow her father's guardsmen; she did so now, however, without compunction, for her sisters' sake. 'Mr Tredinnick,' she said, her tone as much the Princess Royal as she could make it, 'you may wait in the corridor outside, or you may stay here and refrain from interfering, and from revealing to anyone else whatever you may hear. The choice is yours; I suggest you make it at once.'

'Ma'am.' Mr Tredinnick set his teeth. 'I am yours to command, of course.'

She waited long enough for him to decamp, should that be his intention; when instead he settled himself in a corner, perched on a tall stool tucked between two bookcases, she turned back to Gareth and extracted from her reticule the only other possession of Amelia's which she had been able to discover: one of the pair of silver-and-garnet ear-drops given to her by the Professor for her sixteenth birthday, which Katell had found trodden into the thick carpet beneath the dressing-table in the Kingfisher room. The others she had had to leave behind in Jenny's care, if she were not to be required to confess to Jenny – and, worse, to Lady Maëlle and Joanna – that she intended revealing their private trouble to a rank outsider.

'This belonged – *belongs* – to my sister Amelia,' she said, unfolding the handkerchief in which she had wrapped it and holding it out on her flattened palm. 'She has . . . That is, we have reason to believe that she has run away with, with Henry Taylor.' Speaking over Gareth's shocked intake of breath, she hurried on: 'As you knew Mr Taylor in his student days, you will understand why we are anxious to locate her. Gray's sister, as you may know, is a scry-mage of some talent, and she has done her best with some other objects of my sister's, but she has not the training you have, Gareth, as she herself is the first to admit, and so . . .'

Gareth had listened to all of this with a troubled frown, and in silence. If she desired his help, she must ask for it outright.

'And so,' she said, measured and deliberate, 'I should be very much in your debt, Gareth, if you were to consent to scry this ear-ring, though I have not its owner's permission to do so, and tell me what you see of my sister, which may shed any light on her present circumstances or whereabouts.'

After another long, considering silence, Evans-Hughes sighed, leant forward, and reached for the ear-drop in Sophie's hand. 'Your sister would not be the first young woman to follow her own inclinations in marriage, in opposition to her family's,' he said pointedly, 'nor the first to take this means of doing so, and sometimes with good reason. If you had not said *with Henry Taylor*, Sophie, I should refuse to have anything to do with the business, and I should advise you—'

'If Henry Taylor were not in the case,' Sophie retorted, 'or someone very like him, I should be wishing my sister joy of her choice, not joining in the hunt for her. What sort of hypocrite do you think me, Gareth Evans-Hughes? But it *is* Henry Taylor, and therefore—'

'And therefore, I shall do as you ask,' said Gareth. 'Now, be quiet a moment, if you please.'

Sophie clasped her hands in her lap, pressed her lips together, and did her best to keep still.

At length Gareth surfaced from what Sophie could only call a trance and laid Amelia's ear-drop carefully upon the table beside the weighted-down parchment.

'Marshall has gone off to Normandie to look for your sister, I suppose?' he said.

Sophie, startled, recalled that just before introducing them to one another, Gray had ducked his head to murmur in her ear, *Evans-Hughes is a good, solid man, and trustworthy; but you must always bear in mind that he is at least twice as clever as he looks.* And it was not, perhaps, very difficult to draw the necessary connexions in this case. 'Yes,' she conceded.

At least he has not guessed what else Gray is about.

'Not a bad guess,' said Gareth, rather cryptically, 'but not far enough.'

'Gareth—'

'I apologise.' He held up a hand, then, absently, began turning the delicate silver filigree round and round between the fingers of the other hand, studying it as though, having just probed into this object's accreted secrets, he now could not imagine what its original purpose might have been. 'Your sister-in-law has told you, I expect, that . . . May I call her Amelia?'

Sophie shrugged; what could it matter?

'That Amelia, at the time when she was making ready to leave London, believed herself to be bound for Normandie, by way of Portsmouth and then Honfleur?'

'Yes,' said Sophie, 'more or less. Is that—'

'That is certainly what she *believed*, yes. But, as you say, Henry Taylor.' Gareth sighed gustily, and his shoulders sank back against the threadbare damask of his chair. 'Or perhaps—well. Not so far from Honfleur,' he said, recapturing the thread of his narrative after this cryptic digression, 'as the crow flies more or less north – and very near indeed to Dover, as the ship sails – is the port of Calais, in the Comté d'Artois, which presently owes allegiance to the Duc de Bourgogne.'

'And . . . Amelia is going to Calais? Or has gone there?'

'Oh! Certainly. From London to Dover, from Dover to Calais. And from there . . . from there,' Gareth repeated, 'things are murkier; but Bourgogne is known to be friendly with Orléans, though of course it does not follow that Artois should necessarily feel likewise—'

'Gareth,' Sophie broke in, 'my sister?'

He had the grace to look a little sheepish; it made his face suddenly altogether familiar, and Sophie bit her lip to tamp down a wholly unexpected pang of regret for those things at Merlin College which she had loved, and those persons who had welcomed her unreservedly, during her brief and difficult sojourn here – Gareth Evans-Hughes included.

Quickly, before she could lose her nerve once more, she said, 'Amelia left London intending to marry Mr Taylor; did she—have they—'

She scarcely knew which of the two possibilities was the more dreadful. On the one hand, an elopement without some reasonably official form of marriage, should it become known, must materially damage any gentlewoman's reputation and prospects; but, on the other, for Amelia to be the wife of Henry Taylor . . . !

This time Gareth took pity on her stammering. 'In fact, so far as I have been able to see,' he said gently, 'not only has there been no marriage, but from Dover your sister appears to have been . . . to be travelling alone.'

'Travelling alone!' Sophie exclaimed, incredulous. '*Amelia?*'

What to think of this development? Sophie could not imagine. On the one hand, the world was full of perils for a woman – particularly a young and beautiful woman – travelling alone; on the other hand . . .

'Go on,' she said.

'Well,' said Gareth. 'The aetheric echoes attaching to this . . . item' – he gave it another vaguely baffled look – 'have by now been very much attenuated, you understand; but your sister, so far as I can tell, has been thinking very little about Henry Taylor – I fancy he disappointed her, not by refusing to marry her, but by attempting to alter their destination; but that may be only my imagination, you understand – and a great deal about their original plan, in which she was to be reunited with her beloved papa, and of how she might accomplish it for herself, without Taylor's assistance. Also, of the much happier life she shall have, when her papa is a great man again, and when—'

He shut his mouth abruptly, with a guilty look.

Sophie sighed. 'Tell me.'

After some hesitation, he said, '. . . when you are not in it.'

With few exceptions, it was only what Katell had told them, or they had known, already; why should it sound so very much worse now? Sophie sat very still, concentrating hard; a friend Gareth might be, but still she had no intention of going all to pieces in front of him.

'Sophie?' he said hesitantly, after what might have been a moment or half an hour.

With some effort, she forced herself to meet his gaze. 'Where?' she said. 'Do you know, can you tell, Gareth, where this reunion is to take place?'

'Alas, I cannot,' he said. 'And what I *can* tell you, I regret to say, makes no sense at all.' He frowned, shrugged his broad shoulders, dropped Amelia's ear-ring back into the folds of Sophie's handkerchief, and handed it across to her. 'According to your sister, who had the tale from Taylor,' he said at last, 'Appius Callender is presently employed as an advisor to the Emperor of Gaul.'

CHAPTER XX

In Which Gray Reconsiders
Long-Held Prejudices

The passage through the encampment of Lance-Corporal Kerambrun and his passengers drew a considerable number of stares. This surprised Gray – Lécuyer and Ollivier in their owl-shapes must after all be a familiar sight here – till he recollected that only the night-scouts themselves, Colonel Dubois, Mage-Captain Tremblay, and, it now appeared, Kerambrun knew of this particular manifestation of his talent. The rest must all be wondering at two owls' having become three.

Over the course of a long and frankly indolent afternoon largely given over to sleep and games of chance – for Captain Tremblay's night-scouts, it appeared, enjoyed a somewhat equivocal status in their off hours, which were many, as a consequence of performing a difficult and wearing duty in which none of their fellows could replace them – Ollivier and Lécuyer had given him some notion of their *modus operandi*. Though in fact they flew patterns, separately and together, designed to give them sight of as much of the land below them as possible – just as a patrol on foot or on horseback might spread out and quarter their ground, in order not to miss any square foot of it in their passing – their survival might at any time depend on their not appearing to do so. All the scouts, it appeared, had of necessity become scholars of the behaviour, hunting techniques, and flight patterns of birds of prey, so that they might pass for natural, ordinary birds and attract no untoward attention.

'Tanguy had an arrow through his left wing, once,' Ollivier had said, and all of them shuddered. 'Though that was in the heat of battle. He has never been sure whether it was excellent aim or appalling luck.'

Tanguy, Gray found upon enquiring, was one of the company's day-scouts, a *milan royal* in his shape-shifted form, and through a fortunate landing and the immediate assistance of a talented healer, he had survived his ordeal with no lasting ill effects but a slight stiffness of his left arm in damp weather.

'He must have kept his head remarkably well,' said Gray, 'to have stayed aloft long enough to make any sort of landing.'

He was thinking, as from time to time he could not prevent himself from doing, of the occasion when he had himself attempted to go aloft on a badly injured wing; remarking that his companions were looking at him curiously, he discovered that he had clasped his right hand protectively over his left shoulder. Hastily he pretended to be scratching an itch.

'Tanguy is made of quicksilver and cast iron,' said Ollivier, allowing him the pretence. 'Whatever does not rebound from his fortunate hide seems to pass straight through him without leaving a mark. Well,' he amended, 'not much, at any rate.'

He and Lécuyer had grinned, then, and Gray had made himself do likewise, grateful to them for letting the awkward moment pass.

The night-scouts, it must be said, had surprised him – and Mage-Captain Tremblay, too; none of them at all suited his notion of an army officer. Even Colonel Dubois, as seen through the lens of his gruff kindness to young Mr Morvand, was altogether more . . . *human* than Gray had expected. For a moment, even, he caught himself pondering whether his father might not in fact have had his best interests in mind, in purchasing for him a mage-lieutenant's commission and urging (no: *ordering*) him to take it up. Here he was, after all, making genuine use at last of what was otherwise an obscure and largely impractical, if impressive, skill which had cost him a great deal of time and painful effort to attain, in the company of other men who had undertaken the same single-minded – some might say mule-headed – journey; they were, some of their manners aside, not brutish louts but brave and clever men who treated him as a respected comrade.

If they accorded him that respect for all the wrong reasons, well . . .

The plan they had ultimately made, such as it was, would allow Gray to conduct his own reconnaissance, closer to the ground, without much interference from the others, and would assure him of hearing their full reports whilst not committing himself to reveal every detail of his own observations (or his own purposes) in return.

And what, indeed, do you hope to observe that they shall not? he asked himself now, derisively. Both Lécuyer and Olliver had been flying these twilight sorties for years; both had been stationed at Ivry for some months and knew the territory as he could not possibly do. And of course it was not to be supposed that he should happen upon Professor Callender and his cronies, or upon Henry Taylor and Amelia, in the fields and woods round Ivry at night.

To Ivry, Sieur Germain de Kergabet had said, *and from Ivry, to where the trail may lead you.*

In Captain Tremblay's tent, the three owls perched on the scarred and battered poles of a wooden contraption clearly built for this purpose, peering at the map unrolled upon the Captain's desk.

'Here, here and here, you see,' said Colonel Dubois, pointing, 'are the positions of the encampments reported by the scouts of Captain Howells' company this morning, when they returned at the third hour before noon. Tanguy and Fournier reported seeing no movement during the afternoon, apart from the ordinary business – foraging and scouting parties and the like,' he added, aside, in Gray's direction.

Unthinkingly – as though he had been conversing with Sophie – Gray bobbed his head in acknowledgement of this explanation.

Questions were bubbling up in his mind like a pot a-boiling: *What concealing-spells might the armies of the Duchies be employing? Have they airborne scouting parties of their own? How numerous are these nearby encampments, and whose banners do they fly?* – and, less worthily, *If one of us should be injured, or worse, how shall anyone here know of it?* For almost the first time in his life, he would gladly have traded his wings for his human voice in order to ask them. What fool had thought he and the night-scouts ought to be briefed after shifting and not before?

'Steady on, Mr Marshall,' Captain Tremblay murmured, and Gray discovered to his chagrin that he was bobbing anxiously up and down, shifting from foot to foot, in a most undignified manner. He ruffled his feathers apologetically and settled his wings, though inwardly feeling no calmer.

The briefing, such as it was, concluded with an offering to Mithras, the soldiers' especial deity, and to Lady Minerva, whose sacred bird was the owl; and at last by Captain Tremblay's unlocking a battered dispatch-case and extracting from it an equally battered ledger and three small leather bands hung with miniature soldiers' talismans.

'Sixteen,' he said, reading aloud from the inner surface of the first band; Kerambrun made a note in the ledger. 'One-and-twenty. Three.'

Gray cocked his head, eyeing the odd objects in Tremblay's hand and pondering whether they might be charms of concealment such as he had worn once or twice before; Lécuyer and Ollivier, however, put out their left feet and waited patiently whilst the bands were fastened on by Kerambrun. Gray, when his turn came, followed their example.

'Should anything befall you,' said Kerambrun quietly, as his quick fingers worked the tiny buckle about Gray's leg, 'which the gods forbid, any mage-officer in the company, whether or not he has ever laid eyes on you in either form, could work a finding-spell to seek this talisman, and so find you.'

Well, that is one question answered, at any rate. Again Gray bobbed his head in acknowledgement, and hoped that his relief might not be outwardly visible.

The three owls were then conveyed to the camp's forestward edge and up a ladder to the makeshift watchtower, from which – without further unnecessary ceremony – they were tossed out one by one.

Gray knew perfectly well that his attention ought all to be on the ground below him, the forest all around; but after these earthbound months in London he could not help, for the first few exhilarating moments, simply glorying in being aloft. He coasted to a convenient branch – surveyed the forest floor below, seamed by meandering tree-roots and inches deep in leaf-mould – spotted a *belette* creeping from tree-trunk to tree-trunk, and repressed his owl-body's urge to dive after whatever it might be hunting – dropped from his branch again, spreading his wings, and launched himself once more into the night air.

His position was equivocal, his companions temporary, his present task dangerous and of dubious utility; yet a part of him – and no small part, at that – rejoiced, happy as, in all his life, only flying and Sophie's company had ever made him happy.

That night's patrolling – and all the next several nights' – yielded no startling or even particularly interesting intelligence with respect to the troops massing along Britain's frontiers. Their numbers seemed to be increasing, but slowly; they were, to all appearances, as solidly entrenched as their counterparts of His Majesty's army; the juxtapositions of hitherto warring dukes', counts', and viscounts' banners – though certainly baffling – were only what Kergabet had led Gray to expect.

When not aloft, Gray wandered about the camp, taking note of what the officers and men and camp-followers spoke of; striking up an apparently idle conversation whenever he could; and becoming friendly with the sentries, so as better to observe the camps' many comings and goings. Though apparently exploring idly and at random, he had actually been proceeding in accordance with a plan of the camp, consulted almost daily with Colonel Dubois, on which he was steadily marking off each tent, picket, and cookfire – and there were now very few persons in the camp with whom he had not had some contact; yet thus far all his overhearings, all his faux-casual questioning, had revealed nothing more unsavoury than petty thefts and a tendency to lewd and sometimes cruel jesting. Most had heard the name Imperator Gallia; many had specific, often contradictory details to relate; but all dismissed it as the species of rumour always liable to be spread by troops wishing to unsettle and intimidate their opponents.

Unbeknownst to Kergabet – or, at any rate, without telling him of it – Gray had succeeded in absconding with one of Lord de Vaucourt's spelled maps, and throughout his sojourn at Ivry he had been using it to work Cameron's mapped finding, nearly every day – but thus far no trace of Amelia, Appius Callender, or any of the other conspirators had he found.

The situation had, in fact, all the earmarks of a stalemate, and after nearly a se'nnight Gray was on the point of giving it up – was laying plans to move on from Ivry, over the frontier into the territory of Blois, in search of Amelia, the absconded traitors, or both – when the decision was taken out of his hands.

He had come very near to all three garrisons on various occasions – near enough to note the details of banners and to make approximate counts of men and horses – and always had felt, even in owl-shape, the telltale raising of hairs (or, in this case, feathers) up the back of his neck, which warned him of the working of magick. From this evidence together with that of Ollivier and Lécuyer, as well as of the day-scouts Fournier and Tanguy, and of the several mage-officers who took it in turns to accompany Captain Howells' infantry scouts, Gray concluded that the three most proximate enemy encampments almost certainly had mages of their own, and that very possibly these mages had worked (or were presently working) some manner of protection, illusion, or concealment.

And if that is so, he wrote, concluding today's dispatch to Lord

Kergabet, *all of our observations are – or may be – as good as useless, for we cannot know for certain what is truth, and what illusion.*

Having laboriously enciphered his text and burnt the unenciphered original, he sealed the enciphered copy and tucked it into an inner pocket of his very unmilitary coat, locked away his writing-case in the bottom of his trunk, and made for Colonel Dubois' command-post.

Gray had been sleeping badly, alone in his too-short bed amidst the noisy bustle of the camp's daylight hours; he missed Sophie most fiercely not at night, when the twin imperatives of surveillance and survival occupied the lion's share of his attention, but during the long, restless days. They could not correspond except by way of Kergabet – even this dubious privilege was a compromise, which he dared not protest lest it, too, be withdrawn – and to end each day without telling Sophie of its happenings large and small, without hearing in return what had occupied and preoccupied her, unsettled him far more than he judged it ought.

Nevertheless, Sophie and he had learnt many things in the course of their years in Alba, one of which was that their magicks linked them, whether they themselves were together or far apart. Though none of their researches had taught them any means of controlling or influencing this link, by patient experiment they had learnt to see one another's magick, in the same way that every mage sees his own.

His dispatch delivered, Gray ducked back into the night-scouts' tent, shrugged out of his coat and slung it across the lid of the trunk, and carefully folded himself into his borrowed camp bed. Then, closing his eyes, he sank deep into the consciousness of his own magick; having found it – a vast dim autumn rose of blue-green flame – he felt cautiously outwards into the warm dark, seeking the frail bright thread which, at this vast distance, was all he could see of Sophie's. It came, when at last he grasped it, with a faint, aetherial chorus of treble voices – which Gray had half expected – and a bright anticipatory spark of excitement, which he had not.

What are you about, Sophie-of-mine? But whatever it was, at any rate Sophie was not – at this particular moment – sunk in melancholy. *I wish you well of it, love, and may the gods grant us leisure to tell all our adventures very soon.*

Outside, some heavy object fell to the ground with an ominous clatter, and a man's voice shouted, 'Mars and Mithras! Have a care!'

Gray's eyes flew open; Lécuyer stirred in his sleep; Ollivier flung up one arm and let out a single stentorian snore. Gray chuckled wearily, closed his eyes once more, and at last drifted down into sleep.

After a long, unbroken spell of fine weather, that night brought a lashing rain, the occasional clap of thunder, and a tense twilight conference amongst the night-scouts and their captain as to the advisability of a sortie.

'Ollivier cannot possibly go,' declared Lécuyer, folding his arms across his chest; for a wonder, they had both dressed in full uniform, if not very carefully, and Lécuyer wore in addition a vast great-coat which smelt strongly of lavender-oil. 'You know what his feathers are like; he should be waterlogged and in need of rescuing within a quarter-hour, and what good is that to anyone?'

Ollivier glared, but did not attempt to contradict him. Gray was no expert on the physiology of *Tyto alba*, but it was true that the soft feathers which enabled barn owls to fly so silently in dry weather must absorb water to a dangerous degree when it was wet.

Captain Tremblay pressed the bridge of his nose between

thumb and forefinger and sighed. 'I am sorry to say it, Mr Ollivier, but that is certainly true. Mr Marshall' – he turned to Gray – 'what experience have you of flying in wet weather?'

Gray considered this question carefully, listening to the keening of the wind and the drumming spatter of the rain against the canvas roof and walls. A great deal of his flying, in fact, had been done in wet weather, but he had never had reason to go aloft on a night like this one, and it was not the rain but the wind which gave him pause. Too, this lashing rain would impede even his owl's eyes, making reconnaissance difficult if not impossible – even if he and Lécuyer were fortunate enough not to be blown off course or, worse, against a tree.

On the other hand, if I were a general contemplating an invasion, I should make use of any circumstance which seemed likely to shield my movements from the enemy. What might we fail to see tonight, should we choose the prudent course?

'I can give you no promises,' he said at last, 'but I am prepared to make the attempt.'

'Good man!' Tremblay clapped him on the shoulder – the left one, which had ached all day as it always did when the air was damp and chill.

'Captain, is this wise?' said Ollivier.

Gray turned to look at him, startled; he had observed before now that Captain Tremblay's men, and the mage-officers in particular, observed the forms of military discipline only as the humour took them, but never before had he seen any of them issue so direct a challenge.

'Tell me, Mr Ollivier,' said the Captain dryly, 'which of us commands this company?'

'Your pardon, sir,' said Ollivier. He did not look remorseful, however – or even abashed – and Gray was irresistibly reminded of Joanna at thirteen, fearlessly berating persons older and more powerful than herself when she believed them to be in the wrong; she was grown more politic now, and to his surprise he rather regretted the change.

Ollivier, indeed, was not deterred: 'Can the Colonel not wait till morning for the next report?' he said. 'It is a difference of only a few hours, and at what price?'

'Kannig,' said Lécuyer, who looked acutely uncomfortable. 'Hold your tongue, idiot.'

'I shall not, then,' said Ollivier, turning on him. 'And which of us is the idiot, to insist on flying in this unholy mess? Not I.'

They looked ready to come to blows, and Gray was as much relieved as startled when the furious tension between them was broken by Captain Tremblay's saying, in a tone of well-controlled ire, 'Enough. Mr Lécuyer, Mr Marshall, you will make ready to go aloft in half an hour's time. *Mr* Ollivier, you will go back to your quarters at once, and I should advise you very strongly not to be seen outside them before tomorrow morning. Is that clear?'

'As a midsummer sky, sir,' said Ollivier, through gritted teeth. He saluted smartly, turned on his heel, turned up the collar of his coat, and vanished into the driving rain.

There is a story there, thought Gray, gazing after him. Ollivier, in his observation, had no less courage than any of the other scouts, though he was rather less reckless; it was not cowardice or an excess of caution, presumably, which had pushed him to such behaviour.

Gray and Lécuyer, avoiding one another's eyes, turned up their collars likewise and followed Ollivier out into the rain and wind. They were very damp indeed – Gray particularly – by the time they reached their own quarters, and Lécuyer flung off his dripping great-coat and collapsed upon his bed with a theatrical groan, one arm across his face.

Ollivier had shed his regimental coat and wrapped himself in a thick travelling-rug, and was pacing to and fro, already wearing a path in the packed-earth floor. He looked daggers at the oblivious Lécuyer and, when Gray shrugged out of his coat and sat down gingerly on his own bed, at once sat down beside him.

'If you *must* go, do keep an eye on him,' he said, low, before the startled Gray could protest this liberty. 'He is as brave as a lion, and he has no more sense than a rabbit.' He leant closer and added, almost inaudibly, 'And there is something uncanny about this storm.'

'Shut *up*, Kannig,' said Lécuyer. His words were muffled by his coat-sleeve, but his exasperated tone was entirely audible. 'I have not needed a nursemaid these twenty years. You had better take your dry night's leisure and thank Jove for it, than to be making such an almighty row.'

Ollivier, on his feet once more and glaring down at his brother-officer, scoffed. 'You were quick enough to stop *me* from flying,' he said; when Lécuyer made no reply to this, he continued, 'If I hear tomorrow that you have been taking stupid risks, Arzhur, I shall kill you myself. And not quickly.'

Then he curled up on his bed – muddy boots, travelling-rug and all – and closed his eyes. He was still feigning sleep when Kerambrun arrived to collect Lécuyer and Gray.

A sound like a hound's barking caught Gray's ear through the tumult of the storm, away off to the north-east. He pondered it, curving his wings to catch an updraft and gliding perilously above the tops of the trees. It came again – from the general direction of the largest enemy camp, but . . . higher? Yes: not a hound's bark but the call of an eagle owl sounding the alarm. *Lécuyer has found something he wishes me to see.*

There was another possibility, of course, but for the moment Gray resolutely refrained from considering it.

He answered the call with a series of low hoots, and – somewhat to his surprise, for the wind had risen to a sort of keening wail – was answered in turn by another brief volley of barking. Each hearing made the source easier to pinpoint, and before long Gray had sight of his quarry, clinging damp and bedraggled to the bottom-most branch of an enormous oak-tree half overcome with mistletoe. Lécuyer, catching sight of him in turn as he glided in, greeted him with a more usual *oohu-oohu-oohu.* For some time they huddled close for warmth, quite unselfconsciously, Gray's right foot nearly overlapping Lécuyer's left; then Lécuyer tilted his body forward and, with a powerful thrust of his legs, dropped away from the branch. Gray followed him as closely as he dared, skimming close to the forest floor.

They reached the river, swollen by a full day's heavy rain to within a foot of the near bank, and Lécuyer sheered away upwards, climbing high above the rushing water, above the new-felled trees on the far bank, above the camp which for at least a fortnight had flown the banners of lords beholden to Blois, Poitou, Anjou, Artois, and Bourgogne so puzzlingly side by side. New banners had been raised alongside and above them – the number was larger than before – but the lashing rain made them impossible to distinguish.

But this, whatever it might mean, was neither the worst nor the most astonishing discovery to be made that night; for as he followed Lécuyer's circuit of the camp, farther aloft than either of them ordinarily flew, he saw that it appeared to have tripled in size since the previous night – even, in fact, since this morning's report from Fournier and Tanguy – and that yet more troops – foot-soldiers and cavalry, pikemen and archers, teams of horses pulling siege-engines, trebuchets, and huge carriage-mounted saltpetre-cannon of the sort armies use when they have no battle-mages to sow large-scale havoc amongst the opposing force – were pouring towards it along the southern road.

Gray had always found this body less sensitive to the presence of magick than his human one, but down the back of his skull and all along his spine there now crawled a prickling sensation in reaction to someone else's spell-work. Were there mages – trebuchets and cannon notwithstanding – amongst those steadily moving columns of men and horses below? Doing what exactly? Or had Ollivier been correct in supposing that this storm was not of natural origin? If so, were the persons responsible en route to the enemy camp, or were they in residence already?

They circled the camp twice more, attempting to see as much as they could of its drastically altered configurations; the rain grew heavier, harder – solidified into tiny hailstones, striking with painful force – and Gray began more seriously to consider Ollivier's theory. Navigating the increasingly violent wind was becoming exhausting; a sharp ache in his left wing began to demand his attention and quickly grew impossible to ignore. At last, subordinating curiosity to common sense after a particularly punishing buffet of hailstones, he called to Lécuyer, and when the latter had circled back to him, gave the agreed-upon signal for *injured, returning to camp*. Had Ollivier been with them as usual, Lécuyer might have seen him across the river, into friendly territory, and then turned back, but in the circumstances, Gray was not surprised to be escorted all the way back to the eastern watchtower of Colonel Dubois' encampment.

He was surprised, however, at how closely Lécuyer followed him – their wingtips sometimes almost brushing – and astonished by the commotion that greeted their return. It was customary (or perhaps a rule of military conduct) for the scouts to be divested of their identifying leg-bands and returned to their quarters before resuming their natural form, but they had no sooner alighted in the watch-tower than Lécuyer was exploding from owl to man – mother-naked and entirely heedless of the fact – and bellowing, 'A healer, quickly! He has caught an arrow through the wing.'

Oh, thought Gray vaguely. *Those were not only hailstones, then.*

Someone had slung a great-coat about Lécuyer's shoulders; kneeling on the rough boards of the watchtower, he gathered Gray's owl-body gently into his arms, tucked him between the great-coat's overlapping layers, and began to descend the ladder. Gray shut his eyes, wound his talons into the rough wool, and held on.

CHAPTER XXI

In Which Sophie Dispatches a Message, Joanna Commits an Error in Judgement, and Lucia Makes a Discovery

'*Imperator Gallia?*' Joanna repeated, her face folding up into a frown. 'But the Emperor of Gaul is only a rumour, surely – a monster invented to frighten the common soldiers. You do not suppose—'

'Amelia evidently believes in him, at any rate,' said Sophie, rather more crossly than she had intended. 'Unless, of course, one prefers to take the view that my friend Evans-Hughes has invented the tale for his own amusement.'

The two of them were presently in sole possession of the bedroom which Sophie was to share with Lucia, Sophie curled in the room's one armchair and Joanna sprawled across the counterpane. Gareth, who had accompanied Sophie back to the Dragon and Lion and thereafter dined with the party from London, had then volunteered to conduct them on a guided tour of those of Oxford's sights which could be seen in the interval between dinner and dusk. Lucia, Roland, and Gwendolen had received this suggestion with enthusiasm; when Joanna would have joined them, however, Sophie had leant casually towards her and muttered in her ear, 'I have something to tell you about Amelia,' after which Joanna had promptly developed a headache, and elected to remain behind.

'Well,' Joanna sighed, 'of course if anything casts the Professor in a flattering light, poor Amelia will happily swallow it whole. In any case, however, I do not see that that titbit gets us much forwarder. But Dover . . . Dover is very suggestive.'

'It suggests a wish to leave Britain as quickly as possible, certainly.'

'Dover,' said Joanna, pushing herself up on her elbows, 'is the most heavily fortified port along the Manche, precisely because one can very nearly throw a stone across the strait from Calais and strike the ships in the harbour. Its entire garrison is on alert for the fugitives from the Tower, of whom Henry Taylor is one.'

'Seen in that light,' said Sophie, thoughtful, 'it seems a most peculiar choice for him to have made.'

'Exactly,' said Joanna. 'And in fact, according to your friend, from Dover Amelia went on to Calais alone, and neither of them was apprehended – nor even *seen*, so far as we know. Now, of course, the garrison and the local constabulary were on the lookout for the conspirators travelling together, not for one of them with a woman, or a woman alone, but no British ship's captain who valued his livelihood would have given either of them passage to Calais without papers of some sort—'

'Woodville, the forger?' Sophie suggested.

Joanna replied with a noncommittal sort of hum.

'At any rate,' said Sophie, 'this must all go to Kergabet, as soon as may be. If I write my letter at once, shall you have time to help me encipher it this evening, so that one of the guardsmen can deliver it in the morning?'

Joanna yawned hugely and rolled over onto her back. 'I shall help you this time,' she said, 'but after this I shall make you do your own enciphering. Hurry up, then! The light is going.'

Sophie called a globe of magelight, then another, and sent them to hover amongst the rafters. Then she extricated her writing-case from the bottom of a valise and sat down at the small spindle-legged desk, more decorative than practical, to begin her letter.

'I am glad she is not with Taylor,' she said, 'but I do wish she had not gone off all alone.'

Early the following afternoon, in a state of mingled excitement and trepidation and armed with a three-hundred-year-old plan of their quarry, an assortment of tools, and a borrowed ladder, Sophie's party approached the main gate of Lady Morgan College. Constructed from close-set wrought-iron bars, the gate was set in a tall, narrow archway flanked on either side by long wings of dressed Headington stone, whose windowless ground-floor walls were almost less forbidding than the broken-paned casements brooding dark above them. The gate was locked, and a heavy chain, wrapped several times and secured by a large padlock, anchored it to the gatepost. In the interstices of the ivy-leaves, Sophie saw that the whole arrangement had rusted to a near-uniform russet-brown. She ceased to fret that no one knew where to look for the keys to these locks, and began to wish for draught horses and a dredging-hook.

She and Roland and Lucia, however, had unlocking-spells at the ready. Sophie's was one she had learnt from Gray and had never failed her before; perhaps it was made for well-kept locks, however, for its sole effect on the rusted padlock was to strike a few sparks. Roland's brief, emphatic spell made the padlock groan, shedding flakes of rust, but still there came no telltale clicking of tumblers. Frowning, Roland tried it twice more, with the same result.

'The trouble with mages,' said Joanna, coming forward to peer at the lock, 'is that you cannot conceive of a problem to which magick is not the solution. Gwen, come and see whether you cannot pick the lock, as you have such a talent for it!'

'*Joanna!*'

Sophie, glancing over her shoulder, saw that Miss Pryce's face was flushed red.

Joanna, who had not been looking at her friend when she made her careless pronouncement, now wore an expression of dawning horror.

'I believe,' said Sophie – both to draw the others' attention away from the unfortunate Miss Pryce, and because she had herself had an idea – 'that picking locks requires equipment which we have not brought with us. We *have* brought a ladder, however, and Mr Goff has got an axe.'

'Only a wood-axe, ma'am,' said Goff apologetically, 'for doors and the like. It would not do much good against an iron gate, even rusted . . .'

Ceana MacGregor tapped Mr Goff smartly on the shoulder and, when he turned to face her, held out her hand for the axe. He frowned, but surrendered it.

Ceana made for the padlocked gate, then hefted the axe and drew it back up over her right shoulder, the wrong way about, with the sharp edge upwards – which puzzled Sophie until it came down again, powerful and precise, and the blunt end of the axe-head rang against a single link in the great rusted chain. Two more precise blows upon that same link – two more again – a last, and it exploded into flakes of rust and shards of metal. Sophie scratched absently at the bridge of her nose.

Ceana MacGregor propped the axe, head down, against the

wall beside the gate, and with assistance from Goff and Roland began unwrapping the chain. It was a long and noisy business – during which, to Sophie's intense discomfort, a furious whispered argument between Joanna and Miss Pryce continued unabated.

At last the chain was reduced to a heap of rusted links at the foot of the wall, and Sophie and Lucia converged upon the gate's own locking mechanism.

'Hmm,' said Lucia, in an interested tone; shifting (perhaps unconsciously) from Latin into Gaelic, she said, 'there is magick *in* this lock, and I believe it still lives.'

'*Lives?*' said Roland, sceptical. 'Like . . . like the yew-hedge?'

Lucia smiled a little at this cryptic query and said, 'A little like. This iron gate is farther from its roots even than your tamed and trammelled yew-trees, but it has not quite forgotten them; and the lock . . .'

She turned to look at Sophie, a solemn, meaning look. 'Like calls to like,' she said. 'Iron to iron. I shall try my spell, but I think . . . I think the lock's own magick may be—'

'The key?' Roland offered sardonically, stepping up beside Sophie.

Lucia ignored him; she had leant her head against the bars of the gate and was murmuring low and quick. To Sophie's eye, no effect was forthcoming.

'As I thought,' murmured Lucia, stepping back a little.

Gwendolen Pryce had drifted closer without Sophie's noticing, and now said quietly in Latin, 'May I be of any help?'

'Have you a pocket-knife about you?' said Lucia. 'Or a pen-knife? And can you call fire?'

'I have,' said Gwendolen, in a doubtful tone, 'and I can, but why—'

'Well, give it here, then!' Lucia's tone was eager.

Gwendolen hesitated; Lucia thrust out a hand insistently and repeated, 'The *knife*. And call me a small flame to light, to light . . .' She rummaged in a capacious pocket of the riding-habit – split-skirted and tailored above to mimic a man's dress – which she had insisted on wearing for the purposes of this venture, and pulled up a stub of candle. 'This. Here.'

'*Lucia*,' said Roland, urgent. 'Is this wise?' There was no response.

Sophie studied her friend – the quivering tension in her stooped shoulders, the slim fingers wrapped tight round the bars of the gate, the pale sliver of her profile, her one visible eye intent on her work. Lucia meant to give her own blood to the lock in hopes of inducing it to open; so much was clear, to Sophie if not to anyone else. Was this a brilliant or a disastrous notion? Or was it, perhaps – like many a notion of Sophie's own – brilliant or disastrous only as subsequent events might decide?

Sophie nodded once at Miss Pryce, who, though her dark-curved brows rose in surprise, stepped forward with her pen-knife in one hand and took the candle-stub from Lucia.

'The flame must be hot,' said Lucia, low. 'As hot as you can manage. Pass the blade through.'

Sophie only just heard the whispered *Flammo te!* before the wick burst into flame – a tiny flame, blue-hot and precisely controlled. Gwendolen Pryce knew her business when it came to minor magicks, though seemingly incapable of greater ones.

With a steady hand she held the pen-knife's small blade in the flame – one breath, two, three – then wrapped Lucia's splayed fingers about its handle and, abandoning magickal for more prosaic methods, blew the candle out.

Lucia loosed her hold on the gate and with her right hand raised the knife to the pad of her left forefinger. Now Roland at last saw what she had in mind, and Sophie caught him by both elbows just in time to arrest his panicked lunge towards her.

'*Nuair a thig air duine thig air uile*,' Lucia murmured – *what befalls one, befalls all* – as she nicked the pad of her finger.

Roland growled; Sophie gripped his arm to restrain him and dimly registered that Ceana – despite her very evident disapproval of Lucia's proceedings – was doing the same on his other side.

'Whatever she is about,' said Sophie, low, 'we must not interrupt it.'

Lucia regarded her bleeding finger, dripping steadily onto the blade of the knife – then, as though it had been the most natural thing in the world, crouched down and, holding the knife in her left hand, slid the blade slowly into the keyhole.

For a moment, nothing happened. Then came a sudden smell of hot iron; Sophie's nose began to itch, so fiercely as to be almost painful; at almost the same time, Lucia yelped and staggered back from the gate, dropping the knife and cradling her left hand against her chest.

Ceana MacGregor caught her – just – when she stumbled and nearly fell headlong. The rest converged on her in a rush.

'Stay *back*,' Ceana snarled. She was holding Lucia upright with both arms locked about her ribs, but not without difficulty: Lucia – pale as her own candle-stub but still intently focused on the centuries-old lock – was struggling mightily to get free.

'Lucia,' said Sophie, very firmly and as loudly as she dared. 'Lucia, look at me.'

Lucia blinked, blinked again, and abruptly ceased her struggles to escape. Ceana MacGregor eased her hold, though without releasing it.

'The lock needs blood,' said Lucia, as calmly as though she had not been fighting tooth and claw against her own guard captain just moments ago. 'My spell was an adequate substitute for the key, but the locking-spell cannot be broken in that way; it must have blood. Not *my* blood, however; the spell has made that very clear.'

She held out her left hand, palm up, and Sophie saw that the skin of her hand, the palm and all five fingers, was burnt to blisters.

'And yet, why leave even such a loophole as that, if they truly meant it never to be opened again? Why, indeed – as we have asked ourselves before – not knock down the walls and buildings, and make some other use of the land beneath?'

'More to the point,' said Miss Pryce, who had gone back to the gate to retrieve her knife and was wiping it clean with her handkerchief, 'how are we to know whose blood, if anyone's, will appease the spell, and how are we to undertake the trial without anyone else's being hurt?'

Sophie considered. 'Suppose,' she said after a moment, 'suppose that the lock and the spell expect the key and the blood, respectively – as Lucia believes they do – one might . . . er . . . apply the latter to the former, and so provide both at once. And as we have already dealt with the lock itself – have we not, Lucia?'

Lucia nodded without looking up. She had unwrapped Ceana MacGregor's makeshift cold compress from her hand and was studying her burnt fingers.

'Then one might find another object of the same length and circumference,' said Sophie, beginning to look about her. 'A key with no bit, so to speak, to serve the same purpose—'

'But it must be iron,' said Lucia, urgently. 'You are thinking of a tree-branch, Sophie, or something of the sort, but it must be iron, like the lock itself. Not wood or bone – not even steel.' She held up her burnt hand.

'Very well,' said Sophie. She studied the gate, the height of the windows; considered the lower east wall, the height of the ladder. It was growing late in the afternoon, and everyone must be wanting their dinner. No – this problem, alas, would not be solved today.

'A tactical retreat,' she announced. 'We shall return tomorrow, properly armed. Mr Goff, I should be obliged if you would seek out a trustworthy blacksmith; perhaps the innkeeper may tell you where one is to be found.' Using a piece of string, she made crude measurements of the keyhole and noted them down on a page of her commonplace-book, which she tore out and presented to Mr Goff.

He looked deeply dubious, but nevertheless said, 'Ma'am,' and after glancing at the torn-off paper, folded it and tucked it away in a coat-pocket.

'Back to the inn, then,' said Sophie briskly, concealing her restless frustration as well as she was able, 'for dinner, and a healer, and our beds.'

By a variety of stratagems, Joanna contrived largely to avoid Gwendolen during what remained of the afternoon and evening. At last, however, the company retired for the night, and there was no more evading the continuance of the afternoon's dispute.

By now she had, by slow degrees, talked herself out of her self-righteous insistence that Gwendolen ought not to be angry with her, and returned to that first access of remorse; she hoped that Gwendolen's temper, too, might now be cooled, at least a little.

'I am sorry, Gwen,' she began, without other preamble. 'It is true that I did not know how strongly you should object to my saying what I said, but still I ought not to have said it, and I am sorry.'

Gwendolen, leaning against the edge of the dressing-table, arms folded, in a pose of wholly unconvincing nonchalance, gave her a long, measuring look.

'I believe you,' she said at last, unsmiling.

Joanna winced. To be believed was something, but in this case it was evidently some considerable distance from being pardoned.

'You know, I hope, that I should never hurt you by intent,' she said. 'Perhaps, if I understood why—'

Gwendolen cut her off with an impatient huff. 'Can you truly imagine no reason why I should be reluctant to advertise a talent for breaking and entering?' she demanded. 'None whatsoever?'

'I do not see that it is any different from an unlocking-spell,' said Joanna – not for the first time – 'which Sophie and Roland and Lucia had no objection to being seen to work.'

'It is *different*,' said Gwendolen, through gritted teeth, 'first, because very few common thieves can work an unlocking-spell, and second, because powerful mages of royal birth may do any number of things with impunity, which the cast-off daughters of heavily indebted country squires cannot afford even to be suspected of doing. Particularly' – she raised a hand to fend off Joanna's protest – 'if those daughters should happen to be engaged in equivocal and secretive intimate friendships with the protégées of men prominent at Court.'

Joanna closed her eyes for a long, silent moment: *Lady Venus, wise Minerva, guide my tongue, or I shall say entirely the wrong thing once again.*

'You surely cannot think my father any better prize than yours,' she said carefully. 'And I hope you do not suppose yourself any less solidly under the protection of Lord and Lady Kergabet than I am?'

Gwendolen stared at her in frank astonishment. 'Jo, you are Lady Kergabet's sister-in-law,' she said. 'And it is plain to see that they love you for yourself. Of course I am grateful to Lady Kergabet for taking pity on me that day at the Griffith-Rowlands', and for all the rest of it, but—'

'You are quite wrong,' cried Joanna, equally astonished at this thorough misinterpretation of the facts. Seeing Gwendolen's fine dark brows begin to draw together in a frown, she hurried on: 'I do not say that Jenny did not *begin* by feeling sorry for your plight, but how can you suppose *now* that she does not love you? And – and in any case *I* love you, Gwen, and they should protect you for my sake even if they did not.'

Then – abashed at this uncharacteristic eruption of passionate words, and cut to the heart by Gwendolen's expression of wonder at hearing them – she retreated to the washbasin to splash cool water upon her burning cheeks.

When the shades of Gwen's father and stepmother, and of that tyrant Mrs Griffith-Rowlands, are judged in the realm of Hades, I hope they may all be condemned to the fires of Tartarus, for having made my Gwen believe no one but her dead mama could love her.

When at last she turned away from the washstand, still drying her hands on the inn's crisp linen towel, she found Gwendolen standing before her, near enough to touch. Without her conscious volition, her hands came up to clasp her friend's slim shoulders, and Gwendolen stepped forward into her arms.

'You must never doubt it,' Joanna whispered fiercely. 'Not for a moment.'

'Nor you,' said Gwendolen, muffled into Joanna's hair.

Joanna pulled away just far enough to look up into Gwendolen's deep brown eyes. 'And you must never think you have any cause to be ashamed,' she said. 'I ought not to have spoken as I did, without your leave, but a useful skill is always worth possessing, and I spoke from pride in your skill, not . . . not from any other motive.'

Gwendolen swallowed hard, pressing her lips together briefly; then she smiled – a small swift thing, but warm and full of affection – and said, 'I thought, perhaps, your motive was to open that rusted old gate. But perhaps I may be mistaken?'

Joanna laughed aloud, and kissed her.

All the same, she thought, not for the first time, *I should very much like to know what* your *motive was for learning to pick locks.*

CHAPTER XXII

In Which Gray Receives a Message and Makes a Decision

Gray woke to watery late-afternoon sunshine slanting through an open tent-flap, and prudently took stock before attempting to sit up. This was not his too-small camp bed in the night-scouts' tent, but one of many identical ones set in tidy rows in a much larger tent – really a sort of pavilion, a canvas roof and walls which could be rolled up to admit fresh air and sunlight, supported by sturdy wooden posts. The regimental infirmary, then; and to judge from its lack of occupants, whatever offensive action might be contemplated by the force across the river had not yet begun.

Someone had dressed him, not in his own clothes but in a worn linen nightshirt, too small but scrupulously clean. His left arm, bent at the elbow, was bound flat against his ribs with a square of linen folded into a sling, which also held in place the folded bandages padding his shoulder; the shoulder yet ached a little, but the throbbing agony he remembered was nowhere in evidence. His head, on the other hand, felt as though he had spent an evening attempting to outdrink his brother George, and the whole of the succeeding night regretting it.

An arrow through the wing. Lécuyer's words echoed in Gray's mind. There were healers here – very skilled ones, clearly – and Lécuyer had lost no time in delivering Gray into their care; but even so, such a wound could not be recovered from in a single night. *I shall not be flying for some days, I suspect.*

Pinned to the blankets at the foot of the bed with a clothes-peg was a flat object, more or less white and more or less rectangular: a letter? Gray struggled to sit up, to lean down after it. An indrawn breath snagged in his throat, and he coughed. By all the gods, when had he last had anything to drink?

Help arrived in the form of a young man, clad in an odd hodgepodge of uniform breeches and boots and healer's robes, bearing a *cantine* of water. He then insisted on taking Gray's pulse, changing the dressing on his shoulder wound, and testing the motion of his arm, by the end of which operations, his patient was in a very fever of impatience.

'Is that a letter for me?' Gray inquired, low, when the healer had finished and was preparing to take himself off again. 'May I read it?'

He held out his right hand to the healer, who gave him a dubious frown but unpinned the letter and handed it over. Awkwardly one-handed, Gray broke the seal. His brows rose; not Kergabet's hand but Joanna's had enciphered the contents. What could this portend?

Upon deciphering, the message proved brief – a mere few lines, padded out with nonsense. *In Oxford*, it read. *Have consulted GEH; A is gone to Calais, not to Honfleur, and not with T. Means to join Papa, whereabouts unknown, and person styled Imperator Gallia. Not a rumour? Go carefully. S.*

Gray stared at it for some time, questions boiling up in his mind: why should Sophie go to Oxford – or rather, why should her father consent to her going? Calais, not Honfleur; meaning that Amelia sailed from Dover? *Not* with Taylor? Then with whom? Not all alone, surely? And where was she (were they?) going, in the end?

At any rate – all relevant observations having by now been reported up the chain of command, and there being no evidence whatsoever amongst the garrison of conversation with the enemy – Gray had already concluded that he could do no more good in Normandie.

He folded Sophie's letter away and, for lack of a pocket of his own to stow it in, folded his fingers around it. Then – moving slowly at first, until he was certain that he should not fall over – he extricated himself from the camp-bed, climbed to his feet, and went in search of his boots and a pair of trousers, without which he did not quite dare accost Colonel Dubois.

Gray departed the camp at Ivry with even less ceremony than had attended his arrival a se'nnight since – shortly before dusk, on horseback, with a few necessities distributed into a pair of saddle-bags (together with a small purse of coin from Anjou, Orléanais, Picardie, Poitou, and Champagne, helpfully provided by Colonel Dubois); the rest of his possessions he had left behind in the care of Mage-Captain Tremblay. As soon as he could safely do so, he meant to wander into enemy territory in the dark; if, somewhere in one of the Duchies, someone were indeed calling himself Emperor of Gaul, then Gray had only to keep his ears open and his origins and identity concealed, and soon enough he should discover where to seek his quarry.

Or so I hope.

Around him, the camp hummed with preparations – improvements to the regiment's defensive position, chiefly, though

Gray and the rangy grey gelding Colonel Dubois had lent him were also passed by troops of grim-faced grooms shepherding strings of horses in from their picket-lines outside the camp proper. From time to time he received a respectful nod or even, once or twice, a salute; word had spread of the civilian night-scout who had matched the feat of the acclaimed Mage-Lieutenant Tanguy. *My father would be pleased, at any rate*, thought Gray, suppressing an ironical twist of his lips as he gravely returned a passing cavalry-officer's greeting. Not that, should this sortie of his succeed, his father was ever likely to hear anything of it.

Gray had written, enciphered, and dispatched a report to Kergabet – parallel to the official version and, he suspected, rather shorter – giving a detailed account of his observations of the camp on the far bank of the River Eure, in which was enclosed a brief message of thanks to Sophie, together with a précis of his plans. Perhaps more usefully, Tremblay had unlocked his dispatch-case once more and made Gray a temporary gift of one of the talismans stored therein – the one marked *XXI*, which he had worn on his first sortie with the night-scouts; this small piece of insurance presently reposed in an inner pocket of his coat, and Tremblay had proposed a regular rotation of finding-spells by means of which he and Colonel Dubois should be apprised of Gray's approximate location at least once every day, unless and until he reached the limits of the available mages' range.

There, Sophie-of-mine: I am leaving you a trail to follow, as best I may, should . . . anything befall me.

He wished more than ever, now, that she had been here with him; how much more might he hope to accomplish, with two pairs of eyes to observe, two sets of ears to listen, and Sophie's magick to wrap them in unremarkable obscurity? But he had

331

made her a promise to return to her safe and whole, though plainly (he flexed his injured shoulder irritably, and thanked Aesculapius for talented healers) it was too late to return actually unscathed; and Gray hoped he was not a man to break a promise to his wife.

The grey gelding rejoiced in the name of Tonnerre, which in Gray's experience thus far could not have been less à propos to its placid, accommodating temperament. Having passed the outer pickets, they ambled through the gathering dusk in a more or less southerly direction, roughly parallel to but out of sight of the River Eure and, it was to be hoped, any sentries or scouts posted by the force massed on its opposite bank.

The size of that force had more than tripled, the number of siege-engines doubled; the heavy saltpetre-cannon had been added to the array of weaponry visible along the far bank, and new banners to the collection flying from the peaks of tents and pavilions and from the watchtowers facing the British camp. But no sortie had been made, either to attack or to parley. What might they be waiting for?

The lights of Colonel Dubois' camp behind him, Gray dug in his heels, urging Tonnerre into an easy canter.

The night was well advanced, and a gibbous moon lighting Gray's path in black and silver, before it seemed likely that he should be able to cross the Eure without being seen or heard from the enemy camp. Fording the river left him drenched to the hips, chilled, shivering, and at odds with the world at large and Tonnerre in particular – no one had mentioned to him, for reasons best known to themselves, the gelding's particular dislike of running water. But here he was, and a warming-spell repaired the worst of the damage, or at any rate rendered man and horse willing to tolerate one another once more.

By noon they were ambling into a village – middling prosperous, to all appearances, and in most respects indistinguishable from any farming village in Maine or Normandie – and looking about them in search of their breakfasts. The village proved, surprisingly for its size, to possess two inns, at opposite ends of its principal street; their signboards proclaimed them to be, respectively, the Lion d'Or and the Cheval Blanc. Gray, after some thought, chose the former.

Gray's meal was a very long time in coming, and when at last it appeared, was garnished with pre-emptive apologies for its quality – the muster of the Seigneur de Déols had marched through the village three days since, and the inn's cook, indeed half its staff, monsieur, had marched off with them, without so much as giving notice! – which, sadly, proved entirely justified.

The beds at the Lion d'Or, on the other hand, were clean and dry and free of vermin – though Gray, after his night's journey, would gladly have slept on a horse-blanket in the stables.

The following morning, having inadvertently slept all afternoon and most of the night and feeling much the better for it, Gray loaded his saddle-bags, mounted up, and set off again, attempting to look as though he had some notion of going somewhere in particular. He could not, of course, turn back in the direction he claimed to have come from, nor was there any purpose in retracing his actual route – in addition to which, what wandering scholar would ride towards an army when he might so easily ride away from it? But if Amelia, with or without Taylor, had landed at Calais, then his best chance of intercepting her, surely, lay in travelling north-east, to Picardie and Artois. He therefore set his face more or less east once more, towards – eventually – the great River Seine.

The next several villages, with their several inns, offered generally better provisioning but not, in the main, much more useful conversation, and the endlessly repeated finding-spells continued to turn up nothing whatsoever. Gray began to curse himself – very quietly, rolled up in Ollivier's borrowed travelling-rug in shared bedchambers at night – for believing that this wild-goose chase of his might have any other result than his eventually coming to the end of his coin and either starving to death or being hanged as a thief.

On an unseasonably wet and chilly day he arrived at dusk in a village which had no inn as such, but did possess a public-house – denominated Le Bouclier d'Argent – in whose hayloft, for a small price, travellers might spend the night. Here the cook and her minions remained, but the matériel for her art was lacking, having been eaten or simply requisitioned by a passing cavalry troop.

Conversation amongst the half-dozen persons poking dispiritedly at their unappetising dinners, however, showed more promise. Being asked his name and business, Gray declared himself once more to be Guy Marais of Poitiers, in Poitou (which he had judged sufficiently distant that most persons he encountered were unlikely to know it any better than he did himself, from reading histories and travellers' accounts), and to be a scholar travelling the Duchies seeking employment, or, failing that, to visit as many libraries as possible. Having thus persuaded his new acquaintance that he was odd, eccentric, and almost certainly harmless, he assumed an affable and perhaps slightly foolish expression, and for some time let their talk flow over and around him.

Three were merchants from Arras en route to Tours, old acquaintance travelling together for safety and economy. A father and son had been stranded by the recent storm and were now making their way home to their farm near Anet. The sixth man was, so he said, a priest of Ceres, and had been travelling on the business of his temple in Orléans. Like Gray himself, he said little, but unlike Gray he did not try to hide that he was listening attentively to all that the others said. They all spoke in Français, in deference to the farmer, who had no Latin, and his son, who had very little; Gray's Français was as different from the priest's, the Artésien merchants', and the farmers' as they were from one another, but no one, it appeared, remarked it as Normand rather than Angevin.

In the Duchies as in Britain, it seemed, relative strangers taking one another's measure were apt to talk about the weather. In the present case, however, thought Gray, the weather bore talking of – such a storm, the grizzled farmer and his son agreed, had not been seen here for many years, and the cold, wet weather since was out of the ordinary, also.

'Has there been much damage to the crops hereabouts?' Gray enquired, more or less generally, after nearly half an hour's such desultory talk. 'Or is there like to be?'

'With the goddess's goodwill, there will not,' the priest of Ceres replied.

'And without it?' said the farmer's son, with a sardonic half smile. His father frowned at him, and he subsided.

'You are come from Orléans, I believe you said?' one of the merchants said, addressing the priest. 'Have you found things very . . . unsettled along the way?'

Observing the priest covertly, in profile, Gray saw him frown briefly before smoothing his face into blankness. 'Here and there,' he said.

The merchants, severally and together, related at some length their misadventures on the road from Arras with their goods and gear. They had been forced several times to alter their planned route, either to avoid armies on the march or because, the said armies having passed before them and eaten the local populace out of house and home, they could no longer expect themselves, their servants, or their beasts to be lodged or fed; they had heard such rumours of happenings in and around Orléans that they had decided to swing wide around it on their outward journey, and return that way from Tours instead.

'Could you,' Gray ventured, hesitantly – if military strategy was not his strong suit, trade was perhaps still less so – 'might there not be a market for your goods amongst the soldiers themselves? So that you need not travel all the way to Tours after all?'

The eldest of the merchants gave him a pitying look which Gray had seen before. 'When one has woven webs of exchange over many years, monsieur,' he said, in a sententious tone, 'when one's word is trusted by one's associates even at a great distance, because one has never broken it, one does not simply leap at the first opportunity of turning a profit, at the risk of tearing all those webs to shreds.'

'And besides, Médard,' said one of the others, a lean man perhaps in the middle forties, 'there is no great demand for fine tapestries or carpets in a soldiers' camp.'

He grinned. The rest of the table laughed aloud; the butt of all this mirth glared at his friend, but not without a small, rueful chuckle at his own expense.

'I had thought of visiting Orléans,' Gray said, seizing his opening before the conversation could turn again; improvising hastily on a strong ground of truth, he continued, 'on my return journey. I have heard much of the libraries at the temples of

Minerva and Apollo Grannus there. Ought I to avoid it, do you think? And what of Paris?'

'From what we have heard along the road,' said the third merchant, 'Paris is no better.' He was the youngest-looking of the three – not, by Gray's estimation, very much older than himself – but did not seem to lack for self-confidence. 'They are building ships to go up the Seine to Rouen, and out to the Manche.'

There had been, in less unsettled times, some considerable degree of trade between Paris and Rouen by way of the River Seine; by the man's tone, however, this was not the sort of ship he spoke of.

'Oh?' said Gray. 'Er . . . what sort of ships? And who is "they"?'

'Ships with saltpetre-cannon mounted aboard,' the young merchant elaborated. He seemed rather to be enjoying himself. 'As for *who*—'

The priest, Gray saw too late, was giving him a rather more interested and penetrating look than before.

'You are a scholar, monsieur, I think you said?' he enquired. 'In search of some employment?'

'I am,' said Gray – immensely glad, not for the first time, that he had not tried his powers of invention further.

'A scholar of what, if I may ask?'

The truth is safest. 'Of magick, monsieur,' he said.

The priest of Ceres smiled. 'How fortuitous,' he said. 'Monsieur . . . Marais, is it? I believe we may be of use to one another.'

That tone of voice, too, Gray had heard before. It was the tone in which, one very strange day years ago, Appius Callender had invited him to spend the summer in Breizh: the tone of a man disguising a command as a friendly invitation.

But I need not obey this man's command unless it serves my own purposes, Gray reminded himself. He was not that boy of barely one-and-twenty, almost equally lacking in friends and funds, and forced to choose, in effect, between incarceration as his tutor's guest and an accusation of murder. Perhaps most importantly, he had – unlike that frightened, baffled younger version of himself – the full use of his talent, and the certain knowledge that he was not alone in the world.

He returned the priest's smile and leant back a little in his seat. 'Do tell, monsieur,' he said.

So it was that by the following morning, Gray found himself travelling south through the Île-des-Francs in the company of one Charles Durand, priest of the Temple of Ceres, who wished to make him known to the man he called the Emperor of Gaul.

CHAPTER XXIII

In Which Roland Makes
Himself Surprisingly Useful

In the morning, armed with several slim iron rods made to Sophie's specifications by an obliging blacksmith, and sundry other useful tools, they renewed their assault upon the College gate. Sophie and Lucia – her good spirits much restored by the attentions of the talented healer whom Roland had insisted upon summoning from the Infirmary – had sat up late the previous night in their room, racking their brains for some better method than crude trial and error, but, in the almost total absence of information, had been forced to concede defeat. Accordingly, therefore, Joanna produced a wax candle in a brass holder, and held it steady whilst Gwendolen called fire to produce another of her focused, blue-hot flames; Sophie carried a basin, soap, and towels borrowed from the inn; and Lucia extracted from her reticule a bodkin and a stack of clean handkerchiefs collected from the rest of the party, and passed the former through the flame.

'Let me be first to try,' said Ceana MacGregor, predictably.

She did not so much as flinch when Lucia ran the bodkin deep into her thumb, or when she squeezed it to encourage the blood to drip onto the first of the iron rods. But when tried in the lock, Ceana MacGregor's blood, like Lucia's, had no effect upon the spell at all.

There followed a brief debate between Sophie and her guardsmen as to which of them should make the next attempt, which Mr Goff won – only to discover that, alas, his blood was no more to the spell's taste than Ceana MacGregor's.

Mr Tredinnick, Miss Pryce, and Joanna all tried their luck, to the same effect, before any of the others would agree to either Sophie's or Roland's doing so. The morning was wearing on, however, and the discouraging failures (and bloodied handkerchiefs) mounting up; when Joanna was nursing her bleeding right thumb and Mr Goff beginning to talk of calling in the rest of the guardsmen presently off-duty at the inn, and Ceana MacGregor of summoning some of her subordinates, to try their luck, Sophie and her brother exchanged a meaning glance, and Roland said firmly, 'I shall take the next turn.'

At his own insistence, Lucia turned over to him the iron rod smeared with his blood, to be tried in the keyhole. Sophie tensed involuntarily as he inserted it. So much occupied was her mind in anticipating the outcome that she did not register the stiff *click-clank* of the tumblers turning, or even the low groan of the hinges, until Roland said, in a stupefied tone, 'The . . . the gate is opening.'

Through the ivy-covered gateway Sophie went – magick buzzed in her mind's ear like swarming bees, then rippled as a sheet of water falling – and before she quite understood what she was doing, she found herself the first living person in more than two centuries to set foot inside the walls of Lady Morgan College.

She stopped in her tracks, causing someone to jostle her shoulder and someone else to tread painfully on her heel, and stared about her.

Even in the dungeons of remote Castle MacAlpine on the Ross of Mull, she had never seen such thorough dereliction. So high was the frontage that only the verdigris-green dome had been visible from without – or was there magick at work there, too, concealing the true state of things from the casual observer? – but here within, massive oaks and plane trees (and one lightning-split horse-chestnut) spread their branches overhead in a near-unbroken canopy, and underfoot the carpet of leaf-mould and acorns and rotting conkers was ankle-deep in places, interrupted by springy tree-shoots at various stages of growth. Clusters of primrose-yellow and harebell-blue swirled about the feet of the great old trees, like supplicants on their knees before the great gods.

Oak-trees, thought Sophie vaguely, *are sacred to Jupiter.*

With a scraping and a creaking of hinges, the gate closed (or was closed) behind them; and then silence. Utter silence, but for the breathing of the five women and three men who stood just inside the gate, suspended in Sophie's indecision.

Sophie drew a deep, slow breath, shut her eyes, and reached for her magick. The unspeakable relief of finding it just as usual took her aback – she had not understood until this moment how much she had dreaded the reverse, had feared that they might be crossing the boundary of an interdiction – and she stood for a moment perfectly still, steadying her breathing, willing her pulse down from its panicked hammering in her ears. That done, she reached out cautiously, seeking touchpoints in the not-quite-space about her: near at hand the bright red-gold touch of Lucia's magick, to which her own had once been linked; far away, so far as to be nearly undetectable, the deep blue-green thread of Gray's, linked to hers still though the connexion was faint and attenuated by the distance between them. Gray's magick had had a flavour of feathers about

341

it for some time now, and on one recent night the sizzle of stormy weather and a worrying flash of pain; this morning, however, it tasted only of deep sleep.

Easy to ponder the significance of this, to worry at the possibilities like a terrier with a rat, to be drawn aside from the concerns of the here-and-now—

Sophie gave herself a mental shake, drew in her wandering wits, and put forth the tendrils of her magick to prod (carefully, gently) at the barrier which logic suggested must enclose the College grounds. At first she could detect nothing, and frowned in bafflement; had she and her companions, in passing through the circumference of the spell, somehow released or erased it? Such a thing was not impossible – not, at any rate, more impossible than some of the other things they had seen and done since arriving in Oxford – but it would be an odd sort of mage, or group of mages, who so constructed any sort of barrier-spell as to permit some unknown future invader to undo it.

And, besides that, there is *something. I felt it, and I feel it still.*

No, she corrected herself almost at once, remembering: *There are two things.* Two layers of magick – and of quite different magicks, if she had read the signs aright – one encircling and enclosing the other.

Those generations-ago mages, whoever they had been – even this much, none of the books she had found and read could tell her – what had they been thinking, what seeking to achieve?

Following the logic of that thought, and peripherally aware of her companions' soft footfalls all about her, Sophie shifted and broadened the focus of her explorations; it might be a cleverly modified concealment-spell, the thing she sought, but equally it might be some species of warding-spell, of shielding, of protection – all related, of course, but nonetheless distinct from one another. And there, *there*—

That shimmering inner layer followed the exterior walls, she found – unsurprising – but curved high overhead, too, and – astonishing! – deep beneath her feet. A shielding-spell, or the essence of one, a perfect sphere constrained and contorted by the shape of the walls about its middle, like a ball of wool forced through an arm-ring.

The magick tasted familiar, somehow – not like her own, or Gray's, or Lucia's, not *like* that of anyone she knew, and yet . . . and yet. The scent of it echoed in her mind's ear, as though she should recognise it if only she could find just the right angle of observation. She touched it with a tendril of her magick (a single petal of the blue-white flame-flower by which her mind chose to represent her power, pulled out into a fine thread), steeling herself against some hostile reaction. To her astonishment, however, the only response was a brief shiver, rippling outwards from the point of metaphysickal contact like the concentric waves a still pond makes when a small stone is dropped into it; it was not hostility she felt, shimmering back along that hair's-breadth tendril of her magick, but . . . surely it could not be . . . recognition?

Now, the outward layer, on the other hand—

A hand on her arm wrenched her back to the world of leaf-mould and ancient, overgrown trees; she opened her eyes to find Joanna peering anxiously up into her face.

'Sophie,' she said quietly, 'is all well? Ought we to proceed, or . . . ?'

Sophie felt anxious eyes upon her from all sides. She straightened her spine, squared her shoulders, and said, 'We proceed. Mr Tredinnick, the maps, if you please.'

Mr Tredinnick unshipped from his shoulder the heavy cylindrical case which held the rolled-up maps, and which Sophie herself, to her intense irritation, had not been permitted to carry. The map she wanted (actually the plan of the College located by Evans-Hughes at Merlin) was fortunately the outermost; there being no flat surface to hand, Mr Goff offered his own back for the purpose, and Sophie – acutely uncomfortable, but unwilling to risk unnecessary delay – unrolled the parchment and flattened it across his broad shoulders, holding it in place with one palm to each of its short edges.

The others crowded round them, so close that Sophie experienced a strong desire to scream.

'Here we are,' she said, nodding at the point towards the lower edge of the plan which represented the gate. Nodding at it was quite useless, but she had no free hand to point with. 'Miss Pryce, may I ask—'

Miss Pryce's slim hands pressed flat the two corners nearest her, and Sophie retracted her right hand and tapped her forefinger upon the spot where – more or less – they now stood. 'Here is the Shrine of Minerva; here, the Library, and there the Refectory.'

They had planned to investigate the Library first of all, if they should find the buildings still standing – though it had been a long morning already, and the Shrine of Minerva was temptingly near . . .

Lucia rested one forefinger on the representation of the Library; she glanced up from the map, then down again, orienting herself. 'That way, I believe,' she said, pointing. 'But the way is not very clear.'

Indeed, the way was choked with brambles – almost entirely dead for lack of sunlight – and twilight-dark besides, for the canopies of two plane-trees and a horse-chestnut met overhead in that spot, and between them contrived to block almost all the sunlight that elsewhere filtered through the branches.

'Well, then,' said Roland cheerfully, 'shall we begin?'

Either he was quite unintimidated by the prospect before him – buoyed up, just possibly, by his unexpected (and quite unearned) success with the gate – or he was developing into a far better actor than Sophie had hitherto suspected. For her purposes, however, it did not much matter which.

'Certainly,' she said, and began rolling up the map.

The guardsmen obligingly hacked their way through the worst of the overgrown brambles and half-fallen trees. Here and there they found the remains of a footpath by the crunching of gravel under their feet, but the place was so still and silent around them that Sophie could not help feeling, uneasily, that they were treading through a tomb. The others followed; conversing at first in whispers, they fell silent one by one, and went unspeaking, single-file, their footsteps slow and cautious as her own.

The College Library hove into view after perhaps a quarter-hour – at a distance which ought not to have taken half that time to traverse – half buried in ivy and old-man's-beard but instantly recognisable by its two long wings and square central tower. The main doors were easily enough located by reference to the plan, but it took some time, even with three wood-axes to yesterday's one, to hack away the creeping growth that covered them. So oppressive was the pervading silence that the sound of the axe-blades biting into tough ivy-stems and glancing against stone came, perversely, as something of a relief to Sophie.

She started at a brief touch on her arm, but it was only Roland. Drawing in close beside her, he bent his head to speak in her ear: 'Are you quite sure of this, Sophie?'

Sophie stepped back and turned to look at him. 'What makes you ask?' she said. 'You were eager enough this morning, at the gate.'

Roland pursed his lips, wrinkled up his forehead, and scuffed one boot-toe in the leaf-mould underfoot. 'It is too quiet,' he said at last.

'It is that,' Sophie conceded. 'I do not quite know what to make of it.'

'*La belle au bois dormant*,' said Roland. 'That is what I make of it.'

'I believe that cryptic utterance was intended to convey some very deep meaning,' said Sophie, after a long moment, 'but I must tell you, Roland, that I have not the least notion what it might be.'

She surveyed the scene before her, telling herself that she was the captain of this small expeditionary force and was merely gauging its progress. The truth was that since the moment they had all passed in the gate, a cold vague dread had been creeping through her, winding frigid fingers about her heart; sober reason told her that, if any dire fate was to befall any of her party, it could not be avoided by her watchful eye alone, but nonetheless she did not like to let them out of her sight. Mr Goff and Mr Tredinnick were resting from their assault on the ivy, whilst Ceana MacGregor knelt at the foot of the door, prying up matted grass-roots from between the paving-stones with her belt-knife; Joanna and Miss Pryce had spread out the College plan on the lowest step and were discussing it (or something else) in low voices, and Lucia, inexplicably, was picking flowers.

'*La belle au bois dormant*,' Roland repeated, unhelpfully. 'You must know the tale, surely!'

'Joanna knows it, I am sure,' said Sophie, 'but—'

'Knows what?' Joanna raised her head and turned round to look at Sophie and Roland.

'The tale of the beautiful woman in the sleeping wood,' said Sophie.

'No, no,' said Joanna. She sprang to her feet, dusted her hands on her skirts, and descended the three steps in one casual jump. 'It is the woman who sleeps, in the tale; the wood goes on growing for a hundred years – or was it a thousand?'

'A hundred,' said Miss Pryce, descending the steps more sedately in Joanna's wake. 'Surely you remember! You heard me reading this tale to Agatha and Yvon very lately – it is Agatha's favourite at present. The princess pricks her finger on the spindle, and the curse of Alecto, of which she ought to have died, is softened by the blessing of Melpomene, so that instead she falls into a deep sleep, and the whole of her father's palace likewise. They sleep for a hundred years, whilst the wood grows up all about them, until they are freed by the bold and handsome prince who contrives, with the blessings and aid of the Lady Venus, to break through the barrier of the wood and wake the princess.'

'Was it Melpomene, Gwen?' said Joanna, screwing up her face in thought. 'I thought it was Thalia.'

'Oh, certainly, perhaps it might be,' Gwendolen agreed.

Sophie considered this in silence for some moments, and at last, turning to Roland, said, 'The resemblances are striking, I must concede.'

'But the wood,' said Roland. 'The *trees*. That is what made me think of it – that, and the terrible quiet. The prince needs the help of the Lady Venus, you see, because the trees are not merely standing in his way, but waging war against him.'

At this last Lucia, who had wandered into hearing distance

whilst Roland was speaking, looked up sharply from her fistful of wildflowers. 'You hear them?' she said. 'You are quite sure? What do they say?'

'You know it is not like that,' said Roland. He sounded rather cross. 'They do not want us here; that is all I know.'

'Roland, what—' Sophie began, but got no further before Lucia and Roland's conversation went on over and without her.

'Do not want *us* here?' said Lucia. 'Us, particularly? Or—'

'Do not want anyone,' said Roland. 'I think. That is, they wish to be left in peace. That is – truly, Lucia, you ask too much!'

To Sophie's astonishment, Lucia did not dispute this accusation, but only said, 'I am sorry.'

Roland blinked.

'These trees will not speak to me at all,' Lucia went on; Roland's eyes widened, as though this surprised him. 'I do not know why they should, in point of fact; who am I, to the trees of Lady Morgan College?'

'And why should they speak to me?' Roland demanded. 'This was a domain of women – of women *scholars* – and I am neither of those things; why in Hades should the trees speak to me, of all people? Yet they do, more or less. Plainly there is no logic or reason in the case.'

Joanna, edging close to Sophie whilst Roland and Lucia were absorbed in their debate, stretched up on tiptoe and muttered into her ear, 'I confess I do not find this tale of speaking trees more persuasive with repetition.'

'Hush, Jo,' Sophie murmured. Tredinnick and Goff had begun to swing their axes again, and she was struggling to hear anything over the din.

'But it was your blood that opened the gate,' Lucia was saying.

'You cannot deny it – indeed, you were rather preening yourself on it not two hours ago. And if the gate—'

A tremendous cracking sound, and the sharp unsettling shriek of metal striking metal.

'Your Highness,' called Mr Goff, from the top of the steps. 'We are through the door.'

Sophie hesitated – how could she leave that cryptic conversation unexplored? – but the others were surging past her and up the steps to the Library doors, and so she made haste to follow, calling a light to hover over her shoulder as she went, for beyond the splintered oaken doors lay a profound and palpable darkness.

When she would have stepped through the new-hewn doorway, however, the crossed handles of Mr Goff's axe and Mr Tredinnick's halted her in her tracks. 'Begging your pardon, ma'am,' said the latter, 'but you'll not be going first. Anything might be lurking in there.'

'But—'

'Consider our poor nerves, ma'am,' said Goff, politely but firmly, 'and imagine our fate at your honoured father's hands if anything should befall you that we might have prevented through *perfectly reasonable* precautions.'

The heavy stress which he laid upon those two words, Sophie felt, was entirely superfluous to requirements – but it was true that she ought not to force them into such an equivocal position.

'Very well,' she said, graciously enough; 'I concede to you the honour of first setting foot in the pages of history. Give me that lantern,' she added, in a more prosaic tone.

Mr Tredinnick handed it to her, and she chivvied her magelight into it and handed it back.

'I thank you, ma'am,' said Mr Goff, with a little bow which Sophie strongly suspected of irony.

'I beg you will not think of it,' said Sophie.

The two guardsmen turned their faces to the ruined door and, moving confidently but cautiously, in single file, stepped over the threshold. Sophie and the others crowded around the opening – torn into the wall of ivy like a wound – and watched them, or their magelight lantern, away into the deep, dark stillness.

CHAPTER XXIV

In Which Gwendolen Makes a Discovery

After what seemed a very long time – though judging by the movement of the sun, it was no more than a quarter-hour at the most – Goff and Tredinnick emerged once more from the gaping doorway, looking very sober and rather wide of eye, but otherwise none the worse for their experience.

'If it please Your Highness,' said Tredinnick. His jaw tightened briefly. 'There seems no immediate danger within.'

'But?' said Roland, after a moment.

Tredinnick hesitated, and exchanged a worried look with his comrade.

'But there is something within,' said Goff at last, 'that . . . something that may pose a risk to your safety, sir, and to that of the Princess.'

Lucia saw the lift of Sophie's chin and repressed a sigh. Did Sophie's guardsmen, after so many years' close observation, understand her so little?

Then, glancing from Sophie to the two men who stood upon the steps, she saw the expression of betrayal which Tredinnick was directing at Goff – Goff who was, Lucia remembered now, a countryman of Sophie and Joanna's, born and raised in the province of Breizh. For the first time it came home to her that Roland's kingdom might be as rife with shifting and conflicting loyalties as her own, and as difficult to navigate.

'What thing, Mr Goff?' Sophie enquired.

The two guardsmen shifted from foot to foot and looked anywhere but at Sophie or each other. Goff was again the first to yield to Sophie's expectant silence: 'Not . . . not so much a *thing*, ma'am,' he said, speaking miserably to his boots. 'More of a feeling. Er. A feeling of dread.'

Sophie pressed her lips together briefly. 'I see. Mr Tredinnick, do you concur?'

Tredinnick raised his head. 'Yes, ma'am,' he said.

'That does not seem very dangerous,' muttered Gwendolen Pryce.

The next step in the dance was entirely predictable. 'Mr Goff,' Sophie said, 'give me that lantern, if you please.'

Less predictably, Goff descended the steps and did so. He said something to Sophie as the lantern changed hands, which made her smile very slightly and Joanna, overhearing, produce and quickly muffle a snort of astonished laughter.

'Sophie,' said Roland, 'I do not think you ought—'

Sophie spun to face him, eyes blazing, and – as though actuated all by the same impulse – Lucia, Joanna, and Gwendolen hurriedly converged to separate them.

'Sophie, there is no need for that,' Lucia heard Joanna say soothingly, behind her, as she herself caught Roland by the shoulders and said, low and urgent, 'I beg of you, Roland, do not antagonise your sister.'

'I am not *antagonising* her,' he protested, sinking his voice to match hers. 'I am attempting to keep her safe.'

'To hear you,' said Lucia, 'one would think you did not know Sophie at all. Truly, Roland, I can think of nothing more likely to antagonise her than an attempt to shield her from the consequences of her own decisions, in the course of an expedition under her command.'

Roland's brows drew together and his lips pursed up at her military terminology, or perhaps at its use in connexion with his sister. 'Do you have *any notion*, Lucia MacNeill,' he said, vehement through gritted teeth, 'what my fate will be at my father's hands should any harm befall Sophie?'

Lucia had not the patience at present, she decided, to debate with Roland his imagined hierarchy of paternal affection. She dared a look back over her shoulder and found Sophie consulting with Goff and Tredinnick over the draughtsman's plan of the College Library which Sophie's historian friend, Gareth Evans-Hughes, had unearthed from a drawer of uncatalogued plans and charts in the library at Merlin College.

'There is no stopping her,' she said, turning back to Roland, 'short of knocking her flat and sitting on her, which I hope we can all agree to be an overreaction in this case. If you are wishful to keep your sister safe – or at any rate to be on hand to make the attempt—'

'Yes, yes,' said Roland impatiently. He shrugged out of Lucia's grip on his shoulders, caught her hand in his – she drew breath in surprise, and returned his grip with interest – and started up the steps.

* * *

'I hope we may not regret this, Jo,' Gwendolen muttered, her shoulder pressed close against Joanna's in the dark. All about them loomed silent shrouded shapes – bookcases and tables and reading-desks. Outside, the sun had been shining; here the air – as unnaturally still as in the quadrangle – was dry as paper-dust and cold as Midwinter Night.

Joanna, greatly daring, found Gwen's hand and squeezed it. 'We have done many a stupider thing,' she said, 'and lived to tell the tale. What horrors are we like to find in an abandoned library, worse than those we saw on the Ross of Mull?'

Gwendolen (who had been so brave on that dreadful night, so calm and so quick-witted) shuddered a little and pressed closer still. 'But all the same,' she said, 'Mr Goff and Mr Tredinnick are not wrong: I do feel something here, Jo, and it is most unpleasant. As though . . . as though we were not wanted.'

'That is only damp, I expect,' said Joanna stoutly.

The magelight lantern, followed closely by Roland's and Lucia MacNeill's lights, was drawing farther ahead. Gwendolen called her own small globe of magelight and sent it aloft to hover above their heads.

A pale shape, very nearly human, leapt into relief in the light of Sophie's lantern. There was a chorus of gasps and yelps – Joanna's among them – which gave way to a startled burst of laughter from the vanguard when Tredinnick, tallest of the party, held the lantern aloft to reveal a perfectly ordinary marble statue of Minerva with an owl upon one shoulder, set in a raised alcove to the left of a massive set of oaken doors.

Lucia MacNeill's light grew brighter, illuminating the doors and the large square signboard upon the rightmost, which read in large letters, *Closed Stacks*. The doors bore heavy wrought-iron handles, gracefully curving left and right.

Sophie turned to face the others, her eyes alight with a dangerous glee. 'Mr Goff!' she said. 'Opened you this door, in the course of your reconnaissance?'

'No, ma'am,' said Goff. 'In any case I should have supposed it locked.'

'We shall see, then,' said Sophie. Turning away again, she set her hand to the right-hand door-handle.

Joanna, watching with her heart hammering in her ears, saw Sophie's shoulders tense and her elbow draw sharply back an instant before Roland, Sophie, and Lucia MacNeill, in voices taut with dismay, said, 'Oh, *no.*'

It was not surprising, of course, that a college library should contain a very large number of books. Nor was it astonishing, after two centuries' neglect, that the said books should be in a distressing condition. But this was not mere neglect; this was vicious, wanton destruction. The foreboding which had pressed upon her (upon all of them, if Mr Tredinnick and Mr Goff were to be believed) since the moment of entering the building grew abruptly heavier, as though someone had thrown over her shoulders a cloak lined with lead.

For a dizzying, horrified moment, Sophie was transported back to the Master's Lodge of Merlin College as she and Gray had seen it on the night of Lord Halifax's death – a wasteland of torn and half-burnt codices, broken glass and toppled furniture, the hiss and crackle of flames, the thick air choking her – and began instinctively to look amongst the mangled books for a human victim. With an effort she wrenched herself back to the present, gently disentangled herself from Roland's hand gripping her elbow, and advanced into the wreckage of the closed stacks.

She picked her way cautiously amongst the debris, picking up objects more or less at random – here the front half of an edition of Virgil's *Eclogues*, there a single page of Cymric verse – and gently putting them down again. Puffs of dust rose underfoot at every step.

The mutilated books, the overturned chairs and tables and reading-stands, her own hands moving before her, grew blurred and indistinct; Sophie heard someone muttering, louder and louder, *Who could—how could—what monster has done such a thing?*

Only when gentle hands took hold of her shoulders, turning her away from the wreckage, and pressed her face into Lucia's shoulder, did she recognise that the outraged muttering was her own, and that she was weeping.

'I was wrong,' she said, raising her head and surveying her little company. 'I was wrong – Gray was wrong – we were all of us deluded. There is nothing left here, and we shall never be permitted to rebuild it, any of it. I am sorry to have so misled all of you, and wasted so much of your time and – and—'

Sophie turned away from Lucia and sat down hard on the filthy floor, her back against the end of a bookcase, wrapped her arms about her shins, and hid her face against her drawn-up knees. She was distantly aware that she was behaving like a thwarted child, but to have come here with such bright hopes, so have poured so much hard work and will and magick – even, quite literally, the blood from their veins – into the effort to gain access to this place, and then to find it in such a state . . .

'Sophia Marshall!'

Sophie looked up, startled – then farther up, into her sister's furious face looming above her.

'How *dare* you!' said Joanna. 'After – after *everything*, Sophie, how dare you give up, when we have come so far, only because some sheep-witted, ham-handed dolts have made a mess of a few old books!'

Gwendolen stood at Joanna's right elbow, and Roland at her left with Lucia beside him; beyond the circle of their anxious, indignant faces, Mr Goff and Mr Tredinnick hovered, inwardly debating, Sophie supposed, whether this constituted a threat of the sort against which they were meant to be protecting her, or a salutary check upon her temper.

'It is not *a few old books*, Jo!' Sophie protested. She did not trouble to keep her despair from leaking into her voice or from showing on her face. 'It is *thousands* of books – it is *all* the books – there may be some that existed nowhere else. Even to collect up all the fragments would be the work of a month, before we could begin piecing them together, to see what has been lost; and as for repairing them—!'

Lucia MacNeill dropped to her knees in the dust and debris and caught one of Sophie's hands in hers. 'A college is not its books, Sophie,' she said. 'A college is the minds and hearts and voices of its scholars – its Fellows, its students – and the knowledge they make together. This' – she tilted her head at the destruction – 'hurts my heart as it hurts yours; but a library can be rebuilt, Sophie, within as well as without.'

Sophie blinked slowly, considering this. There was a large and obvious flaw in Lucia's reasoning: at present, Lady Morgan College lacked not only books (or, at any rate, books in a condition to be read and used) but Fellows, students, librarians, servants, gardeners, patrons, tutors, and lecturers as well. And what hope had they now of discovering the secrets of the place, if even its ordinary, everyday possessions had been visited by such destruction?

'Sophie,' said Joanna again – her voice not angry now, but sharp with sudden worry. She crouched directly in front of Sophie, hands on her knees for balance, and looked searchingly into her face. 'Sophie, this is not . . . you are not missing Gray again, as you did in Alba?'

This query, at which Roland's brow furrowed in confusion, sharpened Sophie's mind as perhaps nothing else could have done at this moment. 'I,' she said, and bit her lip in concentration. 'No, I think—'

She let her eyes fall shut, reached inwards with practised ease and then, tentatively, outwards – found the thread of Gray's magick once more, and gauged the strength of her own. 'No,' she said positively, opening her eyes. 'He is far away, and, I think, going farther still, but – no.'

The exercise of seeking out her link to Gray, however, had made her senses more awake to the presence of other magicks around her, and it became clear to her now that the foreboding which had dogged all their steps since first they passed the College gate was not a product of anyone's imagination but a real and very nearly tangible thing. That it was, in fact, exactly what some long-dead mage, or mages, had meant subsequent intruders to feel.

Well, then: whoever you are – were – I decline to oblige you. Sophie smiled down at her knees. Then she turned the smile upwards and outwards, let it begin to blaze away the fog of despair in which she had been about to lose herself, and levered herself to her feet.

'My apologies for my outburst,' she said briskly, dusting her hands on her skirts. 'I shall not let it occur again.' *I hope.* 'Mr Goff – Mr Tredinnick – Ceana MacGregor – I believe we have useful work here for your troops to do; you may assign the most careful of them to begin collecting and organising all of this . . . material . . . so that it may be properly catalogued hereafter.'

'Ma'am,' said Mr Goff. Ceana MacGregor nodded.

Sophie looked about her, and found she could imagine the skewed and gaping shelves straightened, repaired and filled with books once more.

Though the mere sight of it very evidently pained her, Sophie insisted – over the protests of the others – upon a full exploration of the ruined library stacks. This proved a fortunate choice, however: the destruction, they discovered, was far less complete than had at first appeared, and they left the closed stacks greatly encouraged, to proceed to the reading rooms.

It was in the Fellows' Reading Room – once a place of ease and comfort, even luxury, to judge by the shapes of the dust-furred sofas and the array of cobwebbed bottles and decanters upon the side-board – that this strange day began to grow even stranger.

'Jo,' said Gwendolen, sending her small magelight up to hover near the ceiling, at the corner formed by the room's south and east walls.

The corner was occupied by a triangular glass-fronted curio-case, well above six feet tall, from behind whose square panes (only one of them broken, for a wonder) could be glimpsed, inter alia, a bronze knot-work buckle, several large shells, a silver welcome-cup entirely black with tarnish, and a small bust of Hypatia of Alexandria. What might be on the top of it, however, Joanna could not possibly determine.

'If you will give me a leg up,' said Gwendolen – as though they had been discussing the logistics of mounting a particularly tall horse – 'I shall be able to get it down, I think.'

'Get *what* down?' said Joanna.

'Once I have laid hands on it,' Gwendolen said patiently, 'perhaps we may discover what it is.'

Joanna, grumbling more for the look of the thing than from any genuine reluctance, took a knee and cupped her hands to boost Gwendolen up the last few inches.

The thing which had caught Gwendolen's eye proved to be a box: a perfectly ordinary oblong box, or chest – such as a lady might use to keep her jewellery in, or her love-letters – of polished wood, with brass hinges to one side and a robust lock to the other. Perfectly ordinary, that is, but that over the course of two centuries it appeared to have gathered no dust.

Joanna and Gwendolen looked at one another, and at Lucia.

'Sophie!' Joanna said. 'Come and look what Gwen has found.'

Gwendolen carried the box to the table by the vast cold hearth on the west wall and set it down very carefully, as though she feared it might burst into flame. Sophie straightened up from investigating the bottom drawer of the sideboard, and they gathered round the table, Roland and Tredinnick having set out to investigate the bindery where once on a time, according to Edwina Antonia Calixta's plan, the College's librarians had maintained and repaired their own books.

The lock resisted first Gwendolen's attempts upon it with a pair of hairpins and Joanna's paper-knife, and then Lucia's unlocking-spell, but opened with a soft *snick* when Sophie laid her hand upon it and murmured, '*Libera quod hic habeant in carcere.*'

The four of them exchanged a look of trepidation; then Sophie carefully lifted the hinged lid of the box – like the lock, the hinges seemed not to have remarked the passage of time, for they swung easily and silently.

Within, the box was lined with crimson velvet, unworn and unfaded by time, and filled with closely written pages; perched atop them, a folded and sealed letter was directed – in a flowing, exuberant hand – *To she who has succeeded in opening the box.*

They stared at it, frozen in a silence pregnant with terror and exhilaration, the length of four long breaths. Joanna could hear the others breathing – fancied, indeed, that she could hear their hearts beating, though it must be only her own pulse hammering in her ears.

Then Lucia MacNeill said, in a sort of strangled whisper, 'That will be you, then, Sophie.'

Sophie made no reply, unless her quickened breathing might be so construed.

'Ought we to read it here?' said Joanna, when the silence had again begun to stretch unbearably. 'Or take it away with us?'

'Ought we even to touch it?' said Gwendolen. 'Is it not likely to be a trap?'

She was staring at the open box, Joanna saw, like a mouse watching a cat: wary and preternaturally still, as though seeking to make herself invisible. *That is Sophie's bailiwick, Gwen; the rest of us had better not attempt it.*

'What sort of trap?' said Joanna, practically.

'It may be poisoned.' Gwendolen looked down at her, brow furrowed with worry. 'Or – or perhaps removing the letter from the box may trigger some other sort of trap, or—'

Her next horrible idea remained unspoken, however, for she broke off abruptly when Sophie reached out, picked up the letter, and broke the seal.

When – contrary to her expectation – no flash of mage-fire or magickal explosion followed, no shriek of pain or sudden swoon, Joanna relaxed minutely; from which she understood, as she had not before, how tightly she was wound. Wincing, she flexed her fingers and shifted surreptitiously from foot to foot.

There was not much else to be done: Sophie was reading the letter – if letter it was – in a tense, breathing silence, whilst everyone else watched her doing so; and though Joanna should not have hesitated, in the normal course of things, to ask importunate questions, peer round her sister's shoulder, or demand that the letter be read aloud, the present atmosphere made all of these possibilities altogether unthinkable.

She could, however, edge closer to the box, the better to peer at the topmost paper in the stack, and this she did – though very slowly, so that Sophie might not remark it.

The swooping hand was the same as that which had directed the letter, and not easily intelligible; Joanna found herself wishing that the document had been only enciphered, rather than written two centuries ago by someone now long dead, and thus impossible to interrogate. Sophie, she supposed, must often have encountered documents of similar or even less recent vintage, in the course of her studies; at any rate, though her perusal of the mysterious letter was by no means rapid, it seemed not to be giving her any particular difficulty. The documents which crossed Joanna's desk in the course of her work, by contrast, were seldom more than a month old. Not for nothing, however, had she spent so much of the past five years in translating the hurried shorthand notes of a variety of persons into legible and consistent fair copies; she had grown adept at spotting patterns, and at leaps of logic premised on nothing more than the vague shape of a word.

And the shapes of the words before her now . . .

No. Surely not.

She blinked – blinked again, hard – but having resolved the swooping whorls and decorative loops and slashes into intelligible words, she could not unsee them.

Being the true tale of the deathe and life of Edward, by the gods favour Rex Britannicus, in the VIth yr of hys reigne

attested this XVth day of May, anno XX Edw. VI R.

by his sisters—

It was a forgery, surely – it could not be what it appeared – could it? *The* death and life *of Edward* – what in Hades could that mean? Joanna's fingers itched to reach for the page, to turn it over so that she might see the next.

She glanced at Sophie, and found her gazing at the last page of the letter as if transfixed.

'Tell me I am not mad,' she said abruptly, thrusting the pages at Joanna, who was nearest. 'Look at these . . . these signs-manual, and tell me I am not mad.'

Joanna stared at it – Lucia MacNeill and Gwendolen crowded in to do the same – they exchanged incredulous glances, and stared still more.

The names were unmistakable, written in letters nearly as

high as the preceding paragraph, and each underscored with a complicated arrangement of interlocking horizontal loops:

Mathilda Julia

Edith Augusta

'Either that is the cleverest forgery I have ever seen,' said Joanna last, 'or this letter was written to you by the Princesses Regent.'

CHAPTER XXV

In Which Sophie Reads a Letter

'Must we stay here?' Roland was pacing – both irritable and irritating – an increasingly rapid circle round the Fellows' Reading Room. 'Whatever this mysterious box has to tell us, can it not be told . . . elsewhere?'

'If you cannot be still, Roland,' Joanna snapped, 'I beg you will at least be *quiet.*' She spun on one heel to address Lucia: 'Can you not knock him down and sit on him?'

Lucia had for some time been resisting a strong urge to do exactly this, not least because she was not entirely certain of succeeding. She shook her head at Joanna, who, with a small huff of impatience, turned back to Sophie. Tempers were fraying on all sides, it appeared.

I cannot knock him down and sit on him, but perhaps . . .

'Roland,' said Lucia quietly, laying a hand on his arm, when next his fretful peregrinations brought him near. He paused, turned, met her gaze; his eyes, blue as the sky at Midsummer, burnt fever-bright, and beneath her hand his arm quivered with tension.

'Can you hear it?' he said. 'It has not stopped since we set foot in this room.' In a tone as near to desperate pleading as she had ever heard from him, he repeated, '*Must* we stay here?'

Lucia heard nothing out of the ordinary – nothing but Roland's quiet near-panic and the others murmuring together as they deciphered Sophie's ancestral artefact – but it was true that the atmosphere in this room was charged as even the quadrangle, with its still air and whispering trees, had not been. *Was* there something in this place, something only Roland could hear? Were Roland's pacing, Joanna's snappish temper, Lucia's own restless anxiety, linked by something more than their strange uncertain circumstances?

'What do you hear?' she said. 'Is it . . . It is not the trees again, surely? I should hear them, I think – at least a little – if it were that.'

'No,' he said, twitching. 'Not trees. Voices . . . voices and *bells*. Why *bells*, by all the gods? Can you – are you quite sure you cannot hear them, Lucia?'

His voice had risen by now from a low murmur almost to a shout, and from behind Lucia there came a furious bellow: 'Roland, *be quiet*!'

The next moment found the five of them gaping at one another in speechless shock, and Sophie – whose bellow it had been – most staggered of all.

There is *something here*, thought Lucia grimly, *tangling us up and bending us awry.*

The question was whether that something resided here, in the College Library – and thus could be run away from – or whether it was tied to that box which only Sophie could open, or to its bizarre contents, and thus would follow them wherever they might go.

'I think,' said Sophie in a quite different voice, high and a little shaky, 'we ought perhaps to resume this conversation elsewhere.'

* * *

366

In the still sun-dappled air of the quadrangle, the trees shivered and rustled, and Lucia and Roland – walking arm in arm, pressed close together, though they seemed not to know it – looked anxiously about them, and started at small sounds.

Sophie carried the box. It seemed to grow heavier and heavier – it was only that her arms were not so strong as she had thought, she told herself firmly – and she was reminded of Gray's midnight misadventures in Oxford long ago, of his description of Henry Taylor cradling the teakwood box which, as Sophie and her friends discovered much later, had held a beating human heart to be used in the Professor's arcane poison. Might the contents of this quite different box, she wondered, prove equally deadly?

They collected their much-reduced bodyguard at the College gate, to which – eventually – they had been persuaded to return and wait, in case of inquisitive passers-by. Mr Tredinnick's eyes widened at the sight of them; Mr Goff and Ceana MacGregor seemed disposed to ask questions but were stared into temporary silence by Joanna.

The return journey to the Dragon and Lion was slow and subdued, as though all of them felt – as Sophie certainly did – far more drained by their afternoon's labours than the nature of those labours warranted.

She surveyed her troops, as she fancied a general might, and made a decision.

'The baths first,' she said firmly, 'and then dinner, and then this horrible box.'

'*In the sixth year of our brother Edward's reign*,' Sophie read, peering down at the manuscript page on the table before her, *a sickness came upon him, which, for the first time, all the skill and all the art of the Royal Healers proved powerless to amend. Then as now, the greatest threat to our kingdom was that of retribution from Ferdinand of Aragon and his allies amongst the other Iberian kings, on behalf of his daughter, the first Queen Catherine; a strong hand on the reins was, and remains, necessary to Britain's survival.*

Our father Henry was – like his patron Jove – impetuous, headstrong, and apt at times to be ruled by the bodily passions, but—

'Jove's blood!' Roland exclaimed, starting up in his chair. 'Do you suppose they dared speak of him so when he was alive?'

'If they did,' said Joanna, sotto voce, 'it was no more than he deserved.'

Too restless to sit still, she had eschewed all of the available seats in favour of loitering before the window, only half seeing the bustle of the inn-yard below. Gwendolen, standing just behind her left shoulder, prodded her reprovingly in the ribs; Joanna ignored her.

'I expect,' said Sophie dryly, 'that had either of the Princesses been in the habit of insulting their father to his face during his lifetime, they should not later have found themselves among their brother's Regents. If I may continue?'

—but he was not a fool; indeed, he possessed both a formidable intellect and an unparalleled grasp of political strategy, though all too often overridden by less noble concerns. In divorcing Catherine of Aragon, he did not act in ignorance of the likely consequences but, rather, in defiance thereof, and in full confidence of Britain's capacity to defend her own interests.

For this reason, when the full consciousness of his impending demise came upon him, he took great care in dictating the terms under which his successor – our brother Edward – should be guided during the years of his minority.

In another kingdom, perhaps, or in other circumstances, Henry might simply have named one of his daughters – both intelligent women; both thoroughly educated in history, politics, and the theory and practice of magick; the elder already of an age to rule, and the younger very nearly – as his successor. Both Eire and Alba, for example, have from time to time been ruled by women of exceptional strength of character, and neither, we feel bound to note, has been rendered a less formidable foe thereby.

Lucia MacNeill produced a small, appreciative chuckle.

Our father, however, Sophie continued, *knew such a course to be politically impossible in Britain, and therefore, in the interests of averting consequences which might well have escalated to the point of civil war, chose what seemed to him the next best course, by appointing both of us – together with Edward Seymour, Earl of Hertford (later Duke of Somerset) and brother of our late stepmother Genevieve Seymour, and Hugh Dudley, Earl of Warwick (later Duke of Northumberland) – as Regents to the child Edward.*

If you, unknown and yet-unborn scion of the House of Tudor, have any knowledge of history, you will of course know what next befell: the attempt by Somerset to install himself as Lord Protector, and of Northumberland to blow up the spark of conflict with Aragon into the full flames of war; their trial, conviction, and execution on charges of high

treason, and our unexpected victory in remaining Edward's
sole regents until his majority; Edward's successive betrothals,
and their various failures; his illness at the age of fifteen, and
the struggles for dominance which ensued; his marriage in the
following year, and – the Lady Juno willing – the tale of his
descendants, down to your own day. What you cannot know –
what no one presently living knows, excepting our two selves,
nor ever will know from our lips whilst we live – is the true
tale of that illness. This we set down here, both as a caution
for others who may suffer the same temptations, and as a
protest against that other precaution which Edward, against
our counsel, intends to take, that of casting into perpetual
oblivion that seat of learning which fed and nurtured us, and
many another young woman of intellect and spirit, and thus
gave us both the knowledge of a means to save him, and the
audacity to make the attempt.

We intend no disloyalty to our brother, to our King, or to
our kingdom. Indeed, in every particular we have acted from
a determination to safeguard both the King's person and the
kingdom itself.

'Yes, but what in Hades did they *do?*' Joanna had spent a great
deal of time, these past several years, in cultivating patience; but
this aggravated avoidance of the point – and perhaps, too, she
grudgingly conceded, whatever mysterious current had so affected
all of them whilst they stood about in the College Library – was
making her skin crawl and her gut clench and her fingers twitch,
not only in impatience but in something very like dread.

'If you will listen instead of interrupting,' said Sophie, 'perhaps
we shall all find out.'

Joanna turned from the window and glared at her, but made a show of pressing her lips tight shut.

If you now hold in your hands this manuscript, and have read so far as this—

'Then you have the patience of Prometheus,' muttered Roland, and Joanna, Gwendolen, and Lucia erupted in entirely inappropriate laughter.

Sophie, frowning, raised her voice and overrode them:

—and have read so far as this, then you have done what Edward and his Privy Council (from which we have long been banished, for the offence of keeping the royal sceptre of Britain safely in our brother's hand) are bent upon preventing: you have opened the gates of Lady Morgan College, gained entrance to the Library, and succeeded in opening the box into which this manuscript will shortly be sealed. We commend your perseverance; we tremble at your temerity. May the gods protect and aid you in confronting whatever dire peril has led you here.

Sophie turned over the page from which she had been reading; before she could go on to the next, Roland said, 'Why should they suppose that we – that is, that the reader of their words – should be in dire peril? I mean to say – of course there is danger to the kingdom, but—'

'Why indeed?' echoed Lucia, stepping in (to Roland's visible consternation) before he could further entangle himself. 'After all, Sophie, you did not suppose any such peril existed when you conceived your idea. And – I am sorry to say it, but so it is – we should none of us be here at all, had your father given you leave to go where the true peril is, or appears to be.'

'One does ask oneself these questions.' Sophie, looking grim, lowered her gaze to the paper before her.

> *Know, then, that this last illness of Edward's did not come near to killing him, as it had done more than once before, but killed him indeed; that we, his sisters, bargained with the gods for his life, and that the bargain we struck gave back his spirit to the world of flesh and blood, in exchange for the lives we should have had, as wives and mothers. Our life's blood flows now in his veins; our three hearts beat in time; we have taken his ills upon ourselves, and our lives are bound up in his. When he takes ship for Elysium at last, we shall go with him – or, as it may be, shall go down to the depths of Tartarus, as punishment for our desperate arrogance, in thwarting the will or whim of the gods.*

> *What we did was done for the best, as we have said, for Edward had no heir – nor even a wife – at the time of his death, and though already he showed promise as a shrewd and even-handed ruler, with much of our father's wit but little of his grosser appetites, we could not predict (or, rather, could predict all too well) what scoundrel, fool, or wastrel amongst the twisted limbs of our family tree might be seized upon to succeed him – or what pretenders might emerge from Bourgogne or Acquitaine, or even from Aragon, to press their suits by claim of law or, worse, by force upon our kingdom's body.*

'What a very unappealing metaphor,' said Lucia, wincing.
'Quite,' said Sophie.

Nevertheless, Edward, upon being told of our great feat and sacrifice when he came of age, declared it a crime against his person (for being in such dire straits, we had not sought to know his wishes, nor sought his consent to what we meant to do) and against the gods (whose will it had clearly been, he said, that he should die on that day, at that hour), and exiled us from his Court. We have taken refuge here, at Lady Morgan College, which has extended to us her protection and welcomed us back within her hallowed walls – but, as we know in our heart of hearts, only so long as nothing is known of our crime, our sacrifice. Edward of Britain and the Fellows of Lady Morgan College agree on very few points, but on the subject of the ancient magick of blood and stone, their views are both alike distressingly rigid.

'"The ancient magick of blood and stone,"' Lucia repeated thoughtfully. 'What can that mean, do you suppose?'

'I have not the least idea,' said Sophie. 'I must say that this is quite the longest and almost the least useful description of a magickal working I have read in my life; the Princesses Regent appear to have modelled their prose style on that of Xanthus Marinus.'

In case Edward should carry out his scheme to consign Lady Morgan College to oblivion – as at present we think very likely – we feel duty-bound to record, for posterity if for no other purpose, what the transgression was that has led to the dissolution of his College and the revocation of its Royal Charter. Had we understood at the time that we should be sacrificing not only our own future, but those of the thousands of young women who might have passed through the gates into this place of learning, of knowledge, of seeking after wisdom, we should have acted, not differently, but with infinitely more regret for this consequence of our choice, which falls not on ourselves but on others. Notwithstanding these regrets, however, it is our considered opinion that to permit our brother's early death to open the way for disorder and strife in the kingdom we love as fiercely as he does himself were the worse betrayal of the two.

Who can say how we may be remembered, if at all? But Edward VI shall be remembered as a good and wise king, and thus we shall have our posterity.

Sophie looked up once more, blinking owlishly. 'And that,' she said, 'is all there is of it. As well that we have no need to replicate their grand mysterious working, for they have told us nothing whatever about it!'

'Sophie, they were writing a deathbed confession, not reporting the results of an experiment for the *Transactions*,' said Lucia MacNeill, much more gently than Joanna could have managed.

'And, as you say,' said Roland, 'we have no need of such a working.'

The four women exchanged a long, meaning look, but made him no reply.

'At any rate,' said Joanna, when the silence threatened to grow impossibly long, 'we have solved your mystery, Sophie. Only, I do not suppose that we ought to make this tale public.'

'We should certainly put paid to any notion of restoring Lady Morgan College, if we did so,' said Sophie dryly.

'*Did* the Princesses Regent die along with their brother?' said Lucia.

'Oh, indeed,' said Gwendolen. 'It is a well-known tale. King Edward perished in the sinking of the frigate *Titania*, en route from Portsmouth to Honfleur, and his sisters on the same day, of a fever, in the infirmary of the Temple of Minerva at Bath – they were old women by then, for Edward's reign was a long one. And now I suppose we know why.'

A shiver seemed to pass through all of them, then, though the day was warm and the inn's sunny sitting-room, with its south-facing windows warmer still.

There was a long, thoughtful silence, until at last Sophie said, in a small voice, 'Suppose Lady Morgan College *is* cursed? Suppose the Princesses Regent *did* thwart the will of some god or gods, and were punished accordingly? Ought we to . . . ought we to interfere?'

'*Think*, Sophie,' said Joanna, in some exasperation. 'If, as their confession claims, they bargained with the gods for their brother's life, then the worst that can be said of them, in that respect, is that perhaps they sought to play one god or goddess off against another, which I daresay most of us have done more than once; it is not a greater crime in this case, surely, simply because the gods in question happened to take notice.

'And, besides,' she added, 'have not whichever god or gods sought Edward's death, if so any of them did, had ample opportunities to kill off his descendants? There have been Tudor kings on the throne of Britain almost without interruption since the time of Henry the Great's father; that does not seem to me a sign of divine disfavour.'

'No-o,' Sophie conceded, her brow crinkling in earnest thought. 'But that this working of theirs was so great a secret that even in confessing to it they should avoid describing how it was done – does that not suggest something very . . . very wrong? Or, at any rate, very dangerous?'

'Or possibly both,' said Joanna, who did not disagree with her sister's analysis – only her conclusions.

'There is another possibility, of course,' said Lucia thoughtfully.

'Oh?'

'Have you never, in making your own notes on a particular working, used some form of shorthand to refer to another working, which you need not explain in detail because you know it well already, or have made fuller note of it elsewhere?'

'Certainly I have,' said Sophie, 'but I should not do so if I were making notes for someone else!'

'Not even if the working referred to were one which that someone else might also be expected to know perfectly well?' Lucia countered. 'That is, if you were to write me out instructions for a sleeping-draught, I daresay you should not begin them with half a page's worth of explaining how to call fire to boil the water?'

'No,' said Sophie again. 'So, then, your theory is that this . . .' She shuffled through the pages in her hands. 'This *ancient magick of blood and stone* is – was – common knowledge amongst . . . whom, exactly?'

'The Fellows of Lady Morgan College, to begin with,' said Joanna, 'as we are told they disapproved of it. They must have known of it in order to disapprove, though of course it does not follow that they *understood* it.'

Sophie chuckled darkly. 'As a particular contingent of the Fellows of Merlin have lately demonstrated,' she said. 'Though, in fairness to them, I am no longer altogether persuaded that *I* understand what we are about in this business.'

'That may be,' said Joanna. 'But I cannot think that, because one pair of female mages once overstepped the bounds of magickal ethics, they – we – must therefore all be forced to piece together what education we can from scraps and fragments, for lack of any organised alternative. After all, to hear Gray tell it, Merlin men have created magickal disasters enough, without their College's being closed and forgotten in punishment for their mistakes.'

'*That* is certainly true,' said Sophie. 'Indeed, not even treason on the part of a Senior Fellow—'

She broke off at the sound of brisk knocking on the sitting-room door, started a little, and began gathering the papers into a stack and stuffing them back into the box. When she had closed the lid and stowed the box away under the table, she snapped her fingers to release her wards upon the room, and called, '*Quo vadis?*'

'An express is come from London for Mrs Marshall.' It was the voice of the innkeeper himself – he who but rarely climbed the stairs on his twisted leg – and Joanna sprang up from her chair to cross the room and open the door.

'Our apologies for having kept you waiting,' she said, and thanked him.

Even before she had closed the door and turned back to the others, Sophie was at her shoulder, reaching for the letter in her hand. Its source was perfectly evident – it was directed in Mr Fowler's hand and bore Kergabet's personal seal – but whether it contained good news or ill was impossible to guess.

Sophie sank down into the nearest available chair, her heart pounding, and broke the seal on Sieur Germain's letter. As she unfolded it, a smaller enclosure fell out, enciphered in a more careful version of Gray's large untidy hand. Which to read first? Sieur Germain's letter was not enciphered, and thus might be read quickly; but a message from Gray . . . !

In the end she could not bear the suspense, and read her

brother-in-law's missive straight through before setting her mind to the task of deciphering her husband's. Neither was long. Sieur Germain wished her to know that Gray had been safe and in one piece when last heard from, but was intending to go into the Duchies in search of the conspirators and Amelia; he thanked her and Joanna once again for the information they had forwarded; and he wished to be told at once should they run across any more.

Then, the first alarm over – *safe and in one piece* might conceal a multitude of hurts, but it was enough to be going on with – she smoothed out the even briefer note from Gray and studied it. He had scratched in the numerals of the date at the top, very small: *That was Mercuriday, and therefore* . . .

'Sophie!' said Joanna, peering over her shoulder. 'You have not *memorised* all the cipher keys?'

'Why not?' Sophie did not look up; the deciphered message was taking shape, and she could not spare the time to argue with her sister. 'There are not so very many. It is no different from getting Greek noun declensions by heart. And it was you who said I must learn to encipher my own letters, Jo.'

Am going carefully, the message read; *the regiment will have a means of finding me.* She smiled at his use of her own words, then said, very low, 'But going where?'

PART FOUR

Orléans

CHAPTER XXVI

In Which Gray Makes
a New Acquaintance

Three days into his journey to the soi-disant Emperor's court, in the company of Monsieur Durand of the Temple of Ceres, Gray had yet to settle in his own mind the question of his companion's motives. Had he seen through Gray's Angevin incognito and pegged him as a spy? Had he, on the contrary, been taken in by it, and seen Gray as a useful recruit to his master's cause? Was he, too, reserving judgement, awaiting some revealing word or act which should sway him in one direction or the other?

And was it his business, truly, to quarter the countryside in search of unemployed scholar-mages whom he might tempt into vowing their service to a man who was, at least at present, Emperor of nothing and nowhere?

From the first their conversation had been subtly guarded; Durand was not inclined to loquacity, and what he did say was not notably revealing. But he had said that the Emperor was gathering scholar-mages to his court; Gray, for his part, played the eccentric scholar-mage to the hilt, discoursing at length on the theory and practice of illusion-spells and quoting all the dullest authorities he could think of, whenever an opportunity offered.

Durand, he learnt, possessed only the most rudimentary magickal talent – capable of calling light and fire, and of small summonings, and no more than that – but he claimed other powers granted by his patron goddess, including that of blessing farmers' crops on her behalf.

Being a priest of Ceres in the countryside, moreover, Durand could command food and lodging gratis, or, rather, in return for blessings and divinations rather than coin, which at any rate spared Gray's increasingly thin purse, though he salved his conscience by trotting out his best mending-spells for the benefit of their hosts. They rode briskly, and soon they were threading their way between one lord's encamped troops and another's, approaching a great walled city on the bank of what proved to be the River Loire.

The city was not under siege, whatever the appearances, Durand assured him; these were the Emperor's own liege-men, gathering here to march with him upon the King of Britain. Gray, lost in frantic calculations (how far was he now from Colonel Dubois' regiment and Tremblay's mages with their finding-spells? How soon, as the owl flew, could he reach them with a message?), replied somewhat at random.

The banner flying from the central tower of the castle keep bore a familiar-unfamiliar blazon: on a crimson field, three vaguely triangular flowerlike emblems in white – the arms of Orléans! *Yes, now I see* – surmounted by three fleurs-de-lys and what looked very like a Roman eagle.

'The banner of the New Empire of Gaul,' said Durand grandly.

Once past the sentries and the walls – thanks to the countersign supplied by Durand – Gray was conducted to the castle keep, surrendered Tonnerre to the ministrations of a groom, and was himself handed over to an unsmiling chatelaine accompanied by two pages. She took in his travel-worn clothing, his dishevelled hair, his general air of road-weariness, and burst into a rapid stream of orders; Gray was borne off to the baths, his clothing was taken away to be laundered, and the rest of his possessions vanished up a staircase 'to the mages' quarters'.

Gray saw them go with considerable trepidation.

Two hours later, however, scrubbed, shaved and barbered, dressed in clothes which, if they did not quite fit him, at least were not caked in the mud of every road, track, and farmer's field between Ivry-sur-Eure and Orléans, he was conducted to a small, bare cubicle – almost entirely like a prisoner's cell, but for possessing clean bedding on the narrow bed, a window out onto the keep's central courtyard, and an open doorway – where he found his saddle-bags slung over the foot of the bed and his own clothes, still warm from the laundress's iron, hung up on pegs on the opposite wall. The saddle-bags appeared not to have been tampered with, though of course a man who was collecting mages might have at his disposal more than one means of effecting a search.

If I am to be kept prisoner again, Gray reflected, *at any rate I shall be kept comfortably this time.*

The notion was no more appealing for that, however.

Yet another page appeared shortly thereafter to conduct him into the presence of the great man.

'You are Monsieur Guy Marais of Poitiers?'

At first glance, Henri-François, Duc d'Orléans and self-styled Emperor of Gaul, was not much to look at – a small man, dark of hair and eyes, clad in buckskin breeches, gleaming boots, and a blue velvet coat adorned with a frankly absurd array of gold braid, and lounging in a massive chair of ornate design which made him appear smaller still – and certainly did not look as though he should inspire terror. The tense shimmering feeling of the air all about them, however, told a different tale altogether; this man fairly radiated power – both magickal and otherwise – and was accustomed to use it without scruple or compunction.

'I am, Your Imperial Majesty,' said Gray. He had thought the address absurd, when Durand instructed him in how to address the Emperor *so that you may not disgrace yourself, or me,* and he thought it so still – what was this man Emperor of, after all, but some thousands of men and a few square miles of town? – but not by any betraying twitch of lip or eyebrow did he show it.

'And you are a mage?'

'I am, sir.'

Henri-François d'Orléans sat back in his chair – or, rather, Gray decided, his throne – and studied him, narrow-eyed, in a manner which suggested that he was looking beneath the surfaces of things. 'There is vast potential here, certainly,' he murmured, after a moment; and then, shifting his gaze to Gray's face, 'Show me.'

Gray blinked. 'Is there,' he said, 'any particular working which you should like to see demonstrated? Sir?'

Orléans waved a careless hand, but his gaze on Gray perceptibly sharpened. 'All those of which you are capable,' he said.

Take care what you ask this man for, thought Gray, ruefully. He did not mean, of course, to reveal *everything* of which he was capable; shape-shifting was too distinctive a working to risk, and no scholar-mage such as he was claiming to be would be expected to have a store of offensive spells at the ready, though some might be capable of a shielding-spell or two.

384

He began by calling an ordinary globe of magelight, then split it into two, then four, and sent them to spin in a circle overhead: a foolish trick, entertainment for children. He asked for a candle and called fire to light it, working as neatly and precisely as he knew how, then drew raindrops from the air (fortunately rather damp) to put it out again. Then summoning-spells: the book from the top of the stack at the Emperor's left hand, then the embroidered handkerchief which one of the Emperor's attendants had just slipped into his pocket. He worked an illusion-spell to create a facsimile of Charles Durand's hat – the *catch*, the necessary clue to distinguish illusion from reality, a sprig of bright orange forget-me-not tucked over one ear. He set strong wards about himself, the Emperor, and his attendants, and invited them all to try whether they could pass through them.

To his secret dismay, Orléans – though none of the others – could, and did, brushing at his shoulders as though sweeping aside strands of cobweb clinging to his coat.

This man is more powerful even than I feared. Had he sprung a trap from which he should not be capable of escape? *We shall see . . .*

'A promising display,' said Orléans at last.

Gray bowed.

'Walk with me a little, Guy Marais of Poitiers.'

Gray, beginning to be sorry he had ever left London, followed him – up to the battlements, as it proved, whence they could see the great River Loire, the great bridge spanning it to give access to the city from the south, the wide flat vista spread out all about them.

'My legions,' said Orléans, his expansive gesture taking in the thousands, tens of thousands, of men encamped outside the walls to the east, north, and west.

'If I may be permitted an observation, sir,' said Gray mildly, 'you appear to be preparing for war.'

Orléans turned slightly, leaning one elbow on the battlement, and gave him a long look. 'Tell me, Monsieur Marais – where have you been travelling of late, that you should only now have arrived at this conclusion?'

Gray attempted a self-deprecating laugh but was conscious of its not succeeding very well. 'My pursuits and those of kings and armies do not often intersect,' he said. 'I confess that when I accepted Monsieur Durand's invitation to be presented to his patron, I did not expect to find myself in the midst of a military campaign.'

'All Gallia is at war at present, Monsieur Marais,' said Orléans gravely, 'or soon will be. For centuries we have fought amongst ourselves, when we ought to have made common cause against our common foes, to recapture the lands lost to Rome and build a new empire.'

Gray swallowed. 'I see,' he said. 'Given such vast and well-equipped armies as you appear to have mustered, however, I confess I do not see what need you have of scholar-mages in your war of empire.'

'*Our* war,' Orléans corrected. How could so soft-spoken a man project such menace? 'I am only the gods' instrument in this matter.'

'The gods of Rome,' Gray said, testing a hypothesis.

'The great and true gods,' said Orléans, confirming it.

Perhaps this may explain his appeal to Appius Callender, thought Gray; like not a few other persons of his class and education, Callender was, or had been, conspicuously dismissive of the local gods whose worship was so much a part of the lives of, for example, his tenant farmers. Though, for the matter of that, flattery and

386

other sops to his self-consequence might explain it equally well. *The mystery is Callender's appeal to him.*

'Nevertheless—'

'Julius Caesar,' said Orléans, 'by the gift of the gods, was a mage of great talent and exemplary skill, by which means he was able to wrest lands and peoples from lesser, undeserving gods, to bring them the gift of the Pax Romana, and so merited the title he bore in life and the godhood he was granted thereafter.'

Gray tried to look as though the connexion between his query and this unprompted and oddly tilted (not to say wildly inaccurate) lecture on Roman history were perfectly clear to him.

'Julius Caesar, Divus Iulius, died at the hands of a conspiracy of traitors' – *as King Henry nearly did, at the hands of Callender and his friends*, thought Gray – 'and in time the empire he built passed into the hands of those whom the gods had not chosen, and thence into decline and irrelevance. But the Roman people – we citizens of the old empire, made worthy by our allegiance to the great gods of Rome – can build a new empire, can reconquer the lost lands, which now are throwing away the power of their prayers and offerings on small, unworthy gods, and create a new Pax Romana for their peoples.'

By killing those peoples' own gods, or those who serve them? Not even the mad emperor Nero ever conceived such a monstrous idea.

Gray was too much appalled to speak (though not too much to wonder what in Hades this man was about, to be spouting these mad ideas to a perfect stranger of whose loyalties he knew almost nothing); fortunately, his companion swept on unheeding: 'The histories tell us that Caesar's sorcerer-centuries were the key to his success in the field; less well known is the key to the sorcerer-centuries themselves: that to every sorcerer in the field were linked two more behind the line of battle – his reserves – to strengthen him and replenish his magick. The barbarians thought them invincible, and often they had only to be seen to take the field in order to win their battles.'

He smiled in a manner that chilled Gray to his bones. 'You wished to know what use I have for scholar-mages? I have built a new sorcerer-century, and am building another, and my sorcerers need reserves.'

'Linked,' said Gray, now fighting a strong urge to leap off the battlements, shift, and fly away – or, as was far more likely, shift and plummet to his death in a hail of arrows. 'Linked, how?'

He could imagine it, he thought, far more easily than this man suspected – a bond like his link with Sophie, but drawing all one way.

'Oh, you understand well enough what I am speaking of, I think,' said Orléans, as though in reply.

Gray controlled a startled exclamation: a reader of thoughts, or a seer of magick? Either was dismaying, in the circumstances. Upon further thought, Gray decided that the latter was most likely; had Orléans truly been capable of hearing his thoughts, he should long since have been clapped in irons, at the very least.

'We need not go so far at present, however,' said Orléans, in what he perhaps imagined to be a reassuring tone. 'Come – you shall see what we are building here.'

Gray could think of few things he desired less, but he had been given a task, and he meant to carry it out. What he had expected to be the most difficult aspect of this ill-advised operation – to persuade the men whom he had helped to convict of murder and attempted regicide that he had decided to throw in his lot with them – took on a rather different aspect, now that he understood what fate awaited them. How had Orléans persuaded them to consent to it? *No — surely they have been tricked, misled, coerced.*

And Amelia — what in Hades has Amelia to do with this mess?

'Certainly, sir,' he said.

The first surprise was that all of them appeared quite contented — even pleased — with their lot. What Orléans called *the mages' work-room* was vast, bright, and warmly sunlit, and the dozens of men in it (they were all men) were engaged in perfectly ordinary pursuits, from the purely scholarly to the more practical — one fellow was distilling some disturbingly bright green solution in a series of alembics, many were reading, and several were debating good-naturedly the merits of several disparate spells of concealment. One or two appeared to have dozed off in their armchairs. Might any of these be Kergabet's missing agents? Impossible to say.

Not one, so far as Gray could determine, was at present working any sort of magick. The atmosphere was busy and cheerful, like . . . *like the nursery at Grosvenor Square, in fact.* Strangest of all was the fact that not one of them took the slightest notice of their master or his companion.

Gray tucked these thoughts away for later contemplation.

He picked out Callender and the healer Lord Spencer almost at once, and he thought he could guess to what employment Orléans had put Taylor and Woodville, strong young men trained in offensive and defensive magicks. What had become of Lord Wrexham, Queen Edwina's brother — the one member of the conspiracy, absent the late Viscount Carteret, entirely without magickal talent — was less easy to guess, but of course wherever he was he should not be in this room. More puzzling was the absence of Lord Merton, erstwhile Fellow of King's College, Oxford, and certainly a mage of considerable power. Perhaps, despite his age, Orléans meant to put him in the field?

Orléans ushered Gray out of the workroom again. 'A thing of beauty, is it not?' he said happily. 'Nothing can disturb them when they are busy about their work. But you, I think, will wish to see the other side of the coin. You are young and strong, and if I do not mistake, you have hidden depths; should you choose to join us, your place will be in the field, not in the workroom.'

Did Gray imagine the sinister ring to that *should you choose*? He rolled his left shoulder, testing its range of motion, and was unspeakably relieved to feel no unusual twinge of pain. *I can fly if I must, then. That is well.*

They found the Emperor's sorcerer-century – not quite a century, in fact, though more than a half-century – conducting manoeuvres in a large flagstone courtyard. Behind them – in the midst of a group of other young ladies seated on a bench along the courtyard's far wall, all watching the mages whilst hemming, or pretending to hem, some long strip of white linen – was Amelia Callender.

CHAPTER XXVII

In Which Sophie Receives a Deputation

The excavation of the library continued through the next several days. Ceana MacGregor ruthlessly organised her forces into salvage and triage parties, depending on their skill with letters and languages, as a result of which the work progressed more quickly than any of the rest had dared hope.

Lucia and Roland took charge of collating texts in Latin and Français, Sophie and Evans-Hughes of those in English and Cymric, and Master Alcuin, recruited for the cause over dinner at the Dragon and Lion, of those in Greek.

Joanna and Gwendolen, for their part, were charged with cataloguing the results of the work of everybody else. They pitched their camp in the library's tiny map-room, whose contents were in comparatively pristine condition. In the intervals of receiving more-or-less complete codices to catalogue, they took out and examined the maps and charts; there were hundreds of these, of which, by the afternoon of the third day, they had examined perhaps five dozen.

'I do not suppose they are much good for any but an historian,' said Gwendolen. She was gazing thoughtfully at a large, intricately decorated map of the Iberian peninsula – at least four centuries out of date. 'But how beautiful some of them are!'

'Not this one,' said Joanna, drawing out a small map of Britain and the adjacent Duchies, badly foxed, which had somehow adhered to the back of a larger one. 'It cannot ever have been as beautiful as yours, there, but it has certainly nothing at all to recommend it now!'

They spread it out, nevertheless, and studied it, standing side by side at the sturdy table. This room was very nearly private, if, as now, one stood out of sight from the half-open door; Joanna dared to lean her shoulder into Gwendolen's, and to tilt up her face to kiss her friend's cheek. Gwendolen tamped down a smile, and nudged Joanna's shoulder in return.

'What on earth *is* it?' she said, after a moment. 'It looks very old – older even than that Iberian one.'

'Yes, I should think it may be,' Joanna agreed.

No well-supplied court cartographer had drawn this map. The rough and ready lines, the cramped script, suggested a military man working in the field, marking out rivers and roads and waggon-tracks, the ponds that might serve to water cavalry and pack-horses, the villages and farms where supplies might be replenished and officers quartered at need, the obstacles and fortifications that must be taken into account in planning and executing a military campaign. Borders had been drawn and then scratched out, till in some long-contested territories – along the River Loire, for example – the map was a palimpsest.

Joanna searched the map for a date, for the name of a king, for any indication of its age, and found none, but the borders of Britain shown upon it – those uppermost, and most recently drawn – were those of the time of Henry the Great, not vastly different from their own.

'What are those red . . . things?' said Gwendolen, leaning close and pointing with one forefinger. 'Here, and along here, and there?'

'I have not the least idea.' Joanna bent closer, too, and peered at them. 'Fortifications, perhaps – the way they are placed suggests it, there along the border of Breizh with Anjou.'

'Well, perhaps. But look there—'

Joanna did. That spit of land protruding from the Breizhek coastline, south-west of Gwened on the Gulf of Morbihan, was surely Kiberon; which, if she did not greatly err, put that oddly placed grouping of red marks – much the largest, for the rest were single or in pairs – square amongst the Stones of Karnag.

'How peculiar,' she said, almost to herself.

'Jo,' said Gwendolen then, fingertips gentle on Joanna's wrist. 'Jo, look at this.'

In one corner of the map, half obscured by a dark stain which might have been anything from strong tea to human blood, was drawn an aggressively straight-sided rectangle, filled to the edges, in an entirely different hand from that which had labelled the map's cities and provinces, with Greek.

'*Not* Greek,' said Gwendolen. 'At least, I think not.'

Greek but not Greek. That rings a bell . . .

Joanna fetched Master Alcuin away from his stacks of dismembered codices and stood shifting from foot to foot whilst he peered at the blotched letters through a magnifying glass and hummed interestedly.

'Not Greek,' he confirmed at last, looking up. 'We have seen this trick before, Miss Joanna, have we not? Some other tongue set down using Greek rather than Roman characters—'

'But, Master Alcuin, what does it *say*?'

He chuckled. 'Patience, my dear,' he said. 'I shall transcribe it for you, and then we shall see.'

Gwendolen fetched him pen and paper, and Joanna a four-legged stool, and they settled down to watch.

To Joanna's chagrin, the message taking shape under Master Alcuin's pen made no more sense in Roman characters than in Greek ones; till, several words along, she recognised that the unnamed annotator had disguised the message not only through the use of the Greek alphabet but also by writing it backwards. 'Start at the end,' she said, and Master Alcuin said, 'Ha!' and did so, tracking his progress through the final-or-first sentence with his left forefinger.

'Sophie!' Joanna bellowed, some two dozen words later. 'Sophie, come here at once!'

The Brezhoneg words were sometimes oddly spelt, but the message was perfectly clear for all that. *This map*, the new transcription read,

> *shows the anchors of the magick of blood and stone, which Argentaela ar Breizh, wife of Nevenoe, devised and sealed with her blood to protect her husband's kingdom, which Ahez daughter of Alan, King of Breizh, brought as dowry to her English husband, which the queens of Britain have preserved as once it preserved us from the longship raiders of the north, from the mage-warriors of the east, from the great golden ships of Iberia to the south. Look to the stones when danger threatens, and may the old gods preserve us all.*

'"Sealed with her blood,"' Sophie repeated. '"The magick of blood and stone." This place is steeped in blood, it seems to me.'

Lucia, Roland, and Evans-Hughes, drawn presumably by Joanna's calling to Sophie, had by now all crowded in at the map-room door.

'It is also steeped in persons who do not explain themselves,' Lucia remarked. 'We may now be said to know what this magick of blood and stone was meant to accomplish, and where it originated; but we are no nearer understanding either what it does, or how.'

'It does sound very like Ailpín Drostan's spell-net, however,' said Sophie – more thoughtful than revolted, now. 'The blood of the rulers, the bones of the land. And its purpose must have been similar. One wonders how the Princesses Regent shaped it to their very different ends, for which it seems to me very ill-suited, and what on the gods' earth gave them the notion to attempt it.'

As the afternoon sun began to dip below the tops of the library windows, the party returned as usual to the Dragon and Lion, there to wash off the accumulated filth of their excavations, change their clothes, and eat their dinner. Ordinarily, they were left to their own devices until the first two of these proceedings had been completed; on this occasion, however, they had not even reached the staircase to the first floor before they were hailed by the innkeeper, who informed Sophie that there were *some gentlemen from Merlin College waiting for you in the parlour, ma'am.*

They looked at one another in consternation.

'Who can it be?' said Gareth. 'Alcuin and I are here already, and none of your other acquaintance, I am quite sure, are in college at present.'

'What does it matter?' said Sophie, gesturing comprehensively at her filthy boots, the streaks of grime down the front of her gown, the hand-shaped smudges where she had tucked up her skirts to climb a ladder. 'I cannot possibly meet anyone at all, looking as I do at present. I was ashamed to be seen in the street.'

The gentlemen in the parlour, having presumably heard the telltale sounds of a large party trooping in at the front door and starting up the stairs, emerged into the corridor. Gareth had been mistaken; with Professor de Guivrée and Professor Langsdale, alas, she was very well acquainted, to their mutual irritation.

'Evans-Hughes!' exclaimed the latter, taking in the filthy canvas overall which Gareth, with his usual foresight, had put on over his own clothes that morning, and was now taking off and folding inside-out over one arm. 'Whatever can you be doing here?'

'He is just going,' said Sophie firmly, giving Gareth's broad back a purposeful shove in the direction of the front door. He attempted to resist; she stared hard at him, and after a moment he relented and, *Thank all the gods!*, went away.

'Professor Langsdale,' said Sophie, turning to her visitors with an unfelt smile and motioning them back into the public parlour. 'Professor de Guivrée. To what do I owe this unexpected honour?'

They eyed her with more than usual distaste – some of it for herself, she supposed, and the rest for the appalling state of her clothes, her hair and very likely her face. She stared back, unblinking, as she drew out her magick to tame her hair and smooth both dust and dismay from her face, for the brief perverse satisfaction of seeing them goggle at the change. She did not invite them to sit down; perhaps they might take the hint and refrain from lingering.

Professor Langsdale cleared his throat. 'We are come on behalf of the Senior Fellows of Merlin College, er, Mrs Marshall, for the purpose of—'

'Magistra,' Sophie corrected him.

'I beg your pardon?'

'As I hold a master's degree in practical magick from the

University in Din Edin,' said Sophie, 'I am correctly addressed as *Magistra Marshall*.' The honorific did not much matter to her in the ordinary way, but it seemed necessary to remind these men of her right to it.

'Er.' *It is sticking in his craw, right enough, the old goat.* 'Magistra Marshall. Am I correct in supposing that you have elected, despite advice to the contrary, to proceed with this business of a college for young ladies?'

Sophie gave him an edged smile. 'You are correct in supposing that you have failed to warn me off, yes.'

'And, er. What is your husband's view of this, er, venture?'

'My husband's view?' Sophie repeated, surprised. 'He supports it entirely. Why should you imagine otherwise?'

'And yet he has, er, has not accompanied you to Oxford.'

'My husband,' said Sophie, her tone as chilly as she could make it, 'has duties of his own.' She paused, and added conversationally, 'Before you continue your representations, professors, it may interest you to know that this venture, as you put it, is under the personal patronage not only of the Princess Royal' – she smiled demurely – 'but also of His Majesty the King.'

As she had surmised, this flummoxed them; to harass and browbeat *her* was one thing, to attempt the same upon their sovereign quite another.

They were not entirely deterred, however, and did not take themselves off until Sophie had pretended to listen to a quarter-hour's worth of variations on the theme *Lady Morgan College was an experiment that failed and need not be repeated* – throughout which she was continually thinking, *If only you knew!* – and allowed them to hand her a petition signed by some number of Fellows of Merlin and other Colleges, which she had no intention of reading. As a result of this visit, or visitation, she arrived at the dinner-table late, wearing mismatched ear-drops, and so cross that Joanna and Lucia began making cautious enquiries as to her well-being.

When, therefore, one of the innkeeper's daughters knocked at her door early the next morning, to inform her that there was *a, er, a gentleman below wanting to see you, ma'am*, her first instinct was to tear off the boots, stockings, gown, and shift she had just put on, resume her nightdress, and go back to sleep.

'Sophie?' said Lucia, her voice blurred and sleepy. 'Is all well?'

'There is another deputation downstairs in the parlour,' said Sophie crossly. They had neither of them slept well. 'With another petition, no doubt. I shall just go and tell them to go away.'

She closed the door behind her, descended the stairs as quietly as their tendency to creak permitted, rounded the turning into the parlour, and stopped dead, her mouth falling open in shock.

The man who stood fidgeting nervously by the fireplace mantel was not another Fellow of Merlin – was not, any longer, an Oxford man at all. A man of her father's age, lean to the point of emaciation, his pallid face surmounted by a sweep of greying hair: Lord Merton, lately of King's College and friend – or, at any rate, co-conspirator – of her stepfather, Appius Callender.

'Mrs Marshall?' said his younger, more solid companion. 'My name is Henry Taylor.'

After a moment's gobsmacked silence, Sophie – without pausing further to consider her approach, or thinking the circumstances through – marched across the parlour, took Taylor by the lapels of his ill-fitting coat, and said, 'What in Hades have you done with my sister Amelia?'

She did not altogether recognise that she was shaking him – and so preventing him from answering her – until a sharply indrawn breath behind her made her pause, turn, and behold Roland and Joanna standing in the doorway.

'I-I-I have not seen your sister,' Taylor managed. He was green in the face and breathing in shallow gasps. 'Not since we parted on the Dover road. I-I tried, I asked her – but she would go.'

Sophie let go of his coat and swung away from him, exasperated.

'Where?' Joanna demanded. '*Where* would she go?'

Henry Taylor could not possibly have been more outraged by this turn of events if he had been truly innocent of all wrongdoing. *He* had never intended to take Amelia to Calais, he said indignantly; *he* had meant to throw himself on the King's mercy, and had only wished to speak to Amelia – to bid her a proper farewell – before doing so.

'How came you to be on the Dover road together, then?' said Joanna, deeply sceptical. 'And what have you been doing with yourself, in all the time since?'

Had she not said all along that Amelia would not have eloped with the unwashed, uncombed, half-lunatic man she and Gwendolen had encountered in the park? But it was not very satisfying, in the event, to be proved right.

'Hiding, chiefly,' said Taylor, his righteous indignation fading into weariness. 'Evading the City Watch. I called at my sister's house, when she was not at home, and helped myself to some of her husband's coin – he will never miss it – and a suit of his clothes. And in the end I came back to Merlin.' He shrugged. 'I had that in common with Marshall, always, though I do not suppose he knew it: we had neither of us any other home.'

Joanna kept her expression impassive in the face of this bid for compassion. *I shall consider feeling sorry for you when we have rescued my sister.* On the heels of this thought came another: that she and Sophie, out in the wide world with their vastly expanded families, had begun to think of Amelia as though she were not the eldest of them but the youngest – and, worse, to treat her accordingly.

Roland, who had quietly left the room whilst Joanna's attention was occupied elsewhere, now returned to stand at her shoulder once more. 'I have asked the innkeeper to send for the Watch,' he said, low; then, a little louder. 'Sophie, come here.'

Predictably, rather than obeying, Sophie turned to glare at him. Roland sighed. There came the sound of footsteps – coming down the stairs, not along the corridor – and then Joanna felt Gwendolen's hand on her shoulder, and Lucia was crowding in behind them, peering around Roland's head.

Roland squared his shoulders and took a step forward. At once Taylor and Merton tensed, wary, and brought up their hands defensively as though to do . . . what? Roland, in any case, seemed quite unintimidated. 'I arrest you in the name of His Majesty the King,' he said firmly.

They goggled at him. Roland had always been a good man in a crisis, Joanna reminded herself; it was in the small ordinary difficulties of everyday life that he tended either to forget, or to make far too much of, the dignity of his years.

'The City Watch has been summoned,' he went on; 'I should advise you to go with them without argument, when they arrive. In the meantime, however, let us sit down like reasonable people and discuss how we may be of use to one another. Sophie, will you set us a ward?'

Sophie blinked at him (*horses, stable doors*, thought Joanna) but after a moment nodded, closed her eyes, and began muttering a spell. Roland waited patiently for its conclusion before turning his earnest gaze squarely on his . . . prisoners, Joanna supposed she must call them. They seated themselves, looking rather like stunned oxen, on two hideous armchairs.

'You have information of value to us,' he said. 'My sister and I have the ear of the King' – the prisoners' eyes widened as, belatedly, they recognised to whom they were speaking – 'and I, at least, will undertake to intercede on your behalf, should you put us in the way of locating Miss Callender.'

'And tell us who it was that abetted your escape,' Joanna added prudently, from the doorway, 'and why.'

'Indeed,' said Roland.

Taylor and Merton conferred in voices too low for Joanna to distinguish. At last Merton said, 'How are we to lead you to Miss Callender when neither of us had any hand in her departure from England?'

'We know,' said Sophie, 'that my sister left London with the goal of rejoining her father at the court of the Emperor of France. Presumably you must know, or at any rate suspect, who is meant by that epithet, and where he has his court?'

'You will speak for us to the King?' said Lord Merton. 'We have your word upon it?'

'You have,' said Roland.

'You sought us out, Lord Merton,' Sophie said quietly. 'You sought *me* out, in fact. Why do so, if not because you have something to say to me? Whatever it is, very soon now you shall have to say it to the Watch Captain, who may be less inclined to compromise.'

'I had hoped,' Merton said, grimacing, 'to retain both my life and my liberty, and to give warning without further risk to myself. I am not a traitor, Your Highness—'

Roland and Sophie exchanged an incredulous look.

'What I did,' Merton insisted, 'I did for the good of the kingdom, as I saw it. I could not have predicted this consequence. I am acting now from the same motive; I cannot speak for any other person.'

'Go on, then,' said Roland. 'And do not be too long about it.'

Merton frowned at him. 'The man who calls himself Imperator Gallia,' he said, 'is the Duke of Orléans, and Orléans is where you shall find him, unless he be now on the march with his armies. He has anointed himself a second Julius Caesar, and aims to unite all of Caesar's Gaulish and Frankish territories, and thereafter to build a new Roman Empire. He is collecting mages, as well as the armies of his followers, because he aspires to control sorcerer-centuries such as those which struck terror into the hearts of Caesar's conquests.'

His auditors digested this for some moments; then Lucia MacNeill ventured, 'Is he mad, think you?'

'Quite mad,' said Taylor positively. 'He – by way of his agent in London, that is – agreed to aid our escape, and promised that we should be granted posts in his court, in return for information – harmless enough information, it seemed at first – until, before we knew where we were, we were all become his liege-men – his creatures, I should rather say.'

'For myself,' said Roland, in a distant tone, 'I do not think I should seek out convicted traitors as my liege-men.'

'That is because you do not understand the circumstances,' Taylor snapped. 'Lord Carteret was Orléans' liege-man before he was King Henry's.'

Does this mean, can it mean, that this self-styled Emperor was somehow behind Carteret's plot? How far down, how far back, does this rabbit-hole extend? And how could the priests of Apollo Coelispex, discerners of truth and falsehood in the minds of men, have failed to discern such a momentous truth as this one?

Into the astonished silence which greeted this revelation, Taylor continued: 'Poor Amelia was the go-between – though she believed she was only sending parcels to her papa, of course, along with her own. By the time the day arrived, I had already made up my mind that I wanted no part of the Emperor's court, and had written to Amelia to beg her to come to London – we should go to Eire, perhaps, I thought, or Alba, or to the Low Countries, and put all of this business behind us. But it was not so easy as I thought to escape from the escape – so to speak – and then . . . well. When the time came to choose, she did not choose me.'

He did not appear to have noticed how widely this version of his intentions departed from his initial protests of innocence. *Wished only to say a proper farewell, indeed,* thought Joanna.

'And you, sir?' said Roland, turning to Lord Merton. 'What is your tale?'

'Whether or not Orléans is mad, I cannot undertake to say,' said Merton. 'But he has certainly an idée fixe on the subject of this restored empire of his, and of the Roman gods. I am a follower of the Roman path myself, like most educated men,' he added, in an explaining tone, 'but to speak of enforcing Pax Romana by stamping out the worship of all other gods is another matter altogether, and an aim to which I cannot lend myself.'

He concluded this speech with a decisive nod and sat back in his chair.

'I confess,' said Roland, 'that I had rather hoped for more concrete intelligence with which to act upon your warning. What are my father's generals to do with the information that their opponent has declared war on the old gods? Does he mean to declare war on Britain? When, if so? Is he likely to be amenable to terms? What numbers has he, and how deployed?'

There was a small, stifled sound to Joanna's left; darting her eyes in that direction, she observed Lucia gazing at Roland in pleased approval. *There's for all your poetical wooing, Roland*, she thought, rolling her eyes. *You had only to talk to her of tactics and strategy, after all.*

Alas, however, neither of their informants had been near enough to Orléans' councils to acquire any of the intelligence Roland sought.

'I have promised to intercede on your behalf,' he said at last, 'and I shall not go back on my word; but when next you decide to throw yourself on the King's mercy in return for information, I should advice you first to build up a greater store thereof.'

It happened at this moment that the Captain of the Watch knocked loudly on the door of the Dragon and Lion, and Roland, glancing that way to gauge the source of the noise, met Lucia's gaze and held it. Joanna saw him register her appreciative expression – saw his cheeks flush and his eyes brighten in response. Then the men of the Watch in their heavy boots were clomping along the passage and crowding through the parlour door, and in the bustle of handing over the prisoners and impressing upon the Watch Captain the importance of their being transported *at once* to London and given into the custody of Lord Kergabet and Lord de Vaucourt, the moment passed.

CHAPTER XXVIII

In Which Lucia Attends a Concert, and Lives to Tell the Tale

Having dispatched both Taylor and Merton, and an explanatory missive on the subject thereof, to Kergabet in London, Sophie's party sat down to eat their breakfast and take stock. They had by now collected and sorted all the damaged codices from the library of Lady Morgan College, and had pieced together and catalogued most of them, but they had still to explore the Shrine of Minerva Sophia. Further discussion decided them, however, that the following morning must suffice for this endeavour, and that thereafter they should return with their prizes to London, where they might study them in more comfort and be in the way of more quickly hearing any news.

The reclaimed books and maps were packed up under Ceana MacGregor's direction into a large number of crates and dispatched in a hired cart, tightly covered in oilcloth in case of rain, to the Royal Palace. The box containing the confession of the Princesses Regent, however, and the mysterious map which seemed to belong to it, Sophie wrapped carefully in layers of clean linens and packed into her own trunk. She was not altogether clear, in her own mind, what she meant to do with either of them, but the letter in the box was directed to her, in a way, and she felt a responsibility for its secrets.

Indeed, its secrets weighed upon her like a cloak of lead.

They arrived in Grosvenor Square to find that Mrs Marshall, disappointed in the matter of Miss Beaumont, had decamped to Glascoombe. Lady Maëlle remained, but to Sophie's eye she seemed reduced, as though the loss of Amelia – in effect, her last child – had altered her in some fundamental way. Sophie and Joanna, feeling guiltily that they, too, had abandoned her in rushing off to Oxford to go exploring, exerted themselves to demonstrate their affection, but though she smiled at them and called them good girls, as though they had been children once again, nothing they could say or do appeared to make the least difference to her melancholy.

Some days after their return to London, the Grosvenor Square family, together with Roland, Lucia, Edward, Delphine, and Harry, attended a concert at the Apollonium. The mood in the city was oddly buoyant, following the very public return of two of the escaped conspirators to the Tower of London, in consequence of which – and of the private knowledge that the others were almost certainly hundreds of miles away – Lord Kergabet had relaxed his strictures on public appearances by Sophie and Joanna. Delphine (who was very fond of music) had lobbied strenuously in favour of this engagement, as had Edward, who was to depart with his regiment but two days hence and therefore was more than usually inclined to indulge his wife.

It was not precisely like being amongst friends; it was not the Royal Palace, however, and the company was in general a younger and more carefree set of persons than were to be met under the careful chaperonage of Queen Edwina. Alas, Sìleas Barra MacNeill had insisted upon Lucia's wearing one of her new gowns, a stiff and thickly embroidered creation in which sitting was uncomfortable (and dancing nearly impossible), but the music, when it began, was very lovely, and it was pleasant – if very odd – to be reunited with the Oxford party, in this altogether less consequential atmosphere.

At the first interval, they rose from their seats and moved out to the terrace. Roland and his brothers trooped off to fetch glasses of wine for the ladies of the party; Sophie, Delphine, and Gwendolen had their heads together, comparing notes on the performances they had just heard, whilst Joanna propped her shoulders against a pillar and studied her programme with an abstracted air. Lucia stepped away from them a little and leant her elbows upon the balustrade, gazing out at the busy River Thames below.

'Lady Lucia?' The speaker, when she turned to look at him, proved to be a dark-haired young man, not much taller than herself, with bright hazel eyes. He wore, if she did not mistake, the uniform of a cavalry lieutenant.

'I am she,' she said, cautiously.

'I beg your pardon,' he said in Latin, with a bashful smile which, despite herself, Lucia found rather charming. 'I know we have not been introduced. My name is Arzhur Kermorgant. I have a most particular reason for wishing to speak with you—'

Lucia did not see the threat until it was very nearly too late: his arms had closed behind her, mimicking a lover's embrace, and what later proved to be the tip of a tiny clasp-knife was nosing gently at the fabric of her stiff, uncomfortable new gown, scraping amongst glass beads and gilt thread and seeking the best opportunity to slide in between her ribs.

It was fortunate – for both of them, as it transpired – that Ceana MacGregor had insisted on teaching her the rudiments of self-defence, and fortunate too that Lucia's instinct, when events moved too quickly for thought, had always favoured magick over force. The heiress of Alba did not panic, did not cry out, did not for a moment lose her composure; she was reaching for her magick, flinging it out around her on the words of a shielding-spell, almost before her conscious mind had acknowledged the danger.

And then her assailant was flat on his back at her feet, the knife (so small, honed so deadly sharp) skittering across the polished floor, and other people (so many people!) exclaiming and running about and shouting for someone to call for the Watch. Lucia stared down at the man who had attacked her, dry-eyed and perfectly steady but for the painful hitching of her breath, and concentrated on slowing her heartbeat.

He lay motionless, his eyes closed. Dead? *He looks very young. Almost a boy.* His chest rose and fell. *Not dead. Hail Brighde!* Lucia did not shrink from the notion of killing, when killing was required – a chieftain who did so (as she had tried to explain to tender-hearted Sophie) was no chieftain at all – but he was so very young, this would-be assassin, and in any case it had *not* been required. *Besides which, had you killed him, he could not answer your questions.*

Running footsteps approached from several directions – the patter of dancing-slippers, the thump of heavy boots – and Lucia raised her head, slow and careful, and took a wary step backwards, then another, pressing her spine against the pillar that interrupted the balustrade.

'Lucia!' Sophie's voice, breathless and worried – then Roland's – Joanna's, Gwendolen's – and finally a gruff familiar baritone: 'My lady! Are you hurt?' Conall Barra MacNeill, Ceana MacGregor's second-in-command. Whose head Ceana

MacGregor would certainly have, and his guts for bowstrings, if any harm came to Lucia through some negligence on his part.

Casting only the merest glance at the stranger who lay insensible upon the floor, Roland strode towards Lucia and reached out to her; she shrank away in spite of herself, and Sophie and Gwendolen caught his elbows and held him back.

'A moment, I pray you,' she said, astonished to find her voice steady. For the ears of the approaching guardsmen, her own and King Henry's both (here because she and Delphine and the Princes were here), she forced into it a note of command: 'I am quite unharmed; there is no danger now. Stand down.'

Conall Barra MacNeill glared the King's guardsmen out of countenance, and knelt by the young man's shoulder to examine him more closely.

A melodic *skrrr* caught Lucia's ear; when she looked that way, there was Joanna Callender straightening up from the floor with some small metallic object in her hand, held between the halves of a folded handkerchief. 'His weapon, I believe,' she said, and Lucia watched her hand it over to the guard captain – Prichard, yes, that was his name.

'I must go and speak to Jenny, and keep her away from . . . this,' Joanna muttered, and strode away, neither asking leave nor taking it.

'Lucia,' said Sophie's voice again, nearer this time; while all this was going forward, it seemed, Sophie had drawn level with Conall and was hovering there, prudently just out of Lucia's reach (though not, of course, Lucia could not help remarking, out of reach of an offensive spell). 'Thank all the gods you were not hurt!'

'Not in the least,' said Lucia. 'Let no one tell you that learning a trustworthy shielding-spell is a waste of effort.'

Now, *now* she heard the betraying tremble in her own voice – *Steadfast in the face of danger*, she thought, in bitter self-mockery, *and undone by a kind word from a friend.*

She put out a hand, thinking to keep Sophie at bay, but Sophie, misunderstanding, caught her hand and held it, and stepped over the stranger's splayed limbs to stand at Lucia's side, curving one arm protectively about her shoulders. In spite of herself Lucia leant towards her a little, feeling chilled and trying very hard not to shiver.

'Lucia, will you not come and sit down?' Roland had escaped from Joanna and Gwendolen and was approaching, with great caution, from Lucia's other side. 'You look—that is, you must have used considerable magick, I think, in defending yourself – Sophie, you will help her to a chair? – I shall fetch you something to eat.'

He turned on his heel and hared off in the direction of the supper-room.

It now occurred to Lucia that her shielding-spell might have used more magick than, had she been thinking at all at the time, she might have intended. Certainly it was comforting, a balm to her pride, to suppose that it was magick shock and not simple cowardice that made her feel chilled and light-headed and weak at the knees.

And clever of Roland to have deduced (or had he only guessed?) what had happened, before she had said anything to him about it.

Lucia and Sophie were still gazing down at the would-be assassin when Roland re-emerged onto the terrace; he was carrying two plates, one piled with strawberry tarts, the other with delicate slices of ham.

'Please, Lucia,' he said again, 'will you not sit down?'

'I will sit down,' she said, turning from Sophie's encircling arm

410

to look him full in the face, 'if you will undertake to ensure that I shall be present when this man is questioned.'

'I—' Roland faltered, then said, 'If it be in my power – yes. You have certainly a right to hear whatever he may have to say for himself.'

He did not altogether like the notion, Lucia could see. She allowed herself to be steered to a chair near the terrace doors, from which she could both observe ongoing events and devour her strawberry tarts and ham.

Having seen her settled, Roland returned to the scene of the attempted crime, where Captain Prichard and Conall Barra MacNeill were concluding a businesslike search of the unconscious youth, now bound at wrists and ankles, and – by their gestures – contesting possession of their prisoner.

The latter interrupted their debate with a low groan, and by stirring and attempting, with no success whatsoever, to sit up.

'I—stay here, Lucia,' said Sophie abstractedly. She patted Lucia's shoulder and darted off.

Lucia took stock of herself – *yes, much better!* – then stood up (gripping the chair-back for the first moment, to be safe) and followed.

Conall Barra MacNeill looked up at her approach and came forward, frowning, in an attempt to head her off. 'There is no use at all in my ordering you back to the Sasunnach castle and to bed, I suppose,' he said.

'None whatsoever,' Lucia. 'Is there any use in my offering you that chair, to spare your knee?'

Conall glowered down at her, his arms folded across his broad chest. 'You may be heir to the chieftain's seat, Lucia MacNeill, but I have not forgotten the time you put a hedgehog in Ceana MacGregor's parade helmet, or the time—'

Lucia held up one hand to signify her surrender.

Fortunately – for Roland, missing the substance and misreading the tone of their rapid, low-voiced exchange, appeared to be on the verge of wading into it in Lucia's defence – Joanna now came hastening back, with Prince Edward in his scarlet coat close on her heels. Delphine, to Lucia's relief, was nowhere in sight.

'Roland!' cried Edward. '*Quomodo vales?*'

Roland – with interjections from Lucia and the rest of the witnesses – explained.

Edward stood over the prisoner, now seated, more or less, with his back against the balustrade – was the young man's regimental coat his own, Lucia wondered, or part of a disguise? – and fixed him with a no doubt forbidding glare.

'Explain yourself, Lieutenant,' he said. 'What is your name? Your regiment? What reason can you possibly possess to attempt such a vile deed?'

'I-I-I am Derrien Robic, C-captain – Your Royal Highness – I serve in Colonel Maheux's regiment, presently quartered north of the River Huisne, in Maine – I—' He gazed about him in what looked like genuine bewilderment. 'M-may I know of what crime I am accused? And . . . I beg your pardon, my lords . . . where I am?'

The gathering erupted at this point into confused debate, which was ended at last by Edward's saying, loudly and very firmly, 'Captain Prichard, take this man to the Palace and confine him to the interdicted chamber, if you please.'

'Sir,' said Prichard, offering a crisp salute.

He signalled one of his guardsmen, and they began to pull Derrien Robic to his feet.

Lucia, however, was not inclined to sit quietly whilst her assailant's fate was decided by others. 'A word, Your Highness,' she said.

Their faces turned towards her, Roland's wary, Edward's astonished.

'Truly, Lucia,' said the latter, 'there is no need to trouble yourself further over this business; my father employs guardsmen and mages for exactly this purpose, and you may be assured that those responsible for this outrage upon a guest of his house – of our house – shall be suitably punished.'

Struggling to keep her temper, Lucia said, 'Your father may impose whatever punishment—' Lucia could see Prince Edward drawing breath to overrule her, and raised her voice a little: '—whatever punishment he sees fit, with my blessing, but first we must know how, and *whom*, and *why*—'

'Lady Lucia' – and Edward's voice was louder still, though quite without any show of temper – 'as a guest of—'

'Ned!' said Roland, between gritted teeth. 'Lucia has every right to know why she was attacked, and by whom.' His composed expression, to judge by the rhythmic clenching of his left hand at his side, was costing him some effort to maintain. 'Her being our guest is rather an argument in favour of her request than not, I should have thought. If *I* had been so used—'

'You are not a lady!' Prince Edward insisted, his voice lower now, but not the less vehement for that.

Lucia blinked.

'No more is Lucia,' said Roland, and, before anyone could protest, 'not in the way you mean. She is the *heiress of Alba*, Ned – or had you forgotten?' His eyes, like his brother's a vivid blue, glinted with ill-timed mischief as he added, 'I am at fault, of course; I ought to have compared Lucia's case to your own, and not to mine.'

The expression of outrage that bloomed over the Crown Prince's face as he digested this statement forced Lucia to clap one hand over her mouth to stifle a sudden, *entirely* inappropriate upwelling of laughter. She had admired Roland's unexpectedly able handling of Merton and Taylor in Oxford, but to hear him taking her part, and with such conviction, was something else again.

His gaze found hers – swift and furtive, seeking her approval, but with an almost-hidden glint of answering laughter in his eyes – and she grinned at him (though only for a moment) as fiercely as she knew how.

'What we need,' said Lucia, 'is a spell-seer.'

'Is it?' said Sophie doubtfully. 'To see what, precisely? Even if, as we suppose, Mr Robic was acting under some manner of compulsion, surely it will by now have passed off – or been broken – and there will be nothing left to see.'

'One of Lord de Vaucourt's apprentices is a spell-seer,' said Roland, 'and not altogether insufferable – Macsen Griffiths, you know. Will I send a steward to fetch him?'

They had, collectively, persuaded both Captain Prichard and King Henry, who could overrule Lord de Vaucourt, to permit the three of them to attend the formal questioning of Robic, though not to lead it. No one had authorised them to invite further persons into the business; but, as Sophie had heard Joanna say more than once, absolution is often more easily gained than permission.

'Yes,' said Sophie. 'Do so.'

They were a party of four, therefore, when they made rendezvous with Captain Prichard and Lord de Vaucourt outside the door to the Palace's interdicted chamber. Vaucourt raised his eyebrows at Griffiths, and then at the other three, but desisted when all four of them returned him the same level stare.

414

Captain Prichard unlocked and unbolted the door and pushed it open, then strode into the room to retrieve the prisoner. Having seen (and occasionally experienced for herself) the consequences to a powerful mage of imprisonment under interdiction, Sophie was prepared for his drooping posture, his miserable expression, and the faintly green hue of his pallid face; Roland, however, looked altogether horrified when Prichard, having bound Mr Robic's hands once more, led him out into the corridor.

She edged closer to him and murmured, 'It will pass off soon enough.'

Mr Robic, for his part, regarded her in mute and miserable appeal. Sophie set her teeth. What in Hades did he suppose her willing (or even able) to do on his behalf, after what he had so nearly done?

Some two hours later, they had begun to conclude that there was nothing useful to be learnt from this exercise. Griffiths had given it as his considered opinion that some faint trace of compulsion indeed lingered about the prisoner, but he could form no impression of the spell's author or of its intent or motivation. Mr Robic himself appeared genuinely to remember nothing of what he had done, or why.

An idea occurred to Sophie, halfway through the third or fourth of these retellings of cavalry manoeuvres, stable duties, disputes among the common soldiers, and supervising the unloading of fodder and other supplies. She could, in theory, by means of a song-spell such as the one she had employed to divert her mother-in-law's attention from Lord Kergabet and Jenny, compel a person to speak the truth; could she also, perhaps, compel him to speak a truth which he did not consciously remember?

Lord de Vaucourt would never permit it, she told herself. But . . .

But what if Lord de Vaucourt did not know? Reaching gently for her magick, she began humming under her breath, weaving melody and magick together into a call for the revelation of hidden truths. Griffiths shot her a sharp sideways glance, but refrained from betraying whatever it was he saw.

The prisoner stumbled once more to the end of his recital. This time, however, the low monotonous voice, beyond even weariness, did not stop at '. . . and reported for patrol duty with my men,' but continued: 'And when we rode out, we were ambushed in our own woods by men of Orléanais.'

Everyone sat up straighter; no one spoke.

As though this one misstep had jarred loose all the rest of the contents of some tight-packed secret cabinet, he went on – and on – in the same hollow monotone.

'There were two officers and six men, none mounted. They strung lines across the trees at chest height, and so scraped us off our horses' backs. Stupid of me not to see it. One was a mage-officer, which in general none of the Duchies' troops employ. Perhaps he was a spell-seer, for he looked at all of us and singled me out, and I was the only one of us able to do more than call light.

'He sent the rest back to camp. Bespelled them somehow, I think, for no alarm was raised. And I . . .' For the first time, he faltered – then swallowed hard – and at last went on. 'I must call myself a deserter, I suppose. The mage-officer . . . spoke to me. I cannot recall even now what he said. But I knew at once what I must do. He gave me . . .'

He paused.

'May I have my hands free?' he said. A humble petition, eyes downcast.

Vaucourt and Prichard exchanged a look.

'Very well,' said Prichard after a moment, and untied them. 'He gave me this,' said Mr Robic. His slim, callused right hand dipped into the pocket of his coat, and brought out what looked like an ordinary copper coin, dull and green with age. 'In case I should be caught, or fail in my task.'

He raised the coin to his lips. Sophie saw what he was about to do in the heartbeat before he swallowed it; she leapt forward out of her seat, shouting, and Lucia and Roland with her – but too late, too late, too late.

CHAPTER XXIX

In Which Joanna Draws Conclusions, and Gray Is Taken by Surprise

Having spent the night of the disrupted concert with Lucia at the Royal Palace, Sophie was returned to Grosvenor Square early the following evening in a state of numb, unspeaking horror which Joanna had seen before.

'What has *happened*?' she demanded, clasping Sophie's chilled hands. Treveur, who had been hovering in expectation of collecting Sophie's hat and gloves, instead vanished momentarily and returned with a woollen shawl, which Gwendolen wrapped about Sophie's shoulders.

Sophie's throat worked; she blinked slowly, once, twice; her lips opened, then closed again.

'You are ill,' Joanna decided. 'Let me take you upstairs and tuck you up in bed, and ask Lady Maëlle to—'

'No,' said Sophie. Her throat worked again. 'Not . . . I am not ill. This morning . . . The young man who attacked Lucia – he had been bespelled—' Her silence being now broken, the words tumbled from her lips faster and faster. 'The interdiction delayed the inevitable, but the effect wore off, I suppose, or—and he remembered. He told us what he knew – what little he knew – but then he – then he—'

This was not a conversation for the front door, but there was no question now of going upstairs, or anywhere else; Sophie was weeping almost too much to draw breath, and clutching at Joanna as though she feared her being snatched away.

The storm at last eased, however, and Joanna and Gwendolen succeeded in spiriting Sophie up to her bedroom via the servants' stairs, so as to avoid for the moment any further necessity to answer questions. Over the course of the next hour, the ugly tale slowly emerged.

'And if I had not made him speak,' said Sophie, 'then perhaps—'

'*No*, Sophie,' Joanna said firmly. 'He was to be punished for his failure, whatever you did or did not do; that much is clear.'

For some little time they all three sat silently contemplating the horror of it.

To fall on one's sword might be an honourable end; but this – this poisoning-by-proxy – had been no more or less than foul murder.

'Orléanais,' said Joanna at last.

'I beg your pardon?' Sophie looked-up, dull-eyed.

'On the one hand we have, by Mr Robic's account, a mage-officer from Orléanais,' said Joanna, 'who bespells a young Breizhek officer to compel him to commit . . . well, both murder and treason, to begin with. And a very *particular* murder, which if successful might have been expected to outrage not only Britain but Alba as well; certainly it must end any hope of alliance between us, and perhaps – very likely – it might constitute an effective casus belli, and thus draw our attention to our northern border and away from the eastern ones.

'On the other hand,' she continued, 'by the evidence of Lord Merton, we have the Duc d'Orléans, who styles himself Imperator

Gallia and desires to control all the former territory of Roman Gaul, principally including, we must suppose, Britain's own three provinces on that side of the Manche. Who seeks to bring all the peoples of this empire of his to the worship of the Roman gods alone. Who has somehow persuaded at least half of his neighbours to unite under his banner, and who apparently is searching the Duchies for mages to train up to his sorcerer-centuries – meaning, I suppose, to erase the only two tactical advantages which we have always had over the armies of the Duchies.

'We know now, in fact – do we not? – where Gray is likely to be, and the Professor and Amelia too.'

Sophie nodded; she did not look comforted.

'I quite see why a man who is collecting mages should be eager to get his hands on Mr Marshall,' said Gwendolen, 'but what should this Imperator Gallia want with your sister?'

Joanna had asked herself this question more than once, and thus far had arrived at no satisfactory answer.

'I think,' said Sophie, after a long moment, 'I think that is the wrong question to ask.'

'What is the right one, then?' said Joanna.

'What I mean is – perhaps it is not a matter of his wanting Amelia, but of Amelia's wishing to go to him. That is, to go to the Professor.' At Joanna's sceptical look, she hurried on, her eyes brightening as she warmed to her theory: 'Amelia was always devoted to the Professor, and he to her, insofar as he was capable of devotion. Certainly he valued her above either of us. She was mistress of Callender Hall, and now she has nothing – or at any rate, *believes* she has nothing – and she told us, in so many words, that she does not believe him guilty. She was in correspondence with Henry Taylor – perhaps secretly but certainly without Cousin Maëlle's knowledge, for I cannot imagine her allowing it – and perhaps even thought herself in love with him, who can say? And he, or the Professor, or this agent of Orléans whom Taylor spoke of, or all three of them, will have filled her head with tales of what a great man her papa is, or will be, at the Emperor's court. It is not impossible, is it, that she should consider the alternatives apparently on offer, and choose that one?'

There was another long silence.

'If that is so,' said Gwendolen at last, 'then . . . ought we to be seeking to rescue her from herself?'

'Perhaps not,' said Sophie. 'Perhaps she is perfectly well and happy with the Professor at the court of Orléans. Or perhaps she has been robbed by highwaymen of all she was carrying, or kidnapped, or has fallen into a ditch and broken both her legs, or perhaps—'

She stood up and began pacing about her bedroom.

'You must not entertain such thoughts, Sophie,' said Joanna firmly.

Her thumbs pricked – Sophie's pacing had taken on a manic edge, her slim hands twisting and untwisting Gwen's handkerchief, and her brow was furrowed in furious thought. *I know that look, the gods help me.*

Amelia! Gray's lips had shaped the first syllable of her name by the time his mind caught up and stopped him from calling out to her. She had not seen him, or had seen him but was choosing to pretend otherwise; she appeared absorbed in her companions and her work.

Orléans stood beside him, observing with satisfaction the, it must be said, admirably well-coordinated manoeuvres of the seventy-odd young mages as, in response to some signal from their leader, they wheeled leftward in unison, disposed themselves in a half circle about a massive straw-stuffed target mounted on a wooden cart, and let loose in a rippling wave with bolts of flame and lightning – and then, when the target was well aflame, drew water from the air to quench the fire.

Orléans shifted slightly, turning from the blackened, sodden remains, and tilted his head to look up at Gray; he was a small man, no taller than Joanna, but by some alchymy of the mind made his own height seem the Platonic ideal, and Gray's an unfortunate defect. It had been years, Gray reflected, discomfited, since he had been so tempted to stoop in an effort to conceal his height.

'A fine sight, are they not, my sorcerer-century?' he said, smiling faintly. 'Though not, as you have justly remarked, quite a century as yet.'

'Indeed,' Gray replied, somewhat at random; he had not said any such thing aloud – or had he?

'I must just speak a moment with my centurion,' said Orléans, and turned away.

Five, six, seven steps; then Orléans spun on his heel, suddenly, and with a minute flick of two fingers, drew a gout of flame out of the air and sent it streaking back towards Gray.

Almost before the threat had registered in his conscious mind, Gray was throwing up a shielding-spell to block it. The flame struck; the shield dimpled slightly with the force of its impact, recovered, and sent it skittering harmlessly away in tiny showers of sparks.

'That was very well done,' said Orléans. 'For an itinerant scholar.'

'The road has its dangers, from time to time,' Gray replied. 'And I have had very good teachers.'

His heart was pounding, not from exertion but from shock at the suddenness of the attack. With an effort, he slowed and deepened his breathing, until at last his pulse slowed.

'So I see.' Orléans stood with feet spread, hands clasped behind his back, and considered his . . . not *guest*, for there had been no rite of welcome; his experiment, perhaps? 'And I see also that I was quite correct in my initial estimation: you, Monsieur Marais, would be altogether wasted in the reserves.'

Gray's thoughts scrambled for purchase on this new cliff's-edge. He had thought the possibility of being yoked to one of Orléans' battle-mages a credible threat; this, now, was a far worse fate which until this moment he had not even thought to dread.

'I . . . do not take your meaning, my lord.'

Another faint smile. 'On the contrary, I am quite certain that you do.'

I cannot aid this man in his misguided war against the old gods, who made these lands, and those who serve them. Not even to speak of the notion of forging a link between his magick and some other person's who was not Sophie, which made his stomach churn. *But if I refuse outright to give him what he wants, I shall have learnt almost nothing of use, and I shall lose all possibility of rescuing Amelia.*

Always supposing, of course, that Amelia was willing to be rescued.

The mages finished their drilling and were dismissed; they dispersed, some sloping away across the courtyard, others lingering to exchange flirtations with the ladies. Several of the younger men paused before Amelia, but she only glanced up at them and smiled briefly – the barest curve of her rosy lips – before returning to her work.

Perhaps it was a matter of rescue, after all. *Time will tell, if I can contrive to gain some.*

Gray turned back to Orléans, plastering a smile over his deep unease, and said, 'I should like to hear more of your sorcerer-century, my lord.'

'Should you, indeed?' said Orléans, with a tolerant smile. 'I regret I have no more leisure to attend you this afternoon, but I shall appoint you a guide. Decurion Rousseau!' he called, fortunately turning away in time to miss Gray's startled expression. *Decurion?*

One of the young mages raised his head, turned; bent again to murmur something to Amelia, then strode towards his . . . master, in fact, if the expression of slavish devotion upon his face were any sign.

'My lord,' he said, bracing before the imperial presence.

'I have brought you a new recruit, Decurion.' Orléans opened his hand in Gray's direction, and Rousseau's gaze followed the gesture – left, then . . . up.

'Monsieur Guy Marais of Poitiers,' said Orléans. 'Monsieur Marais, Decurion Auguste Rousseau, of the second sorcerer-century.'

Gray bowed; Rousseau returned the gesture. Orléans, favouring them both with a benignant smile, said, 'Rousseau will show you about the place, and you shall dine in the officers' mess. *À la prochaine*, Monsieur Marais; *on se reverra ce soir.*'

Shall we, indeed.

Gray and Rousseau stood side by side, unspeaking, until Orléans had vanished through an archway on the far side of the courtyard. Then Rousseau turned to Gray and said, in a not unfriendly tone, 'What brings you to the Emperor's service, Monsieur Marais?'

Go carefully! This man is a true believer in Orléans' idée fixe, or at any rate in Orléans himself.

'I have sworn no oath of service as yet,' said Gray cautiously. 'I am a scholar of magick; I have been travelling in search of some useful employment, and hope to find it here. And yourself?'

'The Emperor is a great man,' Rousseau declared, with a proud smile. 'I am honoured to serve him in advancing his great vision.'

'I should like to hear more of it,' said Gray. 'He is a spell-seer, I think, the Emperor?'

Rousseau perceived some insult in this query, it appeared, for he drew himself up a little and said, 'The Emperor is a master of all kinds of spell-work, and sees many things which ordinary mages cannot. His talents come from the gods themselves.'

'All magick is a gift from the gods,' Gray countered reflexively; and then, seeking to soften what might be heard as a further insult, 'So we are taught. As Gaius Sejanus Domitianus had it, *Magick is the gods' gift to mankind, and their curse.*'

'Ordinary magickal talents are only an accident of birth,' said Rousseau, with the assurance of one reciting a well-learnt lesson. 'The Emperor has been elected by the gods to a great destiny, like Julius Caesar before him, and thus they have granted him extraordinary gifts with which to fulfil it. Naturally one of these gifts is that of discerning those who may best serve him in establishing his great empire and respect for the true gods.'

I have heard that line of argument before. In very similar words, though in a quite different tongue, had the late Cormac MacAlpine justified his forcible kidnapping and enslavement of foreign mages – Gray and Sophie among them – to feed their magick into his distant ancestor's great spell-web. *And talking of spell-seers . . .*

'Then,' said Gray, 'I should imagine he has seen something in me which he believes he can turn to good account.' *As Cormac MacAlpine did before him.*

'I saw the scholar-mages in your master's workroom, earlier,' he went on, hoping to steer the conversation in a more productive (and less hazardous) direction. 'They seemed . . . very much immersed in their pursuits – indeed, I do not think they at all remarked our presence.'

'Well, we have been drilling all this time,' said Rousseau, as though this explained everything. 'The sorcerer-century, that is. So naturally the fellows in the workroom would have no notice to spare for the outside world.'

Gray considered that *naturally*, and found he did not at all like its implications.

Rousseau's tour of the makeshift *palais imperial* – the Château d'Orléans – culminated in a second stroll along the battlements.

'We are just in time,' said Rousseau cryptically, peering over the chest-high battlement wall.

Gray stepped up beside him, rested both palms on the top of the wall, and followed his gaze. Down in one of the camps below, a crowd of men, moving in as graceful a unison as Rousseau and his companions had earlier done, were carrying out some sort of exercise with a dozen saltpetre-cannon, aimed apparently at nothing, in what might once have been a turnip-field.

'What are they—'

His query was cut off by a bludgeoning roar as all twelve cannon erupted into smoke and flying . . . what?

'Horns of Herne!' said Gray reflexively. He rubbed at his ringing ears.

Rousseau glared up at him. 'We do not call upon the lesser gods here,' he said.

Gray blinked, then nodded. 'Your pardon,' he said. 'I was taken by surprise.'

For reasons which Gray could not entirely fathom, this drew a broad grin from his companion. 'Chain-shot,' he said, gesturing down at the cannon-crews now spread across the field like reapers. 'To slice through enemy cavalry.'

By which he means, in fact, my brother-in-law Ned. Gray repressed a shudder. Below, strings of men, their hands oddly overlarge in thick gloves, were gathering up lengths of heavy chain and neatly coiling them.

In the air with Ollivier and Lécuyer, in conversation with Colonel Dubois or Mage-Captain Tremblay, Gray had begun to think that perhaps the military life might have something to recommend it. The mental image of iron round-shot or those heavy chains falling amidst the ranks of men and horses superimposed itself on these memories of camaraderie and mutual assistance like night-soil emptied onto the spread pages of an illuminated codex.

And I am all alone here, he reflected, fixing his gaze determinedly on the activity below so that he should be in no danger of meeting Rousseau's eye. The mages of Captain Tremblay's company might yet be capable of finding him – impossible to say – but there existed no possibility of his communicating with them, except by returning to Ivry.

Orléans might be a spell-seer, but Rousseau certainly was not, and Orléans, at present, was not by. Gray shut his eyes and reached for the thread of Sophie's magick; finding it as bright and strong as ever, he opened his eyes, swallowed hard, and turned to Rousseau with a bright but unfelt smile.

'Impressive, indeed,' he said.

'Impressively noisy,' said Rousseau, 'and useful in its way, but the Emperor's war will be won by the sorcerer-centuries.'

And what is it they do, then, which is worse than this?

'I can well imagine,' said Gray; the lie coming easily now, he added, 'King Henry's army has nothing to match either one, I believe.'

Dinner in the officers' mess was a more formal affair by far than the equivalent in Captain Tremblay's company. Gray made the acquaintance of the Centurion of the second sorcerer-century – an Orléanais man of about Sieur Germain de Kergabet's age, whose dark eyes assessed him with swift calculation – and at least half a dozen more decurions, Rousseau's fellows, as well as a string of officers of the infantry, cavalry, and artillery, also denominated in the Roman style; they dined upon elegantly dressed joints of meat which were, nevertheless, so tough and stringy that Gray shuddered to think what the Emperor of Gaul was feeding his common soldiers, and drank (all but Gray) a very great deal of not very good wine, which led to some disintegration of the aforesaid formality. Gray nursed his first glass until the last bottle ran dry, the better to keep his wits about him.

After dinner Rousseau walked with him back to his tiny cubicle in the mages' barracks and left him there.

Gray sat down rather heavily on the bed (for lack of any other seat) to think things through. *Have I, or have I not, become a soldier in Orléans' army?* He had taken no oaths, made no promises – indeed, had not so much as answered a relevant question in the affirmative – yet here he was, and it was anyone's guess what might be coming on the morrow.

The correct course of action seemed self-evident: to abandon his saddle-bags and the clothes on his back and fly for his life, the moment he could safely do so. He had already collected valuable intelligence on the situation, of which Colonel Dubois (and, through him, Lord Kergabet and the King) ought to be apprised without delay; that done, the next stage of operations would be in capable hands, and Gray might either be of practical use in carrying it out, or, if his assistance was no longer needed, be permitted to return to London, and Sophie.

He rolled his left shoulder once more, experimentally – reached for his magick, to gauge what remained to him following his displays for Orléans – gave sober thought to the matter, and judged it possible. The difficulties lay elsewhere: here, as in the British garrison, one was almost literally never alone. If he were to depart, it must be by night, whilst the greater part of the place was asleep, and the men standing sentry duty presumably focused on threats from without.

Well, at any rate I should do well to catch some sleep whilst I can.

When Gray woke, the barracks were silent around him – or, at any rate, the only sounds to be heard were those of sleeping men. He rose from his bed; disrobed quickly and methodically, folding away his clothes as he went so that he should not appear to have departed in haste; wrapped himself togalike in the darker of the two woollen blankets provided along with the bed-linens; and stepped out through the doorway of his cubicle (it had no door, and only three-quarters of a wall) into the long, narrow corridor.

There was, he had noted earlier, a window at the far end of it, and he made for this on cautious feet, reminding himself that until the moment of the shift, there was nothing for anyone to see which he could not explain away. Nevertheless his heart was hammering in his throat by the time he reached the window, having safely passed two dozen doorways and as many slumbering mages, and discovered it to be shut and locked.

The lock was not a difficult one – no more than a latch, in truth – but it was stiff and recalcitrant, and oh, gods, the *noise*! *O Janus, master of openings and closings, guide my hand* . . .

It was done at last, however, and with no worse effect than a bass-baritone growl of *Great Mithras, not rats* again*!* and a heavy boot tossed in his general direction, which he easily dodged. The window fortunately was just large enough for his human body to squeeze through, so that he might perch on the roof-peak and nudge the two heavy panels inwards with his heels. Of course he could not do much about the latch without magick, and if he were to fly all the way to Ivry-sur-Eure he would need every last iota for that task.

Gray untied his blanket-toga, crouched low along the roof-peak, and draped the blanket over himself once more. Beneath its concealing darkness, the shift went swiftly – he had done almost nothing else for most of a se'nnight, after all – and after a brief struggle with the suffocating folds of wool, he was aloft, setting his face to the north, and home.

'Do I understand correctly, sir,' said Gray incredulously, around a large mouthful of bread and ham, 'that you are ordering me back to Orléans?'

Colonel Dubois regarded his civilian attaché – tousle-haired and heavy-eyed, wrapped in several rough woollen blankets and eating as though he had not seen food for months – with steady patience. 'I have not the power to order you anywhere,' he said. 'I am *asking* you to return to Orléans, observe what the Duc is about with his saltpetre-cannon and his sorcerer-century, and learn what more you can. You are not under my command, Mr Marshall; you are of course entirely free to refuse my request.'

'How should I convey to you whatever else I might discover?' Gray enquired. 'Supposing that I did consent to return?'

If he were honest, half of him wished very much to do just that. The self-styled Emperor both unsettled and intrigued him, and those brief glimpses of Appius Callender, looking contented but strangely oblivious, and of Amelia . . .

'Both Mr Lécuyer and Mr Ollivier, of Captain Tremblay's company, have volunteered to act as your liaisons.' Colonel Dubois produced a small, sardonic smile. 'The distance involved does suggest a relay arrangement, though I should of course have preferred to send a night-scout and a day-scout together.'

Gray frowned, drained his tankard of ale, and frowned again. 'But,' he said, 'you should then have no night-scouts at all.'

'To a man with a hammer,' said Colonel Dubois dryly, 'every circumstance may come to resemble a nail. I, however, have no hammer, and am therefore free to make use of whatever tools are to hand. Ollivier and Lécuyer may be the best night-scouts in this regiment, Mr Marshall, but they are not the only ones. We shall make shift with human scouts by night, as many another regiment of His Majesty's army must.'

Gray was not altogether persuaded; but if the Colonel did not know his business . . .

Gray must be in Orléans again before morning if his flight was not to be discovered, and was therefore in the air again long before prudence dictated – though at any rate his escort consisted of persons experienced in all manner of magickal emergencies. With several stops for rest and refreshment, the three of them reached the wood outside the castle as dawn was lightening the eastern horizon.

'But how will you feed yourselves?' Gray had asked them, in the night-scouts' tent at Ivry-sur-Eure. 'And—'

Ollivier and Lécuyer had looked at one another. 'We are soldiers, Marshall,' said Ollivier. 'We have lived rough in the woods before.'

Gray, having fled with no intention to return, now had no real choice but to return to the barracks as he had left them. To his immense relief, the blanket he had left on the roof-peak was there yet – though damp with dew – and the window had blown open wide in the course of the night; he had only to grasp the blanket in his talons, drag it along the roof-peak until it overhung the window-frame, then dive through the window, shifting as he went, and pull it through after him into the deserted corridor.

How fortunate I am, he reflected, *that not one man in a hundred, when patrolling a battlement, will ever think to look up as well as down.*

He crept down the corridor and into his warm, dry bed, and there lay exhausted but awake until the morning's bugle-call sounded, thinking guiltily of Ollivier and Lécuyer making the best of things in the woods.

CHAPTER XXX

In Which Further Complications Arise

Gray was returning to his sleeping-quarters after a morning spent drilling with the sorcerer-century, so exhausted that he could think of nothing but reaching his bed and collapsing into it, when a pageboy stopped him, executed a bouncing half bow, thrust a folded paper into his hands, and bounced away again across the courtyard.

From a general impulse to conceal his private affairs from potentially hostile observers, Gray pocketed the note and resumed his interrupted trajectory. When he reached his quarters, after pulling off his boots but before collapsing face first into bed, he extracted it from his pocket and, curled on his side with his back to the door, read it through.

Written in a lady's careful, elegant hand, the note contained no salutation and no valediction, but read in full:

> *I must speak privately with you on a matter of urgency. Can you contrive to wait by the fountain in the south courtyard at dusk? If the answer is no, send word by the bearer.*

Gray frowned at it. But he was here to discover all he could, and here, perhaps, was an opportunity. It might equally be a trap of some sort, of course – but in any case it was now too late to refuse.

Dusk found him, therefore, by the fountain in the little-used south courtyard as instructed – more precisely, seated somewhat precariously upon its edge, with his nose in a book of Roman military history. He waited, pulse skittering with nerves, for what seemed an age, though it could not really have been more than a quarter-hour, until at last light, cautious footsteps heralded the arrival of his mysterious correspondent.

Gray looked up and tried to determine whether he was surprised or entirely the reverse. 'Amelia!' he said.

'Mr Marshall,' said Amelia.

She sounded . . . not *pleased* to have found him here, but relieved – as though she had not altogether expected him; at the same time, however, she wore an air of deep chagrin, almost of humiliation. At the necessity of asking Gray, of all persons in the world, for help?

He lifted both hands in a gesture of appeasement and, rather than standing to loom over her, kept his seat on the wide lip of the fountain, looking up at her expectantly. 'I am come as you requested,' he said, 'to hear of your urgent trouble. What is it?'

Ameila gritted her teeth.

'I should not have approached you, if I were not desperate,' she said. 'As it is, I can only throw myself upon your mercy and trust that you will not use my desperation against me, as no doubt you believe I deserve.'

Gray scarcely knew how to reply; he was saved the necessity of doing so, however, by Amelia's immediately going on: 'I came to this place of my own will, but now I wish to leave it again, and cannot. Will you help me?'

To this, on the other hand, there was only one possible answer. 'Of course,' said Gray. 'If I am able. I have . . . trusted friends nearby, by whom I can send a message—'

'And will you help me rescue my father?'

Gray blinked. Not because her request surprised him, exactly – as a devoted daughter, Amelia Callender had no peer, whatever might be Gray's opinions on the object of her devotion – but because he had not the least notion how to reply. To help Amelia – a glorified camp-follower – to escape Castle Orléans was one thing; to extricate Appius Callender from the very centre of the soi-disant Emperor's operations, quite another.

'Does your father wish to be rescued?' he temporised. 'Is he unhappy with his present situation?'

'*I* am unhappy with his present situation,' said Amelia. She was worrying at a hangnail with her teeth, a most uncharacteristic gesture. 'The Emperor made promises to him, which he is very far from having fulfilled.'

'I must tell you frankly, Amelia,' Gray said, 'that your father's welfare is not my chief concern. Not that I wish him ill, but as he has more than once tried to arrange my death—'

'Do you know what they are, the *reserve* mages?' Amelia demanded. 'They are fodder for the rest, feeding them magick – all they have, if need be – they are tied together, and cannot escape.'

Gray swallowed against rising nausea. Surely even Appius Callender did not deserve such a fate?

'You are a mage, Mr Marshall,' Amelia continued, in a sort of furious hiss. 'What do you imagine becomes of a mage whose magick is all drained out of him by another?'

Indeed, Gray could imagine all too well what would become

of them. But he hardened his heart in spite of it, for the lives of many thousands of men, women, and children – and, most immediately, those of Lécuyer and Ollivier, fending for themselves in the wood north of Castle Orléans – might well depend on the intelligence he could gather here, and, much as he disliked the thought, Amelia's desperation gave him an unexpectedly valuable lever to pull.

'I do not know what I may be able to do for your father,' Gray said at last. 'I have not yet sufficient understanding of Orléans' mage-work to gauge what is best, or even what is possible. But I shall try my best. In return, however, I shall expect payment in information. And,' he added, 'a pair of bedrolls, two sets of infantrymen's clothing and kit, and rations of some sort – whatever you can most easily liberate from the kitchens.'

Amelia gaped at him. 'You promised to help me,' she said after a moment, 'not a quarter-hour ago, and now you demand payment?'

'Not at all,' said Gray. The more he thought of Appius Callender, he found, the steadier grew his resolve. 'I promised to aid your escape in any way I can, and that promise stands. The payment is for aiding your father, to whom I have made no such promise, nor ever shall.'

The tension-taut silence which followed was perhaps the longest in Gray's memory. Amelia glared at him – clenching her fingers in the folds of her skirts, as he had seen her do years ago – then hugged her elbows and stared down at her feet. At last she said, low and bitterly defeated, 'I will pay your price.'

Gray had not, in truth, any very great expectations from the bargain he had made with Amelia; it did not seem to him that, placed as she was, and with no knowledge of magick or of military strategy, she was at all likely to run across information of use to Colonel Dubois or Lord Kergabet. At any rate, however, it had bought Ollivier and Lécuyer a reprieve from starving in the woods; once supplied with infantrymen's clothing and gear, they could slip into one or another of the myriad companies encamped outside the castle and feed themselves from the common cookpot.

Once again, however, Amelia surprised him. They had agreed that, as he had the greater freedom of movement and was known to be a scholar, Gray should make a habit of studying in the quiet of the south courtyard every evening at dusk, so that Amelia might meet him there whenever she had news to convey. For nearly a se'nnight of this second sojourn at Orléans, he waited out the appointed hour, reading by magelight, and saw Amelia not at all. But on the seventh night she emerged from the shadows and crossed the courtyard swiftly to perch beside him on the fountain's stone lip.

'The King's spies in the Duchies have been disappearing, did you not say?' she began, without preamble. 'I have discovered what became of them.'

Gray sat up straighter. 'Tell me,' he said.

'Your *p'tite amie* must have got her facts mixed,' Lécuyer declared, leaning his broad back against the boot of an oak-tree. 'Or she is inventing tales to force you to keep your end of the bargain.'

Gray glared at *p'tite amie*, and Ollivier gave Lécuyer a mighty shove in the shoulder and said, 'The young lady is Marshall's sister-in-law, you lout.'

Lécuyer righted himself and waved a dismissive hand, as though the distinction between sweetheart and sister-in-law were quite immaterial. 'The *point* is, that what she told you cannot possibly be true.' He stretched his long legs out before him, displacing Ollivier, who growled at him with no real heat. 'A spell to replenish one's magick by drawing power from talentless folk? How could such a thing possibly work?'

'I have not the least idea,' said Gray grimly, 'but I have known Amelia five years, and if she has the imagination to invent such a tale, I will eat not only my hat but my coat and boots along with it. And there are certainly tales enough circulating about Orléans that I should not be surprised at his proving to be a great deal more like the emperor Nero than like Julius Caesar.'

Ollivier sat up, cross-legged on his folded bedroll, and frowned at Gray. 'Mad, you mean?'

'Well,' said Gray, 'that also, very likely. I meant, however, what the natural philosopher Pliny said of Nero – that no one could be certain whether his madness was cause or consequence of his taking what did not belong to him. It is not known just what Pliny meant by that turn of phrase – there are so many possibilities! – but my friend Evans-Hughes – he is an historian, at Merlin College – believes it to imply that Nero achieved the godlike power he boasted of by stealing it from other mages.'

Lécuyer grimaced, and Ollivier blanched and clapped a hand over his mouth.

'But,' Lécuyer objected, 'even if that were true – which, meaning no disrespect to your friend, I do not see how it can be – it is still not at all the same thing as taking magick from folk who have none!'

Gray – who could not be absent indefinitely without its being remarked upon – was beginning to lose patience. 'You may convey my report to Colonel Dubois with as much commentary as seems good to you,' he said, 'provided that you do convey it to him, and at once.'

'It is my turn, in any case,' said Ollivier, unfolding himself and climbing to his feet. He still looked a little green. 'Have you anything else to report?'

'Only that three more men have joined the second sorcerer-century,' said Gray. 'I have not been up on the battlements for some days; what have you seen, out in the camps?'

'Another company of cavalry rode in yesterday evening,' said Lécuyer, 'but two companies of infantry marched out early this morning, with two of those great saltpetre-cannon on siege-waggons.'

Ollivier by now had stripped down to his drawers; he now stepped out of these, then efficiently shook out and folded his borrowed clothing and stacked it on his bedroll. Finally, he crouched down, toes curled round a protruding tree-root, and between one eye-blink and the next, was looking up at Gray with the heart-shaped face of a barn owl.

Lécuyer bent and scooped him up – Ollivier squawked at the indignity, but again it seemed quite without heat – and muttered, 'The gods go with you, Kannig,' as he tossed the barn owl into the air.

'The gods go with you,' Gray echoed, under his breath.

Two mornings hence, the Emperor assembled his sorcerer-centuries in the castle courtyard for the unveiling of his grand strategy; by the time he had finished, Gray was thankful for the press of bodies all about him, which might conceal the violence of his reaction. Nor was he, he was relieved to discover, the only one who did not much like what he had heard; when after some unguessable period of frozen horror he became able once more to interpret the evidence of his senses, he heard mutterings all about him, low and wary and worried.

It was the remembrance of these mutterings which upheld him through the rousing speeches, the obligatory cheering, the parade round the courtyard and back to the barracks, and which – together with Amelia's tale of dozens of men imprisoned below Castle Orléans, dying breath by breath as their spirits fed the Emperor's magick – gave him the courage, when all these things were done, to return to the castle keep and approach the door of Orléans' private chambers.

His way was barred by not two but four burly men-at-arms who eyed him with a familiar distrust; Gray had remarked how little enthusiasm the common soldiers had for the men of the sorcerer-centuries.

'I would speak privately with the Emperor,' he said, 'if he is not presently occupied with some urgent matter.'

The tallest of the men-at-arms said, 'Wait here,' and paced down the short corridor to rap at the door.

Gray could discern nothing from the brief conversation that ensued, but upon turning away from the door, the guardsman held it open and with his other hand beckoned Gray towards it. Gray followed, concealing his trepidation as best he could, and waited for the door to close behind him before looking up to meet the Emperor's gaze.

'Marais,' said Orléans, his tone curious, but unalarmed. 'You wished to see me?'

'My lord Emperor,' Gray said. His throat was dry – this man could have him killed on a whim, could, in fact, carry out the act himself, if the humour took him. 'May I have your permission to speak freely?'

Orléans smiled at him. 'Certainly, my boy,' he said.

'Concerning the . . . battle plan which we were told of this morning,' Gray began – then stalled, and with great effort gathered his courage to continue. 'If the men of those garrisons can be so easily slaughtered, then surely they can as easily be subdued and taken prisoner.'

'Oh! Certainly,' said Orléans, with a wave of his hand, 'for a given value of *easily*, which, I fear, betrays your lack of experience in the field, Marais.' He leant forward in his chair, forearms braced on the surface of his desk. 'Tell me, how then shall we feed and house these thousands of prisoners, and how guard them to prevent uprisings and escapes, without materially weakening our own forces?'

'And how shall we,' Gray swallowed hard, 'dispose of thousands of bodies, without fouling our new nest? This is not a battlefield from which we can march onward, leaving the fallen for the looters and the carrion-crows; you propose to march *into* a fortress already littered with enemy dead, and then – what, my lord? There are not enough trees in all the forests of Breizh to build so many pyres, and the burning would choke the skies for days. Or had you thought to cast the dead into pits, like refuse? How shall men be chosen for that duty, and what will they think of their glorious new empire after they have carried it out?'

Orléans might be mad, but he was not a fool; surely he must have thought all of these ramifications through. But sometimes, as Gray knew from experience, to hear one's ugliest thoughts spoken aloud by some other person made them too real and too ugly to be waved away.

'You have not lived among the people of Britain, my lord,' said Gray, pressing his advantage, if such it was, 'but I have travelled there, and speak some of their languages, and have come to know them well.

'You suppose that they will be cowed by such a display of savagery as you mean us to inflict upon them, but it is no such thing – we shall only raise their ire, and spur them to more vehement resistance, by making martyrs of their brave-hearted young men. Not to speak of the women and children who will inevitably be caught up in the slaughter.'

He stopped, willing his pulse back to steadiness, when he recognised that his voice had risen almost to a shout – and in the sudden quiet, he heard the sounds of shuffling feet and muttering voices from behind him. Half turning, he beheld all four sentries poised in the doorway – how had he failed to hear the door opening?

Orléans rose from his seat to stare them down. 'Back to your posts, gentlemen, if you please,' he said, icily calm; as he spoke, Gray felt a faint, chill shiver of magick, and the hairs on his neck rose.

The four men turned and retreated, like puppets on one string, and the door fell shut behind them. Orléans sank back into his chair – but the skin-prickling feeling of magick in the air did not abate.

'If you cannot moderate your tone, Monsieur Marais,' he said, 'perhaps you may in future have the foresight to set a ward beforehand. My personal guards are inclined to be protective.'

'My apologies, m'lord,' Gray choked.

With a gesture like a child spinning a top, Orléans muttered something under his breath; Gray nearly stumbled from the force of the warding-spell that shuddered through him, stronger than the most powerful ward he had ever felt Sophie cast.

442

Orléans regarded him thoughtfully. 'You are a scholar, are you not?' he said.

'I am,' said Gray.

'Ordinarily, scholars do not consider it their métier to give unsolicited advice to military commanders,' he said, 'and still less to kings and emperors.'

'As you have remarked yourself, sir,' he said, 'I am not altogether an ordinary scholar.'

To his astonishment, Orléans laughed. 'That is certainly so,' he said. He waved Gray to a chair, and Gray, bemused but relieved, sank into it. His skin buzzed with the aftershocks of the warding-spell. 'I must tell you, Marais,' Orléans continued, 'that I expected an appeal to sentiment. It is fortunate for you that I was mistaken.'

'There seemed no need to appeal to sentiment,' said Gray, now very glad indeed that he had not done so, 'with such a wealth of pragmatical arguments to be made.'

'Indeed. Nevertheless, it bears mentioning: men of sentiment, I have no use for; men apt in the arts of strategy, on the other hand, may go far in my service.

'I shall think on what you have said,' Orléans continued, 'and in return, think on this: when the first sorcerer-century has taken Ivry-sur-Eure, Château-du-Loir, Klison, Vernon-sur-Seine, and the rest, it will fall to the second to take and hold the keystones at Karnag, and you and your fellows must be ready.'

Gray now had intelligence which, so far as he knew, none of the others had – but he could make no sense of it. The second sorcerer-century, so called, as yet numbered only eighty men; but what in Hades was at Karnag that Orléans should send eighty mages after it? *Take and hold the keystones* – the keystones of what? Take them how, from whom, for what possible purpose?

He did not ask any of these highly suspect questions, however; it was a firm rule among the Emperor's people, from his generals to the boys who fetched and carried for the crews of the great saltpetre-cannon, that whatsoever they might need to know, the Emperor would tell them.

Everything he had heard in the course of this day, he should soon be repeating to Ollivier and Lécuyer, to one of whom – it was Lécuyer's turn, if he did not mistake – would fall the task of conveying it to Colonel Dubois. *And perhaps he may make some sense of it.*

'I understand, sir,' he said, therefore.

'So I hope, Marais. So I hope. You are dismissed.' Orléans snapped his fingers negligently to release his ward, and Gray fled the room with as much dignity as he could manage.

We are to be sent to Breizh; I am bound for home at last! From Karnag, it would not be beyond him to disappear into the Breizhek countryside – Gray spoke the local language, as the officers of the sorcerer-century did not – and a few days' travel would take him to An Alre or even Gwened, where he might decant any further discoveries to the garrison commander and then find passage home. Amelia presented a more difficult problem, to be sure – but if Orléans meant to take the battle elsewhere, was she not safest where she was? And Appius Callender . . .

Appius Callender is my concern only insofar as his fate affects Amelia's.

It was only much later that the implication of Orléans' words dawned upon him: to be ready for battle, in terms of the Emperor's soldier-mages, was to be linked to the mages of the reserves. The realisation woke him, gasping and sweating, in the middle of the night, and not until he had calmed his breathing and reached through the aether to find his connexion to Sophie – still stable and persistent across a kingdom and a half, though, in the terms of the peculiar sight-metaphor in which their magicks chose to represent themselves, finer than a single thread – could he even begin to attempt sleep once more.

CHAPTER XXXI

In Which Sophie Attends to Her Geography, and Roland to His Books

The news reached London across the final days of August that armies under a banner which no one in the field could identify, except in its resemblance to the arms of Orléans, had overrun three British garrisons: first Ivry-sur-Eure in Normandie; then Klison, on the River Sèvre in Breizh; and finally the long-disputed Mainois fortress town of Château-du-Loir.

There had been no formal declaration of war, no negotiating for terms – and, for that matter, no battles to speak of, for the attacks had come in the dead of night, and the British forces, felled by some powerful sleeping-spell, woke in the morning to find their arms and fortifications in the hands of the enemy, and themselves prisoners. After the first such assault, it was said, garrison commanders all along Britain's borders with the Duchies – forewarned of the fate of Ivry – had mustered both mundane and magickal defences as best they could; but Klison and then Château-du-Loir had fallen just the same. Whether the intervening positions had fended off the enemy, or whether there had been no assaults there to fend off, was as yet impossible to say – but thus far all the available evidence pointed, bafflingly, to the latter.

Joanna, Sophie, and Gwendolen, who had taken possession of

the Kergabets' library and filled it with crates of rescued books and documents, abandoned their (mostly) systematic study thereof, whenever some new piece of news arrived, in favour of an assault upon Sieur Germain's unfortunately small collection of up-to-date maps.

They knew a great deal about present circumstances on the continent which the general public did not – to begin with, the likely identity of the man behind that mysterious banner, and, if the evidence of Taylor and Merton were to be believed, the Duchies' new foray into magickal weaponry – but the choice of targets remained a source of bafflement.

'Why *those* garrisons?' Joanna wondered aloud, not for the first time, when the news reached them of the fall of Château-du-Loir.

They stood round the large table in the library, studying a map of the Duchies with rivers and lakes picked out in blue ink and borders, so far as they were known, in red. Sophie's fingertip was pressed so hard to the words *Ivry-sur-Eure* that the flesh beneath her fingernail had gone white – Ivry, whence Gray had last reported in before vanishing into the Duchies – but seeing Joanna's gaze upon her, she snatched it away and clasped her hands behind her back.

'There are so many others between,' Joanna continued, circling the table to study the map from a different angle, 'and some a great deal less difficult of access – though I suppose,' she added, 'if the work of subduing our garrisons is being all done by mages, and not by ordinary soldiers, the terrain of the approach does not much signify. But it is very odd tactics, it seems to me, for an invading army to take so few positions, so widely separated.'

Sophie frowned, turned away from the map altogether, and began rummaging through a crate at the far end of the room. She had been skittish and strange since Derrien Robic's death, immersing herself in her centuries-old rescued documents as though she might thus keep the horrors of the present at bay.

'If Mr Taylor is to be believed,' said Gwendolen instead, 'this army is commanded by a madman. Perhaps we ought not to seek logic in his tactics.'

Joanna shook her head. 'A madman he may be,' she said, 'but not a fool, or he could not have accomplished so much. There is some method here, if only we could discover it.'

Farther down the table was a second map on which, by means of pins and coloured wool, Joanna had been tracing the movements of the various armies arrayed against Britain's eastern borders, according to the reports which Lord Kergabet and Mr Fowler, yielding to her pleas not to be left entirely out of their counsels, had been daily bringing home for her. They had given her to understand, most lately, that they now had an agent in the field in Orléans; she was quite certain in her mind that the agent was Gray, though Lord Kergabet refused to confirm or deny this hypothesis.

She itched to be back in the centre of things – but as this was not at present feasible, she should take what she could, and endeavour to be grateful for it.

Leaning close, she studied the line of red wool stretching from pin to pin, following rivers and, where rivers and borders diverged, the borders maintained over the centuries since the last Angevin conflict – except where the taking of Ivry, Klison, and Château-du-Loir pulled the wool into sharply pointed salients. The red shapes reminded her of something, but what . . . ?

In Sophie's corner, the rustling ceased. 'Jo,' said Sophie, in a tone which instantly made Joanna straighten up and wheel away from the table to face her. 'Jo, look at this.'

She was holding in her hands – was it? Yes – the old field-map Joanna had found in the library. Three strides, four, and she was laying it out on the table beside the one Joanna and Gwendolen had been studying.

'There,' she said, pointing with her right forefinger to the salient at Ivry-sur-Eure, 'and there.' Her left forefinger stabbed at one of the mysterious red markings on the field-map – also at Ivry. 'And look—'

'Mother Goddess,' said Joanna.

Gwendolen, peering over her shoulder, breathed, 'Oh, no.'

There were red marks at Klison and at Château-du-Loir, too.

'That cannot possibly be coincidence,' said Sophie. 'Can it? Surely not.' She sounded shaken and uncertain. 'But if it is not . . . the question is, what does Orléans know, that we do not – and *how*?'

'No,' said Joanna positively. 'That is, I should very much like to know what he knows, and how – but for the moment we are strategists, not scholars, and so the question is, *where next?*'

Sophie blinked. 'Yes,' she said, after a moment. 'Yes, of course.'

They bent once more over the two maps, gazes flitting from one to the other. The red markers, if strung together like the pins on Sieur Germain's map, would have made a wobbling, irregular outline of Britain's continental provinces, from the northernmost at Haudricourt-sur-Seine, marching southward along the frontiers of Normandie and Maine, then striking north and west to Martigné-Ferchaud where Maine and Breizh met the lost province of Anjou, then south again to Klison and finally to the unexplained grouping at Karnag, on the Breizhek coast.

'There, perhaps,' said Gwendolen, touching a fingertip gently to the marker at Valennes, 'as it is so near Château-du-Loir and might be taken without spreading his forces too thin. Or perhaps at Martigné-Ferchaud, by sending troops north from Klison and west from Château-du-Loir at once.'

In the event, however, it was neither; the guardsman bearing their urgent missive to Sieur Germain at the Royal Palace crossed

449

with the one he had himself dispatched to tell them of an assault upon Vernon-sur-Seine by ships from l'Île-des-Francs, which now were continuing northward towards Rouen.

His Majesty's Privy Council, in the aggregate, received the theories of the ladies of Grosvenor Square with a degree of scepticism which was not ameliorated by the revelation of their being premised upon a centuries-old document unearthed from the library of Lady Morgan College. Undeniably, however, dispatches from the border garrisons and from the regiments newly deployed to reinforce them did suggest that the Duc d'Orléans appeared – for reasons at present unfathomable – to be working from the same mysterious map.

Alas, none of this brought either His Majesty or the commanders of his troops any nearer to discovering how Orléans might be defeated, or to identifying the spies or turncoats whose intelligence, and perhaps even direct connivance, had facilitated his successes to date.

'The Princesses Regent were in the secret of this *magick of blood and stone*,' said Sophie positively, 'and we know from the Library's records that their papers were given to the College at the end of their regency; and so it follows – does it not? – that *somewhere* amongst this . . . collection of materials' – she gestured comprehensively at the crates and shelves and untidy heaps which presently surrounded her – 'we shall find the things they knew, and which they meant someone to find one day.'

'Unless whoever ransacked the library succeeded in destroying them,' said Gwendolen, at the same time that Joanna said, 'But if they *did* mean us to find them, why in Hades were they not in the box with the other papers?'

'We are strategists, not scholars.' Sophie's face, as she threw Joanna's words back at her, wore a sort of bright-eyed, frantic glee that boded very ill indeed for someone; Joanna hoped the someone might prove to be Henri-François d'Orléans, and not Sophie herself.

Joanna had not fully understood before how much they had all of them been going through the motions. Now they plunged back into their researches with renewed enthusiasm – not to say manic energy – not merely cataloguing and categorising but searching with purpose. Each morning she awoke eager to get through breakfast and begin, and Sophie fairly hummed with the urgency of the search.

'What do you hear from Gray, Sophie?' Joanna enquired, one morning after breakfast, as they bent together over a stack of tattered manuscript pages.

'Hear?' Sophie repeated. She looked up, brows drawn together in bafflement, and Joanna nearly rolled her eyes: *Never expect sensible conversation from Sophie when she is reading something*, she reminded herself.

'Feel, then,' she said. 'See – sense – you do not suppose me to understand anything about magick, I know,' she went on in a rush, at Sophie's deepening frown, 'but I am not a fool, Sophie.'

Sophie's face cleared – not in relief or understanding, but in that terribly familiar way which meant *I cannot bear anyone to guess what I am feeling* – and she said, low and even, 'He is well. Or, at any rate, he is . . . not ill. Not hurt, not . . .'

'I am glad to hear it,' said Joanna. She laid her hand over Sophie's, where it rested on the table between them, and pressed it briefly. 'And . . . and you?'

In one sense, Sophie's quick recourse to her concealing magick, a moment ago, had already given her the answer. But Sophie's magick was not Sophie's heart – or not entirely – and Joanna and Sophie had been guarding one another's hearts too long to change the habit now.

451

Instead of deflecting the question, Sophie looked Joanna in the eyes, produced a small, grave smile, and said, 'Yes.'

Then, much less astonishingly, she rolled her shoulders and tapped one forefinger against the manuscript page before her. 'Now – where were we?'

'I shall go mad, Sìleas,' said Lucia positively.

'Now, Lucia—'

Lucia was genuinely fond of her cousin, but at present nothing could have been more calculated to increase her irritation than Sìleas Barra MacNeill's soothing tone.

'Why must *I* be placed under house arrest,' she said, 'when the fault was not mine, and the threat is past?'

The threat, she reminded herself with a carefully hidden wince, being that unfortunate young man, whose death Lucia should forever have upon her conscience, whatever anyone else might say about it.

'Lucia, put yourself in Henry Tudor's place,' said Sìleas. She had abandoned *soothing*, the gods be thanked, in favour of *brisk and practical* – never her strong suit, but a thousand times more welcome. 'It is a perfectly sensible precaution.'

'My guardsmen,' said Lucia, 'are a perfectly sensible precaution; *this* is absurd.'

'The Royal Palace is hardly a prison, dear heart.'

'Any house becomes a prison when one is forbidden to leave it.'

Lucia paced two circuits of her sitting-room, walking as quickly as she could manage without knocking into any of the furniture. Then she stopped, drew in a deep breath and let it out in an explosive sigh, and clenched and relaxed her hands.

'My apologies,' she said. 'I shall endeavour to be grateful to Roland's papa for his care of me, instead of resenting it. And I shall go and see whether Delphine may be induced to take a turn about the Fountain Court, I think.'

The Princess Delphine, who expected her first confinement in October, was overheated and out of sorts, but was eventually persuaded to try whether a breath of fresh air might improve her spirits. If so, the change was not very evident to Lucia; on the other hand, however, half an hour's concentrated exposure to Delphine's fears for her husband, now somewhere on the Mainois frontier with his regiment, had a salutary effect on Lucia, by reminding her how small and petty were some of her own complaints.

Thus fortified and chastened, she returned Delphine to her ladies-in-waiting and her comfortable settee, and went in search of her betrothed.

Roland opened the door to her himself, looking as cross as Delphine if less fatigued and overheated.

'Lucia!' he said.

He was only half dressed, and upon seeing Lucia he blushed, gathering his dressing-gown more tightly about him as he stood aside to let her precede him into his sitting-room.

'I . . . apologise for receiving you in such a state of disarray,' said Roland, looking at the floor. 'I did not expect—well.'

The circumstances were sufficiently unusual that Lucia stared at him for some time, forgetful of what she had intended to say to him. The spell was broken, however, when Roland pushed the door to and crossed the room to peer into her face.

'Lucia,' he repeated, 'what—'

'Can you not make your father see reason, Roland?' said Lucia, cutting him off before the earnest, bewildered worry in his eyes could spill over into awkward sentiment of some sort.

'Not notably, to judge by past experience.' Roland pulled a face.

'But will you try?' Lucia persisted. 'I fear I shall run mad if I am mewed up here much longer.'

Roland sighed. 'I have scarcely seen my father since Ned's regiment left England,' he said. 'Talking of *mewed up* – he is always closeted with Lord Kergabet and the rest, and it seems I am not welcome in their counsels; certainly I am not welcome to interrupt them to talk of . . . of other matters.'

Another grimace. Lucia was reminded that Roland and Harry and Delphine and their mother, too, were confined to the Palace until further notice – though Delphine and Queen Edwina had at least their ladies-in-waiting to bear them company, while Roland seemed to have no one at all. Not even – she looked about her curiously – his valet or any of his usual guardsmen.

'Have you sent all your minions away?' she enquired.

Roland's flush deepened, and he thrust his hands deep in the pockets of his dressing-gown. 'Yes,' he said, hanging his head. 'I had rather they did not see me sulking like a little boy.'

In spite of everything, Lucia laughed. 'If you will not negotiate my release from captivity, Your Royal Highness,' she said, 'perhaps you will at least give me a game of chess?'

Roland returned her a sheepish, lopsided smile. 'Certainly, m'lady,' he said.

The crucial document, when at last they discovered it, was an unprepossessing assemblage of foxed and tattered pages, scattered more or less at random throughout the strata of unsorted and uncatalogued detritus in a crate labelled *Miscellaneous manuscript.* For two days Sophie, Joanna, and Gwendolen, with occasional assistance from Jenny and once, briefly and after much cajoling, from Lady Maëlle, painstakingly sorted through the lot, with a relatively innocuous section from the Princesses' Regent account of their brother's illness pinned to the edge of the reading-stand for reference, and perhaps for inspiration. Their first find – not obviously relevant or useful, but undeniably written in the same hand, and therefore at any rate worth remarking upon – came in the afternoon of the first day; it was not until the following morning, however, that Joanna ran across a second, in which appeared the tantalising words *pierres de Carnac*, and by the time the sixth and, so far as they could deduce, final page surfaced – in fact, it was the beginning of the sequence, for they had located what appeared to be its end some time before – Treveur had rung the bell warning the household to begin dressing for dinner, a foot-high stack of miscellaneous papers plausibly attributable to one or other of the Princesses Regent had been assembled in the centre of the table, and the crate was nearly empty. Jenny had long quit the field, for the paper-dust made her sneeze, and Lady Maëlle, pleading fatigue (in Sophie's opinion, it was less fatigue than melancholy), had retired for a rest before dinner.

Sophie was all for ignoring the bell, and dinner itself, in favour of sitting down at once to the reconstruction of the document which mentioned the Karnag stones; how could she, how could anyone, think of food or conversation at such a time? Joanna and Gwendolen, however, flat refused to have anything to do with the enterprise until dinner had been served and eaten. When Sophie attempted to argue the point, they took her by the elbows and marched her up the stairs to her bedroom, then watched her dress for dinner, herded her into Gwendolen's room, and required her to sit on the edge of the bed whilst they did the same.

For a wonder, there were to be no guests for dinner, and Kergabet and Mr Fowler were not expected to return until late in the evening from their latest council of war. They sat down therefore only five at table for what passed in Grosvenor Square for a simple family dinner, and the conversation, except when Treveur and Harry the footman were actually bringing in the dishes, consisted almost entirely in speculation as to the progress of events across the Manche, on the one hand, and the possible contents of Princess Edith's and Princess Julia's papers, on the other.

'I wish we might be assured that should we find some manner of help therein, the Privy Council may be amenable to accepting it,' said Joanna. 'But experience suggests—'

'There is no sense in planning to lose your battles before you have fought them, Jo,' said Gwendolen bracingly.

Jenny raised an eyebrow at this military turn of phrase but made no comment aloud.

And besides, Sophie thought, *if the Privy Council will not do what is needful, why should not we do it ourselves?*

For obvious reasons, she said none of this where Jenny or Lady Maëlle might hear.

Assembling the fragments of their find into the correct order took more than half an hour, for two of the pages had been torn in half, one crossed in two different hands, and several covered on both sides; on the verso side of one of the latter Gwendolen found what appeared to be notes for an essay on the theory of spells of concealment, in yet a third hand quite different from the other two, which muddied the waters for a few moments. At last, however, they were satisfied with their reconstruction, and Sophie carefully shuffled the pages into a stack and began to read aloud.

Since the days of Ahez ar Breizh, the queens of England have held the secrets of the magick of blood and stone, have taught those secrets to their daughters-in-law so that the kingdom might be shielded from the assaults of its enemies. In the reign of our father, the eighth Henry, this chain was broken; for though Queen Elinor did her duty by the Princess Catherine when she married our father's elder brother, Prince Arthur – then heir to the throne – Arthur did not outlive his father, and all know what became of poor Catherine thereafter.

But if Queen Catherine, as she for some years was, was fated never to have a daughter-in-law to whom she might bequeath her knowledge, she did have a daughter; and it was to the Princess Julia – not to her successor, Queen Adwen, or any of King Henry's subsequent wives – that she taught Queen Elinor's secrets. The Princess Julia, whose love of her kingdom exceeded her resentment of her father, had every intention of guarding the knowledge for the sake of her brother's wife, when he should be of an age to marry; young Edward took the throne at the tender age of nine, however, and but a few years later, Mathilda Julia of Britain was called upon to use the magick of blood and stone in a manner which no prior keeper of its secrets could have foreseen.

'Why do they write of themselves as if they were strangers?' said Joanna. 'What a very irritating affectation.'

'Hush,' said Gwendolen; very quietly in Joanna's ear, she added, 'You are quite right, love, but if we are forever interrupting, we shall never come to the point.'

Joanna subsided; she leant her shoulder against Gwendolen's arm, and let her head tilt down to rest on Gwendolen's shoulder, as Sophie read on:

Thus did Edith Augusta of Britain also become a sharer in the magick of blood and stone, and thus was the chain broken in truth, for Edward rewarded his sisters' love and loyalty by exiling them from his Court and—

Sophie stopped. 'We have had this part of the tale already,' she said, running her eyes down the page; 'I think we need not hear it again. Ah! Here we are.'

As we cannot fulfil our duty by bequeathing our knowledge to our brother's queen, we set it down here, in defiance of long custom and in the hope that it may one day come to the hand of her successors, and thus be ready at need in defence of Britain's eastern frontiers.

Joanna and Gwendolen exchanged a look.

She who would wield the magick of blood and stone need not be Queen, but she must be a loyal subject of the Kingdom of Britain, and a mage of some talent and skill. She must possess the map of the keystones, and the spell that wakes their power to rouse the kingdom to its own defence.

'And here is the spell,' said Sophie, holding up the page, the remainder of which appeared to be written in verse. 'The *map of the keystones*, I suppose, is the one we have already – at any rate, I hope it may be so.'

But it falls to the kings of Britain to ensure that the magick of the stones is replenished, at the turning of the year, by that of the kingdom which it protects from harm.

'Mother Goddess!' Joanna exclaimed. 'What in Hades does *that* mean?'

Sophie looked up from the manuscript, frowning. 'I have not the least idea,' she said. 'And I suspect that my father has not either.'

'By which you mean that no one has replenished the magick of the stones since the time of Henry the Great,' said Joanna, her heart sinking, 'and there is no use in our having found the map, or in your learning the spell, because no power remains to be called upon.'

'Wait,' said Sophie. She held up a hand, frowning now *at* the page before her, rather than over it.

> In the reign of Edward Longshanks, whose obsession with conquering Alba led him to neglect the defence of his territories across the Manche, the magick of the stones was not replenished for some years. Following the final defeat of Edward Longshanks at the Roman Wall, it fell to his sole surviving son and heir to repair the damage wrought by his father's neglect. Though a misfortunate monarch in most ways, Edward II did succeed in this one task, for which he is to be commended. Posterity may well record as a noble deed his enterprise in setting down in his private diary the method by which the task was accomplished, for it may be that at some future date another King of Britain shall find himself in need of it.
>
> A copy of his account, dating from the tenth year of his reign, is appended—

'But it is not here,' Sophie concluded, sounding defeated, as she raised her eyes from the page. 'Gods and priestesses! Of all the ill luck—'

Joanna and Gwendolen were already shuffling through the larger stack of royal papers, armed now with a greater certainty of their goal, when Sophie said, in an entirely different tone, 'Oh! Listen – under this blot on the verso: *made from the original in the Royal Archives.* If we cannot find the copy, why should the original not still be where the Princesses found it?'

Joanna looked up. 'Why indeed? But how are we to go to the Archives and look for it, when both Lord Kergabet and your father have decreed that we are none of us to leave this house?'

For what seemed the first time in months, or possibly years, Sophie's face lit in a broad, genuine smile. '*We* cannot go looking for it, but Roland and Lucia can.'

Lucia was kicking her heels in Delphine's sitting-room, amongst a gaggle of young ladies whose laudable attempts to divert Delphine from her melancholy thoughts about Prince Edward by talking very cheerfully of gowns and shoes and millinery had, after more than two hours, begun to set her teeth on edge, when a knock at the door heralded the arrival of a page bearing a message from Roland.

> *I am in the Archives*, it read, *on a commission for Sophie, and should be grateful for your assistance.*
> *— R*

Even had the words *Archives* and *Sophie* not set her heart beating faster, Lucia had been longing for escape this hour and more; she retained self-control enough to rise from her seat and beg Delphine's pardon with grace and dignity, rather than leaping up and running out of the room without explanation, but only just.

'Lucia!' said Roland, his face lighting in pleased surprise, when at last she ran him to earth in a poorly lit back corner of the Palace Archives – not at all his natural habitat. He was halfway up a library-stair, using both hands to wrangle a box off a shelf at about the level of his shoulders; his hair was dusty and more than usually rumpled.

'I thank you for that timely rescue,' she said. 'What are we seeking for Sophie in all this dust?'

Roland smiled sunnily down at her. 'The private diaries of King Edward the Second,' he said.

Lucia perched on the edge of the long, narrow table that ran down the middle of the long, narrow aisle. 'Whatever for?'

'That,' said Roland, puffing a little as the box finally came free, 'Sophie was not willing to entrust to the eyes of the guardsman who brought her letter to me; she knows as well as I do that nearly all of her correspondence is opened and read at present, for my father still fears that she will run off after her husband, with or without his consent. And I daresay she should do,' he added, 'if she knew where to find him.'

He was descending the ladder now, slowly and carefully, the box tucked under one arm.

'If *my* husband were missing in enemy territory in time of war,' said Lucia, 'I hope I should not wait for anyone's consent to see him found and rescued.'

Then she remembered to whom she was speaking, and flushed hotly with embarrassment.

'I am happy to hear you say so,' said Roland gravely – was he laughing at her, beneath that solemn expression? It irked Lucia that she could not tell – as he set the box on the table. 'But of course your position and Sophie's are quite different.'

And that – as she ought not to have needed Roland to remind her – was perfectly true: whatever privilege and indulgence Sophie might enjoy by virtue of being her father's daughter,

Lucia had real power in her father's kingdom, and would have more hereafter. *But then, Sophie also possesses other sorts of power which I can only dream of.*

'Have you found them, the diaries of . . . Edward the Second, did you say?' she enquired, nodding at the dusty box, in lieu of pursuing this line of thought. 'He was the son of Edward Longshanks, the would-be conqueror of Alba, was he not?'

'He was,' said Roland, 'and wisely did not attempt to follow in his father's footsteps – not in that respect, at any rate. These are some of the diaries, or so I hope; the archivist who labelled the boxes was apparently not a believer in writing a clear hand.'

He levered the box open with an alarming creak of the hinges, and they peered into its interior, which indeed was packed tight with ledgers bound in faded red calfskin.

'Sophie wishes us to find the entries from the tenth year of Edward's reign,' said Roland. 'There are a dozen boxes at least marked *Edwardus II Rex*; he reigned twenty years, so I have begun somewhere in the middle.'

It was a sensible approach, assuming that the long-dead archivist had been more skilled in organising his materials than in labelling them.

'You are not such a bad scholar as you believe yourself to be, you know,' said Lucia.

Roland shifted uncomfortably from foot to foot. 'I ought to be with Ned in the field,' he said at last, with the air of one airing a long-held grievance. 'Or in the field in Ned's place. He is the heir; he ought not to be risking himself so.'

'I am sure he will not be put into unnecessary danger,' Lucia ventured.

Roland's expression made clear, however, that his objection was at least as much to being left behind himself, as to his brother's being sent into battle. 'Shall we begin with this box?' he said, producing a falsely bright smile that defied her to either commiserate or advise. 'Or will I fetch down another now, to save time later?'

They fetched down the two boxes on either side of the first and went through them methodically from either end; the contents proved frustratingly disorganised, and eight boxes were open upon the table before at last records from the tenth year of Edward II's reign began to turn up. Roland would have packed the unwanted volumes back into their original boxes, but Lucia insisted upon sorting them into chronological order, insofar as was possible, and fetched pen and ink and labels and paste-pot from the archivist on duty – to the latter's great bafflement – in order to do the thing properly.

The real fruits of their labours – the box now labelled *anno x Edw. II R.*, containing fourteen ledgers dated to that year, which they had found scattered amongst half a dozen boxes – they took away with them, which occasioned further baffled looks from the archivist on duty but, Roland being who he was, no outright protest.

At the door to Lucia's rooms, they were relieved of their prize by a disapproving Conall Barra MacNeill, presently on duty there.

'Your cousin Sìleas is in a terrible fret over you, Lucia MacNeill,' he said.

'Why should she be?' said Lucia, startled. 'What harm does Sìleas imagine could befall me, when I am not permitted even to walk in the outer gardens?'

Conall shrugged eloquently. 'Not for me to say,' he said. 'But when next you take it into your head to disappear, perhaps you may think to tell someone where you are going.'

Lucia sighed. 'My apologies,' she said. 'And I shall apologise to Sìleas also, never fear. I have a task for you, however.'

Roland and she had agreed, in the course of their journey from the Archives, that they could not in good conscience ask any of King Henry's household guard to smuggle a box of purloined diaries from the Palace to Grosvenor Square.

'Brìghde's tears, Lucia MacNeill!' said Conall, when she had explained the matter to him. 'What tangle have you got yourself into now?'

Roland was looking from one of them to the other with eyebrows raised, but, Lucia was pleased to see, more amusement than offence in his expression at Conall's less-than-subservient tone.

'No tangle at all,' she said bracingly. 'Sophie Marshall requested Roland's help and mine with a foray she is making into historical enquiry, as she is also presently under house arrest' – she could not resist giving Conall a hard stare, for his wholehearted connivance at her own imprisonment – 'and therefore cannot come here to search the Archives herself.'

'An innocent bit of scholarship, is it?' said Conall. Lucia thought she had never seen a man look so disbelieving.

'What else should it be?' Lucia demanded.

'Considering the source,' said Conall Barra MacNeill, who had stood with Lucia and Ceana MacGregor in the shambles of Cormac MacAlpine's yew-grove whilst Sophie worked epic and invisible magicks all about them, 'I should not be surprised if it were any sort of mad enterprise, up to and including armed insurrection.'

'There is certainly no question of armed insurrection,' said Lucia firmly; shifting into English, she said, 'Roland, open the box and find me something very dull to show him.'

Roland, concealing a smile, opened the box and took out the first volume that came to his hand; Conall frowned at him, and then at Lucia.

'Here you are,' said Roland, handing over the open codex.

Lucia took it from him and read – slowly, translating from Latin into Gaelic as she went – '*Luneday, the fourth of April, in the tenth year of King Edward the Second. Court remains at Gloucester. Weather very unsettled. Faucher has sent report that*, er, *Lightning has been delivered of a healthy foal. The entertainment this evening consisted in a troupe of players from Shrewsbury, or so Gloucester said, who gave us the tale of—*'

'Very well,' said Conall Barra MacNeill, waving a hand at her. 'I shall see your dusty old books delivered to Sophie Marshall.'

'You are a treasure among guard lieutenants,' said Lucia, and startled Roland by standing on tiptoe to kiss Conall's grizzled cheek.

CHAPTER XXXII

In Which Joanna Counsels Prudence, and Sophie Receives a Gift

The diaries of King Edward II arrived in Grosvenor Square in a crate whose nominal purpose was to convey to Sophie a gift from her friend Lucia MacNeill: to wit, a large and impressively hideous statuette depicting Lady Minerva with an owl. Sophie stared at this astonishing object for some little time before her eye was caught by the corner of a folded sheet of notepaper, protruding from the statuette's base.

> *Sophie*, it read, *we have found you something we hope you shall like, and with it a few books to help you pass the time.*
> *– L & R*

There were fourteen leather-bound ledgers in all, all of them heavy and some a trifle damp, and all – as requested – dated to the tenth year of Edward's reign. Stacked on the library table, they made rather a daunting sight: a full year's worth of his cramped, crabbed hand to pore through, perhaps, before they found what they sought.

If we do find it, which is by no means certain.

Having summoned Joanna and Gwendolen – she had decided already that neither Jenny nor Lady Maëlle could be permitted to assist in this stage of the project, nor to understand its urgent character, for they were neither of them fools and must very quickly have discovered what she was about – she set a ward upon the library to prevent interruptions and then arranged the diaries in order and divided them into three.

'Research,' she said vaguely, when Jenny enquired over dinner as to what the young people presently had in train. 'I may perhaps write something for the *Proceedings of the Society for the History of Magick*.'

'That *you* should bury your head in a stack of books for days at a time does not at all surprise me,' said Lady Maëlle, 'but Joanna?'

'Gwendolen and I have nothing else to do at present,' said Joanna – more gently than Sophie might have expected, but after all, Lady Maëlle had Amelia on her conscience, or thought she had – 'as you may remember; and research makes a change from needlework.'

'And it is quite interesting, by times,' Gwendolen chimed in, then added, as though regretting her small burst of enthusiasm, 'though *very* dusty.'

By design or fortunate happenstance, she sneezed.

Jenny grimaced. 'I shall leave you to it, then, I think.'

It was Gwendolen who found the first clue, about the second hour before noon on the third day, in the diary covering the month of September.

'Jo,' she said sharply. 'Sophie. I think—'

They looked up – Joanna from the second volume of January, Sophie from May – and left their own researches to peer around Gwendolen's shoulders.

x September

Roazhon, en Petite-Bretagne

> *Expect to be at Karnag before the Equinox, and am assured
> that all shall be in readiness there. It remains to pray that the
> gods may forgive me my father's neglect of this duty, and smile
> on my efforts to rebuild what he allowed to fall to ruin.*

'Oh, well spotted!' cried Sophie. 'Now, you must read forward from the tenth of September, and I shall read backwards from the end of August, for he may have set down something of his plans; and, Jo, here is July—'

Three hours later, they had assembled a précis of King Edward's expedition to the Stones of Karnag, and Sophie was aquiver with ideas and plans.

'We shall need half a dozen mages, according to Edward,' she said, scribbling shorthand notes on a scrap of notepaper, 'to replenish the magick of the stones; and if we are to reach Karnag before it is too late to do any good, we shall have to go by ship – shall not we, Jo?'

'Sophie, you cannot be seriously considering—'

'How long have you known me, Joanna Callender?' Sophie demanded, low and fierce. At Joanna's shoulder, Gwendolen shivered – perhaps sensing some magickal exudation which Joanna herself could not. 'What did you imagine we were about, in searching through this rubbish-heap, if not to use whatever treasure we found for some good purpose?'

'And haring off into the midst of a pitched battle between the armies of two kingdoms, entirely without support of any kind, is your notion of *some good purpose?*'

'Certainly not,' said Sophie indignantly.

Joanna exhaled relief, but too soon, of course, for Sophie continued, 'Our *purpose* is to defend Britain against Orléans, and to rescue Amelia, and to find Gray and bring him home. Haring off into the midst of a pitched battle is merely the means to that end.'

'And is there truly no other means available?' said Joanna, after a moment of gobsmacked silence. 'None which does not require you to risk your own life, break your sworn word to your father, deceive Jenny and Kergabet—'

'Suppose,' said Gwendolen, arresting Joanna's increasingly manic momentum with gentle hands on her shoulders, 'suppose that we took the results of our researches to Lord Kergabet, or to His Majesty, and explained what is needed?'

'Yes,' said Joanna, with more confidence than she felt. 'Lord Kergabet has great faith in your judgement in magickal matters, Sophie.'

'But Lord de Vaucourt does not,' said Sophie bitterly. 'And it is Vaucourt who must be persuaded – Vaucourt and my father – if the Crown is to dispatch so many Court mages to Karnag on such a mission. And the Court mages themselves, of course, who are nearly all in Vaucourt's pocket.'

'But Lord de Vaucourt and his fellows could work the spell?' Gwendolen persisted. 'If they could be persuaded?'

'I – I do not see why not,' said Sophie. 'But—' She fell silent, biting her lip; after a moment, she continued, 'but if they cannot be persuaded, they will know – or must suspect – what we are about, and will be the more able to prevent us from doing what they refuse to do.'

Which, Joanna conceded, was entirely true. Nevertheless—

'Nevertheless,' she said aloud, 'we are not irresponsible children, Sophie; we must try, at the least, to do as we ought. There is a name for persons who withhold vital military intelligence from those who have most need of it, and it is not a pleasant one.'

Sophie's face twisted into a thunderous scowl. Sophie was in general disposed to be truthful, however, and Joanna was therefore unsurprised when she made no effort to disagree.

'What a fascinating theory,' said Lord de Vaucourt, leaning his chin upon his folded hands. He turned from Sophie to Lord Kergabet and continued: 'Such imaginations as these young people have! I am all admiration.'

The Sophie who had arrived in London all those years ago at the age of seventeen might well have incinerated Vaucourt's study and everyone in it with the force of her outrage and indignation. The Sophie of the present moment possessed a hard-won level of self-control which permitted her instead – though not without effort – to smile thinly at her antagonist and say, 'I assure you, my lord, that no admiration is necessary – unless, that is, you meant to express admiration of our investigative efforts. There has been no imagination in the case.'

Vaucourt had turned back to her when she spoke to him – according her that show of respect, at any rate, if he could not bring himself to do more – and now returned her edged smile with one of his own. 'You must not think, ma'am, that your desire to assist in the defence of the kingdom is unappreciated,' he said. 'I am sure, however, that you must be aware how much your enthusiasm outstrips your practical experience.'

'Must I?' said Sophie. Vaucourt, who did not know her well, returned her gaze impassively; Joanna, who did, laid a restraining hand on Sophie's, clenched in her skirts beneath the table. 'Tell me, Maître Vaucourt—'

Lord Kergabet, also well acquainted with his sister-in-law, chose this moment to intervene: 'My lord,' he said, touching Sophie's shoulder in silent apology, 'it is a grave mistake, I assure you, to underestimate Magistra Marshall's practical experience in matters of . . . unusual magick.'

'You will forgive me, my lord, I am sure,' Vaucourt returned, 'if I decline to take your word upon it.' He smiled, half apology, half superior smirk. 'It has been my duty to advise His Majesty on all such matters these ten years and more; and I do not presume to usurp *your* authority in matters political.'

The worst of it was, thought Joanna bitterly, that Vaucourt scarcely even *tried* to veil his insults, even when speaking to Lord Kergabet – as His Majesty's chief Privy Councillor, arguably the most powerful man in Britain, save one.

But nearly as bad was the recognition that, in fact, Vaucourt was not altogether wrong; very likely Kergabet's support was based as much on his own faith in Sophie *qua* Sophie as on any sober and rational assessment of the process by which she had drawn her conclusions, and undeniably he was as ill qualified to opine on any magickal question as Joanna was herself.

'My lord,' said Sophie, her hand shaking under Joanna's but her voice admirably even, 'what is your own theory as to the Duc d'Orléans' choice of military targets?'

'The man calls himself Imperator Gallia and has forbidden the worship of any but the gods of Rome in the territories under his control,' said Vaucourt at once. 'He is mad, or at any rate is in the grip of some idée fixe, and his military strategy is that of a madman. We should be foolish to seek reason or logic in it.'

Gwendolen had said something very like this, not so long ago –

she remembered it too, Joanna guessed from her guilty half glance at Sophie – but it had not stung as Vaucourt's easy dismissal did.

'I disagree,' said Sophie. 'His logic may be that of some particular madness, yet logic all the same, capable of being reasoned through by a sufficiently patient opponent, and circumvented before its worst conclusions can be reached. I have seen it before.'

The logic of some particular madness – she has Cormac MacAlpine of Alba in mind, yes.

Joanna and Gwendolen exchanged a brief but meaning look.

'You refer, I suppose, to that scuffle in Alba three years ago?' said Vaucourt.

The three ladies bridled at *scuffle* – could an incident be called a mere scuffle, in which so many persons had so nearly lost their lives? – but when Sophie spoke, her voice remained calm and even: 'I do. Cormac MacAlpine's attempt to claim the chieftain's seat of Alba relied on his belief that his clan alone could restore the spell-net which his distant ancestor had created to unite the warring clans, and that any action which might further that aim could be justified by reference to it. Considered in that light, his behaviour was logical from first to last, though no person who had not fallen prey to the same, as you say, idée fixe could have dreamt of acting in such a way.'

She paused, looking expectantly at Vaucourt.

'Unless I have been very much misinformed,' he said slowly, 'the resolution of that . . . tangle was a matter more of luck than of logic.'

Sophie grimaced a little. 'That is true,' she conceded. 'But only because we lacked the information necessary to draw the correct conclusions. Whereas in *this* case—'

'In this case,' said Vaucourt, impatient now, 'you have drawn conclusions on the basis of information whose accuracy cannot be verified, and you propose to risk the lives of half a dozen trained and powerful mages – men of incalculable value to the kingdom – in hopes of demonstrating your own cleverness. I call that self-serving and cowardly, *Magistra.*'

'Lord Vaucourt!' said Kergabet, frowning dangerously.

Down the table, Gwendolen gasped.

'I do not ask anything of any other mage which I should not be prepared to undertake myself,' said Sophie tightly, 'were I permitted to do so. If you know anything at all of the Cormac MacAlpine affair, my lord, surely you must know *that.*'

'With respect, ma'am,' said Vaucourt, 'the lesson of your . . . *adventures* in Alba is, rather, that what you lack in judgement, you make up in reckless disregard for the good judgement of others.'

'Were it not for my *reckless disregard for the good judgement of others*,' Sophie retorted – Joanna could feel her trembling, now, with the effort of remaining calm – 'my father would be dead, and my brother reigning under the influence of a conspiracy of regicides; and the gods alone know what Cormac MacAlpine might by now have done to Alba. Do you tell me, Maître Vaucourt, that I was wrong to take those bulls by the horns, wrong to give my help where it was needed?'

'What I tell you, Your Royal Highness, is that you owe your past successes to sheer good fortune; and Dame Fortune's wheel turns. You must understand—'

'Vaucourt.' Kergabet rose furiously to his feet. 'You forget yourself.'

But Vaucourt stared unflinchingly back at him and said, 'His Majesty will not thank you for encouraging his precious child in her dangerous fancies.'

'That may be so,' replied Kergabet, low, 'but it is not I who have committed that error today.' He straightened to his full height and gathered up Sophie, Joanna, and Gwendolen with a gesture; they collected their documentary evidence – for all the good it had done them – and followed him out of the conference-room without a backward glance, all, Joanna was quite certain, equally seething within.

The ladies of Grosvenor Square were leaving the breakfast table, several days later, when the next blow fell.

At first Sophie thought she had put a foot wrong, turned an ankle, stumbled over her own feet as she occasionally did when lost in thought. But the momentary disorientation persisted, and catching the back of a chair as she passed it failed to arrest her dizzy downward momentum. When next she blinked her eyes open, the view was of Joanna's and Gwendolen's faces, wide-eyed with alarm; behind them, Lady Maëlle's, bending closer; behind her, the ceiling of the breakfast-room. Some great invisible weight pressed down upon her lungs; her pulse thrummed in her throat, in her ears; the room dimmed, brightened, dimmed again; an oppressive silence closed in about her, broken only by a sharp shock of distress which, after a frozen moment, she recognised as Gray's rather than her own.

The pain was vicious but short-lived, but the relief of its going was entirely eclipsed, for with it went her faint but ever-present sense of her own magick.

Panicked, she sank deeper, forgetting such mundane concerns as sight and sound and breath in the frantic search for this one quintessential thing. At last, farther down and farther in and smaller and fainter than ever before, but still unmistakably *there*, she found what she sought, and the relief of it nearly shattered her concentration. But Sophie's experience of magickal catastrophe had heavily featured not only her own magick but Gray's, too; and so, having reassured herself that the one remained intact, if strangely subdued, she could not help also seeking after the other.

This took longer – or so it seemed; she had no real sense of how much time might be passing, or how little, whilst she swam these half-familiar depths – but by narrowing her focus again, again, again, she at last perceived the faint, fragile thread of Gray's magick, thrumming the same reassuring deep blue-green. But even this was not quite as it ought to be; shivering up the fine-drawn link, as she listened, there came a note of some altogether alien magick.

No: not one note, one magick, but *many*.

Gray, I thank all the gods that you are alive and well; but what in Hades are you about?

'Sophie, thank all the gods!'

Sophie let her eyes close briefly, then opened them again, confused and assessing: her own bed in Jenny's house; Joanna at her bedside, hollow-eyed with lack of sleep; a bright stripe of morning light through the narrow gap in the window-curtains. *Tomorrow morning, then.*

Her head ached, and the rest of her felt limp and worn out, but her vision was undimmed, Joanna's voice came clearly to her ears, and best of all, when she felt for her magick, she found it near at hand and burning brightly. The link to Gray's magick, too, was easily found and tested, and seemed to have regained its former strength.

But the sense of some other persons' presence was undiminished, and the jarring note spoilt the otherwise perfectly expected harmony between Gray's magick and her own.

'Sophie!' Joanna's tone of real alarm disturbed the fragile equilibrium Sophie had only just succeeded in re-establishing.

'What is it?' she said, wallowing up from the pillows to look her sister in the eyes.

Joanna blinked. 'You . . . were not answering me,' she said, after a moment, sounding a trifle sheepish. 'For a *very* long time, Sophie. I did not know where you had gone.'

'I was looking inwards,' said Sophie, 'and looking for Gray. I am sorry to have alarmed you.'

Reaching out, she caught Joanna's hands in hers.

'Looking for Gray?' Joanna said. 'Looking, how?'

How to explain it to Joanna, who could experience magick only from the outside – and not always then?

But Joanna waved an impatient hand. 'Never mind! You found him, I must suppose – where is he?'

'If I were capable of discovering his whereabouts from this distance,' said Sophie, 'even very approximately, I should have said so long before this. But something has happened, Jo – something happened yesterday; it *was* yesterday?' Joanna nodded. 'What it was, exactly, I cannot tell, but there is something else – someone else – woven in with Gray's magick now, which was not there before. Like—'

'Like Lucia MacNeill's spell for sharing her magick!' Joanna exclaimed.

'Yes,' said Sophie, 'and . . . no – for Lucia's magick was a welcome relief to me, and this . . .' She shivered, remembering the phantom weight on her chest, the dimming of her eyes – the sharp distress sizzling along the link between Gray's magick and her own. 'This was not.'

'Sophie—'

476

'I may be able to gain some better notion of where Gray is – in what direction, at any rate – once we are across the Manche,' Sophie continued. 'And of course then it will be worth our while to begin trying a finding-spell – from here it would be useless, for the distance aside, open water is a dreadful dampener of finding-spells. And—'

'*Sophie*—'

'Whatever the Duc d'Orléans is about, it is gathering speed.' Sophie pushed back the bedclothes, swung her legs over the edge of the bed, and cautiously stood.

'But how can you know—'

Sophie could not explain, in rational terms, how she knew, and therefore did not try. 'We have wasted too much time already in trying to persuade Lord Vaucourt and my father to act,' she said instead. 'I do not intend to wait any longer. We know what is needed.'

A frankly enormous breakfast and a nearly scalding bath, undertaken at Joanna's stern insistence, made Sophie feel much more herself, but produced no change in her opinion on the necessity for swift action.

'Then we shall act,' said Joanna simply. 'But *not* by creeping away the moment the night is dark enough. You may be incapable of learning from past experience, but *I* am not; this expedition will be properly planned and provisioned, or we shall none of us have anything to do with it.'

Sophie sighed, but could scarcely argue with this eminently sensible pronouncement.

Their planning was made more difficult by Lady Maëlle's solicitous care of Sophie, and by the fact that Lord Kergabet and

Jenny plainly anticipated some attempt at escape; having largely left them to their own devices whilst they sorted and catalogued the voluminous results of their expedition to Oxford, and even during their furious interrogation of the diaries of Edward II, Jenny now seemed cheerfully determined to keep them under her eye, or busy about some other business, at all times.

They were forced at last to enlist the help of Katell, once more sworn to secrecy – all of which smote Sophie's conscience to a degree which might have been insupportable, had there been less at stake – and to pool their coin for the hire of a carriage to take them to Oxford, which must be the first halt on their journey.

More delicate still was the problem of communicating their intentions to Lucia and Roland, as all written correspondence was liable to be opened and read – for their own safety, naturally. But the first thing necessary to their present mission was a sufficient complement of mages; and Roland and Lucia, surely, were among the least likely to reject their proposal out of hand.

Sophie had made a list of likely candidates at Merlin – headed, of course, by Gareth Evans-Hughes; she did not like to involve Master Alcuin, whose age and health militated against his participation in such an uncertain venture even as his skill and knowledge recommended it – but quailed inwardly at the thought of the time that would be spent, and perhaps wasted, in explanation and persuasion, all because the thing could not be done openly and officially, by the issuing of royal commands.

All the same, a small party of travellers could move more quickly than an army.

The next piece of news was that a fleet of ships flying the banner of the pretended Emperor had been seen departing Tours, sailing down the Loire towards the city of Naoned and, ultimately, the Breizhek coast – directly south and east of Karnag.

Sophie set aside her dignity, therefore, and wrote a pleading letter to her father, asking his permission to make a visit to the Palace, both to escape the four walls of Lord Kergabet's house and to speak with him and with Lucia. His reply arrived sooner than she had dared hope – together with a carriage and a quartet of Royal Guardsmen for her safe conveyance thither.

'I hope you are not come with some idea of further badgering Lord Vaucourt with wild tales culled from the ravings of Edward the Dishonourable, my dear,' said His Majesty, when Sophie and he were settled on opposing sofas in his private study. 'You know, I hope, that if there is any need for a rescue mission, you have only to tell me so?'

Things had gone so far beyond the need for Gray to be rescued that Sophie scarcely knew what to say to this. 'I have no intention of importuning Lord Vaucourt, Father,' she said at last. *Though only because I know very well it would do no one any good.*

She had, it was true, had some hopes that her father might be a more receptive audience than Lord Vaucourt; but clearly they were not to be fulfilled.

'I have no reason to fear for my own health,' she said instead, 'nor to believe that Gray is in more danger now than at any time since he left England.' He had, after all, been in grave danger all along, in one way or another. 'My meeting with Lord Vaucourt was unrelated to either possibility, I assure you.'

His Majesty smiled. 'I am glad of it.'

Sophie drew a deep breath. 'I do have a favour to beg of you, however,' she said carefully. 'If I may not – if I cannot be of any use to Maître de Vaucourt, or to Lord Kergabet, then I should wish to return to Oxford, and continue the work already begun there. If I may be permitted to go, I mean to ask Roland and Lucia to go with me, for I know that they are as weary of confinement as I am myself.'

The King considered her proposal at such length, and in such an imposing silence, that Sophie began to despair of success.

'The Lady Lucia has certainly made her displeasure plain,' he said at last, 'and so, as a result, has your stepmother. I expect that Lucia should be glad of some practical employment, and Roland ought not to be moping about as he has been doing.' He regarded Sophie intently, as though searching her face for some sign of subterfuge; Sophie breathed very steadily, and prayed very hard to wise Minerva, and schooled her features into an expression of hopeful patience.

'Provided that you are adequately guarded,' said the King, 'I suppose there can be no harm in it.' His lips twisted in a rueful not-quite-smile. 'Indeed, on present evidence London would appear the greater danger, for the Lady Lucia at any rate. I must tell you, my dear – for I know you shall not repeat it – that I was astonished at her choosing to remain here, having been subjected to such a gross violation of the laws of hospitality. She certainly does not lack for pluck.'

Pluck, thought Sophie wonderingly, did not come even vaguely near to the truth of Lucia, but for present purposes, it would do well enough.

'I thank you, Father, very much indeed,' she said, rising from her sofa and bending to kiss his cheek. She straightened. 'May I go now to deliver my invitation to Lucia and Roland?'

He waved her away with a kindly smile.

In the corridor outside her father's private study, Sophie ran against Lord de Vaucourt – almost, but not quite, literally – striding purposefully in the opposite direction to herself, with a stack of dispatches in his arms.

It was the work of a moment to decide to listen at the door, and a journey of less than half a dozen steps to put her decision into practice, against both her conscience and her better judgement.

Alas, however, the door was very thick, and Maître Vaucourt highly skilled in the working of warding-spells; and so all that came to her pricked ears, before the two circumstances combined to muffle all sound from within past distinguishing, was the single word *Haudricourt*.

It was enough.

CHAPTER XXXIII

In Which Sophie Breaks Her Word

Sophie ran Lucia to earth in the Fountain Court, reading an historical account of Edward Longshanks' defeat at Berwick with great determination and very little success, and Roland in the music-room, irritably picking out a melancholy tune upon his mother's pianoforte.

'I am come to dragoon you into another expedition to Oxford,' she said, with determined cheerfulness, for the benefit of anyone who might happen to overhear their conversation.

Then she herded them both into Lucia's sitting-room, set the strongest ward she could upon it, and, over the ensuing hour, explained all that had been going forward in Grosvenor Square since their last meeting.

'And the answer – the method of renewing the spell-stones – it was in those old diaries?' said Lucia eagerly, when Sophie related the disappointing discovery that the defensive magick they had hoped to wield had almost certainly fallen prey to two centuries' neglect.

Sophie blinked in surprise – but they were neither of them fools, and they must of course already have concluded that her request for those specific volumes had not been an arbitrary one.

'Yes,' she said. 'And that is why I need your help – both of you. Not to go to Oxford – that is, Oxford *first*, but after that, by ship to Karnag.'

She described her conversations with Lord Kergabet, with Maître de Vaucourt, with her father; described the bizarre experience of feeling some other person's magick invade her link with Gray, and her conviction that Orléans' plan was coming to a head (Roland made to object to this reliance on gut instinct; Lucia said firmly, 'If Sophie says it is so, then that is enough for me,' and he subsided); and concluded with her attempt at eavesdropping on the King and his chief mage, which, they all agreed, might plausibly be taken to support their theory as to Orléans' intentions.

'And King Edward's method requires half a dozen mages,' she said at last. 'Gwendolen Pryce and I are two, but her talent is modest and she is largely untrained. You two, on the other hand—'

Sophie fell silent, gazing determinedly at her toes and chewing her lip in nervous anticipation. From the corner of her eye, she could perceive Roland and Lucia muttering together.

Lucia, who owed no allegiance to anyone on either side of this conflict, save Roland and her own friends, was very ready to be persuaded to quit the increasingly stifling confines of the Royal Palace for a highly unauthorised jaunt across the Manche to Breizh.

'And it is not as though we shall even be going near the fighting,' she pointed out, tracing possible routes on the map – an ordinary map of Britain, this time – which Sophie had prudently brought with her from Grosvenor Square. 'Or . . . not *very* near, at any rate.'

'Not yet,' said Sophie. 'But I think it is only a matter of time, if we go to Karnag, before the fighting comes to us.'

Roland, as Sophie had expected, was a more difficult

undertaking; for him as for herself, what she proposed to do was a matter not only of genuine risk to life and limb but of defying both father and King – if the bones so tossed fell wrongly, in fact, a matter of treason.

But Roland had already been stinging from being made to stay safe at home when fell the dual blows of Derrien Robic's attempt on Lucia's life and successful taking of his own; he was, it seemed, feeling sufficiently useless, reckless, and unjustly stymied that his thoughts made more fertile soil for Sophie's ideas than she had at all allowed herself to hope.

This is only the barest beginning, she reminded herself sternly, when euphoria threatened. *And we may already be too late.*

But Roland and Lucia were looking at her expectantly, and begining to talk of logistics and supply, and she could not help a very small smile.

The chief difficulty to be overcome, Lucia recognised early on, was not that of slipping away from the escort of Royal Guardsmen told off to accompany them to Oxford – no very difficult matter, when one travelled in company with Sophie Marshall – but, rather, that of ensuring that the said guardsmen, once evaded, should neither come to harm as a result of Sophie's deception nor immediately raise the alarm and thus put the expedition at risk.

The offer of a solution came, to Lucia's surprise, from little Master Alcuin – Sophie's former tutor, it transpired, and before that, Gray's – who, though he did not look it, proved to have been a mage-officer in His Majesty's army in his youth, and to be adept at spells of illusion and misdirection.

'If we could have a se'nnight's start on whatever pursuit my father may choose to send after us,' said Sophie eagerly, 'it would be enough, I think; we ought to be able to reach the coast in three days – I shall not tell you where, Magister; you understand? – and once we are aboard ship we shall not be quite so easily found.'

'A se'nnight,' the little don mused. There was a faraway look in his pale-blue eyes, and he tugged absent-mindedly at the end of his beard. 'Yes, it might be done, I think, with a little ingenuity.'

There followed a moment's thoughtful silence before he rose abruptly from his chair, muttering unintelligibly into his beard, and began searching his bookshelves. After some unsuccessful attempts to recapture his attention, Sophie rose also, and tugged Lucia up by the hand. 'Come along,' she said. 'We have other fish to fry.'

The rest of these fish were also Fellows of Merlin College – young men all, though none so young as Sophie herself – with the exception of one graduate student. The field was necessarily limited by its being still, for some weeks more, the Long Vacation; but the Marshalls' particular friends, it appeared, were as fond of their books and their comfortable quarters as the Marshalls themselves.

Their first call was to Gareth Evans-Hughes, who had been of such material assistance on their previous visit to Oxford, and by whose gifts as a scry-mage Sophie set such store. They had not asked permission to wander about Merlin College; instead, disconcertingly, Sophie had simply caused the Porter on the gate to find them unremarkable, and they had walked in on the heels of a fair-headed young man in a blue coat (who took no more notice of them than the Porter had done) and made directly for Master Alcuin's staircase. Lucia had never before seen this power of Sophie's so clearly on display, and in a way it was more terrifying than any of her more dramatic magickal undertakings: the effortlessness of it, as though to make herself and Lucia essentially invisible were a matter of no more account than calling light!

'Gareth is not the most powerful of mages, in the ordinary way,' Sophie explained, low-voiced and in Gaelic, as they crossed a grassy quadrangle. 'But he is sensible and clever, and has been one of our most loyal friends, and I *hope* that he may be persuaded to forgo common sense for the sake of that friendship, if for no other.'

'And,' said Lucia, with a sidelong look, 'we may perhaps have need of a scry-mage?'

'Yes,' said Sophie. 'That, also.'

If Gareth Evans-Hughes proved astonishingly persuadable, Guillaume d'Allaire, Reader in Magickal Theory, was not.

'*This* is your plan,' he said flatly, when Sophie had finished explaining herself. His pale eyebrows had vanished entirely under his untidy, straw-coloured curls. 'This . . . this hodgepodge of legends and speculation. I must tell you, Magistra, I expected better of you.'

Lucia was struck speechless by the man's effrontery, but Sophie – who had named him a friend! – merely pressed her lips together briefly before returning to the fray.

'It seems absurd to you, I know,' she said patiently, 'and I cannot altogether disagree. But it is by no means the strangest defensive magick I have seen at first hand; if it works as it ought to do, we shall be doing a great service to the kingdom, and perhaps saving a great many lives which must otherwise have been laid down in defence of it.'

Guillaume d'Allaire sighed. 'And how, precisely, do I figure into your scheme?'

He looked reluctant and sounded put-upon, but for all that, there was a certain look in his slate-blue eyes which Lucia – her father's apprentice in matters political since her childhood – had seen before.

Unlike Sophie, therefore, she was entirely unsurprised when, at last, d'Allaire agreed to join their clandestine expedition to Karnag.

By the time their party set sail – by night, aboard a smuggler's craft, from the unlovely fishing village of Bognor, upon the Sussex coast – it numbered fully a dozen persons: not only d'Allaire and Evans-Hughes but two more Fellows of Merlin, Henry Crowther and Séverin Proulx, and Gray's former student Rhein Bevan – and (at their own insistence) Ceana MacGregor and Conall Barra MacNeill. It was thus far larger than Lucia considered either necessary or advisable, but she could not deny that the effect on everyone's spirits of travelling with eight mages of some power (and it would not do to discount Gwendolen Pryce, either, she reminded herself) was a cheering one. Of course this was largely an illusion; in fact, it was Sophie's magick which protected all of them at present, and the more persons Sophie must conceal, the greater the drain upon her magick and, thus, the greater the danger to them all.

The company of Royal Guardsmen dispatched to Oxford along with Sophie, they had left to the care of Master Alcuin. His promise to procure Sophie's party a se'nnight's start, to ensure that no harm came to any of the guardsmen, and to pay their tariff at the Dragon and Lion from the purse of coin Sophie had left with him for the purpose, was less reassuring than it ought to have been, from the circumstance of his having refused to tell any of them precisely how he meant to carry out the first of these undertakings.

'I trust Master Alcuin,' Sophie had said, very firmly, but Lucia had wondered whom, exactly, she had been hoping to persuade.

'Lucia?' said Roland, hushed and tentative, at her left shoulder.

Half turning from the taffrail, Lucia saw that Roland had brought her a shawl and was preparing to drape it round her shoulders.

487

'I thank you,' she said, low.

Roland ducked his head. 'You were shivering.' He shifted into halting Gaelic to say, 'Do you think that Sophie's . . . plan has any chance to succeed, truly?'

Lucia did Roland the courtesy of considering this question seriously. 'If I thought we had no chance at all,' she said, after a moment, 'I should not have agreed to be a party to it. It seems . . . a bow drawn at a venture, I will concede, but I have seen Sophie do some very astonishing things.'

In the darkness, Roland nodded. 'And so have I,' he said. 'It is not that I lack faith in Sophie! It is only that . . . well . . .'

Lucia chuckled. 'That her plan has all the hallmarks of madness, and is founded entirely upon instructions found in the diaries of a mad king whose funeral pyre was cold ashes centuries before any of us were born?'

'Well,' Roland repeated, scuffing at a knot in the decking with the toe of his boot. 'Since you ask me, yes.'

'And that this Duke of Orléans has a very large army at his command, and we have not.'

'That, also.'

Roland shivered, and Lucia, greatly daring, unwound the shawl from the left half of her body and wrapped it, and her left arm, about his waist. He tensed briefly; then, perhaps deciding that the proprieties of his father's court need not be scrupulously observed on the deck of a smuggler's craft, drew the shawl up over his left shoulder and settled closer to Lucia at the rail.

'The last time I followed Sophie halfway across a kingdom,' she said pensively, 'I had an army at my back – though only a very small one. I should have reached her much sooner without it, but I was glad of my little troop when we arrived.'

488

'Did you . . . Did your father . . .' Roland's voice trailed off uncertainly.

'I made off with a detachment of my father's household troops without asking his leave, yes,' said Lucia, taking pity on him. 'On the principle of its being easier to beg his pardon than to persuade him. He was *very* angry with me, I am told, but he had regained his temper by the time we next met face-to-face, and only subjected me to a detailed and scathing critique of my conduct – from a military perspective, you understand.'

Roland produced a disbelieving chuckle.

'Should you think less of me,' he said, looking resolutely away from her, 'if I confessed to being a little afraid of your father?'

'If closer acquaintance does not alter your opinion,' said Lucia, 'I shall be very much surprised.'

And if Duncan is not frightened of him, how on earth should you be?

'*My* father will say I ought to have stopped her,' Roland continued unhappily. 'As though I *could*.'

'Roland, your father himself tried to stop Sophie from leaving England, and could not; three years ago, he attempted to stop her from remaining in Din Edin, and could not do that either. And he is not only her father but the *King of Britain*! You surely do not imagine that he expects more of you then he can accomplish himself?'

Roland shrugged, his shoulders hunching.

'Roland.' Lucia inched closer, so that they were pressed together from shoulder to hip, and spoke in Latin, near his ear: 'You may not have seen your father's face – or perhaps you may not remember it – after our adventure in the maze, when he was frightened for you, and declared himself in my debt; but I saw it, and I swear to you on the bones of my mother that you are as much beloved as your sister.'

He did not speak, nor turn to look at her, but his stiff posture gradually relaxed, and they stood shoulder to shoulder at the taffrail until the sun began to warm the eastern horizon.

Breakfast was followed by a council of war to discuss the latest intelligence – not so very recent now, but better than none at all.

'If it were only the troop-ships moving down the Loire,' said Lucia, 'that would be one thing; he might only be aiming at Naoned, which would be perfectly rational – a bid to control the provincial seat, if I understand correctly, and the whole of the river from Orléans down to the sea.' She peered at the map, head tilted, and measured the distance with her spread fingers from the Loire to Naoned. 'But he has a force at Klison already, which is far better placed to besiege Naoned.'

'Exactly,' said Joanna. 'If the reports received thus far are accurate, there are more than enough men at Klison to hold it and march on Naoned besides. But if he can sail *past* Naoned—'

'My uncle's troops will stop him if they can,' said Sophie loyally.

Roland glanced sideways at her. 'Of course they will,' he said, 'but we must allow for the possibility that they cannot – as the garrisons at Klison and elsewhere could not.'

CHAPTER XXXIV

In Which Edward the Dishonourable Disappoints, and Gray Reflects upon the Recent Past

Sophie's party were landed at dawn on a wide-curved beach on the Bay of Kiberon, almost due south of Karnag. They splashed through the surf barefoot, with trouser-legs rolled and skirts tucked up, and collapsed all up and down the empty shingle, with bag and baggage, to wait for the sun to rise.

Then, having set their clothing to rights as best they could, they reassembled themselves as a party of travellers visiting the sights and the holy places of Breizh, located the road to Karnag, and walked the two miles to the village of Le Ménec, on the far side thereof, and its one inn, the Ship at Rest.

The innkeeper beamed when Sophie and Joanna spoke to her in Brezhoneg. Yes, she had good, soft beds to offer them – they should find the rooms small, but bright and clean, never fear! – but such a large party, she hoped they should not object to share their rooms? – no, there had been no Orléanais soldiers hereabouts, no soldiers at all in fact, and glad enough she was of it, for there is nothing like a troop of soldiers for eating a person out of house and home! Well, if there was to be war, she only hoped that whichever side was fated to win it might do so quickly, and not drag the frontier to and fro a dozen times, to the harassment (and worse) of ordinary folk on both sides of it.

Joanna and Sophie looked at one another and refrained from translating this last for the others.

That evening, for the first time, Sophie's finding-spell produced the faintest tug of awareness of Gray's location – almost due south, at the very edge of her perceptive range – and she went to bed in good spirits, for all that the Duke of Orléans was advancing on their position, also, and from two directions at once.

After breakfast the next morning, they trooped out of the inn-yard and through the tiny hamlet of Le Ménec. All but Joanna and the two Alban guards were bleary-eyed and yawning; Sophie herself had scarcely slept.

The bleary eyes opened wide when at length they reached their goal, and stood at the westward end of a vast field planted with massive stones, gazing east along the long, almost mathematically straight rows at the rising sun.

'Apollo, Pan, and Hecate!' breathed Bevan.

Sophie felt very much the same herself; it was one thing to know of the existence of this ancient wonder, and another thing entirely to stand in its presence, feeling the vast aetheric echoes of its past.

'But there are hundreds of stones,' said Joanna, her voice oddly strangled. *'Thousands.* How are we to know which of them are important to the spell?'

'Hush, Jo,' said Sophie absently. She closed her eyes and pressed her palms flat over her ears, the better to hear the thing just beginning to tug at the edge of her perception.

Was this what had kept her awake last night? It seemed the most likely explanation. And if the sounds were not aural but aetheric, then *that* would explain both Joanna's easy energy and her own ill temper, for Joanna might very well have slept like a top.

Sophie moved through the rows of stones with her eyes and ears still stopped, hearing their outlines in her mind as faint, shimmering shapes of dull crimson – not radiating magick, but . . . *soaking it in*; and there, *there*—

'That one,' she said, pointing at the stone to her immediate left, which shimmered sluggishly in a shade of scarlet so intense that it hurt her ears. 'There are six, and that is the first.'

A line of . . . *something* . . . ran between that first stone and the next in the sequence, faint and stuttering but unmistakably *there*. It had a scent like wet limestone and old blood and the air after lightning, and Sophie was growing dizzy with the strangeness of it, which at the same time did not feel nearly so strange as it ought.

There had been rain in the night, and the turf beneath her feet was soft and yielding.

She followed the tugging trail to the next stone – laid both palms against its rough-smooth surface – felt something buzz distantly under her hands and beneath her feet.

It was not like riding the blue-fire magick of Ailpín Drostan's ancient spell-net – to begin with, it was still perfectly clear to her where her own body ended and the rest of the world began – but perhaps, perhaps, the long-dead mage-queen who devised this spell had drawn inspiration from Alba.

As the map had suggested, there were six scarlet stones among the dull crimson ones, straggling vaguely southeastward – in, that is, the approximate direction of Klison, the first link in the chain. Upon opening her eyes, Sophie discovered that each now had a human attendant.

'Yes,' she called, cupping her hands to either side of her face to amplify her voice. 'One mage to every stone.'

There was a brief-scuffle just out of sight amongst the stones.

'Do you mean to begin at once?' d'Allaire called back, from halfway along the chain.

'Have you some better notion?' This from Gareth, farther off still. 'We have not come all this way for a picnic luncheon.'

Sophie rolled her eyes (for none of them could see her, after all), then stood very straight and drew a deep breath, for optimal volume. 'Who has the first stone?'

'I have,' called Lucia MacNeill.

'Then you must begin,' said Sophie. 'Jo, where are you?'

Joanna emerged from beyond the northernmost row of stones, trotted towards Sophie, and said, 'Here.'

'Will you go back to Lucia now,' said Sophie, lowering her voice, 'and give the signal to Gareth when she has finished, and so on? I did not think the keystones would be so far apart.'

Joanna nodded eagerly, and trotted away.

And now there was nothing to do but wait in silence for Lucia – then Gareth, then d'Allaire, then Roland, then Bevan – to take their turns, so that she might cap the spell. *And then we shall have nothing left to do but hope we have succeeded.*

She could hear nothing, and could see very little, of how the others went on, but that did not stop her from imagining each of them in turn pricking one finger with a pen-knife or paper-knife, smearing a drop of blood on the stone, and speaking the invocation, so that by the time her own turn came, every muscle ached with tension.

The little knife was so sharp that she did not feel the sting of the wound until her thumb was pressed against the stone's rough face, and then she nearly jerked it away in surprise at the sudden sensation of *pulling*.

'*O gods great and small,*' she recited, '*O gods above and gods below, gods who made the bones and flesh of my kingdom and made men of bone and flesh and blood to walk upon its beloved soil, protect us. O gods who bring the seasons in their proper time, protect us. O gods who gave magick to mankind, defend us. O gods who wear many guises, defend us. With my blood, with my magick, for the sake of my kingdom and all who dwell there, be renewed.* Do ut des.'

She brought her hand away from the stone, staring at the smear of blood where her thumb had been.

She closed her eyes, stopped her ears, reached for her magick – and found everything precisely as it had been before.

Exhaustion and disappointment rolled heavily over her, and she turned her back to the stone and sagged against it.

'We must have done something wrong,' Sophie sighed, as they made their dispirited way back to the inn. 'Perhaps the spell truly cannot be worked except "at the turning of the year", and we ought to have waited for the Equinox—'

'And the arrival of enemy troops?' said Joanna. 'If that is so, then there is nothing to be done about it, Sophie.'

'Or perhaps the words of the invocation – perhaps I was not careful enough in transcribing it – did I misunderstand Edward's instructions? Not that they were instructions, as such—'

'Perhaps at a different time of day,' said Henry Crowther, clapping her encouragingly upon the shoulder. 'Noon, perhaps. Or midnight? Some spells are more efficacious at midnight, you know, or can be worked only then . . .'

It was kindly meant, but surely if the time of day had been a vital component of the spell, the diary must have said so? Sophie sighed and managed a smile at Crowther.

'I move we make another attempt after dinner,' said d'Allaire.

'Seconded!' said Bevan. 'All in favour of dinner?'

There was a good-naturedly derisive chorus of *Ayes*.

They returned to the stones towards dusk, some of their confidence restored by the inn's simple but excellent dinner, and Evans-Hughes, d'Allaire, Crowther, Proulx, Bevan, and Sophie took up positions at the six stones. At first, either the alteration in the choice and sequence of mages or the time of day appeared to be making the difference, for Sophie, at the end of the chain, could feel the stones farther upstream gathering in magick and beginning to radiate it outwards, as they had not done before. But the momentum died with Bevan, and when Sophie herself nicked her thumb and spoke the invocation, it was with the sinking feeling that nothing she now did, or did not do, would have the slightest effect upon the outcome.

Weary and dispirited, they collected themselves, called a flock of magelights, and began to make their way back to the inn.

'Sophie,' said Evans-Hughes quietly, falling into step beside her as they turned into the inn-yard, 'may I see the diary?'

'Of course,' said Sophie. 'I shall fetch it down for you.'

The next two hours were spent by Gareth in close study of Edward II's diary, and by Sophie and Gwendolen in attempting to repair the damage inflicted upon everyone's clothing by most of a day spent tramping about what was essentially a muddy field.

Sophie was mending a rent in Lucia's petticoat, and Gwendolen progressing steadily through a heap of stockings in want of darning, when there came a knock at the door of Sophie and Lucia's bedchamber.

'The answer is in the names,' said Gareth, quite without

preamble, the moment Gwendolen opened the door. 'The names of the mages. Edward did not think to be more explicit, I suppose, because he thought it clear enough. Look—' He thrust the diary almost under Sophie's nose, and Sophie, perforce, did look. His broad forefinger touched each name as he spoke it, moving along the line of cramped, faded script; did he hear in his mind's ear the voice of a king five centuries dead? 'Arzhur of Dinan. Guillaume Forestier of Bayeux. Guy d'Ernée. Melyor Penrose of Lamorna. Richard of Lincoln, called Blythe. And Edward himself, of course. Do you see?'

Sophie did not see, at first. She read the names over again, however, and a pattern began to emerge. A Breizhek name, then two which were more Français than English; Bayeux was in Normandie, of course, and Ernée . . . yes, in Maine. A Kernowek name, and a very English one, from an English town. But—

She shook her head. 'I thought I saw the pattern,' she said, 'but I was mistaken; there is a second English mage, here' – she tapped Edward's name – 'where I expected a Cymric one.'

'Oh, but Sophie, you forget your history,' said Gareth reproachfully, and Gwendolen exclaimed, 'Of course! Edward of Caernarfon!'

'Of . . . ? *Oh!*' Yes, Edward Longshanks' fourth son had been born in Caernarfon Castle. But did that make him, this long-dead Plantagenet king, a man of Cymru? Surely not – or did it?

It was an absurd method; it was dreadfully impractical; it was . . .

It was, thought Sophie with an inward sigh, just exactly the sort of fail-safe which a mage might conceive of, in an attempt to control some very powerful working otherwise apt to grow dangerously out of hand.

She revolved the matter in her head, surveying the resources at her command. Two English mages – Roland and Crowther – and three Cymric ones – Gareth, Bevan, and Gwendolen. Lucia, whose magick she had been relying upon as the most powerful after her own, was suddenly removed from the equation altogether. Guillaume d'Allaire was Normand and Séverin Proulx Mainois, entirely by luck, and she herself was Breizhek enough for this purpose, surely?

But the pattern had a gap in the shape of Melyor Penrose of Lamorna, Edward's Kernowek mage, and how was Sophie to fill it?

Had she dragged all these men and women across the Manche – and into something very like treason – to no good purpose, after all? *Minerva, Lady of Wisdom, how am I to untangle this knot?*

Before settling down to sleep, she worked the usual finding-spell, ignoring – or attempting to ignore – Lucia's silent sympathetic gaze. To her surprise, the result this time was strong and immediate: Gray had grown closer since yesterday, much closer, and the direction of the pull had altered.

If Gray is coming here . . .

Was Gray, whose parents were English but who had been born at Glascoombe, near Dowr Carrek, sufficiently a man of Kernow to stand in the place of Melyor Penrose of Lamorna?

The small fleet of ships bearing the second sorcerer-century – such as it was – down the River Loire and across the Bay of Kiberon had sailed all day and all night, whenever possible, to cover the distance more quickly. When they came in sight of the long, shallow curve of the beach where they were to go ashore – standing afar off, to be on the safe side, for though the passengers might trust to the Emperor's spells of concealment, the crew did not – the sun was hanging low in the western sky, and Gray watched as the crew prepared to lower the boats over the side of the *Coulèvre* with a strange tight thrumming in his chest.

All through the journey, the signs had been there which told him that he was growing nearer to Sophie (or she to him). He had done his best not to dwell on what this must mean, for knowing Sophie to be safe and well and, above all, out of danger from Orléans' armies had been a comfort to him, but so unmistakable were the sensations of proximity now that there was no denying it: She had, in fact, somehow put herself directly in their path. Why should she do so? And, by all the gods, how had she managed it?

This is British soil we are landing on, he reminded himself; *it is she who has every right to be here, and Orléans' troops who have not.*

In the ordinary way, there was no reason why Sophie should not come to Breizh whenever she liked. But nothing about the present circumstances was ordinary, and so . . .

So, then: Sophie was very near. Sophie had given her father her word not to attempt to follow Gray to Normandie, and her presence in Breizh certainly violated the spirit, if not the letter, of that promise. Sophie could be impetuous, true, but she would not lightly break her word to her father.

Certainly there were few enough things he could trust at present, and few enough people. The other mages treated Gray with a more or less friendly condescension, except when actually engaged in some manner of drill or rehearsal of joint manoeuvres. Only twice – in silent shared horror on the occasion of Orléans' original announcement of his campaign plan, and poorly concealed relief at its subsequent revision from hingeing on wholesale slaughter to making use of spells for deep sleep, immobility, and concealment – had any real fellow-feeling subsisted between the others and himself. How odd that after half a day's acquaintance he had been prepared to trust Ollivier and Lécuyer with his life, yet here . . .

'Marais!' Bertrand jostled Gray's shoulder. '*T'es encore dans la lune, hein? Allons, on descend.*'

Gray mumbled an apology for his inattention, and followed Bertrand and Girard over the starboard rail and into the next boat.

Two young crewmen rowed in near silence by the faint light of magelight lanterns. Crammed in beside Gray in the stern of the boat, Girard tilted up his head and murmured, 'What do you suppose the Emperor wants with this godsforsaken place?'

Gray liked Girard well enough, most of the time – he was not much given to cruelty, and had once helped Gray rescue one of the kitchen-maids from the unwanted attentions of a drunken comrade – but confiding in him was quite impossible. And, in any case, what did Gray know? *Take and hold the keystones at Karnag*, Orléans had said; though it was more than any of the others – save, presumably, their commander – had been told, it did not answer the questions *why*, or *how*, or *to what purpose*.

'I suppose that we shall be told what his purpose is when he deems it necessary,' said Gray, therefore – but not reprovingly. Girard was very young, and it was perfectly natural to be curious, and even apprehensive, in the circumstances.

Girard sighed. 'Yes,' he said. 'I suppose so.'

He subsided, leaning gently against Gray's arm and shoulder, and Gray sank back into thought.

When word had come that the sorcerer-century was to sail from Orléans in three days' time, Gray had come near to pleading with Amelia to allow Ollivier and Lécuyer to engineer her escape, but to no avail, for she refused categorically to abandon her beloved papa. Gray could appreciate the integrity of her position – but the problem of the reserve mages' mysterious compulsion, which ebbed and flowed with the strength of their connexion to the field-mages, was a more complex task even than he had anticipated, and a solution unlikely to materialise in the time remaining to him. He bore Amelia's recriminations on this point without protest but equally without concession, until at last she said, 'Even if I were to leave Papa, what would become of me then? I followed him here because, for all his faults, he loved me and needed me; but now he is fallen under the Emperor's spell, and I have nowhere else to go – no one else to go to.'

'How can you say so?' Gray exclaimed. 'Your sisters and your cousin Maëlle were half sick with worry for you, when last I saw them in London, and dreading what might have befallen you in Taylor's company. Why else should I so readily promise to help you?'

Amelia blinked at him, tears beading on her long lashes, and caught back an emerging sob. 'Truly?' she said, in a very small voice.

'Of course,' said Gray, nonplussed.

Amelia sat down heavily – and with an uncharacteristic lack of grace – on the lip of the fountain. 'But why?' she demanded. 'Why should they take me in, any of them? I have been rude to Joanna, and cruel to Sophie – I am a burden to Lady Maëlle, and likely to remain so—'

'I do not pretend to understand even Sophie, let alone Joanna or Lady Maëlle,' said Gray, by now rather desperate to stem this tide of self-recrimination, 'but love need not be rational. Your sisters, I dare say, remember a time when you were better friends; and as for Lady Maëlle . . . well, she has no children of her own . . .'

'And – and she would take me back, after . . . all of this?' An expressive wave of her hands indicated their surroundings.

'I have not the slightest doubt of it,' said Gray truthfully.

Gray had seen many things, but he would not soon forget the sight of Miss Amelia Callender, erstwhile chatelaine of Callender Hall, weeping into her hands in a moonlit courtyard in Orléans. He reflected, not for the first time, that nearly all of Amelia's behaviour in Grosvenor Square, and most of Sophie's and Joanna's, could be explained very tidily as a means of self-defence – each attempting to wound the other before she could be fatally wounded herself.

The storm of weeping was intense, but mercifully brief; and when its aftermath had been assuaged by means of first Amelia's own handkerchief, then Gray's, she had sat up straight on the fountain's edge, folded her hands in her lap, and said quietly, 'Very well, Mr Marshall—Gray. I am at your disposal.'

Ollivier had smuggled her out of the castle courtyard the following evening, dressed in yet another purloined infantryman's uniform, and by now she might already be safely over the Mainois border, or so Gray hoped.

The boats deposited their passengers on the fine shingle, then at once put out again towards the *Couleuvre,* now nearly invisible in the gathering dusk. The sorcerer-century formed up into small, relatively inconspicuous groups for the brief march inland – the stone-fields of Karnag were only a few miles distant – and Gray, one of very few speakers of Brezhoneg present, found himself in the first group to depart, together with Bertrand, Guillemeau, Dolet, and Decurion Rousseau's particular crony, Antoine Martel.

The high, sweet thrum of Sophie's magick sang louder and louder in his blood as they climbed up from the beach and strode along the road. The strength and the nearness of it both comforted and alarmed him: *Sophie is here!* sang one part of his mind, triumphant, joyful, whilst another gibbered, *Sophie is in terrible danger!*

As the link between his magick and Sophie's tugged him in one direction, his links with the mages of the reserves in Orléans tugged resolutely the other way – each in itself a small and fragile thing, but collectively a weight upon his spirits.

For his own sanity, he had still to avoid recalling too closely the process of forging those links. What Rousseau and Girard had described as mildly unpleasant, on the order of a mild headache or a case of indigestion, Gray – whether because of his existing link to Sophie or because of his violent, if unexpressed, objection to Orléans' modus operandi – had experienced as excruciating pain. He had lost consciousness only briefly (or so he was afterwards assured), but the feeling of disorientation, the skin-crawling sensation of something *wrong*, had taken days to fade, and even then had not vanished but merely subsided.

Worse than all of this was knowing what the links were *for*. Talk amongst the sorcerer-century confirmed Amelia's claim that nothing in the linking-spell prevented a reserve-mage's magick from being entirely drained, should the field-mage's need be sufficiently great. Some drew confidence from this notion; a few had confessed, though quietly and obliquely, that the implications troubled them; but the majority expressed no opinion in either direction. Did they simply take the reserves for granted as insurance against difficulty or disaster, or did they harbour objections which they were too afraid to voice even to one another?

And if, as it was said, only Orléans himself could forge those links between a mage of the sorcerer-century and his reserves, was the reverse also true? Must Gray now pass the rest of his days with half a dozen strangers' magicks uncomfortably twisted up with his own – and, worse, with Sophie's?

Gray wrenched his thoughts away from this distressing tangent, focusing as narrowly as he was able upon the here and now: the sounds and scents of the night air, already hinting at autumn's chill as the Equinox approached; his companions' footfalls, their quiet voices, all about him; the silver glint of moonlight on Martel's dark hair, on the buttons of Bertrand's coat; the precise spot where his own boot was rubbing a blister on his left heel.

When he was calm again, within as well as without, he allowed himself to consider once more how to go on from here. The easiest and least risky choice was to slip away once the first few groups of men had reached the rendezvous point between Karnag and Le Ménec and settled in for the night; if he volunteered to take the first watch, then he should have only one sentry to subdue or outwit, rather than two. By awaiting the next morning's promised briefing, on the other hand, he should have more precise intelligence to carry to Sophie, or to the nearest British garrison, if he should stumble across the latter before finding the former. But what if that small delay should make the difference in his ability to escape, or if it should mean that the intelligence came too late to do any good?

And what in Hades does it mean, *that Sophie is here?*

CHAPTER XXXV

In Which Gray Seizes His Opportunity

The following morning, the whole of the party followed up their breakfast with a largely undirected ramble about Le Ménec, so that they might speak more freely without setting wards. They paused for a quarter-hour's rest in a coppice-wood on the far side of the stone-fields, and at Sophie's insistence she, Gareth, and Lucia worked yet another set of finding-spells. This time, they were pulled so strongly towards Gray that Sophie had to be physically restrained from following her finding at once.

'He may not be alone, or free,' Lucia pointed out reasonably. 'He went into the Duchies to investigate this Imperator Gallia, as well as to search for your sister; we cannot know what schemes he may have in train, and we should do no one any good by interrupting them.'

Sophie, now resting with her back against the trunk of a tree, bounced one knee in suppressed frustration. 'I can go to him without being seen,' she said. 'I have done such things before, as you may remember' – here a pointed look at Lucia, as though Lucia might perhaps have failed to remark how entirely their journey from London to Karnag had depended on Sophie's particular talents – 'and if Gray is in need of rescuing—'

'If he were in need of rescuing,' said Joanna, 'should you not have known it already, now he is so nearby?'

'Well,' said Sophie, looking at her feet. 'Yes, very probably I should. But—'

'And if you can find him,' Joanna continued, 'then *he* ought also to be able to find *you*? He must know already that you are here, just as you have known for some time that he was travelling towards us?'

'Yes,' said Sophie. 'But—'

For a long moment the sisters faced one another in silence, conversing, it appeared, in some language made up entirely of pointed looks.

At last the contest, whatever its precise nature, was resolved in Joanna's favour; Sophie turned away, clasping her elbows and curling in her shoulders, and said, 'Very well.'

Joanna sighed, looking not at all satisfied with her victory.

'I know how eager you must be to see Gray, Sophie,' said Lucia, clasping her shoulder. 'I should be frantic, in your place. But if he is not in any danger . . .'

'It is not only that,' said Sophie.

Lucia mentally chalked up a point to herself, for provoking her friend into speech. *It is a fact of human nature*, her father was fond of saying, *that we are loath to let a wrong statement go unchallenged.*

'This is what Gareth and I wished to explain,' said Sophie, 'here, away from the inn and whoever else may be in it. We need a Kernowek mage, in order to renew the magick of the stones; and Gray is . . . the nearest available approximation.'

'Why?' said d'Allaire blankly.

'Because he was born in Kernow,' said Sophie. She frowned at him.

506

'Not—' d'Allaire scrubbed a hand across the back of his neck. 'I meant – why do we need a mage from Kernow?'

'The diary,' said Gareth. His sideways glance at Sophie held some exasperation; he himself, Lucia suspected, would have begun at the beginning. 'Edward the Second was born in Cymru, and when he came to Karnag to replenish the magick his father had neglected, he brought with him mages from each of Britain's other provinces. If Sophie and I are correct, we shall not succeed unless we do the same.'

'What an odd requirement!' said Crowther. 'You are certain of this, are you? It seems . . .'

'We can be certain that both of our previous attempts failed,' said Evans-Hughes.

'And the first, I think, failed almost straight away,' said Sophie, 'but the second . . . the magick *was* settling in the stones, as it ought to do, until we reached Bevan's stone, and then the . . . the flow reversed itself. Which suits Gareth's theory perfectly, because Gareth had the first stone in the chain, and so you, Rhein, represented a doubling-back to Cymru.'

Bevan nodded thoughtfully.

'I agree with Lucia and Joanna, that we ought to wait for Marshall to seek us out,' said Roland. 'In case he may be occupied with something which ought not be interrupted. But if you had rather not wait, Sophie, could you not use a drawing-spell to bring him here? He is very near now, you said?'

'Very near,' Sophie agreed, 'and to the south. Roland, have you ever *felt* a drawing-spell? Or seen one?'

'No,' said Roland, a little defensive. 'It is not a very common magick.'

'At this distance,' said Sophie, 'it would be very difficult to resist, and quite impossible to explain.'

'A last resort, then,' said d'Allaire, with a wry smile.

The light drizzle which had begun whilst they were debating Evans-Hughes's theory was now thickening into rain of the sort which demanded to be taken notice of.

'If our plan at present is to wait quietly for Marshall to grace us with his presence,' said Crowther plaintively, 'let us at least wait within doors, and out of the damp.'

The slow and stealthy reassembly of the Emperor's troops in a fallow field a few hundred yards from the stones of Le Ménec was accomplished a little before midnight; and when the tents had all been pitched, the latrines and fire-pits dug, and the ring of concealment-spells, wards and shielding-spells set in place, the sorcerer-century retired to its bedrolls. From the tent he shared with Bertrand and Girard, Gray could hear the occasional low murmur of voices from the men standing the first watch, the chirping of crickets, the wind singing through the lines of stones. Soon Girard and Bertrand were snoring to either side of him; Gray lay long awake, however, contemplating the bizarre turn his life had lately taken.

By the time the watch changed, he had dozed and awoken several times, and was forced to concede that Morpheus had chosen not to favour him with restful sleep tonight. Very well, then; he was not likely to find anything more like privacy than this. He closed his eyes, settled his thoughts as best he could, then reached deep for his magick and, holding in his mind's eye an image of Sophie's face, sent it out on the quiet words of a finding-spell: *O amisse reperiaris! Verba oris mei ad te eant. Remitte ea ut me ad te adducant.*

The returning flow of magick was immediate and almost

overwhelming – Sophie was very near now, and he had failed to compensate for the proximity of her magick. He had not been aware of any ebbing of his own power, but now it strained towards hers, clamouring in tandem with the finding-spell to pull him up out of his bedroll and southward towards the village proper. He could follow it – could nudge aside the tent-flaps and crawl out from under the canvas, tug on his boots and creep between the tents and out of the camp – but tomorrow, tomorrow he should discover what Orléans was about with this manoeuvre, and then he should not have spent all this time and effort to no purpose.

Tomorrow.

He rose at dawn having slept scarcely at all, performed his morning ablutions, fell in with the others, and waited for their commanding officer to speak. Beyond their wards and shields, and beyond the woods ringing the field in which they had pitched their camp, some heavy cart or waggon rumbled past along the road from Le Ménec. The Centurion, so called, was ordinarily a man of terse orders and brief but rousing extempore speeches; when instead he drew from his uniform coat several folded pages of writing-paper, a murmur passed through the ranks of mages. It subsided as he began to speak, but rose again, baffled, when he said, 'Once we have taken possession of the stone-fields of Karnag, our empire will hold the reins of a great and ancient magick, older by far than the Kingdom of Britain from whose grasp we must reclaim the remaining lands of Gallia Romana.

'Our brothers of the first sorcerer-century now hold all of the line of fortress-stones, but the wellspring of the magick is here: three thousand stones, three thousand repositories of power, sleeping since the days of Divus Iulius. When we possess the stones, we shall wield unimaginable power. Our task now is to secure the stones – no great matter, as the local people are ignorant of their power, and suppose them no more than an historical curiosity – and then to wake them.'

'To *wake* them?' muttered someone, close enough for Gray to hear. '*Three thousand* stones?'

And how, exactly, does one wake a stone?

Gray did not have long to ponder this question; the answer went some way towards explaining why the half-trained and undermanned second sorcerer-century, and not any of the large, well-equipped infantry regiments presently mustered at Orléans, had been sent to Karnag: to wake the power that slept within the stones, it appeared, required an infusion of magick from without. But how much magick? There were three thousand stones, so said the Centurion, and but eighty mages; how long could each of them keep feeding their own magick into stone after stone after stone, before – reserves or no reserves – they came to the end of themselves?

But he had what he needed now, more or less; there was little to be gained by staying longer.

'When our task is done, the Emperor himself will come to take possession of the legacy of Divus Iulius. All hail the Emperor of Gaul!'

'All hail,' Gray muttered along with the others.

They departed their camp as they had entered it, in twos and threes, and as they filtered into the long field of standing stones, he cast about for some opportunity of escape, placing himself deliberately on the right edge of the field.

From afar, the stones in their long straight rows had looked more or less uniform; close to, however, they varied in size from the height of Gray's knee to well above his head, and were far more irregular in shape than he had supposed. Here and there one had fallen on its side; Gray wondered whether it would be part of the mages' task to right these deviants from the regimented pattern, and, if so, how the Centurion proposed that they do so. Moss and lichen patched their surfaces, particularly on the north faces and in the deep clefts that marked some of the larger oblong stones, bright and pale and deep greens, brown and gold and rust-red. Around their feet, grasses still green or autumn-gold stirred gently in the breeze.

Towards the middle of the sea of stones, a particularly large specimen, just barely taller than Gray and three times as wide at waist height, offered him temporary cover, and whilst the men to his left advanced, he slipped away into the trees to the south. Once out of sight amongst the trees, he moved more quickly – sometimes, when the way was relatively clear, breaking into a run – and when he judged he had got clear, he settled down with his back to a large tree-trunk and repeated his finding-spell.

Sophie was away to the west, now – not because she had moved much, Gray judged, but because he had come so far east since the previous night's attempt. His possessions were scattered across three separate military camps in two kingdoms; he owned, at present, absolutely nothing but the clothes on his back and the meagre contents of his pockets; but the relief of simply following where the finding-spell led him, as he had done hundreds of times in his life (though seldom for so high a stake), was indescribable, and a weight seemed to lift from his shoulders as he strode along the lanes towards Le Ménec.

* * *

'A gentleman to see you, ma'am,' said the innkeeper to Sophie, not a quarter-hour after Sophie had left the breakfast-table and retreated to her bedchamber. Sophie's heart leapt; she quashed the feeling firmly. *But who else could it be?*

'Please show him up,' she said, and folded her trembling hands in her lap. She chanced to be quite alone at present, for Lucia and Roland and Joanna and Gwendolen had developed an unexpected passion for long, exploratory walks about the village and the countryside, which they were presently indulging, and none of the Oxford men had yet emerged from their rooms. When the door opened again and Gray walked through it, she thanked all the gods for the blisters on her heels.

'Thank you, Mrs Cariou,' she managed to say. 'You may leave us, if you please.' At the innkeeper's frankly dubious expression, she added, 'It is most irregular, I know; but this gentleman is my husband, who is just come from England to join me and our friends.' *Without bag or baggage, and looking as though he has been sleeping under a hedge.*

'Very good, ma'am,' said the innkeeper, with the air of one who has many questions which she has decided not to ask, and finally, *finally* went away.

'Sophie,' said Gray, in a voice thick with exhaustion and relief.

He held out his arms, and she ran the length of the room on her blistered feet to fling herself into them, clinging as tight as though she had suspected him of wishing to escape.

By the time Lucia, returning from her walk, pushed open the door of their shared chamber, Sophie had subjected Gray to a hot bath, two helpings of breakfast, and other things not for public consumption; had demanded an accounting in the matter of Amelia, and attempted to come to terms with the revelation that his 'rescue' thereof had apparently consisted in sending her off into the Orléanais countryside with a pair of Breizhek mage-officers; and was well along in explaining how she, her brother and sister, her sister's intimate friend, the heiress of Alba, and five Merlin men had come to be filling up all the guest-rooms of the Ship at Rest in Le Ménec.

'Gray Marshall!' cried Lucia, grinning widely. 'Brìghde's tears, you are a sight to see!'

Footsteps thumped along the corridor, and Joanna, Gwendolen and Roland crowded in behind her. After the barest greetings, Sophie shushed all of them, in order to carry on with her tale.

'And so,' she concluded, 'now that you are come, we ought to be able to make the spell work, and renew the keystones, so that the magick of blood and stone can help my father's armies to repel Orléans.'

'But, Sophie, I have been thinking,' said Joanna. 'We have not got a mage from Breizh, either.'

'We have got Sophie,' Gwendolen objected. After a further moment's thought, however, she exclaimed, 'Herne's horns! What if Jo is right?'

Sophie felt very cold, suddenly, though a moment since she had been warm and contented, pressed against Gray's side with his arm wrapped firm about her shoulders.

'Sophie is more Breizhek than I am Kernowek,' said Gray. 'I shall go and round up the others for another attempt, before—well.' He was on his feet now, and crossing to the door. 'I shall have

513

to explain as we go. But, Sophie, it will not overtax your strength, to conceal all of us at once?'

'No,' said Sophie firmly; of that, at least, she was quite certain. 'Not now.'

Navigating the standing stones and the seventy-odd mages now wandering about in them – thank all the gods, and Ceana MacGregor's plea to see *something besides those gods-accursèd stones*, that their morning's walk had taken them in the opposite direction! – was a new and nerve-stretching undertaking. It was not, of course, that Lucia did not trust Sophie's magick to conceal them from unwelcome notice; there was always the danger of running against someone emerging from behind a stone, however, not to mention the unknowable consequences of success, or of failure, with upwards of half a hundred hostile mages all about them who might well be able to detect the effects of the spell they were presently attempting.

Sophie arrayed her forces – Bevan, then Roland, d'Allaire, Proulx, Gray, and last of all herself – and told off Joanna, Gwendolen, and Evans-Hughes as signalmen between them, and Lucia to make sure that Gray spoke the invocation correctly. Then she paced out an irregular sort of ellipse encompassing all six keystones and set a ward around it, so powerful that when the magick rippled through Lucia's consciousness, she staggered with the force of it.

For all of them but Gray, the spell was by now tiresomely familiar, and they were not so long about it as they had been the first time, or even the second. Unfortunately, however, the results were more or less the same.

'It *was* working,' Sophie insisted, near tears with exasperation.

'Better than the second trial; all of the stones but mine responded, this time.'

'Which means, I fear,' said Gareth Evans-Hughes, 'that birth and not descent is the deciding factor, and we are still short one mage born in Breizh.'

Joanna was listening intently to this exchange, her expression growing increasingly grim.

'Your spell, the one you worked on Sophie in Din Edin,' she said, low, edging closer to Lucia. She caught Lucia's wrist and held it; her grip was surprisingly strong, for all that her hand was scarcely bigger than a child's, and Lucia was reminded that Roland had described her as *a thorough horsewoman*. 'You cannot give your magick to the stones, but if you will share it with me, then—'

'*No*,' said Lucia, almost simultaneously with every other person present.

'But do you not see? If birth is the criterion,' Joanna insisted, 'then we have no other choice. Sophie was born in London, but *I* was born in Breizh, and the only obstacle is—'

'Joanna, the spell does not work that way,' said Lucia, helplessly. 'It is meant for one mage to share magick with another, not—'

'Has it ever been tried?' Joanna demanded.

'I—'

'*Has* it? And, more importantly, can we afford not to make the trial now?'

'The danger is—'

'We are *all* in danger already – we are, quite literally, surrounded by the enemy! – and the kingdom, and everyone in it – and all of those "reserve mages" held prisoner at Orléans, and Kergabet's spies—'

Lucia tried to pull away, but Joanna held fast; her grey eyes had gone a little wild, an impression not hindered by the mad tangle of chestnut-coloured curls about her face, and Lucia suspected that she looked rather wild herself.

'What makes you suppose that the magick will answer to you?' she said. 'How shall you know how to wield it? Joanna, no one has ever done what you ask of me, that I know of. I do not know whether it *can* be done, or, if it could, what the consequences might be. We cannot properly control the parameters of the experiment, and—'

'Whatever the consequences,' said Joanna, 'they cannot be worse than allowing the Duc d'Orléans to march the armies of the Duchies over Britain's borders and declare war upon our gods.'

She was not wrong; but nor was Lucia.

Lucia tried again to wrench her arm away; this time, Joanna let her go. She resisted the urge to cast a beseeching look at Sophie, at Gray, at Roland – in the course of her debate with Joanna, the rest of the party had surrounded them, and giving the choice over to someone, anyone, else would be all too easy. *When you sit the chieftain's seat of Alba, Lucia MacNeill,* she told herself sternly, *it will be your task to make difficult decisions. Had you not better begin as you mean to go on?*

But this did not feel like a decision that ought to be made by one person alone.

'I am willing to try the spell,' she said at last, slowly, making sure to meet each person's eyes as she looked about her, 'but only on condition that all of us agree.'

Sophie's betrayed expression – there and gone in the instant before the blank bland mask descended – was terrible to see. Gray interposed himself between them and drew her into his arms, bending his head to speak into her ear; Joanna, wisely, kept clear of this conversation.

'I should not ask this of you – of anyone – if I thought there were any other choice,' she said, looking up at Lucia with both defiance and apology in her wide grey eyes.

'We are *in Breizh*,' said Lucia. 'Surely we ought to be able to find a Breizhek mage?'

The five Oxford mages exchanged a look.

'What have I said?' Lucia tried to make her voice flat, uncompromising, but did not altogether succeed.

There was another exchange of looks, the upshot of which, it appeared, was to elect Guillaume d'Allaire as spokesman.

'The stones,' he said, with a vague one-armed gesture, 'are a sort of sink for magick; it is a matter of record – though the local people naturally do not like to advertise the fact – that no mage has been born within thirty miles of them these past two hundred years.'

'And that those who come from elsewhere tend to go away again after no more than a year or two,' Evans-Hughes added. He ducked his head and scratched absently at the back of his neck. 'Now, I suppose, we know why.'

'Do we?' This from Bevan, the young graduate student. He looked both horrified and fascinated by the notion of a magick-sink, and stared at Gareth as though expecting him to produce a physical artefact of some sort to demonstrate.

Lucia was about to echo him when at last the pieces fell into place in her mind. 'You mean,' she said, 'that the stones became a magick-sink only when their own magick was allowed to decay.'

'Yes,' said Gareth, smiling at her in spite of everything, like the patient tutor he undoubtedly was, pleased with a student's acuity. 'Exactly. Of course, it is a theory that may take generations to test—'

Crowther jostled his shoulder and said in an exasperated tone, 'Do shut up, Gareth, there's a good chap. The point is, Lady Lucia, that there are likely to be no Breizhek mages within anything like a reasonable distance.'

Lucia sighed. 'I have truly not the least notion whether Joanna's proposal will work,' she said. 'I should not be at all surprised if it did not. But if it were only that—'

'This spell of yours,' said Rhein Bevan. 'How long do its effects persist?'

'It depends,' said Lucia, 'or, rather – for *depends* implies a cause, and I know of none – it *varies*, for no apparent reason; but I have never heard of its lasting longer than a se'nnight.' She glanced about her anxiously, then lowered her voice still further: 'This magick has been used in my clan for a dozen generations at the least, but only ever between one mage and another; I have truly no means of predicting—'

'But,' said Henry, 'how can any field of enquiry advance, except by experiment?'

'I am a great believer in the value of experiment,' said Lucia tightly. 'That is, of controlled experimental trials. What you propose is – is not that.'

'*I* do not see,' said Joanna, evidently deciding that she had kept her prudent silence long enough, 'why, if the risk is mine, the decision should not be mine also, if Lucia is willing.'

'Do you not?'

Joanna turned sharply at the sound of Gwendolen Pryce's voice, tight with some barely contained emotion. The Oxford men regarded them curiously – all but Gareth, whose mouth crimped tight in sympathy.

'Oh,' said Joanna, in a very small voice.

Gareth turned to Lucia and said, a little more loudly than strictly necessary, 'How does the spell work, if I may ask? Professional curiosity, you know.'

This drew the others' attention as perhaps nothing else could have done, and Lucia – watching from the corner of one eye as Joanna and Gwendolen slipped away from the group to the shadow of the nearest great stone – was grateful for it, though already bracing for their inevitable disappointment.

'It is Clan MacNeill magick,' she said. 'I should never be forgiven for revealing its secrets outside the clan, and still less to – my apologies – Sasunnach mages. That is' – she held up a hand to forestall the inevitable objections – 'British mages.'

'And no other clan has ever devised a similar spell?' Crowther enquired.

Lucia shrugged. 'Not to my knowledge – though they would scarcely advertise the fact, if they had. We may be a united kingdom now, but the clans and clan-lands still keep their own counsel on some matters, and clan magicks are one such.'

Gwendolen, towing Joanna by the hand, strode back to the circle, followed after another moment by Sophie and Gray, both wearing expressions of grim resignation.

'Well?' said Lucia, looking round the circle of faces. 'What say you all?'

Though none of them looked happy at the prospect, none objected, and almost before she had time to regret her rash promises, Lucia was seating herself against a hip-high stone and calling fire to a candle-stub to heat her knife.

CHAPTER XXXVI

In Which Joanna Rises to a Challenge

Though her arguments in favour of this course of action had – of course – all been entirely rational ones, that part of Joanna's mind which was always unflinchingly honest could not deny that the prospect of *knowing*, once and for all, what it was to have magick was part of its appeal. She put out her hand for Lucia's knife willingly enough, and watched with interest as Lucia, after wiping the tiny blade and passing it through the candle-flame once more, nicked her own thumb and pressed the two bleeding digits together.

Then hot sharp fizzing panic swept through her, and the world glowed red and gold and upended itself, and for some indeterminable time she was entirely incapable of observation, analysis, or even coherent thought.

When next she opened her eyes on an intelligible vision of stones, long grass, sky, and anxious faces, everything was rimmed with the same faintly glowing aura of crimson and gold.

'Jo,' said Sophie anxiously. 'Jo, are you all right?'

'Yes,' said Joanna at once, though she was not at all certain that she was telling the truth. She had the bizarre impression of feeling her blood flowing through her veins, even the smallest of them; her body felt much too large for the skin meant to contain it; and her head seemed to vary in size according to some pattern of its own devising.

Clutching Gwendolen's left hand and Roland's right, she struggled to her feet, then leant heavily on Gwendolen's arm, panting, until the horizon steadied again. Walking was a frustratingly strenuous exercise, for her feet seemed at once larger than usual and farther from the ground; but at last Gwendolen and the hovering Roland delivered her to what had until now been Sophie's stone, and she sank to her knees beside it.

Her thumb was still bleeding sluggishly; she had the invocation by heart, having heard it several dozen times in the past two days, but how in Hades did one persuade magick to flow out of oneself and into an inanimate object, or, indeed, to do anything whatsoever?

Sophie and Gwendolen knelt on either side of Joanna, each clasping one of her hands; she was pathetically grateful for these tethers to the world of solid and observable things.

'You have only to do one thing,' said Sophie, 'and I shall tell you how to go on.'

Joanna nodded, then at once wished she had not.

'Keep your eyes shut,' Sophie said. Her voice was low, soothing, as though Joanna had been a child waking from a nightmare. 'Breathe deeply and slowly, and listen for the beating of your heart.'

Breathing slowly was an effort, but Joanna's heartbeat was already thudding in her ears. She forced herself to focus on it, however, and felt it slow and steady as she brought her rapid breathing under control.

'Now,' said Sophie, 'go deeper – imagine you are diving to the bottom of a pond, and rising out of the muck and weed is something beautiful – in your case, I should imagine, something shining in gold and scarlet—'

All of these instructions were entirely incomprehensible, and impossible to carry out, until, quite suddenly, the black nothingness behind Joanna's eyelids was interrupted by a gleam of gold. The gleam grew – slowly, then by rapid bursts – into a maelstrom of fire, scarlet and gold and almost too bright to look upon.

'Yes,' she breathed, clutching Sophie's hand. 'I see it, like a fiery whirlpool.'

'Well done,' said Sophie, her voice warm with relief. 'We are nearly there, Jo. Now, can you reach into the whirlpool – gently, now – and pull out a thread from it – wrap it about your wrist, I think, so as not to lose hold of it – and now back up through the water—'

Joanna's metaphorical hand was wrapped about with shining streamers of magick; her physical hands – indeed, the whole of her body – thrummed with a weird amalgam of nervous and magickal energy. What might be happening in the world around her, she could not begin to imagine, so strange and vast and inexplicable was the terrain of her own spirit.

Her left hand was moving – Gwendolen was lifting it – her thumb pressing against rough lichen-covered stone.

'*O gods great and small*,' Sophie prompted gently, and Joanna repeated the words, ran through the whole of the invocation without pausing for breath. The magick flowed out into the stone – was *pulled* out, spiralling down into a yawning chasm which, she saw at once, would take and take and never be filled; and then, in an eyeblink, it *was* filled, was overflowing, was not a chasm but a wellspring, and the air was humming with a sound like bees in a clover-field in summer, and there were arms about her and the laughter of relief, and the ground fell away and her face was pressed into the smells of wool and sweat and woodsmoke and sea air.

'I shall go to sleep, I think,' said Joanna.

* * *

Sophie could never afterwards recall the details of their journey back to the inn on the afternoon of the Autumn Equinox; the whole of it was a blur of triumph, terror, and a determined focus on evading the notice of Orléans' legions of mages. She walked beside Gray, clutching the tail of his coat, so that she should not have to look where she was going; Joanna hung limp in Gray's arms, her sturdy boots and one plump little hand swinging with the rhythm of his stride.

They had succeeded this time, that was the important thing; the magick of the keystones had been replenished, and so the spell could now be used as its makers had intended. But what, precisely, were they to do with a defensive boundary, now that the enemy was on the wrong side of it?

They deposited Joanna in her bed, leaving her to the care of a pale and grim-faced Miss Pryce, and foregathered with the remainder of the party in the cramped private dining-room which Mrs Cariou, the innkeeper, had provided for their use. Lucia had taken the precaution of ordering a substantial meal, in case of magick shock, and they applied themselves to their bread, hard cheese, ham, and apple-tart with cautious enthusiasm.

'Well,' said Roland at last. 'We have brought the spell back to life – the magick of blood and stone – and now what are we to do with it?'

There was a general chorus of *what, indeed?* around the table, and a ring of expectant stares in Sophie's direction.

'*She who would wield the magick of blood and stone need not be Queen,*' Sophie recited, '*but she must be a loyal subject of the Kingdom of Britain, and a mage of some talent and skill. She must possess the map of the keystones, and the spell that wakes their power to rouse the kingdom to its own defence.* That is what we are to do with it – to rouse the kingdom to its own defence.'

They looked at her doubtfully, as though she had not told them all exactly this, not so very long ago in Oxford.

Bevan and Roland (who appeared to have forgotten for the time being that he was a prince) cleared away the remains of the meal and stacked the dishes on the sideboard, and Sophie spread out the map on which the magickal stones were marked in red and the manuscript page containing the relevant spell. The writings of the Princesses Regent on the subject of the magick of blood and stone were frustratingly cryptic – or, more probably, relied on the context of the time to convey their meaning – but both map and spell were mentioned as requirements. A spell, as Sophie had been told often and often, is merely an *aide-mémoire,* a means of focusing mind and magick on the desired working or its outcome; the difficulty here was that they had no real notion of the nature of the spell, or of what it was meant to do.

'Perhaps,' Roland suggested, oddly diffident, 'the spell will do whatever you wish it to do. Within the limits of its capacity, that is.'

'That would be a very useful spell,' said Gareth.

'And unimaginably complex to design,' said Proulx, frowning thoughtfully. 'But more easily worked than a collection of simpler spells designed to produce the same outcomes, and less prone to error.'

'Queen Ahez knew what she was about, I am sure,' said Sophie, with some asperity.

'If *I* were designing such a spell,' said Lucia, 'if I knew how, which alas I do not, I should give the land and the people the power to resist invasion, and leave to them the choice of means to do so. After all, the same tactics are unlikely to be equally useful against longship raiders and siege-engines.'

'And sorcerer-centuries,' added Roland. Lucia smiled at him, and laced their fingers together atop the tablecloth.

'Indeed,' said Sophie. 'But—'

'It seems to me,' said Gray, leaning forward with his chin in his hands, 'that as the stones are now all in the hands of Orléans, the most important thing is to prevent him from making use of them. He supposes, apparently, that waking all the stones of Karnag – there are three thousand altogether – will give him dominion over the whole of Roman Gaul.'

'How?' said d'Allaire, bewildered. 'And . . . how?'

'That information,' said Gray, 'was not conveyed to the rank and file, alas. For myself, I do not greatly care, so long as he is stopped. It is any ruler's right to seek to expand his territory by conquest, of course, but to declare war on the gods who were worshipped here before the Roman Conquest, and to enslave men, not to mention mages, by compulsion to risk their lives for the sake of victory in battle – *no*.'

There was a general shudder around the table; Sophie, who (with Roland, Lucia, and Joanna) had heard all of this in more detail already, flinched and swallowed back nausea at the thought of those mages linked to Gray who, in the wrong circumstances, could be drained of their magick without warning and through no will of his.

'In any case, it scarcely signifies what his foul purpose may be,' said Lucia, 'if we can prevent whatever it is by invoking Queen Ahez's spell. Sophie, you are the only one who can wield the magick, or so the Princesses Regent tell us; you need not wait for the rest of us to conclude our debate before acting as you see fit.'

Sophie glanced round the table again, and was heartened to see no censure or disapproval of this last remark. 'Very well,' she said. 'I shall do my best.'

They fell silent, waiting – they were all of them mages, after all, and knew the value of a quiet room. Sophie read over the spell again, twice more, so as not to stumble, and focused her mind on what seemed to her the desired outcome: the absence of the Duc d'Orléans, his mages, and his troops from all of Britain's provinces; peaceable borders between Britain and the Duchies; and peaceful coexistence amongst the old gods and the new.

She found Gray's hand and clasped it, skin to skin, and felt their magicks well up to meet one another.

Then she closed her eyes, let her magick flow out into the aether, and spoke the spell.

The magic of the stones raged through Sophie like a river in flood through an opened sluice-gate, vast and old and terrible – but there and gone in the space of two heartbeats.

'Sophie?' Gray's voice by her ear; Gray's large warm hand curling over her shoulder.

Somewhere, the sound of a door slamming.

Sophie peeled the side of her face from the table and sat up as straight as she could.

'Hallo the house!' came a voice from the inn-yard below the window, calling loudly in Français.

Roland jumped up to peer through the window, followed in short order by every other person in the room, apart from Sophie herself. Gray went last of all and was back almost at once, cursing under his breath.

'He is *here*,' he said, low and urgent in Sophie's ear. 'He was to come in triumph when we had awakened the stones – all three thousand of them – but surely—'

'Who?' said Sophie, in hopes of making him explain. She felt slow and stupid, as though her thoughts were swimming through treacle.

'Orléans,' said Gray, as though it had been obvious. 'Come and see.'

She levered herself upright, with one arm wrapped tightly about Gray's waist, then made her way to the window and peered down into the forecourt.

Sure enough, there stood in the forecourt of the Ship at Rest an elegantly caparisoned black horse and, holding its reins, a small man, resplendent in a blue coat trimmed with gold braid and positively radiating power.

Sophie straightened away from Gray's side; half turned, grasping the windowsill for balance; and beckoned to Roland to stand beside her. 'We are the generals of this little army, I think,' she said, low, in her brother's ear. 'We stand on the battlefield, face-to-face with the enemy. What say you – will we challenge him?'

Roland's hand caught hers and squeezed it tightly. She glanced aside at him and found him wearing a broad, exultant grin. Lucia stood at his other side, her hand on his shoulder, and Evans-Hughes and Crowther behind him; Joanna clasped hands with Sophie on one side, and Gwendolen Pryce on the other; behind the three of them stood Gray, Bevan, d'Allaire, and Proulx.

Sophie gently detached her hand from Joanna's, flung open the windows, and let go her mother's magick before reaching for her sister's hand once more.

'Monsieur le Duc d'Orléans!' she called. 'We are the Kingdom of Britain, and we and our gods defy you.'

He looked up at their first-floor window and stared at them in outrage; his voice boomed out so loud that Sophie repressed a yelp: 'I am Imperator Gallia. I command legions such as the world has not seen since the great days of Rome; I wield the power of two sorcerer-centuries and of Divus Iulius himself. You, it appears, command an army of eleven. You are a brave and noble band of warriors, I have no doubt, but I need hardly cast the auguries to predict the outcome of this contest.'

'I urge you to reconsider your plan of campaign,' said Roland. His shoulder trembled against Sophie's, but his voice was steady. 'We are not alone; we have the whole of Britain at our backs, and she is waking in anger at the threat to her sons and daughters, and to her gods.'

Orléans stared up at them, frowning – not in anger, if Sophie read his face aright, but in bafflement at this bizarre and inexplicable turn of events.

Then he shook his head, half turned from the window, and began to speak some spell; a spell it was, Sophie felt quite certain, for the very air shivered with the force of his magick drawing in. The air darkened – or were Sophie's eyes failing under the onslaught? – she swayed and staggered against Roland's shoulder, and Joanna's stumbling threatened to pull her off balance from the other side – the air grew thin and hot, and bruised Sophie's throat as she gasped for breath—

—until, between one breath and the next, the cobbles of the forecourt cracked across, with a sound like thunder, and Orléans' horse stumbled and slid, its hind legs sinking hock-deep into the resulting chasm. Orléans himself, stumbling too, backed away from the struggling horse, and the buzz and burn of his gathering magick abruptly ceased as he sat down hard upon the cobbles.

'Oh,' Sophie gasped, her stomach churning. Had her spell done *that*? And not even to the enemy she had meant it for, but to a beast which had no choice in the matter? Or was this the effect of whatever magick Orléans had himself been working?

'Lady Epona,' she whispered, 'let not the blow fall on the innocent.'

It occurred to her then – whether in answer to this prayer, or by sheer happenstance, she could not have said – that here was a use for the drawing-spell she had feared to use yesterday. She drew a deep breath, fixed her gaze on the foundering horse, and began quietly to hum a jaunty march.

The horse's hindquarters rose very slightly; it found its feet just long enough to scramble out of the crack in the cobbles, and stood for a long moment on trembling legs before lifting its head and walking towards the front door – no, the front *window*. Sophie abruptly ceased humming and let the magick go, sighing with relief when the horse lost interest and wandered away to browse in Mrs Cariou's herb beds.

'We have Orléans at our mercy here,' said Lucia quietly, gesturing at him; he was picking himself up, dusting off his elaborate coat. 'This war, the ugly means of prosecuting it, his mad notions about the gods of Rome – cut off the monster's head, and the body will fall to pieces of itself.'

Sophie recoiled in horror.

'Lucia is not suggesting cold-blooded murder, Sophie,' said Roland hastily.

'Well,' said Lucia, 'I—'

Roland gave her a meaning look, and she swallowed, then went on: 'Could not the spell which drew that poor horse out of the crevice in the courtyard also draw our uninvited guest into, for example, the inn's root cellar? And hold him there until further reinforcements can be summoned?'

Sophie blinked at her, considering this, and at last smiled a little. 'Yes, that is a very good notion,' she said.

She was still reaching for a suitable melody, and wondering how to overcome the problem of the locked door, when Orléans got his second wind. His brush with the abyss had not diminished either his power or his determination to use it against his opponents, it appeared, for he was snarling as he spread his hands and began chanting another spell. The magick seemed to come at them from everywhere at once – pressing in upon Sophie's skin, her eardrums, the top of her head – the air like treacle, thick and clinging – *Arachne's Web*, thought Sophie, for she had felt something like it before, but surely Arachne's Web could not be cast on such a scale?

Gray's hands descended on her shoulders, thumbs pressed to the bare skin at the nape of her neck; magick thrummed between them. Sophie straightened her spine, clutched Roland's hand and Joanna's, and held on.

'Mother Goddess, bountiful and kind,' she said aloud. The roaring air swallowed her prayer, but the words came tumbling past her lips, faster and louder: 'Gods above and gods below, gods of the rivers and woods and stones, gods of the Britons and gods of the Gauls, gods who made this land and gods who guard it, hear me!'

'You have no dominion here!' Orléans roared. 'Take your petty gods and your hangers-on and begone!'

The floor trembled beneath Sophie's feet with the force of his spell, whatever it was; the rafters groaned; before her eyes, the window-frame sagged out of true. The floor tilted, the shutters began to splinter and crack.

'Hear me!' cried Roland.

'Hear me! Hear us!' the others echoed, over and over as the staggering heat and pressure of Orléans' spell built up around them, driving them one by one to their knees.

Sharp pain exploded through Sophie's head as her ears gave in to the onslaught; she swallowed back a shriek, and with it the warm iron tang of blood running down over her lips. Her back bowing over, she struggled to regain her feet – fell to her knees again – cracked her chin against the window-sill.

If I am to die here, she thought defiantly, *at any rate I shall not die alone.*

She opened her mouth – it was an effort, by now – and repeated the words of the spell, the Brezhoneg and English and Cymric and Français and Kernowek phrases tumbling over one another (she could not hear her own voice over the tumult of noise and pressure and pain) as her magick and Gray's, Roland's and Lucia's, Gareth's and all the others', rose up to meet the magick of the stones.

Sophie spoke the last word of the spell, and the gathered magicks erupted.

Another teeth-rattling thunder-crack resounded through the house, and another chasm opened in the forecourt – this one immediately behind Orléans' heels, so that he stumbled and nearly fell headlong into it.

From the middle distance – northward, in the direction of the stone-fields – came a series of what sounded like small explosions, accompanied by the occasional pained yelp or howl.

On her knees on the floorboards, Sophie peered over the warped and splintered window-sill. 'Mother Goddess,' she breathed, as the implications began to dawn upon her: the enemy was not only at this particular gate, and therefore Queen Ahez's spell would not be so restricted, either. 'Mother Goddess, what have we done?'

CHAPTER XXXVII

In Which the Fellows of Merlin Change Their Mind

The death toll, in the end, was so low as to beggar belief, and His Majesty declared a feast day throughout the kingdom in thanksgiving to the gods for the carnage spared. The third and last of the minor earthquakes at Karnag claimed the life of Henri-François, Duc d'Orléans, before Sophie could carry out Lucia's scheme to lock him in the cellar of the Ship at Rest; at Klison, the flood that swept away the invaders' weaponry and siege-engines also killed two men of His Majesty's army who had been taken prisoner; and a similar flood at Ivry-sur-Eure carried off two men and their mounts who happened to be crossing the bridge.

The suspicion of many in Britain that Orléans' followers had been under the influence of some magickal compulsion, though never unequivocally verified, was borne out by the startlingly high proportion of soldiers and officers who deserted or surrendered in the aftermath of the earthquakes, fires, floods, lightning-strikes, rock slides, and sinkholes which Sophie had called forth by invoking the magick of blood and stone. Many claimed to remember nothing of what they had done, thought, or said during the previous year – for most a safely unverifiable claim, but not without a kernel of truth. As a result, the men who had first conspired to murder King Henry, and later provided aid and intelligence to the enemy, were not condemned to death, but only returned to a more secure imprisonment.

Joanna recovered without incident from her encounter with magick, rather pleased to have had the experience of seeing magick use from the inside but infinitely grateful to be spared repeating it in the foreseeable future. Amelia, whose journey across Orléanais and Maine had resulted in a thorough change of heart on several points, returned to London to make her peace with her sisters and her guardian, and was invited, together with Lady Maëlle, to continue in Grosvenor Square at least until after the royal wedding. Over the course of that autumn and winter, her quiet beauty caught the eyes of many a young man, but her heart was won, in the end, by a gentleman of five-and-thirty who confessed that he had heard her playing upon Lady Lisle's pianoforte, and singing a Breizhek love-song, some time before he ever saw her face (for he was rather short-sighted), and been inspired by the sincerity of her performance to seek an acquaintance with her.

Some two months after what the public insisted on calling the Battle of Le Ménec – though there had been no battle in the ordinary sense – the Princess Royal and her father received identical copies of a letter from the Fellows of Merlin College, which after the usual salutations read as follows:

> *Whereas trustworthy reports from the scene of the battle*
> *indicate that the actions of female mages, though appearing at*

the time to be ill-advised and based in pure speculation, in fact spared the kingdom much of the expense of prosecuting a costly war and saved countless lives on both sides;

Whereas the contributions of the said female mages are reliably reported to have been integral and even indispensable to the strategy which accomplished these feats;

Whereas the female members of the expedition to Karnag are reliably reported to have conducted themselves with bravery, resourcefulness, intelligence, fortitude, moral courage, and a spirit of enquiry in the course of the said expedition, equal to those of their male counterparts; and

Whereas, in light of these and other facts, it seems high time to revisit the policies and attitudes of the past several centuries with respect to higher education for young ladies,

We, the undersigned Fellows of Merlin College, Oxon, do hereby endorse and support the re-establishment of a college for women on the site of the former Lady Morgan College, Oxon.

The signatures of some half-dozen Fellows remained conspicuously absent from this missive, but these absences were very effectively overshadowed by the signatures of every other Fellow of Merlin and several Fellows of other Colleges.

The marriage of Prince Roland of Britain and Lucia MacNeill, heiress of Alba, was celebrated in London in October, and in Din Edin in December, of the year of the Hundred Days' War. It was rumoured in Britain that they had been secretly handfasted at some time during their unauthorised journey to Breizh; the rumours were never confirmed or denied, and speculation continued for some time. The royal couple's first child, a daughter, was born in the following October, and was named Maeve Edwina Sophia Joanna MacNeill, for her two grandmothers and her aunts.

In the autumn of that same year, the newly established Regents' College opened its doors to its first matriculating students.

CHAPTER XXXVIII

Thereafter

Joanna was well accustomed by now to being among the oldest in her year – second only to Gwendolen and to Mathilde de Courcy – but the feeling was magnified, somehow, by the experience of seeing young ladies several years her junior shake hands with the College Mistress and receive degrees exactly equivalent to her own.

'To Mademoiselle Joanna Claudia Callender,' declared the Mistress of Regents' College, 'is awarded the degree of *Artium Baccalaureus, cum laude.*'

Polite applause from the assembled guests was drowned out entirely by the cheering and, not to put too fine a point on it, hooting of Joanna's particular friends; and, diploma in hand and flushed with both triumph and embarrassment, Joanna retreated to her seat beside Justine Beauvois to watch Mathilde, next in the queue, take her turn before the multitude.

This first matriculating class had been a small one, and had grown smaller as the years progressed, so that by now only one-and-twenty young women remained to receive their degrees; no more than another quarter-hour had passed, therefore, before Mademoiselle Gwendolen

Cornelia Pryce was awarded the degree of *Magicēs Baccalaureus, summa cum laude*, together with the prize (established by the Fellows of the College) for coming first in the practical examinations for the said degree. Joanna beamed up at the stage, and at Gwendolen blushing prettily at the centre of it whilst Mór MacRury stepped forward from the ranks of Fellows to ambush her with a congratulatory embrace, until she felt her face would split in two from the joy of it.

At dinner in Hall, the atmosphere was buoyantly triumphant, the hum of conversation almost painfully loud, and the hall itself packed to the rafters with Fellows, students, and their families and friends. Joanna, so tightly wedged between Sophie and young Agatha that she could scarcely manage her knife and fork, had almost no attention to spare for missing Gwendolen: Agatha was ecstatic to be granted the honour of sitting down to dinner with the grown-up ladies and gentlemen, and expressed her elation by chattering nineteen to the dozen all through dinner; Sophie was full of plans for her summer in Alba, and was attempting once more to persuade Joanna to make one of the party ('Should you not like to meet Roland and Lucia's little daughter, before she grows taller than either of us?'), before she should return to London to take up her official post as Secretary to the Chief Privy Councillor; Amelia was anxiously seeking advice from Jenny on the rearing of little boys. Joanna had only to look up and along the table to her right, however, to see Gwendolen sitting between her father and her sister Branwen, quietly glowing with pride in her own accomplishments and, more unusually, with pleasure in her family's being by to share them. It was odd, after all these years, to see her in such company – and her father, at least, could not have looked more awkward and ill at ease had he set out to be so – but in a way that warmed Joanna's heart and made her smile.

After dinner they walked about the grounds with their guests, and at last saw them off at the College gate, whither they should return to their lodgings at the Dragon and Lion.

'I could not be prouder of either of you, if you were my own children,' said Sophie, not for the first time, embracing first Joanna and then Gwendolen with undiminished enthusiasm. Gray shook their hands solemnly in the Alban manner; then the two of them strolled away towards their own rooms in the Senior Fellows' wing, hand in hand and heads bent together.

Joanna watched them go, and smiled.

'Jo,' said Gwendolen softly, 'what are you thinking of?'

Joanna turned a little and looked up at her. 'I hardly know,' she said honestly. 'We are come to the end of something, today; but I cannot regret it, for I hope it may be the beginning of something better still.'

Gwendolen, laughing, tangled her long fingers with Joanna's amongst the mingled folds of their skirts. 'From your lips to the gods' ears,' she said.

ACKNOWLEDGEMENTS

This is the last book of a trilogy whose first book I began writing a decade ago, and thanking everyone who has contributed to its (and my) success would require a whole 'nother book. Still, I'll give it a go!

Many, many thanks to my fantabulous family (immediate and extended) and friends, my terrific day-job colleagues, and the lovely and supportive members of Kol Rina Women's Choir, the Orpheus Choir of Toronto, and Congregation Darchei Noam for general and particular cheerleading and encouragement; to Anne Marie Corrigan, Alex Hunter, Tawnie Olson, Luisa Petroianu, Antonia Pop, and Kim Solga for walks, plot talks, and milkshake summits; to Jeannie Scarfe for late-night text conversations and beta reading; to Stephanie Sedgwick for equestrian consulting (and the owl colouring book!); and to Michael Appleby for emergency Latin support. All remaining errors are my own. For much of the writing of this book I was digging my way out of a not-so-nice brain-space, and I appreciate every. single. person. who offered hugs, tissues, encouragement, chocolate, and/or a listening ear when I needed it.

Thinks to my amazing agent, Eddie Schneider, and his colleagues at JABberwocky Literary Agency for everything they do and for a delicious Indian dinner in a pub in London this spring, as well as to John Berlyne of Zeno Literary Agency in the UK. Thanks to my equally amazing and very patient editor, Jessica Wade (without whom this book would be much longer and nothing like as good), and her able assistant, Miranda Hill; to Amy J. Schneider for helpful copy-editing, and Christina Griffiths for the hat trick of gorgeous covers; to Cortney Skinner for mapping the world of the series so beautifully; and to Michelle Kasper, Jennifer Myers, Kayleigh Webb, and Kim Burns for shepherding the book the rest of the way into your hands. A huge thanks also to the team at Allison & Busby for bringing the trilogy to readers in the UK! And a shoutout to the fabulous Toronto Public Library system, and particularly to the North York Central Library, where at least half of the words in this book were written. Writing was fuelled by Kicking Horse Coffee, the Second Cup Coffee Co., DAVIDsTEA, and Adagio Teas.

It's not easy living with someone who's writing a book while also holding down a full-time job! So all the thanks to Alex and Shaina Hunter, who have been putting up with me (and all the weirdos who live in my head) for twenty-four and fourteen years respectively; and to my mum, Luisa Petroianu, my baby brother, Dan Izzo, and the rest of the mishpacha (and mishpacha-of-choice), who have been putting up with me for even longer. *I love you all so much!*

The necklace and earrings Joanna lends to Gwendolen are modelled on a set made for me by Anne Marie Corrigan; Amelia's silver-and-garnet eardrops, on a pair given to me by Deborah and Sam Appel. The Kergabets' bigger, fancier house in Grosvenor Square has many sofas, chairs, and chaises longues, but the green-and-gold-striped sofa in the morning-room is a close cousin of the silk-upholstered one which my mother inherited from her parents, on which (unlike the rest of the furniture) many generations of cats have been forbidden to sleep.

Although 'Duc d'Orléans' was a real title in pre-revolutionary France (a title reserved for members of the French royal family, rather like 'Prince of Wales' in the UK), Henri-François, Duc d'Orléans, is an invention of my own. Similarly, Nevenoe (in French, Nominoë) and his wife, Argentaela, are real historical people, and Nevenoe really is considered the first king/duke of Brittany, but almost everything else this book states or suggests about either of them is completely 100 per cent made up.

I have also, of course, played fast and loose with the history and geography of France and its neighbours. The territories and places mentioned are, or at some point in history were, real ones; most of their alliances and allegiances, however, are fictional. Exceptions to the former are Ivry-la-Bataille, which I have renamed Ivry-sur-Eure (not to be confused with Ivry-sur-Seine); and the territory around Paris, historically known as l'Île-de-France, which, because no kingdom of France exists in the world of this book, I have renamed l'Île-des-Francs.

Most of the songs in this book echo those in the two previous books. The exceptions are 'The Oak and the Ash' in Chapter IV and the two Welsh songs ('Suo Gan' and 'Llywn On', known in English as 'The Ash Grove') and the Scots song 'O Whistle and I'll Come to Ye' in Chapter XI. 'The Oak and the Ash' is the contemplations of a young woman from the north of England who wishes she weren't living in London; 'Suo Gan' is a lullaby; and the others are both love songs, though they could not be more different in character. The story mentioned in Chapters XV and XXIII is, of course, the French fairy tale 'La Belle au bois dormant' by Charles Perrault (1628–1703), better known to English speakers as 'Sleeping Beauty' – judiciously adjusted for congruence with the Midnight-verse.

SYLVIA HUNTER lives in Canada with her husband and daughter and their slightly out-of-control collections of books, comics, and DVDs. She works as an editor and writer, sings in two choirs, reads as much as possible, knits (mostly hats), and engages in experimental baking.

sylviaizzohunter.ca
@sylwritesthings